By *Robert Newcomb:*

THE CHRONICLES OF BLOOD AND STONE

The Fifth Sorceress
The Gates of Dawn
The Scrolls of the Ancients

The Scrolls
of the
Ancients

The Scrolls of the Ancients

VOLUME III

of

THE CHRONICLES OF BLOOD AND STONE

Robert Newcomb

DEL REY

BALLANTINE BOOKS • NEW YORK

A Del Rey® Book
Published by The Random House Publishing Group

Copyright © 2004 by Robert Newcomb

All rights reserved under International and Pan-American
Copyright Conventions. Published in the United States by
The Random House Publishing Group, a division of Random House, Inc., New York,
and simultaneously in Canada by Random House of Canada Limited, Toronto.

Del Rey is a registered trademark and the Del Rey colophon
is a trademark of Random House, Inc.

www.delreydigital.com

Library of Congress Control Number: 2004092243

ISBN 0-345-44896-0

Text design by Mary A. Wirth

Manufactured in the United States of America

First Edition: June 2004

2 4 6 8 9 7 5 3 1

*This one's for
my hugely supportive agent, Matt Bialer,
and my amazingly understanding editor, Shelly Shapiro.
Without them, my books might never have seen
the light of day.*

Contents

The Scrolls

of the

Ancients

Prologue:
Relinquishment

"And there shall come unto Eutracia one who shall willingly forsake her first-born . . . And the child cast away shall haunt her dreams for her entire life. Yet it shall be this same child, temporarily lost and alone in the maze that is the craft, who shall also become known as one of its greatest wielders."
—PAGE 866, CHAPTER TWO OF THE PROPHECIES OF THE TOME

"Do not tell me your name, my dear. But by what name shall we call the child? And remember, first name only, please."

The matron's voice was neither condescending nor harsh. She waited patiently, her squat, bulky frame blocking the doorway to the building behind her.

But the young mother standing before her in the rain had no ready answer. She had not given her child a name, for doing so would only further cement the bond she already felt with him and make the act she was about to perform even more impossible. Tightening her arms around his little body, she lowered her eyes in sadness and shame.

She had come here to give up her baby.

As she tried unsuccessfully to protect the squirming infant from the driving rain, she craned her neck to peer over the matron's shoulder. An inviting glow emanated from the rooms beyond, and she could hear the sounds of laughing children. The smells of warm food drifted to her nostrils, reminding her of how long it had been since she had eaten. Perhaps if she could just go inside for a moment, she might feel better about it all . . .

"May I come in before deciding?" she asked.

"No, my dear, it is forbidden," the matron responded. Her older, wiser heart was breaking, just as it always did for the sad, desperate ones who journeyed here. But the wizards had made their conditions very plain, and as headmistress of this place she had to respect them.

"If you are here to give us your child, surely you must know that you cannot enter," she added gently. "Not now, not ever." She extended her arms. According to Eutracian law, once the baby was handed over, there could be no going back.

Still, the young woman hesitated. She pulled the infant closer to her breast, attempting to cover him further with the worn blanket she had wrapped around him.

"And which of the three categories of blood does this child possess?" the matron asked, hoping to move things along. "Fully endowed, unendowed, or partial?" The weather was worsening, and if this was to be done, she wanted the baby protected from the elements as quickly as possible.

"Fully endowed," the young mother responded quietly.

The matron raised an eyebrow. It had been some time since she had been offered a child of fully endowed blood. Giving one up was a rare thing, usually indicating that the mother's situation was dire, indeed. "And do you have the child's verified blood signature to prove this claim?" she asked.

The mother nodded. From beneath her hooded cloak she produced a parchment, which she handed to the woman before her. Backing away from the rain, the matron unrolled it. She glanced at the blood signature, noted the child's date of birth, then verified that two of the consuls of the Redoubt had witnessed the formation of the signature, as required. The black ink stamp in the shape of the Paragon—the stone that powered the craft of magic—was in place, proof that the child was illegitimate. At last she checked the blood quality rating, also stamped at the bottom of the document. Its numerical value indicated the highest blood quality she had ever seen. Stunned, she simply stood there for a moment. Finally she found her voice.

"And the required parental blood signatures?" she asked, trying to mask her surprise.

The younger woman produced two more parchments. The matron looked intently at them. After noting their signed confirmations by the consuls, she carefully compared them to the first document.

"Very well," she said finally, "I accept the fact that the child is of fully endowed blood. He will be treated accordingly."

Except for the actual handing over of the infant, their business was concluded. All of the permissible questions had been asked and answered, and the necessary documents provided.

The young mother trembled, clearly torn.

The drops from the sky combined with those from her eyes to run down her reddened cheeks. The baby had fallen asleep; the only sound was the cold rain splattering down on the street and the unassuming house that hid so many secrets.

Turning, the young mother looked hesitantly to the rain-soaked carriage-of-four that had brought her here. She saw the kind, elderly faces of her parents as they sat inside, waiting for her to decide.

She thought back to when she had first met Eric. He had swept her off her feet, and she had fallen madly in love. At first her parents—simple commoners—had approved of him: handsome, charming, and of fully endowed blood, just as she was.

But then he had shown his true colors. Upon learning of her pregnancy he had abandoned her, never to be heard from again. Despite his cruel treatment, she still missed him, and feared she always would.

That had been the first time her young heart had been truly broken. Standing here, on this anonymous stoop in the rain, trying to make her fateful decision, was the second.

The voices had come just after she had discovered she was pregnant. *You must abort the child,* they had said.

But she had defied them, carrying the baby to term and then giving birth despite the terrifying warnings searing through her mind. The voices had grown stronger and more insistent, continuing to demand the death of the infant. They had finally become so resonant and powerful that she thought she would go irretrievably mad if the child stayed with her; she was terrified that such madness would cause her to harm the baby, despite her love for him. And so she had come here—to this place many knew about but few talked of—to give her firstborn away.

"I ask you a final time," the matron said. "What name shall be given to this child?"

Tears streaming down her face, the young mother looked down into her baby's face for what she knew in her heart would be the final time. She saw his wispy, sandy hair, and the small mole at the left-hand corner of his mouth. With trembling hands, she handed the infant over to the matron. She thought for a moment.

"Wulfgar," she whispered at last. She covered her face in grief.

"Then Wulfgar it shall be," the matron answered compassionately. Her face hardened slightly. "You are never to visit here again, nor try to discover the whereabouts of the child. Do you understand? The wizards' penalties for disobeying can be quite severe."

The young woman standing before her could only nod.

"Go now," the matron said quietly, her voice kind once more. "And may the Afterlife look over you." Turning, she carried the infant into the house, closing the door behind her.

Sobbing, the young mother collapsed.

She felt her father's strong arms lift her to her feet, felt herself being carried back to the carriage and placed upon the seat. She continued to cry as her mother stroked her hair, as their driver, snapping his whip, charged the horses noisily down the slick, cobblestoned street.

Morganna of the House of Desinoor wept in her mother's arms. Then she felt her mother press something into her hand. It was a lock of sandy-colored hair tied with a red ribbon. It had been cut from the head of her son only this morning, and was now all she had to remember him by.

It would be another three years before she would meet and marry Nicholas of the House of Galland, the true love of her life, and become queen of Eutracia. She would then go on to have twins, whose birth would be heralded by a strange, azure glow and watched over anxiously by ancient wizards.

The carriage plunged on through the night.

PART I

Recollection

THIRTY-FOUR YEARS LATER

CHAPTER

One

And a great calamity shall befall the nation after the second earthly death of the Chosen male's seed, for the endowed and the unendowed alike of the already beleaguered land shall find themselves in chains, with little hope of return.
—PAGE 553, CHAPTER ONE OF THE PROPHECIES OF THE TOME

Whump! . . . whump! . . . whump! . . .
        The two massive sledges came down on the large, simple block of wood in perfect unison, one after the other, monotonously marking out the beat. Its cadence rarely varied. A sledge in each hand, the awful, barely human creature continued to bang out the mind-numbing rhythm as the filthy slaves seated in rows before him toiled endlessly.

Whump! . . . whump! . . . whump! . . .

Built for war, maneuverability, and speed, the ship was unusually large. Christened the *Defiant,* she carried four full masts and a hundred oars. The cramped oaring stations lay one deck down, and smelled of sweat, urine, and slow death.

Fifty such rows stretched down the dark interior of the hull, a single, wide walkway separating them into two equal halves. Six male slaves toiled in each of the divided rows, making six hundred of them on this deck alone. They had few breaks. They were forced to row whenever the wind was directly behind them, or the ship was in the doldrums, or simply, it seemed, when impatience overcame their new taskmasters.

And even when they were allowed a few moments of rest, they remained chained in place, unable to stretch their muscles to rest their weary backs.

The slaves wore nothing but soiled loincloths. Their callused, bleeding hands were chained together and their feet were in shackles, communally chained to the deck. Escape was impossible. Even if one or more of them somehow freed themselves of their bonds, there would be nowhere to go except overboard, to drown in the icy waters of the Sea of Whispers.

They had been at sea for fifteen days. Legend had it that no ship had ever sailed farther than that—ships that tried never returned home.

One of the slaves looked down at the number carved into his oar handle. Number Twenty-Nine. That was his name now—a number, assigned by his captors. It was meant to be dehumanizing, he was sure, but he had seized on it as a symbol, a reminder that his life was not his own, that the slave manning this oar was not his true self. Twenty-Nine. He would use that as his name as long as he remained captive. But someday, somehow, he would be freed, and then he would take up his family name once again with pride.

He glanced out the small oar slot near his station. More ships like this one were out there. Occasionally he could see them, their sails full and their oars slicing through the restless, froth-tipped waves—an inexplicable armada of shame.

His muscles on fire, Twenty-Nine pulled relentlessly on the accursed oar. His hands cramped sharply. Once they had been those of an accomplished artisan. But he knew they would no longer be capable of such specialized work. He could barely straighten his fingers anymore, on those rare occasions when they happened to be removed from the handle.

Seething with hatred, Twenty-Nine looked up at his taskmasters, the monsters who had captured him, chained him, and forced him to labor on their ship.

They were horrific. Once they may have been human—but no more. They were tall and muscular, and their skin was pure white, alabaster, almost translucent. Even when there was a deficit of light, their pale, flawless flesh seemed to shine, as if their bodies carried no blood whatsoever. Twenty-Nine had often wondered if they would bleed, if cut.

The four fingers and thumb of their hands ended in long, pointed talons, rather than fingernails. Their powerful chests bare, each of them wore an odd, black leather skirt, floor length, and divided down the front for walking. The toes of their black leather boots protruded from beneath the hems. A spiked, black leather collar encircled each one's neck.

Each creature carried a short sword in a scabbard hung low behind his back in an ingenious arrangement that allowed the hand to reach naturally down along the outer leg to draw the blade. Twenty-Nine had already seen several of them do so, and their speed had been staggering. Somehow they managed never to catch the swords in the bright red capes that were attached to their spiked leather collars.

Their faces were grotesque. The heads were long, angular, oversized. A shiny metal skullcap covered the top of their white, hairless craniums, ran down between the eyes, then split down either side over the bridge of the nose. Each half extended down the sides of the cheeks to the jawbones, running back to encircle each ear before joining again with the top, leaving the creatures' eyes, mouths, and ears exposed. The ears that protruded from the gaps in the masks were exceptionally high, pointed, and seemed to hear everything. A variety of earrings dangled from them. The wide, wrinkled mouths held black tongues and dark, pointed teeth. For eyes, they had long, narrow slits hiding orbs that were solid white, without irises or pupils, and quite vacant. Still, they missed nothing.

Setting the cadence, the beatmaster among them continued to pummel his twin sledges down on the solitary block of wood as the slaves pulled relentlessly on their oars. Pacing between the rows, others of the blanched monsters moved up and down the shifting, pitching deck. Carrying knotted nine-tails or long-handled tridents, they would without hesitation lash or stab any slave they felt to be shirking his labors. The slaves called these guards "bleeders." The deck of the ship was stained with the blood of those who did not keep up the pace.

"Water," number Twenty-Eight suddenly begged, falling over onto the deck. Twenty-Nine tried, despite his short wrist chains, to help him back onto the bench before any of the bleeders saw what had happened, but he knew he had to continue rowing or be beaten himself.

He looked up to see one of the creatures approaching. It was then that he felt the warmth, smelled the stench. Closing his eyes briefly, he tried to blot out what was happening, but could not. Twenty-Eight was vomiting bile on his feet.

Twenty-Eight retched again, curling his trembling body around one of Twenty-Nine's vomit-soaked feet. "Help us . . . ," he sobbed. "Why won't anyone help us . . ."

The bleeder was standing over them. Without hesitation he shoved the three prongs of the trident into Twenty-Eight's left calf. The blood gushed forth, flowing down the slave's leg in bright rivulets. For a long moment, Twenty-Nine thought he might be sick.

Giving the trident a vicious twist, the bleeder yanked it from Twenty-Eight's leg.

"Back onto the bench—now!" the bleeder shouted. His voice was low, guttural, and commanding. He was standing so close that Twenty-

Nine could smell his putrid breath. Somehow Twenty-Eight did as he was told. Seated on the bench once more, he bent over and retched again. His empty stomach had nothing left to expel.

"If this happens again, the prongs will go directly into your worthless eyes," the bleeder hissed. "Do you understand?" He pointed his trident at the strange brand on Twenty-Eight's shoulder. "You are not of endowed blood, *Talis*. Therefore, you are quite expendable. You live only to serve this ship."

With a sneer, the creature continued down the bloodstained aisle to abuse another man who had fallen behind. Functioning on fear alone, Twenty-Eight somehow resumed rowing.

Twenty-Nine looked over to the left shoulder of his friend, at the word that had been branded into his skin. *Talis*. He had no idea what it meant, but he believed it to be from a long-lost language his father had told him of, something he had called "Old Eutracian." His father and his father's father had all handed down tales of a mysterious, beautiful language, now long since abandoned.

The same word had been branded into the left shoulder of almost every oarsman just before they were forced to board the vessel at the coastal city of Farpoint. The rest were marked with a slightly different word: *R'talis*. He had no idea what either word meant.

Pulling on his oar, he glanced down at the aisle dividing the rows of slaves. Latticed gates lay flush in the floor, held fast with huge iron padlocks. They led to the lower decks, where still more slaves—men as well as women—were held.

At the docks, the women and the men had been herded together. Twenty-Nine had been puzzled to see that they were all about the same age: somewhere between thirty and thirty-five Seasons of New Life. Then, after a small quantity of their blood had been taken, they had been branded. Those given the designation *R'talis* had been carefully boarded first and were treated marginally better. For example, he had never seen an *R'talis* forced to toil at the oars.

Lost in thought, he let his mind drift just a bit too long. Before he realized that his pull on the oar had slackened slightly, the knotted ninetails came whistling out of nowhere.

Snapping loudly, its leather straps seared their way into the naked skin of Twenty-Nine's back, making him scream. Trying to regain his focus, he screamed again, perhaps more loudly than was truly warranted.

It was good enough for the bleeder with the whip. Apparently satisfied, the creature turned his white, opaque eyes to someone else, weapon arm raised.

Suddenly a latticed doorway in the deck above opened and a stairway descended with a crash. Sunlight and sea air streamed in as a figure slowly climbed down. Twenty-Nine narrowed his eyes. He had seen this being only one other time since boarding the slave ship, and knew him only by the private name he had silently bestowed on him: the Harlequin.

Even though the slaves continued rowing to the mind-numbing beat, every pair of eyes was now focused squarely on the Harlequin.

As had been the case the other time Twenty-Nine had seen him, he was absurdly dressed. His long-sleeved, black-and-white-checked doublet was fastened down the center with shining gold buttons. Highly padded epaulets broadened the shoulders, and short, white ruffles on the raised, circular collar and cuffs of the doublet lengthened neck and arms. The almost obscenely tight, bright red breeches ended in black, square-toed shoes with raised heels and highly polished silver buckles. Rings adorned almost every finger, and a matching gold necklace hung to his breastbone. The long fingernails were also red.

Strangest of all, his face was painted.

The effect was chilling. His face was stark white; his lips were deep scarlet. A bright red painted mask surrounded dark, piercing eyes. Angular and foreboding, its edges swept back sharply from the eyebrows and lower lids into the stark white field surrounding it. The haughty, prominent nose was severely aquiline, the jaw surprisingly strong. An inverted red triangle was painted beneath the lower lip.

His hair was dyed a bright red, and was pulled back tightly from the widow-peaked hairline to the rear of his skull.

Fastened to his belt was a device that looked like two small iron spheres, one black and the other white, attached to either end of an alternating black-and-white knotted line. The line was coiled up and hung neatly from a hook on his belt at the right hip. Sometimes, usually when he was deep in thought or watching something he found to be particularly stimulating, the Harlequin would reach down and grasp the twin spheres, then gently rub them together, producing a soft clinking sound. There was something unnerving and perverse about the action, and Twenty-Nine cringed whenever he saw it.

Taken as a whole, the Harlequin looked like a freak on view at a province fair rather than the leader of the fearsome taskmasters controlling the oarsmen. But whomever he turned his eyes on quickly learned the truth. This was no fair, and his intentions were sincerely deadly.

The Harlequin whispered something to the bleeder keeping time, and the monster stopped pounding on the block of wood. As they had been trained, the oarsmen immediately ceased their labors. The silence was deafening.

"Raise oars!" the bleeder shouted. Immediately all of the slaves pushed down on the handles of their oars, raising them up out of the restless Sea of Whispers.

"Ship oars!"

The slaves dutifully began to pull their oars into the ship and lay them down in the aisle separating the rows. Gasping, exhausted, they tried their best to remain quiet.

"We have arrived at the first of our destinations," Harlequin said to the bleeder. "I shall need forty of them." He placed his hands upon his hips. "You may have the honor of selecting them for me." His eyes hardened. "Make sure you take *Talis* only," he added.

"As you wish," the master bleeder answered. Rising from his seat, he began walking down the length of the bloody aisle, pointing to slaves seemingly at random.

A cold sense of dread shot through Twenty-Nine as the blanched creature stopped directly before his row. His broken, bloody hands were trembling. He held his breath and kept his head down and eyes lowered.

"You," came the simple command.

Twenty-Nine looked up. The bleeder was pointing to Twenty-Eight. Feeling guilty, Twenty-Nine let out a long breath.

Other bleeders began unchaining the chosen forty. They were forced to stand; many at first went crashing back down to the bloody deck, their legs too weak and cramped to hold their weight. Eventually all of them, including number Twenty-Eight, began shuffling stiffly toward the stairway where the bizarre Harlequin stood waiting. Twenty-Nine tried to give his seatmate a look of encouragement as he walked away, but Twenty-Eight wasn't looking at him. As the slaves began climbing the stairs, the Harlequin examined each of them closely.

Another of the chosen men was weeping openly. He was pulled out of the line. The Harlequin drew him closer.

"Do not fear," he said, almost compassionately. "You go to a far better place." With that he released the man to the bleeders, and they forced him up the stairway. "Choose two more." The bleeder did so, and the Harlequin followed the last of them up the stairs.

It was at that moment Twenty-Nine realized things had changed.

He could sense no movement: The ship was no longer rocking back and forth in the sea, as one would normally expect. There was no creaking of the ship's sides. There was, in fact, no sound whatsoever.

And then the temperature began to change.

It started to become cold—impossibly so. The slaves in their meager loincloths began to shiver; their breath turned to clouds of vapor.

Twenty-Nine bent over, trying to conserve body heat. Then he had an idea. Sliding as far into Twenty-Eight's vacant seat as his chains would allow, he peered across the shivering bodies of the other four slaves in his row, trying to get a better look out the small oar slit.

What he saw did not encourage him. The ship seemed to be in the grip of an impenetrable gray fog, the likes of which he had never seen. Growing up in the coastal city of Farpoint, he had seen fog banks roll in, to be sure. But this was decidedly different. As if it had a life of its own, the fog began to slither into the boat, tendrils reaching in through the oar slits and falling down the stairway from which the Harlequin had descended. It quickly filled the deck. As it increased in density the fog replaced the smell of the salt sea with a cleaner odor, such as one might inhale on land after a brisk, cold rain.

Then came the voices: many voices whispering as one.

"Pay us our bounty or we shall first take your ships, and then your bodies."

Almost immediately Twenty-Nine could hear desperate, tormented cries from above. Then everything became eerily silent again. The ship continued to sit motionless, but at last the fog still surrounding them began to thin, and he could see the terrified faces of his fellow oarsmen.

Craning his neck, Twenty-Nine saw that the sun shone brightly once more. Then the splashing noises began.

Instinctively, he started counting them. As he watched through the narrow slit, he could see the occasional bloodied body plunging into the sea. There were forty splashes in all.

Then he heard snuffling, snarling, grunting sounds. They reminded him of one time he and his father had been ocean fishing. Twenty-Nine had been young, and had made the mistake of accidentally tipping an entire bucket of bloody fish offal overboard. Sharks had swarmed.

As had happened then, eventually all went quiet. Straining to get the best possible view, Twenty-Nine could see the red, spreading stain of blood as it stretched across the surface of the impossibly placid sea.

Then the topside deck hatch opened noisily again, and the Harlequin reappeared. Blood dripped from the hem of his doublet. Gently wiping it off with an embroidered handkerchief, he descended the stairs and walked to the master bleeder.

"Fill the vacant seats with replacements from below," he said casually. "*Talis* only. And be quick about it."

Several bleeders moved aside the oars and unlocked the grates in the aisle floor, then descended into the darkness. Soon the replacements came up and out, furiously blinking their eyes in the brighter light of the oar deck. They were assigned to their stations and roughly chained into place.

Twenty-Nine tried to smile hopefully into the face of the frightened, confused slave now seated next to him.

Then he felt the great ship rock and heard the accompanying creaking of her sides. He heard the scurrying noises of the topside bleeders as they went about their labors above. Slowly, the *Defiant* began to make way.

The Harlequin looked to the pacemaster. "Battle speed," he ordered. "We have time to make up for."

"Very good," the pacemaster replied. But an unusually worried look had crowded in upon the corners of his face. "But before we commence— are we safe?" he asked. "Are we through it?"

"Oh, indeed," the Harlequin answered casually.

"And the human offerings?" the pacemaster inquired, taking up his twin sledges. "Their numbers sufficed?"

"Oh, yes," the Harlequin answered, walking to a comfortable-looking chair placed before the slaves. He smiled. "I think it safe to say they all disagreed with something that ate them!"

The bleeders broke into raucous laughter. Reclining into the softness of his upholstered chair, the Harlequin threw a leg up over one of its arms.

As the slaves slid their oars into the restless sea, the pacemaster resumed the beat, and the *Defiant* truly began to make way. Reaching down, the Harlequin took the twin iron spheres into his hand and began clinking them together, exactly matching the pacemaster's beat.

On the same ship, another slave lay shackled to the floor, one of hundreds packed cheek by jowl in the lower deck. His eyes were hazel. His straight, sandy hair was pulled back from his face into a tail that was secured with a bit of worn leather string and ran down almost to the center of his back. Before being chained down he had been branded with the word *R'talis,* as had many of the others imprisoned with him. He was strong and in the prime of his life, but in the darkness of this hold it didn't matter. Nothing did.

With no way to raise himself up, there was precious little escape from the constantly nauseating stench of human waste, not to mention the ever-present vomit from those who continually succumbed to seasickness. All the slaves marked *R'talis* were fed and hydrated enough to keep them alive. Still, his lips parched and his clothing soaked, his hollow stomach felt long past the point of hunger. He had no idea that his ship was part of a large flotilla of slavers. Nor did it matter. All he wanted was his freedom.

A few hours earlier, the ship had inexplicably stopped, then suddenly resumed course. He did not know why.

He could do nothing but listen to the moaning and sobbing of his fellow captives as the ship pitched sickeningly through the violent Sea of Whispers. Trying to keep from vomiting, he closed his eyes. His parched tongue reached out to touch the dark mole at the left-hand corner of his mouth.

Two

"Dried tulip of Rokhana," the old woman said in her raspy voice, pointing to the smoke-colored bottle. Never in her life had she seen so many rare, wonderful herbs collected in a single place. The sheer quantity and selection astounded her. She watched anxiously, as a greedy child might, while the man in the two-colored robe took the fragile bottle down from the shelf. He carefully placed it into the saddlebag alongside the others. The woman smiled, revealing the absence of several teeth.

"And sneezeweed!" she added gleefully, clapping her hands together. She pointed to another container. "We must have sneezeweed!" Again the man complied.

The small, thatched cottage they were plundering was in the Hartwick Woods, just east of the town of Florian's Glade, in the south of Eutracia. An ancient herbmistress lived there. At the moment she cowered within the glowing wizard's warp the man in the robe had conjured after breaking into her home.

"What about this one?" he asked casually. He held a small, fluted bottle of shredded blue leaves before the light of the fireplace.

"Bah!" the old woman grunted with a disparaging wave of her ancient hand. "What you now hold is a bottle of the ground flowers from a shammatrass tree. They bloom only once every twenty-three years, and must be picked within hours of their appearance, or they are no good. It is used for medicinal purposes only—not at all something that we need."

She smiled wickedly. "It is, however, exceedingly difficult to come by," she continued. "It probably took the herbmistress there her entire life to collect the meager amount you now hold in the palm of your hand." Turning, she cast a jealous eye to the woman trapped behind the azure bars of the cage.

"Really?" the man asked nastily. "How interesting." With that he removed the cork and cast the bottle's contents into the fire. The flames roared colorfully for a moment before finally settling down again. The herbmistress cried aloud and slumped to the floor.

Smiling, the man in the two-colored robe looked over at her. "After I have finished here, I will visit the lead wizard," he said softly. "I will gladly give him your regards." He began to laugh, but his laugh quickly decayed into an all-consuming cough.

Hacking relentlessly, he placed a cloth before his mouth. When he took it away, it was covered with blood that was moving across the cloth, tracing his endowed blood signature. His lips twisting angrily, he stuffed the rag back into his robes. He stood there quietly for a moment, trying to reclaim his breathing.

"Are you sure there is nothing in this place that would help me?" he whispered to the crone as she went about selecting more of the precious bottles.

At last she stopped her search and turned her green eyes to him. "As I have told you before, Krassus, there is nothing of this world that can help you now. As you yourself have said, your illness is of the craft. What you have swirling inside was given to you by your previous master, the dead son of the Chosen One. What shall be shall be." She turned her attention back to the shelves. "The items we take today should, however, help me locate the scroll you seek. And hopefully before it is too late," she added softly.

Hours after they had gone, the wizard's warp finally dissolved, leaving the crying herbmistress free to face the task of cleaning up her smashed, looted home.

Three

"Dreng!" the wizard Faegan shouted happily from his chair on wheels. "That's another two hundred points!" Using a feathered quill, he made an exaggerated show of noting the tally down on a small pad. Smiling coyly, he sat back and stroked Nicodemus, his blue cat, as he waited for the inevitable outburst from the lead wizard. It didn't take long.

"Once again I say you're cheating! You must be!" Wigg shouted back. His jaw stuck out like the prow of a ship. "You're using the craft! I don't know how you're managing it, but I'll find out! No one gets a full dreng on only two hands! Not even you!"

Wigg, onetime lead wizard of the Directorate, was becoming more furious by the minute. His craggy face was red, and he glared at Faegan with the mighty, all-consuming surety of his convictions.

Grabbing up the cards to shuffle them and deal out another hand, Faegan only smiled.

Tristan of the House of Galland, prince of Eutracia, sat at the rectangular, upholstered gaming table listening to the two ancient wizards bicker. It had been this way for the better part of an hour. He normally found it comic when they were at each other's throats, usually over something trivial. Today it was starting to annoy him.

Six of them were playing the card game dreng, and the score was tied. Wigg captained the team consisting of himself, his daughter Celeste, and Tristan. The team sitting across from them was made up of Faegan, Geldon the hunchbacked dwarf, and Princess Shailiha, Tristan's twin sister. Morganna, Shailiha's baby, sat on the carpet, batting at some scattered toys.

At first Wigg had not wanted to play, arguing, as usual, that there were far more important matters to attend to. In truth he had probably been right. But after some stiff cajoling by Shailiha and what Tristan thought to be comic but shameless outright begging by Celeste, the lead wizard had finally given in.

These two strong-willed women had become Wigg's and Faegan's soft spots, and everyone in the palace knew it. There was in fact very little in this world that the two women could not get either of the wizards to do, especially if they both asked at once—a strategy the women had been quick to learn, and to capitalize upon.

Tristan cast an eye across the table toward his sister, and gave her a slight smile. Shailiha smiled back, her long blond hair and hazel eyes as lovely as ever. She then looked at Wigg. The lead wizard's face was red, and a vein had begun throbbing in his right temple. Suddenly unsure about the relative wisdom of purposely engaging the two irascible wizards in a competition, she looked back over at her twin brother.

Tristan ran a hand impatiently through his dark hair. He stretched back in his chair, uncoiling his long legs, and glanced at the floor, where he had placed his dreggan—the nasty curved sword he had taken from one of his deadliest enemies—and the quiver of throwing knives that he usually wore across the back of his right shoulder. Despite the fact that the palace was relatively secure, he always made it a point to never be far from his weapons. Life had been far too dangerous of late.

The room in which they were playing was sumptuous—one of those that had been recently refurbished by the Minions of Day and Night, the winged army Tristan commanded. The marble of the floor and walls was of the palest gray, shot through with streaks of indigo. A huge oil chandelier hung in the center of the ceiling, giving off a soft, comforting glow.

It was nearly dinnertime, and Tristan was hungry. Despite the distance from this game room to the palace kitchens, he had almost convinced himself he could smell the aroma of the warm, inviting food that would soon be served by the gnome wives. He sighed. A glass of wine would be especially welcome.

Gazing over at the open balcony window, he saw the sun setting down into the western horizon. It had been four months since he had witnessed the death of his son Nicholas and the destruction of the Gates of Dawn. Nicholas had planned to use the gates to rend open the heavens, allowing the return of the Heretics of the Guild, masters of the Vagaries who would then use the dark side of the craft to rule forever. An anomaly in Nicholas' blood had killed him just before he had been able to accomplish this feat. At that point, the Gates had collapsed and the Heretics had once again been confined to the heavens.

As Tristan had predicted, the recent Season of Crystal had been unusually harsh, with heavy snowfall and ice-cold winds. But now the Season of New Life—his personal favorite—was coming into full bloom. Flower buds and green grass were springing up, and the air was full of the many wonderful scents that only nature's rebirth could provide. The last few days had been wonderfully warm. So warm, in fact, that today they had been able to leave the balcony doors open for the first time.

A shout from Faegan brought the prince's attention back to the gaming table. Faegan, the impish, three-hundred-year-old rogue wizard, protector of the area of Eutracia known as Shadowood, was the keeper of many secrets. He possessed the very rare power of Consummate Recollection, which allowed him to recall instantly anything he had ever seen, read, or heard. He was also the only living person to have completely read the first two volumes of the Tome, the great book of the craft. His gray-black hair, carelessly parted down the center, fell almost to his shoulders. Over his loose-fitting black robe he wore the Paragon, the bloodred jewel that helped sustain the craft of magic. Amazing gray-green eyes set in an intense, commanding face only hinted at the awesome power lying behind them.

He was flanked by Geldon and Celeste. Loyal, intelligent, and kind, Geldon had contributed mightily to their survival over the recent past. A slave of the sorceresses for nearly three centuries, he had been instrumental in defeating the Coven and helping to destroy Nicholas' Gates of Dawn.

For the thousandth time, Tristan turned his dark eyes toward Celeste.

Over three hundred years old, protected by time enchantments that kept her forever youthful, she was the long-lost daughter of Wigg and the first mistress of the recently defeated Coven of sorceresses, Failee. Celeste had finally discovered her true identity by bravely escaping Ragnar, the mutated blood stalker who had endowed her with time enchantments and kept her as his slave in the Caves of the Paragon for more than three centuries. She was originally to have been Failee's fifth sorceress; her blood quality was supposedly second only to that of Tristan and Shailiha, the Chosen Ones of prophecy.

Dark red hair parted on one side fell down to Celeste's shoulders. Her sapphire eyes showed both intelligence and compassion. The hint of a cleft in her chin gave her the appearance of personal strength, even though her talents and confidence in her new world above ground were still developing. Whenever Tristan was near her he could smell a hint of myrrh, and it had been her scented, embroidered handkerchief that he had carried into battle to defeat his son Nicholas.

"I still say you're cheating!" Wigg said to Faegan, distracting Tristan.

"No, I'm not." Faegan sniffed. "I don't need to, especially considering the amateurish way you're laying down your cards."

With a smile, he winked at Tristan, then levitated his cards in a straight line, just above the surface of the table.

Wigg shook his head angrily, laying down another card. "*Must* you show off that way?" he huffed. The knight card he had just played would trump Faegan's page, and the lead wizard knew it. Thinking he finally had Faegan's team on the run, he smiled wickedly.

Played with two-sided cards, dreng was a notoriously difficult game to learn, and an even more difficult game to play with any degree of expertise. Played in teams, it could easily develop many unexpected twists and turns—something that Wigg was being increasingly reminded of.

"I'm sorry, Lead Wizard, but that simply will not do," Shailiha said with mock compassion, placing a card down on top of Wigg's. "Dreng!" she said happily, easing herself back into her chair. Faegan's team had easily taken the hand.

Wigg's first reaction was to turn angrily around and search for Caprice, Shailiha's giant butterfly. The violet-and-yellow flier of the fields was never far from her mistress; sure enough she was perched quietly on a bookcase behind Shailiha, calmly opening and closing her wings. It was obvious that the flier could not have been reading Wigg's cards, silently informing the princess via the mental bond they possessed. Still unable to find evidence of Faegan's cheating, the frustrated lead wizard scowled menacingly.

Tristan was an excellent dreng player, but his interest was quickly waning. Hopefully Shawna the Short would arrive soon, announcing in that no-nonsense way of hers that dinner was served.

"Admit it!" Wigg insisted.

One corner of his mouth coming up, Tristan looked over at the lead wizard's craggy profile. At the back of Wigg's neck, the gray hair was pulled into a short braid. His "wizard's tail" had been sadistically cut away by the first mistress of the Coven during her vicious torture of him, the first time he and Tristan had visited Parthalon. Tristan had long suspected that Wigg would grow it back out of respect for the members of the Directorate, all of whom had perished at the sorceresses' hands, and he had been right.

"How do you know Faegan is cheating, Father?" Celeste asked, interrupting the prince's thoughts. He caught her giving a secret wink across the table to Shailiha. "Just what is it you think he is doing?"

"He is no doubt employing the craft to deal invisibly from the bottom of the deck." Wigg sniffed, narrowing his eyes as Faegan again took up the cards.

Faegan dealt the cards out once more. He then looked briefly at both sides of his cards, arranged them to his liking, and cast his sharp eyes over at Wigg's hand. Then he smiled impishly.

"If I wanted to change the nature of your cards, I wouldn't choose such a banal, pedestrian method of doing it," he said. "Instead, I would probably do something more inventive. Something like this . . ."

He closed his eyes, and a soft, azure glow began to surround Wigg's cards. In a matter of mere moments, all of the courtly characters displayed upon them, dressed in their customary finery, had been drastically altered.

They were now quite naked, leaving very little to the imagination.

Everyone around the table broke into raucous laughter—except for Wigg.

"This is the last straw!" the lead wizard shouted, tossing his useless cards to the table. "I think it's high time I—"

Then, quite suddenly, Wigg stopped talking. At first Tristan thought it was out of pure frustration. But then the lead wizard stiffened and rose up a bit in his chair. Raising one hand to silence the table, he tilted his head.

The prince glanced over at Faegan, to see a concerned look darkening his face, as well. Faegan looked at Wigg and nodded. Tristan had seen this signal pass between the two wizards before, and it usually meant only one thing: They had sensed the presence of endowed blood—unfamiliar endowed blood.

Reaching down to the floor for his dreggan, Tristan slid the blade from its scabbard.

A glow was forming.

In one of the far corners of the room, where the ceiling formed a joint with two connecting walls, the familiar azure glow of the craft was coalescing. When it took up the entire corner, its outline started to sharpen.

Standing slowly, Tristan raised his sword. Faegan, his back to the glow, turned his chair to see whatever it was. Finally everyone in the room was gazing on the anomaly.

The image continued to form hauntingly. Finally, the azure glow faded away and the shape became clear.

A man hung there like a spider, face to the card players, the fingertips and balls of his feet touching the ceiling and walls behind him.

Suddenly he spread his arms wide and launched himself from the wall, landing upright in the exact center of the table. Playing cards went flying high into the air. Shailiha and Celeste recoiled back into their chairs.

Tristan didn't hesitate. He swung the dreggan for all he was worth, sending its razor-sharp edge whistling through the air in an attempt to cut the intruder's legs off at the knees.

The figure before them only laughed and jumped into the air, easily avoiding Tristan's blade.

Both Wigg and Faegan had raised their arms to employ the craft, but the man standing before them was too fast. Another glow had already begun to form, engulfing the entire table and everyone around it. Tristan tried to lunge at the intruder—only to discover that he was frozen in place. All he could move was his head. He could hear, and he somehow felt sure that he still commanded the power of speech. But he could not move a muscle from his neck down. A glance at the others told him that they, too, were caught in the paralyzing warp. Tristan wondered frantically. He could not fathom how the man had so silently, invisibly breached the security of the palace, evading the hundreds of Minion warriors who were camped outside.

The intruder was tall and gaunt, with a face to match. Straight, stringy locks of pure white hair fell down from the crown of the man's skull. It was somewhat longer than shoulder length, except for the ragged bangs that covered most of his forehead. But despite the white hair, his age did not seem advanced. Studying the face, Tristan guessed the man to be no more than forty-five Seasons of New Life.

His skin was pale, almost gray. Dark brows arched over piercing eyes; the cheekbones were high and elegant. The nose was large, and aquiline. Thin lips formed the straight slash that was his mouth. The cheeks were deeply creased and hollow; the jaw was strong. Taken as a whole the face conveyed tightly controlled intelligence and power.

The man was dressed in a full-length robe of two colors, divided down the center. The left-hand side was gray, the color once worn by the Directorate of Wizards and still worn by Wigg. The right-hand side was the dark blue worn by the Brotherhood of Consuls.

Unexpectedly, the man began to cough.

His hacking began softly, but quickly built in intensity. He finally produced a rag from his robes and covered his mouth briefly. It came away bloody. The sudden sign of illness in the same man who had just executed such clever acrobatics and the lightning-swift construction of a powerful wizard's warp seemed contradictory indeed.

"Forgive me, Wigg," the man said sarcastically once his coughing had subsided. Looking down at the lead wizard, he placed his hands into the opposite sleeves of his robe. "My entrance was unexpected, I know.

But given the numbers of Minion warriors camped outside, it seemed the only sensible way. I may be ill, but I have no desire to die sooner than necessary. And what I have come to say will not take long." His voice was controlled and deep.

Wigg gazed at him in amazement. Working his jaw, he found he was being allowed to speak.

"Krassus," he whispered. "So you live." He narrowed his eyes, taking in the man's strange, two-colored robe. "And you still wear the robe of first alternate. Can we therefore assume it is you we now have to thank for so many of our problems?"

Tristan could move his eyes just enough to look over at Faegan. It was clear that the ancient crippled wizard did not know this man.

"That is correct," Krassus said. "But our relationship does not have to be adversarial. I have, in fact, come to offer you a truce. That part of it will depend entirely on you, Lead Wizard. I have come for information, and I intend to have it."

"Who are you?" Faegan broke in. "What do you want?"

Krassus looked toward the voice, and a brief smile of recognition crawled across his face.

"Faegan," he said softly, almost reverently, as if he could not believe his eyes. "It *must* be! The recently departed Nicholas told me you had returned to Tammerland. Until then, I had thought you had passed from flesh and blood into myth. Your power and knowledge are legendary. But forgive me, for you and I have never been properly introduced. I am the consul Krassus. I was at one time both first alternate to the dearly departed Directorate of Wizards and the servant of Nicholas, son of the Chosen One. It is indeed an honor to finally meet you."

Krassus looked down at Tristan and smiled. "And the Chosen One himself is also in attendance." He then admired the sword Tristan still held. "He truly is as impulsive as they say, isn't he?"

Looking to Shailiha, he added, "We are honored by the presence of the princess, as well. How nice." His gaze flicked briefly over Geldon, then settled on Celeste.

"And who is it we have here?" he asked. "Had I ever met a woman as beautiful as this, I would surely have remembered."

Celeste did not respond, but her expression hardened almost imperceptibly.

"What do you want?" Wigg demanded again, purposely interrupting Krassus' disturbing examination of his daughter. "From what you say, I take it you are the new leader of the supposedly rebellious brotherhood?"

"Indeed I am," Krassus answered. "But as I said earlier, I am willing to put the recent hostilities behind us and start over. I will allow everyone in this room to live, and I have already ordered the consuls to remove the bounty on Tristan. I will even bring the remaining consuls back into the fold, so to speak. All I ask in return is unencumbered leadership of the consuls—and some information. If you refuse, you will make me your enemy for life. The Chosen One's son may be dead, but certain aspects of his cause are not. True, the number of consuls had been radically reduced, but it should be enough."

"Enough for what?" Faegan asked.

Krassus smiled. "You see," he went on, "I'm afraid the death of Nicholas and the destruction of the Gates are only the beginning of your problems. Unknown to you, the son of the Chosen One had already placed other plans into motion—plans designed to pave the way for the Heretics to ensure that the Vagaries will rule as the sole arm of the craft. With Nicholas gone, this sacred duty falls to me. I do not intend to release the Heretics from the heavens, as Nicholas tried to do. As you have no doubt discerned, I am fatally ill. Thus, I do not have the time for such endeavors, much less the training or quality of blood required. No—the Forestallments imbued into my blood by my late master are not all-powerful, as his were, but they provide me with ample skills to finish the more earthly aspects of his plan. All I need is the proper information. If you resist me, before you perish you shall learn there remain other methods of making sure the Vagaries solely rule the craft."

Krassus lowered his eyes and focused them menacingly on the lead wizard. "You can either be a willing partner in what I do, or you and your little group here will die. It is no more complicated than that."

"Surely you must realize that if your goal is to promulgate the Vagaries, I will never help you," Wigg answered adamantly. "Nor will Faegan. Every person in this room would gladly give his or her life to make sure the Vagaries never rule the land."

"I have no need to ask Faegan the first of my questions," Krassus responded calmly. "Only the second. Faegan may be the greatest keeper of knowledge, but you, Lead Wizard, are the greatest keeper of secrets, and always have been. I know you have the information I seek, because I now travel with a partial adept who is a blaze-gazer as well as an herbmistress. And she is never wrong."

Wigg suddenly appeared as if his entire world had just collapsed. But his look of defeat quickly turned to one of anger.

"If you have harmed her, I will kill you," he snarled. "Slowly."

Tristan had no idea who they were talking about, but Wigg was clearly incensed.

"Oh no, my friend," Krassus responded almost kindly. "It is not *she* with whom I travel, but another. I did, however, visit the home of the one you refer to, to collect a few things my partial adept shall eventually need. You might want to go and see your old friend after I depart. I left her in a rather bad way."

Krassus bent over slightly, placing his face closer to the lead wizard's. "Now then," he said softly. "For the first of my two questions: Where is Wulfgar?"

Wigg's face went completely white. His eyes widened briefly with amazement, then narrowed again in a poor attempt to disguise his shock. He then glanced at the questioning faces of Tristan and Shailiha, and his heart was heavy with the realization that he might be forced now to break yet another of his promises to their parents.

"I don't know who you're talking about," he answered adamantly.

"That's not good enough," Krassus whispered. His fist came around like lightning, smashing into the side of Wigg's face. Tristan had never seen such superhuman speed. The lead wizard reeled drunkenly for a moment, a trail of blood snaking its way down his chin, curlicuing into his blood signature as it went. Celeste cried out for her father, and tears welled in her eyes.

Slowly collecting himself, Wigg looked through half-closed eyes at the consul. Somehow, he smiled.

"Is that the best you can do?" he asked drunkenly. "Even the first mistress of the Coven struck me harder."

"As I told you, I'm ill," Krassus answered sarcastically. His fist came around again, smashing into the point of Wigg's chin and driving the wizard's head into the back of his chair.

"Stop it, you bastard!" Tristan screamed. He tried again to move his sword arm, but it was no good. Looking for a glimmer of hope, he turned his eyes to Faegan. But all the great wizard could do was shake his head back and forth angrily.

"And the two Scrolls of the Ancients," Krassus went on blithely. "I suppose you know nothing of them, either? Actually I need only find one. The other, the Scroll of the Vagaries, is already in my possession." A nasty grin spead slowly across his face.

"I have no idea what you're babbling about," Wigg answered thickly. "Perhaps all of your time with Nicholas has . . . addled your brain . . . So you now apparently detest the Vigors." Exhausted from his beating, he ran out of breath, and his chin slumped forward to his chest.

Krassus bent over Faegan. "And you, cripple," he said insultingly. "I suppose you also know nothing of either Wulfgar or the scrolls?"

Summoning up all of the saliva he could muster, Faegan spat it at the hem of Krassus' robe. "That is the only answer I shall ever have for you," he whispered venomously. "Go find whatever it is you're looking for by yourself! Assuming, of course, you're intelligent enough to do so."

Straightening, Krassus smiled. "The famous wizards, recalcitrant to the end!" His laugh turned into a single, short, diseased cough. "Very well, then. It seems I shall have to find out for myself whether the two of you are lying."

He closed his eyes, and a soft glow began to surround the wizards' chairs, slowly increasing in intensity. Suddenly Wigg's and Faegan's heads simultaneously snapped back. Their eyes were wide open, but seemed to observe nothing. Watching, Tristan realized that Krassus had succeeded in entering at least a portion of their minds—testing them just as they had once tested Geldon, before allowing Tristan to go to Parthalon to rescue Shailiha from the Coven. They desperately fought the intrusion by the consul. Sweat broke out on each of the three struggling faces as Wigg and Faegan fought to keep from having their minds violated, and Krassus tried desperately to enter. After several long, agonizing moments, the glow faded away, and the consul opened his eyes. Wigg and Faegan were breathing heavily in total exhaustion.

"So," Krassus said softly, half to himself. "It seems Wigg still does not know the location of Wulfgar, after all. Such a pity. Now I must find him the hard way. But that's why I travel with a partial adept, isn't it?"

He turned to Faegan. "Such a strong mind," he said in a conversational tone. "I have never experienced its like. You were partially successful in blocking my intrusion, weren't you? No matter. Although you are aware of scant references to the scrolls, I can tell you have no real knowledge of either where they may be, or of their vast importance. And you, unlike the lead wizard, have absolutely no idea who Wulfgar is."

Krassus made a sarcastic, clucking sound with his tongue. "Don't the two of you know that it isn't polite to keep secrets from each other? Even the Chosen Ones do not know of Wulfgar! How deliciously ironic!"

Wigg summoned the strength to look up at Krassus. His face was already swelling. "But why?" he asked, still sounding drunk. "Why do you turn your back on your teachings . . . follow the darkness of the Vagaries? And how is it that you have defeated the death enchantments put on all the consuls? They should have killed you the first time you attempted to practice the Vagaries." The battered lead wizard paused to catch his breath. "A prospect that I must say would no longer disappoint me," he added softly.

"Ah, so you wish to make a guessing game of it, do you?" Krassus asked nastily. "Very well then. Let's play!"

He leaned over again and placed his mouth close to Wigg's ear. "Tell me, Lead Wizard. Each time a creature of the Vagaries or one of the Coven died, do you *really* know why there were such strange atmospheric disturbances? The wind howling until you thought your ears might burst, and lightning across the sky so bright that night seems as day? You always taught us that it was simply to mark their passing into the Afterlife. Not true! And do you know why I seek Wulfgar, the lost one? Again, the answer is no. It seems that even the lead wizard of the not-dearly-departed Directorate still has a great deal to learn about the true workings of your nation, and your craft.

"Because you refused to help me, we are now enemies," he continued brazenly. "I know I do not possess the strength to destroy both of you here today at the same time. Therefore I am forced to wait. But your individual times will come, I promise you. And one last thing: Should any of you doubt the seriousness of my words, I suggest you take a little journey to Farpoint, three days from now. What you shall witness there is of Nicholas' planning and my execution, and should be of great interest to you."

Krassus paused for a moment, obviously relishing his temporary dominion over them all. "Still so much for you to learn, Wigg. And so little time for either of us to accomplish our ends. You, because part of the plans Nicholas imagined still remains in motion. And I, because I will soon perish. My duties done, I will then gladly go to the Heretics— the reward promised to me by the son of the Chosen One."

Smiling, he stretched out his arms. "And now I am forced to bid you all farewell," he said quietly. "Until next time."

The azure glow of the craft began to form again. Amazed, Tristan watched as the consul melted away into nothingness, the glow disappearing with him. He could hear the sound of the intruder's boot heels as they defiantly marched across the gaming table and jumped to the floor. Then, as if completely of their own accord, the balcony doors swung wide open, closing again after a brief pause.

No one had to tell the prince that Krassus had just escaped the palace as easily as he had entered.

The warps surrounding them disappeared, Wigg fell unconscious from his chair, landing hard on the cold marble floor.

CHAPTER

Four

She had lain there on the stone floor of her cottage for some time, sobbing softly. The cruel man in the two-colored robe and his equally cruel companion had departed, and slowly the wizard's cage surrounding her had dissolved. Her home was a wreck of smashed and battered vials, jars, bottles—even furniture was broken—and she knew it would take many days to repair the damage. But the most difficult task would be replacing the herbs, roots, blossoms, and seeds they had stolen. Some represented the work of more than three centuries, now vanished in a single day. The intruders had known exactly what to take, and her loss was unimaginable.

But because she was the recipient of time enchantments, time was the one thing on her side.

Abbey of the House of Lindstrom slowly came to her feet. After brushing off her burgundy peasant's dress, she stoked the hearth and decided first to prepare herself a cup of nerveweed tea.

Looking to her shelves, she hoped it would still be there. Then she saw it and let out a sigh of relief. The herb had long been known for its calming effects, and she could use a good dose of it just now.

After placing the water into the pot and hanging it over the gathering fire, she righted the table and chairs and sat, despondently, before the hearth. Soon the bone-soaking warmth and sooty smell of the flames started to give her some small measure of comfort. She looked down at her hands and saw that they were still shaking. Closing her eyes for a moment, she tried to fathom the meaning of what had happened here today.

Why would anyone do such a thing? she wondered. *We who possessed these esoteric arts were so few, even before the Sorceresses' War. And now, three centuries later, our numbers have surely dwindled even farther due to the ban by the Directorate. I should have recognized the woman, but I didn't.*

The whistling teakettle suddenly interrupted her thoughts. Removing it from the flames, she set it on the table. Then she filled a tea basket with dried nerveweed leaves and lowered them into the kettle to steep.

Something glinted on the floor, and, bending down, she identified it as a rather large shard of broken mirror. She picked it up and gazed into it. The face reflected back to her was awash with great sadness, and even greater confusion.

Although her dark hair was streaked with gray, she remained a very handsome woman. Gray eyes looked back at her with intelligence, and the dark eyebrows arched highly, almost seductively over them. Her jaw was strong yet feminine; her cheeks were still blessed with the rosy bloom of her long-faded youth. Sighing, she carefully put down the mirror.

Interesting, she thought for the thousandth time. The one man on earth she still cared for was also the one who had tried to force her into abandoning her art. She had thought of him so many times over the centuries, even employing her art to regard him from time to time. Despite his recent travails, she knew he was well. Many were the times she had been tempted to go to him, to offer her forgiveness. But that would have caused him nothing but more trouble. It was better, she supposed, to simply live with the memories of those long-ago days than to go chasing after what could never be.

She poured herself a cup of the dark, harsh tea and drank, relishing its warmth as it went down. The nerveweed would soon take hold, and she would then begin the business of straightening up her house. Looking around the thatched cottage, her mind went back to the time she had first come here. She had been alone, ashamed, and angry.

That had been more than three centuries ago. But after the exile of the Coven to the Sea of Whispers, the newly formed Directorate of Wizards had banned all partial adepts—both male and female—from practicing their arts. Hurt and confused, they had been ordered to scatter, no two being allowed to go in the same direction. And so she had finally chosen this place to be alone, and to carry on in secret. But not before one of the wizards—the one who still had a place in her heart—had secretly granted her the time enchantments, tearfully wishing her well.

Abbey's heart skipped a beat. *My gazing flame!* she thought anxiously. *Is it still burning, or did they destroy that, too?*

She put her teacup down and bolted from the cottage.

Outside, she hiked up her skirt and began running as fast as she could through the woods. Even though the sun had set, the path before her shone clearly by the light of the three red Eutracian moons.

With huge relief, she saw that the smooth, flat rock was still in place. Chest heaving, she stood before it. She breathed deeply to calm herself, and closed her eyes. Silently, slowly, the rock began to slide to one side across the dewy grass. Opening her eyes, she held her breath.

Almost immediately a high, golden plume of flame erupted, casting a magnificent light into the dark of the night. Letting out a great sigh, she stood there silently for a moment, blessing her good fortune.

The single, golden flame coming from the earth was approximately one meter wide, and three meters tall. It was flat and broad. The glade surrounding it had long ago been cleared of all trees and shrubs, and Abbey lovingly saw to it that it remained that way.

Abbey of the House of Lindstrom was many things, but first and foremost she was a blaze-gazer.

Reaching into one of the pockets of her dress, she produced a very small bottle. Its contents were so rare and precious that she always carried it on her person, no matter the circumstances. Thankfully, that very habit had kept it safe from the intruders.

But they had known exactly what to take, and her remaining supply of herbs needed to sustain the flame had gone with them. What was contained in her locket would provide just enough for one more viewing, and no more. When she finished, her flame would slowly die, because she would have no more herbs to replenish it. Even so, she could think of no better time than now to use them up. After what the man in the two-colored robe had told her about the lead wizard, she simply had to know.

Opening the top, she emptied the bottle into the palm of her hand. Carefully, she walked closer to the roaring fire.

Raising one arm, she commanded the flame to split into two branches, one far larger than the other. As she curled the index finger of her outstretched hand, the smaller of the branches obediently approached her. As always, the searing heat of the gazer's flame threatened to scorch her face and dress.

Quickly, she pointed her hand to the right. The flame flattened out and began to flow horizontally. Its edges licked dangerously close to her outstretched hand. With great discipline she dropped the herbs into the waiting flame.

The effect was immediate.

The two branches suddenly rejoined and shot back up toward the sky. Abbey backed away from the searing heat. As she did, she reached for the pendant she wore around her neck. Opening it, she withdrew a short braid of brown hair and held it high. Then she looked back at the flame.

Midway up the body of the flame, a rectangular, azure window began to form. Closing her eyes, she concentrated intently. Opening them again, she gazed deeply into the chasm surrounded by the roaring flame.

Her eyes widened. She was not at all pleased with what she saw.

CHAPTER

Five

Faegan sat in his chair by Wigg's bed, eyes closed, a concerned frown on his face. His ancient hand gently covered the lead wizard's forehead. Tristan, Shailiha, and Celeste stood behind him, equally concerned. Caprice perched on Shailiha's arm, slowly opening and closing her wings. Morganna, Shailiha's baby daughter, had been given over to the care of one of the gnome wives.

"Will he be all right?" Celeste asked nervously.

When the wizard didn't answer, Tristan touched Celeste on the arm. When she looked at him, he placed an index finger to his lips, telling her to remain quiet. From prior experience the prince knew that whatever Faegan was doing, he would be far more effective if silence reigned. Understanding, Celeste nodded.

Faegan remained that way for some time, his only movement the occasional touch of his palm on a different area of Wigg's skull. After what seemed an eternity, he removed his hand and opened his eyes.

"He has been through a great deal," the old wizard said sadly. "The endowed physical blows were bad enough. When the spell attacking his mind was enacted, he fought it with everything he had. The mental and physical beating together proved more than Wigg could bear, and he went unconscious, his mind shutting down as a protective mechanism. In many respects, it was probably for the best."

Tristan looked down at his friend and mentor of so many years. His hands balled into fists, and his knuckles went white with anger at the one called Krassus. So many questions had been purposely, cruelly left unanswered by the consul. But one thing was clearly certain: The lead wizard alone held the answers to many of them.

"How bad is it?" Tristan asked anxiously.

"He will recover," Faegan said with certainty. "But it may take several days for him to regain his strength completely."

At that, he replaced his hand on Wigg's forehead, and the room went silent. Faegan closed his eyes. After a time Wigg's lids began to flutter; then his eyes slowly opened.

Opening his own eyes, Faegan peered down at Wigg. He then turned to Tristan and smiled.

"I still say you cheat at cards," Wigg said weakly, frowning up into Faegan's face.

Faegan smiled. "I never actually denied it," he answered softly. "Someday I'll show you how it is done."

Bending over, Celeste hugged her father and gave him a kiss. "I was so worried," she whispered. "I don't know what I'd do without you."

"Do you think you are strong enough to answer a few questions?" Faegan asked, his usual curiosity returning. "There is much for us to discuss."

Wigg nodded. Then, quite unexpectedly, he began to cry.

Taken aback, Tristan realized that there was much more to Krassus' visit than he had imagined.

"I can see that this is difficult for you, old friend," Faegan began with uncharacteristic tact. "But the question simply must be asked." He paused for a moment, then inquired, abruptly, "Who is Wulfgar?"

Gathering his resolve, Wigg looked at Tristan and Shailiha. He lowered his eyes for a moment, then slowly raised them again.

"Wulfgar is your lost half brother," he whispered to them.

Tristan's eyes went wide, his jaw slack. Shailiha gasped. Even the usually unflappable Faegan was taken by surprise.

It was a moment before anyone spoke. Then Faegan broke the silence.

"You said *half* brother," he murmured. "Do you mean to say—"

"That's right," the lead wizard interrupted, wanting to approach it in a gentler way than the more analytical Faegan might. "Wulfgar is illegitimate," he continued. "He is Morganna's first child, four years older than the Chosen Ones, and also of very highly endowed blood. Wulfgar's father was named Eric. Upon discovering Morganna was with child, Eric refused to marry her. He disappeared, leaving her heartbroken. Morganna gave the baby up for adoption at one of the wizards' orphanages scattered throughout the realm.

"Despite the deep secret Morganna always carried, Nicholas loved his queen unconditionally," he finally added. "They were two of the most amazing people it has ever been my pleasure to know."

Tristan looked at Shailiha. As if touching his sister could somehow ease their mutual shock, he took her hand. "But why would Mother give her baby up?" he finally asked, his voice cracking.

The lead wizard sighed. "Because she heard voices," he said quietly. "Voices telling her to destroy the child before it came to term."

"Do you mean to tell us that our mother was mad?" Tristan whispered.

"No," Wigg answered adamantly. "And I wish to make that point abundantly clear. But at the time, you can understand how she might have believed herself to be. The voices grew even stronger after the birth, this time telling Morganna that she must kill her child."

"But apparently she could not bring herself to do it," Faegan said.

"No," Wigg said. "Her heart wouldn't let her. She could neither destroy her unborn child nor murder her baby. But Morganna was afraid that the voices in her head might eventually make her even more deranged, even though such was never actually the case. It was her fear of this unexplained madness that finally drove her to give up her child, rather than risk harming him because of what she perceived to be her decaying mental state."

He paused, then looked at the prince and princess. "All of this occurred before Morganna met Nicholas, the common smith who eventually became king of Eutracia, and Tristan and Shailiha's father.

"The Directorate had no idea of any of this when Nicholas, after we selected him to be king, took Morganna for his bride. But later that year, Morganna and Nicholas came to me, telling me her secret. A simple check of Wulfgar's signature in the Hall of Blood Records confirmed their tale. Aside from the head matron of the orphanage, only Morganna, Nicholas, the queen's parents, and I were aware of this. I was never to reveal this secret, at least until Wulfgar could be found. We have been searching for him ever since. This was yet another of the tasks of the consuls of the Redoubt, and another of the reasons they were taught how to examine blood signatures. As for Wulfgar, presumably he has no inkling of who he really is." Wigg paused for a moment, letting his words sink in. "And, despite our best efforts, I still have no idea where he may be." He looked down at his gnarled hands.

"And what would have become of Wulfgar if he had been found?" Shailiha asked anxiously.

"We would have been forced to train him in the craft, even before Tristan," Wigg whispered. "If his training went poorly, it was agreed that other arrangements would be made."

The blood rushed from Tristan's face. He moved his chair closer to the lead wizard.

"But that contradicts everything you have always told me," he said, thoroughly confused. "It was always my understanding that I was to be trained first, followed by Shailiha, should I die or fail in my eventual attempt to join the two sides of the craft. The Tome says so."

"The Tome says a great many things," Faegan interrupted, "and at first glance much of it can seem highly contradictory." Sighing, he shook his head. "I suggest we allow the lead wizard to continue."

"We came to believe that the voices speaking to Morganna were those of the Ones Who Came Before," Wigg went on. "We knew that the Ones were the original practitioners of the Vigors—the benevolent side of the craft. Therefore, their demand that she destroy this child, we reasoned, could only be of the greatest importance. They had no direct way to force her, but their constant beseeching was literally starting to drive your mother insane. Once we ordered the consuls to find Wulfgar, the voices blessedly stopped, never to return."

"But what about the Tome?" Tristan pressed. "It says I am to be trained first, does it not?"

"Correct," Faegan answered. "But unless I miss my guess, the lead wizard was about to remind us of the fact that the Tome was written long before the birth of Wulfgar. For reasons we still do not understand, the Ones knew of the eventual coming of you and your sister, and which parents would give birth to you. But Wulfgar's birth was apparently an unexpected surprise, even for the Ones." He rubbed his brow, thinking.

"And your mother told us that no azure glow appeared at Wulfgar's birth, as it did when you and your sister were born," Wigg added. "Wulfgar was born of a different father. We know from that Tome that Nicholas and Morganna were destined to find each other, and only from that union would the Chosen Ones be brought forth. And there is another reason why Wulfgar could never be one of the Chosen Ones." He paused, then took a deep breath and let it out slowly before resuming.

"You see, Wulfgar's blood signature is left-leaning."

Even more confused, Tristan, Shailiha, and Celeste looked to Faegan for the answer. But the crippled wizard's mouth hung open with astonishment—a rare sight indeed.

"Do you mean to say—"

"Yes," Wigg said.

Speechless, Faegan leaned back his chair. "Both Tristan and Shailiha's signatures are right-leaning, of course," he muttered, half to himself. "As were those of the king and queen. Therefore Wulfgar's left-leaning signature is a result of Eric, his endowed father."

"What are you talking about?" Tristan demanded. "What is a left-leaning signature?"

"Simply put," Wigg answered, "if one draws a perfectly vertical axis through the exact center of a blood signature, a trained eye can determine that each and every one leans slightly either to the left or to the right of center. Signatures leaning to the right indicate the possessor shall be more naturally attracted to the practice of the Vigors. Conversely, a left-leaning signature indicates that the possessor shall be far more inclined to want to follow the Vagaries. Additionally, the degree of deviation from the vertical axis tells us just how much influence, one way or the other, there shall be. Wulfgar's signature was the most severe left-leaning example ever recorded."

A deafening silence fell over the room.

"Do Forestallments change the lean of a signature?" Tristan asked at last.

"As far as we know, they do not," Wigg answered. "Forestallments are merely spells that remain dormant until being activated at a later time. The signature lean is hereditary. A child inherits the lean of his parents' blood signatures. If their leans are oppositional, then the stronger blood prevails. For example, my blood was stronger than Failee's, and thus Celeste's signature leans to the right. During the Sorceresses' War it was rumored that a spell existed that could actually change the lean of a blood signature, but none was ever found."

Shailiha finally found her voice. "Then Failee's signature was left-leaning, was it not?" she asked.

"Yes," Wigg answered.

"Are you telling us that Wulfgar, should he be trained in the craft, would be even more enamored of the Vagaries than the first mistress of the Coven?" Shailiha leaned forward, her hazel eyes intent.

"Yes," Wigg replied. "Even more so than Failee. The firstborn child of the woman destined to bear the Chosen Ones remains loose upon the world, with a left-leaning blood signature that knows no equal."

Something the lead wizard had mentioned struck Tristan as odd. The more he thought about it, the greater became his sense of dread. His nerves coiled up, almost as if he were about to go into battle.

"What were the 'other arrangements' regarding Wulfgar to have been?" he asked bluntly.

Again looking down at his hands, Wigg sighed.

"If we were fortunate enough to find him, it was decided we would first try to train him in the craft," he answered slowly. "The entire Directorate would be informed of Wulfgar's identity and sworn to secrecy. Together we would then do all we could to help him ignore the temptations of the Vagaries. But if the pull toward the dark side of the craft had proven too strong for him to resist, even with our help, the king, queen, and I had agreed upon other measures."

Tristan's heart went cold. "And they were?" he asked softly.

Wigg's aquamarine eyes looked straight into Tristan's with an unusual mixture of sadness and determination.

"It would then fall to me to take his life," the lead wizard whispered.

Tristan stared at Wigg in disbelief. "How could you do such a thing?" he breathed. "From what you tell us he is an innocent. Not only does he not know who he really is, but he remains untrained, as well. I cannot believe my parents sanctioned your ghastly idea."

"It wasn't my idea, Tristan," Wigg answered. "It was your mother's."

Speechless, the prince half sat, half fell back down into his chair. It seemed to him as if the world he had once inhabited with his parents had just been turned completely upside down—as if Nicholas and Morganna had somehow suddenly become people he had never really known at all.

"But why?" Shailiha whispered. It was all she could do to get the question out.

"Have you not been listening?" Wigg responded. "Wulfgar is very close to possessing the highest blood quality ever known, second only to that of the Chosen Ones—the two of you. In addition, his left-leaning blood signature is without question the most severe ever witnessed. This combination is unprecedented. Trained by an unscrupulous master, Wulfgar could eventually wield power that only Tristan's son Nicholas has to this date demonstrated. To allow him to roam loose in the world would be disastrous."

"But to kill him . . ." Tristan said softly. "How could Mother have even dreamt of such a thing?"

"Morganna realized that Eutracia and the Vigors must come first, even at the expense of her losing her firstborn child all over again," Wigg told them. "It was not out of selfishness or shame that the queen made this decision. It was out of sacrifice."

"But why bother to train him at all?" Celeste asked. "Left untrained but in your care, he would have been harmless, would he not?"

Wigg smiled. "One might first come to that conclusion," he replied. "But he still might have been irresistibly called eventually to abandon us. Untrained, he might not be completely aware of what it was he was searching for, but the pull might be irresistible. Better to train him ourselves, and then do what we must, rather than leave him as raw clay for someone else to mold."

"Then why not train him and also imbue him with death enchantments, as the consuls were?" Tristan suggested. "That way, if he ever practiced the Vagaries, his death would be a certainty. At least he would be allowed to live for as long as he could hold out against their temptations. That would seem far more fair, not to mention more compassionate."

"Well done," Wigg answered. "And that possibility was considered. But in truth, it would have been far too cruel."

"What do you mean?" Tristan asked.

"First," Wigg explained, "suppose for some unknown reason the death enchantments were to become unraveled, as seems now to be the case with the consuls. Wulfgar would then be not only trained, but completely unbridled, as well. And second, when the death enchantments are activated, the transgressor's demise is particularly ugly and painful: yet another deterrent to the practice of the Vagaries. Morganna would have none of that. No, far better for me to have ended Wulfgar's existence painlessly, under our control, than to leave him to the inevitable torment of the death enchantments."

Thinking of all he and his family had been through, Tristan lowered his head.

"Does it never end?" he asked softly.

Recognizing the prince's pain, Wigg gave a rueful half smile.

"No," he answered. "Not so long as the Vagaries exist as an art unto themselves and there are those of endowed blood unable or unwilling to resist its temptations. The Tome says that only the Chosen Ones can end the struggle, by combining the two sides of the craft for the good of the world. Even though we still do not know how this is to be accomplished, we believe that is why you and your sister were put upon the earth. Your parents believed it, too, and were willing to sacrifice everything toward that goal. Even themselves."

"And Wulfgar was never found," the prince said sadly.

After a long silence, Faegan changed the subject.

"Who is Krassus?" he asked.

"As Krassus said, he is a consul," Wigg answered, a bit of guilt beginning to crowd in upon the edges of his craggy face. "Or I should say 'was.' And without doubt he was the most powerful of them. Perhaps even more powerful now, if Nicholas imbued his blood signature with certain Forestallments before he died. As with those that you and Shailiha carry, they can bequeath on the bearer many exotic abilities. Krassus was first alternate to the Directorate of Wizards. That meant that should one of us have died, Krassus would be the one to take his place. His unique two-colored robe signified his position in the hierarchy. But until such time as he would have been called upon to join the Directorate, Krassus had no vote or involvement. His duties were strictly those of a wandering consul. You would not have known him."

"But if this Krassus truly wants you and Faegan dead, why didn't he take the opportunity to kill you today, while you were both in his warp?" Tristan asked.

"Because maintaining a wizard's warp takes a great deal of energy,"

Faegan answered. "To attempt to kill one of us would be to risk losing control of the warp, thus allowing us the chance to fight back."

"And he wants Wulfgar," Celeste said. "But why?"

"No doubt to use his enormous potential to fulfill whatever portion of Nicholas' dream he vowed to complete," Faegan answered.

"We must find Wulfgar first," Tristan said adamantly. He knew he was stating the obvious. But for him it had been as much a statement about his family as it was one regarding the welfare of his nation, or the craft.

Wigg thought for a moment, then looked over at Faegan.

"Tell us, old friend," he asked. "What are these Scrolls of the Ancients that Krassus kept referring to?"

Faegan closed his eyes, his brow furrowing with concentration. Tristan could tell that the master wizard was about to employ the gift of Consummate Recollection to find the answer.

" 'And the survivors shall discover two parchments, each replete with the workings of the acts delayed,' " he began, quoting from the Tome. " 'They shall be of indescribable value—the keys enabling the descendants to partially unravel the mystery that is the craft. But in the hands of those practicing the Vagaries, the Scrolls of the Ancients shall become as potent a weapon as ever witnessed in the history of the world.' "

Faegan opened his eyes. It was clear that after the draining experience of having Krassus invade his mind, the effort of using the gift of Consummate Recollection had fatigued him. "That was the first such quote from the Tome regarding the scrolls," he said tiredly. "When I am more refreshed, I will attempt to recall the others."

"What are the 'acts delayed'?" Wigg asked him. "Does this refer to the art of Forestallments?"

"That is my initial impression," the master wizard answered. "And if that is true, the scrolls would teach us much. I have an almost infinite number of questions about the Forestallments. For example, how does one place them into the blood, and how can we tell whether they are event or time activated? Once placed there, can they be removed? Can one discern whether they are open ended and lasting forever or are closed ended and therefore limited in duration? Is there any way to tell from one's blood signature what the gifts shall eventually become? For that matter, do the scrolls hold these answers, or are we altogether wrong in assuming that they refer to the Forestallments? The study of Forestallments is without doubt the most frustrating and at the same time most fascinating aspects of the craft I have ever encountered. But why does Krassus want these scrolls so badly? And what do they have to do with Wulfgar?"

"Krassus said that we should go to Farpoint, three days from now,"

Tristan interjected. "That something would happen there—something that would convince us of his desire to carry on Nicholas' work. Do either of you know what he might be talking about?"

Both Wigg and Faegan shook their heads.

"I have no inkling either, but I will go," the prince announced.

Closing his eyes, Wigg rubbed his forehead. His heart wanted to warn the prince about the wisdom—or lack thereof—of traveling to Farpoint, the very place Krassus had dared them to visit. But he also did not possess the strength to argue the issue. Especially now, with the everheadstrong Tristan.

"Wigg, I know you are tired, but I have one more question," Faegan pressured gently. "Krassus said he was traveling with a partial adept. Do you mean to say that their kind is still roaming Eutracia?"

Tristan looked curiously at Shailiha and Celeste. They seemed to be as baffled as he was.

"In truth, I do not know," Wigg said with finality, closing his eyes. His tone and facial expression hinted either that he was trying to keep something secret—which would be just like him—or that he simply did not wish to discuss the matter just now.

"What is a partial adept?" Shailiha asked.

Sighing, Wigg opened his eyes again. "A partial adept is a specially trained man or woman of the craft, whose blood signature shows up as a 'partial,' like baby Morganna's does. They had only one endowed parent and so are not fully endowed."

"I thought people were either endowed, or they weren't," Tristan pressed.

"That's true, and it isn't," Wigg said. "It's a long story. And one I am too tired to discuss." As if there were nothing left to say about the matter, the lead wizard closed his eyes again.

Raising an eyebrow, Tristan looked skeptically at Faegan. The wizard in the wheeled chair sighed. It was clear to them that they would be hearing little more from the lead wizard this night.

Suddenly the door to Wigg's quarters blew open, revealing a rather put-out Shawna the Short. As usual, the hard-working gnome wore her gray hair tied back in a tight, unforgiving bun. Her dress was simple and clean; her no-nonsense shoes were flat and sturdy. In one hand she wielded a large mixing spoon the same way a warrior might wield his sword.

Tristan suddenly realized how hungry he was.

"I can explain," he began, giving her a hopeful smile. "You see, the lead wizard is rather indisposed—"

"I don't care what the lead wizard is!" she snapped back, in the kindly but stern manner it seemed only she could master. "Dinner is served! And don't blame me if it has gone cold!" With that she haughtily turned and stomped away.

Despite all that had happened, Tristan snorted a laugh down his nose. "I suppose we had all best obey," he said. Taking Shailiha and Celeste by the arms, he started for the door. Faegan began wheeling his chair along behind them. Then Celeste stopped, turning back to Wigg.

"I will return later with a tray of food for you, Father," she said. "Sleep well."

"Thank you, my dear," Wigg murmured without opening his eyes.

Entering the hallway, the group closed the door behind them, leaving the lead wizard alone. It was only then that his aquamarine eyes opened. He was lost in thought.

Had Krassus harmed Abbey? Wigg could count on one hand the number of days she had not entered his mind over the last three centuries. If Abbey lived, and was somehow a part of all this, how could he ever hope to explain her to the others? What in the name of the Afterlife was going on?

Out of sheer fatigue, Wigg closed his eyes again. Blessedly, sleep began to separate him from his thoughts.

CHAPTER

Six

"Raise oars!"

The grotesque pacemaster finally stopped beating out the incessant rhythm and placed his twin mallets on the floor. Number Twenty-Nine thanked the Afterlife that he had survived the horrific pace, and, along with the other slaves in his row, pushed down on the heavy oars, lifting the paddles from the Sea of Whispers. Blood was dripping from his palms; every muscle in his body felt as if it might literally crack in two.

"Ship oars!" the pacemaster shouted.

Using whatever remaining energy they could muster, the slaves who could still move drew their long oars into the frigate and laid them in neat rows down the length of the aisle. Many of the oarsmen had collapsed during the final, brutal day. Some had simply died of heat and exhaustion where they sat. Those had been unchained and thrown overboard, to be replaced by another *Talis* from the decks below. The deck was bathed in vomit, urine, and blood.

As usual, the Harlequin and the pacemaster seemed to take it all in stride. For much of the day the Harlequin had sat in his upholstered chair, watching the slaves labor as he sipped what seemed to be a bottomless glass of red wine.

Oars finally secured in the gangway, Twenty-Nine collapsed on the filthy, bloody deck. After what seemed only moments, the bleeders came around again, using their tridents to prod the helpless slaves upright. Coughing, Twenty-Nine managed to regain his seat and used the opportunity to peer out the oar slit in the side of the hull. His gaze fell upon a sheer face of gray, slick rock, and he realized they had struck land.

Smiling, the Harlequin stood up, arms akimbo. "Unchain them," he ordered.

The white-skinned bleeders in the strange skullcaps immediately began to unchain the slaves from one another, but left wrist manacles and foot shackles in place, drastically limiting movement.

"Where are they taking us?" the slave next to Twenty-Nine whispered, trembling with fear.

Twenty-Nine glared at him angrily.

"Do not talk, you fool!" he muttered furiously. "This is no time to invite attention! And as you go by the Harlequin, lower your face!"

The bleeders then began prodding them to their feet. It took many painful attempts to get cramped and atrophied legs to stand, but eventually, after a smiling, almost kindly gesture from the Harlequin, they all began shuffling toward the bow, their manacles clanking as they went.

Twenty-Nine reached the stairway and followed his comrades up onto the deck above. The first thing he saw were hundreds of slaves of both sexes standing before him, waiting to disembark. They had been divided by gender. The women, dressed in simple, one-piece frocks, had apparently fared little better than the men. Most looked ill; many were coughing.

Trying to adjust his vision to the relative darkness, Twenty-Nine rubbed his stinging, bloodshot eyes. Blinking, he finally saw where he was.

Their ship seemed to be docked in some kind of subterranean stone harbor. The flat, rough-hewn wharf had apparently been carved directly from the walls. A great deal of activity was taking place. The noise of the clanking manacles and the shouting of frightened slaves echoed hauntingly back and forth between the cavern walls and ceiling. Wide enough to easily anchor several ships like the *Defiant,* the saltwater bay was open to the ocean at only one end. The tunnel-shaped portal was easily wide enough and high enough to allow the passage of the great ships in and out.

Looking more closely, Twenty-Nine saw the sunlight beyond the cavern's outer edges come streaming down from the sky. Dappling the surface of the sea beyond, it tantalizingly reminded him of the freedom from which he had been so unbelievably, inexplicably taken. In the distance, his eyes could just make out the white, graceful sails of two more ships.

The stone pier before them was huge, easily large enough to allow several hundred persons to stand upon it. Numerous gangplanks had been lowered from the *Defiant* to the pier, and slaves were already filing down them. Dozens of bleeders stood there waiting.

As he looked closer, he could see beyond the crowd of disembarked slaves several dozen men sitting at long tables. They wore dark blue robes. As the slaves approached them, the men wrote with quills and ink in large, leather-bound journals.

Turning around, Twenty-Nine could see that the seawater here looked murky and cold as it gently lapped up against the rock walls and the sides of the ships. Numerous stalactites snaked down from the ceiling, covered with and surrounded by moss and mildew. The chamber smelled of a strange combination of mustiness and sea salt.

The only light, aside from the sunshine streaming in at the curved entrance to the harbor, came from various wall sconces and larger, standing lanterns dotting the edge of the stone pier. Their combined glow cast spectral shadows across the slickness of the walls. The air was full of the sounds of snapping bullwhips, crying, and still greater confusion.

Twenty-Nine looked down the pier and saw that two other ships were also docked quietly along its length. They floated there gently, their graceful lines and somehow comfortingly creaking hulls belying their horrific, inhuman purpose. Their waterlines rode high in the sea, revealing that their human cargoes had already been ordered ashore.

Twenty-Nine lowered his head in shame. Averting his eyes from his soiled loincloth, he regarded his tortured, shackled hands. Once beautiful, they had easily commanded the highest of compensation for his chosen trade of weapon making. Now they were bloodied and broken, and he doubted they could ever demand such sums again, even if somehow given the chance. Painfully, he tried to straighten out his fingers, but they stubbornly refused to obey, as if they had become appendages belonging to someone else. As they defiantly clung to the shape of the oar handle, he suddenly realized that even though he no longer held the oar, its mastery of him might remain a part of his being forever. Raising his face back up to the strange subterranean harbor and the wailing of his fellow innocents, he felt tears come to his eyes.

It was while standing there, waiting his turn to walk down the gangplank, that Twenty-Nine first noticed the slave directly to his right.

The man was very tall, and unlike most of the other slaves, he somehow stood defiantly erect. Broad-shouldered and stocky, the man was heavily muscled, making it clear that he was quite used to manual labor. The level, intelligent-looking eyes were hazel. Smooth, sandy-colored hair was tied behind his neck with a short strip of leather and fell long down his back. A dark mole lay at the left-hand corner of the man's mouth. Although not what many would call classically handsome, the slave carried with him a great sense of strength and personal fortitude. He looked to be approximately thirty-five Seasons of New Life.

On the man's shoulder Twenty-Nine could easily see the still angry, partially healed brand *R'talis.*

All the captives grouped with this man had been branded with the same word, Twenty-Nine noticed. He also quickly realized that this particular group of men and women was noticeably smaller than the others, almost as if they had been singled out for some reason.

Just then the cat-o'-nine-tails came whistling out of nowhere.

The knotted strands of leather lashed into Twenty-Nine's naked back. He screamed, falling to the pier. For the briefest of moments he looked up, fire in his eyes, his anger tempting him to lash out at his attacker. Taking a breath, he wisely relented.

The bleeder responsible grabbed him by his dark hair and wrestled him to his feet. Twenty-Nine suddenly realized why he had been whipped. In his examination of the slave standing next to him, he hadn't kept up with the moving line.

The bleeder struck him in the back, forcing him to close ranks. As if understanding, the slave he had been regarding turned his face to him and gave him a nod. Through his pain, Twenty-Nine tried to manage a little smile back.

Reaching the *Defiant*'s gunwales, they began marching down the gangplanks and onto the stone pier. After what seemed an eternity, he finally took his turn at the tables where the men in the hooded blue robes sat waiting. He could now see that the robed ones were seated in dozens of pairs, one pair before each line of disembarking slaves. Twenty-Nine faced the pair in front of him, and they looked up at him disinterestedly.

"Turn to the right," one of them said. Twenty-Nine did so.

"*Talis,*" the other one said, looking at the brand on his shoulder. "Your number?"

"Twenty-Nine."

Refilling his quill with ink, the man scribbled something in his ledger.

"And your given name and house?" the man asked. As Twenty-Nine told him, he again wrote in the book.

"Hold out your right hand," the other one said flatly. Looking around, Twenty-Nine tentatively did so.

One of the seated men narrowed his eyes, and a strange blue glow began to surround Twenty-Nine's tortured hand. Startled, he tried to pull it away. But then the bleeder assigned to these two robed men grabbed his wrist, forcing it back into position over the tabletop. A small, almost painless incision somehow formed in his fingertip. Then a single, controlled drop of his red blood obediently plopped down onto a sheet of parchment lying on the table. As the glow around his hand dissipated, the bleeder let Twenty-Nine's wrist go.

Then one of the men picked up a small vial and poured a single drop of what looked to be red water from it. The drop of water also landed upon the parchment, a short distance away from Twenty-Nine's blood. Leaning over, the two men at the table watched closely as Twenty-Nine's blood drop on the parchment began to dry up. He looked back up at them.

"Lack of blood activity confirmed," one of them said perfunctorily, again writing in his ledger. "*Talis.* No blood assay or Forestallment map required."

The man next to him reached over to a large pile of books. Selecting one, he rifled through its pages.

"*Talis* section," he said, looking up at the bleeder. A notation was made in this book, as well.

Ready to escort him away, the bleeder took Twenty-Nine by the arms.

But before the bleeder could push him into motion, a loud hubbub started to come from the line to Twenty-Nine's right. The man he had been studying earlier was standing before another pair of robed men. They seemed very excited, and their voices were rising in volume. Even the bleeder holding Twenty-Nine and the robed ones seated at the desk before him stopped their duties to listen.

"Say your name again!" one of the agitated blue-robes shouted at the slave. "And your house!" It was clear he was extremely eager to have his answer.

The man looked at them with defiance. "I already told you," he said. "I am Wulfgar, of the House of Merrick; son of Jason and Selene. What do you want of me?"

One of the robed men before him looked up to the bleeder stationed by his side. "Take his wrist," he ordered. The bleeder obeyed.

The robed one seated on the right looked back up into the man's eyes. "This will not hurt," he said softly. Twenty-Nine was surprised by his sudden change in tone.

Almost immediately an azure glow formed around the slave's hand. An incision similar to the one created in Twenty-Nine's finger opened. A single drop of his blood fell softly onto the blank parchment lying on the table.

Then the two robed men did something curious.

From a leather case, one of them produced a strange-looking object—

actually two objects, housed side by side in some kind of open frame, Twenty-Nine soon realized. One of them appeared to be a clear beaker, the other an hourglass. Both were small in size.

The beaker contained a small quantity of thick, red fluid that seemed to move about inside it in little waves, as if it had a life of its own. At the bottom of the beaker was a small spigot.

The hourglass was the smallest Twenty-Nine had ever seen. Its lower, teardrop-shaped globe contained what looked to be no more than a dozen small black spheres. Looking closer, he couldn't possibly imagine why one would need to measure the extremely limited period of time such a small amount of sand would allow.

The beaker and the hourglass were fastened upright, side by side, in a simple frame of wood without front or back panels.

One of the blue-robes very carefully moved the device into place on the blank sheet of parchment. By now everyone in the immediate vicinity—slaves, bleeders, and hooded ones alike—had become very still, wondering what would happen next.

Slowly, carefully, the man slid the odd device across the parchment, bringing it to rest near the blood drop. The beaker was nearest the blood, the hourglass positioned on the opposite side.

From his bag he then produced a piece of string marked in bright red near either end. Stretching the length of string out on the parchment, he very carefully adjusted the position of the device until one of the string's red marks lay exactly across from the blood drop, the other directly beneath the beaker spigot. Finally satisfied, he replaced the string in his bag.

"Are you ready?" he asked, turning to the robed one beside him.

"I am," the other replied seriously, grasping the hourglass.

"You realize they must be exactly timed," the first man said, holding the release handle of the beaker spigot.

"Of course," the other said eagerly. "Begin the count."

"On my mark," the first man said. "Five, four, three, two, one, now!"

Simultaneously, the two men moved, one turning over the hourglass, one hand hovering above it, the other releasing a single drop of the strange red fluid from the beaker down onto the parchment.

Almost immediately, the two drops of fluid flowed toward each other across the parchment and joined in a single, larger drop of red. The man holding the hourglass waved his hand. A blue glow formed around the device, and the black spheres stopped falling—one of them in midair. Twenty-Nine gasped. Then, wide-eyed, he turned his eyes back to the red drop to see that it had begun to trace a design onto the surface of the parchment. After it finished forming its design, the fluid began to retrace its path over and over again atop its original lines.

Amazed, Twenty-Nine looked over at the man whose blood had accomplished this marvel. The man looked stunned.

The robed one on the right then produced a single piece of parchment from his case. He spent what seemed to be a great deal of time nervously looking from one sheet to the other, and back again. Finally, he raised his eyes to his associate.

"They match!" he shouted. "It is he! We have found him!"

His partner turned to him. "How many spheres?" he asked eagerly.

The other narrowed his eyes, and stared intently at the glass. His mouth fell open.

"Only one and one half!" he whispered in awe, barely able to croak out the words. "The second sphere didn't even reach the bottom! I have never seen such blood assay quality!"

Barely able to contain his joy, his colleague again reached into his case. This time he produced a thick magnifying lens mounted on a tripod. Unfolding the tripod's three legs, he carefully placed it over the strange red design. Standing, he closed one eye, using the other to peer down through the lens. He remained that way for some time.

"A left-leaning signature!" he announced. "And the angle is the most severe I have ever encountered!"

"And there are no Forestallments to map!" the other said. "His blood is unadulterated, just as Krassus predicted! We could not have asked for more!"

Stunned, the two men sat back in their chairs. The one on the right looked up in awe at the confused slave. Then he nodded to a nearby bleeder.

"Take him," he ordered. The bleeder immediately stepped behind the man and grasped him by both arms. "Should any harm befall him, you forfeit your life!"

"I understand, my lord," the bleeder answered obediently.

The man behind the table then turned to another bleeder. "Go and fetch Janus," he said. "Tell him we have good news. And for the moment, none of the other slaves are to go anywhere."

"Yes, my lord," the monster answered. In a flash he was gone, easily wending his bulky form through the crowd.

Twenty-Nine looked back down at the tabletop, and to the design on the parchment, and the weird devices the two men had used in their examination of the slave's blood. He shook his head, understanding none of what had just transpired.

The man named Wulfgar was faring no better. Confusion and hate filled his eyes as he stood there gripped from behind, waiting for the one called Janus.

Finally, the crowds of slaves began to part. Turning, Twenty-Nine looked to see who it was.

It was the Harlequin.

Ignoring everyone but the men seated at the table, he strode forward to face them. "What is it?" he asked.

"We have finally found him, Janus," one of them said proudly, as if having just obediently returned with a bone thrown by his master. "The blood signature is conclusive."

Janus picked up the two parchments. He gazed back and forth between them for some time. Finally he returned his red-masked eyes to the ones behind the table.

"You are sure?" he asked sternly. Turning, he looked briefly at Wulfgar. "Trust me when I say that Krassus will not be amused should he again return to this forsaken place, only to find this to be yet another false alarm."

He turned back to the robed ones. "What did the blood assay reveal?" he asked.

"A blood quality of one and a half," one of them replied promptly. "We have never seen its like. That is, of course, with the exception of the Chosen Ones."

"And the craft tendency?" Janus asked.

"Left-leaning," the man seated on the right answered. "To a degree never before seen."

"You don't say," Janus mused. Removing his fancy handkerchief from a pocket, he dusted off the lens atop the tripod. Placing his eye to it, he examined the design on the parchment for some time. Finally, he raised his head back up.

"Very well," he said finally. "I stand convinced."

The painted freak turned toward Wulfgar. "All of that magnificently endowed blood, just waiting to be trained," he mused. Grasping Wulfgar's chin, he examined the slave's face as he turned it this way and that in the dim light of the torches.

"And you are so beautiful, as well," he added. Then, letting out an exasperated breath, he backed away, all the while staring with revulsion at the slave's soiled, torn loincloth and filthy, bare feet. Reaching into a pocket, he produced a small, golden tin of snuff. With careful movements, he held a pinch up to his nose and sniffed hard. A sudden, forceful sneeze followed. Then he smiled.

"No matter," he said, sniffing twice again. "Your disgusting aroma can be remedied. And beautiful you are, my dear Wulfgar, despite your current state. You are living proof that the licentious tart that was your mother somehow always managed to vomit forth impressive children, no matter the quality of the fool she laid with. How nice."

The slave's answer was immediate: He summoned all the saliva he could and spat it directly into Janus' face.

Slowly Janus wiped the spittle from his face with his embroidered handkerchief. "So much defiance," he said softly. "And how like your half brother and sister you seem to be."

Confusion flashed across Wulfgar's face.

"Ah, but you don't know about them yet, do you?" Janus asked nastily. "All in good time. We'll see to it that the demonslavers watch over you well."

Twenty-Nine looked over to the white-skinned monster on his right. *Demonslavers.* So that was what they were called.

Janus turned back to Wulfgar and looked into the slave's hazel eyes. "Assign this one to Krassus' personal quarters," he ordered the ones at the table. "And keep the door securing our new charge locked at all times. See to it that he is bathed and properly fed. Nothing but the finest for our friend, wouldn't you agree? Also see to it that our guest has some finery to wear. His forthcoming station shall require it. Otherwise, he is not to be disturbed unless I order it." He smiled again. "I want him to be sleek and happy when he first meets his new teacher." The robed men nodded.

Wulfgar struggled in vain to free himself from the demonslaver's iron grip. "What do you want of me?" he growled. "What is it that I am supposed to do for you?"

Janus smiled. "Be at peace," he cooed softly. "For the time being, all that matters is what we shall be doing for *you*."

It was at that point that a single, defiant voice rang out from the crowd of slaves.

"Leave him alone! He has done nothing to you!"

Turning quickly, Janus narrowed his eyes and searched among the slaves. "It seems we have a wolf among the sheep!" he said loudly. "How wonderful! Come and show yourself!"

A man stepped out of line and began shuffling toward the table. The nearest demonslaver moved to strike him down, but backed down at a quick gesture from Janus. With a cavalier wave of one hand, Janus beckoned the loinclothed slave forward.

The man had served on the oaring deck. Twenty-Nine had never been afforded the opportunity to speak to him, for their stations had been too far removed from each other. But he did know that this slave had been one of the most quarrelsome. He had purposely given the demonslavers a great deal of trouble, sometimes even mocking them. Many of the others manning the oars had looked up to him. The grisly evidence of the demonslavers' love for both the nine-tails and trident showed over much of his lean, hard body, and yet this man, like the slave named Wulfgar, had somehow managed to keep not only part of his strength intact, but also most of his dignity. As he walked slowly forward to face Janus, the demonslavers grudgingly made way.

"You are in no position to give orders," Janus said, looking the man up and down. He grinned as he fingered the black-and-white spheres at his hip, rubbing them together in a circle around his palm. Twenty-Nine cringed at the perverse, metallic sound of their clinking together.

"Turn your left shoulder to me," Janus ordered. The man obeyed. Janus narrowed his eyes.

"*Talis,*" he said approvingly. "Good. Your death shall be no particular loss. I'll tell you what I'll do. I'll give you a head start—say, twenty meters. Run as fast as you can toward the edge of the pier, where the ships lay docked. If you make it, I'll let you live. And if you don't, well, let's just say that you will be saved the unpleasant experience of this place."

After an indication from Janus, one of the demonslavers unlocked the slave's manacles. The slave rubbed his tortured wrists in disbelief.

Smiling, Janus took the black-and-white rope from the hook on his belt and slowly began uncoiling it. Then he grasped the line at its center, letting the small iron spheres at either end hang down almost to the stone floor. Casually, he looked up into the eyes of the slave who had dared defy him.

"I suggest you start now," he said softly.

The slave turned and began running toward the ships docked at the end of the pier.

Calmly, almost slowly, Janus raised the checkered line high over his head and began to swing the spheres around in a circle. The line and spheres sang hauntingly as they tore though the air—faster, faster, until they were a glimmering pinwheel of black and white.

And then Janus let go.

The weapon wheeled unerringly toward the running slave. He never had a chance.

The midpoint of the checkered line caught him in the back of the neck. Instantaneously the lines on either side wound around and around his throat.

The twin spheres closed ranks, smashing with a great cracking noise into his head—one into his face, the other into the back of his skull. Blood and brain matter exploded from his crushed cranium, and he crashed to the ground just before reaching the end of the pier. A hush came over the crowd.

The victim groaned.

"Don't tell me he still lives!" Janus sneered. "How remarkable!"

The Harlequin strode to his victim and uncoiled his bizarre weapon from the slave's mangled neck. The slave groaned one last time as the heartless butcher stood over him, watching him expire.

With a smile, Janus bent over to dip the spheres into the sea to clean them, then replaced them on his belt. He looked over to several demon-slavers who had crowded around the body. Suddenly his smile widened.

"I think it safe to say he no longer has the head for this business!" And he gave a sarcastic laugh.

The slavers standing near him broke into raucous laughter.

Twenty-Nine lowered his head in shame. Then his shame quickly turned to anger, filling every corner of his heart. He looked down at his broken hands. Clenching his jaw, he turned to glare at the freak standing so proudly over his bloody victory.

"What shall we do with the body?" one of the demonslavers asked.

Thinking for a moment, the Harlequin turned back to the crowd of slaves and beckoned. Immediately the air became filled with the sounds of snapping nine-tails as the slavers forced the crowd toward the edge of the pier, where the slain slave lay.

"Hear me!" Janus shouted. "For those others of you who might defy us, know that what happened to this slave is perhaps the most lenient of consequences. There exist far more ingenious methods of obtaining your cooperation, I assure you! Your loved ones back in Eutracia know you are gone, but have absolutely no idea of where you have been taken. Nor shall they ever. Rescue is quite impossible. And should any of you be thinking of plotting an escape, also know that you are on an island. Should you try to leave us, only death awaits you in these waters. Allow me to demonstrate!"

Janus calmly turned to several of the slavers standing beside him. He pointed to the mutilated corpse. "Hack the body into pieces, and throw them in," he ordered simply.

Two of the demonslavers came forward, sliding their short, broad swords from the scabbards hanging low on their backs. With amazingly fast strokes, the body was quickly dismembered. Blood ran slowly toward the edge of the pier and dripped into the sea.

Two of the demonslavers grasped the bloody parts and tossed them into the ocean just aft of the *Defiant*. Then Janus turned to look down into the murky depths and held up a painted hand. The entire crowd went silent.

"Wait for it," he said quietly. Then, slowly, something began to happen.

There was a disturbance in the water.

An area of the sea surface started to glow with the color azure. It began to writhe and churn. Deepening whirlpools, each several meters across, could be seen forming in various spots on the gloomy sea of the subterranean harbor. Everyone stood transfixed, waiting to see what would happen next. And then, almost as if with a single mind, the crowd recoiled.

From the midst of the azure whirlpools, squat, menacing heads silently began rising up out of the sea.

The long, flat skulls were covered with dark red scales. Slanted, yellow eyes, with vertical black irises, darted from side to side as the heads turned menacingly this way and that, searching for whatever had disturbed the surface of the sea. Several of them began slithering hungrily toward the pieces of severed corpse, portions of their long, smooth bodies intermittently rising and submerging as they went. Their strangely forked tails rose silently from the water, only to submerge again. In the center of their backs a spiny fin occasionally swept up in a gentle curve only to fall again, to lie against the sinuous spine.

Dozens of them were rising silently to the surface now, slithering over and under one another, writhing and twisting in the dark sea. The only sound was their eager hissing.

Some of them had reached their meal, and they opened their jaws wide. Astoundingly long pink, forked tongues flashed out to entwine the bloody body parts. Then the tongues retracted, pulling the meat into waiting maws. In each mouth, four long, white fangs—two at the top and another pair at the bottom—flashed as they bit down. With snorting, snuffling grunts of pleasure the monsters swallowed.

The sea became a whirling riot of activity as the grisly feeding frenzy continued unabated.

When the dismembered corpse was finally consumed, the beasts, silent now, slithered back into the depths. The surface of the sea stilled; the azure glow faded away. The bloodied, soiled loincloth of the dead slave floated to the surface of the murky water—all that was left of the man who had dared defy Janus.

Smiling, the Harlequin turned back to the gaping crowd.

"They are called sea slitherers," he said. "Created by my esteemed master. They number in the thousands, and completely surround the waters of these isles. As I said, escape is impossible."

Twenty-Nine stood numbly, unable to believe what he had just witnessed. He turned to look at the man called Wulfgar. It was clear he had given up struggling with the slaver holding him.

Gloating, Janus sauntered back from the end of the pier.

"Enough fun for one afternoon," he said casually. "Our little object lesson is now concluded." He looked commandingly at the two robed ones still seated at the table, then pointed to Wulfgar.

"Have him taken to his quarters," he ordered, "and see to it that my other commands are carried out to the letter. His well-being is paramount. Should any harm befall him, you will have to answer to Krassus himself."

The men behind the table nodded obediently.

"Also see to it that the two parchments carrying his endowed signature and blood assay are securely locked away in the vault of the Scriptorium," he added.

He looked back at the hundreds of filthy slaves standing in the dim light of the torches. "In the meantime, keep processing these vermin," he added. "And be quick about it. Two more ships are approaching, and will be in need of docking berths." He turned on his heel and walked away.

As Janus left, several demonslavers gathered around Wulfgar, presumably forming a security squad to escort him to his quarters.

Strong hands suddenly gripped Twenty-Nine from behind. A knee was slammed into his back, and he was muscled around the end of the table.

His foot shackles rattling, he was herded roughly toward the far wall, where two dark, stone doorways waited. Over one was carved the word *Talis*. Over the other, *R'talis*. A steep stairway led upward from each, curving around and out of sight.

Just before being shoved through the door marked *Talis*, he forced his head around one final time to look at Wulfgar. Perhaps he could give him a look of hope, as Wulfgar had done for him.

But Wulfgar was already gone.

A trident at his naked back, Twenty-Nine began climbing the steep, rough-hewn stairway.

Seven

"**O**x sorry," the huge Minion said, wringing his hands. "Ox should been inside palace with Chosen One, not outside with troops. Not happen again. Ox promise."

Tristan smiled over at the slow-witted but loyal Minion, knowing full well how ashamed the warrior felt. The prince had repeatedly tried to reassure him that what had happened had not been his fault, and that Krassus would have slipped by the Minion troops anyway. But as Tristan's supposed bodyguard, Ox hadn't agreed and had continued to castigate himself.

Deciding there was little more he could do to change the warrior's opinion, Tristan uncoiled his long legs and looked out the window, admiring the Eutracian landscape as it flew by below.

The prince, Ox, Shailiha, and the wizard Faegan were sitting inside one of the Minion litters, being carried through the sky by six of the winged troops. Another six warriors flew alongside as guards. They had been traveling this way for several hours, and it would take at least two more to reach the coastal city of Farpoint.

Sitting directly across from Tristan, Shailiha was obviously nervous. She did not like traveling by flying litter, even if it was with her brother. She would occasionally stick her head out, trying to adjust to the fact that she was soaring along so quickly, several thousand feet above the earth. Tristan gave her a wide smile, reassuring her it would be all right. She smiled back tentatively.

Faegan had immediately fallen asleep—or so it seemed. But Tristan doubted that the wily wizard was actually dozing, suspecting that Faegan was instead absorbed in his wizardly contemplations. The Paragon hung around Faegan's neck, its vibrant, red light shimmering from within as always.

Three days had passed since Krassus had breached the security of the palace. To the wizards' dismay, Tristan and Shailiha had insisted on traveling to Farpoint to witness firsthand whatever it was that Krassus had taunted them about. Wigg, although improving daily, was still too weak to make the trip with them. And so Faegan had come; both to protect them, if necessary, and to lend his experienced wizard's eyes to their observations. Celeste had stayed at the palace to tend Wigg.

The plan was to have the Minions drop them in the woods just outside the city. They would walk into town, and once there, would hire a carriage and tour the streets anonymously, trying to find out what they could. Ox and his Minions would stay in the woods with the litters, waiting for their return.

Tristan rubbed his face, not liking the thick, dark beard Faegan had conjured for him. He had never really had a full beard, and he would be glad to be rid of it.

Faegan had given Shailiha a change of hair color, from blond to black. A simple plaid peasant's dress replaced her gown. These changes in appearance were the results of new craft calculations the old wizard had been trying to achieve, but the calculations were still limited in scope, as were their applications.

Thinking back to the day of Krassus' attack, Tristan scowled. Not only had the traitorous wizard invaded the palace with ease, but his doing so had resulted in several amazing revelations. Over the past three days, Wigg and Faegan had adamantly refused to elaborate on these mysteries. That would be like them: to hold back information, at least until they had figured out more of the pieces to the puzzle.

But Tristan sensed there were other reasons for the crusty wizards' silence. And if Wigg wouldn't talk, perhaps Faegan now would—especially since the lead wizard wasn't here to listen.

Tristan stretched out one leg to nudge Faegan's foot.

"Faegan," he said gently, "are you awake?"

"Of course," the master wizard answered rather sourly, his eyes still closed. "Bouncing along in one of these contraptions, thousands of feet in the air, who could possibly be asleep?"

Looking at Shailiha, Tristan grinned.

"I have a question for you," he said to the wizard.

Faegan sighed, "What is it?" he asked grumpily. The ancient, gray-green eyes remained closed.

"Are partials endowed?" Tristan asked. "I always thought that people were either endowed, or they weren't."

Faegan's left eye suddenly opened, to stare directly at the prince. With another sigh, he opened the other eye and sat up, shaking off his previous thoughts. Taking a deep breath, he raised his arms and stretched his back. "It's not that simple," he said with a smile. "And I suppose that without Wigg here to castigate me, you expect to hear all about it, don't you?"

Tristan grinned, realizing that Faegan was about to give him at least some of his answers—if for no other reason than to eventually annoy the lead wizard.

"Partials are not endowed in the classic sense," Faegan answered, "but given the proper training, some of the more powerful of them can perform certain acts that unendowed persons cannot."

"Such as?" Shailiha asked.

"Skills such as blaze-gazing, or being able to force someone to reveal the truth, even against his or her will. Healing or causing illness. Also, it is rumored that some could perform several arcane forms of beast-mastery. All of these talents require the use of some form of organic life, such as that which comes from the ground or the water. The most gifted of them often became what we called herbmasters or herbmistresses, using specific combinations of plants, herbs, and oils to refine and strengthen their craft even further. Most wizards had little to fear from them, as partial adepts—as we called those partials who practiced the craft—were not particularly powerful."

"But why would a partial's gifts be limited to only certain aspects of the craft?" Shailiha asked. "That doesn't make sense to me."

"I can understand your confusion," Faegan replied. "As is true with so many things of magic, the answer has to do with the Paragon." He held the square-cut, bloodred stone up for inspection.

"If you were to count the facets of the surface of the Paragon, you would find there to be twenty-five in all," he told her. "Just as there are twenty-five major facets of the craft, such as the Kinetic, the Sympathetic, and the Formative. The facet, for example, allows the practitioner certain dynamic uses of the craft, such as the throwing of azure bolts. The Sympathetic facet allows the user certain gifts associated with sound, touch, and vibration. And as you might well guess, the Formative facet has to do with the conjuring and altering of things—or their disappearance. These are but three of the twenty-five."

Neither Tristan nor Shailiha had ever heard this, and it put the Paragon in an entirely new light.

"How do you know all of this?" Shailiha asked.

"This information came to us from the preface to the Tome," Faegan answered. "The Ones Who Came Before constructed the jewel as the living passageway between endowed blood and the orbs of the Vigors and the Vagaries—the two fountainheads of all that is the craft. The twenty-five facets that the Ones cut into the stone represent what they considered to be the most important disciplines of the craft."

"But that still doesn't explain why a partial adept's gifts are limited, and vice versa," Tristan pressed.

"That is because the Ones granted those of fully endowed blood sole access to all of the facets save for one," Faegan told them. "The arts of that one facet are divided between those of fully endowed blood, and the partials."

"What is that facet called?" Tristan asked.

"The Organic," Faegan answered.

"And what aspects of the craft does the Organic facet control?" Shailiha asked.

"Those arts that are made possible only through the use of such organics as herbs, oils, plants, water, and so on," Faegan explained. "These arts have the greatest effect of all on the plant life, water, and air of the world. The Ones Who Came Before channeled some of the arts of the Organic into the weaker blood signatures of the partials, and the rest into the blood of the fully endowed. A wizard has access to a far greater number of skills, and has much greater power, but partial adepts have access to some Organic skills that we do not."

"But why would the Ones do that?" Tristan asked. "Wouldn't they want the fully endowed to have all the gifts, so that they could be used to their greatest advantage?"

"Enabling one group to employ all of the arts of the Organic discipline to their utmost was precisely what the Ones were trying to *avoid*," the wizard said.

"But you still haven't answered why," Shailiha pressed.

"It seems that what the Ones wanted most, second only to the preservation of the craft, was to prevent any future recurrence of their war with the Heretics of the Guild. The preface to the Tome tells us that during their War of Attrition, as they called it, vast areas of the world became scorched and lifeless. If they couldn't preserve the land, air, and sea for future generations, humankind ran the risk of becoming extinct." He paused for a moment in thought.

"People are replaceable, I suppose, should one care to characterize things in such a manner," he went on, as their litter continued to bounce along through the air. "But the earth we walk upon, the water we drink, and the air we breathe is not. And without them we would soon perish, taking the craft with us. For in the final analysis, our endowed blood is the ultimate resting place of the craft, and our lives the instruments by which it is passed down through the generations, thereby making it timeless. That is why the Ones devised the Organic facet of the Paragon the way they did: gifting some of the most dangerous of these arts only to those of partial blood. That way, they hoped, no one would ever be able to use them again in a manner that was so destructive."

"But if these Organic gifts are so potentially destructive, why allow them to be used at all?" Shailiha asked.

"Because their potential to be used for good is just as strong," Faegan answered. "If all these aspects of the craft had not been preserved, knowledge of them would have died with the Ones. Even now we have no way of knowing how many of their arts may have vanished with the Ones' passing from the world."

Suddenly something Faegan had said earlier began gnawing at the back of the prince's mind. "What is a blaze-gazer?" he asked.

Faegan pursed his lips. "A blaze-gazer is a partial adept who is able to use herbs to see events that are occurring some distance away. Or so goes the myth. That art is said to be very rare, and almost always the province of women, rather than men."

"Can you blaze-gaze?" Shailiha asked.

"No," Faegan answered testily. True to form, he was becoming irritable at the questioning of his abilities. "Nor can any other wizard I have ever known—including Wigg. I would love to learn to blaze-gaze, but it is doubtful that a partial adept would ever share such knowledge with an outsider, or even that the Paragon would allow me that skill."

"And Krassus now travels with a partial adept," Tristan mused. "Or at least he claims to."

"Yes," Faegan agreed. "If what he said is true, that does not bode well for any of us."

"Krassus said that Wigg knows one," Shailiha commented. "And the lead wizard became very defensive when we asked him about it. Could it be true?"

Faegan raised an eyebrow. "First of all, it is Wigg's nature to be defensive," he said. "You know how secretive he can be. When he does not wish to speak about a subject, even wild mules can't pull the words out of him." A bit more somber now, Faegan looked out the window again.

"You know, part of what Krassus said is quite valid," he mused.

"What part?" Tristan asked.

"He said that although I am the greatest keeper of the craft, Wigg is the greatest keeper of secrets," Faegan said softly. "That is so true. When thinking of Wigg, always remember that he has survived over three centuries in the maze of politics and magic that is Eutracia. The things he has seen and the secrets he still keeps may well be uncountable."

Tristan sat back in the seat, thinking. Something Wigg had told them that day still haunted him.

"Is it true?" he asked the ancient wizard. "Would Wigg have really done it? Would he do it still?"

"Do what?" Faegan asked.

"Would he truly kill Wulfgar, should our brother be found and his left-leaning blood signature induce him to the Vagaries?"

Faegan's expression darkened. Removing his hands from the opposite sleeves of his robes, he leaned forward. "Would Wigg obey the orders of a dead queen, and kill your half sibling in order to protect the craft? Or for that matter, would I? And even more importantly, would the two of you let us? Or could you stop us, should you choose to try?" His gray-green eyes narrowed.

"Those very thoughts have consumed my mind ever since Krassus revealed himself to us," the wizard said. "All I know right now is that we must find Wulfgar before he does, or none of it will matter. Not to mention these scrolls he searches for."

Suddenly there came a harsh, insistent pounding upon the side of the litter. Ox stuck his head out the window.

"Speak!" he ordered the Minion officer flying close by.

"Farpoint approaches, sir!" the Minion shouted. "You ordered us to let you know when we neared!"

Ox looked back questioningly at Tristan.

"Tell him they should land us about one quarter league from the outskirts of the city," the prince ordered. "Place us down in the woods, if possible. We must not be seen."

"I live to serve," Ox replied, and shouted Tristan's orders to his warriors. The litter began to tilt downward. Faegan's manner suddenly became even more serious.

"It was only after much discussion that Wigg and I agreed to let you come here," he said. "In truth, I doubt we could have stopped you, anyway, short of using a wizard's warp on you both. But that doesn't mean that we think this is a good idea. If it is to be done, it will be done our way. I have not visited Farpoint for many years, but I remember it as an exceedingly rough place. Eutracian fishing towns always are. Tristan, I want you to push my chair for me. If questioned, you are to say that you are my bodyguard, and my ward. Shailiha, you are to pretend to be my nurse. Remember, we are here only to observe, not to participate." He pursed his lips.

"One other thing," he said, sounding solemn. "Tristan, should anything untoward happen, I want you to employ your skills to protect us, rather than my resorting to the use of the craft. I don't want anyone here to know I am a wizard unless it becomes absolutely necessary. For all we know, Krassus may even be here. He has already sworn to kill Wigg and me. At the very least he is probably expecting us to take the bait by simply coming here. Therefore, I will be cloaking our endowed blood—a job that, because of the combined, exceedingly high quality of our blood, shall take a great deal of effort. Only in the direst of circumstances will I drop the cloak and employ the craft. Otherwise, it is your duty to protect us. And let me do the talking. The first thing I want to do is to find a carriage for hire. It will be faster and safer than walking the streets. Do you understand?"

Both the Chosen Ones nodded.

Faegan sighed and shook his head. "Then may the Afterlife watch over us."

The six Minion warriors gently landed the litter in a small glade surrounded by fir trees. Then the other six landed, dreggans drawn, and formed a protective ring. The four occupants descended from the litter and onto the soft grass of the forest, the Minions handling the wizard's chair for him.

"Stay here, out of sight," Tristan ordered Ox. It was plain to see by the look on the warrior's face that he was severely disappointed not to be coming along.

"Sorry, my friend," the prince said with a smile. "But your presence in Farpoint would cause a commotion, to say the least! Light no fires. And send no sentries into the sky, as you normally would. Do, however, post guards in the woods. If you are found and must defend your lives, do so. But if your attackers are simple townsfolk, try to subdue them, rather than kill them. I do not know how long we may be gone, but wait for us. There is food and water stored in the litter."

Ox clicked the heels of his boots together. "I live to serve."

Tristan nodded back. With that he and Shailiha grasped Faegan's chair and began wheeling him out of the forest.

Pushing the wooden chair through the thick undergrowth was very difficult. Faegan could have levitated it, of course, but they could not risk being spotted using the craft. At last they came upon a hardscrabble road, which was smooth enough that Tristan could manage the chair without Shailiha's help. Tristan longed to have Pilgrim, his dappled gray-and-white stallion, beneath him, but it was also good to stretch his legs, especially after the hours aboard the flying litter.

The prince had made several official visits to Farpoint when his father and mother were alive, and he had to agree with Faegan that the fishing town was a rough-and-tumble place. The seafaring folk were a stern, tough, and uncompromising lot. They worked hard. And when they returned to town with their clothes full of the stink of fish and their pockets full of gold coins, they drank too much, gambled too much, and fought too much.

It was not much longer until they entered the outskirts of the city, and Tristan, with Shailiha at his side, wheeled Faegan's chair down one of the streets he felt would most likely provide adequate livery service. His magically acquired beard itched.

Several empty hansom cabs stood waiting on one side of the wide, cobblestoned boulevard. Tristan wheeled Faegan toward the first of them, and the old wizard turned his gray-green eyes up to the man sitting atop it.

"Good day," he said politely. "Are you for hire?"

"I don't be sittin' up here for my health, cripple," the driver snarled back. He spat, narrowly missing the wizard's feet.

Faegan remained unperturbed. "How much?" he asked.

"How far?" the driver countered, his careful eyes examining the old man in the wheeled chair.

Faegan took a slow breath. "We heard there is to be some special activity here today," he said. Then he winked conspiratorially up at the driver. When the driver remained silent, Faegan pressed, "You know the kind of activity I mean. And we have money to spend. But we are new here, and we do not know the way. Now will you take us there, or do we have to go to one of your competitors?"

Blatantly craning his neck to look over at the next carriage, Faegan conjured some kisa—the gold coin of the realm—into one of his robe pockets. Reaching in, he jangled them together loudly.

Scowling, the driver rubbed the salt-and-pepper grizzle on his chin. Then, looking down from his seat, he gestured toward Tristan.

"Except for that nasty-looking bastard with the sword and the knives, you don't look like the usual lot who goes there," he said cautiously. "Not only that, but if the two younger ones know what's good for 'em, they won't go there at all. The white ones will be there, ya' know."

This piqued Faegan's interest. "How much?" he demanded.

"All right, all right!" the driver said. "Don't get your robe in a twist! Twelve kisa should do it."

"Six!" Faegan countered.

"Eight!" the driver hollered down.

"Done!" the wizard said.

"Get aboard." The driver sighed, reaching for his whip. It was abundantly clear from his posture that helping Faegan in was not going to be part of the bargain.

Tristan opened the hansom door and helped Shailiha in, then walked around to the back of the coach. He was dismayed to see that there was no storage compartment large enough for Faegan's chair, and no way to secure it on top of the carriage.

"Go ahead," Faegan said, giving Tristan a wink. "You're strong enough. I know you can do it."

Smiling, the prince suddenly understood. Reaching down, he grabbed the chair, wizard and all, just as the driver finally decided to come down from atop his seat to berate them for taking so long. The man approached just in time to see Tristan smoothly, effortlessly lift both the wizard and chair and place them through the open door of the coach as though they weighed no more than a feather.

The driver's eyes went wide; his grizzled jaw dropping with disbelief. "How in the name of the Afterlife did you do that?"

As Tristan climbed into the carriage, Faegan poked his head out the window. "As I said, he's very strong." He winked mischievously.

Scratching his head, the bewildered driver clambered back atop the carriage. With a whistle to his horses and a snap of his whip, the coach started rumbling down the streets of Farpoint.

Despite the danger of their situation, both Tristan and Shailiha began to laugh.

" '*He's very strong?*' " Tristan asked the wizard. "I thought you weren't going to use the craft!"

"I couldn't resist." Faegan chuckled. "The driver deserved it after all he put me through. I sensed no endowed blood nearby, so I dropped our cloak momentarily. We had to get me into the carriage somehow, didn't we? Besides, what is the good of being a wizard if you can't have some fun once in a while?" He cackled gleefully.

Shaking his head and turning to look at his sister, Tristan had to laugh again. Traveling with Faegan was certainly different from traveling with the lead wizard!

Looking out the carriage window, Faegan grew more serious. "Pay close attention as we go down the streets," he ordered. "If you notice anything unusual—anything at all—tell me right away. Remember, we still do not know where we are going, or what we will find when we get there."

"Faegan, who are 'the white ones' the driver spoke of?" Shailiha asked. "He seemed to fear them."

Faegan shook his head. "I have been wondering the same thing," he replied.

Tristan looked out the window of the carriage. There were few people on the streets for this time of the day, he mused. Perhaps that was due to the fact that they were still on the outskirts of the city.

At first that seemed to be the answer: As they continued farther into town, he began to see the usual smattering of elderly and middle-aged people going about their business. There were children, too, and the usual groupings of teenagers. But then he began to notice something else, and his blood ran cold.

The city seemed to be completely devoid of people his own age.

The longer he looked, the surer he became. He saw no one who looked to be between the years of twenty to forty Seasons of New Life.

He told himself he was imagining things, that as they continued on, he'd certainly start to see more people of *all* ages. But he didn't.

Then he noticed something else. Most of the people he saw seemed weary and downtrodden. Some were even sobbing. It was as if some great pall had descended over the town.

He looked over at Faegan. "Do you see it?" he asked quietly. "Or am I dreaming?"

Faegan looked somber. "This is no dream," he replied. "Something dark has come over this place, and we must find out what it is."

He thought for a moment. Then he spoke again. "Tristan, I want you to go up and sit with the driver. He probably won't be happy about it, but be cordial. Try to get as much information out of him as you can without raising his suspicions. If you see anything untoward, return at once and inform me."

Tristan nodded. After giving Shailiha a reassuring pat on the hand, he swung open the door and quickly hoisted himself up onto the driver's bench.

Surprised, the grizzled driver glared at him. "What do you think you're doing?" he snapped. "You shouldn't be up here—especially not now. For the life of me I can't understand why you and the girl would want to do this. Hasn't the old cripple told you what's going on here? Is he insane, or just stupid?" He spat down loudly into the passing gutter.

Tristan grinned. "The old one doesn't tell us a lot," he answered. "The sick old fool only hired me for my sword. The woman is his nurse. Truth be told, I don't know why we're here, either."

He let several precious seconds go by. Then he put on his most innocent expression and asked, "Why don't you tell me what's going on here?"

As if finally willing to answer Tristan's question, the driver turned to him. But just then, something seemed to catch his eye. Drawing a quick breath, he pulled the team of horses up short. The carriage came to an abrupt stop. Raising a finger, the driver pointed to a corner down the street.

"Do you see them?" he whispered. His hands shook; his face was blanched with fear.

Snapping his head around to look, Tristan caught sight of several strange-looking figures walking hurriedly away. They were tall, with white, almost translucent skin—but that was all he could make of them before they rounded the corner and vanished from sight.

"Demonslavers," the driver whispered, so quietly that Tristan barely heard him.

"What?" Tristan asked. The man's obvious terror was unnerving.

"This is as far as I go!" the driver shouted, jumping down from his seat. "Everybody out!"

Running around to the side of the carriage, he violently jerked the door open, grabbed Shailiha's arm, and literally pulled her out. By the time Tristan got there, the man was screaming at Faegan, ordering him to get out.

"Very well, very well!" Faegan shouted back. He looked at Tristan. "If you would," he said.

Understanding, Tristan reached in, retrieving the old one and his chair the same way he had placed them inside. But this time the driver didn't care about Tristan's supposedly amazing feat of strength. All he wanted was to leave, and quickly.

"If you value your lives, go back to wherever you came from and forget this place!" he shouted frantically. "No power in the world can help this accursed town! If you remain foolish enough to carry on with this madness, the place you are searching for is the docks! But you would be insane to go there!" He climbed back into the carriage seat as fast as he could.

With a crack of his whip, he wheeled his team around. "And if you know what's good for them, you'll get those two off the street before it's too late!" he hollered at Faegan, while pointing to Tristan and his sister. With another lash from his whip he charged his team back down the way they had come, the horses' hooves colliding noisily with the cobblestones. In mere moments, he was gone.

"What do we do now?" Tristan asked the wizard.

A crowd had started to form. Some of the onlookers were staring oddly at the prince and Shailiha, as if they weren't human. Some started pointing. Many of them seemed to be angry.

"The last thing we need is attention," Faegan whispered urgently. "For the time being, we'll get off the street. Any of these shops will do. I suggest we hurry!"

Tristan saw a storefront with a sign in the shape of a mortar and pestle. The sign said "Apothecary—Drugs and Compounds." Swiftly he wheeled Faegan's chair around and, with Shailiha, made for the door.

The double doors closed behind them with finality, a little bell at their top happily announcing the fact that the shop's proprietor had customers.

Tristan looked around. They seemed to be the only people in here.

The shop was quite large, lined with shelves and littered with tables all filled with multicolored bottles and jars. Everything was covered with a layer of dust, as if the merchandise hadn't been touched for years. A long counter stretched from wall to wall at the far end, with yet more wall cabinets behind it.

A massive, circular oak chandelier hung by a rope over the center of the floor. The rope ran through a pulley in the ceiling and on to a hook attached to the far wall, a system that allowed for the raising and lowering of the fixture for the filling of its oil sconces. The chandelier was not lit.

There was no sign of the proprietor. The place smelled of dust, lack of use, and countless exotic compounds.

Wheeling himself up to one of the tables, Faegan picked up a bottle and examined it. Removing the cork, he smelled the contents. His eyes lit up.

"Ground blossom of rapturegrass!" he cackled, triumphantly smacking one hand flat upon the arm of his chair. "I'd stake my life on it!" He appeared to be quite delighted. "I haven't seen this for decades!" He held the bottle up for Tristan and Shailiha to see. "Good for the libido," he added with a wink.

With a sigh and a slight shake of his head, Tristan looked over at his sister. She was watching Faegan with an expression of disbelief. As one corner of his mouth came up, Tristan reminded himself that she was not as familiar with the wizard's eccentricities as he was.

"Faegan," Tristan asked, "have you ever heard of something called a demonslaver?"

"A *what?*" Faegan asked, his full attention firmly locked upon the prince. Then Tristan heard someone clear his throat.

"May I be of assistance?" a different voice suddenly said.

Turning, Tristan, Shailiha, and Faegan looked behind the counter to see a thin, ruddy-faced man wearing wire spectacles that seemed far too large for him. Watching him push the spectacles back up the sweaty bridge of his nose, only to see them slide back down again, Tristan guessed that the automatic gesture had become a lifelong habit. The shopkeeper wore an apron covered with multicolored dust, and he appeared unusually nervous.

But when he saw the faces of the prince and princess, he turned absolutely white.

"Get out!" he shouted immediately. "You shouldn't be here! I don't want any trouble!"

"Nor do we," Tristan said courteously, taking a single step toward the counter. "All we want are the answers to a few simple—"

The twin doors to the shop suddenly blew open with such force that they banged into the walls beside them. Their etched-glass windows shattered, cascading to the floor in thousands of shards of prismed light. Moving instinctively, Tristan whirled around, reaching behind his back and drawing his dreggan. The ring of its razor-sharp blade resounded through the musty air of the shop.

There were five of them, and they were something out of a nightmare. The only way they seemed to differ from one another was in the various weapons they carried: in addition to swords, one of them carried a whip, another a trident.

Black leather skirts, slit down the front for walking, fell from their waists to the floor. Their chests and shoulders were bare. Their fingers ended in talons, rather than fingernails. Bright red capes cascaded down their backs. Short swords hung low behind their backs, almost to their knees. Tristan's experienced eye took quick note of the unique way the baldrics were hung, immediately sensing the ease and speed with which the things would be able to draw their swords. But it was their faces that were most unsettling.

Their skin was pure white—almost translucent—and seemed to shine. Polished metal caps covered their skulls and swept around their eyes and ears. The ears were long, pointed things, with earrings dangling from some of them. Their white, opaque eyes held no irises, but somehow seemed never to miss a thing.

Tristan's heart pounded in his chest, and his right hand tightened around the hilt of his dreggan. He heard the shopkeeper scream, followed by the sound of running and the slamming of a door. The prince knew better than to turn and watch the man run away.

He sized up the situation, and his heart fell.

He had never before faced five at once, he thought nervously.

Faegan wheeled his chair slowly toward the counter. Shailiha walked behind Tristan and over toward the far wall.

"What do you want?" Tristan barked. "Go away and leave us in peace!"

Two of the monsters walked closer. "We want you," one of them said as he approached. "You and the woman. We do not require the old man in the chair." The monster smiled, showing dark, pointed teeth.

"I don't think so," Tristan growled. He raised the tip of his sword a fraction.

In a blindingly fast motion, the other creature drew his sword. It was the quickest use of a blade Tristan had ever seen. Had his dreggan not already been drawn, he would surely have died on the spot.

The two gleaming blades clanged together with a force so powerful they sent sparks flying. As was his habit, Tristan quickly backed off, trying to gain some maneuvering room. But suddenly he stopped, realizing that he did not want to bring his attacker any closer to Shailiha than he must. He began hacking viciously at his foe. But the monster was as skilled as he was, and he could find no opening. Then at last, he saw the chance he had hoped for.

Teeth bared, his opponent suddenly screamed and rushed forward, his short sword raised high over his head. His intention was clear: to strike straight downward, cleaving Tristan's skull.

Just as the thing reached the zenith of his swing, Tristan rushed dangerously in and reached up, grabbing his attacker's sword wrist. And during the split second in which he held the monster's blade in place, he shoved the point of the dreggan to the thing's throat, angling it up.

He pressed the hidden button in the dreggan's hilt, and the blade shot forward the extra foot, entering just beneath the point of the thing's jaw and exiting the top of the head. The monster died immediately. Pressing the button again, Tristan retracted the blade and pushed the body off him.

Enraged, the second of them drew his sword as surely as had the first and with a scream, he rushed at the prince. But this time Tristan had the distance he needed.

Without hesitation he tossed the heavy dreggan from his right hand over into his left. Reaching back, he gripped the handle of his first throwing knife. With a whirl of his arm, the blade twirled unerringly toward its target and buried itself in the center of the thing's forehead with a sickening thud, stopping him in midstride. Stunned, the attacker simply stood as a trail of bright red blood snaked its sure, silent way down over his damaged skullcap and onto his white face. As if trapped in some impossible dream, the creature ran his fingers through it, then blankly examined it before staring back up at the prince. His sword slipped from his fingers and clanged noisily to the floor.

The white eyes closed, and he fell over onto his back, dead.

Chest heaving, Tristan glared at the remaining three. He tossed the dreggan back into his right hand, and his fingers tightened around the hilt.

He didn't have to wait very long.

Suddenly the huge oak chandelier came crashing down in a cacophony of noise, glass, and lamp oil. It smashed directly onto the heads of the three would-be attackers. All three collapsed, as glass shattered and oil spilled as the long rope pooled atop the mess. Blood mixed strangely with the oil and ran across the floor and into the cracks between the floorboards.

Tristan hesitated in shock for an instant, then rushed in and ran each body through. Two were already dead, and the third could not have been far from it—his neck lay at an odd angle, clearly broken, and he was unable to breathe. Tristan's blade was a blessing.

Once done, Tristan turned, and his eyes went wide.

Shailiha had untied the rope holding up the chandelier.

Letting out a great sigh of relief, Tristan uncoiled. Shailiha, arms akimbo, stared intently at the beings she had just killed.

This was the first time she had ever taken a life, Tristan realized as he went to her.

The moment he put his arms around her, she dropped her defiant stance.

"Are you all right?" he asked gently as he looked into her eyes.

"Yes." Her voice was strong and calm. She looked past Tristan's shoulder at the bodies lying beneath the chandelier. Faegan had wheeled his chair over to the tangled mess to examine the creatures.

"And just what were you prepared to do while all of this was going on?" Tristan growled at the wizard, raising a skeptical eyebrow.

"After you killed the first two, even I doubted you could have handled the next three all at once," Faegan said with a smile. "I was of course prepared to use the craft to help you. But then I saw the princess had other plans."

"What in the name of the Afterlife *are* these things?" Tristan asked. Walking over, he reached down and wiped the blade of his dreggan clean with one of the victim's black leather skirts. Satisfied, he slid the sword back into its scabbard. Then he retrieved his throwing knife and repeated the process with it.

Shailiha walked up behind him and took his hand. "I have never seen anything like them," she said quietly.

"Do you remember your question to me about the demonslavers?" Faegan asked, his eyes alight with curiosity. "Well, I think you have just found your answer."

"But where do they come from, and why did they want *us*?" asked Shailiha.

"They are without question some product of the Vagaries," Faegan answered seriously. "But as to how they were produced or who they may have originally been, I cannot say. They may be mutated wizards, as are the blood stalkers. Or perhaps they are something else entirely. Only time will tell. These beings may have been hunting under Krassus' orders. He did, after all, literally dare us to come here to see what was taking place." He paused, rubbing his chin. "I fear, though, that we may have only scratched the surface of our troubles."

"What do we do now?" Shailiha asked.

"First," Faegan answered, "Tristan needs to drag the bodies out back and hide them behind the shop. We have been fortunate, but I believe we have yet to see whatever it is Krassus taunted us about. We must still make our way to the docks—the roughest part of all Farpoint.

"We're within walking distance. Tristan, we leave as soon as you have finished."

Eight

"Are you quite certain you should be doing this, Father?" Celeste asked nervously.

Wigg stepped over another fallen log as he made his way carefully through the forest. "Yes, my dear," he answered patiently. "I am quite all right."

Truth be known, he loved the way she looked after him. He smiled as he realized just how long it had been since anyone had taken care of him: more than three centuries.

He stopped for a moment to get his bearings. An equal number of years had passed since he had visited this section of the Hartwick Woods, and he wanted to be sure of his way.

Walking up beside him, Celeste took her father's hand. "Just the same, let's rest for a moment," she suggested softly.

Looking around, Wigg saw a small clearing and headed for it. They sat in the shade of a hibernium tree. As was the old wizard's custom, he picked a blade of grass and began shredding it with his long, elegant fingers.

The day was still young, the sun just rising above the tops of the trees as they swayed gently back and forth in the wind. The dark green grass was soft and fresh, as were so many of the living things now bursting forth from the Season of New Life. The songs of the birds made a comforting, familiar background refrain.

Wigg turned to look at his daughter—the daughter he had only so recently found. He loved her more than his life, and would do anything to protect her. Although she seemed outwardly normal, Celeste was just beginning to come to grips with all that she had been forced to endure. He had spent hours discussing the matter with Faegan, who had sadly agreed that no matter how intelligent or how high the quality of her endowed blood, Celeste would need a great deal of care and guidance to set things right, if indeed they ever could be.

Both Wigg and Faegan had a great deal of collective knowledge regarding such psychosexual trauma, for they had witnessed firsthand the various abuses of the Coven during the Sorceresses' War of three centuries earlier. But this was different. This time the victim had been the lead wizard's only child, and his stake in her healing was acutely personal.

Lying down in the soft grass, Celeste closed her eyes. Shawna the Short had wisely seen to it that her gown and slippers were replaced with attire more suitable for walking through the forest: a brown leather jerkin over a close-fitting blouse of black silk with sleeves that gathered at the wrists. Trunk hose rose to just above her knees, and she wore soft, brown knee boots. Her dark red hair spread out upon the ground like a luxurious fan. Looking at her, Wigg could easily pick out the fine features she had inherited from her mother, Failee.

No matter what she wore or how distressed she became, her beauty always shone through, the old one thought. In that way, she was much like Shailiha. Yet, in so many ways, she was also very different. Suddenly forced to wipe away a tear, he continued to contemplate the various psychological stages of healing the young woman would be forced to endure.

She was in denial, he knew, and this very uncertain mental stage would presumably be followed by others. Eventually would come her anger, then her eventual acceptance of what had been done to her. And finally, if she was lucky, a form of personal resolution would befall her, truly allowing her to lead a relatively normal life out in the world.

His thoughts floated back to three days earlier, when Krassus had so suddenly appeared. The rogue wizard had said many things that stunned Wigg that day, but none so much as his reference to the partial adept living here in these woods, and his mention of having visited her. Wigg had no doubt that Krassus' motives for doing so could certainly not have been harmless.

The lead wizard had spent the last three days in bed thinking, and trying to regain his strength, before finally deciding to venture into Hartwick. The Minion litter and armed guard of winged warriors that had transported him and Celeste waited patiently just to the north. Wigg sighed. He had come because he knew in his heart he needed to see this person from his past—if indeed she still lived.

Celeste stirred, coming up on one elbow. "You still haven't told me why we're here," she said, smiling at him.

"We have come to see someone," he told her.

"Who?"

He pursed his lips. "Someone I knew a long time ago—someone Krassus referred to that day when he appeared to us in the game room. A woman I was . . . friendly with . . . just after the Sorceresses' War."

For several moments he explained to her the world of the partial adepts, just as Faegan had done for Tristan and Shailiha. He also went on to discuss how their kind had, for better or worse, been banished by the Directorate, both the women and the men. When he finished, Celeste's sapphire eyes were alight with curiosity.

"But why did you bring me with you, Father?" she asked. Sitting upright, she wrapped her hands around her raised knees and placed her chin upon them. "You know how much I love to be with you, but wouldn't you have preferred to see her alone? Especially after all these years?"

"If she still lives, I want her to meet you," he answered. "And truth be known, you and I have had precious little chance to be alone. Besides, if there is anyone in the world I would wish to share this encounter with, it is you."

Deciding to change the subject, Wigg selected another blade of grass to worry. "You care for Tristan very much, don't you?" he asked.

At her father's blunt, unexpected question, Celeste blushed. Then the rose of her cheeks faded, and her expression became more somber, perhaps even bordering on mild confusion.

"I care for all of you," she answered simply. "You know that."

Gently grasping her chin, Wigg turned her face to his. "But you care for the prince in a different way than you do for the rest of us, do you not?" he asked softly.

Celeste lowered her eyes. "I would like to," she said hesitantly.

She tilted her head slightly as if in pain, not knowing how much her next words would sear her father's heart. She was trembling, and tears came to her eyes. "Yes, I would like to care for him. But, you see, I really don't know how," she whispered, so softly he could barely hear her.

Grasping her shoulders, Wigg pulled her close. "I know," he answered.

For a long time they sat that way in the grass, simply holding each other: the father who had never known he had a daughter, and the daughter who had never learned how to love.

Finally, Celeste lifted her face. She looked across the glade, alert, head cocked. Narrowing her eyes, she asked, "Tell me, Father, do you hear that?"

"Of course." He smiled. "I first heard it when we sat down. I have wizard's ears, remember?"

"What is it?"

Across the clearing, a swarm of bees anxiously tended a massive comb nested in the crook of a tree branch. Each of the bees was at least the size of a man's fist. As they swirled and danced in the air, the familiar green-and-purple striping upon their backs was highlighted by the climbing sun.

"They're Eutracian honeybees," he said, smiling again. "They're protecting their hive. They are usually not dangerous, so long as they are left alone."

"What's honey?" she asked.

Realizing anew just how many things Celeste had not experienced that the rest of the world took for granted, he leaned in conspiratorially. "Watch," he whispered. His right hand came up.

As she watched, an azure glow began to form around the comb, trapping the bees inside. They started buzzing even more furiously. Then a nearby dried branch on the grassy floor of the glade rose to penetrate one of the openings in the comb. It withdrew then, one end covered with a sticky, amber-colored substance that dripped lazily to the ground. Then the branch slowly coasted across the clearing, coming to rest patiently in the air before them.

The glow surrounding the comb slowly began to dissipate, finally vanishing altogether. The honeybees went about the business of repairing the rent in the comb.

Wigg grasped the clean end of the branch and held the sticky end out to her. "Taste it," he said with a smile.

"Really?" she asked, her eyes alight with curiosity. "Is it good?"

Still holding the branch, Wigg made a mocking little bow and chuckled. "On my honor as lead wizard of the Directorate."

Celeste took the branch, and tentatively touched her tongue to the honey. Her face lit up.

"I have never tasted anything so wonderful!" she exclaimed brightly. Enjoying the moment, the lead wizard smiled.

But it was that single, innocent action that would cause Celeste's world, and the world of her father, to be changed forever.

Celeste dropped the branch and gripped her throat. Shaking violently, she convulsed into Wigg's arms, her hands reaching up to his face in a pitiful, beseeching gesture of helplessness.

The lead wizard was stunned, unsure of what to do or of what could be causing such a violent reaction. He narrowed his eyes, about to use the craft in an attempt to relieve her suffering.

But he never got the chance.

The sound of snapping branches startled him, and he looked up from the face of his struggling daughter to see the tall grasses across the glade gently, slowly part. Then a large, bulky form emerged from the woods. Wigg froze, and a shiver went down his spine. He heard a soft, menacing growl.

A large, sandy creature, walking on all fours, gracefully stepped from the edge of the clearing, not far from the swarming honeybees. It glared at Wigg with yellow eyes as he tried to quiet his stricken daughter. Lifting its head, the beast flared its nostrils, testing the air; then it leveled its deadly gaze once more at Wigg and Celeste and snarled again, this time more loudly.

It was a saber-toothed bear.

The vicious creatures had roamed Eutracia for centuries. They resembled an odd cross between a bear and a lion. Two long, upper fangs ran well down below the lower jaw. A bearlike face, snout, ears, and intense, yellow eyes made up the head. The leonine body had padded feet with long, pointed claws. The long, slim tail ended in a small ball of fur. The mottled tan-and-black hide had long been prized by Eutracian hunters—provided they lived to tell the tale. Few did.

Unlike many other creatures of these woods, many of the sabertooths were man-eaters—an acquired, not natural, taste. Once one had devoured the meat of a human being—usually out of desperation—it rarely, if ever, returned to its previous feeding habits. Its heightened sense of smell and unusually keen eyesight were legendary. This one was clearly a male, by far the heavier but not necessarily the deadlier of the two sexes.

It seemed clear that this saber-tooth had already feasted upon humans at least once, and wished to do so again.

And then, quite unexpectedly, the saber-tooth's mate quietly, smoothly appeared at the opposite side of the glade. She padded silently to a spot just inside the circle, and crouched in the grass, her long muscles clenched. Her hungry, yellow eyes missed nothing.

Wigg held his breath, trying to remain as still as possible with the struggling Celeste in his lap. He had heard tales of unarmed woodsmen who had come upon these beasts, only to remain stock-still and have them blessedly saunter away. But now, with the female squarely at the opposite end of the clearing, Wigg knew that his luck had run out. He had heard enough about them to know that first the male would attack, grasping his victim in his jaws. Then the female would rush in from the opposite direction to deliver the deathblow—either with a powerful swipe of her claws, or by impaling the prey on her curved, white fangs. After that, their prize secure, the leisurely feasting would go on for a long time.

Then the sudden realization hit him: It was the honey that had brought them! What an idiot he had been to break open the comb!

If they were to have any chance of surviving this, he must act immediately. It was highly unlikely he could kill both animals, even using the craft. He wouldn't have the time.

Standing and sliding Celeste down to the grass behind him, he cautiously raised his right hand toward the male.

The saber-tooth charged.

Bounding across the field, its teeth exposed in a vicious snarl, the monster leapt into the air.

Wigg loosed an azure bolt from his hand. It struck the creature squarely in the forehead. With a loud crack the saber-tooth's skull parted. Dead, he crashed to the earth just feet from where the wizard stood.

Wigg whirled around, robes flying, and raised his arm again. But the female was already on the move. He was too late.

Suddenly several azure bolts came soaring out of nowhere, crashing into the female saber-tooth. They were the most brilliant, powerful beams Wigg had ever seen. Striking the beast almost simultaneously, they literally ripped her apart. Her head exploded, her legs were severed from her body, and then her torso blew apart, blood and innards flying across the field. What was left of the creature skidded sloppily to a stop less than a meter from his boots. Whirling around again, Wigg looked to see who had commanded such awesome power. His jaw dropped.

It was Celeste.

She stood before him, swaying, with a strange, determined look on her face. Her sapphire eyes had rolled up into their sockets. Her skin was pale, her body shaking. The fingertips of her right hand were scorched and black. Smoke was rising from them, drifting away on the morning breeze. She took a single, weak step forward.

"Father . . ."

And then she collapsed.

Wigg scooped her up in his arms and began running back into the forest as fast as he could, in search of the one person he hoped might be able to help.

Nine

By the time Tristan had hidden the dead demonslavers in the alley behind the apothecary shop and the three travelers were ready to go on, the streets seemed even more deserted. The few people who did venture out glared and pointed at the prince and his sister, as if the two of them had no right to be any part of the city's population.

Faegan searched out a clothing shop and, leaving Tristan and Shailiha waiting in the shadows of a nearby alley, went in alone to purchase two hooded robes to cover the bodies and heads of the Chosen Ones. Not perfect disguises, but the best he could do without the aid of the craft. Tristan worried that the robe covered his weapons, making it nearly impossible for him to grasp them quickly, but he kept his concerns to himself. There seemed little other choice.

They then proceeded to a stable, where Faegan was forced to pay the suspicious stablemaster handsomely for three run-down horses, a dilapidated cart, and extra tack. Tristan harnessed one of the mounts to the cart and hoisted Faegan atop its seat, and at last the three of them made their way to the harbor area of Farpoint.

Although the sun was beginning to set, the docks were alive with people. A large crowd had gathered here, and it was clear they were eagerly waiting for something to happen. The air was full of the smells of salty sea air and freshly caught fish.

Tristan slid off the swaybacked roan mare, and as Shailiha dismounted her aged gelding, he went around to the back of the cart and got out Faegan's chair. Shailiha held the chair while Tristan lifted Faegan from the buckboard seat and got him settled.

Then he turned to study the inn where Faegan had directed them to stop. Many of its shutters were broken and peeling from the constant exposure to the strong, salty winds. Some of the windows were cracked, and the steps to the lobby were in disrepair. The place had clearly seen better days.

"Why are we stopping here?" Shailiha asked. She was eager to get to the oceanfront. "The carriage driver said we needed to get to the docks. Can't we just quietly wend our way through the crowd?"

"No," Faegan answered adamantly as he looked around. "This inn is perfect for what I have in mind—the kind of place where few questions will be asked. Besides, Krassus may be near, not to mention more of the demonslavers. Tristan, I want you to go around back and tell me what you find. In particular, I want to know whether there is any way up to the roof, and a secure place where we might tie the horses."

Tristan nodded. After a smile to his sister, he was gone.

The alley behind the inn was inconspicuous enough, with the usual iron rings embedded in the building's rear wall to secure bridle reins. Several mounts were already tied there, telling the prince that the shopworn inn had at least a few customers. An iron fire ladder reached from the ground all the way to the roof, with platforms at each of the inn's four levels. Backing farther into the shadows, Tristan observed the inn quietly, branding the scene into his memory. Finally satisfied, he returned to the street.

"Bridle rings *and* a ladder," he said quietly to the wizard.

"Does the ladder go all the way to the roof?" Faegan asked.

"Yes."

"And does the roof appear to be flat?"

"From what I could see, yes."

"Good," Faegan answered. Tristan and Shailiha could see mischief coming to the ancient wizard's eyes as his plan continued to form.

"I want you and Shailiha to walk the three horses around back," he said. "Leave your two saddled. Unharness the cart and put it to one side. Take the extra saddle and bridle from the cart and put them on my horse. Tie all the horses to the wall. Then return. Do it quickly."

Tristan and Shailiha carried out the wizard's orders as swiftly as they could, then returned to the front of the inn.

"Is it done?" Faegan asked. Tristan nodded.

"Very well," the wizard said. "Follow me into the inn. Whatever you do, do not lower your hoods. Stay quiet, and follow my lead. Try to act as though you do not exist." He pointed to one of the loose boards of the inn steps. "Tristan, if you would?" he asked.

Understanding, the prince reached down to tear the wide, loose board away from its few remaining nails, then inclined it against the steps of the inn. It made a serviceable ramp. After briefly testing its strength, he wheeled Faegan's chair up and through the door into the lobby, Shailiha right behind.

Inside, the inn was dingy, dark, and unappealing. The large front room held several chairs, tables, and a long bar with a mirror behind it. Sullen-looking men, some obviously fishermen, sat hunched over the tables and bar, drinking quietly. Several scantily dressed women walked among the tables, flirting with the men. For hire, no doubt, Tristan thought with a slight shake of his head.

The thin, greasy-looking man Tristan took to be the innkeeper sat at a small desk in one corner, making notes in a bound ledger. A tankard sat before him. He did not look up. Indeed, no one took any great notice of the newcomers at all, save for a few furtive, curious glances at Faegan's chair. With a smile, the wizard calmly wheeled himself toward the proprietor.

"Three rooms, please," Faegan said politely.

The man looked up from his arithmetic. His eyes were dark and distrustful.

"The only rooms I have left are on the top floor," he said rudely, "but taking you up and down the stairs isn't included in the rent."

Some of the customers laughed aloud.

Faegan graciously ignored the insult. "Thank you for your worry, but my bodyguard will take care of that. He's quite used to it, in fact. Now then, how much?"

"How many nights?" the innkeeper asked. He took a sloppy gulp of stale-smelling ale, then set the tankard back down on the desk. Letting go a wet belch, he wiped his mouth with a stained, gartered shirtsleeve.

"Three rooms, one night each," Faegan answered.

"Twelve kisa," the man replied. "Fourth floor. The washing facilities are at the end of the hall. Take it or leave it."

Twelve kisa was a steep price for such a place, Tristan thought, but clearly Faegan thought it better not to bargain. Reaching into his robes, the wizard took out the necessary kisa and dropped them on the desk. After counting them, the innkeeper produced three keys, which he handed over to the wizard. Saying nothing more, Faegan turned his chair to the stairs, Tristan and Shailiha following behind.

At the foot of the steps, Tristan leaned in, putting his lips to the wizard's ear. "Are you joking?" he growled quietly. "Four flights of stairs?"

"No." Faegan smiled. "Actually, I'm hoping there will be five." Looking over to Shailiha, he gave her a wink. She smiled back quizzically.

"What do you mean five?" Tristan argued.

"We have no friends here, and this is no time for a debate," Faegan answered urgently. "Let's go."

Sighing, Tristan began pulling the wizard's chair backward up the steps. After what seemed an eternity, they finally reached the fourth floor. Tristan looked around cautiously. Nothing seemed amiss.

"What are our room numbers?" Shailiha asked Faegan as Tristan leaned over, breathing heavily from exhaustion.

"We won't be using the rooms." Faegan smiled and looked up at the ceiling. "That was just for show."

Before either of the Chosen Ones could ask the obvious question, the wizard found what he was looking for. In the middle of the ceiling was a wooden framework, from which hung a rope ending in a pull handle.

Faegan wheeled himself to the rope and gave it a tug. Stairs to the roof slowly descended on a pivot, revealing the first stars of the evening twinkling through the opening. Faegan grinned at the prince.

"As I told you, there are five," he said impishly. "But again you must pull me up without my using the craft. There might still be people about."

Tristan nodded. With a determined grip he pushed the chair to the stairs, and, with some help from Shailiha below, managed to pull it up and onto the roof. Shailiha scrambled up behind them, then pulled the duplicate rope on the other side, wisely lifting the pivoting stairway back into place.

The gray slate roof was large and flat. The wind had risen, and the smell of the sea came to them again. From here the prince could see much of the city, the flickering streetlamps casting macabre, dancing shadows along the sides of the buildings and down the cobblestoned thoroughfares.

"Quickly, Tristan," Faegan whispered. "Lift me from my chair and put me down by the east edge of the roof. Then both of you come and lie next to me, one on either side."

Tristan did as the wizard ordered, and Faegan lay on his stomach, peering over the edge toward the docks. Tristan and Shailiha lay down beside him.

Down on the stone piers that formed the breakwater to the sea, hundreds of people were milling anxiously about. Three large ships, their sails furled, lay tied up in docking berths, their white, salty waterlines riding well above the waves. Even Tristan's inexperienced eyes could guess that meant the ships were empty of cargo.

A raised wooden platform had been placed in a cleared area between the crowd and the water's edge. A short series of steps ran down from one of its sides to the ground. Alongside the platform a long, crude, rectangular table sat upon the pier. Seated behind it were at least a dozen men in dark robes. Consuls' robes, the prince thought. On the table before each man lay several objects, but Tristan could not identify them from this distance. The men behind the table sat patiently, as if waiting for something.

Before the table stood two large, black kettles with strange, curved iron handles. An orange-red glow emanated from each of their circular tops. Tristan assumed that the strange auras were being produced by glowing, red-hot coals deep within them. Black smoke rose lazily from the kettles' glowing embers, vanishing into the growing darkness of the evening sky.

Near the kettles, two pillories had been constructed. The orange glow from the black kettles mixed with the light from the dozens of oil lamps to cast strangely flickering shadows across the hulls of the silently waiting ships and the stark, empty pillories.

Then Tristan saw the white-skinned demonslavers lining the inner edges of the clearing, keeping the burgeoning crowd from approaching the raised platform by the constant threat of their nine-tails and tridents. Then Krassus came into view. The people in the crowd began to shout invectives and wave their arms in anger. Krassus didn't seem to care.

Slowly he walked to the platform in his blue-and-gray robe. An elderly woman with frizzled gray hair and dressed in a shopworn black robe followed along behind him. As they approached, the demonslavers kept the crowd back. Without fanfare Krassus and his unknown companion walked to the side of the platform and up the steps. They remained silent.

Tristan looked over at Faegan. "Is that woman the partial adept Krassus talked about that day in the palace?" he asked urgently. "Do you know her?"

"From here, I can't tell who she might be," Faegan whispered back, not shifting his eyes from the scene. "But it is obvious she has importance for him."

Tristan expected Krassus to speak. But he didn't. He simply stood there, the woman by his side, as if he, too, waited for something.

Suddenly Tristan heard the sound of shod hooves rattling harshly against the same cobblestoned street he, Faegan, and Shailiha had just come down. Turning, he crawled on his stomach across the slate roof to its northern side and looked carefully over.

At least a dozen carriages-of-four were approaching, their teams trotting down the street and toward the docks. But as they neared, Tristan could see that the vehicles were really not carriages at all. They were more like bizarre, wooden-slatted cages on wheels, and they were being driven by yet more of the demonslavers. Finally he could see them better, and his heart skipped a beat.

They were full of people.

Each of the rough-hewn cages contained perhaps twenty or more people, men and women alike. They sat crammed upon what looked like piles of soiled straw, and he could make out black iron manacles here and there.

The cages continued rattling up the street toward the docks. Tristan crawled back across the roof to lie beside Faegan. Below, the demonslavers on the pier barked out orders, and the crowd reluctantly parted to allow the vehicles to pass.

The cages came to a stop before the long table. A group of demonslavers promptly went to one corner of the clearing, and from a pile lying there each of them took up a device that seemed to be a long iron rod with a ring at one end. Another group of demonslavers began unlocking and opening the cage doors.

One by one the rod-wielding demonslavers approached the open cages. With a quick twist of the rod handles, the rings at their ends clanged open. The open rings were shoved into the cages and forced up against the throats of the captives. With another twist, the rings closed viciously around the prisoners' necks. One by one, the men and women were dragged out, kicking and screaming.

With the captives finally free of their cages, Tristan could see them much better. It was then that he began to get an inkling of why he and his sister had been regarded so strangely all day.

All the slaves were about the same age as he and Shailiha!

Tristan looked back to Krassus. The wizard had yet to speak, but his dark eyes missed nothing as the prisoners were hauled from their cages and forced to move toward the table where the robed men sat waiting.

"Can you tell what's happening?" he asked Faegan quietly. All he could make out was that the robed men were busy doing something that involved the occasional azure glow of the craft, and were making notations in some kind of large books.

"I can see part of it," the wizard responded softly. "And yes, I believe I have a good idea of what is going on. But let us not speak of it now."

There was a distinct sadness in the old man's tone. Shailiha looked to her brother and placed an index finger across her lips. Tristan nodded back.

One by one the prisoners were hauled away from the table by their necks and locked into one of the two pillories. Two demonslavers pulled the rods from the black kettles; the ends of the rods came out glowing bright red. Branding irons.

Before each of the slavers pressed his hot iron to skin, he looked up to Krassus, waiting for a sign. And each time, before giving his blessing, the wizard in the two-colored robe would look down for an indication from the men at the tables. Then he would indicate with either his right hand or his left.

As the demonslavers pressed the heated irons into the left shoulders of the prisoners, screams resounded through the night. Many if not most of them fainted away in the stocks, and were dragged by their necks to separate areas on the pier. When one prisoner was finished, another immediately took his or her place. As the excruciating process continued, Tristan saw that one group of slaves was becoming noticeably larger than the other.

Faegan lowered his head. Shailiha closed her eyes, brushing tears from her face. Only Tristan's eyes remained locked on the gruesome scene, his hands balled up into fists and his jaw clenched with the frustration of not being able to take action. Finally he, too, could take no more, and he slowly closed his eyes against the spectacle.

Those prisoners were his people, the prince realized in shame and horror, and there was absolutely nothing he could do to help them. Was that what Krassus' taunts had meant? What in the name of the Afterlife was it all about?

At last, blessedly, the branding stopped, all of the prisoners having been marked with a rod from one kettle or the other. The moaning and crying of the victims was softer now.

Those who had fainted were revived by having cold seawater splashed in their faces. Then the two groups were marched down the piers to the waiting frigates and forced up the gangways. Full of despair, Tristan lowered his head.

Suddenly a long, silent, moonlit shadow flowed darkly across the roof between him and his sister. Then came another, and yet another. Tristan tugged silently on the sleeve of the wizard's robe, slid the dreggan from its scabbard, and smoothly rolled over onto his back. He was on his feet in a flash, his dreggan in a strong, two-handed grip.

Three demonslavers stood near the ladder at the other side of the roof, the rose-colored moonlight glinting off their alabaster skin. Each of them held a short sword. Two of them smiled.

Just then Shailiha turned to see why Tristan had risen, and the air left her lungs in a rush. Turning over, Faegan also looked. But before anything could be done, all three slavers charged at once.

Tristan ran across the roof, his dreggan slashing as he went. The first of the slavers he met died quickly, its head cleanly severed from its body.

But the next two would not be so easy. They hacked savagely at Tristan, who fended them off as best he could, his sword almost a blur. But inexorably they came on, forcing him to keep backing up toward the wizard and the princess, as the three blades clanged coldly, harshly against one another.

Shailiha looked aghast at Faegan, silently beseeching him to intervene with the craft, no matter the consequences.

The demonslavers were closing on Tristan, and it was plain to see that the prince was tiring. Faegan relaxed his mind and stopped cloaking their endowed blood.

Just then Tristan lost his footing on the slick roof and fell hard on his back. Sensing victory, the two monsters rushed in, swords held high. Faegan raised both his arms.

Twin azure bolts tore across the roof directly over Tristan. He could feel the searing heat, see the blinding azure light, and sense the rush of the wind as the force of them ripped at his hair and clothing and almost tore the dreggan from his hands. Turning his head and gritting his teeth, he held on to the sword with all his might.

Shailiha glanced down at Krassus and saw him suddenly stiffen. With a smile, he motioned to a group of about twenty demonslavers, then pointed to the roof of the inn.

Faegan's bolts struck each of the slavers squarely in the chest. Tristan, his eyes still closed, heard their bodies being ripped apart; he felt and smelled the sickening offal, blood, and sinew splattering down on him. In a matter of seconds, it was over.

He opened his eyes and saw one of the monsters' short, shiny swords lying quietly beside him in the moonlight.

But where was the other?

Wildly turning his head to the sky, he saw the shiny, silver point of the second sword. Launched skyward by the explosions of the wizard's bolts, it was free-falling straight down at him.

He started to roll to one side, realizing even as he moved that he was too late.

Suddenly an azure hand grasped the sword only inches from his throat. Wasting no time, Tristan rolled away, coming to his hands and knees in the slick, bloody mess. As the glow of the craft disappeared, he watched the sword fall harmlessly to the roof with a clang. He picked it up with his free hand and ran to Shailiha and Faegan.

The wizard was already seated in his chair, but the look on his face was far from reassuring. Tristan shoved the demonslaver's sword into Shailiha's hands. "Do you remember your fencing lessons?" he shouted urgently.

Smiling, she nodded.

"There is no time for talk!" Faegan growled, pointing toward the opposite side of the roof. "By now Krassus will surely know we are here! Make for the horses!"

Tristan, sword still in hand, looked briefly into his sister's eyes. Then they both sprinted across the slippery, blood-soaked roof. Faegan levitated his chair and soared ahead of them.

The wizard reached the edge first and looked down. Other than the tied horses and the abandoned cart, he saw nothing, but he knew that the relative peace of the alleyway wouldn't last much longer. He swung the chair back near the prince and his sister.

"Both of you—onto my chair, now!" he ordered.

Somewhat bewildered, the two of them did as they were told. Shailiha sat on the wizard's lap; Tristan clung to one of the chair arms. Then Faegan steered his chair over the side of the roof.

On the way down Tristan saw about twenty demonslavers working their way through the crowd and up the side street, viciously using their whips, swords, and tridents to clear a path.

Faegan hurried his chair downward as fast as he could safely manage. About one meter above the backs of the horses, he stopped and looked frantically at the prince and his sister.

"Jump!"

Tristan immediately let go, falling the remaining distance to the ground. As he ran to untie their horses, out of the corner of his eye he saw Shailiha drop directly into her saddle, the demonslaver's sword still in one hand. She masterfully whirled her horse around.

Faegan levitated himself from his chair and, with a wave of one hand, let it go. The centuries-old chair fell to the ground, smashing into pieces. Ignoring it, he lowered himself into the saddle atop the third horse. Tristan leapt into his saddle and wheeled his mount around, his back to the wall of the inn, to look down their escape route toward the end of the alley.

The rear door of the inn opened a crack. A gleam of soft, yellow light cut through the darkness of the alleyway, spilling out onto the ground.

It was the greasy innkeeper. Raising a demonslaver sword high in both hands, the point forward, he charged at the prince's back.

Shailiha noticed the sudden light and raised her sword. Spurring her horse forward, she used the momentum to shove her blade directly into the man's throat; it went through his neck and came out the back. She pulled her weapon out hard and swung it.

Tristan wheeled his horse around just in time to see his sister swing her stolen blade in a perfect arc, taking the innkeeper's head cleanly off at the neck. The headless body remained standing for a moment, as if it were still somehow in control of itself. Then what was left of the innkeeper fell forward, into the alleyway in front of Shailiha's horse. Blood poured from the ravaged neck into the thirsty dirt.

Without pause the three of them turned their horses and charged side by side for the end of the alleyway. Tristan held his breath, wondering if they could make it to the street before the passageway filled with demonslavers. But even before their horses could break into a full gallop, the prince had his answer.

The monsters flowed down the street like a river, blocking the way to freedom. There had to be at least one hundred of them. Waving swords and tridents, they shouted and hissed as they formed what seemed to be an impenetrable wall at the entrance to the street.

Tristan turned frantically around in his saddle. He looked behind him, only to be reminded that the way back was a dead end. Charging through the slavers was the only way to freedom, but he knew in his heart that it couldn't be done.

Holding up his hand, Faegan brought his mount to a skidding stop; Tristan and Shailiha followed suit. The alleyway became strangely quiet, as the slavers stopped shouting and began walking purposefully, menacingly toward them. Tristan turned frantically to the wizard.

"Can you kill them?" he asked.

"Some," Faegan answered quickly, his eyes trained upon the monsters as they came. "But there are too many, and no doubt even more are following behind them." Then a knowing look crossed his face, and he turned to the prince and princess. "Killing them is not the answer."

"Then what is?" Shailiha asked urgently.

"Avoiding them. Follow me single file, and don't look back," he ordered. "Whatever happens, don't be surprised at what you see, and just keep on going. When we finally reach the street, whip your horses for all they're worth, and stay with me. Do you understand?" His last sentence wasn't a question. It was an order.

They both nodded.

Whipping his horse with the reins, Faegan charged down the alley, Shailiha behind him, Tristan bringing up the rear.

At first the prince thought he must be seeing things. Glowing a brilliant azure, something took solid form.

It was a bridge.

Barely wide enough to allow a single rider at a time, it arched from the dirt of the alleyway, and climbed over the heads of the slavers, touching down again on the other side. Caught off guard, the demonslavers stood in confused wonder.

At the sight of the glowing bridge, all three horses skidded to a stop and reared in fright. Several precious seconds passed as Faegan fought to bring his mare under control. Only when he got her moving again did Tristan's and Shailiha's mounts settle down and obey their commands to approach the bridge.

Faegan's horse reached it first, his mare's hooves banging down loudly upon the embodiment of the craft as she carried him to its apex and then started down the other side. Next came Shailiha. Following close behind, Tristan's horse approached the glowing ramp.

But upon placing her first, poorly shod hoof onto the glowing bridge, Tristan's mare stumbled, and went down hard on both front knees.

Tristan was launched forward. Her front legs broken, the mare fell over onto her back, screaming wildly. Somehow Tristan managed to keep hold of his dreggan, but the slavers charged him immediately. He staggered drunkenly to one knee, then finally to his feet. Forced to use both hands, he raised his sword weakly, but could only get it as high as his waist.

From where he stood, he could see nothing but slavers coming toward him, their awful faces and the whiteness of their skin strangely highlighted by the glow from the azure bridge.

On the other side, Faegan and Shailiha wheeled their horses around to look. Shailiha screamed and would have spurred her gelding back over the bridge, but Faegan grabbed her reins, forcing her horse around. Some of the slavers near the bridge were already coming their way, and there was no time to lose.

"No!" he shouted. "We have to go! There is nothing we can do for him now! We will return for him, I promise!"

Shailiha cried out as she lost sight of her brother. The glowing bridge dissolved, leaving only the mob of angry slavers as they crowded in around the prince.

Shailiha turned her terrified eyes back to the wizard. Finally she lowered her head and nodded. It was without question the hardest single decision she had ever been forced to make.

Following Faegan's horse, Shailiha thundered down the cobblestoned street just as another wave of the sword-wielding demonslavers rushed in.

Stunned and bewildered, his hands and body covered with blood from the battles on the roof, Tristan tried his best to swing his dreggan at the first of them. But the heavy blade was too much for him, and its momentum took him to his knees.

Then a blinding white light seared through his consciousness, and he collapsed to the dirt.

Ten

Abbey walked down through the gently sloping field of flowers. The light of day was gone, and the stars had come out. Moonlit shadows created by the yellow-and-turquoise-leaved chirithium trees slowly lengthened out over the waving grasses, blossoms, and herbs she walked through on her way home. Carried by the wind, light, fluffy clouds danced to and fro in the night sky, as if struggling to escape their banishment into the darkness. The blooming fragrances of the Season of New Life swirled everywhere about her.

She stopped for a moment to tie up her gray-streaked dark hair, and smiled, taking in the smells, the colors, and the breeze. Then, gripping her straw basket a bit tighter, she continued up the hill.

She had been out foraging today, just as she had done for the last three days, trying to replace at least some of what the mysterious robbers had taken from her. It had been a good day, and her large, hinge-topped basket was full. When she returned home, she would meticulously dry, store, and catalogue what she had reaped. But first she'd enjoy a cup of sallow blossom tea, she decided.

Abbey had no idea who the intruders had been, or how they had found her, but she was concerned that she had not recognized the cruel woman who had so obviously been an herbmistress. So few of their kind remained, and they had always tried to stay in contact with one another. Even more astonishing was the fact that the unknown woman had been traveling with a wizard. After all, the wizards had banished those of her kind—both males and females alike—from their presence long ago.

As she crested the hill, her cottage came into view. She took a quick breath.

Smoke was curling up from the chimney, and light shone from the cottage windows.

She stood in the field for some time, trying to figure out what to do. She could run, but there was no safe place nearby that she could easily reach. Finally she decided to approach the cottage from the rear, where there were no windows, then creep around to one side and try to peek in without being seen. Walking over to the edge of the field, she entered the dense cover of the drooping chirithium trees and started down.

The glade surrounding the cottage seemed deserted; she saw no horses tied nearby. She carefully set down her basket by a tree, then made her way as silently as possible to the rear wall. Keeping low, she crept around the corner and squatted beneath the first of the leaded windows. Slowly she raised her head up as far as she dared and looked in.

A young, beautiful woman with brilliant red hair was lying on Abbey's bed. Her eyes were closed; her face was very pale. The staggered rising and falling of the thin blanket that covered the woman told the experienced herbmistress that the stranger was having great difficulty breathing. A man's hand, with long, elegant fingers, rested flat on the woman's forehead. Abbey could not see the rest of him.

Slipping quietly around the back of the cottage, she retrieved her precious basket and then made her way to the front. She gathered her courage, took a deep breath, and walked in, allowing the rusty door hinges to announce her entrance. The man sitting by the bed turned to face her.

Abbey dropped her basket, and its contents spilled to the floor. Her hands flew to cover her open mouth.

"Hello, Abbey," the man said gently. "It's been a long time. Please pardon my intrusion, but I very much need your help."

Abbey, her eyes locked on his face, staggered toward a chair and sat down clumsily. It was difficult for her to speak, to think, or even to breathe as a flood of conflicting emotions coursed through her.

Wigg waited, maintaining an outward calm. But inside, he, too, was bubbling with unexpected emotions. But as he watched, her expression changed from one of astonishment to anger.

Finally Abbey pointed to the woman in the bed. "Who is she?" she asked. She was chagrined to hear her voice crack. "After all these years, why are you here?"

At first Wigg did not answer. He pointed to the basket and the plants lying on the stone floor. The scattered clippings rose into the air and floated over to the basket, where they fell into a neat, contained pile.

The refilled basket floated up to the table beside the stunned herb-mistress and came to rest. Wigg took another long breath, letting it go slowly before placing his hands into the opposite sleeves of his robe.

"Her name is Celeste," he answered softly. "She is of endowed blood, and has been adversely affected by the craft. In all my years I have seen this phenomenon occur only one other time—quite recently, in fact—to another woman who means just as much to me. The other woman, however, managed its effects much more handily. I cannot be sure, but I think it was because of the greater strength of her blood. In any event, this woman needs our help. I have been unable to awaken her by myself, and I fear that if she does not return to consciousness soon, I may lose her for all time. Will you help me?" The wizard's eyes were shiny with unshed tears.

Abbey stood and walked to the bed. First she looked into each of Celeste's eyes; then she cautiously examined her strangely scorched fingertips.

"Her mind has gone deep. For the moment she is stable," the herb-mistress told Wigg cautiously, "but she is in a bad way. Although I am not sure how much help I can be, I will do what I can. But hear this first, Lead Wizard." Her gray eyes bored directly into Wigg's. "What I do, I do for her, and her alone. Not for you."

"Thank you," Wigg said gratefully. "And I cannot blame you for the way you feel." Silence reigned for a moment.

"First I want to know who she is," Abbey said. She wanted to prepare a tea, but the fire had gone down. She walked to the hearth and bent over to stoke the flames. But before she could, Wigg pointed, and the logs blazed again. Then two more from the nearby pile rose into the air and floated over to fall upon the ones already burning.

Abbey sighed. "I had almost forgotten how much easier life can be for certain trained males," she commented as she began to prepare some tea. One corner of Wigg's mouth came up: He could hardly disagree.

"I asked you a question," she added without turning around. "Who is she?"

"She is my daughter," the lead wizard answered softly, knowing the effect his words would have.

For several long moments Abbey stopped what she was doing. "So you finally remarried," she said softly, once more busying herself with the teakettle. Wigg thought he heard her voice crack again.

"No," he answered gently. "Failee was apparently pregnant when she left me. Celeste was protected by time enchantments and is nearly as old as you and I." He paused. "A great many things have transpired in our land since we were last together. Much of which, I'm sure, you remain unaware of. It would be a very long story."

Abbey, her face emotionless, placed two cups of tea on the table and took a seat. She beckoned Wigg to join her. "You and I are each blessed with the enchantments granting eternal life," she said flatly. "I think we can spare the time."

Wigg's mouth came up into a short smile.

As succinctly as he could, the lead wizard told her of the workings of the Paragon. He also described the Tome and its several volumes. After explaining the importance of Tristan and Shailiha, he then told her of the unexpected return of the Sorceresses of the Coven, and how he and Tristan had ventured across the Sea of Whispers to defeat them in the previously unknown land of Parthalon. He told her everything: the story of Nicholas, Ragnar, and Celeste, and the destruction of the Gates of Dawn.

Abbey listened intently, searching for any scrap of information that might help her unravel the secret to helping Wigg's stricken daughter. He explained the recent discovery of the Forestallments in the blood signatures of Shailiha, baby Morganna, Tristan, and Celeste. These spells took the form of crooked branches leading away from the main pattern of the blood signature, and had apparently been placed into their blood by the Coven—for what purposes Wigg and Faegan could only guess and would likely never know. It had been such a Forestallment that had resulted in Shailiha's highly unusual ability to commune with the fliers of the field. And the Forestallment he had unwittingly helped activate in Celeste had enabled her to save their lives by killing the saber-toothed bear.

At the mention of Celeste's Forestallment, Abbey's eyes lit up. She stood and walked quickly back to the bed. Lifting Celeste's hands, she again examined her blackened fingertips and broken nails.

"You say the bolt she sent against the bear—this 'Forestallment,' as you call it—was unusually strong?" she asked. "And that it happened just after she began to convulse?"

"Yes," Wigg answered. "Her bolts were the most powerful I have ever seen; they literally ripped the creature apart. Then she collapsed. And now . . ." He paused, one eyebrow rising, "I think I know why."

"Explain," Abbey said, returning to the table.

"You just said it yourself," he replied. "Her first use of a Forestallment came quickly, immediately after its activation, so her blood had no time to adjust to its new state. No doubt it was Failee's intention to activate Celeste's gifts one by one, and train her in their use gradually, in a controlled environment. But given the desperate situation, Celeste acted instinctively. This proved to be too much for her untrained blood, and plunged her into this deep, twilight state." He turned sadly, looking back over at the bed. "There is another wizard with me at the palace. His name is Faegan. He would have been able to help, for he is also an herbalist. But your cottage was much closer."

"And so you brought her here," Abbey answered skeptically. "But what were the two of you doing in these woods to begin with?"

"We were coming to see you about a different matter," Wigg said rather apologetically. "I was hoping, after all of these years, to gain your help. Eutracia needs you."

Abbey shook her head slowly. "It seems you suddenly require a great deal of help, Lead Wizard," she replied stiffly. The herbmistress thought for a moment. Then she leaned closer, her face dark.

"Tell me," she said sternly, "after more than three hundred years of surviving without my services, how is it that the lofty nation of Eutracia suddenly needs one of those who was so summarily banished?"

Trying to think of a way to broach the subject, Wigg looked around the unkempt cottage. Bottles lay overturned and shelves had been torn down; much of the glassware that should have contained Abbey's hard-won treasures was conspicuously empty. His eyes went back to the herb-mistress. "I don't remember you being such a poor housekeeper," he said simply.

"What does that have to do with anything?" she shot back.

"This mess is not like you, and we both know it," Wigg said gently. And then he took a breath and asked, "He was here, wasn't he? The man in the two-colored robe. And he had a woman with him—a partial adept, possibly trained both as an herbmistress and a blaze-gazer. They took much from you, didn't they? Not the least of which was a sizable portion of your rather infamous pride."

The herbmistress' hard shell seemed to crack a bit, and a tear came to one eye. Taking a chance, Wigg placed one of his hands over hers. Surprisingly, she did not pull away.

"Did they hurt you?" he asked softly.

"No," she said, looking down. "But the woman knew exactly which herbs and compounds she wanted. Many of them were among my most prized. I cannot say for sure whether she was a gazer, since she practiced no such art in my presence. But given her knowledge of my stores, she was certainly an herbmistress. The man was ill with some disease of the lungs. He put me in some kind of bizarre, glowing cage, and I couldn't stop him. All I could do was watch as they destroyed a lifetime of work." She raised her face back up. "But how did you know?"

"His name is Krassus, and he was once first alternate to the Directorate of Wizards," Wigg answered. "Ironically, I appointed him to that position myself. He is now apparently a full wizard of some power, his gifts perhaps imbued by Nicholas through Forestallments. But we do not know who the woman is. Krassus claimed she is a blaze-gazer, but we have no proof of that. He came to the palace demanding information. He searches for a man named Wulfgar. His other quest is for something called the Scrolls of the Ancients. Tell me, are you familiar with either?"

"No."

"When I could not answer his questions, he beat me and violated my mind," Wigg said angrily. "He also gloated about having been here, and leaving you in a bad way. Then, after promising to kill Faegan and me, he left. I simply had to come, to see if you were all right. But I must admit that I had other reasons for visiting you."

"I knew you lay ill," she said unexpectedly.

Wigg's eyes sharpened at Abbey's unexpected statement. "What?" he asked.

"After they left, I went to my gazing flame and searched for you," she answered. "I admit that it was not the first time I have done so. You were lying in a bed, with people standing around you whom I did not know."

"So you have a gazing flame here?" Wigg asked.

Abbey nodded.

"But what is there of mine that you could possibly have kept all of these years?" he asked, clearly puzzled. "Don't you need something personal of your subject in order to properly view the image?"

Abbey reached for the locket around her neck and opened it. Curled up inside was a short braid of dark brown hair. She placed it on the table. Wigg's eyes went wide.

"Mine?" he asked. "But how could that be?"

"I took it from you in bed one night, more than three hundred years go," she answered, placing the braid back into the pendant and locking it again. "You always slept so deeply." A slight smile finally appeared on her face: the coming of some memory, perhaps. But then it was quickly overtaken by another look of anger.

"And then you voted with your brotherhood to banish all the partial adepts," she whispered angrily. "Yet another of the Directorate's knee-jerk reactions to anyone or anything of the craft not directly controlled by them." She turned her face away. "You hurt me deeply, Wigg. You hurt all of us with partial blood. To this day I am not sure I will ever be able to forgive you. It was so unfair . . ."

Wigg sighed. If he could have taken back parts of those days, he would.

"I voted for my nation," he said sadly. "In hindsight, I've come to see that many of our decisions were wrong. But both Eutracia and her monarchy were new, and still in great distress. The survival of our land and the foretold coming of the Chosen Ones were far more important than the two of us, or what we may have wanted for ourselves. Surely you can see that. And like you, I have suffered much. I'm not naive,

Abbey, so I won't ask you to forgive me. But the best, most personal gift I could bestow upon you before you left was the time enchantments. Had the Directorate discovered what I had done, there would surely have been a great scandal; perhaps even my own banishment from the Directorate, given the harsh, reactionary attitudes of those days. But now all of my friends of that august body are dead."

He paused, wondering how his next words would be received, then laced his long fingers together and placed his hands on the table.

"As I said, Abbey, we need you," he continued softly. "When I leave here, I want you to come back to Tammerland with me."

Stunned, she looked at him with wide eyes.

"No!" she said flatly. "I won't do it! Why should I? My life is good here, and the people here have come to rely on me for healing. Here, at least, I am allowed to practice my arts in peace."

"Until four days ago, that is," Wigg reminded her gently. "I can make you come back with me, and we both know it. I won't do that, but hear me out. If Krassus truly has a partial adept with him, and if we are ever to even the odds of defeating him, then we must have one, too. I have a feeling these scrolls he referred to are extremely important, and that if we don't find them and Wulfgar before Krassus does, our world may irrevocably change—for the worse. And what if Krassus comes back? With us you would be far safer."

The twinkle returned to his eyes, and he smiled knowingly. "Besides," he added, "wouldn't you like a chance to get even?"

Abbey thought for a time, her jaw clenching. "I will consider your words," she said finally. "But how could I be of help, while all of my stores and books remain here?"

"My friend Faegan has a great many herbs growing in an atrium in his mansion in a place called Shadowood," Wigg told her. "And we can have all of your books and charts brought to Tammerland." He smiled, thinking of the Archives of the Redoubt. "And you'll have more scrolls and books than you can imagine at your disposal."

Wigg smiled to himself. If he could convince Abbey to come, it would be very interesting to see someone teach Faegan something for a change. Abbey turned to look at Celeste, though, and her face darkened.

"We have talked too long," she said urgently. "We must attend to your daughter."

Celeste's breathing had become more labored, and beads of sweat stood on her pale forehead.

The herbmistress thought for a moment. "It's the honey," she said at last, half to herself.

"Of course," Wigg answered. "Her ingestion of the honey was the trigger that activated her first Forestallment. So simple an act . . ."

"No, no—you don't understand," Abbey said. "There is more to it than that."

"What do you mean?"

"Honey is the key to our problem," she told him. "But first I must find my charts of opposites."

Perplexed, Wigg watched her walk to the far wall of the cottage. She pushed on one side of it, and the entire wall rotated on a hidden pivot to reveal a bookcase lined with ledgers, texts, and scrolls. A much smaller room could be seen beyond, containing a desk and many piles of reference materials, as well as a store of additional herbs and oils. Luckily, this room seemed to have been untouched by Krassus. Abbey selected a text from one of the shelves, blew the dust from it, and returned to the table. The binding read *Charts of Opposites, Letters H–I*.

Wigg waited patiently as she leafed through the book. Finally she stopped, running one finger down a dog-eared page. On it was a drawing of a wheel divided into equal-sized, pie-shaped sections.

"What are 'charts of opposites'?" Wigg asked.

"Just as the craft has its dark and light aspects, every other thing existing in the universe also has its direct opposite," she answered. "And in some cases, more than one. Look at this."

She passed the book over to Wigg. "This page is only one of dozens whose words begin with the letter 'h,'" she said. "Run your finger around the circle until you find the word 'honey.' Then go directly to the opposite side, and read aloud what it says."

Wigg did as she asked, finally finding and speaking the words "powdered tetturess," and "oil of hibernium: Leaf Only." He looked up at Abbey.

"Are you saying these two substances are nature's direct opposites to honey?" he asked skeptically. "How can you be so sure?"

"By way of hundreds of years of careful experimentation," she answered simply. She raised an eyebrow. "I wrote this book myself."

Walking to her shelves, she began her search. After some time, she returned to the table with a green bottle. When Abbey uncorked it, Wigg saw that it contained a violet oil.

"I still don't understand," he said, furrowing his brow. He watched as she began measuring out a portion into a thick porcelain cup. "This problem is of the craft. How are these substances going to help?"

"The honey she ingested is no doubt still in her bloodstream," Abbey answered as she concentrated intently on her work. "And from what you told me, it was the catalyst that set everything else in motion. The direct opposites of honey are hibernium—just the oil squeezed from the leaf, mind you, not from the wood—and powder of tetturess blossom. They are even more potent when combined. If she ingests them in both the proper ratios and amounts, they should neutralize the honey in her system."

As she spoke, she finished measuring out the oil. Then she looked around her smashed cottage, and her face darkened.

"This oil remained safe in the other room," she said. "But my bottle of tetturess blossom was taken by Krassus. Turn to the back of the book until you find the pages labeled 'Diagrams of Substitutions,' and tell me what the substitution is for tetturess blossom. I could probably guess, but I'd rather be sure."

Wigg thumbed to the back of the book and found the diagram. "Dried stalk of widow's wart," he answered without looking up. "It also says that if widow's wart is not available, then flakes of dried newt's skin will also suffice."

Abbey nodded. "My widow's wart was also taken," she said angrily, "but I think I still have the newt's skin. The widow's wart would have been better, but we'll just have to make do with what we have."

Rising from her chair, she walked to one of the shelves that was broken at one end and had half fallen to the floor. After a good bit of rummaging around she finally produced a small tin, which she brought back to the table. She opened the lid and removed what appeared to be a small, square patch of dried leather. It was gray, with pink spots. She scraped some of the skin off with a knife, and dropped the resultant flakes into the cup with the oil. Satisfied for the moment, she looked back at Wigg.

"We are fortunate that the necessary ingredients for this potion survived the destruction here," she commented. "Still, that is only half the battle."

Wigg understood. "As the mixture counteracts the honey, I must also use my powers, trying to bring her consciousness back to the surface," he mused.

"Correct."

Abbey went to a sideboard to retrieve a copper pitcher, and filled it with water. She transferred the ingredients from the mortar into an iron pot, poured in a measure of water, and stirred it slowly with a wooden spoon. Then she placed the iron pot on the hearth hook and swiveled it over the flames.

She went back to the bookshelves and picked out another volume. As she brought it to the table, Wigg glanced at the title: *Combinations and Potions: Times and Instruments for the Application of Heat and Cold, and the Subsequent Reactions Thereof.* She began to read.

"Now what are you doing?" he asked. His interest in the process had gradually become more genuine. But Abbey, her thoughts obviously lost in the volume, didn't answer.

She finally put down the book. "White feather of male highland goose," she said softly to herself. "It seems nothing else will do. Now where did I put those?"

Busily wiping her hands on her apron, she returned to the shelves. After some looking, she reached up to grasp a pewter canister. She opened the top, peered inside, and pulled out a long, white feather. She then went to her writing desk and retrieved a quill pen and a small bottle. Finally she returned to the table.

She opened the bottle. Taking up the quill, she filled it with red ink. She then laid the white feather flat on the table. About two-thirds of the way to the top, she slowly began drawing a straight, red line across it.

"What in the name of the Afterlife are you doing?" Wigg asked, completely at sea. He was beginning to grow anxious. He turned back to look at Celeste.

"Still the same old Wigg," Abbey said, her eyes remaining locked on her artwork. He almost thought he saw a hint of another smile. "With an attitude like that, you must drive this Faegan you speak of to absolute distraction."

Saying nothing, Wigg pursed his lips.

Finally she finished and blew on the feather, drying the ink. Then she walked back to the hearth, swung the pot toward her, and carefully lowered the feather down into it, so that the ink line showed just above the rim. Almost immediately the portion of the feather just above the mixture began to brown from the heat of the potion. She turned back to Wigg.

"Bring two chairs over here," she said.

"What good does the feather do?" Wigg asked curiously.

"Tell me something, *Lead* Wizard," she said, her eyes still locked on the feather. "Despite all of your knowledge of the craft, without the goose quill, how would you know how long to let the mixture cook?"

Smiling, Wigg nodded. "When the brown color reaches the ink line, the temperature is right," he mused. "Very clever."

"There's more to it than that," she answered. "Not only does the right temperature activate the potion, but it also assures that we will not burn her throat."

Saying nothing more, the two of them watched quietly as the brown stain gradually climbed higher and higher. When it finally met the ink line, Abbey swung the pot around and took it off the hook. She very quickly poured the entire potion into a cup.

"Now!" she ordered. "Before it cools! You understand what you must do?" she asked. "As soon as the potion starts down her throat, begin your work. And be warned, she may become difficult to control."

He nodded quickly and went to his daughter. He tilted up her head and carefully parted her lips.

As Abbey poured the mixture into Celeste's waiting mouth, he employed the craft, attempting to reach into the depths of his daughter's consciousness. At first, things seemed to go well. After a few moments Celeste began to stir and moan. Then, unbelievably, she opened her eyes, looked beseechingly up at her father, and started to cry.

It was just then that Wigg suddenly realized what both he and Abbey should have done, but had not.

Coming partly out of her stupor, Celeste suddenly bolted upright. Her eyes wide, she screamed, and her body began shaking uncontrollably. As if possessed, she began to raise both trembling hands at once. Understanding, Wigg tried to force her hands back down, but she was too strong for him.

"Hold her!" Abbey shouted.

Wigg briefly thought of using the craft to hold Celeste, but that would mean stopping the flow of his power into her, to help her. With a final, purely physical effort, Wigg was able to force Celeste's arms back down onto the bed. But suddenly her wrists turned up. Just as the azure bolts shot forth, Wigg let go of her, grabbed Abbey, and threw the herb-mistress to the floor. Covering her body with his own, he closed his eyes, knowing that all he could do was continue to aid Celeste's mind and hope that it soon would be over.

A deafening cacophony of destruction came from every corner of the house: the sounds of breaking glass and falling stone.

Then, blessedly, it was over. Wigg carefully stood and gave Abbey a hand up. He found himself choked by dust. As his eyes cleared, he looked around.

The devastation was amazing. Only two of the walls were still standing, but one of them suddenly gave up the effort and collapsed inward, crashing to the cottage floor. Most of the roof was gone, revealing the stars twinkling innocently in the early evening sky. In the dim light he could see that the vast majority of Abbey's bottles and other containers had been blown out of the house and lay broken or open, scattered haphazardly across the nearby woods and fields. Wigg realized that they were probably quite unrecoverable. Almost every stick of furniture was demolished, and even the hearth had been rent in two, its bricks scattered across the floor like abandoned children's toys. Most of the chimney somehow still rose toward the sky like a crooked, broken finger, trying to point to the stars.

Miraculously, the wall still standing was the one holding the shelves full of Abbey's books, scrolls, and ledgers. For the most part, they and the others scattered about behind them seemed unharmed. The wind began whistling coldly through the remains of the cottage, swirling the dust and debris into little maelstroms as it went.

Celeste had collapsed on the bed. Her eyes fluttered once, then twice, before finally staying open. Rising weakly up on her elbows, she looked aghast at the remains of the cottage. She looked down at her fingertips and began to cry.

Wigg instinctively knew that she was crying not because of her physical pain, but at the sudden, inescapable realization of what she had done. Abbey—walking stiffly, mechanically, through the rubble of what had once been her home—was also crying.

Standing shakily, Celeste embraced her father. He held her tightly, knowing how close he had come to losing her.

"I did this, didn't I?" she asked, looking around again in horror. "Somehow, I just know it. But the last thing I remember is having tasted some honey. Did that really happen?" She looked quizzically around the smashed cottage once more.

"Where are we, Father?" she asked softly. Then her eyes closed again, and she collapsed into his arms.

Laying her back down on the bed, Wigg placed a palm on her forehead. For a time he closed his eyes, then smiled. He and Abbey had done it. This time Celeste's sleep was genuine, natural. When she finally awakened, she would be herself again.

With the exception of her first activated Forestallment, he mused. He would have to train her in its proper use as soon as possible.

He went to Abbey. In her trembling hands she was clutching a dusty book she had retrieved from the floor. He put a hand on her shoulder.

"I don't know what to say," he said softly. "I'm so sorry."

Abbey turned to him, her eyes wet. Then she did something unexpected. Stepping nearer, she put her arms around him and lay her head upon his shoulder. His gray robe soon became soaked with tears.

They stood that way for some time as the wind rustled through the remains of the cottage and the sounds of the night creatures came softly to their ears. Finally she took her head from his shoulder and looked into his eyes.

"It seems I will be coming with you after all," she said, her voice so small he could barely hear her. "I never expected to see you again."

Wigg pulled her closer.

"Nor I, you," he said softly. "Nor I, you."

PART II

Revelation

Eleven

*It is within one of the Scrolls of the Ancients that those of the Vagaries shall
procure a great weapon. The reading and employment thereof shall bring a shift
in all things, including the lives of the Chosen Ones. Just as those who find and
control the Scroll of the Vigors come yet another step closer to combining the two
sides of magic, those controlling the Scroll of the Vagaries shall also be nearer
their goal of complete, never-ending rule over the craft.*

—PAGE 774, VOLUME II, OF THE VIGORS OF THE TOME

W ulfgar turned over luxuriously in the great bed. Even though
he remained a prisoner, he could escape into his dreams of
better times.

"And how are you this evening, Traveler?" his dream-self asked.
Pushing aside the stallion's forelock, the boy briskly rubbed the horse's
white-starred forehead. The black stallion snorted softly, eagerly stretching his neck for yet more of his keeper's attention.

From behind his back, Wulfgar produced a bright red apple. Traveler
snorted again, and his ears pricked up. Wulfgar was about to play a game
with him, and the horse knew it.

Wulfgar backed away slightly and held the apple higher, just out of
Traveler's reach. The stallion pushed forward against the unforgiving oak
door to his stall and let go a loud, impatient whinny.

Wulfgar smiled. "Not so fast," he said gently. "You know what you
have to do first."

The horse impatiently shook his head, forelock and mane flying haphazardly. Finally there came the sound of a single shod hoof banging loudly, one time only, on the floor of the stall.

Smiling, Wulfgar produced a folding knife and began slicing the apple into pieces. As he held the first of the apple slices out, Traveler took it between his long, uniform teeth and munched contentedly.

Turning away from the stall for a moment, Wulfgar took a piece of apple for himself and looked down the length of the barn. For as long as he could remember he had loved the sights, smells, and sounds of this place more than any other.

His father, Jason of the House of Merrick, owned these barns and presided over the combination of stables and blacksmith shop. Thanks to the Directorate of Wizards, peace and prosperity had reigned for more than three centuries, and Jason's business was good. Even so, the Merrick family was by no means wealthy. But father, mother, and son were happy in the ways that money could not buy.

The young man of thirteen looked down the length of the barn. It was full to capacity. Yellow straw lay everywhere, and the smell of green hay, amber grain, horses, and saddle soap combined with the sooty smoke and char of the blacksmith's hearth in the next room to create a familiar scent he breathed in gladly. A soft, low light came from the many lanterns lining the aisle between the rows of stalls. To his ears came the occasional snorts and whinnies of the horses and the comforting double clangs of his father's hammer on the anvil. These sounds and smells had become an integral part of his life.

Wulfgar gave Traveler another piece of apple. Then he noticed that the clanging of his father's hammer had ceased. Turning, Wulfgar saw his father approaching. Jason looked tired, but he grinned affectionately at Wulfgar as he approached. His weathered face and hands were covered with dark soot, as was the worn leather blacksmith's apron tied around his middle.

"Enough for one day," he said, his voice gravelly and strong. He smelled like hot charcoal. As usual, his massive strength was both comforting and familiar to Wulfgar, like standing next to a favorite old oak tree.

"Dinner must be ready by now," Jason added as he folded his apron and looked out from the barn. Warm, inviting lights came from the small house lying just beyond. "You know how your mother gets when we let her creations go cold." He winked.

"I'm not hungry," Wulfgar countered gamely. "Besides, I still have tack to polish. The customers will expect it done by morning, when they arrive for their mounts."

Jason smiled. "There's another reason why you don't want to leave the stables, isn't there?" he asked.

Wulfgar looked down at some straw near the toes of his boots and didn't answer.

"The tack can wait until morning," his father said. "You still have schoolwork to do, and that must come first. Given the fact that we're full up, if some of the tack doesn't get polished, I'm sure the customers will understand."

Wulfgar's face fell. He liked his lessons well enough—indeed, he was one of his school's best students—but he had always been something of a loner, with a fiercely held sense of independence that set him apart from the other boys. Having schoolmates was fine, but it was the horses that continually came and went from these barns that truly possessed his heart.

"Suppose I told you that dinner tonight is veal pie—your favorite," Jason said, as he draped a muscular arm over his son's shoulders and turned the boy toward the far doors of the barn. Sighing, Wulfgar nodded. With a final look back at Traveler, he tossed the remains of the apple into the stall. Then, side by side, father and son left the barn and headed for—

Wulfgar suddenly started awake, all of his senses coming alive at once. He shot upright. Sweaty and breathing heavily, he glanced wildly around the room, trying to remember where he was.

He had been dreaming again, he realized, rubbing the back of his neck. He wished he had not woken up. The dream was infinitely preferable to his current reality.

He had been locked within these rooms—supposedly the personal quarters of the one called Krassus—for the last four days. During that time, he had seen no one, save for the demonslavers who supplied him with food, toilet articles, and clean clothing. Not one of them had spoken to him.

Swinging his legs over the side of the bed, he retied his long sandy hair behind him with the worn leather strip and then turned to look out the open balcony doors. Morning was dawning, the sky sunny and clear.

Reluctantly he took the frantically patterned silk robe from the settee at the end of the bed and put it on. He felt like a fool. He acutely missed his simple leather breeches, boots, and matching sleeveless shirt, the one that had been so forgiving when he used to swing the heavy hammer down on the anvil. He walked sleepily to the spacious balcony and sat down in one of the overstuffed chairs.

His velvet cage—as he had come to think of his prison—was indeed sumptuous, but there was absolutely no way to escape it. The only exit was through double doors of solid marble, locked from the other side. Two armed, white-skinned slavers stood perpetual guard in the hall.

The chambers consisted of a bedroom with a gigantic four-poster bed, an adjoining drawing room with shelves full of books and a large fireplace, and a huge, ornate bath. The rooms were of highly polished marble, as was the open, low-walled balcony where he now sat. Below, the sea crashed against the nearby shore, and he could smell the crisp, salty sea air.

Looking toward the west and out over the seemingly endless Sea of Whispers, he was again reminded that his quarters were hundreds of feet in the air, and surely comprised but a small part of the massive building in which he was being held. One corner of his mouth came up knowingly. No one guarded him on this side of his quarters, for there was no need to. The exterior walls were slick and smooth. Any attempt to escape that way would mean a fall and certain death on the jagged rocks that lined the shore.

Tall, white-sailed ships arrived daily—no doubt transporting yet more slaves—and each time the swaying masts and graceful sails appeared on the horizon, the view steeled his resolve to escape—someday, somehow. But not before killing Janus, he promised himself, and as many of the grotesque slavers as he could.

During the last four days there had been little to do except sit and watch the restless ocean. He had tried to read the books in the drawing room, but they were all written in a beautiful-looking but utterly foreign language. The only words he recognized were *Talis* and *R'talis,* and they seemed to be repeated over and over. He was alone with unanswered questions. Why was he was being treated like a king, while his fellow slaves were supposedly confined somewhere else, somewhere far less comfortable? Why had such excitement accompanied his arrival at the docks? Things had been said and done to him there that he couldn't even begin to understand.

Shame washed over him, and he closed his eyes.

The darkness momentarily brought back his dream, and his thoughts turned to his home in the coastal city of Farpoint, and the parents he loved with all his heart. As far as he knew, Jason and Selene were still alive and well, though surely they missed him. Jason still worked in the stables, but no longer performed the difficult manual labor required by his trade. Wulfgar, now thirty-five Seasons of New Life, had stayed on, taking over the blacksmith shop. His strong, hard body showed the years of hard work, his muscles sculpted by so many strikes of the hammer to the anvil. Although there had been several women in his life, he had yet to marry.

He had been abducted in Farpoint while making a trip to order grain for the stables. Rumors of the abduction of men and women his age had been circulating for days, but always the independent skeptic, he had ignored them and ventured into the city anyway. It was at the mill that several of the awful, white-skinned things had come at him at once. Sadly, he had been unarmed.

Nonetheless, Wulfgar had fought back like a lion, badly injuring several of them with his fists and feet before being rendered unconscious. He had awakened to the fire of a branding iron on his shoulder and was then bound in the darkness belowdecks on a ship that tossed its way through the Sea of Whispers for sixteen excruciating days.

He craned his neck to look at the brand on his left shoulder and was heartened to see that it had almost completely healed. He shook his head again at the insanity of it all. It had taken him three days of twice-daily bathing before he had felt truly free of the filth and stink of the ship's hold. But he would never be free of the bizarre brand.

As he continued to stare out over the ocean, his thoughts turned to Eutracia, and to the royal family. Most people believed the king and queen to be dead, along with the Directorate of Wizards. It was widely rumored that they had perished in the royal palace on Prince Tristan's coronation day. Some even said that the king had died at the prince's own hand.

Questions about the survival of the royal twins had stubbornly remained. But if they lived, as so many people thought, why weren't they coming to the aid of their citizens?

No one seemed to know. But if the other rumors were indeed true about the winged ones that had come and murdered both the royal family and the entire Royal Guard, then perhaps even Tristan and Shailiha could do little to stem the tide of the slavers—especially without the powers of the Directorate to help them.

His thoughts were interrupted by the sound of the bolt sliding, and the double doors of his bedroom swung open. Breakfast time.

Two demonslavers entered, swords drawn. A third slaver pushed the now-familiar silver cart loaded with food and drink into the room. Then, unexpectedly, two other persons came through the door. Wulfgar stood quickly and came in from the balcony.

Janus stood there proudly, dressed in his usual flagrant clothes. The twin iron spheres dangling, as always, from his right hip clanked together menacingly as he walked. The dark eyes surrounded by the red, painted mask surveyed the room cautiously.

Beside him stood a woman. Janus roughly shoved her forward, as though displaying her for Wulfgar's approval.

She was beautiful. Tall and shapely, she wore her long, brunette hair in ringlets that twirled down to her shoulders. Her eyes were wide, and bright blue. A magnificent yellow taffeta gown trimmed with white lace draped gracefully from her bare shoulders to the floor, the hem just reaching the tops of her matching silk slippers. On her left shoulder was an angry, healing brand: *R'talis.*

As Janus took a few steps closer, Wulfgar cringed. Janus looked Wulfgar up and down, and then nodded his approval.

"You clean up nicely," he cooed. "A vast improvement over that day at the docks, I must say."

Without looking around, he raised one hand and snapped his fingers. The two demonslavers immediately grabbed the woman and tossed her onto the four-poster bed as though she were a toy. Surprisingly unafraid, she glared back at them with hate in her eyes.

"As you might have already guessed, she's for you," Janus said calmly, as if he were giving Wulfgar a birthday gift. "*R'talis,* of course. Nothing but the best for our honored guest. She pleases the eye, does she not? After four days of boredom, I thought you could use some 'companionship.' In any event, do with her as you will."

Wulfgar turned to look at the beauty on the bed, then looked back at Janus. "I don't know how to thank you," he said sarcastically.

"Think nothing of it," Janus answered. "There are many more where she came from, should she displease you."

He removed his gold snuffbox from a pocket of his doublet and snorted a pinch up one nostril. An explosive sneeze followed. He looked Wulfgar up and down another time, then cast his masked eyes back to the woman on the bed.

"Why am I here?" Wulfgar demanded. "What is this place? And why have I been granted such special treatment?"

Janus sighed. "I often forget how truly uneducated you are," he said softly. "No matter. As soon as Krassus arrives, he will help you overcome your handicap. He is due to arrive in a matter of days. Then we will see just how strong you really are."

"What is this place?" Wulfgar asked again.

"As I told everyone that day on the pier, you are on an island. It is a very special place. It has existed secretly for eons, under one master of the Vagaries or another. Even the Wizards of the Directorate did not know of it. It is called the Citadel, and for good reason."

Wulfgar had no idea what Janus was talking about. He seized on the one idea that made sense. "No one can sail farther than fifteen days into the Sea of Whispers," he countered. "How do you manage it?"

"Yet another secret you shall eventually learn," Janus answered. "But, as I already said, Krassus is the one best suited to answer your inquiries. He will be most delighted to learn that you are finally here. We have been looking for you for some time. Others have searched even longer."

"Why?" Wulfgar demanded. "I don't even know this Krassus. He's nothing to me. Why should he care about my welfare?"

"He cares because of an oath he swore to one of your distant relatives just before the man's unfortunate demise," Janus answered. It was clear that he was enjoying his riddle.

"Ironically, he was murdered by yet another of your relatives. But you wouldn't know about that yet, would you?"

"That's impossible!" Wulfgar snarled. "My relatives are not murderers!"

Janus shook his head knowingly. "Oh, but they are," he answered. "Yet another fact you will soon be forced to deal with."

He snapped his fingers again. From a shelf beneath the food cart, one of the slavers produced an hourglass and handed it to his master. Janus looked first to the woman on the bed, and then back to Wulfgar. He turned the hourglass over and placed it on a nearby table.

"You have one hour to do all you would like to this woman," he said nastily. "Then we shall come back for her. Should she not please you, tell me when I return, and I will see to it that she is appropriately punished. As I said, nothing is too good for our very special guest." The painted monster smiled again.

"And now I must bid you good-bye," he said. "Enjoy her, Wulfgar," he added. "I must say I envy you." He gave them both a short, sarcastic bow.

With that he turned and walked purposefully out of the room, the twin spheres at his side clinking together ominously, the demonslavers behind him. As the massive marble doors closed with a decisive thud, Wulfgar heard the bolt slide into place on the other side.

Turning, he looked at the beautiful woman on the bed.

CHAPTER

Twelve

"You had best be successful this time, Grizelda," Krassus said sternly. "I am growing tired of your failures."

Swaying on her knees, the haggard herbmistress looked up at Krassus. As she did, her stomach lurched again.

She had been seasick for the last four days, and even a dose of nerveweed had not helped. But she was not too ill to understand that the next few moments could mean either the continuance of her life, or a torturous death at the hands of the wizard, should she displease him.

After vomiting into the nearby bucket for what seemed the thousandth time, she slowly wiped her mouth on the sleeve of her tattered robe. Regaining her composure, she surveyed the shifting deck of the *Sojourner*, her lord's flagship, as she made her way east across the Sea of Whispers. Alabaster-skinned demonslavers hurried about their duties, crewing the ship and keeping the hundreds of slaves chained belowdecks under tight control. *Sojourner's* bright, white sails were full, and seawater occasionally splashed up over her decks as she pitched up and down in the restless sea. Two other frigates, the *Wayfarer* and the *Stalwart*, followed in her wake.

After the herbs and potions Krassus and Grizelda had stolen from Abbey's cottage had been loaded aboard, the three ships had departed Farpoint. They were making good time running before the steady, westerly winds.

Krassus turned to the demonslaver standing next to him. The monster immediately came to attention.

"Make sure all the crow's nests remain manned upon each of our vessels," Krassus ordered. "Signal them to continue keeping an especially sharp lookout, not only on the sea, but also in the sky. With the capture of the prince, I have no doubt that the wizards have sent their Minions after us. I believe we are already well beyond their flying range, but Wigg and Faegan are nothing if not resourceful."

The demonslaver nodded curtly. "My lord," he answered with a bow. He then left to fulfill his orders. Krassus returned his attention to the woman on her knees.

He and Grizelda were on the aft deck, the mizzen sail having just been furled. This would reduce their speed somewhat, but it couldn't be helped. What Grizelda was about to attempt was hazardous, especially with a full sail directly overhead: an uncontrolled fire on board ship in the middle of the Sea of Whispers was something to be avoided at all costs. Besides, performing these rituals in the confines of the chambers belowdecks was unthinkable.

When Tristan had been rendered unconscious in the alley by the slavers, he had been immediately taken to Krassus, then placed aboard the *Sojourner*. There Krassus had induced a deep sleep over him, and the prince was being force-fed liquid nourishment. The beard Faegan had conjured for him had since disappeared, and in its place there was now a shorter, two-day growth of dark, natural stubble. Still dressed in his usual clothes but his weapons gone, he lay peacefully belowdecks in a windowless stateroom guarded by demonslavers.

Krassus smiled. Capturing the prince had been an unexpected treat—a gamble risked and won. Satisfied, he took a deep breath of the nighttime sea air. But the cold, clear saltiness was too much for his lungs, and he let go a small cough. Several droplets of his blood spewed forth to hit the deck, where they immediately began twisting their way into familiar signatures. Sighing angrily, he wiped them away with the sole of his boot.

Thinking, he turned again to look out over the whitecapped ocean, where waves danced continually in the moonlight. Although Tristan was still untrained in the ways of the craft, Nicholas had warned Krassus that the prince's blood—the strongest in the world—possessed Forestallments that had been placed there by Failee, the failed first mistress of the Coven.

Krassus had been well trained by Nicholas in the art of imbuing Forestallments. The powers imparted thusly into the blood were delayed, or "forestalled," to be brought to life later, either activated at a predetermined time or catalyzed into being by the performance of certain specified acts by their possessor. If the Forestallment was time activated, there was no way to know when it might show itself, unless one knew the nature of the spell to begin with. If it was event activated, it could manifest at any time, provided that the correct action or sequence of actions had been taken by the person in whose blood the Forestallment had been placed. Krassus had no way of knowing the nature of the Forestallments that Failee had placed in Tristan's blood. Her did not want to accidentally activate one of those as-yet-untapped gifts. He would have to be exceedingly careful in his handling of the prince.

His plans were proceeding well, but he could not afford to become complacent. The two ancient wizards of the Redoubt remained very powerful. To defeat them and also accomplish his other goals, he would have to be very clever indeed. And he would have to get his hands on both the Scrolls of the Ancients and Wulfgar, Morganna's bastard son.

True, he still did not have the Scroll of the Vigors, and leaving Eutracia without having found it gave him great pause. But he had the Scroll of the Vagaries, and the work of his consuls back at the Citadel needed to begin. Besides, once his herbmistress was finally able to view the other scroll, he could always instruct his demonslavers to retrieve it for him, wherever it might be.

"The prince continues to sleep belowdecks?" Grizelda asked, breaking into Krassus' thoughts.

Krassus placed his hands into the opposite sleeves of his blue-and-gray robe. "Yes," he said. "Although untrained, he can still be quite dangerous, as he has so adeptly proven a number of times. As a precaution, I have decided to have him transferred to one of the other ships. Under no circumstances shall the Chosen One and the Scroll of the Vagaries be allowed to continue sharing the same vessel. Should the scroll fall into the hands of the wizards in Tammerland, our cause might be lost."

He smiled again. "I wonder if the good prince knows how to row," he added nastily. Suddenly impatient, his dark gaze bored its way into her.

"Now then," he said. "I suggest you get on with it."

Krassus smiled. He was gradually finding himself a reluctant admirer of the old woman's talents. Before finding her, he had located several partial adepts, but none had the particular combination of talents he hoped would help him fulfill his oath to Nicholas. As a precaution, he had killed them on the spot. He wished he had killed Abbey, too. But he hadn't dared, fearing he might need her as leverage with Wigg. Should she ever cross his path again, he swore, he would not make the same mistake twice.

In order to accomplish his goals, he needed to find Wulfgar. In addition, there was no telling what other persons or things of the craft he might need to collect while on his path to victory. For this, only a well-trained partial adept would do. He immediately set out to locate one.

He had finally discovered Grizelda in the city of Warwick Watch.

She had been doing sleight of hand and other, lesser aspects of her arts for the amusement of the crowds, apparently living on whatever meager offerings they might deign to throw into her bowl. He had watched her for some time, then closed his eyes and reached out to her blood with his specialized senses. Finally sure, he waited until the small crowd had dispersed and the shadows of the day were beginning to lengthen. Picking up her meager things, the haggard woman counted her coins carefully, then tied them up in a dirty rag and scurried into the depths of a nearby alley.

Following her, Krassus saw her stop at the end of the alley, near the protection of its angled, dead end and the large wooden box that sat against one wall. A few rusty cooking utensils lay nearby. Crouching, she set down her makeshift coin bag and began to light a small fire.

Silently, Krassus came to stand before her.

She did not see him until the length of his shadow crawled toward the flames. Looking up, she snatched her coin bag to her breast and scrabbled back toward the false security of the dilapidated wooden box.

Krassus regarded her carefully. She was very old. Her long, gray hair fell crazily over her shoulders, and her face was weather-beaten, presumably from living for so many years out of doors. Wrinkling his nose, he wondered how long it had been since she had bathed. Her plain, black robe, tattered and worn, covered a thin, unremarkable figure.

"Who are you?" she demanded. Her piercing, dark eyes betrayed a sharp intelligence. "What do you want?"

"I know what you are," he answered quietly. "You may fool the simple, unendowed peasants in the streets, but not me."

"What are you talking about?" she shot back. "Go away and leave me alone."

Krassus smiled. "This is what I'm talking about, crone," he answered. He raised one hand, and the azure glow of the craft appeared about her. As he moved his index finger slightly, a small incision began to form in her right palm. Several drops of her blood fell to the floor of the alleyway. Looking down, Krassus watched them twist their way through the thirsty dirt, forming signatures.

As he had suspected, they were partials.

Only the softer, curvier halves revealed themselves. The woman's mother had been her only parent with endowed blood.

"You're a partial," he said calmly. "And because your blood reveals a signature without the aid of waters from the Caves, it is also clear that you have been trained. That makes you a partial adept. Tell me, what are your skills? I may have need of you." He was becoming more certain of his find by the moment.

The old woman shook her head. "I have no such skills," she said sullenly. "I am but a poor street performer, trying to make a living. Go away and leave me be." She inched farther backward a bit, closer to the wooden box. Her knuckles whitened from her tight grip around the coin bag.

"Oh, you are far more than a simple woman of the street," Krassus countered. "The blood signatures prove that." His jaw hardened. If he was forced to use violence against her in order to learn the truth, then so be it. All he cared about was getting his answers. "What is your name?" he asked harshly.

"Grizelda. What of it?"

"Tell me, Grizelda, are you really what you seem?"

No answer came.

"Are you a trained herbmistress, perhaps?" he asked.

Again, only silence reigned.

His patience growing thin, he took another step closer. "Are you a blaze-gazer, as well?"

"The answers to your questions depend," she said, sensing an opportunity. She stood up, and he saw that she was taller than he had first thought.

"On what?" he asked, knowing full well what her answer would be.

She took a step toward him. "On what you're willing to pay," she answered craftily. "As you can see, I do not eat well. My stomach has long pressed emptily against the insides of my ribs." For the first time, she smiled crookedly at him.

Krassus had suddenly had enough. He raised his arm, and the familiar azure glow of the craft appeared in the air between them and coalesced into a recognizable shape: a human hand.

With a twitch of one of Krassus' fingers, the hand tore across the remaining distance to the woman and wrapped its glowing fingers around her wrinkled throat. The force of the impact was so great that it lifted her off her feet, slamming her hard against her wooden box. She began to choke. Drool frothed at one corner of her mouth, spilled over to snake crazily down her chin. Her body shook with the convulsions rattling her starving lungs.

Twisting and turning his hand slightly, Krassus pointed to her shoes. The laces began to untie themselves. Then the shoes slowly slipped from her feet and fell to the ground. With a simple turn of his head, Krassus caused the small fire the old woman had lit to rise slowly into the air and come to rest just below her. Burnt-orange shadows darted across the darkness of the alleyway.

Krassus turned his hand again, and the flames licked upward at the soles of her feet. Her scream came out as a rasp.

"Now then," he said quietly. "Let's try again. Are you a blaze-gazer?"

The old woman nodded.

"Very good," Krassus answered. "You are now one-third of the way toward staying alive. Tell me, and do not lie. Believe me, you don't have the time. Are you a trained herbmistress?"

Again came a single nod. Her face was turning from red to light blue, and her toes were twitching involuntarily, trying to escape the flames.

"I'm impressed," he said. "Two out of three." Just to see her suffer, he paused before asking his final question. The moments ticked by slowly, dangerously, as the flames scalded her naked feet.

"And are you protected by someone's time enchantments?" he asked intently.

She shook her head.

Finally satisfied, he extinguished the flame and let her go. She tumbled hard to the dirt of the alley, her feet badly burned and her lungs crying out for air.

"You'll do," he said simply. "You're coming with me. I have need of your services." With the toe of one boot, he lifted her chin. "Provided, of course, you have been telling the truth," he added. "But that we will discover later, won't we, Grizelda?"

The haggard herbmistress managed to come to all fours. "How do you . . . know . . . I won't run . . . away?" she gasped. With a cry, she collapsed again and curled up on the dirt of the alley, protectively gripping her tortured feet.

"That's simple," Krassus answered almost politely. "I traveled halfway across Eutracia to find you. Do you really believe I could not search you out again, especially given the short distance you might travel before I discovered you had fled? We have a great mission to fulfill, you and I. Disobey me, or fail in the demands I shall make of you, and you will die. Do as I say, remain successful in the arts you have admitted to possessing, and you shall live."

All she could do was give him a short nod.

From that moment on, she was his. He had then gone on to use the craft to heal her feet. Not because he wished to be kind, but because a partial adept who could not keep up would surely prove more of a hindrance than a help. And there remained a great deal to do.

"I am ready, m'lord," the herbmistress said now, breaking into the wizard's reveries once more. He turned from the sea to look at her.

Several open bottles of herbs sat on the table next to her, their contents spilled out and combined into a pile in the center of the large iron bowl next to her feet.

"You may begin," Krassus said. "But first, tell me: Will we be able to hear what they say?"

"No," she said with certainty. "For that, I would need something truly personal of one of those we wish to view. And we still do not know who possesses the other scroll."

She reached down into the basket again and produced steel and flint. Without hesitation, she struck them together, and the pile of herbs came ablaze.

Krassus watched as the flame grew into a bonfire. Grizelda motioned with one hand, and part of the fire separated itself from the main body— a lesser offshoot that would allow her to work in closer proximity to her creation. That arm of fire lengthened, and flowed parallel to the deck of the ship. Grizelda tossed a few more herbs into the branch of the flame.

Standing as close to it as she dared, she held out a piece of blank parchment recently taken from the Scroll of the Vagaries. Then she closed her eyes.

Almost immediately, an azure window began to form in the main body of the flame. The partial adept opened her eyes and stared into the window in the fire.

Eager to see the results, Krassus stepped up beside her and looked in. What he saw disappointed him, and his mouth twisted into a sneer.

As had been the case every time before when trying to locate the Scroll of the Vigors, all that the gazing window revealed was blackness.

CHAPTER

Thirteen

T win azure bolts, so strong and brilliant that they could barely be looked upon, seared across the expanse of the courtyard and smashed into the upright marble column with an earsplitting explosion. The ground shook from their impact.

Once again the target had been destroyed, rent in two by the sheer force of the magic. As the smoke and dust cleared, it could be seen that the two huge chunks of marble had been thrown several meters apart. Many smaller fragments lay nearby, their shattered ends still smoldering from the heat.

"Well done," Wigg said. "But your control over the bolts is still not all it could be. Remember, they are malleable, and their shape can be altered to suit your needs. Once you have mastered this stage, it will serve as the foundation for the finer applications of your gift, such as slicing through an object, manipulating an object, or even actually grasping something and lifting it into the air." In truth, he was stunned by the amazing progress his pupil had made in so short a time.

"Now then, let's try again," he pressed. "But I want you to attempt a smaller target this time; say, the piece of column lying on the right." Smiling, he gave her a wink.

"And this time," he continued, "use only one hand. Fold the thumb and last fingers of your right hand inward, and point only the remaining three. Using those three fingers alone, try to sustain the life of the bolts and *slice* the marble column into three equal segments, rather than simply destroying it. Remember," he added, "almost anyone trained in the craft can use the bolts to destroy. But only a master can employ them in a useful way, to create something that was not there before." A short smile graced his lips. "Whenever you're ready," he said quietly.

"Yes, Father," Celeste answered.

The early-morning sun shone down on the courtyard of the royal palace, where she and her wizard father stood. She was growing tired, and Wigg knew it. But he also knew that her fatigue was an invaluable part of her learning that would serve to build her endurance.

Celeste raised her right arm and trapped her little finger beneath her thumb. Aiming the three remaining fingers at the piece of marble, she loosed three azure bolts, one from each fingertip.

Concentrating, she turned her head slightly as she forced them to change shape, turning them into slim, razor-sharp edges of gleaming azure. They tore across the courtyard in a flash, easily finding their marks. Straining with every fiber of her being, she guided the bolts up and down against the column's fluted surface, trying to slice through the marble, rather than destroy it.

For a short time she continued to move them successfully up and down against the polished, unforgiving surface of the stone. But then her aim slipped, and with it, her concentration. The bolts widened out again, and the column exploded loudly. It shattered into a thousand tiny pieces that flew high into the air before finally falling to the earth like dry, dusty rain.

Exhausted, she sighed and lowered her arm.

Shailiha walked up. Caprice, her violet-and-yellow flier of the fields, sat perched on her right forearm, the way a hunting hawk might.

"You almost did it that time," she said, trying to reassure Celeste. "Surely it won't be long now before you grasp it."

Celeste looked back at Shailiha with tired eyes. "Somehow, it doesn't feel that way," she answered back. Knowing the pain Shailiha was suffering over Tristan, she tried to give her a reassuring smile.

Then she looked down to examine her fingertips. They were red and sore again. The effect would lessen over time, her father had told her. But right now it was one of the prices to be paid for learning to control her gift.

Wigg put an arm around her shoulder. He knew he must take the time to teach her to control her Forestallment as quickly as possible. Under no circumstances could he allow another disaster such as the one that had occurred at Abbey's cottage. But it was hard for her to concentrate these days—and hard for him, too. Worry for Tristan filled all their hearts.

When Wigg and Celeste had learned of Tristan's capture, their shock had given way to tears, their tears then pushed aside by anger and frustration. Faegan and Shailiha could offer no idea as to where the prince might be, or what he might be enduring at the hands of Krassus and his slavers. Worse yet, they didn't even know whether he still lived.

After Tristan's defeat, Shailiha and Faegan had fled back to the campsite and their Minion guards, knowing the demonslavers couldn't be far behind. Upon learning of the prince's fate, Ox had gone nearly wild with grief. He begged to take his troops, few as they might be, and fly straight for Farpoint. In his rage he vowed to tear the town inside out, if necessary, to find the prince.

But despite how much he desperately wished to see Tristan returned, Faegan couldn't allow it. A dozen Minion warriors, no matter how brave and skillful, would have had little chance against the untold numbers of demonslavers under Krassus' command. Besides, there was no time. As it was, the Minions had lifted their litter into the sky just as the slavers entered the moonlit glade, swords waving. With heavy hearts the winged warriors had flown north, safely returning the princess and the wizard to Tammerland.

After everyone had returned to the Redoubt and told their stories, the lead wizard introduced Abbey to the group. The others did all they could to make her feel welcome, but it was obvious that she was wary of her new situation. Clearly, her trust was something that would have to be earned.

Minion warriors were dispatched to her smashed cottage, and they returned with her entire collection of books, scrolls, and ledgers. Simply cataloguing them again had taken the better part of the last two days.

Their first priority was to find Tristan. Abbey was the key, Wigg knew, to viewing subjects over great distances. But the herbs she required to ignite her gazing blaze were in short supply here in the Redoubt, despite the various species Faegan had growing in his atrium. For the last several days he and the partial adept had been trying to discover the most efficient way to overcome the shortfall.

The wizards had of course considered sending squadrons of Minions aloft to scout for the ships that Faegan and Shailiha had seen at the docks in Farpoint, in case Tristan might be aboard one of them. But if and when they did sight a ship at sea, what were they to do? It had been too dark even for Faegan to read the names of the vessels that night in Farpoint. Having the Minions fly over and board every ship that plied the Sea of Whispers was not only impossible, but might also provoke unnecessary confrontations between the winged ones and what would surely be the terrified, confused seamen who saw the fearsome warriors suddenly descending on them.

Nonetheless, several thousand of them, with the indefatigable Ox at their head, had volunteered to do just that. Out of sheer desperation, Wigg and Faegan had finally agreed. For the last six days the Minions had flown as far out over both land and sea as they could, only to return exhausted and disheartened, having seen no sign of the prince.

Suddenly the voice of Shannon the Short broke into his thoughts.

"Begging your pardon, Lead Wizard," he said, "but Master Faegan and Abbey have asked that you and the ladies join them in the Hall of Blood Records." Smoke billowed from the corncob pipe held between his teeth.

Wigg took in the gnome's red hair, matching beard, and dark eyes. Shannon was dressed, as always, in his red shirt, blue bibs, and upturned shoes. A black watch cap sat atop his head, and his ever-present ale jug was firmly clamped in one hand. Shannon took a deep, irreverent slug of his brew, then wiped his mouth on his sleeve.

Despite his outward courtesy, there was always a hint of comic disrespect on the little one's face—especially where Wigg was concerned. Ever since the lead wizard had met Shannon, there had never been any question that the gnome accepted none but Faegan as his master.

Wigg had never been fond of the gnomes, but he had to admit grudgingly that they had become trusted allies. Their courage had impressed even the lead wizard when they had helped defeat Nicholas' birds of prey in the invisible valley that guarded Shadowood, the home they had shared with Faegan for more than three centuries.

Shannon cleared his throat. "They say it's important," he said.

Wigg raised an eyebrow. Faegan and Abbey had been meeting almost nonstop for the last several days. Much of that time had been spent with Abbey showing Faegan her resource materials and explaining what she would need in the way of herbs, blossoms, and roots, while the crippled wizard tried to ascertain whether they were immediately available.

Wigg sighed. They needed Abbey's abilities desperately just now. He hoped with all his heart that they were about to hear good news.

*W*hen they reached the Hall of Blood Records, they found Abbey and Faegan engrossed in fervent conversation. Both looked tired; neither noticed the arrival of the others.

Faegan was sitting in a newly constructed chair on wheels at the magnificent mahogany table in the center of the room. Abbey stood by his side, looking over his shoulder at a document. Every inch of the huge table was covered with Abbey's parchments, scrolls, and ledgers. Numerous blood signature documents had also been pulled, their storage left open, drawers yawning rudely before the imposing majesty of the room. Dozens of bottles of dried herbs sat on the table, many of them also open. Their combined odors spoke both of magic and of the ephemeral hope of success.

Scowling, Wigg looked first at the argumentative Abbey and Faegan, then back to Shailiha and Celeste. Shaking his head slightly, he rolled his eyes.

For three centuries he had wondered what might happen if the proud partial adept and the eccentric wizard in the chair ever met. He realized he was about to get his answer.

While Abbey's and Faegan's voices continued to rise, Wigg sat down at the table and cleared his throat loudly.

It didn't help.

"And I'm telling you that blossom of sintrinium is no substitute for nectar of oleaster!" Abbey shouted. She threw her hands into the air. "It just won't work, no matter how much you'd like it to! If any substitutions are made, then either the gazing flame will burn too hot, thereby clouding the view, or there will be nothing to see at all! Trust me; I know what I'm talking about! These are time-honored formulas, and they must be respected! Half of the palace could go up with your tinkering!"

"And I say you're wrong!" Faegan countered angrily, slapping one hand down on the arm of his chair.

Looking at them, Wigg was absolutely certain that this had been going on for some time now, and it showed no signs of stopping.

"If your charts of similars say sintrinium will work, then why won't it?" Faegan's jaw stuck out like the prow of a ship.

"Because 'similar' does not mean 'equal'!" Abbey exclaimed. "This is a delicate process, not a parlor trick! We're trying to ignite a gazing flame, you old fool, not make rabbits scurry out from under your robes!" Exasperated, she ran one hand through her dark, gray-streaked hair.

"Why don't you come and sit down?" Wigg asked Abbey. Startled, she glanced at him at last, and he pulled out the chair next to him.

With a loud sigh, Abbey relented and walked over. Just before she sat down, she placed her lips next to Wigg's ear.

"And I used to think that *you* could be difficult," she whispered.

Fighting back a smile, the lead wizard turned his eyes to Faegan. "Is there a problem?" he asked politely.

"Indeed," Faegan answered. "It seems your herbmistress is being uncooperative regarding my proposed substitution of certain ingredients needed for igniting her gazing flame. After careful review, it seems we do not possess all of the required elements. I was only trying to save us a trip back to Shadowood, where my selection of such goods is far greater. And I need remind none of you that time is not on our side."

"Is he right?" Wigg asked Abbey. "Can we make substitutions to save time?"

Abbey's attitude softened a bit. "At first glance, I can understand how Faegan might jump to that conclusion," she said. Leaning forward, she placed her forearms on the table. "But what both of you must realize is that the ingredients don't just help create the flame—they also serve as its ongoing fuel. The formula must be perfect. In addition, if you wish me to perform the ritual more than once, I shall need quite a lot of these substances. If substitutes are allowed, it simply will not work."

Leaning back in her chair, she looked at the group. "It seems someone must go to Shadowood, wherever that is," she said simply.

"This means that we must wait even longer before Abbey can use her gift to find Tristan, doesn't it?" Shailiha asked. Her lovely face had grown hard with frustration and anger. She was sick of waiting, and she was willing to do anything, risk anything, to bring her brother back.

Wigg looked at her. Shailiha had always been strong-willed, but until the recent past there had been very little reason for her to display that trait. Now, especially with Tristan missing, things were vastly different.

First had come the awakening of her Forestallment allowing her to communicate with the fliers of the fields. Then she had accompanied Tristan and Faegan to Farpoint, fighting alongside them as well as any man could have. She had taken her first lives, and Wigg suspected sadly that they would not be her last.

Shailiha tossed back long, blond hair and turned her determined eyes to Faegan. "I'm tired of hearing you blather on about herbs and roots," she countered. "If you and Abbey must go to Shadowood, then do so, and quickly. But first I have questions, and I want the answers now."

"As always, Princess, I will do my best," Faegan answered respectfully.

"First of all," she began, "that night at the docks. I know the slaves were being branded, but why? What did the two branding irons say?"

Pursing his lips, Faegan laced his gnarled fingers and tried to think of where to begin. "Wigg and I think we have part of the puzzle pieced together. But certainly not all of it," he said.

"Please go on," the princess said.

"One of the branding irons—the one that was used most often—said *Talis*. That is the Old Eutracian word for 'unendowed.' The other one read *R'talis*, or 'endowed.' The men in the blue robes sitting at the table were no doubt consuls of the Redoubt; some of those who were turned by Nicholas and swore allegiance to him. They are now unquestionably under the leadership of Krassus. We also believe that the person with Krassus that night was his partial adept—the one he bragged about the day he infiltrated the palace and attacked Wigg. When I described her to Abbey, she agreed that the woman sounded like the one who helped Krassus ransack her cottage."

"What were the consuls at the table doing?" Shailiha asked.

"Testing the blood of the slaves," Faegan answered. "If he or she was unendowed, as most of them would be, they were branded accordingly. If they were endowed, they were branded with the other iron."

"But the consuls were doing more than that," Shailiha remembered. "There were strange tools on the tables before them. I couldn't make out what they were."

"Tools like this?" Faegan asked. Unlacing his fingers, he reached under the table, and brought out two odd-looking objects.

The first was a wooden frame holding an hourglass and a small vial. The vial contained what looked to be the vibrant red water of the Caves of the Paragon. The hourglass held what seemed to be no more than a dozen tiny black spheres.

The second device was a three-legged wooden tripod, about half a meter in height, with a magnifying lens at its top. Embedded into the lens were dark, wire crosshairs. The two upper quadrants created by the wires were marked off on each side by degrees, from the vertical axis outward.

Stymied, all the princess could do was look and wonder. She turned to Celeste, but the look on Celeste's face made it plain that she was as lost as Shailiha.

Wigg pointed to the frame holding the hourglass and the vial. "This is called a blood criterion. Its purpose is to assay the quality of endowed blood. The lower the assay number, the higher the quality of the blood that is being examined. The plans for this device were found in the Tome of the Paragon during Faegan's first reading of it. The Ones Who Came Before, through their dictates in the Tome, ordered us to construct it and assay your blood immediately following your births. Just like the azure glow surrounding your deliveries, your blood ratings were further proof to the Directorate that you and Tristan were indeed the Chosen Ones."

At the mention of Tristan, Shailiha's face darkened again. "How does it work?' she asked.

"It's really quite simple," Wigg explained. "First, the criterion is placed upon a piece of parchment. Then a drop of the subject's blood is placed on the parchment a specific distance from the criterion. The hourglass is turned over at the exact moment a single drop of cave water is released from the vial and lands on the parchment. As you have already been taught, endowed blood and water from the Caves immediately attract, but to varying degrees, depending upon the quality of the blood.

The stronger the blood, the faster the two seek each other out and join to form a signature. The number of spheres that drop in the time it takes for the two fluids to meet equates to the number of the blood quality."

"Ingenious," Celeste said.

Shailiha reached out and drew the tripod device toward her. Standing, she closed one eye and looked down through the lens.

"Although simpler in design, this tool is as valuable as the criterion," Wigg went on. "The plans for it were also found in the Tome. Called a signature scope, it is used to determine whether the blood signature on the parchment beneath it leans to the left or the right, and to what degree. A high blood quality rating, coupled with a severe degree of lean one way or the other, results in a person of very great potential power, indeed."

Reaching out, Shailiha took up one of the parchments on the table that held a blood signature. Sliding it beneath the tripod, she squared it up as best she knew how, then looked down again. Sure enough, she could see a slight tendency to the right. She raised her face back up to Wigg.

"And you have said that both my signature and Tristan's lean to the right," she mused.

"Correct," the lead wizard answered.

"And Wulfgar's blood signature leans as far to the left as you have ever seen."

"Regrettably, also correct. And his blood assay is one and one-half—equal to yours and second only to your brother's, which has a blood-quality rating of one. Wulfgar's blood, given these particular traits, is most probably the most dangerous in the world."

"Is there a copy of his signature registered here?" she suddenly asked.

Nodding, Wigg caused the appropriate drawer to slide open. But this time, instead of only the parchment floating over to the table, the entire drawer did. As it landed, Shailiha could see that it contained not only a copy of a blood signature, but a lock of sandy-colored hair bound together with a red ribbon.

She picked up the lock of hair. "This came from Wulfgar, didn't it?" she asked.

Wigg nodded. "It was taken from him the morning of the day your mother gave him up," he replied softly. "It was one of her most prized possessions, and she felt it rightly belonged here, alongside his blood signature."

"Wulfgar is the reason why the *R'talis* are being taken, isn't it?" she asked. "They are searching for him."

"Yes," Wigg said, "we believe so. In truth, they may already have found him."

"But why also take the unendowed?" Celeste asked, looking over at her father. "Or the endowed women, for that matter? If Wulfgar is the only one they seek, then what they're doing doesn't make any sense."

"That is still unknown," Faegan said. "But considering all of the effort it takes, they must have a reason."

"Why Farpoint?" Shailiha mused quietly.

"What?" Wigg asked.

"Why Farpoint?" Shailiha repeated. "Why would Krassus concentrate his search there, and not elsewhere?"

"We don't know that he has," Wigg answered. "But your question is a good one. For the moment, we can only suspect that Nicholas told him to search there, just before he died."

"And where did the demonslavers come from?" Celeste asked. "From what everyone tells me, their like has never been seen in Eutracia before now."

"Another unknown," Faegan answered. "But from what the princess and I saw that night in Farpoint, I think it safe to assume that though they appear to be a product of magic, they have no command of it. Much like the Minions, they represent only a blunt instrument—one that is most useful when wielded by others. They may be what remained of the consuls, mutated by Krassus. Or they may have sprung from another source entirely—conjured, perhaps. Be that as it may, it is abundantly clear that they serve only him." He paused and sighed. "Unfortunately, only time will answer your questions. And as I said, time is not on our side."

Something suddenly occurred to Shailiha. "Can Abbey locate Wulfgar?" she asked quickly. "If he has already been captured, perhaps he and Tristan are together."

Wigg raised an eyebrow. "Well done," he answered. He turned to Abbey. "Can you view Wulfgar from the blood dried on this certificate, or from the lock of his hair? I'm afraid it's all we have of him." He passed them over to her.

Abbey looked intently at them. "Perhaps," she answered. "How old are these samples?"

"Thirty-five years," Wigg answered.

Abbey sighed. "I won't know until I try. Blood tends to lose its vibrancy far more quickly than hair, so the latter will afford the better chance of success."

Gently touching the locket that hung around her neck, she gave Wigg a coy smile. A slight blush spread across the lead wizard's face.

"But as I said before, all of this is academic until I have a sufficient quantity of the right ingredients," she added.

Wigg looked at Faegan. "Clearly, our first priority must be to secure from Shadowood the goods Abbey needs to construct her gazing flame."

"There is something else that must be done," Shailiha said adamantly. "I want to lead a party of Minions to Farpoint. We'll turn the city upside down, if we have to, to find my brother and bring him home—if he's still there." Sitting back in her chair, she angrily folded her arms over her breasts.

Wigg looked at Faegan. They had been expecting something like this from her, and they also knew that under no circumstances could they allow it. In the first place, should Tristan already be dead, it was vital that they not put Shailiha in harm's way. And second, it might well be exactly what Krassus wanted: the opportunity to capture the second of the Chosen Ones, and perhaps to take the palace, which would be far too vulnerable without sufficient Minion guards to protect it.

Taking a deep breath, Wigg placed his hands flat on the table and calmly explained to the princess why they could not go through with her plan. As he did, it was easy to see the anger and frustration build in her face once more.

For a long time she sat there seething. Looking down, she gently touched the gold medallion lying around her neck. Then she finally spoke.

"Very well," she said softly. "But I refuse to sit here and do nothing while my brother is out there somewhere, and in danger." She looked at Abbey, and the herbmistress felt Shailiha's hazel eyes go straight through her.

"Give me a list of things you need, and I'll go to Shadowood myself," the princess said. "I've already been there once—the gnomes know me. The journey is safe enough. Even you and Faegan can agree with that much, I should think!"

"And I will go with her," Celeste announced enthusiastically. "Together we will be stronger."

A slight smile came to Shailiha's lips.

"Absolutely not!" Wigg thundered. He glared at the two women as if they were completely mad. The telltale vein in his right temple had begun to throb again.

"I can use my gift to protect us, if need be," Celeste said quickly. "And if we employ Faegan's portal, we won't be gone long at all. What could be safer?" Smiling, she mischievously tugged the sleeve of her father's robe—a gesture she knew always softened his heart.

"You'll never even miss us, especially given the fact that you now have an old friend here to keep you occupied, so to speak," she added coyly. At that reference to Abbey, Faegan grinned widely.

Wigg blushed, and the vein in his temple throbbed even harder. "You still do not know how to use your gift effectively!" he argued.

"Really?" Celeste asked. "I already used it once to save *your* life, didn't I?"

Wigg looked beseechingly at Faegan. "And what say you to this madness?" he asked.

Faegan smiled. "Actually, I say 'yes.' Abbey and I will send along a list of our needs to Lionel the Little, the caretaker at my mansion, along with a letter of permission from me to give what we need to the ladies. You will be bringing back only dried herbs, not fresh ones. If time permits, we may send you back for fresh herbs later."

"Why do you want only dried herbs?"

"With rare exceptions, herbs must be dried before they can be of use in the craft," Faegan answered. "And unlike the process used by ordinary cooks, the drying of herbs for magic can be long and meticulous in its stages—and our needs are immediate. In addition, dried herbs are far easier to mix. I'm sure once you reach Shadowood, Lionel will be happy to tell you more. He can be amazingly talkative."

For the first time in days, Shailiha grinned.

"Very well," Wigg said reluctantly. "But this little errand of yours should take no more than a single day. If the two of you do not come home on the appointed hour, I am coming to Shadowood myself to get you. Understood?"

Sighing, the lead wizard sat back in his chair and looked at the two women who had just bested him.

Fourteen

The woman on Wulfgar's bed looked him up and down in his robe, her eyes filled with hate.

"I see you're already dressed for the occasion," she said nastily. "Just do whatever you want to me, and get it over with." Her voice was defiant.

Wulfgar looked at her. Despite the fact that her sea voyage had made her thin, she remained beautiful. Dark ringlets curled down over her breasts. Her taffeta gown—no doubt supplied by Janus—was stunning, and the yellow complemented her deep blue eyes. Given her situation, he might have expected her to cower before him. But she did not. Only anger showed. He immediately found himself respecting her for it, and wanting to know more about her.

"No harm will befall you here," he said quietly. "I'm a slave, just like you."

She let go a short, derisive laugh. "Don't lie to me, as well as abuse me." She looked briefly around the room and then shook her head. "No slave has quarters such as these."

Taking another step, Wulfgar pulled down the left shoulder of his robe. At first she recoiled, but then she saw the brand—the exact duplicate of her own. Her mouth dropped, and she began to relax a little.

"We may have to be slaves for them, but we don't have to be for one another," he added gently. He gestured to the silver table full of food. When he did so, her eyes greedily followed his.

"Would you like something to eat?" he asked. "You look very hungry."

She nodded, but it was abundantly clear that she wasn't ready to trust him.

Sensing that she might feel less threatened out on the spacious balcony, Wulfgar walked over to the breakfast cart and pushed it out into the sun. Sitting down in one of the upholstered chairs, he gazed out over the ever-restless ocean.

"Come and eat," he said casually. "I promise not to harm you."

She stood tentatively and walked to the balcony. After a cautious look at him, she stared straight down over the balcony wall. Then she raised her eyes and looked out to the west, toward Eutracia, and tears began to form. For some time she stood still, the only movement the gentle swaying of her ringlets in the salty sea breeze.

"Please sit down," Wulfgar said. He fixed a generous plate of food and handed it to her. Before she had even sat down, she snatched it from him and then bent over her prize protectively, the way a starving animal might, tearing into it as though she hadn't eaten for a lifetime. Smiling slightly, Wulfgar waited. As she continued to look warily at him in between bites of cheese, warm rolls, and fruit, Wulfgar poured her a cup of tea. She took it from him greedily. Still trying to gain her trust, he smiled again.

"What is your name?" he asked. "Where are you from?"

"I am Serena," she answered cautiously. Another bite of roll went quickly into her waiting mouth. "Of the House of Winslow."

"Winslow?" Wulfgar asked. She nodded.

"From Farpoint?"

Another nod.

Uncrossing his legs, Wulfgar leaned forward in his chair and looked intently into her face. "Is your father by chance Simon Winslow, the animal healer?"

Surprised, she stopped chewing for a moment. "Yes," she answered. Then her eyes narrowed. "How did you know?"

"I know Simon well," he said, smiling. "We do business. His practice is on the west side of town, is it not? On Baylor Street. I take horses there whenever I am unable to cure them myself. Your father is very good at what he does—the best in the city, as far as I am concerned. My parents are Jason and Selene, of the House of Merrick."

Finally starting to believe, she stopped chewing and put her plate down for a moment. Her eyes searched his face. "The Merrick Stables?" she whispered incredulously.

"Yes," he answered. "I am their son, Wulfgar."

She relaxed a little. "My father has spoken often of you," she said. "He respects you and Jason greatly."

Wishing he could talk to her forever, a sudden, darker thought crossed Wulfgar's mind. Standing and walking from the balcony, he went into the bedroom to fetch the hourglass Janus had left behind. It was the only gauge he had to tell him when the painted freak and his monsters would return. When Serena saw it again, her face hardened.

"Why are we here?" she asked. "And how is it that you are being treated so differently from the rest of us?"

"I don't know," he answered. "They made a great fuss over me when they took my blood at the pier, and then I was immediately brought here. They are waiting for someone called Krassus to arrive. Apparently he will tell me more." He thought for a moment.

"Tell me," he said. "How much of this building have you seen? Did you notice any way out?"

"I'm sorry, but I saw no exits," she answered honestly. "And I viewed little, compared to the gigantic size of this place. I have heard some of the slavers refer to this structure as the 'Citadel.' All of us with this *R'talis* mark, the men and women alike, are kept in gigantic cages. They give us just enough food and water to keep us alive. New *R'talis* prisoners arrive every day. We have no idea where the people with the other kind of brand are being held, or even if they still live. Every morning Janus and his slavers come and take a different selection of us away. Those taken never return. It is all very strange."

Wulfgar looked at the hourglass. More than half of the contents of the top globe had already spilled down.

"What happened this morning?" he asked.

"Janus came to us early. I now know that it was to select one of the women for you," she said ashamedly. "But none of us knew that then. We thought that he was simply taking more of us away. When he chose me, I was terrified. He had me taken to other quarters, rather like these. This gown was laid out on the bed, and there was a room for bathing." Then her face lowered.

"He watched the entire time as I bathed myself and changed into this dress," she whispered. "All the while he was smiling, and clinking those strange spheres of his in one hand. It sent shivers down my spine. Then he and his slavers brought me here. Along the way I saw many dark hall-ways, lit by torches, and a very large, open courtyard. But most of the time was spent navigating stairways. The walk was very long, and hun-dreds of demonslavers filed by us in the halls. I also saw a few of the men in the dark blue robes. I can tell you that this place, this Citadel as they call it, is very well guarded."

Wulfgar's heart fell. If there was any way to escape, he still hadn't found it.

"There was something else about my walk here," she added softly, taking him away from his thoughts. "Something horrible."

"What?" he asked anxiously.

Serena closed her eyes. "The screaming," she whispered.

"Please go on," he said. He could tell she was upset, and a part of him hated having to press her further.

"One of the halls we went down was lined with huge marble doors," she said, shaking her head. "From the other side came horrible, insane screaming, from men and women alike. It went on and on, until we finally rounded the corner and it faded away. It didn't seem to bother Janus at all." She paused to wipe away a tear. "I can't begin to imagine what was going on behind those doors."

Silence passed for a time. When Serena felt like talking again, they spoke of Farpoint and told each other more about their families. They ate a bit more, and sipped more tea.

When Wulfgar turned to look at the hourglass, he saw that very little time remained. He looked into Serena's eyes. "Do you trust me?" he asked urgently.

For a moment she hesitated, then seemed to decide. "Yes," she finally said.

"Good," he answered back. "You were brought here to please me. And Janus said that if you did not, he would punish you. I can't allow that to happen."

"Come with me!" he ordered. Then he stood and led her back into the bedroom, where he pushed her gently onto the bed.

Going back to the balcony, he retrieved the hourglass and replaced it on the table in the bedroom where Janus had left it. Then he pushed the food cart back into the room. Hurrying back to the bed, he sat down next to her and looked into her eyes.

"If you want to survive this day, you must do as I tell you," he ordered. "Stand up!"

Wulfgar quickly pulled the bedspread and silk sheets apart and purposely tangled them. Then he mussed up the pillows. "Turn around!" he ordered.

To her surprise, he quickly began unlacing the back of her gown. After it was partially undone, he whirled her around to face him. Then he grasped the bodice of her gown with both hands and tore it down the front, partially exposing her breasts. Ordering her to lift first one foot then the other, he removed both her slippers and tossed them aside. He ran his hands through her ringlets, making a mess of them. Then he did something even more unexpected.

Reaching down, he quickly captured her right hand tightly in his. Then, before she could protest, he placed her fingernails hard against his left cheek and scratched himself. Drops of blood began running from the three scrapes, and he purposely did not wipe them away.

Horrified, Serena looked up into his face. Tears came to her eyes once more. Taking her by the shoulders, Wulfgar shook her, trying to get her to focus on what must be done. He felt her suddenly go limp, as though she had almost given up.

"Listen to me!" he whispered. "Your life depends on it! The bolt on the other side of the door will slide open at any moment. When it does, I'm going to kiss you. Kiss me back like you mean it! Don't stop until I do, and then let me do all the talking! Be surprised by nothing I do or say! Do you understand?"

Slowly, the strength he had first seen in her eyes came back. She nodded.

Wulfgar took her into his arms and held her tightly. Untying the sash of his robe, he let it fall open, pressing his naked body against her. He tried as best he could to give her a smile of encouragement.

Turning to look at the hourglass, they both saw that the last few grains of sand were sliding into the lower globe. For several moments the room went silent, the only sounds the beating of their hearts and the waves crashing on the rocky shore below.

Right on time, the bolt on the other side of the double doors began to scratch its way across. Wulfgar turned to look into Serena's eyes a final time. They both held their breath.

Just as the doors opened a crack, he bent her deeply beneath him and put his mouth down on hers.

The double doors burst open, and Janus and his slavers walked arrogantly into the room. Ignoring them, Wulfgar kissed Serena hard, letting his hands explore her body as if he owned her. Understanding, Serena obeyed him and responded passionately, running her hands through Wulfgar's long, blond hair. Widening her stance, she moaned and pulled him harder against her. For a moment Wulfgar stopped kissing her, and bent her back even farther to slowly bury his face in the torn bodice of her dress.

"Well done!" Wulfgar heard the painted freak call out.

As if angry to have been interrupted, Wulfgar slowly, reluctantly stopped what he was doing. Breathing harder than he needed to, he turned his damaged cheek toward Janus, so the freak could get a good look. But he did not let go of Serena. Her body locked tightly against his, he felt a quick shudder of fear go through her.

Janus walked over to them and ran his index finger across Wulfgar's bloody cheek. "So she can scratch, as well," he mused. "But it looks as if you have tamed her—at least for the time being." He smiled. "Tell me," he asked conspiratorially. "Was she good?"

Wulfgar let Serena go. "Good enough for me to want more," he growled as he closed his robe. "As you can see, I had a bit of trouble getting her to disrobe the first time. I was about to take her all over again, but you returned before I could." He gave Janus a wicked, knowing smile. Then he looked back to Serena.

"It's just like breaking a horse," he said nastily. "After the first ride, they're usually far more willing." He smiled again. "It's always better when they help."

Smiling, Janus gave Wulfgar a nod. Then, suddenly, his eyes narrowed and he took a menacing step closer to Serena.

"But if you were going to take her once more, why did you let her dress herself again?" he asked.

Wulfgar thought his heart might stop. He hadn't considered this. Then he remembered something Serena had told him about her captor.

He smiled. "I like to watch. Don't you?" Then he shot Serena a nasty, disparaging look, as though she were the lowest whore in creation.

"Oh, yes," Janus said. "Indeed I do." Apparently satisfied, he motioned two of his slavers forward. "Take this trollop back where she came from," he ordered. They immediately grasped Serena by both arms and began roughly shoving her toward the door.

"Wait!" Wulfgar interjected. As he took a brazen step forward, one of the slavers drew his sword. What he was about to dare was risky, he knew. But he had to try.

"What is it?" Janus demanded.

Wulfgar let go another leering, brutish smile. "Bring her to me again in a day or two," he said adamantly. "I want more." Wryly rubbing the scratches on his face, he looked Serena up and down again.

"And give this she-cat something better to eat," he added commandingly. "I like them with a few more curves on their bones."

His demands had been a gamble, to be sure. Despite the lustful look on his face, his heart was pounding with worry, wondering how the painted freak would react.

Raising an eyebrow, Janus took two quiet steps closer, reached down to the twin spheres hanging from his belt, and began clinking them together. Janus' closeness made Wulfgar want to cringe, but he held his ground. The freak turned to study the woman once more, then looked back at Wulfgar. As he smiled, the painted red mask crinkled menacingly at the outer edges of his eyes.

"You are clearly in no position to make demands, Wulfgar," he said. "Surely you know that. Yet I commend your courage. I suppose what you request could be granted." He smiled again. "Until next time, then."

Saying nothing more, he went out the double doors. As the slavers pushed Serena toward them, she turned to give Wulfgar a final glance. There were tears tracing down her cheeks. He knew she dared not speak, but it didn't matter. The thankful look on her face said it all.

As the great doors closed with finality, Wulfgar heard the bolt scratch its way across on the other side.

His chest was heaving. Closing his eyes, he took a deep breath. He stood there that way for some time, listening to the crashing of the waves as they broke on the rocky shore hundreds of feet below. For a short, delicious moment, he thought he could still smell the perfume she had been wearing. Then he opened his eyes and walked to the balcony.

Looking down, he saw the plate and teacup Serena had just used. As if it could somehow bring her back, he took a sip. It was still warm.

Even so, his loneliness was already again so great that it was almost as if she had never been here. He hung his head for a moment. Some of what he had just said and done to her sickened him, but it had been necessary. And despite it, he still had no idea whether he would ever see her again, or whether he had helped her plight.

Looking out over the sea, he watched sadly as the white-sailed masts of yet two more ships broke over the western horizon.

Fifteen

Krassus looked at the ancient parchment lying on the table before him. The oil lamp hanging from the ceiling cast its golden light down upon it as it countermatched the ceaseless, rhythmic swaying of the ship. The beautiful script on the dry, ancient document seemed to call to his blood, beckoning him to enter its timeless, infinite wonder.

The fabled document was truly majestic, just as Nicholas had promised. About one meter long and half a meter in diameter, it was rolled around a solid gold rod with a fluted, golden knob at each end. A wide gold band engraved in Old Eutracian secured the massive document around its middle. Heavy marble bookends kept it from rolling off the table.

He stood and stretched, then walked across the sumptuous room and swung open one of the stained-glass windows that lined the curved, graceful stern of his flagship. Dappled sunshine bounced off the froth-tipped waves, and the salty sea air immediately invaded the room. The air was brisk, and the *Sojourner* was making good time as she ran before the wind.

He smiled. He already had the male of the Chosen Ones—and the Scroll of the Vagaries. Two prizes remained to be secured: Wulfgar, the bastard son of Morganna, late queen of Eutracia, and the Scroll of the Vigors.

Obtaining the first scroll had been simple enough. Indeed, had its mate been there with it as Nicholas had promised, he would now have them both. But when he had finally found and entered the glowing, enchanted base of one of the destroyed Gates of Dawn, he had been shocked to find only the Scroll of the Vagaries present. The other had obviously been taken, but by whom? And why hadn't this one been taken, as well? The gold that made up their center rods and end knobs alone was worth a king's ransom. These confounding questions had plagued him ever since that fateful day, and he meant to have his answers.

The mystery had led him to two frightening conclusions. First, whoever had taken the other scroll probably had no idea of its overall importance, or he would have returned to steal the second one. And second, if the thief truly did not know what he had, then the missing scroll could be in grave danger—the gold in it melted down, for instance, and the pages tossed away or destroyed outright.

His need to find the other scroll intensified with each passing day. But he also needed to get to the Citadel as soon as possible, to begin the other part of his task.

Only one loose end remained to be dealt with. As he had learned when invading the wizards' minds, there was yet another place in Eutracia where the herbs, blossoms, and roots used in blaze-gazing had been collected in abundance—and his plan for that problem would be accomplished this very day, far away from where the *Sojourner* sailed toward the secret island in the sea.

Turning from the window, Krassus looked at the two other persons in the room. Grizelda sat in a chair on the opposite side of the table. She looked tired and worn. Under Krassus' orders, she had been using her gazing blaze to try to locate the Scroll of the Vigors. Her approach had been to employ bits of blank vellum taken from the edges of the scroll already in their possession in the hope that they would be enough of a match to let her view the whereabouts of its mate. So far she had been unsuccessful.

This greatly angered Krassus, for it might also mean that there was no way to find the missing scrolls from a distance. Or, worse, it might indicate that the scroll he sought had already been destroyed. These were not scenarios he was willing to accept.

The other person seated at the table was Tristan. Bound to his chair, he was still unconscious due to the spell cast over him. He looked pale and drawn, and the dark stubble on his face was becoming thicker by the day. His head slumped down toward his chest.

Krassus looked back at Grizelda. "I think it's time for the good prince to rejoin the world," he said simply.

The herbmistress' face darkened with worry. "Begging your pardon, my lord, but are you sure this is wise? You said yourself that he can be very dangerous, even though he is still untrained. And the scroll is here, in this very room. Do you really want him to see it?" Her face suddenly pinched with fear that she had just overstepped her bounds.

"What difference could it possibly make?" Krassus replied confidently. "Given his situation, he cannot possibly harm us. And I want him to see it. I want the Chosen One to know how close we are to vanquishing his wizards before he is forever confined within the purgatory that is the Citadel." Pausing for a moment, Krassus' face became harder.

"Besides, he is of little importance," he continued. "If he dies, he dies. And if he survives the voyage, he will live out his days as a slave on the Citadel—unless I finally decide to kill him, of course. Either way, I win."

With that Krassus narrowed his eyes, and the glow of the craft began to surround the prince. Moaning softly, Tristan began to stir.

Weakly, he lifted his face. His eyes were glazed, and his jaw was slack. Drool dripped from the corners of his mouth.

"Welcome back, Chosen One," Krassus said quietly. "You have been gone five days. You are groggy, but you are basically well, and should suffer no lasting effects from my ministrations. I trust your dreams were pleasant."

Trying to focus his eyes, Tristan looked blankly around the room. Through the haze of his vision he saw Grizelda, and the scroll resting on the table before him. But his first concerns were not for them, or for himself.

"Faegan . . . and Shailiha," he croaked anxiously, his throat so dry it might have been made of paper. "Are they—"

"Dead?" Krassus smiled. "No, I'm sorry to say they are not. But it wasn't for my lack of trying. The bridge Faegan so cleverly conjured allowed them to get away, but it seems the poor quality horse you were on didn't make it to the other side. Your sister and the crippled wizard were lifted into the air by your Minions just as my slavers began to corner them in the woods."

Tristan turned his attention to the haggard woman seated next to him at the table. "And this must be your partial adept," he rasped. "The woman you bragged about . . . in the palace . . . She was with you on the docks. She's lovely . . ." His head slumped forward again.

"How droll," Krassus said. "But I suggest you save your sense of humor. Where you're going, you will surely need it." As he smiled, the creases in his thin cheeks deepened.

Raising his head, Tristan tried desperately to clear his mind. He looked at the majestic scroll on the table.

"The Scroll of the Vagaries?" he asked.

"Yes," Krassus answered simply.

"And my brother, Wulfgar?" Tristan asked. "What of him?"

"Unfortunately, he still eludes my grasp." Krassus sighed. "But it is only a matter of time until we find him."

His mind finally clear, Tristan thought for a moment. Looking down, he saw that he was bound hand and foot with heavy strands of rope, and he could not reach his weapons. That was when he first realized that either the room was rocking, or his mind still was. Then the oil lamp swinging from the ceiling and the sounds and smells coming from the open window finally told him they were at sea. As his powers of concentration strengthened, so did the anger in his heart.

He focused his eyes on Krassus. Something the wizard had just said had sparked a question within him.

"You mentioned Farpoint," Tristan said slowly. "What makes you think Wulfgar is there?"

Krassus smiled. "I see no harm in answering that," he said. "Your son Nicholas told me to search there, just before he met his untimely death atop the Gates of Dawn. Surely you remember that day."

Tristan's brows came together in a frown. "How could Nicholas have known?"

"The Heretics of the Guild told him," Krassus said. "Your esteemed son's magnificent powers allowed him mental communication with the Heretics—or didn't you know that?" The wizard's expression was one of wicked glee.

"From their place in the heavens, they see everything," he added. "In fact, due to my illness I will soon be joining them. It is a reward I look forward to."

"Where are you taking me?" Tristan growled.

"To a place that is almost as old as the craft itself," Krassus answered. "Nicholas told me of it, and it is said that many of magic's greatest secrets can be found there. Some even say it is one of the places where it all began. If the winds hold, we should arrive there in less than a fortnight."

Tristan tried to twist his hands back and forth, testing his bonds. They were completely unforgiving. He turned his eyes back to Krassus.

"This ship is full of slaves you branded that night on the Farpoint docks, isn't it?" he asked.

"Of course."

"And the consuls seated at the tables—they were testing the slaves' blood, weren't they? Then you ordered them branded accordingly, so that it would be easier to tell them apart later on."

Smiling, Krassus turned to Grizelda. "See, my dear," he said. "I told you he was clever." He turned back to Tristan. "Meet Grizelda, Chosen One. She is my personal partial adept, blaze-gazer, and herbmistress. She is the one who will find the Scroll of the Vigors for me."

"Unless Wigg and Faegan find it first," Tristan said menacingly.

"Oh, that will be quite impossible after today," Krassus answered happily. "Before we sailed, I ordered something be done in Eutracia. It is happening as we speak, and it will change everything."

Tristan's blood went cold. "What are you talking about?" he demanded. No reply came. "Tell me, you bastard!"

"Oh, no, Chosen One," Krassus said gently, almost as if he were talking to a child. "That would be revealing too much." Silence settled over the room for a moment.

"Why do you need all of these slaves?" Tristan finally asked. "Of what possible use could they be to you?"

"For much the same reason I require your brother." Krassus smiled. "But you will probably go to your death never having learned the answer." Then the look in the wizard's eyes intensified and he leaned forward, lovingly placing his hands on either side of the massive scroll.

"You have yet to ask the one question that I thought would be foremost in your mind, Chosen One," Krassus said.

"And that is?" Tristan asked skeptically.

"Why I allow you to live," the wizard answered quietly.

For a time, Tristan continued to glare at Krassus. Then he glanced at the haggard herbmistress. Grizelda only smiled back wickedly, exposing the absence of several teeth.

"Very well," Tristan finally said. "Why?"

"Because I want to bear witness as you pay for your sins," Krassus hissed softly. "The sin of killing your only son, Nicholas, the messiah who was also my master. That's why we're having this little talk. As you find yourself suffering by my hand today and in the future, I want you to know why."

Tristan's jaw hardened. The wizard's continual mentions of Nicholas conjured up conflicting emotions within him. He glared hatefully at the wizard across the table.

"I would see him die a thousand times again, if need be," Tristan whispered venomously. "He was of my seed, that much I cannot deny. But he was conceived in an act of violence, and against my will. His azure blood was adulterated with Forestallments placed there by the Heretics of the Guild, forcing him to cherish only the Vagaries. Much the same way I suspect he tainted your blood."

Seeing the anger rising in Krassus' face, Tristan smiled. Having nothing to lose, he decided to press. "But in truth, how perfect could Nicholas have been? After all, his blood failed him just when he needed it most, did it not?" He again paused for a moment, allowing the import of his words sink in.

"I didn't kill Nicholas," he finished. "I didn't have to. His own imperfections did that job for me, while I watched. And I enjoyed it."

Krassus' temper suddenly reached the boiling point. Standing up, he pointed an angry finger at the prince.

"Liar!" he screamed. Standing, he walked around the desk.

He slammed his fist into Tristan's face with a force so great that the prince's head hit the back of the chair. Azure blood snaked down from one corner of Tristan's mouth as he shook his head, trying to clear his mind. Grasping Tristan's hair, Krassus violently jerked the prince's face up to meet his. Tristan's eyes fluttered open. Bruises were already showing beneath the dark stubble.

"You're . . . very good at beating people who . . . can't fight back . . . aren't you?" Tristan croaked. "Why don't you just use . . . the craft . . . to do it, traitor?"

Krassus bent over the prince until their noses almost touched. "Because sometimes this is far more enjoyable," he whispered. "And as I told the lead wizard that day in the palace, I've been ill."

"I will kill you," Tristan snarled through his pain. "I swear it. You represent nothing but evil, like Nicholas . . . I will watch you die, just as I watched him. And I will enjoy that, too."

Krassus wrenched the prince's head up farther. "Evil?" he replied. "He who has yet to be trained dares to call *me* evil? Don't you know that there is no such thing as 'good' or 'evil,' Chosen One? There is only the Vigors or the Vagaries. There is still so much your wizards have not told you. But I would have thought your experiences with the Coven of Sorceresses would have taught you something. Tell me, dear prince, do you really believe Failee was 'evil'? Or was she simply doing what she was born to do, compelled to do? Given the undeniable call of her left-leaning signature, did she truly have a choice? Don't you see, you fool? It is the same with me. I'm not 'evil.' I don't even know the meaning of the word." Once again, he smiled wickedly. "You see, my dear prince, I simply have a different point of view."

With that, Krassus again slammed his fist—with a force supplemented by the craft—into Tristan's face. This time the blow was even harder. It launched the chair off its feet and sent it crashing backward to the floor. The prince immediately went unconscious.

Wasting no time, Krassus walked to the door and violently threw it open. Several demonslavers entered immediately, swords drawn.

"Get this abomination of the craft out of my sight!" Krassus ordered them, pointing down at the prince. "Signal the *Wayfarer* and order her to come alongside. Transfer this refuse to her. I want him immediately ordered to the *Wayfarer*. He is to man an oaring station. And keep him in his clothes—I want him easily singled out from the rest. It should be most interesting to observe how that famous azure blood of his holds up." Looking down at the bloodied prince, the wizard smiled again.

"We'll see how much he likes to row," he added softly.

"Begging your pardon, my lord," one of the slavers said. "What shall we do with his weapons?"

As Krassus looked at the prince's dreggan and throwing knives, his lips came up into a sneer. "Strip him of them," he answered. "Have them transferred to the other ship. I want nothing of this bastard left around to remind me of him."

Untying Tristan from his chair, the slavers lifted him up as if he were a rag doll and dragged him from the room on his toes.

CHAPTER

Sixteen

S hailiha came awake first. Groaning slightly, she shook her head and opened her eyes to the sky above.

The weather was unsettled in Shadowood, with dark, slow-moving clouds randomly checkerboarded among the white. The breeze was fairly strong, waving the new grass to and fro, and carried with it the unique, fresh smell of coming rain. Shailiha took a deep breath and sat up slowly, trying to clear her mind from the effects of Faegan's portal.

Not far from her, Celeste was stirring in the grass. Rising to her knees, the red-haired beauty lowered her head and shook it back and forth lightly before tossing back her long hair. She gave the princess a sly smile.

Shailiha smiled back. Of course the wizards would never have allowed her to lead the Minions against Farpoint. She and Celeste had known that from the start—just as they had known that making that request was likely to result in the granting of a second request. Neither woman was willing just to sit by like some dainty lady-in-waiting. Doing anything was better than nothing, even if that meant going herb hunting for a three-hundred-year-old partial adept.

Both women were dressed in black trunk hose, knee-high riding boots, and leather jerkins, with long, close-fitting sleeves. Shailiha's was brown, Celeste's dark gray. The jerkins were gathered at the waist by broad leather belts. On their hands they wore tight, black leather gloves, and daggers hung from their right hips in sheaths that were tied around their thighs. Shailiha also carried a short sword at her left hip; upon the sword's gold hilt was engraved the lion and the broadsword, the heraldry of the House of Galland.

Reaching beneath her jerkin, the princess searched for both the list of goods that Abbey had given her and the letter of permission that Faegan had penned for Lionel the Little. To her relief, they were both still there.

"It seems we have finally made it after all," Celeste said. "We had best hurry, though."

"You're right," Shailiha answered as she readjusted the baldric that held her sword. Then she paused, taking a sniff of the air. For a moment she had thought she smelled smoke . . . but no, she must have been mistaken. As she rose to her knees, she smiled again at her friend. "For a moment there, I thought the vein in Wigg's temple was going to—"

She stopped in midsentence. Holding one hand out to indicate silence, she wrinkled up her nose again. This time the smell was unmistakable.

Placing one finger vertically over her lips, Shailiha indicated that Celeste should follow her on all fours through the grass. Wigg's daughter nodded back. The short ridge that lay just uphill would look down onto the area where the gnomes lived. Casting her eyes to the sky, the princess could now see the dark, acrid smoke that was finding its way to her nostrils. She began to crawl, Celeste right behind her.

As the women approached the ridge, they went down on their stomachs and wriggled the final distance to the top. As Shailiha cautiously raised her head to look down, the air left her lungs in a rush.

Tree Town was on fire.

At least half of the beautifully intricate houses and the huge, magnificent trees that held them were wildly ablaze. Flames shot up toward the darkening sky. Thick black smoke billowed out of collapsing roofs and smashed windows like dark, undulating rivers, rising to lay over the town in a gloomy cloud. Gnome children ran about, screaming for their parents. The adults had formed bucket brigades from the well in the center of the glade, but without their master Faegan here to help them with the craft, they were clearly fighting a losing battle.

Holding her breath, she tried to peer through the smoke and locate the distinct roofline of Faegan's mansion. Finally seeing it, she let out a small sigh of relief. Somehow, it seemed unaffected by the fire.

And then, out of the corner of her eye she saw the demonslavers.

Dozens of the awful monsters were pouring around a corner, screaming and waving swords, torches, and tridents. Laughing wickedly, they tossed their torches into an area of still-intact homes. Immediately the dwellings burst into flames. Armed with pitchforks and knives, a group of male gnomes started bravely for the demonslavers, but were hacked to death amid the fire, blood, and screaming. Some of the white-skinned monsters were walking about in triumph, holding up their tridents with dead gnomes impaled upon them.

Lowering her head for a moment, Shailiha was sure she was about to be ill.

But abruptly, unexpectedly, the sounds of havoc stopped, leaving only the snapping and roaring of the flames and the crying and moaning of the gnomes. Shailiha risked another look.

The demonslavers had gathered the surviving gnomes into a group and forced them to their knees. One of the slavers shouted a command. Then another group of slavers rounded a corner, carrying dozens of large canvas bags, stuffed full and tied shut. They piled three of the bags on the ground and gleefully touched their torches to them. The odd-looking bags went up in flames, emitting a riot of unfamiliar odors and colors.

As the flames went higher and the bags were consumed, more were thrown on the burning pile. Shailiha knew it wouldn't be long before all the remaining bags had been turned to ashes.

Then a realization seized her, and she closed her eyes. The slavers hadn't been sent here simply to kill gnomes, or to destroy Tree Town. She and Celeste had to act, and act soon.

She turned to speak to Celeste, but suddenly a sharp, penetrating scream forced her eyes back down to the horrifying scene.

Two of the slavers had stepped forward, taken hold of one of the male gnomes, and were swinging him over the burning bags. The more he screamed the closer to the fire they lowered him.

Then his clothing erupted into flames, and, laughing, they dropped him in.

Shailiha turned desperately to Celeste. "Can you kill them?" she whispered urgently.

At first a look of concern came over Celeste's face, but then she nodded. "I can try," she said. "But I cannot be sure I will not kill some of the gnomes, as well!"

"Better that only some of the gnomes die quickly at your hand, than all of them die that way!" Shailiha responded. She looked down in horror to see that the two slavers were dragging another screaming gnome— a female this time—toward the burning bags.

"When you see me coming out of the woods at their right, stand up and do your best! Then run down the hill as fast as you can, continuing to kill any of them that might have survived! I'm sorry, but that is as much of a plan as I have, and there is no time!" Silently she drew her sword. "And whatever you do, try your best not to kill *me!*" Before Celeste could say anything more, the princess was gone, crawling off to the right through the grass.

Celeste raised her head up a bit. She tried to follow Shailiha's progress, but the brown leather of the princess' jerkin made her blend in with the surroundings. And then, finally, Celeste saw her, standing just inside the edge of the woods at the bottom of the hill.

Her chest heaving and her palms wet, Shailiha stood with her back against a tree, her sword held upright as she tried to steady herself. Slowly, silently, she turned her head to look.

The two demonslavers were laughing and swinging the screaming gnome over the fire as the others cheered them on, and it seemed that they might drop her in at any moment. Embers were already teasing the hem of her dress and threatening to burst it into flames. Looking up at the ridge, Shailiha caught a sliver of Celeste's red hair just over the tops of the swaying grasses. Thinking of Tristan and Morganna, she closed her eyes for a moment, gathering her courage.

And then, her sword held high, she ran out into the glade.

Celeste acted immediately. Standing straight up, she raised her right arm and pointed her fingers. A magnificent azure bolt shot from her hand in a continuous stream, just as it had yesterday in the courtyard with her father looking on. The bolt screamed down over the grassy field, straight toward the demonslavers taunting the gnomes. Continuing to sustain the bolt, Celeste ran down the hill as fast as her legs could carry her.

Sawing into a group of slavers, the bolt exploded. Dozens of slavers flew into the air, their torsos blown apart, organs and blood splattering all over the glade. The surviving slavers scattered, looking around for the source of the magic. Still running down the hill, Celeste manipulated the bolt by turning her hand, trying to avoid the gnomes and kill the straggling slavers. Many of the horrible monsters went down.

But not all of them.

Screaming, Shailiha ran at the first of the two who had been torturing the gnome. A surprised look came to the slaver's face. Then his white eyes went wide with horror as he realized he was already too late. With a single, perfect stroke, Shailiha took his head off at the shoulders. Blood erupted everywhere and the scalded gnome went flying, landing to one side in the grass.

Just as Tristan had taught her, she wasted no time gloating over her victory and instead spun on her heels like a dancer, searching for the other slaver. But she was not as experienced as her brother, and she was too slow.

Had her sword not already been raised she would have died there and then, as the second slaver's blade came singing down at her. The two swords clashed together, sparks flying from their razor-sharp edges, and the princess immediately knew she had lost the upper hand. Turning, she backed up on the balls of her feet as quickly as she could to afford herself some maneuvering room. But her opponent was just as fast.

The tall, white-skinned monster slashed relentlessly, raining down blow after blow, forcing her to keep backing up. She nearly panicked when she felt the heat of the fire licking at her back and realized she had nowhere left to go. As the monster's blade came whistling through the air yet another time, she knew she had only one option left.

Raising her sword with both hands, she purposely fell to one side before the roaring fire. The monster's blade flashed over her head, its edge coming so close that she felt it tearing through the ends of her long blond hair. Just as her right hip touched the ground she brought her blade around with all her strength, slicing through the slaver's calves. Screaming wildly, he fell to the ground next to her.

Coming quickly to one knee, Shailiha raised her sword high and rammed its point straight down between the slaver's eyes and out the back of his head, impaling his skull. She stood, put one boot against his face, and pulled back hard on her sword, freeing it. Blood dripping from her hands and blade, she quickly looked around.

Dead slavers and gnomes lay everywhere. Celeste's bolts had ceased, and an eerie quiet descended over the glade, punctuated only by the snapping of the fires and the somewhat more subdued crying of the surviving gnomes.

Turning frantically to search for Celeste, the princess found her alone at the edge of the glade, her right hand still outstretched. The tips of her fingers were badly scorched.

Before her knelt three demonslavers—apparently the last of those remaining alive. Disarmed, their weapons in a pile a short distance away, they glared up defiantly with a hatred that made Shailiha's blood run cold.

Shailiha walked to Celeste and gratefully placed a hand upon one of her shoulders. "Are you all right?" she asked. Without taking her eyes off the slavers, Celeste nodded. "If any of them make the slightest move, kill them all," Shailiha said sternly.

One corner of Celeste's mouth turned up. "Love to," she answered, her eyes never wavering.

Shailiha walked back to the site of the battle. Some of the survivors had begun to gather up their dead and wounded, while others remained bent over the victims' small, broken bodies and sobbed. It seemed to Shailiha that the wailing might never stop. Another group of survivors had formed bucket brigades, and they were furiously working on the fire. She was heartened to see that some of the homes might be spared, after all.

Seeing her coming, some of the stunned gnomes stepped tentatively forward. A few of them fell at her feet, kissing her bloody boots. Some others wrapped their arms around her legs, weeping openly. As the gnomes gathered around her, Shailiha lowered her head.

Looking at what was once Tree Town, she saw that the houses that had been set alight were all but gone, the charred ash of their remains cradled strangely in tree branches that stretched forth like dark, skeletal fingers. But about a third of the houses seemed to have been spared, including Faegan's mansion. About a dozen of the canvas bags that the slavers had been burning remained untouched. She turned back to the gnomes.

"I am Shailiha, princess of Eutracia," she said loudly. "Some of you might recognize me from the last time I was here. Tell me, does Lionel the Little still live?"

At first no one spoke, no one moved, and Shailiha's heart fell. Then the crowd parted slightly to allow an old gnome to pass through. His head was bald and shiny, with a single island of gray, wispy hair growing in the center of where his hairline used to be. Sharp, highly intelligent-looking eyes stared back at her. He was dressed in dark, torn trousers, a matching shirt and vest, and upturned shoes. He came to stand before the princess and bowed his head briefly.

"I am Lionel," he said. "On behalf of all of us, I would like to thank you for what you have done, I would," he said oddly. The gnomes standing around him buzzed with agreement.

With a bloody hand, Shailiha reached beneath her jerkin and retrieved both the letter Faegan had written, and the list Abbey had provided. She gave him the letter first.

Seeing Faegan's familiar red wax seal on the back of the envelope, Lionel took it from her eagerly. Reaching into his vest, he produced a pair of cracked spectacles. Pinching them as best he could into place near the end of his nose, he broke the seal on the envelope and opened the letter. As he read, Shailiha gave another quick, anxious glance back at Celeste and the captive slavers. Nothing had changed.

"I understand, yes I do," Lionel finally said, refolding the letter. For some reason he looked even more crestfallen than before, and Shailiha was reasonably sure she knew why. "And your list?" he asked quietly. The princess handed it to him.

"This will be nearly impossible, you know," he said apologetically as he scanned the list. "In the end, there may be little I can do, yes, very little."

"I understand, but it is imperative that we try," Shailiha answered. She turned to look at the slavers, then faced Lionel again. "Please take your survivors away from here," she half asked, half ordered him. "You may come back later for your dead. We will join you at Faegan's mansion. But first there is something I must do, and your people have already seen enough."

Understanding, Lionel carefully folded the list and tucked it into a vest pocket. "I will await you both, I will," he said simply. "In the meantime, I will do what I can."

After an indication from the diminutive caretaker, a few of the male gnomes picked up the remaining canvas bags. Then as a whole the crowd began to trudge tiredly out of the glade.

Still holding her bloody sword, Shailiha walked back to the three slavers. Celeste's arm was still raised, poised to let go another bolt. The demonslavers continued to glare at them with their strange, white eyes.

Without speaking, Shailiha came to stand before the first of them. Bending down, she wiped her sword in the grass, cleaning its blade of demonslaver blood, and slid it back into its scabbard. Then she drew her dagger from the sheath on her right thigh.

After blatantly running his white eyes up and down her body, the demonslaver leered up at her. Smiling, he ran his black tongue up and over his lips. "You're pretty, bitch."

Shailiha's eyes narrowed. "You aren't."

With a quick, unforgiving stroke, she slashed the dagger across the slaver's throat. Blood rushed out, cascading down his chest. At first his eyes registered surprise, then glazed over. Raising her right boot, Shailiha kicked him beneath the chin, launching him over onto his back.

She stood there for a moment, listening to the desperate gurgling sounds as the life force poured out of him.

She walked before the second of them. Placing the dagger hard against one of the thing's lower eyelids, she gave it just enough of a nudge that a single drop of blood ran slowly down the dagger's blood groove and onto the handle.

With her free hand, she pointed to the slaver she had just killed. "That was an object lesson," she said quietly. "I want some answers, and I want them now. Krassus sent you here to eradicate Faegan's stores of herbs, didn't he? That's what was in those canvas bags you were burning. Tell me, how much of it did you destroy?"

The second slaver just looked up at her. Then he spat all the saliva he could muster into her face.

With a single thrust, Shailiha drove the point of the dagger upward, cleaving the monster's eyeball. Blood and vitreous fluid poured out of the ruptured orb as the point of the knife continued on, slicing into his brain. As she pulled it back out, his face contorted into a mask of pain, and he fell facedown at her feet.

She stood there quietly for a moment watching his tortured death throes and listening to the last bit of breath rattle from his lungs. Calmly, slowly, she stepped before the third of them.

"Hopefully you are bright enough to have learned by example," she said, pressing the bloody point of her dagger up against the base of his right eye. "I'll keep this simple," she snarled. "Where is my brother—the man you took away that night in the alley fight in Farpoint?"

The slaver smiled up at her. "He is off to the place that is the most horrible on earth," he said softly. "Some even say it is the birthplace of the craft. It is a place from which your brother will never return. And even if he did, you would find him quite unrecognizable, *Your Highness.*" He paused for a moment and smiled again, showing pointed, black teeth.

"So kill me if you must," he hissed, "for I will tell you no more. No death by your hand could ever match the horrors that would be visited on me by Krassus should I talk."

Her mind made up, Shailiha took a step backward. Resheathing her dagger, she drew her sword and grasped it with both hands. Then she walked around behind the slaver and raised the sword high.

Swinging it down and around with everything she had, she beheaded the thing with a single stroke.

Celeste dropped her tired arm, and they looked at each other. Shailiha held her sword limply, its point hanging toward the ground. Thunder rumbled softly across the sky. Then the wind picked up, blowing the debris of the battle around in little maelstroms.

Shailiha cast her tired eyes upward. The clouds had become darker, and the rain suddenly began. As the water collected on the ground, it swept up the fresh blood of both the tortured and the tormentors into little red rivers flowing through the grass.

Shailiha sheathed her sword, and then she and Celeste walked into the charred remains of Tree Town.

CHAPTER

Seventeen

"You're worried, aren't you?" Abbey asked.

Wigg took a deep breath and let it out slowly. He had, of course, known that Celeste and Shailiha had been trying to maneuver him into letting them go to Shadowood. He knew, too, that his eventual agreement to their request had perhaps not been altogether prudent. But he also understood their frustration at being virtual prisoners here in the palace while Tristan remained missing. And so, knowing how much each of them cared about the prince, he had finally relented.

Wigg sighed. On the surface of it, letting the two strong-willed women go alone had at first seemed safe enough, especially given the emergence of Celeste's Forestallment. In his more than three hundred years of experience in the craft, he had never seen bolts so dynamic as those his daughter could now command. While it was true that she needed more training, the degree of power she already possessed was unmistakable. But now that they were gone, he was having misgivings about his decision.

He scowled. If Celeste and Shailiha did not exit Faegan's portal tomorrow by the end of the appointed hour, he would enter the enchanted passageway himself and bring them back by their ears, if he had to. Would that retrieving Tristan could be as simple.

Four Seasons of New Life before, Wigg had himself chosen Krassus for the position of first alternate—a fact that added heavily to the lead wizard's increasing sense of guilt. At the time, Krassus had been everything the wizards could have asked for. He was very powerful and learned for a consul, and seemed humbly, steadfastly devoted to the exclusive practice of the Vigors. Famous among the Brotherhood for the number of good deeds he had performed, he was well known for his compassion and patience—so much so that Wigg had nominated him to the post without the slightest reservation.

The Directorate had heartily agreed, installing him into the lofty position by unanimous vote. Even when Nicholas had begun abducting the consuls to help him construct the Gates of Dawn, Wigg had hoped that Krassus might be among those who had eluded his grasp.

But all that had changed that day in the gaming room when Krassus appeared with his evil demands.

The Krassus that Wigg had observed that day had been far more than simply evil. He had also been angry, impatient, and quick to employ force without thinking—much the same way the sorceresses of the Coven had been. Not only had he become far more powerful than ever before, but he clearly now had a wild, unpredictable side, making him the worst possible kind of enemy. And his new illness—the sudden, violent coughing up of endowed blood—remained a mystery.

The memory of the unmistakable glint of depravity in those eyes made Wigg more fearful for Tristan's welfare with each passing moment. They simply had to have the goods from Shadowood as quickly as possible if there was ever to be any hope of finding the prince and bringing him home alive.

"A kisa for your thoughts," Abbey said, breaking into his reveries.

Turning over in Wigg's huge, four-poster bed, she raised herself up on one elbow and smiled. Lifting his left hand, he gently ran the backs of his fingers down her cheek.

"You surprised me this night," he said softly. "Although I cannot say I am disappointed."

"Three hundred years is a long time, Lead Wizard," she teased, "in spite of the time enchantments." Moving her face closer to his, she smiled again. "A girl shouldn't have to wait forever, you know, simply because forever has been made available to her."

Wigg smiled back at her.

It was well after midnight, and from the open doors of his balcony came the gentle peeping of the tree frogs and the sound of the breeze as it rustled through the palace's once well-tended gardens. The night sky was clear, and the stars twinkled brightly, as if winking to the lovers that the heavens knew of their secret, and approved. Occasionally the form of a silent, patrolling warrior could be seen eerily silhouetted in black, flying across the triplet spheres of the rose-colored moons.

In his worry over Tristan, Shailiha, and Celeste, Wigg had been unable to sleep. It had already been late when the door to his chambers had unexpectedly opened, then quietly closed again. He had sat up in bed and raised his arm, ready to defend himself. Then he'd seen Abbey's form move silently across the doorframe of the open, moonlit balcony.

He had tried to speak, but she'd moved to the bed and placed a finger delicately across his lips. She'd dropped her robe to the floor and stood for a moment, her body shining in the rose-colored light. Then she lowered herself into his bed. Wigg had taken her into his arms, and their three hundred years of separation had finally, truly come to an end.

Turning, Wigg looked into her eyes. "I am most worried about the prince," he said. The herbmistress felt warm next to him, and she smelled pleasantly of the many fragrances of her art. The long-missed sensations were both familiar and good. "Tell me truly," he asked. "If you have the right supplies, will you be able to find him?"

Narrowing her eyes with thought, she shook her head and sighed. "It would be far better if I had something truly of his body, like a lock of his hair or a clipping of toenail," she answered. "But he and the princess are twins, so her hair may be sufficient. Or perhaps a drop of her blood. But remember, even if the flame allows us to see him, unless you or the others can identify some landmark or city, we still will not know where he is. I will do all I can, of course, but it may not be enough."

"And this ancient scroll Krassus spoke of—what of that?"

"Viewing that will be much more difficult. Even impossible, I daresay. I would need something of the scroll itself, and we do not have such a sample. Attempting to view that document will be like trying to find a needle in a sneezeweed stack, while wearing both a blindfold and pair of mittens."

"And Wulfgar?"

"Hopefully, the lock of his hair will work. I will only know for sure once I try. I know this is not what you wanted to hear, but that's how things are, nonetheless." Silence reigned for a moment as they each retreated into their private thoughts.

"They love each other, don't they?" Abbey asked unexpectedly.

"Who?" he asked back.

"Tristan and Celeste," she replied. She smiled again. After having known the lead wizard for so long, she could easily tell when he was being purposely obtuse, and she wasn't about to let him get away with it.

"Only a fool could miss the attraction they have for each other," she went on. "Although I am not sure even they realize how strong it is. Oddly, it is sometimes the lovers themselves who are the last to know, wouldn't you agree?"

Wigg remained silent for a moment; then one corner of his mouth turned up.

"Yes," he answered softly. "You're right. About a great many things."

"But still they do not act upon it," she said. "Why is that? Do they think it might displease you?"

"It wouldn't," Wigg answered. "In fact, I would welcome it. To see Tristan, the male of the Chosen Ones whom I have loved with all my heart, and Celeste, the daughter I have only just discovered, finally unite would truly be one of the most joyous days of my life. But part of the reason Tristan does not act on his love for her, I think, is because he fears it might change his relationship with me. And it no doubt would, but not in the ways he probably imagines. The greater worry in this is Celeste, and she troubles me deeply. Tristan understands this other concern, as well. I can see it in his eyes. And I suspect it is yet another reason why he hasn't tried to more deeply enter the recesses of her heart. In short, he is being a gentleman."

Lowering herself down, Abbey laid one side of her face on Wigg's chest. "I don't understand."

"Tristan is waiting for her psyche to heal," Wigg answered sadly. "And that may never happen. Celeste never speaks of the abuse she suffered at the hands of Ragnar. It is as if she believes that by denying it, she can erase that part of her past. But until she voluntarily admits those horrors to herself, embraces them as an indelible part of her past, and then finally lets them go, she will never stop hiding behind the shield of denial that she carries. The same shield, I suspect, that bars Tristan from coming closer. I saw all too much of this during the aftermath of the Sorceresses' War, three hundred years ago. I never believed I would ever have children, but I felt sure that if I did, as lead wizard I would be able to protect them. How wrong I was!" Wigg paused for a moment, thinking. "I have two other, equally deep regrets, you know," he said softly.

"Tell me," Abbey found herself saying, even though she was quite sure she knew what at least one of them would be.

"The first of them is you," he answered quietly. "You know that. I should never have voted with the Directorate to ban the partial adepts. It was cruel and unnecessary, as were so many of our decisions of those days. Instead, I should have resigned my seat and gone away with you. We could have had the last three hundred years together, and the Directorate could just as easily have gone on without me."

Raising her head, Abbey looked deeply into his eyes. "No," she said adamantly. "You're wrong. Everything happens for a reason. Your destiny was to rule the Directorate and oversee the birth and growth of the Chosen Ones. And then, with Tristan's help, to save Shailiha and the Paragon from the depravity of the Coven. Just as it was mine to live alone and hone my arts in the Hartwick Woods so that I might return to help you when you needed me most. Had you voted against the Directorate and then deserted Tammerland, the world would today exist only as a plaything of the sorceresses. In your heart you know that. You stayed here because it was your fate; just as we now find ourselves together again, through a different yet similar act of fate. That is clear to me now, and forgiving you is unnecessary. You did what you had to do. Don't you see? And now all is finally as it should be."

She moved her body a bit closer to his, to ward off the breeze wafting in from the balcony. "Even if it did take you three hundred years to come around," she added impishly. Wigg laughed softly.

"And the other regret?" she asked.

"Wulfgar," Wigg said. "The late king and queen charged me and the consuls with the burden of finding him, but we never did. I made a secret pilgrimage to the wizard's orphanage that gave him away, of course, and I spoke to the head matron. But by the time I arrived at the address she had given me, the family had moved, and I never found their trail again. That's understandable, I suppose, given the size of the nation and the passage of time. But I can feel Wulfgar's presence out there somewhere, just as I can feel Tristan's. And my heart tells me that they are both in grave danger. Their paths may even cross someday, without either of them knowing who the other truly is. I must find them both, before it becomes too late."

Wigg lay back into the luxurious sheets, thinking. "I can only hope that if I find Wulfgar, circumstances will not make it necessary for me to kill him," he said in a low voice. "It is an order from my queen that has plagued me for decades, and I don't think my heart could survive it."

They lay there together quietly for a time, listening to the wind.

"So many secrets," Wigg finally said, half to himself. "And each of them more a burden than a blessing, I assure you."

Abbey smiled knowingly. "And still so many you have yet to share with us, I'm sure."

"Oh, yes," Wigg answered simply. "Many secrets indeed. There is still so much that Tristan, Shailiha, and especially Wulfgar do not know about themselves. Things that only time will allow me to teach them. And time is running out."

"And what about our secret?" Abbey asked. "The one we formed here this night. Shall we tell the others?"

Wigg thought for a moment. "No, I think not," he said, smiling at her. "I have been without you for over three centuries, and I would like to keep this part of our relationship to ourselves, if we can. Call me overbearing if you wish, but you are new to both the palace and the Redoubt. The others will find out soon enough. There is no need for us to hurry that day forward. And when they do discover it, rest assured that their teasing will be merciless. In fact, Celeste and Shailiha have in some ways already started." His infamous right eyebrow arched up, driving home his point.

"Very well," she said sleepily.

Wigg lay silent for a moment, thinking. "Faegan will know without being told, of course," he mused.

"How?" Abbey asked softly. Sleep had finally come padding to her on silent cat's paws, and her eyes were closing.

As Wigg ran his hand through her long hair, he listened to her breathing deepen. "He's a wizard," he whispered to her softly as she drifted off in his arms. "And wizards always know."

CHAPTER

Eighteen

*W*hump! . . . whump! . . . whump! . . .

The incessant sound of the beatmaster's hammer seared through Tristan's head like a dagger as he pulled hard on his oar. The heat in the galley was overpowering, as was the stench. Bound in chains, weaponless, he found himself surrounded by other men in the same straits, trying to row as best they could lest they suddenly be struck with either the lash or the trident.

For some reason he had been allowed to remain in his clothes, rather than being forced to don the shabby loincloth all the others wore. And the food they gave him was better than that given to the others. This had caused furtive, distrustful glances from his fellow slaves, making him feel like an outcast. Worse, in the increased heat his clothes made him more fatigued and dehydrated. By now he actually envied the others the simple, almost indecent rags they wore.

As he rowed, doing his best to keep up, sweat poured off him and his muscles felt as if they were about to crack apart. He watched with hatred as the white-skinned slaver before them hammered out the incessant, mind-numbing beat. Other slavers strode arrogantly up and down the alleyway, using their gruesome weapons with impunity. He had not been struck yet, but knew it would only be a matter of time before that happened.

Tristan was positioned in the front row, in the first seat to the immediate right of the alleyway. As he pulled the oar to his chest over and over again, he looked down at the number that had been so crudely carved into its handle. *One.* Despite the desperate nature of his situation, his mouth turned up slightly at the irony.

Suddenly a wave of nausea rolled over him. He had no choice but to bend over toward the pitching deck and just let it happen. By now this had occurred so often that nothing but clear bile emerged. The sounds of sick men retching were almost continual, and the unrelenting stench— a combination of vomit, blood, and urine—only added to his queasiness.

Tristan had not been surprised when he first became seasick, for he was completely unaccustomed to being on the water. In fact, he knew very little about oceangoing vessels. Since the end of the Sorceresses' War more than three hundred years earlier, the monarchy had sponsored no navy. Given the fact that the Sea of Whispers was supposedly un-crossable from any direction, and that no other nation at that time had been known to exist, a seagoing force had been deemed unnecessary.

But the unexpected return of the Coven and the revelation of how they had crossed the ocean had changed all that. For some time, Tristan had been acutely aware of the vast importance of the Minion armada anchored just off the coast of Parthalon—an armada that he now sup-posedly commanded. But the ships might as well have been moored on one of the three moons for all the good they could do him. The view out the oar slit in the hull told him that the ship was traveling east. But to where? Parthalon? What in the name of the Afterlife was Krassus try-ing to accomplish?

Tristan looked down at his chains. They bound him not only to the deck floor, but to the rest of the oarsmen. Each of them had the word *Talis* seared into his shoulder. Tristan had not been branded, but he had the distinct impression that they were all expendable, including him. The chain system made that point: should the ship founder, the slaves, linked together as they were, would never be able to get out in time.

Number One, he thought as he pulled the heavy oar to his chest. Here he was no longer the crown prince of Eutracia, or even the Cho-sen One. Just Number One. And Number One would be granted no special favors or undue mercy. As of yet, no one seemed to have recog-nized him. He was simply one of the slaves, trying to stay alive another day. And here there were no wizards to help him escape.

Just then a demonslaver came down the stairway from the deck above. "Raise oars!" he shouted. At once, the relentless pounding of the hammer stopped. As a group, the slaves lifted their oars from the Sea of Whispers and held them still, just a few feet above the waves.

Tristan knew what was about to happen, for he had seen this ritual before. A fresh beatmaster had come to take the place of the one who had just served. It seemed to happen every four hours or so, during which time the slaves did not row.

Tristan obediently pushed down on the handle of his oar as best he could, muscles burning, keeping the paddle well out of the ocean. He wanted no undue attention, and the only way to ensure that was to keep doing an especially good job.

Tristan's dark eyes watched as the seated beatmaster laid down the two great hammers and the other slaver walked across to replace him. In truth, Tristan had been waiting and hoping for this precise moment.

He harbored no illusions about escape. He knew there was no way he could ever overpower the slavers, and freeing himself from his chains was impossible. But this rare moment would provide the precious seconds of quiet distraction that he needed. He simply had to know the answer to the mystery that had plagued him ever since he had awakened here, and the time to find out was now.

Slowly, he turned his head toward the slave seated on his right. The fellow was balding, sullen, and perpetually quiet. They had said very little to each other, and Tristan had immediately distrusted him. He had no choice, though. Soon the incessant pounding would begin anew, and Tristan's chance would be lost. He would simply have to make his attempt, and trust to luck.

Feigning another attack of nausea, Tristan forced his weight onto the handle of the oar, at the same time surreptitiously slipping his right hand free of the handle and down toward the top of his right boot.

As Tristan had intended, the man next to him turned his head away from the sight of a fellow slave going through another bout of seasickness while trying not to drop the oar.

Straining with everything he had but not wanting to hurry, Tristan let go another series of false retches, at the same time gradually moving his hand closer to the top of his boot. Turning his head slightly, he could see that he was nearly there.

Finding the top of his boot, his first two fingers slipped inside.

Tristan froze. There was nothing there.

Unsure of what to do, he nearly panicked. But with yet another great effort, he pressed the oar handle a bit lower, allowing his fingers deeper access inside the boot. Raising his eyes, he saw that the beatmaster had risen from his seat. Only seconds remained before the new slaver would call out the order to lower oars, and he would have to begin rowing again.

And then his fingers touched metal. The brain hook—the slim, razor-sharp stiletto with the tiny, curved hook at the end—that he had carried hidden in his right boot ever since the death of Nicholas and the destruction of the Gates of Dawn was still there, undiscovered by Krassus and his demonslavers! Tristan was overjoyed.

But then, just as he was about to grip it, his fingers touched something else—something pliable and scratchy. It was tucked away farther back, near his calf. Whoever had put it there probably hadn't noticed the brain hook, driven so far down as it had been.

Risking everything, his muscles straining to the breaking point, he captured its upper edge between his fingertips, lifted it gently to the top of his boot, and looked down.

It was a piece of vellum, and he immediately recognized it as being a fragment of the Scroll of the Vagaries, the ancient document Krassus had had lying on his desk aboard the *Sojourner.*

Who would have put it in his boot? And why?

But there was no time now to ponder this new mystery. Muscles shaking with fatigue and effort, he leaned against the oar while using his fingertips to push the piece of parchment back into the deep recesses of his boot.

But the strain of holding the oar in place for so long with only one hand finally became too great. Just as he started to sit back up, the oar handle slipped from his grasp, and the other slaves in his row cried out as they attempted to keep the oar in place without his added strength.

The demonslavers immediately snapped their heads around and leveled their vacant eyes at him, and several of them trotted over to where Tristan sat chained, trying to catch his breath.

The demonslaver who was to have become the new beatmaster reached him first. He smiled, showing his black, pointed teeth. When Tristan looked up at him, he saw a large ring of keys hooked to the top of a leather belt running around the monster's waist.

"Krassus told me you would become a problem, Number One," the slaver said softly, menacingly. "And so you have. It didn't take you long to live up to our expectations, did it?"

Reaching out, he took a nine-tails from one of the other slavers standing nearby and began coiling it up slowly.

"You shall of course be punished," he said. "And the best method I can think of is to give you something that will remind you of your new place in life every time you bend forward to pull on your oar. We still have a long way to go, and with every new stroke you will be reminded of me." He smiled again.

Tristan looked up hatefully. "You aren't as good as you think you are, you know," he growled. "I killed several of your kind back in Farpoint. It was easy, and I enjoyed having their blood on my hands. There will be many more of you dead before I am finished, I swear it. And you will be one of them."

The slaver placed the handle of his whip beneath Tristan's chin and viciously forced the prince's face up. "Really," he mused. "Tell me, how many of my brothers did you kill?"

Tristan's reaction was immediate. "At least five," he retorted without thinking. It was only after saying it that he realized his mistake.

The thing standing before him smiled again. "Thank you," he said, almost politely. "Then five it shall be." Removing the whip from beneath Tristan's chin, he nodded shortly to the slavers standing next to him.

Two of them grabbed the prince's hands, while another of them began to unlace the ties at the front of his black leather vest. Before he knew it, the vest had come over the top of his head, and was lying on his forearms. Then he was grabbed again and forced to bend over at the waist. Everyone had gone silent, and the only sound was the creaking of the *Wayfarer's* hull as she rocked back and forth on the Sea of Whispers.

Tristan knew what was coming, and there was nothing he could do to prevent it. All he had to fight them with was his mind. For every lash of the whip, he decided, he would think of someone he cared for. And whatever happened, he would not give these abhorrent monsters the pleasure of hearing him scream.

The nine-tails whistled through the air and broke the skin of his naked back. The leather strips sent shock waves through his body, causing him to convulse.

Shailiha, he thought, *the sister I brought back from Parthalon.*

Again the lash came down, rupturing the skin at a right angle to the first cuts. Crossroads of azure blood began to drip down. His body jangled like a marionette.

Wigg, my teacher. The one who will someday instruct me in the ways of the craft.

The nine leather strips came yet again, opening up part of his lower back. Glowing, azure blood ran down in earnest now, collecting eerily upon the rough-hewn, wooden seat and the unforgiving, rusty chains that bound him.

Faegan . . . the rogue wizard from Shadowood . . . with his violin and his blue cat . . .

Again the strips came around, this time deepening the first set of gashes. Gritting his teeth desperately, he almost cried out. Sweat dripped down his face, and his breath came in short, ragged puffs. He closed his eyes, trying to brace himself for the next assault.

Geldon, my friend . . . so small in stature . . . but with so . . . great . . . a heart . . .

The fifth and final stroke came down with the greatest intensity of all, sending azure blood splattering wildly across the slaver's face and hands. Smiling, the monster began to retract the whip, coiling it up slowly. As the bright, glowing blood flowed from Tristan's back down onto the deck, slaves and demonslavers alike stared at the strange, wondrous substance as if it had just come from another world.

And Celeste . . . my love . . .

Suddenly he felt an unexpected rush of cold, salt-laden seawater splash against his wounds. It was more than he could bear.

Groaning softly, Tristan lost consciousness and collapsed to the filthy deck.

Nineteen

"Welcome to the herb cubiculum!" Lionel said without turning around. Faegan's diminutive caretaker seemed to be searching urgently for something. "Now where on earth did I put my equalizing spoons?"

He began rummaging about anxiously on the top of the broad, cluttered table. "If I can't find them, it will make things far more difficult for us, yes it will," he chattered nervously. "And I know Master Faegan has a deadline, that he does."

Pulling with frustration at the single tuft of hair on the top of his head while at the same time trying to keep his broken spectacles in place, Lionel the Little jumped down off the stool that seemed far too high for him and began scurrying about the room on his short, bowed legs as though everyone's lives depended upon it. In many ways, the princess thought, perhaps they did.

After Shailiha had killed the slavers in the glade, she and Celeste had made their way to Faegan's tree house mansion. There they were directed to a secret door in the trunk of the ancient, gnarled tree, and had come up the spiral staircase to the foyer. They were greeted immediately by a rotund, gracious gnome who curtsied, then politely introduced herself as Samantha the Squat. Beckoning them to follow her, she turned and led the way down a series of dark, highly polished, wooden-paneled hallways. The mazelike quality of the place reminded Shailiha of the Redoubt—albeit a smaller, wooden version. After climbing two flights of stairs, another hallway led at last to a set of double doors of inlaid mahogany. Samantha knocked twice. After hearing a welcoming call from Lionel, she smiled, curtsied again, and took her leave.

Shailiha and Celeste opened the door and walked into the room, then stopped and gazed about, wide-eyed. The huge room seemed to take up the entire third floor of the mansion. The ceiling was constructed of curved, clear glass, its various sections separated by leaded panes. Outside, the rain had stopped, and rays of sunlight streamed down between the parting clouds.

The herb cubiculum, as Lionel called it, was part nursery, part laboratory, and part library. One of the long walls was filled from floor to ceiling with bookcases holding texts, charts, and scrolls. Charts carrying esoteric symbols covered another of the walls.

The nursery area took up about half of the floor and was full of short tables littered with potted plants of innumerable colors, shapes, and sizes. In many cases their leaves, branches, and vines had grown long enough to reach the floor and even to snake their way down the narrow aisles between the tables. Some of the hardier, gnarled vines had found their way to the walls and pillars, which they were climbing in their continued quest for the sunlight that streamed in through the glass ceiling.

The remainder of the cubiculum was given over to a laboratory. The tables there held strange-looking instruments and containers. Beakers burbled and bubbled, cauldrons steamed, and through crisscrossing lines of glass tubing flowed brightly colored, swirling fluids. The air was warm and fetid; but conversely, its odor was light, airy, and herbal, as if thousands of exotic petals had just bloomed, releasing their scents only moments before.

But a part of the laboratory area was in terrible disrepair. An entire wall of shelving had been pulled down, spilling hundreds of jars and vessels. Dried herbs lay scattered across the floor among shards of broken glass and weathered labels. Oils had run together into shiny, multicolored puddles. Not far from the mess, the canvas bags that had been rescued from the slavers' fire lay in a heap next to a large vat.

"I must find my equalizing spoons, I must." Lionel continued to chatter as he searched the room, the boards of the hardwood floor occasionally squeaking beneath his feet as he went. "They are absolutely necessary, don't you see? If I have lost them I will be very vexed, yes, terribly, terribly vexed!"

After watching Lionel's distraught antics for a moment, Shailiha gave Celeste a questioning look. Shaking her head slightly, Wigg's daughter raised an eyebrow, much the same way her father would have. Sensing their lack of understanding, Lionel turned to them.

"Well, don't just stand there gawking!" he said anxiously, waving them into the room with one of his short, stubby arms. "There is much to do! Come, come!" Doing as he asked, the two women stepped deeper into the room.

Shailiha pointed to the canvas bags. "Those contain herbs, don't they?" she asked. "That's why Krassus sent his thugs here—to destroy as much of Faegan's stores as possible, thereby making it far more difficult for us to employ the services of our herbmistress."

"Quite right," Lionel said, still waddling briskly from table to table in search of his mysterious spoons. "Master Faegan explained your predicament to me in his letter. A true quandary, I agree. But now things have gone from bad to worse, I must say, yes, they certainly have."

"Please explain," Celeste said.

Stopping at another table, Lionel began rummaging around under some papers. Then he squealed with delight. "I have found them!" he hollered.

Waddling back to Shailiha and Celeste, he proudly held up what looked to be an ordinary set of cook's wooden measuring spoons, fastened together by a brass ring. But then his expression darkened.

"Don't you see?" he said worriedly. "The coming of the slavers has changed everything, oh, indeed it has."

"But why?" Shailiha asked anxiously. Her impatience was clearly beginning to seep through. "We saved a lot of the herbs, didn't we? Why can't we just take them back to Eutracia and be done with it? Forgive me for being abrupt, but we have no time to waste. Tristan is missing, and we need those things to find him!"

"But you're forgetting something, Princess, yes, you are," Lionel countered. One of his stubby little index fingers went imperiously into the air as he emphasized his point.

"And just what is that?" Celeste asked.

Reaching into the pocket of his vest, Lionel pulled out a piece of paper. "Abbey's list," he said. "Given the fact that the bags aren't labeled, even if you take them back with you, how can you be sure that they contain what you need? Many or all of her requirements could have already gone up in smoke, in the bags that the slavers burned. And this vat presents the same problem—full of a mixture of oils, but which oils? Most of the individual containers have been spilled. I'm afraid that's only the beginning of the problem, yes, it is," he added.

Shailiha's heart fell. What was to have supposedly been a simple mission had quickly turned into a nightmare. If she and Celeste didn't return to Eutracia with the ingredients Abbey required for her gazing flame, then none of them might ever see Tristan again, much less find Wulfgar, or the other Scroll of the Ancients.

"And the other problem is?" she asked, not altogether sure she wanted to hear what the gnome's answer would be.

"Not only are the bags and the vat not labeled, but their contents have been mixed," Lionel explained sadly. "If you were to dip into one of them, you would come back with a fistful of herbs or a cupful of oil, to be sure, but you would have absolutely no idea what they were, or in what ratios they had been combined. Don't you see? If you better understood the art of herbmastery, you would know that this is without question the greatest tragedy that could befall us. Second only to the complete destruction of the cubiculum, of course, of course."

Suddenly both Celeste and Shailiha fully understood what it was that Lionel was trying to tell them.

"Why would the slavers go to all that trouble, mixing everything, dragging it out to the fire in the glade?" Shailiha asked. "If all they wanted to do was destroy what's here, then why not just set fire to the mansion, sit back, and watch everything go up in flames? Wouldn't that have been far easier?"

"Easier, yes," Lionel agreed as he walked back to the high stool and laboriously climbed up. "But there was more to their mission, yes, much more. And setting fire to the mansion so soon would have been counter-productive to their goals, yes, it would."

"How so?" Celeste asked.

"You're forgetting something again," Lionel answered. He pointed to the far wall. "Those texts and scrolls represent more than three hundred years of Master Faegan's research in the art of herbmastery. They are without doubt the single greatest such collection in existence, and are among his most prized possessions. Surely this Krassus fellow would have wanted them. Apparently the slavers' orders were to make certain that the herbs and oils were destroyed first, and then to abscond with the research materials. I can only assume that the demonslavers decided to take the herbs and oils to Tree Town, to use them to feed the fires and put even greater fear into the hearts of the gnomes. Then they could take their time removing the research. I also have no doubt that some of the slavers would have stayed behind to kill off the rest of us and set fire to the remainder of the town. Including, of course, the master's mansion. But then you two arrived, and stopped them." Lionel paused as a look of deep gratitude came over his face. "Master Faegan doesn't know it yet, but he has much to thank you for." Then he paused again. "But there is still something else to tell you, yes, there is," he said sadly.

Shailiha wasn't sure she could take hearing any more. She closed her eyes briefly. "What is it?" she asked softly.

"When the demonslavers, as you call them, first invaded the mansion, they came upon me here in this room. Strangely, they had their own list of requirements, just as you do. Then they held me as they went about selecting various herbs and oils, packed them up, and took them away before the mixing started. It took some time to search them all out. But in truth the job was not difficult, since all of the vessels were clearly marked. Master Faegan is nothing if not organized, you know. Then this group of slavers left quickly with their stolen goods, and I think they may have escaped you. And if that is true, then Krassus is now in possession of the very items you came here to procure. I suspect Krassus' herbmistress is either running low on stores, or she wishes to try new ingredients in her quest to view Wulfgar and the scrolls. Either way, she now has the means to do the job. He is a very clever fellow, this Krassus, yes, he is."

"But how could Krassus have known all of this was here?" Celeste asked. "Shadowood was supposed to have been one of the Directorate's greatest secrets, was it not?"

"I already know how," Shailiha answered sadly, shaking her head. "That day in the palace—the day Krassus materialized out of nothing. It is something I shall never forget. Remember how he violated Wigg and Faegan's minds? From Wigg he gleaned the existence of Shadowood. And from Faegan he learned the whereabouts of his stores and library. He claimed he was searching their memories for information about Wulfgar and the scrolls, but he found much, much more, and he never ever let on."

Suddenly thinking of Tristan, Shailiha's heart fell. But then something began prodding the back of her mind—something that had been bothering her ever since she had first seen the slavers in the glade.

"But Shadowood is protected from the rest of Eutracia by enchantments," she mused, "including the invisible canyon that surrounds it, the deadly forest, and the tunnel of bones. Isn't that so? And the slavers can't fly. Or at least I have never seen one do so. So how did they get here safely? I can't imagine the wizards' protective mechanisms all failing at once. It doesn't make any sense."

"If your assumptions are true about Krassus more completely violating my father's mind than we first thought, then he would have known about those dangers, as well," Celeste said, rubbing her brow. "But that still doesn't explain how he overcame them."

"I think I know," Lionel said quietly.

"How?" the two women asked in one voice.

"I believe the slavers came by sea," Lionel answered, "rather than overland, through Eutracia. When Shadowood was created during the Sorceresses' War, the wizards of the Directorate were far more concerned about invasion from the land side than from the ocean. Remember, at that time the sorceresses of the Coven were their great concern, and the Coven's armies were approaching from the west. The only safe-guard on the eastern side is the Sea of Whispers, and the invisible canyon. If Krassus already knew of the canyon, getting his slavers over it might not have been so difficult. Especially if he is now as powerful a wizard as Master Faegan's letter suggests. Remember, the canyon was made to keep out those who didn't know it existed, rather than those who did. It's invisible only to the untrained. There are many ways that an accom-plished wizard might cross it, though Master Faegan would know much more about that than I."

He paused for a moment.

"The slavers that took the goods are now long gone," he finally added. "In fact, there is most probably another ship still anchored just offshore, waiting for the ones that you killed."

Suddenly it all made perfect, tragic sense. Seething in her newfound knowledge, Shailiha yearned desperately to rush right to the coast, where Celeste could use her powers to blow that ship out of the water, along with any demonslavers that might still be aboard. But she knew that she couldn't. Gathering up whatever herbs and oils which were still salvage-able and getting them safely back to Faegan and Abbey simply had to take priority. Krassus, she realized, had bested them at every turn. She turned back to Lionel.

"So what do we do now?" she asked urgently. "Are any of these mixed herbs or oils still useful?"

Lionel sighed. "Some, yes. But the rest must first be separated again, then tested to see how and to what extent their potency has been altered. Even then I cannot be sure how they will react if used. Something like this has never happened before on so grand a scale."

Curious, Celeste walked over to one of the canvas bags. Bending down, she untied the cinched rope at its top and reached in. She came back with a handful of what appeared to be ground-up, multicolored leaves. "Isn't there any way to tell what these herbs are?" she asked the gnome.

"Bring them over to me and I will try," Lionel said. "But don't ex-pect too much, no, do not."

Celeste carefully emptied her handful of herbs onto the tabletop. From another area of the table, Lionel produced a magnifying glass. Peering through the glass, he pushed and prodded at the herbs. Then he bent over and sniffed at them. His face fell.

"This is even worse than I thought, yes, it is," he said, shaking his head. "There is an absolute riot of colors and odors in this handful alone. Too many to even try to count." Lifting his small head, he looked for-lornly at the canvas bags lying on the opposite side of the room.

"This could take years, perhaps even lifetimes to unravel," he added.

"And from what I glean from Master Faegan's letter, we don't have that kind of time. Still, even on a small scale it is worth trying before I send you back."

Reaching across the table, he picked up what he had referred to earlier as his equalizing spoons. Unhooking the ring that held them together, he placed them on the table in a neat row. There appeared to be about a dozen of them. He put a small amount of the herb mixture into each one, then sat back and closed his eyes.

"*E'masteratu, ventricumtitas, didebfan, sente!*" he chanted deeply. Almost immediately, the spoons began to move.

Shailiha and Celeste watched, spellbound, as the line of spoons rose into the air over the tabletop. Lionel opened his eyes. "Watch carefully," he said.

The wooden spoons began to shake back and forth, spilling some of their precious contents onto the table. As they did, they rose a bit higher, each to a different level. Then they came to hover in a neat, level row once again. When they had finally all stopped moving, Lionel spoke again.

"*R'santos, tenticualrem, wensicat!*"

The spoons obediently lowered themselves back down to the table. Curious, Shailiha and Celeste looked down into them.

There was now a different color and amount of herb in each spoon.

"Each spoon now only contains one kind of herb, doesn't it?" Shailiha asked. "But gnomes don't have endowed blood. How could you make this happen?"

"And that was Old Eutracian you were speaking, wasn't it?" Celeste interjected. "How does a Shadowood gnome come to know Old Eutracian?"

Lionel chuckled. "Master Faegan is indeed wise," he answered. "He took the liberty of enchanting these spoons centuries ago, for just such an emergency as this—namely, the untangling of mixed herbs. They are enchanted to react to anyone who recites the proper phrases in Old Eutracian. One need not be of endowed blood to make them work—one need only be able to say the commands correctly. There are other items here in the herb cubiculum that the master enchanted so that I might be able to use them if need be. And it certainly seems our day has come. Still, this only solves part of the problem, and only to a very minor degree. I'm afraid the most difficult part is yet to come."

Hopping down off his stool, Lionel beckoned the women to follow him over to what appeared to be a bare wooden wall. He raised his hands.

"*P'intastoretas, vintostmante erasdeat tomirenticas!*"

A vertical line appeared down the center of the wall, dividing it into equal halves. Then the gap grew wider as the two sections slowly slid to opposite sides, eventually revealing another wall covered by a gigantic chart.

The chart was arranged in dozens of horizontal rows. Each row held hundreds of individual squares, and each square was its own color. The color of each row darkened slightly in hue as it ran from left to right.

As Shailiha looked up, she saw that the top row was all descending hues of violet, each of the squares becoming lighter as one's eye followed along to the right. And as one looked down the rows from top to bottom, the colors of the rows changed gradually, following the order of a rainbow. After the violet rows came others in blue, green, yellow, orange, and finally red. Each of the individual, colored squares seemed to be labeled. A ladder was propped up over the chart, topped with wheels that lay in a track running along the entire length of the chart.

"I give you the Chart of Herbal Hues," Lionel said proudly. "Master Faegan and I created it."

"It's beautiful," Celeste said. "But what is it for?"

"It uses the color of the herb to help us identify the family it comes from," he explained.

From the top of the table he took up a clear glass globe that had a wooden, vertical handle mounted at its bottom. In the center of the globe could be seen a vertical rod with what looked like a miniature weathervane mounted at its top. Carrying the odd globe upright, Lionel walked to the ladder and climbed about halfway up.

He pointed to the equalizing spoons that still lay on the table. "Please bring me one of those," he asked. "For our purposes just now, any will do."

Celeste retrieved one of the spoons and handed it up to Lionel. The color of the herb in the spoon was a soft yellow-green. Lionel looked down at the herb, and then he raised an eyebrow.

"Not an altogether simple one to start with, but it should prove an interesting challenge," he mused. Asking Shailiha to push the ladder, he directed her to a spot about midway across the face of the chart. Placing the spoon down carefully on one of the ladder steps, he used both hands to twist the handle at the bottom of his globe. It popped open. Carefully, he sprinkled a pinch of the yellow-green herbs into the base of the open handle, then twisted it closed again. He handed the spoon back down to Celeste.

"Now we shall see what we shall see," he said with a wink.

Holding the device before one of the many rows containing the yellows and greens, he closed his eyes.

"W'ntesirare ostumae, ventarntateratu, oderastic!"

Almost at once the familiar glow of the craft began to surround the globe, and the little weathervane within it began to spin slowly. Lionel held it still for a moment, then he started to move it horizontally, along one of the yellow rows. As he did, the vane started to turn more rapidly; then it went faster still, until it revolved so quickly that it became a blur. He kept it in place for a moment, taking note of the spot on the chart. Then he moved the device a bit to the right, and the vane began to slow. When he moved it back to the left, it sped up again. Lowering the globe, Lionel took note of the writing beneath the colored square before which the vane had spun the fastest. The azure glow surrounding the globe finally faded and disappeared.

"Y267," he muttered to himself as he climbed down the ladder and waddled back to the stool at the table. Hopping up on it, he placed the globe on the tabletop, next to his equalizing spoons. "Y267, yes, it is," he chattered to himself, as if he were in danger of forgetting it. Quickly he made a note of the letter and numbers on a sheet of parchment. Only then did he seem to relax.

"What did you just do?" Shailiha asked. Bursting with curiosity, both she and Celeste walked over to the table and bent over to examine the odd globe.

"That device is called a hue harmonizer," Lionel said simply. "Yet another invention of the master's. It senses the color of the herb in its handle, then matches it to the one most closely represented on the chart. It is enchanted to make allowances for the passage of time, since once the herbs are dried and ground their colors generally fade somewhat. This can, of course, also be attempted by the human eye, but the results are far more vague—oftentimes even dangerous. Anyway, once the correctly colored square is found, one makes a note of the code written below it. In this case, our herb is of the yellow family, square number 267. Interesting, is it not? But we are not quite finished."

He looked to the wall containing the vast library. "*Source Book of Herbal Families,* please," he said loudly. "Yellow Family, code numbers two hundred through three hundred."

Almost immediately a dusty, ancient book slid out and came soaring through the air. It landed gently on the table in front of him. The thick, gilt-edged book looked as old as time itself.

Thumbing through the text, Lionel finally found number 267. "Ah, at last," he announced proudly. "Yellow number 267 is the blossom of the witherwood tree—a rarity employed primarily for the relief of pain in the joints, particularly in the upper extremities. Probably nothing that Abbey needs, but with herbmistresses, one never knows." Then he looked at the bags lying on the floor.

"Perhaps after having seen these procedures, you can better understand the immense nature of the task ahead," he said sadly. "Yes, the herbs can be isolated. But do you you realize how long it took to identify a pinch of just one? There are thousands of herbs in those bags, and they are all mixed together. And making things even more difficult is the fact that Abbey has a particular list of things she requires, and she needs them now. But because they are so mixed up, there is just no way to give priority to searching for the ones she wants. We must simply go through all of the bags, one by one, and trust to luck that we come upon those she needs, and soon enough to be of help." He shook his head for a moment.

"Frankly, the task is monstrous," he added quietly. "And I'm glad I'm not the one who has to explain all of this to my master."

Shailiha looked skeptically at Celeste. All Wigg's daughter could do was shake her head.

Then the princess saw a curious look come over Lionel's face.

"But we still do not know the effects upon the witherwood's potency from having been mixed with so many other herbs," he said. "It would be most interesting to find out, don't you think? And it would provide a ray of sunlight for Master Faegan, to be sure, oh yes, to be sure. Being able to tell him the potency of at least one of them might soften his mood when he hears about all of this, yes, it might."

Taking another small pinch of the dried witherwood blossom from the spoon, he eagerly walked to another table at the far end of the laboratory. There he dropped it into a flat, gold pan.

"One of the best ways to determine an herb's purity is to test the sample with fire," he called back to the women. "The amount I have here is far too small to cause much reaction. Still, it should tell us something."

Striking a common match against his trouser leg, he held the small flame to the herbs. Celeste and Shailiha cringed instinctively.

As the match burned, the top of the tiny pile of herbs began to singe and smoke a bit, but nothing more. Finally the match went out.

Smiling, Lionel turned to them. "See," he shouted triumphantly. "I told you so! The potency must be so weak that—"

The explosion that followed sent Lionel flying through the air. He landed hard onto the tabletop near them. Beakers overturned and fragile glass tubing shattered, their contents pouring out as the gnome came to rest on his back in the slick, multicolored mess. Flames shot upward into a giant red ball, its concussive force so great that it shattered a section of the ceiling, sending smashed glass raining down. The roiling smoke was at first so thick that Shailiha couldn't see a thing.

Fearing for Lionel's life, she held her breath and waved her arms madly as she tried to make her way to the table she had seen him land on, the glass crunching beneath her boots as she went. By the time she got there, Lionel was sitting up, holding his head.

Bits of glass fell from him. His spectacles were more shattered than ever, and lying halfway off his nose. He was wet and sticky from head to toe, and part of his vest was still smoldering. Shailiha quickly began patting Lionel down, making sure that he was not truly on fire. In the final analysis, he somehow didn't seem too much the worse for wear.

Then the doors to the herb cubiculum blew wide open and an anxious group of gnomes burst in carrying buckets of water. Seeing that the fire was already out, they simply stood there, glaring at Lionel. Then an obviously indignant Samantha the Squat marched straight up to Lionel, threw her hands into the air, then pushed one of her stubby index fingers at his stunned, sooty face.

"How could you do this again!" she shouted at him. Shailiha couldn't decide which was more merciless: Samantha's shrill voice, or her imperiously wagging finger. "You know you aren't supposed to experiment unless the master is present! He has told you that countless numbers of times! What in the name of the Afterlife is the matter with you? Are you deaf, as well as stupid?"

Aghast, the princess and Celeste turned to Samantha. "Do you mean to tell us that this has happened before?" Celeste asked.

"Oh, yes," Samantha answered angrily as she lifted one of Lionel's eyelids to examine an overly dilated pupil. "You just love to impress folks with your supposed knowledge of this room, don't you, Lionel?"

Smiling stupidly, Lionel looked back at her, his eyes partially glazed over. *"I can't hear you!"* he screamed. Shailiha and Celeste recoiled at the loudness of his voice.

"You know it's like this every time there is an explosion!" he shouted as he swayed back and forth, animatedly gesturing to one of his ears.

Beginning to wonder whether Lionel's hearing had suddenly become selective, rather than simply impaired, Shailiha turned to look around the room. Although the entire herb cubiculum was a slippery, tangled mess, the canvas bags of herbs blessedly remained unharmed, as did the vat of oils. But how in the world were she and Celeste going to manage getting them to—and through—Faegan's portal? Not to mention the Chart of Ascending and Descending Hues and the massive library that Faegan and Abbey would now apparently require.

And then there was the matter of Lionel. She couldn't leave the curious gnome here, free to conduct more of his "experiments" without Faegan's guidance. Only the Afterlife knew what might come of it.

There was only one solution: She would have Celeste and Lionel help her hide the bags, the vat, and as many of the books as possible before Faegan's portal opened the next day. Then all three of them would go back through the portal. That way, in the event that other slavers returned they would find neither the missing items nor the princess and Wigg's daughter. She hated the idea of leaving the rest of the gnomes defenseless, but she could see no other way.

She shook her head as she tried to imagine the wizards' reactions when she walked out of the portal with only Celeste and a sooty, over-confident gnome who had just blown up Faegan's herb cubiculum.

Wigg and Faegan would not be pleased.

Twenty

"Such a beautiful boy you are," cooed the aging woman in the ragged red dress. As if in defiance of her advancing years, there was a suggestive slit running a bit too high up one side of her frock, and her cheeks were overly pink with rouge. Her eyes were sharp, but her voice was old and cracked, much like the lines in her skin. She smelled faintly of cheap perfume and body odor. Running a gnarled hand over the boy's curly red hair, she bent forward slightly, so as to examine him better. He felt her coarse fingers grip his chin, then turn his face first one way, then the other.

"Would you like to come and work for me?" she asked coyly. "You look like you could do with a hot meal, and it is warm and dry where I live. Not cold and wet, like here."

She dragged her long, painted nails gently down one of his grimy cheeks, leaving odd-looking, contrasting rows of what had once been healthier, cleaner skin. He cringed. "You do trust me, don't you, dearie?" she asked sweetly.

Her face only inches from his own, she widened her mouth and kissed him lightly on the lips. With the kiss came the smell of garlic, wine, and half-digested fish.

His back hard against the brick wall, Marcus cringed. His foray to steal some food from this still largely unknown city had inadvertently led him to one of its darkest and most crime-ridden niches. Bargainer's Square, he had heard someone call it.

Night was falling, and the light cast from the oil streetlamps had begun to spread silent, shadowy fingers across the sidewalks and streets, morphing the silhouettes of passersby into twisted, misshapen monsters. Halfway into this human wasteland he had realized his mistake and tried to turn and leave. But by then the aging harlot had cornered him in the alley, and it had been too late.

Having just turned twelve Seasons of New Life, he was streetwise enough to understand what it was the old whore was trying to entice him into. He had heard stories about purveyors like her. She was one of those who sold young people to older ones, and every fiber of his being told him he wanted no part of it. He had to get free of her quickly, before any of her friends might appear and help her abduct him outright.

Because if that happened, 'Becca would be alone. And 'Becca needed him.

But just as he thought he might be able to give the old woman a sharp push and run around her, a shadow loomed.

Marcus raised his face to see a man—a large, dirty man—come up behind the woman. He had a thick beard and long, tangled hair. He wore a dark cloak around his shoulders, and huge, knobby boots. From where Marcus stood, the man's hands seemed the size of small hams.

"What'cha got here, Allison?" he asked in a heavy, gravelly tone. The woman just smiled.

The man studied Marcus. "A good one," he said approvingly. "Nice and fresh. With him in the stable, we can sit back and make a pretty pile of kisa, that's for sure." A yellow, broken smile spread across his bearded face. "And he's never been touched, I'd wager. I wouldn't mind breaking him in myself! But I won't, for his first time should bring a tidy sum. Might even be able to get an auction going, and get the losers to pay to watch his debut. Just like we did with that little blond girl we took from her screaming nanny on Highbridge Street last season. Now that was a night to remember, eh?"

With surprising speed the bear-man turned his great bulk and took a quick look around. There was no one near—no one, at least, who would be willing to help. He looked confidently down into Marcus' frightened green eyes.

"So are you going to come with us peaceable-like, or do I have to rough you up? Trust me, you little bastard—if you resist, you won't fare the better for it. And we don't want any bruises on that pretty face, now, do we?"

Marcus glanced back at the woman. She was smiling.

As the bear-man stood there staring greedily at him, Marcus realized that if he didn't act now, he would lose his only chance. Casually sliding his hand into his right pocket, he grasped his spring-loaded knife and ran his thumb over the button on its handle. He had never used his knife on a person before, and he knew he was about to do something awful—but it was unavoidable, if he wanted to stay alive and return to 'Becca.

He forced himself to smile.

"I am not so inexperienced as you think," he said slyly, while fingering the comforting coolness of the knife handle. "I've lived my entire life on the streets, and I know what it takes to get along. In fact, I like it. But I'm tired of foraging for myself, and I do need someone to look after me." Sick inside, he smiled again. "Before I go with you, would you like to see what I can do?"

The old harlot's face lit up. "Of course," she purred. Then she tilted her head back toward bear-man. "Why don't you prove your talents on him first? I'll watch."

Marcus' mind raced. This was exactly what he had been hoping for, but there would be only once chance—one razor-slim door of opportunity. If he failed, his failure would last forever. And then there would be no one left to take care of 'Becca.

He took a few steps forward, then went to his knees. Holding out his left hand, he crooked a finger suggestively at the man standing before him.

With an eager grunt, the huge man stepped nearer. The dark cloak parted. Large, meaty hands unbuttoned the front of his breeches. His face, looming over Marcus, was split in a wide grin.

Trying to control his revulsion, Marcus grinned back in kind and moved closer yet. Inside his pocket, his right hand closed carefully around the knife hilt. With his left hand, Marcus reached out toward the man's groin. The leering brute groaned and closed his eyes.

Better yet, Marcus thought. The knife felt cold and hard, just like his heart. With one swift movement, he slipped it from his pocket and pressed the button on the hilt.

Click.

At the sound, the man's eyes popped open and he recoiled, but it was too late. Marcus had grabbed the exposed privates and pulled hard. With a single, relentless slash he cut straight down.

Marcus cringed, feeling the sensation through the blade as it first struck home, ripped its way in, and then finally broke free. The amputated entities in his left hand suddenly felt warm, soft, and sticky, and he dropped them to the ground.

Even before the man could scream, Marcus was back on his feet, turning on the harlot. With a single slash of the knife, he cut the right side of her face from ear to chin. Then he whirled and ran, leaving behind the earsplitting, inhuman screaming of his victims.

Marcus ran from the alley and down the long, dark streets, until he thought his lungs would burst. Finally he stopped, his chest heaving, and leaned against the wall of a closed rug shop.

He was on one of the more widely used boulevards. Numbly, he wiped the knife off, folded it, and returned it to his pocket. Then he looked cautiously around the corner of the shop. Not far from him, a dark alley loomed. As he walked toward it on unsteady legs, he suddenly felt queasy. The moment he entered the alley, he fell to his knees and vomited, retching over and over until he thought it might never stop.

And then, finally, he curled up on the ground in a little ball, thought of 'Becca, and cried silently, shoulders shaking, until at last sleep came.

*R*ebecca of the House of Stinton was shivering. The fire in the abandoned one-room shed had gone out hours ago, and even the embers had long since faded away. She couldn't light another, for she had no more wood. Besides, Marcus had told her never to do so on her own, no matter what. And Marcus always knew best.

And so she remained hungry and cold in the little dilapidated shack while she waited for his return. Watching the shadows from the single oil lamp creep silently across the clapboard walls, she wondered what would happen when their dark, twisting fingers finally reached her. The cold hearth smelled acridly of spent wood, soot, and charcoal, and her hands were shaking. Curling up on the single cot, she felt terribly alone, and began to cry.

She was very frightened. Marcus had never been gone this long before. Her stomach growled as she pulled the single thin sheet closer around her shoulders. She had not eaten since the previous morning, and even that had been meager. Almost past the point of caring, she reached down to touch her belly. As she did it growled again. Then she suddenly saw the glow, and she froze with terror.

The strange, blue light beneath her cot had returned. All the other times this had happened Marcus had been with her. But he wasn't here now, and the thought of being left alone with it horrified her. Pulling her head under the dirty sheet, she cowered, hoping the strange light would simply go away. But the light didn't stop—it just kept getting brighter.

The glow continued to strengthen. She thought she should look under the cot, but at first couldn't summon the courage. Finally forcing herself to get up, she went to the ground on her knees before the light. Despite her fear, she knew exactly where the strange light was coming from.

The thing she and Marcus had stolen was glowing again. Dozens of pinprick-sized rays of azure light streaked up through the soft dirt where it was buried, hauntingly illuminating the underside of the cot and the walls and roof of the shed with their shimmering, ethereal glow.

Ever since she and her brother had found the object in the midst of the rubble, she had begged him to leave it behind. Having it always with them made her so nervous. But Marcus had remained adamant about keeping it, telling her that he thought it had to do with magic. It might be valuable, he'd said. And so they had kept it, and secretly brought it to the only place they knew where such a thing might be coveted.

She just wanted the rays of light to stop. She began clawing at the earth, trying to gather up more dirt in the hope of covering up the frightening, invasive light. But the more she tried, the more the glow just kept coming, seeping up through the ground like a silent, never-ending ghost. Frustrated and frightened, she began banging her fists on the ground as the tears ran down her cheeks. Finally she gave up and fell to the dirt beside the cot.

It was just then that she heard the rusty hinges on the door creak, and she turned around. Sitting up and wiping her dirty, tear-streaked face with one hand, Rebecca looked up hopefully.

Marcus stood there with a bag in his hand. He looked like he had just been through a war. He appeared distraught and tired, and parts of his clothes were splattered with what looked like dried blood. Closing the door quietly, he walked into the room and placed the bag on the table.

Getting up on her good foot, she limped to him and held him tightly. They stood like that for some time, saying nothing. The azure rays of light mixed oddly with the yellow flickering of the solitary table lamp.

Finally he let her go and looked meaningfully over to the cot. "How long has it been this time?" he asked tiredly.

"Not long," she answered. "It started just before you came in. I was terribly afraid . . . I'm so glad you're back."

Studying him more closely, she saw that his hands were bloody. "What happened?" she asked nervously. "Are you hurt?"

"I had some trouble, but I'm all right," he answered as casually as he could manage.

He took a moment to look at her. At seven Seasons of New Life, 'Becca was tall for her age, with a bright smile, long dark hair, and deep brown eyes. But she had been born with a clubfoot—something that she had always managed to shoulder with grace and dignity, despite her awkward, halting gait. She had a lot of strength, and he loved her for it.

It had always been her dream that their parents might one day save enough kisa to make the pilgrimage to Tammerland and seek help for her at the royal palace. Once there they would gladly have waited for as long as it might take to gain an audience with the king and his wizards in the royal chamber of supplication. Then, if she was lucky, the king might order one of his wizards—perhaps even the lead wizard himself—to heal her. But the money for the trip had never come. Now the king was dead, and it was widely rumored that all the wizards of the Directorate had been slain, along with the entire Royal Guard.

As Marcus looked down at 'Becca's tattered plaid dress, grimy face, and clubfoot, his heart ached. Their parents were dead; all they had was each other. He did not enjoy stealing, but they had no money, and the way to Tammerland had been hard. That was why he was so determined to hold on to the amazing thing they had found. If there was any place in Eutracia where it might have value, he reasoned, it would be where the wizards had once lived, and where the craft was said to flourish. Even if he found no buyers for the object itself, he could at least sell off the gold.

They had actually found two of the things, but had been forced to leave one behind. 'Becca had not been strong enough to carry off the other by herself, and he had not possessed the stamina to handle both at the same time. They had returned later to try to take the twin, but by then it was already gone.

At first he had stolen it just for the gold. But when it had started glowing, he had immediately become convinced of its potentially greater value. As for what purpose of the craft it supposedly served, he had absolutely no idea. But if he could find someone who would pay enough for it, he might be able to secure a healer to help with 'Becca's foot. And perhaps even have enough left over to help them start a new life here, in the capital.

But they were strangers in Tammerland, and in the absence of the royal guard, the city had become a very dangerous place. That lesson had been abundantly proven today, when he had wandered into the wrong part of town. Being no fool, he understood all too well that he needed to be supremely careful, for what they had buried beneath the cot could just as easily get them killed as set them free.

"Is there food in the bag?" Rebecca suddenly asked, taking him away from his thoughts.

"Yes," he answered. "This time I was able to get enough to last us for two days. Chicken stolen from a store, and bread taken from a window-sill."

"Can we eat now?" she asked eagerly. "I'm so hungry, Marcus!"

He smiled. "You go ahead. I have something to do first. Just be sure you leave me some! I know what a piglet you can be!" Then his eyes turned again to the blue light beneath the cot.

Rebecca's face fell. He was going to dig it up again. He did so every time it glowed, to make sure nothing had happened to it. And every time he did—which seemed to be happening more and more frequently—it made her nervous. But her hunger was greater than her anxiety, and the lure of the bag on the table was too great, so she turned her back on her brother and went to eat.

Marcus knelt and peered under the cot at the narrow rays of light shooting up and out of the loose dirt. This was the seventh time it had glowed since he had stolen it, and each time its illumination had increased in strength. That was a large part of why he had decided to bury it, but clearly that was no longer working.

Even before uncovering it, he could tell that this time would be the brightest yet. Narrowing his eyes against the azure light, he began slowly moving the dirt aside. Soon their treasure was exposed, filling the room with its brilliance.

He did not touch it, but instead examined the scroll as it lay there. About a meter long and half a meter wide, it was secured in the middle with a gold band. The rod running through it was gold as well, as were each of the fluted end knobs. The writing on the parchment was in a beautiful script that looked utterly unfamiliar to him, which added to the mystery. The scroll appeared to be unharmed. He sat back on his heels, thinking.

One thing was certain. He needed to find a buyer soon, for the glow was becoming too difficult to hide. He had no money to purchase any kind of container for it, and he'd buried it as deep as possible before hitting bedrock beneath the shack. As far as he was concerned, the sooner he turned it into kisa, the better.

Quickly, he covered the scroll back up. As he did the glow began to extinguish itself of its own accord, just as it always did. He did not know why the glow came and went, but was glad to see it die for the time being. When it was completely covered, he stood and walked to the table.

Her mouth and fingers covered with chicken grease, 'Becca beamed up at him and handed him a piece of bread.

Standing on the mizzen deck of the *Sojourner,* behind Grizelda, Krassus was greatly encouraged by what he was seeing. It was a clear, starry night; and the three moons were out, bathing the ship and the sea in their familiar, rose-colored light. Though there was little wind, the *Sojourner* continued to make good time as she plowed her way east through the restless waves. The lights of the other two ships running alongside them twinkled in the night. Thinking of the Chosen One pulling on an oar, Krassus smiled.

Grizelda selected some herbs from her bag and tossed them into the gazing flame. Hissing, the fire shot higher, and the viewing window in its center grew just a bit clearer. In his desperation to find the other scroll, Krassus had been forcing her to perform the ritual often, and by now both Grizelda's stores of herbs and her own energy were running very low. But finally this time she had been more successful.

The view was cloudy, but for the first time she actually had something to look at. Holding up a small piece of vellum taken from the Scroll of the Vagaries, she tried to make the scene unfolding before her clearer.

The Scroll of the Vigors came into view. It was glowing with azure light, and a pair of hands were starting to cover it over with dirt. Then the hands pulled away, and all that remained in the viewing window was a dirt floor that could have been anywhere. She dropped her arms to her sides, and the flame lowered accordingly.

"We have done it, my lord," she said with a smile. The sea wind snatched at her long, gray hair, and she hooked a portion of it behind one ear.

"I now know why we have had such trouble trying to view the scroll," she went on. "Whoever took it is hiding it, burying it in the dirt. Only when it is exposed may we view it—which may not be often. Whoever is in possession of the scroll knows nothing of the craft—of that much I am certain. If it were with the wizards of the Redoubt, they would be busy trying to decipher its secrets, rather than burying it."

For a moment she looked perturbed, but then she smiled again. "When the herbs and oils you promised me arrive at the Citadel, I will be able to do much better—even from that far away."

Krassus looked down at her. "You may retire now," he said simply. With a short bow, Grizelda picked up her bag and started for her cabin.

Turning, the wizard in the gray-and-blue robe walked to the gunwale and leaned his forearms on it as he looked out to the ever-shifting sea. The wind had picked up a bit more, and the waves were frothy and whitecapped.

Soon, he assured himself. Soon he would have the Scroll of the Vigors, and there would be nothing the wizards in the Redoubt could do to stop him. And once he had Wulfgar, the world would see wonders of the craft that had not been witnessed for eons.

Twenty-one

"**G**et up! Now, you *Talis* pigs! Time to get back to work!"

The chorus of harsh voices, shouting the same thing over and over again, rang in his ears. He just wanted them to be quiet, so he could go back to sleep. Didn't they know they were being rude, shouting like that? He would have to remember to speak to the lead wizard about it, after he got up and had his breakfast. Determined to sleep, he started to turn over on his side, but something tugged at him, preventing him from doing so.

Suddenly the searing pain in his back returned, bringing him fully awake. His nostrils were immediately assaulted by the stench of his surroundings.

He opened his eyes to darkness. Then faint light began to push away the shadows, and he saw that demonslavers were moving about, hanging flaming oil lanterns on the columns supporting the deck above. Other demonslavers were starting to unchain their captives from the floor. As the light in the hold increased, Tristan's situation slowly came into focus.

He didn't remember being brought here, or being chained. All he could recall was passing out, just after one of the slavers had poured salt-water on his wounds.

He looked down the length of his body. His hands and feet were still bound together by the same shackles he had worn while rowing. Additional chains lay across his chest and lower legs, securing him to the deck. Raising his head as best he could, he saw row after row of his fellow slaves, all male, also chained down like animals. It seemed their numbers took up every inch of the filthy deck. As they were unchained one by one, they stood awkwardly, blinking their eyes against the light.

The pain in his back was excruciating. His vest had been put back on him, its laces retied in the front. His wounds must have begun to scab over, because they now itched, as well as hurt.

One of the slavers sauntered over to him and looked down with life-less, opaque eyes. Without warning the monster kicked Tristan in the ribs, knocking the wind out of him. Pain burned in his side. Then the slaver raised his trident high over Tristan's face. Wondering if he was about to die, Tristan made a last promise to himself not to flinch. He kept it, even as the trident came down at him with unbelievable speed.

The three silver points of the trident buried themselves loudly into the deck, just inches from Tristan's head. Then the slaver let out a laugh.

"If you give us any more trouble, I have permission from Krassus to add to the artwork on your back," he sneered. "And I beg you to try, dear prince. For I would love another such excuse."

Tristan looked defiantly up into the white eyes. As he did, he noticed the ring of keys hanging from the slaver's side. Then he remembered: This was the same one who had whipped him; he was sure of it.

The monster unchained him from the floor. Still shackled hand and foot, Tristan was pulled roughly to his feet and shoved into the line of slaves waiting their turn to climb the stairway to the deck above.

After being chained to his seat, Tristan looked out his oar slit and decided it was early morning. He then turned to watch as the rest of the slaves were chained down. The slaver who had beaten him was using one of his keys to close the massive padlock that secured the single chain running through all of the slaves' shackles. The key that fit it was the largest of them, and lay in the center of the ring normally hooked on his belt. Tristan filed this information away in his head, even though he realized that, given the tight security of the slavers' system, such knowledge would be unlikely to help him.

One by one, the exhausted, weak-kneed men they were replacing were herded to the trapdoor between the rows and forced down the stairway. Several slavers followed them down, to chain them to the floor in the same filthy spots the fresh rowers had just vacated. Then the pace-master started pounding out the mind-numbing beat, and Tristan and the others began to pull on their oars.

Despite the searing pain, he rowed as best he could. He had no other choice: He wasn't sure he could survive another savage beating from the slaver. As he rowed he felt his wounds rip open, the pain cutting through his back like hot knives.

He looked up to see the slaver who had beaten him staring coldly at him, as if waiting for him to make another mistake. Pulling determinedly at his oar, Tristan drew comfort from the thought of the brain hook hidden in his right boot.

As all of the unfortunates pulled on their oars, the *Wayfarer* began to plow faster through the Sea of Whispers.

*T*he demonslaver manning the crow's nest aboard the *Sojourner* twisted the third cylinder of his spyglass as he tried to confirm what he had seen with his naked eyes. He had no wish to suffer the consequences of making a false report to Krassus. Peering across the sea, he scoured the horizon.

There they were: Three frigates, sailing as a group and making a direct line from the north. They were running quickly before the wind, while *Sojourner* and her two sister ships were wearing out their rowers to stay on their easterly heading.

He ran his glass over them carefully. They were not part of Krassus' fleet, judging by the way their spars and masts had been lengthened to carry more sail. They were a fast lot—of that there was no doubt. Faster than the *Sojourner* could be even if she weren't loaded down with slaves. And at their present course they would soon be upon the three slower, heavier slavers. But who were they, and what did they want?

Searching for an identifying flag, he turned his glass to the lead frigate's rigging. Finally he found what he was looking for. It was high atop the mainmast, fluttering back and forth proudly. Turning the cylinder on the spyglass again, he brought it into focus.

At first he thought he must be seeing things. Taking his eye from the glass for a moment, the slaver stared across the ocean and drew a quick breath. He put the device back to his eye. So it was true, after all. The blue-and-gold banner carried both the lion and the broadsword, and every man, woman, and child in Eutracia knew what it represented.

It was the royal battle flag of the House of Galland.

He rang the alarm bell. Almost before it had finished pealing, another slaver had climbed up the rigging to a spot just below him. Pointing out to sea with one arm, the spotter relayed the message. The other slaver climbed back down and ran to find Krassus.

He found him standing on the stern deck by the ship's wheel, looking over some charts. His herbmistress was there with him. The slaver came to attention.

"Begging your pardon, my lord," he said urgently. "But the crow's nest has spied three ships, frigate class, on a direct course to intercept us from the north. Their speed is great. They run the blue-and-gold battle flag of the House of Galland."

Krassus froze. Snatching up his spyglass from the table before him, he turned to look north. There he saw the three ships plowing directly toward them, running before the wind with unusually large sails. He moved the lens up to the enemy ship's rigging and saw the blue-and-gold flag. His mind racing, he slowly lowered the spyglass. They were clearly after him, but who could they be? The wizards of the Redoubt, perhaps? But the Redoubt had no standing navy. Still, who else but the wizards would have the gall to run the royal battle flag?

Then it hit him. These could be vessels of the Minion fleet, under the assumed command of the wizards. But those vessels were rumored anchored off the coast of Parthalon, at a port far to the north of his present position. How could Wigg and Faegan have gotten word to them, supplied the ships, and had them catch up to his present position in so short a time? The logistics simply didn't work. And if it was indeed the Minions, then why were there only three ships?

Still, there they were. And he knew he had to take action quickly, or all might be lost.

Lost in thought, he stared out over the sea. He would have preferred to stand and fight, throwing bolts at the three enemy ships and blowing them out of the water. But he could do that only by letting them come much closer, and thereby losing his precious lead. And if Wigg and Faegan were aboard them, they could presumably throw twice the number of bolts at him as he could at them. Then there was the problem of whether the Minions were aboard the enemy ships. If so, they could board him at any moment simply by flying to him.

No, the distance between the *Sojourner* and the enemy frigates had to be maintained. The only way to do that was to sacrifice the other two slavers sailing with him, to buy him time. True, one of them could be carrying Wulfgar. But they were transporting countless slaves in many sea crossings; the odds of Wulfgar currently being aboard either of his two sister ships was not great. He would just have to risk it. Besides, for all he knew Wulfgar might well be in custody already. And he could allow nothing to stand in the way of getting the scroll to the Citadel. He turned to the waiting demonslaver.

"Hear me well, for our lives depend on the next few moments," he ordered. "Call for my first mate. And tell him to bring my lantern. He'll know the one. Have every *Talis* slave, except those currently manning the galley and one equal-sized number to relieve them, brought topside. They are to be immediately killed and thrown overboard to lighten our load. The *R'talis* captives are not to be touched. And order the slaves to stop rowing—they'll only slow us down. Go now! And be quick about it!"

Immediately, the slaver was gone. Soon the first mate appeared holding a lantern.

"You are familiar with the situation?" Krassus asked abruptly. The slaver nodded.

"Good," Krassus said. Taking the lamp, he closed his eyes. The lamp began to glow with the blue of the craft. He handed it back to his first mate.

"Take this to the stern gunwale and signal our situation to the *Wayfarer* and the *Stalwart*. They are to come about and intercept the three frigates while we sail on. They are to stop the enemy at all costs, and kill everyone aboard. Do you understand?"

The first mate nodded.

"Very well," Krassus said. "Go now."

Looking astern, Krassus saw the *Wayfarer* and the *Stalwart* following in their wake, saw the alternating beams of azure light shooting toward them from the lantern, giving them their orders. He turned to Grizelda.

"Now we shall see what we shall see," he said quietly.

The herbmistress' face showed concern. "Surely my lord has not forgotten that the Chosen One is still aboard the *Wayfarer*," she said questioningly. "He could be killed."

Before answering, Krassus turned to see the additional sails being raised, and the first of the *Talis* slaves coming topside, blinking their eyes in the sunlight. A gang of slavers stood waiting, swords drawn. As the slaves appeared up the stairway one by one, the slavers stepped up behind them quietly, cut their throats, then tossed the bodies over the gunwales and into the sea.

Sharks swarmed, snaking through the increasingly bloody water. Krassus turned his dark eyes back to the three enemy frigates, ignoring the screams of the dying slaves as if they weren't there.

"Of course I haven't forgotten," he said quietly. "If he dies, he dies. In the end it doesn't really matter. As I have already told you, for what I have planned, his blood signature is of no use to me. But if he should be rescued, I have arranged a little surprise for him and his wizards—one that could be very much to our advantage. So you see, there is no need to worry about him."

He watched intently as the *Wayfarer* and the *Stalwart* began to alter course, heeling hard to port, to take on the three advancing frigates. Hundreds of demonslavers could be seen on their decks, swords waving in the air.

As the *Sojourner's* extra sails snapped open she began to pick up speed, distancing herself from the impending calamity.

*T*ristan pulled hard on his oar while trying both to keep one eye on the commotion coming from the deck above, and to ignore the searing pain in his back. They had been rowing at battle speed for the last quarter of an hour, ever since the *Wayfarer* had made a sharp, unexplained course change. Looking out his oar slit, he was sure they were now headed north. As the pacemaster continued to pound out the impossible beat, slaves began groaning and collapsing at their stations, and the lone guard—all the other slavers had been ordered topside—was using his nine-tails with abandon, trying to force them back to work.

For the first time, Tristan noticed a hint of concern in the faces of the two remaining slavers. Then the *Wayfarer* lurched to port, leaning over hard. As she did, one of the oarsmen on the other side of the ship suddenly dropped his oar, pointed out the slit in the hull, and began babbling wildly.

"Ships!" he screamed, his eyes alight with hope. "Three Eutracian ships! And they fly the war banner of the monarchy!"

Picking up his trident, the demonslaver mercilessly stabbed the man through the abdomen. Then he pulled the prongs out viciously, twisting them to maximize the damage. The man was dead before he hit the deck.

But he hadn't died in vain.

Almost every slave in the galley let go of his oar and craned his neck to look outside. Shouting and pandemonium reigned as the slaver tried in vain to whip them back into submission. Tristan could see nothing on his side of the ship but empty sea. Nonetheless, he was stunned by the slave's words. There was only one answer.

They had finally come for him.

Part of the Minion fleet had arrived, and Wigg and Faegan might even be aboard. His heart sang with the promise of escape. And of killing Krassus and his herbmistress, and taking as many of his horrific captors to their graves as he could. They might even be able to recover the Scroll of the Vagaries. There were debts to repay, and he meant to have his revenge.

While the slaver who had beaten him was preoccupied with trying to whip the excited oarsmen back into submission, Tristan reached into his right boot and slid out the brain hook. Cupping it in his hand, he laid the blade up along the underside of his forearm, then placed his arm down by his side. The blade felt sharp and comforting against his skin.

He knew this would have to be a very closely run thing, for his chains did not allow much freedom of movement. He would only get one chance, and it had to be right.

Hungrily he eyed the ring of keys hanging from the slaver's belt. The large one in the center was still there. Amid the screaming and confusion, Tristan willed the slaver to come to him.

Almost as if he had heard Tristan's silent pleading, the slaver turned, glared at the prince hatefully, and began walking to the front of the ship. Summoning up all the saliva he could muster, Tristan spat toward him and then smiled.

The slaver took another step. Then another. Finally he was directly alongside Tristan. With a smile, he raised his trident.

But suddenly the *Wayfarer* collided with something. A massive blow struck hard against the port side, and the hull tipped hard to starboard. Losing his balance, the slaver slipped to the right.

As the prongs of the trident came down, Tristan slid toward the bow and grabbed the handle of the trident, using the ship's momentum to pull the surprised slaver down into his lap. In one smooth motion he grabbed the slaver by the throat and shoved the point of the brain hook into the thing's ear.

The slaver screamed and began to struggle. With a vicious twist, Tristan yanked out the hook. The slaver was dead, blood pouring from his ear.

Tristan shoved the brain hook back into his boot. Then he snatched the key ring from the slaver's belt and pushed the corpse off him, into the aisle.

The gigantic pacemaster was already on his feet, waving a hammer and coming toward Tristan. Finding the large key in the center of the ring, Tristan shoved it into the padlock lying on the deck and turned it.

Nothing happened.

A quick glance told him that the pacemaster was nearly upon him. Again he turned the key in the rusty lock. The lock sprung open.

As fast as he could Tristan pulled his chain free, which allowed him to move his feet. But his wrists and ankles were still shackled together, and there was no time to pick up a weapon. The pacemaster, hammer raised, was looming over him.

As the great hammer came down, Tristan slipped to the right, dodging the heavy blow. Then he slid back in, placed his hands together, and swung them around, slamming his wrist shackles into the slaver's right cheek and eye. Blood sprayed, and the slaver crashed to the deck atop the other one's body.

Praying that the same key would unlock his shackles, Tristan shoved it into the lock binding his feet together and turned it. This time the lock sprang open immediately. The same proved true for his wrist shackles. Smiling, he turned and passed the key to the man seated behind him. There were tears in the fellow's eyes. Tristan started to speak, but suddenly realized that words were not necessary.

Reaching beneath the body of the first slaver, Tristan recovered the thing's short sword. He darted for the stairway, then stopped and purposely slowed his breathing.

Picking up the gold medallion that hung around his neck, he gazed at it for a precious, dangerous moment and thought of all his loved ones. Then he dropped the medallion back to his chest, raised the cool blade of the sword vertically to his forehead, and closed his eyes.

From the way the hull of the ship had been impacted and the sounds of battle coming from the deck above, no one had to tell him that they were being boarded.

Holding his sword before him, Tristan ran up the stairway and into the light.

CHAPTER

Twenty-two

Serena felt like an outcast as she looked down at the sumptuous plate of food. She sat alone at a dining table that was very well appointed, complete with candlesticks and wine. She was dressed in yet another lovely gown picked out for her by Janus.

Starving, clothed in rags, her fellow slaves stared out at her from their bondage. It made her nervous, fearful for her safety every time she finished such a meal and the demonslavers put her back into confinement with the others. Two slavers armed with swords sat nearby, watching carefully.

Although hungry, she didn't really want to eat, for it seemed so cruel to the others. But Wulfgar had told her she must do so when she could, and over the course of the last week she had come to trust his judgment. So she tentatively took her first bite of the delicious veal, trying as best she could to ignore the ravenous, envious glares of her fellow captives as they watched from inside the barred cages.

This bizarre, unexplained treatment of her had been Janus' doing; she was sure of it. Janus was apparently not willing to honor Wulfgar's request to feed her more without twisting it into something evil. Shaking her head, she thought of the insane, sadistic nature of her predicament. She felt naked and alone as she sat there with her fancy meal, and suddenly she realized that the only time she was ever at ease was when she was with Wulfgar, in his quarters.

She gazed around the great hall. It was without doubt the largest room she had ever seen, constructed of smooth, beige marble; lit by numerous, open skylights; and otherwise quite stark. All that the chamber contained were the many large cages holding the other *R'talis* slaves.

She had never been in a position to count the cages, but assumed their number to be in excess of one hundred. Each of the glimmering, silver coops stood alone, separated from the others by several meters. The cages contained people, cots for sleeping, and buckets used for waste. The buckets were not emptied often enough, and they filled the chamber with their stink.

None of the captives knew why they had been brought here, or what their eventual fate might be. Even Serena—the only one allowed out of here, had not been able to figure out the answers to those questions.

She had so far made four more trips to see Wulfgar, each time at his request. She enjoyed visiting him, and found herself growing to like him more and more. He had a strong, understated quality that always made her feel safe, even in this horrific place. Sometimes she wished she could simply stay there with him, but she doubted that Janus would ever grant such a request. He wouldn't want to give up the pleasure of seeing her squirm as she ate in front of the others, and watching them suffer as she was forced to eat the delicacies provided only to her.

Just then a door opened in the far wall and Janus sauntered in, the twin iron spheres on his belt clinking together as he walked. Serena cringed as he sat down in the chair opposite her and poured himself a glass of wine. Then he placed his legs on the table, crossed one over the other, and leaned back. The painted red mask contorted as he smiled.

Looking down at her plate, he feigned an expression of disappointment. "You really must eat something, my dear," he said unctuously. "Or, if you prefer, I could have something else brought in." He raised his eyes to her with a menacing, almost envious stare. "After all, nothing is too good for Wulfgar's whore."

Laying down her fork, Serena glared back at him. "I'm not his whore," she said softly. "We care for each other. Something I doubt you could ever understand."

Janus placed his free hand sarcastically over his heart. "I'm touched; I really am," he sneered. "In any event, he asks for you again. You must be very good at what you do. Perhaps if Wulfgar tires of you, I might take a turn . . ."

Serena remained silent, filled with hatred.

Standing, Janus picked up a fork and casually stabbed it into a slice of Serena's veal. Then he walked over to the nearest cage and waved it back and forth in the air, sending its enticing aroma toward the slaves. Like starving animals, they pushed to the front of the cage, and hands and arms stretched pleadingly out from between the bars. Turning back to her, Janus smiled.

"Food," he mused. "Simple, everyday food. Curious, isn't it? To assume power one need not torture, or even kill. One need only withhold simple sustenance, to suddenly become a king among men. Such an interesting, simple, elegant form of punishment and reward, wouldn't you agree? There really is no equal."

Tears welled up in Serena's eyes. Although she knew that none of this was her fault, she couldn't help feeling as if she were to blame.

"Stop it!" she begged. "Isn't it bad enough that you force me to eat this way before them? Must you add to that torture? How can you be so cruel?"

"Cruel?" Janus asked. He seemed genuinely perplexed. "You find this cruel? This is not cruel, my dear. This is merely . . . theater. But what is happening to the other slaves—those branded *Talis*—now that could truly be defined as cruel. Those poor bastards have simply become a means to an end."

Serena was about to ask him what he meant by that, but she stopped herself. Not only did she doubt that he would tell her, but she also wasn't sure she could bear hearing the answer. She lowered her face and placed her hands on her lap.

Janus smiled again, and waved the piece of meat higher. "You!" he shouted out to a tall man in front. "Show me how far you can reach! Perhaps you will be rewarded!"

The slave eagerly stretched one arm out, his fingers waggling desperately. Janus walked up to him and carefully placed the veal on the floor, several inches past the end of the man's reach—just close enough to tempt, and just far enough away to make touching it impossible. Then, apparently satisfied, he walked back to the table. Serena buried her face in her hands.

"Now, then, shall we go?" Janus asked her politely. "We mustn't keep your whore-master waiting."

Serena rose on shaky legs and followed him toward the door. Despite how badly she felt for those in the cages, she desperately wanted to put this place behind her.

Pausing before two demonslaver guards, Janus pointed at the first of them. "You," he ordered. "Come with me." Then he bent down, placing his mouth next to the other slaver's ear. "You stay here," he whispered softly, just loud enough for Serena to hear. "If one of them actually reaches that meat, take him out and kill him."

The slaver turned his white eyes to the cage, and the desperate, crushing mob within. He smiled. "With pleasure." With that, Janus, the other slaver, and Serena walked out the door and into the hallway.

Night was falling in the Citadel, and the hallways were brightly lit by wall torches. The walk was long, but by now Serena could have negotiated her way to Wulfgar's quarters alone. As they went down one of the hallways, she heard the insane screaming that seemed ever-present in this area of the Citadel, and she suddenly realized that this might be what Janus had been referring to when he mentioned the plight of the *Talis* slaves. She shivered.

Finally Janus stopped at Wulfgar's door. At a nod from him, the two slaver guards on duty there slid back the bolt.

"This is where I leave you, my dear," Janus said simply. "I am needed elsewhere. Do enjoy yourself."

The two guards escorted her inside, then walked back into the hall. She heard them swing the door shut again and slide the bolt across, locking her in.

It was quiet and cool in the rooms, a direct contrast to the horror of what she had just left. Hearing her enter, Wulfgar came in from the balcony and came to her. As his strong arms closed around her, she began to cry.

He started to speak, but decided not to. Instead he just held her, placed his face against her long, dark ringlets, and let her weep.

When the tears finally stopped, she wiped her eyes and looked up into his rugged, comforting face. Then she led him over to the bed and pulled him down to sit beside her. Taking both his hands in hers, she began to speak.

She told him of how the painted monster had teased the other slaves, then ordered the slaver to kill whoever might manage to get hold of the prize laid before them on the floor. As he listened, Wulfgar's face darkened, and the muscles in his jaw clenched tight. When she had finally finished, her tears came again.

Wulfgar held her close. She looked pleadingly into his hazel eyes. "I cannot go on like this," she whispered sadly. "I know Janus will keep humiliating me this way. He enjoys it far too much to let it stop." Ashamed, she lowered her face again. "What can I do?"

Wishing he knew what to say, Wulfgar stroked her cheek, wiping away some of the tears. "I don't know," he answered truthfully. "I feel sorry for the others, but my heart also wants you to survive as best you can. Is that selfish of me? Perhaps." He paused for a moment, thinking.

"For some unknown reason I seem to be important to those in power here," he said at last. "When this leader named Krassus finally comes, I might be able to persuade him to let you stay here with me."

Placing a finger beneath her chin, he raised her face back up to his. "Would you like that?"

For the first time in days, Serena managed a smile. Her heart was sure of this strong, gentle man.

She took one of his hands in hers and placed it on her breast.

Understanding, Wulfgar looked into her eyes. "Are you sure?" he asked gently.

Smiling, she reached behind him and freed his long, sandy hair from its worn leather band. She watched his mane fall down around his shoulders and ran her fingers through it slowly.

Narrowing his eyes slightly, Wulfgar gently laid her down on the bed. His breathing had quickened, and there was a strong sense of command about him that she desperately wanted to surrender herself to.

As his mouth met hers, her body rose to meet him.

Twenty-three

"You did *what* to my herb cubiculum?" Faegan shouted. Shailiha had never seen him so angry. As if the loss of Tree Town and so many of the gnomes he loved hadn't been enough, now he had just learned that his cubiculum had been partially destroyed. His face was bright red, and his gray-green eyes were practically bulging out, a rare sight indeed. The Paragon swung from its gold chain around his neck, refracting its bloodred light about the room.

Lionel the Little sat at the table, his little body trembling. His broken spectacles hung off the end of his nose; the singed tuft of hair was bathed in sweat and stuck flat to his forehead. He suddenly wished he had never, ever, heard of herbs.

"But the explosion was a small one, Master," he countered lamely. "Not as large or destructive as the two others, and I—"

"There have been *others*?" Faegan exploded. He slammed both his hands down on the armrests of his chair on wheels.

Shailiha, Celeste, and Lionel had returned on schedule, after hiding the bags of herbs and the vat of oils, and cleaning up the laboratory, as best they could. They had spent one night in Shadowood, during which time there had been no sign of any other demonslavers. When they finally exited Faegan's portal, they found Wigg, Abbey, and Faegan waiting anxiously for them.

Seeing that the women's jerkins were bloodied and that they had none of the herbs or oils Abbey had requested, the wizards had demanded an explanation. But first Shailiha anxiously inquired about Tristan, only to learn that there was still no word. After hearing what

Shailiha and Celeste had to say, the wizards then ordered everyone to the Hall of Blood Records to discuss the situation further.

At the table sat Wigg, Faegan, Abbey, Shailiha, Celeste, and Lionel. Shailiha had requested that Morganna be brought to her, and she now held her baby happily in her sling. Atop a pedestal in one corner of the room sat the Tome of the Paragon.

With a great sigh Faegan leaned forward, placing his hands flat upon the table. He looked directly at Shailiha. As he did, she could feel his immense power.

"Do you mean to tell me that every remaining bit of dried herb and refined oil left in my cubiculum has been contaminated?" he asked.

"Yes," she answered sadly as she rocked her child. "We arrived in time to save most of the gnomes from death, and some of Tree Town from fire. But not in time to keep the slavers from stealing what they needed and mixing together the remaining herbs and oils. Had we not arrived when we did, there would most probably be nothing left to use at all. I'm sorry we didn't do more."

"Don't be sorry," Wigg said compassionately from the other side of the table. "If it hadn't been for the two of you, we would have lost everything. We're very proud of what you have done." Smiling at them both, he placed an affectionate hand over his daughter's.

"Yes, they are indeed to be commended," Abbey added. "And thank the Afterlife for Celeste's Forestallment. But do any of you fully understand how much more difficult our task has just become?" The herb-mistress was clearly frustrated. Sighing angrily, she ran a hand back through her gray-streaked dark hair.

"What was once considered arduous has now become virtually impossible," she continued. "And we are still no closer to finding Tristan, Wulfgar, or these scrolls you speak of. Not to mention discerning what Krassus' eventual goals in all of this might be."

Celeste looked over at Faegan. "If only a small bit of one herb blew up the laboratory, then why is it that all of Tree Town didn't go up when the demonslavers were burning the herbs by the bagful?" she asked.

Faegan scowled. "I can only assume that is because they were so well mixed. I have never experimented with mixing *all* of my herbs together, because I feared what might happen." He rubbed his chin thoughtfully.

"So now we know," he said in a soft voice. "Still, this was a terrible way to have to find out."

Shailiha looked to Wigg. "There is absolutely no word of my brother?" she asked. "None of the Minion search parties have turned up anything?"

The lead wizard shook his head. "I am sorry," he answered sadly. "But they continue to search, and they won't give up. Several days ago we sent Geldon and Traax to Parthalon, to activate the Minion fleet. They have been on patrol since, plowing the Sea of Whispers in an attempt to intercept Krassus' supposed fleet and recover the Chosen One. We have yet to hear from them."

Shailiha and Celeste looked wide-eyed at the two old wizards. "So you sent the fleet out anyway?" Celeste asked incredulously. "Why didn't you tell us?"

"Because you weren't needed, and there wasn't time for us to endure yet another of your blatant pleadings to go along with them," Wigg said, trying to keep his tone light. "You are both very strong, valuable allies, and we thought your considerable talents might be better used for other things. As it turned out, we were right."

Shailiha glared at the wizards as she tried her best to be angry with them. But in the end, she couldn't. She and Celeste had been so sure they had manipulated them, but in truth it had been the other way around. She was once again reminded that there was always more to dealing with Wigg and Faegan than first met the eye.

"So what do we do now?" she asked the table in general. Morganna cooed, and the princess gave her a little hug.

"Abbey and Lionel shall eventually go back to Shadowood to try to unravel the riddle of the herbs and the oils," Faegan answered. "The bulk of the Minion forces will remain here. After all, we cannot be sure that Krassus and his demonslavers aren't still in Eutracia. We must make sure the castle and the Redoubt are well protected." He paused.

"There is something else I wish to tell you all," he added after a moment, "and this must come first, before anyone returns to Shadowood. I have been doing research into the Tome, to see if I might come up with something more to help us with these problems of the herbs and oils. And after hearing your story, I am most glad that I did."

Raising one arm, he commanded the Tome to come to him. It rose into the air and floated across the room to come to rest on the table. Narrowing his eyes, he employed the craft to open it to a particular section of the text. Then he looked back up at the lead wizard.

"Tell me," he asked Wigg, "have you ever heard of the Chambers of Penitence?"

"No," Wigg answered skeptically. "What are you talking about?"

"At first I did not remember the phrase either," Faegan replied. "But when I used my gift of Consummate Recollection to scan the Tome for the words 'herbs' and 'oils,' a strange thing happened. I also kept seeing the words 'Chambers of Penitence' in my mind. Not just once, mind you, but over and over again, until they started to crowd everything else out. It was as if the Tome was desperately trying to tell me something. Heretofore the text had only been a silent, static entity. But now it was as if it had suddenly come alive, just as the Paragon has its own other-worldly form of existence. It was astounding. So I decided to actually read the pages, rather than simply rely on my memory. And when I did, further references to these chambers kept popping up, taking me to other related pages in the text. And after crisscrossing back and forth in the text this way, I was finally led here, to a specific volume of the Vigors. By itself, the passage would be confusing. But now, after having been led here from its many sources, the meaning is becoming more clear."

"And just what does the passage say?" Wigg asked.

Faegan looked down at the page. " '. . . *And there shall be discovered many Chambers of Penitence, which shall both help to guide their way in the craft, and also ensure the existence of the Vigors. Each chamber shall be different in its secrets than the last, but each shall reveal aspects of the craft so complex that they must be hidden within the earth. But be forewarned, for the psychic price of such knowledge shall be dear, perhaps even mortal.' "*

Faegan looked up from the great book. "Do you see?" he asked excitedly.

Wigg leaned forward, intensely interested.

"Let me show you," Faegan went on. Narrowing his eyes again, he commanded more of the pages to turn to another part of the text. Running his finger down the page, he finally found what he was looking for.

" *'If it be of the herbs and oils of the craft that one seeks guidance, it shall be found in one of the Chambers of Penitence. Within the chamber they shall find the Floating Gardens of the Craft, eternally guarded by the watchwoman of the waters. But the cost of such knowledge shall be dear indeed, and it should be searched out only in times of great distress, for the risk is great. At the base of the Woman of Stone, one shall begin to find the answers. But only with the help of the Paragon, for it alone shall light the way.' "*

"The Woman of Stone?" Celeste asked. "What is that?"

"The Woman of Stone is a rock formation on the coast, not too far from here," Wigg answered, rubbing his chin. "Over time, the waves have carved the profile of a woman into the rock wall overlooking the Sea of Whispers. It has supposedly existed for eons. Long enough, it would now appear, for the Ones Who Came Before to know of it as well, and use her as a landmark by which to leave one of these so-called Chambers of Penitence." Pausing for a moment, he looked back over to Faegan.

"But what of these floating gardens?" he asked. "And who is this watchwoman who is supposedly eternally guarding them? And what does the Tome mean by the 'psychic price to be paid'?"

"We won't know until we go there, will we?" Faegan cackled. His expression and posture reminded Wigg that nothing so entranced his old friend as an unexplained secret of the craft, especially if he was the only one to possess the answer.

"I think we should depart first thing in the morning," Faegan added.

Wigg looked over to Abbey to see a hint of disappointment in her eyes. It seemed they would be separated again, after all. Then he looked back at Faegan and sighed.

He hoped the master wizard was right.

Twenty-four

Raising his sword high, Tristan narrowly parried the sharp strike from the demonslaver's blade. The guard had rushed from the deck above to confront him, even before he had ascended the last two steps of the stairway.

Struggling against the ceaseless blows, he somehow made it topside and gained some badly needed maneuvering room. As his opponent raised his sword yet again, Tristan finally sensed an opening. Sliding in on the balls of his feet, he swung the blade around in a flat, perfect circle. The tip of the sword sliced the slaver's abdomen open, and the monster fell to the deck.

Trying to ignore the desperate pain in his back, Tristan stole a precious moment to get his bearings. There were five ships involved in the struggle. The *Wayfarer* and the *Stalwart* lay next to one another in the water. Two of the still-unidentified frigates flanked them. The third lay before their bows. The three mysterious frigates had employed heavy grappling hooks to pull all the ships together and hold them there. There was nothing for the monsters to do but stand and fight. All five of the vessels' decks swarmed with combatants.

Many of the slave ships' sails were torn and hanging down, while their masts had fallen, shattered, to the decks. Rigging lay everywhere, making fighting all the more difficult. Small fires had broken out here and there, dark smoke rising to blur vision.

Suddenly Tristan realized what was wrong about it all.

There were no Minion warriors about. Not a single one. The fighters who were struggling alongside him and his fellow slaves seemed to be a ragtag, unorganized lot at best. Each of them fought with skill and abandon, as if every moment were his last. They seemed to have precious little fear of the demonslavers, and relished killing them, almost as if they all had personal scores to settle. Amid the blood, the screaming, and the clashing of weapons, Tristan found himself stunned and confused.

A trident came whistling through the air, to bury itself directly beside his head in the thick mast that stood just behind him. Instinctively he reached behind his right shoulder to grasp one of his throwing knives, only to remember that they weren't there.

Cursing, he finally saw the demonslaver that had thrown the trident. He stood a little way across the bloody deck, glaring at him. Sword in hand, the monster smiled and nastily beckoned the prince forward.

On impulse, Tristan raised his sword high and ran toward the slaver across the slippery deck. As he neared, though, he caught a glimpse of yet another slaver running around the corner of the wheelhouse, and realized he was trapped. Tristan knew he couldn't possibly take them both—especially without his usual weapons at his command. So he kept going for all he was worth, intent on cutting down at least the first of them.

Holding his blade in a one-handed grip straight out before him, Tristan ran in and roughly pushed the slaver's sword arm to one side with his free hand. Then he plunged the point of his sword directly into the demonslaver's throat. He turned the edge of the blade sharply, then raised one foot and pushed the body off his sword. Blood rushed from the slaver's neck as he fell to the deck.

Tristan turned around as fast as he could to face the one rushing up behind him. If he died this day, so be it—at least he would have the satisfaction of knowing that he had taken several more of the awful demonslavers to their graves with him. But what he saw surprised him.

A great bear of a man had come up behind the other slaver and taken it around the neck with one of his huge arms. The man's other arm was pushing on the back of the demonslaver's head, forcing it down and forward. Suddenly the man gave the slaver's head another forceful shove downward, and Tristan heard the neck snap like a dry tree branch. Then the giant picked up the dead body and threw it a good five meters across the deck, as if it weighed nothing. Tristan couldn't help but stand speechless for a moment, looking into the eyes of the fighter who had just saved his life.

He was the largest human being the prince had ever seen—even taller and heavier than most of the Minion warriors. Easily topping seven feet, he wore torn, bloody breeches and nothing else—no shoes, shirt, or weapons of any kind. He seemed to be a bit older than Tristan, and his eyes were dark. His head was clean-shaven, and his hugely muscular body was covered with scars of every description, one of which ran diagonally down across his forehead, over his left eye, and onto his cheek.

Tristan watched in awe as yet another demonslaver, his sword held high, rushed toward the giant. With a speed Tristan would have thought impossible for one so large, the man turned and grabbed the slaver's sword arm, giving it a sharp twist. The arm broke, blood and splintered bone erupting through the white skin. As the slaver screamed in agony, the giant picked him up easily and then let him fall straight down onto his raised right knee. Then he lifted the dead body up into his arms as if it, too, were weightless, and it went flying across the deck.

After giving the prince an expressionless look, the giant turned away, searching for another victim.

Tristan looked around but could find no immediate enemy. The battle was clearly subsiding, and it seemed that his mysterious saviors had won the day. Exhausted, chest heaving, Tristan lowered his sword.

His first impulse was to find the *Sojourner*, but clearly she was not here. Turning to the east, he squinted into the sun and let his gaze pan across the horizon. Finally he found it: The white speck of sail in the far-off distance that meant Krassus and his herbmistress had escaped. Angrily he turned back to the now-quiet battle scene.

Bodies—human and demonslaver alike—lay everywhere in impossible poses. The *Wayfarer* and the *Stalwart* lay low in the sea, and the fires upon them were still flaring up here and there. Groups of the still-unidentified crew were busy trying to put them out before the flames licked their way over to their own ships. Weapons, bone, and organs littered the decks, which were awash in blood. Slaves walked vacantly amid the carnage, staring at nothing. Others simply sat on the bloody decks, sobbing in horror and gratitude. Some of the victorious fighters were already looting the two slave ships, loading their bounty of humans, food, and water aboard the three mysterious frigates.

In one corner of the aft deck of the *Wayfarer*, part of the crew that had saved them were busy lining up the surviving captive slavers, forcing them to their knees, and beheading them one by one. The bodies and heads were thrown overboard. Drawn by the blood, packs of sharks had begun to form, their dorsal fins curving ominously through the waves.

At first Tristan's heart recoiled at the casual beheading of the demonslavers, and he gave momentary thought to trying to stop it. But then he remembered that he wasn't in charge here. He finally decided that after witnessing all of the brutality the slavers were capable of, he simply didn't care what happened to them.

He walked on, deciding that he had to discover who was in command. Surely this group of saviors would have a captain, and Tristan was anxious to meet him.

Then one of the men who had helped free them began rounding up the slaves. In a firm, controlled voice he told them to walk to the bow deck of *The People's Revenge,* the ship still barring their way. There they were to await further orders. Tristan soon found himself among a trudging crowd of slaves as the pitiful mass of humanity slowly made its way across a gangplank and aboard the mysterious frigate.

The crowd quickly became huge, and at first Tristan couldn't see what was occurring. After a time he could tell that the slaves were being asked to come forward one by one, to be viewed by the captain, who was seated in a red-upholstered, high-backed chair that had been brought up on deck. After the captain had carefully looked at a slave, he would then motion him or her to one side, to receive food, water, and better clothing.

Tristan desperately wanted to tell the captain who he was and request that he take him to Tammerland as soon as possible. However, he was reticent about revealing his identity to a stranger. As he neared, he decided to ask for a private meeting.

At last Tristan's turn arrived. He stepped forward, he looked up, and his jaw dropped.

The captain was a woman.

Stunned, Tristan looked again. He had at first mistaken her for a man, due to her short hair and manner of dress. She sat very casually in the high-backed chair, with one long leg thrown up over one of its arms. She wore battered black knee boots. Tight breeches of brown and tan vertical stripes ran high up her waist, ending just short of her breasts. One of the demonslaver's short swords hung low on her hips, from a wide leather belt that stretched suggestively from the top of the right hip to the lower part of the left. Blood still dripped from its hilt, telling Tristan that she had done more than simply give orders this day. Her stiff, brown leather jacket was buttoned about halfway up. It was topped with an open, equally stiff collar that ran up around the back of her neck in a semicircle that reached almost as high as her earlobes.

Her face was pretty, but also conveyed a strong sense of power. Dark, fine brows, arched over large, expressive blue eyes with exceptionally long lashes. Her nose was short and straight; her lips were red and full. The unusually short, dark brown hair was some sort of outrageous, urchinlike affair that went every which way. It was almost as though she either had no conception of how to wear it, or didn't much care how it looked. For some reason, Tristan thought it was the latter. From each of her earlobes dangled large gold hoops. The scarred giant who had saved

Tristan's life stood obediently by her side, his arms folded over his great, barrel chest.

She looked the prince over quietly for a moment, taking in his unusual clothes, scraggly beard, and dark blue eyes. Apparently unimpressed, she then motioned for him to move to one side and join the other slaves she had already examined. But Tristan knew he must speak to her now, or he might never get another chance. For better or worse, he decided to stand his ground.

"I must speak with you, Captain!" he said loudly as one of her crew tried to lead him away. At first he didn't resist. He still had the sword, but he didn't want to cause trouble unless he had to. "I have information that is vital to us both! You simply must hear me out!"

She leveled her blue eyes at him. "I feel sorry for you all, but have no time to hear individual stories," she said calmly. Her voice was smooth, and had a sort of smoky sensuality about it. With a nod from her, two more of her crew began to take him away.

But as they turned Tristan around and began to push him to one side, he heard her voice ring out.

"Wait!"

Her crewmembers immediately stopped, and Tristan turned toward her again.

Stepping down from her chair, she walked around behind him. She closely examined the glowing blood that was dripping from his back, then placed a finger under his vest and touched one of his wounds lightly. Tristan cringed, but held his ground.

Removing her hand, she looked at the bizarre, azure blood on her fingertips. Saying nothing, she turned and motioned for the giant to come to her. He was there in an instant. As he leaned over, she whispered something in his ear. The giant nodded and took Tristan by the arm. Looking up at the colossus, Tristan knew there would be no escape from him. With a single twist of his free hand, the giant took the prince's sword away and tossed it to the deck.

"This man is called Scars," she told Tristan quietly. "The reasons why should be obvious. He is my first mate. He will escort you to other quarters, where you will bathe and shave. Then I will speak to you."

Tristan tried to take a step forward, if for no other reason than to test the strength of the one called Scars. But it was like being locked in an iron vise. "I don't need to be treated any differently than the others," he protested. "But it is imperative that you and I speak." He looked back up at the giant, then at the captain again. "Preferably in private."

He thought he saw a hint of a smile cross her lips. But if so, it vanished just as quickly. Saying nothing more, she indicated to Scars that the prince should be taken away.

Scars lifted Tristan to his toes as if he weighed nothing, and literally danced him across the deck like a marionette. As he took the prince down a stairway leading to the lower decks of *The People's Revenge,* the captain took her chair and resumed her odd process of reviewing each and every slave.

The quarters Scars led Tristan to were humble, but after life as a slave, they seemed as luxurious as anything in the royal palace. There was a bed, a tub, and a washstand containing shaving things. There was also a mirror and a porthole. After some crewmen brought water and filled the tub, the first thing the prince did was remove his right boot and make sure he still had the brain hook and the piece of mysterious parchment.

Setting the weapon aside, he unrolled the parchment and turned it to the light of the window.

There was no writing on it. It was very old and yellowed, and he felt certain somehow that it had come from the Scroll of the Vagaries. But who had put it there?

However it had gotten there, he knew it must be taken to the wizards at once—and it was up to him to find a way to make that happen, without letting anyone else know that it existed. Wondering how he would ever manage such a thing, he carefully replaced both the brain hook and the parchment back into the boot.

Then he removed his other boot and the rest of his clothes and set about shaving and bathing, trying to pay special attention to the wounds on his back. Tending them hurt terribly, but it had to be done. Just as he was finishing he felt *The People's Revenge* lurch, and he knew they were leaving the scene of the battle.

As he dressed, he wondered two things. First, he wanted to know where his own weapons were. Had they been found? He always felt naked without them, and now was no exception. Second, was Scars still outside in the hallway, waiting for him? That question, at least, was easily answered. Opening the cabin door, he saw the giant standing there quietly, arms folded over his huge chest.

Seeing Tristan, Scars solemnly pointed back the way they had come, and shortly they were topside again. The sunlight and breeze felt good on the prince's freshly shaven face.

Things had changed drastically in the short time he had been below. *The People's Revenge,* flanked by her two sister ships, was headed west at full sail, her ragged crewmen swarming over her like an army of busy ants. Back to the east, clouds of smoke billowed on the horizon. Tristan respected this female captain, whoever she was.

As Scars led him aft, he looked over the men who had saved his life. They were definitely a ragtag group. Their clothes were torn and bloodied, and many of them wore colorful bandanas on their heads. Earrings occasionally dangled alongside their faces, which were more often than not covered by beards and mustaches. Each man seemed to bristle with weapons, and most of them had the hardened, weathered look of those who had spent most of their lives at sea. Tristan had never heard of pirates running the Sea of Whispers. These men certainly looked the part, though.

Scars led Tristan past the ship's wheel and down another flight of stairs. Finally the giant stopped before large double doors. After knocking once he waited for the reply, then opened the doors and ushered Tristan inside.

The prince was surprised at the size and beauty of the room. Curved, stained-glass windows lined the entire stern wall and had been opened, filling the space with dappled sunlight bouncing off the waves. Ornate, gilt-edged scrollwork lined the corners of the ceiling and the window frames; the floor was covered with patterned rugs. A huge desk and several chairs sat just forward of the windows. A luxurious four-poster bed filled one wall, next to the open door to what looked to be a private washroom. The room smelled faintly of wine, smoke, and fresh salt air.

The captain sat at the great desk, poring over several charts. Her sword and baldric were slung over the high, upholstered back of her chair. On the desk were a large wheel of cheese with a knife stuck in it and a broken loaf of bread, accompanied by a half-consumed bottle of red wine. Tristan suddenly realized how long it had been since he had last eaten.

Finally, the captain looked up. Saying nothing, she indicated an empty chair on Tristan's side of the desk.

"I'd rather stand," he said wryly. "I've had quite enough of sitting down for a while."

The captain gave Scars a look, and the giant picked Tristan up in both arms and unceremoniously dumped him into the leather chair as if he were a rag doll.

Wincing at the fresh pain in his back, the prince scowled. "Doesn't he ever talk?" he asked angrily.

The captain actually smiled. She looked up at Scars. "You may leave us," she said simply. "I think I can handle whatever might arise."

"Are you sure, Captain?" the giant replied. His speaking voice was unexpectedly elegant. "His manner seems quite uncivilized to me."

Scars' diction was eloquent and educated, at odds with his rough appearance.

"Yes, I'm certain," she answered. "But if it makes you feel better, you may stand just outside the door."

Scars gave Tristan a distinct look of warning, then went to the double doors. As he walked through them, his body seemed to take up the entire doorway. Then the doors closed quietly behind him, and Tristan and the captain were alone.

She wasted no time. "Now, then, who are you?" she asked. "You clean up nicely. But I have never seen blue, glowing blood before. It's quite unique."

Tristan thought for a moment. Something inside still made him reticent about telling her who he was. But he suspected that if he was ever going to get home, he would probably have to be at least partly honest with her. Taking a deep breath, he looked intently into her eyes.

"I am Tristan, crown prince of Eutracia," he said firmly. "Son of Nicholas and Morganna, now dead. My blood glows because I am of the craft of magic."

This time the captain's smile was followed by outright, derisive laughter. "But of course you are! The crown prince—here on my ship! How amazing! Perhaps I should bow!"

He scowled. "You don't believe me."

Her face suddenly became more serious. "Actually, I do," she answered. Opening a drawer, she produced a parchment. It was rolled up and tied with a ribbon. She casually tossed it across the desk. Reaching out, Tristan took it and opened it.

It was a copy of one of the wanted posters of him that his son Nicholas had ordered distributed across Eutracia before he died at the Gates of Dawn. Tristan looked back up at her.

"It's a good likeness, don't you think?" she asked. "And we've recovered some weapons like those shown in the portrait." She paused for a moment, thinking. "This proves an interesting situation, I must say. I might just turn you in and claim the reward myself. One hundred thousand kisa is a great deal of money, and my men have not been paid in some time."

Tristan tossed the awful warrant back onto her desk. "I'm sorry to disappoint you, but the reward no longer exists," he answered. "The one who was distributing the posters is now dead."

"Really?" she asked. It was clear she remained unconvinced. "What happened to him?"

Tristan's jaw hardened. "I found him first."

Unperturbed, the captain put one long leg up on the desk, then crossed the other over it. Reaching out, she grasped an ornate, inlaid wooden box and pulled it toward her. From the box she produced a cigarillo rolled of some type of dark plant leaf. Pulling an oil lamp near, she placed the tube in her mouth, lit the end, and blew the smoke down through her nose. Finally she looked back at him.

"From what city were you taken?" she asked. "And tell me, is it really true that you murdered your own father, and also oversaw the murders of the entire Directorate of Wizards, as this poster says? My, my, but you *have* been a bad boy. You might fit in well here."

Tristan was growing angrier by the moment. Despite the fact that she had saved him and the other slaves, that wasn't enough to make him trust her. He was tired of her insults, and he desperately wanted some answers of his own.

"You first," he said. "Who in the name of the Afterlife are you? And what gives you the right to fly my battle flag?"

Calmly drawing in more smoke, she raised her face and blew it toward the ceiling. As she did, Tristan watched it disappear into the salt-laden air. "I am Teresa of the House of Welborne," she answered calmly. "My friends call me Tyranny."

"Tyranny?"

"Yes." She smiled. "Apparently I was quite a handful when I was growing up. My late father jokingly bastardized 'Teresa' into 'Tyranny,' and it stuck. My mother never forgave him. But then again, I always was more tomboy than dainty little girl."

Leaning forward in his chair, Tristan decided to press. "You're look-ing for someone, aren't you?" he asked. "That's why you and your ships are out here, plowing up and down the Sea of Whispers. It's also why you lined up all the slaves—in hopes of finding whoever it is you're looking for."

He could tell he had struck a nerve. But he also realized that if he ever wanted to get home, now might be a good time for some flattery.

"And by the way," he added quietly, "the blood I saw on the hilt of your sword tells me that you do more than simply give orders. Well done."

Tyranny's eyes narrowed. "You catch on quickly," she answered. "My older brother was taken by the demonslavers one night. Both my parents were killed trying to fight them off and give me time to escape. We lived in Farpoint—where most of the slaving activity seems to be taking place. My father owned the largest fleet of fishing vessels in the city, and I used to work with him. I have been looking for my brother ever since, and I won't stop until I find him."

"That explains your familiarity with these waters," Tristan mused. "And Scars?" he asked. "I have never seen anyone quite like him. Where did he come from?"

"Scars was one of my father's most trusted employees," she answered. "We grew up together. He got his wounds and his huge muscles from wrestling live sharks out of the sea for fun, from my father's boats. He loved my father dearly, and he would die for me. And he can tear a demonslaver apart with his bare hands."

"Tell me," Tristan asked, "do you know how to safely cross the Sea of Whispers? Have you ever done so?"

"I do know," she answered. "And we have. We tortured the information out of one of the captured demonslavers. They're a tough lot, but time spent with Scars can be very effective. It seems that with the death of the Coven of Sorceresses, the Necrophagians are now willing to accept their grisly tribute from anyone who wants to cross—provided the dead bodies are sufficient in number, of course. We used the demonslaver bodies as payment, but we have only done so once. And I certainly don't recommend it." Casually, she lifted her glass and took a sip of wine.

"Would you like some?" she asked, and nodded toward an empty glass. It seemed her demeanor was starting to soften.

Too thirsty to stand on ceremony, Tristan took the glass and poured himself some wine. He drank it down in a single draft, then poured another and sat back in his chair.

"Where did this crew of yours come from?" he asked. "How do you pay them? And how did you come by these ships?"

"My crew is a combination of my father's old employees and other men who asked to join us after my reputation began to grow," she answered. "As you might imagine, many of them are also looking for lost friends or relatives, and what better way to do it than this? They have become a ruthless and determined lot, I can assure you." Pausing, she took another sip of the wine, then another lungful of smoke. She hissed what remained of the smoke toward the ceiling.

"As for their pay and food, both come from the kisa and provisions usually given us by grateful family members, when we return their loved ones to them," she continued. "I don't demand such payment, but I don't refuse it, either. After all, this operation has to run on something besides altruism, wouldn't you agree? How I got my ships is another story. The first belonged to my father. We renamed her *The People's Revenge* and went from there. The two other frigates that now sail alongside us are both slaver conquests."

Tristan stared at her, even further impressed by this strong-willed woman. He thought for a moment, and then decided to take a risk.

"Do you know a man named Krassus, or a woman named Grizelda?" he asked. "Or have you ever heard of documents called the Scrolls of the Ancients?"

Tyranny shook her head.

"Have you ever encountered a slave named Wulfgar?"

"No," she answered. "Why do you ask?"

"They're people and things I am searching for, much the same way you search for your brother," he said as nonchalantly as he could. He decided to change the subject. "Do you know why these demonslavers are taking our people?" Again she shook her head. Then Tristan thought of something else.

"Have you ever heard of a place called the Citadel?" he asked. He fully expected her to say she had not, but her face darkened.

"Not only have I heard of it, but I have seen it," she answered solemnly. "It's an island to the east, with a huge stone fortress atop it—a massive, forbidding place hewn directly from the living rock that makes up the island. It looks ancient. We learned of its location from a captured demonslaver. I have even charted its location on my maps. We decided to go there, and actually got to within half a league of it before being forced to turn back. The waters surrounding the Citadel are swarming with slaver ships. After they saw us, we came about and barely got away with our lives."

It was clear that despite her bravado, Tyranny's experience with the Citadel had had a strong effect upon her. And Tristan was by now quite sure she was a woman who was not easily frightened. Fascinated, he leaned forward in his chair.

"Could you lead another fleet there if you had to?" he asked eagerly. "Do you really know the way?"

"Of course," she answered. "I know this ocean as well as anyone alive. But hear me well: Going there is blatant suicide."

Tristan looked at her for a long moment, absorbing all that he had just heard. The breeze from the open windows wafted through the room, gently moving her scruffy dark hair, and her blue eyes continued to regard him with confidence. A slight smile came to his lips. "So you're really a pirate?" he asked.

Tyranny smiled. "We prefer to think of ourselves as privateers, doing the work that the vanquished monarchy no longer can. We would, of course, prefer to do so under authenticated letters of marque, but the king and the wizards who might have granted them to us are now all dead."

"Letters of marque?" Tristan repeated quizzically.

"For the crown prince of Eutracia, you don't seem to know much about your own history," she quipped. "Letters of marque were papers granted by the wizards to privateers during the Sorceresses' War. These documents gave official sanction to the raiding of the Coven's vessels and the killing of their servants. They also allowed the privateer to legally keep a portion of any of the booty recovered. It was a very nice arrangement, actually. The wizards didn't have to dirty their hands, and a brave, enterprising privateer could do very well. It was almost impossible to take a ship that had a sorceress aboard, of course. But if one could be found manned only by blood stalkers or unendowed humans who had been pressed into the Coven's service, it could be a great prize indeed, for the sorceresses' ships often carried treasure. But those days are long gone, I'm afraid."

"How do you know all of this?" Tristan asked.

"Some of the original privateers of the Sorceresses' War were my forebears," she answered, then inhaled more of the smoke. Leaning back, she arched her back like a cat and adjusted her slim frame slightly in the chair. "When the war ended, their continuing love for the ocean turned them into fishermen. Not as exciting, but infinitely safer. You also might enjoy knowing that the *Resolve,* the vessel the lead wizard supposedly used to banish the Coven to the Sea of Whispers, was owned by the last of my privateering grandfathers and was loaned to the newly formed Directorate for just that purpose. Her ship's wheel was taken from her and handed down through the generations. It means a great deal to me, and is now the same one that guides this ship."

Tristan smiled and shook his head. "And you run my battle flag," he mused. "The lion and the broadsword. Where did you get it?"

"That was simple," she replied. "Unfortunately, since the destruction caused by the Coven, your flag can often be found needful of a place to fly. Besides, what other banner should we run in our fight against the demonslavers? I love my country."

Leaning forward, Tristan placed his glass on the desk. He wasn't sure he could trust her, but he had no other choice. He looked meaningfully into Tyranny's wide, blue eyes.

"How would you like to make more kisa than you've ever seen in your entire life?" he asked quietly.

"Just now you're in no position to pay such a sum," she answered. "And you're in no position to ask for any favors, either." Another puff of bluish smoke poured out her nose.

"But my wizards are," he answered. "And all you would have to do is take me to the Cavalon Delta and release me. From there, you and I could easily make our way to Tammerland, where you would be paid. No harm would befall you, and my wizards would be most appreciative, I assure you. With a word from me, they could conjure enough kisa to sink this ship; certainly more than enough to allow you to continue to look for your brother, and to do so for as long as you need to. We might even be able to help you find him."

Tyranny removed her long legs from the desk and sat upright in her chair. She ran a quick hand through her short hair, tousling it even further. "The wizards are all dead; everybody knows that," she answered skeptically, shaking her head. "This is just a trick to secure your release."

"The reported deaths of the wizards were not entirely true," Tristan countered. "Wigg, the lead wizard, still lives. As does another named Faegan. In fact, I believe they would be happy to hear about what you have been doing. I might even be able to convince them to give you your letters of marque and recognize you officially, if it means that much to you."

Then he sat back, desperately hoping his offer was enough. He simply had to get back to Tammerland and give the wizards the scrap of parchment hidden in his boot.

He could see that Tyranny was sorely tempted.

"If I were to do this thing, my price would be the one hundred thousand kisa that were supposedly offered by the warrant," she said craftily. "And I would also require some form of collateral against the possibility that you're lying. In that regard, I think the medallion hanging around your neck would do nicely. The quality of its gold appears to be particularly high. Melted down, it would go a long way toward convincing me."

Tristan looked down at the medallion. He saw that he had little other choice. He looked back up at Tyranny with determined eyes.

"I agree," he said quietly. "But I have conditions."

"Conditions?" Tyranny asked. "I could just have Scars come in and take the medallion from you, you know, then set sail for any place I choose."

"Yes," he answered. "But I don't think you will. Something about honor among thieves."

Silence reigned for a moment, their eyes locked together in a battle of wills.

"What are your conditions?" she asked finally, leaning her arms on the desk.

"No detours—we sail directly to the Cavalon Delta," he answered. "If other slave ships are sighted on the way, you do not engage them. You are also to return my weapons to me, and keep my real identity a secret on this ship. In addition, when we reach the palace you will draw a chart for my wizards, showing them the exact location of the Citadel. And there is one other thing," he added.

Tyranny's blue eyes narrowed. It was clear she wasn't used to demands. "And that is?"

"You allow me to wear my medallion until our business is concluded, either one way or another."

Tyranny leaned back in her chair. "You demand a great deal," she said.

"One hundred thousand kisa is a great deal of money," he answered. He purposely let his words hang in the air for a moment. "From our current position, how long before we could reach the delta?"

She looked down at one of her charts. "If the winds hold, six days."

Silence engulfed the room. Tristan held his breath, wondering what her answer would be.

Finally she stood. Raising her right hand, she spat into her palm and held it out. "Done," she said. Standing up as well, Tristan looked at her quizzically.

"It's the way a privateer's bargain was sealed in the old days," Tyranny said with a wry smile. "And it remains the best." She held her hand out a bit farther.

Smiling, Tristan spat into his right hand, and took hers into it. "And done," he answered back. For the first time since entering the room, he thought he might be able to trust her. But only time would tell.

Tyranny pulled a small piece of parchment toward her, took up a quill, and began to write out their agreement. She handed it over to Tristan, and he read it. Like its author, it came straight to the point. Picking up the quill, Tristan signed it with a false name, then handed it back to her.

Studying the fresh signature, Tyranny raised an eyebrow. "This is not who you said you were."

"I also told you that I did not want your crew to know who I am," Tristan replied calmly. "You've already shown me the warrant and threatened to turn me in for the reward. What kind of fool would I be if I added my real signature to your documents, as well? Don't worry— there's no place for me to run to. When you come before my wizards, you will have your kisa, I assure you. And if I'm lying, you and that monster first mate of yours can easily kill me. You still have a fortune to win and nothing to lose. Take it or leave it."

After thinking for a moment, Tyranny finally countersigned the agreement, folded the parchment, and slipped it between her breasts. She then called for Scars. The double doors blew open, and the giant was by her side in a flash.

"Return this man's weapons to him," she ordered. "He is one of us now. And change course for the Cavalon Delta at full sail. We have new business there." Then she looked at Tristan.

"Here's the first rule of *The People's Revenge*," she said. "If you are going to eat our food, you must work for it—regardless of what other circumstances might prevail between us. Scars, take him topside and feed him. Then give him something to do. Perhaps we can make a privateer out of him yet."

"Agreed," Tristan answered.

Without further fanfare, Scars escorted the prince from the room.

Standing, Tyranny went to the windows and looked out on the restless sea. Sensing *The People's Revenge* heel over to her new course, she smiled.

Twenty-five

Twenty-Nine watched as his fellow slave pounded the hammer down on the glowing strip of red-hot metal. Then he heard the hiss and saw the steam rise as the man plunged the strip back into the brackish water, tempering it again. The emerging blade would soon become the business end of a short sword and be added to the heap of homely but effective weapons already lying in the far corner of the room.

Other slaves went about fashioning hilts and guards, while still others sharpened and polished the blades. Then the parts would be assembled into the double-edged, razor-sharp swords carried by the demonslavers. On the opposite side of the room, another group of slaves sat fashioning leather into scabbards and baldrics. Periodically a slaver would come in to choose a weapon from the pile of new swords, and tridents.

Twenty-Nine hung his head, still unable to believe that he was plying his craft—which had always been his pride and his passion—for the benefit of these evil monsters.

The simple stone chamber in which he worked was very large and had been hewn directly from the rock, just as the docks had been. A great hole had been fashioned in its ceiling to allow the escape of the smoke generated by the ever-busy hearths. Light was supplied both by the massive oil sconces on the walls, and the surging glow of the orange-red coals. The raucous clanging of the hammers against anvils never seemed to stop, and armed demonslavers paced slowly, watching every move of the hundred or so slaves who toiled here. The room smelled of sweat, soot, and hot iron.

Twenty-Nine remembered when Janus and several of his monstrous servants had first come to where he and his fellow *Talis* slaves were being held, and demanded to know what their various trades had been. It was a day he would never forget. If they were leathersmiths or weapons makers, the freak had said, then their lives could soon become much easier. There was no point in lying, he had added, for the men in the dark blue robes could enter minds and read the truth. Punishment would be instant death.

And so, hoping that Janus' promises would somehow hold true, Twenty-Nine and a number of others had raised their hands. It was not long until they all wished they had not.

He looked down at his gnarled, broken hands, knowing that even though he could never properly wield a hammer again, he still carried within him an exquisite, uncommon knowledge of the craft of sword making. Even at the relatively young age of thirty-three Seasons of New Life, he had amassed far greater skill than most of the graybeards who had been fashioning swords their entire lives.

He had owned one of the most prestigious weapons shops in all of Eutracia, and had employed over one hundred artisans, all of them serving under his personal mentorship. He had been one of the largest suppliers of arms to the royal guard, and had even been asked from time to time to craft special ceremonial weapons for the royal house. But those days were long gone, due to the destruction of the Royal Guard at the hands of the winged ones that were rumored to have come from across the sea. Without the continued support of the monarchy, his shop had fallen on hard times.

Then he had been captured and brought to the Citadel. Ironically, some of the very men he had employed in his shop now labored with him here in this living nightmare. And knowing them as he did, Twenty-Nine could tell that they were as ashamed of their work as he was. But once a person was assigned to this area, there was no going back. And Janus had lied to them, for this was a harsher existence than the one they had left behind in the cages.

When they had first been brought here and told that it would be their job to produce arms for the demonslavers, many of them had refused—himself included. Janus had simply smiled and marched in another group of fresh *Talis* slaves. Then he had calmly ordered his demonslavers to behead them, as casually as though he had been speaking about the weather.

From then on, he had said, every time a craftsman slowed in his production or objected to his duties, the number of deaths would double, and then double again. And so they had grudgingly gone about their work. After repeated questioning by Janus regarding their various histories and abilities, Twenty-Nine had been singled out to oversee the labors of all the others and take ultimate responsibility for the quality of the weapons they made.

He yearned to fight back, but he didn't know how. He knew his ruined hands could never effectively employ a sword against the slavers. Even if he and his fellow slaves did manage to take up arms, there were more than enough guards stationed in this room alone to cut them to ribbons. But there was one way to hurt them, he realized.

He would take his own life.

For he was the glue that held the workers together and kept them productive. Without his presence the quality of the weapons would suffer drastically. That would not only hurt the demonslavers' cause, but perhaps even take a few of them when it came time for them to fight. How he wished he could see that day! But he would have to be satisfied with merely taking such knowledge to his grave.

His mood darkened even further as he looked around. Twenty-Nine had always been an honorable man, making superb weapons for the justifiable defense of his nation. This was different. This was the forced production of homely, crude instruments meant for little more than outright butchery of the innocent. And he would have no more of it. Today would be the day.

He began making his way toward the pile of finished weapons in the corner. He was careful to give the appearance of wanting to inspect several of them, as had become his custom. It would not raise any suspicion until it was too late.

Picking up one of the short swords, he felt as much as saw the watchful eyes of several of the demonslavers on him. Taking a deep breath, Twenty-Nine drew the sword and dropped the scabbard to the floor.

Holding the weapon between both palms without wrapping his fingers around it, Twenty-Nine let the blade's point fall to the floor and bobbed it up and down a bit, testing its balance. Then he grasped the hilt as best his damaged hands would allow, turning it this way and that so as to inspect the crazing on either side of the blade. Satisfied, he gently ran his thumb over one edge at a time, testing the sharpness. Finally he grasped the handle and turned the blade around, extending it as far from his body as he could, its point squarely directed toward his chest and only inches from his skin. Then he made a great show of examining the blood groove for uniformity, just as he had already done hundreds of times before in this awful place. By now his tortured hands had begun to shake, and he desperately hoped he wasn't about to give himself away.

As he closed his eyes he held the sword as rigidly before him as possible and let his knees collapse.

But as he started to drop a strange whirring passed by his right ear. He felt a huge impact against the blade of the sword; heard an awful, ear-splitting clang.

Surprised, he opened his eyes and stopped his fall just in time to see the blade go flying against the far wall, then crash harmlessly to the stone floor. Janus' black-and-white iron spheres, tangled with it, had not only pulled the sword from his hands, but had also cleanly broken its blade in half. The weapon that was to have been both his salvation and his personal revenge on the demonslavers now lay in a broken, useless heap.

Demonslavers grabbed him by either arm and held him tight. He knew what to expect. Janus was standing on the opposite side of the room, gloating. Twenty-Nine hadn't seen him there.

Saying nothing, Janus walked over to where the damaged sword lay and unwound his weapon from the broken blade. Smiling again, he coiled up the black-and-white line and replaced it upon his belt.

With a single, vicious swipe, Janus struck Twenty-Nine across the face. Groaning softly, Twenty-Nine hung drunkenly between the slavers, trying to regain his focus. Janus grasped Twenty-Nine's chin and raised the slave's face up to his own.

"Did you really think it would be so easy?" he asked sarcastically. "You will never be allowed to die until we dictate it, of that I can assure you. But have no fear. Before we are finished with all of you, you will beg us for your deaths. And we will give them to you."

He looked at the two slavers holding Twenty-Nine.

"From now on, his hands are to be bound behind his back at all times," he sneered. "Even when he is sleeping. The others shall hold the weapons for him to inspect. When it comes time for him to eat, one of you shall feed him." Then Janus turned to look at a door at the far end of the room. "As an added incentive to behave, I think we should show this one a bit more of what actually goes on here behind closed doors."

Janus sauntered to the heavy stone door and opened it. "Bring him," he said casually over his shoulder.

The slavers lifted Twenty-Nine and dragged him toward it on his toes. As the remaining slaves and demonslavers watched, the four of them went through. The door closed behind them.

Still dazed, held upright by the slavers, Twenty-Nine at first couldn't make out the scene before him. But he could hear the insane pleading and screaming well enough. It was coming from men and women alike, and never seemed to pause. As his vision swam into focus, he raised his head and looked.

The first thing he did was scream. Then warm urine ran uncontrollably down the insides of his thighs, forming a puddle at his feet.

Closing his eyes, Twenty-Nine tried desperately to free himself from the slavers and bolt for the door, but he was powerless in their grip. He began to tremble, and then to cry.

"Hold him!" Janus ordered. Removing an ornate dagger from his belt, he came to stand before Twenty-Nine and placed the cool, sharp tip of the blade to the blacksmith's throat. Cold sweat beaded on Twenty-Nine's forehead.

"Either look at what I brought you here to see, or join those in this room," Janus said softly, menacingly. "The same fate awaits you should you shirk your labors or try to take your life again. Do you understand?"

Twenty-Nine opened his eyes. As he did, the men in the dark blue robes he had seen at the docks looked calmly back at him from their slow, deliberate labors. Several of them smiled.

Another, even more terrified scream came from him, mixing with the others still echoing horrifically through the room.

Finally he could take no more. He felt his mind slipping, and he fainted away, hanging limply in the grasp of the demonslavers.

Smiling, Janus put away his knife.

PART III

Regret

Twenty-six

"Regret . . . such a simple, easy word to say. And yet—for so many of us—so difficult to dismiss from our memories. What other single word conjures up not only such sublime sorrow, but also the sweet, forlorn loss of what might have been? Act upon act, regret upon regret, turning with the time enchantments forever. Even so, it is not the wise man who casts away such memories, but rather the foolish one."

—FROM THE PERSONAL DIARIES OF WIGG, ONETIME LEAD WIZARD OF
THE DIRECTORATE OF WIZARDS

"Lately I have noticed a distinct twinkle in your eye that I had not seen since my return to Tammerland," Faegan told Wigg wryly, with a wink and a smile as the Minion litter bounced them along through the sky. "My compliments, by the way. While it's true she and I have had our differences regarding the art of herbmastery, Abbey is certainly a lovely and intelligent woman. You're a very lucky man."

Wigg pursed his lips, then turned from the window to scowl at the wizard sitting across from him. The morning air was cold at this altitude, and Wigg defiantly thrust his hands into the sleeves of his robe to warm them. He hoped they would arrive at the coast soon.

Wigg had expected Faegan to bring up the subject of his relationship with Abbey long before this, especially given the way the other wizard loved to tease him. At least Faegan had chosen a private moment between them to broach the subject.

Sighing, Wigg pushed his tongue against the inside of one cheek. "Is it that obvious?" he asked back.

"Oh, yes," Faegan answered happily. "There is a boyish spring in your step and a recurring smile on your face that I have not seen for three centuries. The others may not notice, but I do."

"Abbey and I would very much like to leave the others uninformed. At least for the time being," Wigg said sternly. His face reddened uncharacteristically.

"I understand completely," Faegan said, smiling mischievously.

Shaking his head, Wigg gave a short, derisive snort and returned to watching the ribbon of the Sippora River snaking through the landscape far below.

They had been traveling for the better part of two hours and were very close to their destination. Their goal was to reach the coast by midday. Ox flew point a short distance ahead, while six other Minions carried the litter through the air and four more flew guard. The morning was bright, cold, and cloudless, and the lush greenery of the Eutracian landscape passed below them peacefully, belying the many troubles the nation still suffered.

Suddenly the litter banked to the left and began to lose altitude. Through the window, the jagged coastline could be seen, stony cliffs constantly bombarded by the froth-tipped waves of the Sea of Whispers.

Then Wigg finally saw it: the smooth formation of stone that legend said had been carved out by the restless sea. Shouting out to the Minions, he ordered them to fly up to it and hover just above the waves.

Both wizards gazed silently at the dark, majestic stone face. It was not a new sight for them—the Woman of Stone had long been an attraction of some note for Eutracian citizens—but no matter how many times one had seen it, viewing it was always an eerie, awe-inspiring experience. Especially now, given the revelation that the image before them apparently held far more secrets than anyone had previously imagined.

Wigg opened the door of the litter and stepped out into the air, using the craft to hover just above the waves by the imposing edifice. Faegan levitated his chair, exited the litter, and glided up alongside him. The roaring ocean below splashed constantly against the slick stone, and the sea wind pestered the wizards, snatching at their robes and hair. Looking up, Wigg beckoned to Ox to come lower.

"Order the litter to the cliffs, and wait for us there," he shouted against the sound of the sea. "There's no telling how long we might be. If the provisions in the litter run out, order some of the warriors back to the palace for more, or hunt for what you need. But I want at least enough of you here at all times to carry the litter when we come back out."

Wigg looked back to the edifice, and his jaw hardened. "*If* we come back out, that is."

Nodding, Ox turned away to carry out his orders. The cold, salty wind continued to whip at the wizards as they hovered just feet above the angry waves. Wigg looked at the Woman of Stone again.

The face was large—at least ten meters high and another four or five meters across—and impressive. Beautiful, but at the same time commanding. Long strands of stone hair hung down past the shoulders to descend into the sea, and the huge eyes lay peacefully closed behind heavy, seductive lids. The nose was slim; the lips were both sensuous and inviting; the cheekbones were high and elegant. Black as night and polished to a smooth luster by the sea, she seemed the very picture of serene, detached femininity.

Whether a face of such elegance and detail could have been carved naturally from the waves had been a great subject of debate for as long as Eutracia had existed. There was a distinct minority who insisted she must be a purely natural phenomenon—a freak of nature, as it were. Most, however, argued that she was far too refined, far too perfect to be an accident, and must therefore be the result of some arcane use of the craft from eons earlier. Wigg was entirely convinced it was the latter.

Wigg looked over to Faegan to comment on the beauty of the face, and stopped, stunned.

The Paragon was glowing.

The square-cut, bloodred jewel of the craft lying about Faegan's neck had always seemed to have a life of its own and tended to be faintly luminous no matter the time of day or the circumstances surrounding it. But this was incredible. The jewel was glowing with blinding red light.

Suddenly, without warning, two narrow, perfectly straight beams shot from the Paragon and tore toward the Stone Woman's eyes. Wigg and Faegan hovered, speechless, wondering what would happen next.

Then, as abruptly as they had appeared, the beams vanished, and the jewel returned to normal. Baffled, the two wizards looked at each other, then back at the Stone Woman.

The eyes were beginning to open.

Slowly, the huge, heavy lids parted, revealing piercing eyes of the most intense azure. The eyes regarded them calmly for a few moments; the lids gently blinked. And then the lips began to move.

"You are of the craft," the Stone Woman said, her words coming to them quite clearly over the pounding waves. Her voice was compassionate, yet strong. "You carry the Paragon, and so you may see me for what I truly am. Welcome, and well done."

Wigg found his voice first. "Who are you?" he asked. "Are you the watchwoman of the floating gardens?"

"No," she replied. "She awaits within. I am but one left by those you call the Ones Who Came Before. I oversee the first of the tests required to successfully enter and leave this Chamber of Penitence. Do you wish to enter?"

The lips closed again, and the amazing azure eyes continued to regard the two wizards in silence.

Fascinated, Faegan floated closer to the beautiful, dark face. "Yes," he said simply. "We wish to enter."

The stone lips parted again. "And do you both know that there is a psychic price to be paid for what can be learned here? Be warned, for it may be a demand that your human minds find too dear to survive."

"What is this psychic price?" Faegan asked.

"That is not my place to say," she answered softly. "The watchwoman of the gardens will tell you more, should I deign to let you enter."

"And how may we enter?" Wigg asked.

"You must pass my test," she answered. The beautiful face remained expressionless. "I must first be sure that you are not practitioners of the Vagaries. The knowledge kept within must never be allowed to pass into the hands of those who would prefer to practice the darker aspects of the craft."

For the first time she showed emotion, her lips turning up slightly at the corners. "There is still so much neither of you understand about the craft, or the true history of this land," she answered softly.

His eyes gleaming with curiosity, Faegan leaned forward in his chair. "Tell us more," he implored. "I beg you."

"No," she answered. "Educating you is not my mission. It is now time for you to be tested."

"What is it we must do?" Wigg asked.

"Nothing," she answered. "I shall do it all. Each of you please expose one of your wrists."

Wigg and Faegan did as she asked. Almost immediately the familiar, azure glow of the craft coalesced around their bare wrists. In each, a small incision appeared painlessly, allowing a single drop of blood to escape. As the incisions closed and the azure glow disappeared, the two blood droplets, hovering in the air, immediately began twisting into their respective blood signatures.

The eyes in the black face then narrowed slightly, and the glow of the craft appeared again, this time surrounding the two blood signatures. The signatures began to enlarge, until each of them was about two meters across in length.

Spellbound, the wizards stared in awe until the huge blood signatures faded and then disappeared.

"Clearly, you are both of the Vigors," the Stone Woman said. "So now it is time for you to decide. Do you still wish to enter this Chamber of Penitence?"

Faegan turned to the lead wizard. Wigg took a deep, apprehensive breath, then nodded. Faegan looked back into the lovely, azure eyes.

"We do," he said.

"Very well," she answered. "Behold."

Her mouth opened wider, exposing perfect, white teeth. Farther and farther her lips parted, until the opening was about two meters high. Only fathomless darkness could be seen beyond, its depths occasionally interrupted by haunting, eerie flashes of azure light, like lightning across a night sky. Then her eyes closed, and she remained still.

Faegan again looked at Wigg, who responded with a raised eyebrow. Without speaking further, the two wizards glided forward, entering the Chamber of Penitence.

From where they stood on the sea cliffs above, Ox and the other Minions of Day and Night watched in horror as the wizards disappeared into darkness and the lovely stone mouth closed behind them.

Twenty-seven

"I'm afraid, Marcus," Rebecca said quietly. "I've never done anything like this before. Are you sure this is going to work?"

She shivered in the cold of the early morning, as she held tightly onto her brother's strong, comforting hand. Her stomach growled again. She hadn't had enough to eat this morning, and this place Marcus had led her to scared her. Hoping her brother knew what he was doing, she limped alongside him through the human carnival known as Bargainer's Square.

With the demise of the Royal Guard, Bargainer's Square had become a hotbed of vice and crime. It seemed to Marcus as if all of the wicked of Eutracia had for some reason suddenly descended on this single spot. It had been Bargainer's Square where he had accidentally found himself the night he had narrowly evaded the old harlot and her partner, running for his life down the dark, lamplit street. But from that wayward experience had also come an unexpected blessing: the rug shop where he had finally stopped running to catch his breath.

He had taken little notice of it at the time, but now, two days later, he had suddenly realized how the little shop might be of great help with his problem regarding the scroll. And so he had visited the shop once it was open and had formulated his plan. Yesterday he had brazenly stolen the contents of the canvas bag now slung over his shoulder. Today he would act. Looking into 'Becca's trusting brown eyes, he gave her an encouraging smile.

"I know it's scary here," he said as he led her through the bizarre maze of people, noises, and vice. "And I'm sorry. But you must trust me.

I haven't steered us wrong yet, have I? Now stay close to me, keep your head down, and try not to talk. We don't need any undue attention."

Nodding and biting her lip, Rebecca tried to smile.

Bargainer's Square was actually a huge, circular plaza, paved with cobblestones. A great many streets opened onto the gathering place from various directions.

Shouting, cursing, and the smells of bad food and cheap liquor wafted on the breeze. Street vendors, each of them trying to holler louder than the next, filled the area. Virtually all of the men and many of the women were armed in some fashion. Seeing two children walking alone in this part of town was highly unusual, and many furtive, lecherous glances came their way. Whores, pimps, and male prostitutes stood on the corners, their leering smiles tacitly promising sex for money. Cockfights and dogfights could easily be found in the alleyways, with men and women crowded around them, eagerly throwing their money away.

Marcus gripped Rebecca's hand tighter, and they continued on.

When they reached the rug shop, he guided Rebecca to the other side of the busy street and into the opening of a relatively quiet alleyway. Peering out, he verified that the store was indeed open for business. From what he could see through the parted double doors, the shop already had a smattering of patrons inside, which he considered a good thing. When the time came, he would need all the distractions he could get.

Kneeling down before her, he pointed to the store. "That's it," he whispered. "I'll go inside first, while you wait here. After a few moments, if you don't see me come back out, walk in and begin doing as I instructed you. Keep one eye on me. When you see that I have gone, make your way out and meet me where I told you to, all right?"

Trying to be brave, Rebecca nodded. Giving her a final, encouraging smile, Marcus started across the street.

He approached the shop casually, and entered as nonchalantly as he could. Inside, the proprietor was going from one patron to another, eagerly explaining to them why he or she simply could not live another moment without one of his beautiful, most certainly inexpensive rugs. He was a stout man whom Marcus was sure wouldn't be able to run very well—yet another plus for choosing this place.

Marcus ambled over to a pile of rugs in one corner, his eyes going to the back of the shop. There was a short counter that ran partway across the back, leaving a space for access to the rear door. A brief smile crossed his lips: everything was in perfect order.

The rear door of the shop was wide open to allow a cooling morning draft for the heavy, already sweating proprietor, just as it had been the last time Marcus had visited here. The owner, it seemed, was nothing if not a creature of habit. Feeling the weight of the bag across his shoulder, Marcus thought of its contents and smiled again. Then, turning his head toward the door, he saw 'Becca enter the shop. She looked scared to death.

As her brown eyes finally found him, he winked at her, letting her know that he was about to proceed. Biting her lip again, she nodded back and walked near the proprietor, just as her brother had told her to do. Marcus then walked to one side a bit, to a little oasis of bare floor.

Slowly, carefully, he took the canvas bag from his shoulder. Making sure his back was to the others, he untied the top of the bag and turned it over. As the contents came falling out to the floor, he tossed the bag aside and quickly looked over at 'Becca. Then he winked again, telling her to start.

It has often been said that the high-pitched, earsplitting scream coming from a young girl is unequaled, and Rebecca's proved no exception. Taking great lungfuls of air, she screamed for all she was worth, sending shock waves through the little shop. The outcry was so piercing that at first Marcus thought the glass panes in the double doors might burst.

"Snakes!" Rebecca shrieked, pointing frantically across the room and jumping up onto one of the piles of rugs. She pointed again. "Big snakes!" Then, her eyes wide with false terror, she put her hands up to the sides of her head, jumped frantically up and down atop the pile of rugs, and let go another insane scream.

Pandemonium immediately engulfed the shop. A woman screamed and clambered onto the pile of rugs with Rebecca; then another joined them. Just as Marcus had hoped, the snakes quickly separated and began slithering across the floor, trying to find refuge among the piles of rugs or make for the freedom of the open doors. The startled patrons scattered. Women screamed; men simply stood there, frozen in horror.

The snakes Marcus had freed from the canvas bag were especially large, hungry, and highly agitated.

Long, thick, and brightly patterned, these snakes were known as slickribbons, and they were very quick. Marcus had boldly stolen an entire wire cage full of them from the front shelf of one of the exotic animal vendors in the square, and then had run for his life, narrowly avoiding being caught. Black, shiny, and menacing-looking, slickribbons had triangular yellow markings on their backs, making them highly prized for their skins. They were not venomous or harmful to humans in any way, but right now the terrified people in the shop didn't care about that. All they wanted to do—the proprietor included—was get out.

As the customers swarmed toward the front door, Marcus calmly picked up the rug he wanted. It was rolled up and secured by twine, but he guessed by its thickness and the length of the roll that its size would do for what he had planned. Hoisting it over one shoulder, he sauntered through the open back door and went out into the alley.

Walk, he reminded himself. *Walk as if you own this rug. Whatever you do, don't run.*

Suddenly enjoying herself immensely, Rebecca let out another ear-splitting scream just for fun, jumped down off the pile of rugs, and joined the rush for the open doors.

CHAPTER

Twenty-eight

Seated at the ancient, ornate desk in the Scriptorium of the Citadel, Krassus took a moment from his labors to enjoy the feeling of success. Four uneventful days of sailing had passed since he had cleverly avoided the unidentified frigates bearing down on him on the Sea of Whispers. Only an hour earlier he had descended the gangway of the *Sojourner* and been told by Janus that his consuls believed they had finally identified the bastard son of the late Queen Morganna. Overjoyed, Krassus had immediately come to the Scriptorium to examine the supposed authenticity of the blood signature for himself before going to view the prize from which it had come.

He carefully drew the tripod toward him yet again, then adjusted the parchment squarely under the crosshairs of the lens. This was the fourth time he had done so, as if with each new attempt the results would somehow change. But of course they hadn't. Having already compared the upper and lower shapes of the signature to those of Queen Morganna and Eric, her onetime lover, he looked down through the lens, no less stunned at what he saw this time than the times before.

Nicholas had told him that Wulfgar's signature would be a thing of wonder. But nothing had prepared Krassus for the likes of what now lay before him.

Never before had he seen such a left-leaning signature. Only two others were known to deviate so widely from the vertical axis. Those belonged to the Chosen Ones themselves, and they both leaned to the right.

Taking his eye from the lens, he looked at the assay mark written on the corner of the parchment: 1½. The blood quality was equal to that of Princess Shailiha, and second only to that of Tristan himself.

Krassus smiled. Janus and his consuls had been right. The slave this signature came from was indeed Wulfgar, the bastard son of Morganna.

Krassus now possessed not only the half sibling of the Chosen Ones, but also the Scroll of the Vagaries. Much of his work could finally go forward. If and when he got hold of the Scroll of the Vigors, he would be unstoppable.

He looked around this part of the Scriptorium. Built of the palest tan marble, the room was light and airy, and its floor was partially covered with highly patterned rugs. The stained-glass windows—now open to let in the sun and the salt air—were numerous. Bookcase after bookcase lined the walls. The texts and scrolls on their shelves were dusty from long neglect, but they would not remain that way much longer. The Scroll of the Vagaries lay nearby on another desk, the engraved gold band around its middle still tightly imprisoning the knowledge contained within.

Smiling, Krassus rose and walked out to the spacious balcony that overlooked the ocean. Standing there feeling the wind on his face, he thought of how honored he had been when Nicholas had told him of this place and what his mission would be. It had been eons since the Citadel had been inhabited and used for purposes of the craft. His endowed blood sang with the excitement that was soon to follow, and his pride at having been chosen as the new master of this fortress isle knew no bounds. For a moment, his mind turned back to the circumstances that had made it so.

He had been captured one day by Nicholas' great birds of prey, and then taken to the Caves of the Paragon, along with other consuls of the Redoubt. But as sole first alternate to the late Directorate of Wizards, Krassus had been kept isolated from Nicholas' other servants, and his blood imbued with the Forestallments required to turn him to the Vagaries.

Krassus' instructions had come to him the very day the Chosen One and Nicholas had first met, deep in the bowels of the Caves. Not only had Nicholas asked Tristan to join his cause, but he had also promised him a lifetime of ecstasy practicing the Vagaries. But in his ridiculous loyalty to the insipid Vigors and the inferior wizards he commanded, the prince had not only refused Nicholas' gracious offer, but had threatened to kill him, as well.

And Krassus had been there the entire time, hiding in a small alcove to one side of the room, listening to every word. After the traitorous prince left, Nicholas had bid his new servant to join him. For Krassus, it had been like standing before a god.

"You heard?" Nicholas asked simply. Incensed by the words of the foolish, traitorous prince, Krassus had nodded angrily.

Nicholas placed a hand on one of Krassus' shoulders. "So now you understand how it is I am treated," he whispered. "My own blood means not only to stop what I have planned at the Gates of Dawn, but to see me dead in the bargain."

It was then that Nicholas had first told him of the Scrolls of the Ancients, and Krassus had begun to understand that the construction and employment of the Gates were but one facet of his master's plans. Then Nicholas had dismissed him, and had never spoken to him again.

And so, after hearing of his master's failure at the Gates of Dawn, Krassus had zealously begun his work. He had sought out the glowing base of one of the Gates, just as Nicholas had ordered. Finally finding it, he had been infuriated to see the secret door in its side already open, and only one of the fabled scrolls present. Luckily, the one remaining was the scroll he needed the most.

Then he had used his new powers to create the demonslavers, steal a fleet of ships and begin capturing slaves in his search for Wulfgar. At the thought of all those *Talis* and *R'talis* slaves, his mouth turned upward at the corners. When all was said and done, those hiding in the Redoubt of the Directorate would pay, and pay dearly.

Taking himself away from his memories, he looked quietly out over the sea. It was midday, the sun having just reached the zenith of its golden, luminescent arc. Sighing, he took a great breath of salt air. But then, as his lungs convulsed, he realized it had been too much for him.

Coughing up blood, he reached for the cloth in his robes and covered his mouth. Several small drops escaped, however, and fell to the marble floor to twist their way into his familiar blood signature. Cursing under his breath, he wiped them away with the sole of his boot. Looking back out to sea, the reccurring, frightful realization once again gripped his heart.

He was dying.

He knew he must complete his work before he succumbed, his lungs eventually drowning in their own blood. And to be absolutely certain of success, he had to have the other scroll.

Suddenly there came a knock on the door. Krassus wiped his face and stuffed the bloody cloth back in his robes before answering it.

The wide, double doors at the opposite end of the Scriptorium opened, and Grizelda and Janus walked in, accompanied by two demonslavers. Janus seemed to be especially pleased for some reason. As they approached the desk, Krassus came in from the balcony and sat back down, at the same time motioning his guests to chairs on the opposite side. The armed slavers retreated to take up guard in the hallway, closing the doors behind them.

"I have more good news, my lord," Janus said excitedly. "The frigate loaded with the herbs and oils taken from the raid on Shadowood has just arrived—well ahead of schedule. The goods are being unloaded as we speak." Then his painted smile melted into a partial frown.

"I am told that some of the slavers in the raiding party never returned," he added glumly. "Those remaining aboard their frigate waited as long as they dared, then finally set sail. It is possible that the missing slavers were intercepted, perhaps even killed by the Chosen One's wizards."

Scowling, Krassus considered Janus' news carefully. True, it was possible that Wigg and Faegan had interrupted the raid. But if they had, it appeared they had been too late to keep his slavers from taking what his herbmistress required. The loss of a few more of his servants made no difference one way or the other.

He looked back at Janus. "And our very special guest?" he asked. "How does he fare?"

Janus smiled again, the edges of his red, painted mask crinkling up as he did so. "Very well," he answered. "He remains quite rebellious, however, just as we expected from one of his unique bloodline." He looked eagerly at the tripod and parchment on Krassus' desk. "You have had time to examine the document, my lord?" he asked. "Is he really Wulfgar?"

"One and the same," Krassus replied. "And the woman named Serena—the two of them have become close?"

"Indeed," Janus assured him. "As planned, she is reviled by the other slaves for the superior treatment she receives during mealtimes, and Wulfgar has asked that she be allowed to stay with him at all other times. I have allowed it, of course."

Satisfied, Krassus turned to Grizelda. "Now that you have the herbs and oils you require, I will expect you to successfully view the Scroll of the Vigors and give me some reference point in Eutracia from which to begin the search. Then I shall send you, Janus, and a group of my best slavers to recover it, no matter where it might be. Is that understood?"

Bending forward slightly in her chair, Grizelda smiled greedily. "It shall be an honor, my lord."

"Very well," Krassus replied. Standing up, he made it clear that the meeting was over. "I go to converse with Wulfgar." His smile deepened the creases in his hollow cheeks. "He and Serena are about to begin understanding the nature of their fates. Their reactions should prove to be most interesting."

The three of them walked to the double doors and went out into the hallway. Janus left to escort Grizelda to what would soon become her new workplace, while Krassus went down the opposite length of the hall.

On and on Nicholas' servant of the Vagaries went, as he wound his way up through the labyrinthine halls and spiral staircases of the Citadel. Tiring, he resorted to the craft to carry him up the remaining flights.

Then he continued on to the marble doors that marked the entrance to Wulfgar's quarters. At a single nod from their master, the guards slid back the iron bolt. Then, before he could enter, one of the slavers spoke.

"Forgive me, my lord, but the man inside is very strong. Shouldn't at least one of us accompany you inside?"

Krassus simply smiled. "I am a wizard of the craft," he said patiently, as if he were addressing a confused schoolboy. "What can he do to me that I would not allow?"

With that Krassus opened the double doors and walked into the room. Behind him, he heard the doors close and bolt.

Surprised by the sudden entry of a stranger, Wulfgar and Serena looked up from the balcony.

CHAPTER

Twenty-nine

The wind in his hair and the sea air in his lungs, Tristan leaned against the pitching gunwale of *The People's Revenge* as the great frigate plowed her way west through the Sea of Whispers. His dreggan and his throwing knives had been returned to him, and it felt good to have them lying across his back again.

The ship seemed amazingly alive, the seamen and the many grateful slaves she was bringing home swarming over her decks. Tyranny's crew did all they knew how for the newly freed captives. But her men were not professional healers, and their gifts in such matters were limited. Now, after having had the opportunity to look them over more closely, Tristan sadly concluded that many of these poor souls would not survive even the relatively short voyage to Eutracia, no matter how well the crew cared for them.

So far, Tyranny seemed to be keeping to their bargain of heading straight for the Cavalon Delta. But the winds had proven fickle, and the frigates had been forced to tack in order to stay on course, something that Tristan soon learned would make the voyage longer.

Four uneventful days had passed since he had made his bargain with the highly interesting sea captain, and sometimes his great desire to be home convinced him that he could almost smell the rich, fertile soil of the Eutracian coast. Soon he would set foot on dry land and see his loved ones again.

One corner of his mouth turned up as he thought of parading the brash Tyranny and the huge colossus named Scars unannounced through the royal palace and finally introducing them to everyone. Then he would live up to his part of it, demanding that the wizards not only pay her a ransom of one hundred thousand gold kisa, but that they award her with the letters of marque she so valued. In his mind's eye, he could already see the vein in the lead wizard's right temple throbbing, and Faegan's ever-curious, gray-green eyes flashing with mischief.

Tristan had encountered Tyranny often during the last four days as she inspected the decks and spoke with both her crew and the slaves she had rescued. Sometimes it seemed to him that she had spent time with every slave aboard, and he thought he knew why: She was trying to glean from them any information she could about her lost brother. Twice she had graciously invited him to take his evening meal with her in her quarters, where they had talked at length about their respective backgrounds. Tristan had used the opportunity to tell her about his past, and bring her up to date with all that had happened in Eutracia since the return of the Coven. He soon found that he not only respected this rather admirable outlaw, but genuinely liked her, as well.

Perhaps he had promised her too much, he suddenly realized. He gave a quick, derisive laugh. Too much or not, he was sure that taking her and Scars before the crusty, indomitable wizards would be worth it.

But despite how badly he wanted to get home, he had swiftly come to love the sea, complete with all of its whims and dangers. After Scars had finally come to the conclusion that Tristan was indeed not one of the enemy, he and the prince had arrived at an uneasy truce. The surprisingly eloquent giant had taken him under his wing, instructing him in the ways of the great boat. Tristan had certainly not become a seasoned crewmember, but he was fascinated by what Scars was teaching him; and each day he found himself eager to learn more.

He now understood the differences between the various sails, spars, and booms, and how the rigging and sheets worked to help steady them and raise and lower the sails. He had learned the various types of maneuvers the ship was capable of, such as running before the wind, tacking, and being in irons. Tristan had even gingerly climbed the rigging all the way to the crow's nest, to gaze out over the ocean and feel the splendid, exaggerated motion of the ship as she pitched and rolled beneath him, dozens of meters below. Seeing his battle flag flying high atop the mainmast had done his heart good.

To his great surprise, Scars had suggested that Tristan take the ship's wheel for a time—under the giant's watchful eye, of course. If what Tyranny had told him was true, it was the same wheel that had once steered the *Resolve,* the vessel Wigg had used more than three centuries earlier to banish the Coven of sorceresses from Eutracia. As Tristan had placed his hands on the worn, curved grips that graced the wheel's outer ring, he almost thought he could feel the gnarled, ghostly hands of those who had gone before, turning it with him. Sensing the great ship obey him had been an experience he would never forget.

He had found a small plaque mounted below the wheel. On it was inscribed the name of every single person who had commanded the various vessels the wheel had served over the course of the centuries. Toward the top, he had seen Wigg's name. And the last name was Tyranny's. Smiling, Tristan shook his head and wondered how many other names would be added to the plaque before the wheel was finally lost to the sea or otherwise destroyed. He found himself hoping that would never happen.

Turning to look toward the bow, he felt the sharp, pulling sting of the whip marks across his back. They were healing, but they still hurt. He knew that when he returned to the palace, the wizards would gladly enact an incantation of accelerated healing over them, and they would soon mend. But in truth he had to admit that it was neither the vicious beating by the demonslaver nor the healed scars that would forever remain on his back that now plagued him so.

There had recently come to him a new, unexpected form of mental, rather than physical anguish. It was something that had been building inexorably in his soul ever since that fateful day in Parthalon when his blood had suddenly turned from red to azure. It was a foreign, insidious feeling, and one that had finally come to fruition for him not only at the savage whipping, but when Tyranny had pulled him out of the ragged line of slaves to speak to him.

As the contradictory, rather frightening thought went through his mind, he closed his dark blue eyes for a moment. The unthinkable had happened.

He was coming to curse his glowing, azure blood.

He was not distressed by the fact that his blood was endowed. That much of it was his natural heritage, his birthright. But that his blood now glowed, that it had turned the same color that always accompanied any significant use of the craft, was just too bizarre.

His azure blood kept him from learning the craft, because the wizards were concerned with the unknown ramifications of such a thing, should they try to instruct him. That angered and frustrated him, for his desire to learn burned within him as hotly as ever. Even the Tome, the great book of magic, stated that the male of the Chosen Ones *must* be trained, so that he could attempt to join the Vigors and the Vagaries together into a single art, thereby putting an end to the eons-old conflict between the two sides of the craft. But as things stood now, even Wigg and Faegan were at a loss over what to do. And with all of the problems that had been thrust upon them since the unexpected return of the Coven, using valuable time to begin his training had clearly been out of the question. Worst of all, he felt guilty because he was no closer to fulfilling his destiny, as the Tome said he must.

Sometimes his unique blood made him feel very isolated. Every time he was wounded, no matter how slight the insult to his body, if his blood was drawn, his enemies would be able to recognize him immediately. They wouldn't even need to examine his blood signature to know who he was, for the color of his blood would tell it all. Then he remembered Faegan's warning, spoken that night in his mansion in Shadowood, not so long ago.

"Although it does not say how, the second volume of the Tome affirms that he may be forever, inalterably changed. You must be on the lookout for this change, whatever it is to be."

And his own silent vow: *"I will not rest until I have discovered who has poured such endowed blood into my veins, and why. I shall know why I have become the vessel that contains the blood of the fates . . ."*

He stared out over the sea, yearning for home, for the company of his sister and his friends—and especially for Celeste. He had fallen deeply in love with the beautiful, red-haired daughter of the lead wizard, and he knew it. But he also knew her psyche wasn't ready to accept his affection on that level, and he had no choice other than to accept it. He could only wait, hoping that one day they could be truly together.

Engrossed as he was in his thoughts, he didn't hear Tyranny's footsteps until she came to a stop directly alongside him. Smiling slightly, she laced her fingers together and leaned her forearms on the rail.

"Tell me about her," she said simply.

"Tell you about who?" he asked.

Tyranny responded with a wry, knowing smile. "Don't be coy," she replied. "It doesn't suit you. You're the straightforward type, just like me. Besides, you forget that I have been sailing these waters in the company of men for the majority of my life. I know their every mood, and the expressions and gestures that go along with them. You miss someone special. A woman—I'm sure of it. And you miss her very much, but not in the same way you miss your sister, the princess. After some of the interesting things you have told me about yourself, I must admit that I'm curious about the kind of woman it takes to hold your heart." She looked around, then conspiratorially lowered her voice. "So tell me, crown prince of all of Eutracia, what is she like?"

Smiling and shaking his head, Tristan looked back out to sea. "It's a long story," he answered honestly. "Three hundred years in the making, in fact. Which also happens to be how old she is."

Turning back, he looked into Tyranny's wide, blue eyes and watched as the wind moved through her haphazardly cut hair. It was the first time since knowing her that he had seen real surprise cross her face. True to form, however, she recovered quickly.

"My, but you do like them mature, don't you?" she teased. Then her expression softened a bit. "Still, it's nice to have someone who wants to share the same rainbow's end, isn't it?"

Before Tristan could frame an answer, they heard the unmistakable peal of the warning bell high in the crow's nest.

Drawing her sword, Tyranny looked up to see one of her crew already climbing the rigging. Scars appeared by her side, and only moments later, the crewman who had scaled the rigging was back again.

"Screechlings!" he shouted at the top of his lungs. "Three separate maelstroms of them, about to rise no more than half a league off the bow!"

Confused, Tristan followed Tyranny and Scars as they ran frantically forward. Standing with them at the bow, Tristan could just make out three huge, dark circles that seemed to lie atop the waves. His first thought was that at last he was seeing the legendary Necrophagians—the monsters that made the Sea of Whispers impassable to all but those who were willing to make the necessary sacrifice. But something about what he saw told him that was not the case. Perplexed, he turned to Tyranny. She stood still, brandishing her sword with one hand, holding her spyglass to one eye with the other.

"What is it?" he asked.

"A nightmare," she responded tensely, not taking the lens from her eye. "Creatures of the sea, said to be of the craft. No one knows for sure, for they have only recently begun to appear. What we *do* know is that they hunt in packs." Then she lowered her spyglass, and Tristan clearly saw the worry on her face. "I know of no vessel that has ever survived an onslaught of three maelstroms, but I refuse to go down without a fight!"

"Maelstroms?" Tristan repeated. "What are they? What can I do?"

"You will understand all too soon," she answered, her right eye squarely against the spyglass again. "Try to stay near me or Scars! It seems that you are finally going to get your chance to show us how well you use those unusual weapons you carry across your back!"

"Can't we outrun them?"

"No," she said adamantly. "No ship ever built could outrun them at this range—not even *The People's Revenge*. The only course now is to stand and fight, and hope we can survive them." Then she barked out some orders to her crew, and everything began to change.

Turning to look behind him, Tristan saw that the ship had become even more alive with furious activity. Shouting crewmen were forcing the confused slaves belowdecks, while others frantically tried to close and lock all of the remaining deck hatches and stairwell doors. The rigging was covered in seamen frantically reefing the sails. One man was hurriedly tying off the ship's wheel. Tristan was only a novice sailor, but he knew enough to realize that with all of her sails reefed and her wheel tied off, *The People's Revenge* would be dead in the water, rocking back and forth at the mercy of the waves. After having been told repeatedly that speed was often the only thing that kept them alive, he was completely stymied.

He turned to look out over the bow again. Stunned by what he saw, he quietly drew his dreggan from its scabbard.

A vast area of the ocean lying before them had come alive. Three whirling spouts of swirling, foaming seawater had risen from the ocean, dark and foreboding. On and on the huge waterspouts rose, spinning and rising with dizzying speed. About one-eighth of a league ahead of the bow, they were already nearly the height of the ship's mainmast, and they were climbing still.

Then they began to glow strangely from within, circling colors that spun in a continuous riot of alternating hues. Had he not been told the maelstroms were deadly, he would have considered them one of the most beautiful things he had ever seen.

Suddenly the glowing maelstroms flattened out at their tops, gained some distance between themselves, and then careened with impossible speed in a straight line toward the three unmoving ships. Tristan heard Tyranny's voice ring out beside him.

"Come on then, you bastards!" she screamed, holding her sword high above her head. "You filthy scavengers! Come to me! Let's see how many of you I can kill on the first pass!" When they finally reached her she began swinging her sword with abandon, and thin, watery, bright red blood began raining down.

When the first of them buzzed by his head, Tristan thought he must be seeing things. As it passed, he heard the unmistakable sound of teeth snapping together and realized that his hesitation had nearly cost him his life. Making insane screeching noises as they came, another flew by him, then more still, until their numbers finally became so great that they blotted out the sun and covered the deck of the frigate with their shadows. Viciously they attacked both the crewmembers and the rigging, tearing away those sails that had not already been reefed.

Swinging his dreggan, Tristan missed the first one, then finally managed to take one down. It was a glancing, not a killing blow, but as the dazed thing lay bleeding at his feet, he finally got a look at it up close.

He was amazed to see what appeared to be some kind of very large, very strange, fishlike creature. It was almost two meters long, half a

meter deep, and very brightly colored with what seemed to be luminescent stripes running down along its sides. Instead of fins, it had three
oddly shaped, scaly wings, one on either side of its colorful body, and a
third rising vertically from its spine, just forward of its large, wide tail. As
he watched, its mouth opened, revealing a multitude of razor-sharp
teeth. Seeing that brought Tristan back to the reality of the battle raging
around him. With a single stroke of his dreggan, he beheaded the monster. But he had lost precious time.

Pain seared through both his shoulders, as he was swept off his feet
and flown toward the starboard gunwale. Horrified, he realized that two
of the vicious, powerful things had their teeth in him and were carrying
him away. He tried to use his sword, but the pain in his arms was too
great. And as the gunwale grew closer, he realized what was about to
happen to him, for he could see the same thing happening to a host of
other screaming, defenseless crewmen.

The monsters were about to fly him over the side and drown him in
the Sea of Whispers.

The sea surrounding the ship was already swirling with the bodies of
those who had gone over before him. Some were still alive, flailing
about, trying desperately to swim back to the ship, only to be dragged
under by snapping jaws. Screaming and twisting wildly against his captors, Tristan almost passed out from the pain. But it was no use. In mere
seconds he would be over the side, lost forever.

Then two massive hands reached out to take hold of the thing on
Tristan's right side and muscle it down to the deck. Tristan landed hard
on his back, the teeth of the other creature still embedded in his shoulder. But his right arm was free. Trying as best he could to ignore the
pain, he dropped his dreggan and reached back for one of his throwing
dirks. Turning wildly to his left, he plunged the point of the dirk directly
into the monster's left eyeball, killing it instantly. With its death, Tristan
finally found himself free of its jaws. He threw it to one side and dragged
himself to his feet to see Scars standing near him, the other beast still
screaming and writhing in his awesome grip.

With a single grunt, Scars tore the screaming thing in half and threw
the two pieces to the deck. Giving the prince a short nod, he immediately went about finding more of the things to kill.

Wasting no time, Tristan began using his dreggan to hack the things
out of the air as best as his injured shoulders would allow. Many died at
his hands. Somehow he managed to avoid being taken again. After what
seemed an eternity, he saw that the struggle was finally abating. His chest
heaving, he walked to the gunwale and looked over. A mass of torn
clothing and dead bodies bobbed on the surface of the water. Then he
turned back to look at the ship.

Bodies—human and monster both—lay everywhere, and the deck was awash with blood. Several of the ship's spars were broken and dangling awkwardly from their ropes. Sails lay in tatters, completely beyond repair.

Looking across the sea, he saw that the other two ships had fared no better. The stench of blood filled the air, and a terrible silence engulfed the stricken vessels as they rocked listlessly from port to starboard and back again. After all of the screaming and noise, everything seemed strangely quiet.

Looking across the deck, his azure blood still oozing from each of his shoulders, Tristan searched for Tyranny. He finally found her standing on the mizzen deck, her face down, her sword hanging from one hand as though she no longer had the will or the strength to raise it. She was covered with blood, and as he started toward her she slowly turned to him and looked him in the eyes.

Just as he reached her she collapsed, and he quickly hoisted her limp body into his arms. Holding her there, he looked sadly at the bloody, mangled ship and wondered what would become of them now.

CHAPTER

Thirty

S tirring from her nap, Celeste yawned, then stretched her back and
arms as she lay on the huge, four-poster, canopied bed. The large
hourglass on the nearby stand told her that a little less than two hours had
gone by since she had left Shailiha and Abbey to make their way down
into the Redoubt and to the Hall of Blood Records.

She rose up on her elbows and looked out through one of the four
open, stained-glass windows lining the exterior wall of her private quarters. The soft indigo that always preceded dusk had begun to encroach
on the turquoise edges of the sky and would soon overtake it altogether.
Then the many lights from the Minion campfires would begin to flicker
like stars in the night. Beautiful and reassuring. But then the usual frightening thoughts crowded in again, and she lay back down on the bed,
staring at the red velvet canopy above her.

She was desperately worried, as was everyone remaining here at the
Redoubt. Tristan had been gone for days, and there had been no success
in the search launched by the Minions. Even Ox's hopefulness seemed to
deteriorate with each passing hour, despite the fact that he was trying to
act like a warrior and not let his concern show.

Wigg and Faegan had not returned from their journey to the place
the Tome called the Chamber of Penitence, and her fear for her newfound father and the crippled wizard was great. But it was Tristan upon
whom her heart dwelled the most.

She rose from the bed and padded in her slippers to the other side of
the room to retrieve her pearl-handled hairbrush from the dresser, then

mechanically began brushing her hair, her worry for Tristan still filling her thoughts.

She wanted desperately to be near him again, to see him, to know that he was safe. Sometimes she thought she might burst with the conflicted feelings that surged through her whenever the prince was near. But it was easy to simply miss him and worry about him when he was gone, especially now that he was in danger.

As she ran the brush through her long, deep red hair, she heard the evening wind comfortingly rustling the trees outside her window. Then she heard the squeak of a window hinge. The wind was stronger than she'd thought, and she turned to shut the windows, in case a storm was rising.

Her heart leapt into her throat, and she dropped the brush.

Three of the four windows were shut and locked, and the last one was hauntingly closing by itself.

Before she could run for the door, an azure beam appeared out of nowhere, snaked itself around her waist, and threw her across the length of the room, back onto her bed. She raised an arm to counter with a bolt of her own, but the glow had her pinned to the bed. She was caught in a wizard's warp, she realized, just like the one Krassus had used against them all that day in the card room, when he had assaulted Wigg and violated the wizards' minds.

She tried to scream, but found to her horror that her voice carried no sound. Terrified, she turned her eyes as best she could to look over at the windows.

The last of them had finished closing, and the latch was slowly coming down, locking itself into place. Her heart pounded relentlessly as she waited and watched, unable to do anything else.

Now another glow was building in the room, growing brighter and brighter until it began to take on a shape. Her terrified mind convinced her that it must be Krassus, come back to the palace for some reason. But as she looked closer, she began to recognize the shape standing so dangerously close to the edge of her bed. Tears welled up in her eyes and cascaded maddeningly down her cheeks.

The thing spoke.

"Hello, my darling," it said in a deep, melodious voice. "It has been far too long since we have lain together. I have missed you dearly."

She was going to faint—she knew it. But then her mind was touched by that of the being standing before her, and she was fully conscious once more.

It was Ragnar, the half wizard, half blood stalker who had for over three hundred years kept her his prisoner, abusing her incessantly.

She saw the bald, shiny head, dangling earlobes, and the long, yellow incisors that that jutted down just below his smiling bottom lip. His white robe was untied and slightly open down the center. He was clearly aroused. The mad, bloodshot eyes looked up and down her body with a hunger that seemingly knew no bounds. The small wound in the side of his head was still there, and as a drop of yellow ooze dripped from it, he reached up to wipe it away. Then he placed the wet fingertip into his mouth and smiled.

"So many questions, aren't there, my love?" he asked, lowering his awful face closer to her own. The smell of his fetid breath brought back horrible, mind-numbing memories of her times with him.

"Did you and the wizards actually believe that Nicholas, my beloved master, would really want me dead?" he added. "Or did any of you, as you reveled in the destruction of the Gates of Dawn, actually see my corpse? No. I now serve Krassus, and together he and I carry on a part of Nicholas' glorious work. But first I am going to take you back to the Caves with me. And this time you will never leave, I promise you."

As he spoke, he ran the long, pointed fingernails of one hand down the side of her face. "You always were my favorite." Then a strange look came over him, and he lowered himself even closer.

"And one other thing, my love," he added softly. "Krassus has very kindly imbued me with the Forestallment that, after three hundred years of failed attempts, shall finally grant me the power to make you pregnant. I can't wait to see what our children will look like." He stood up again, his robe falling open obscenely.

"Before we leave here together, I shall take you right here in this very bed," he added menacingly. "A fitting insult to Wigg, my dearest enemy, don't you think? To luxuriate in his only daughter yet again, in the very seat of his power! With both the wizards and the Chosen One gone, there is no one left here of any consequence to stop me. And who knows—you might even conceive here in the royal palace this very night! Deliciously ironic, wouldn't you agree?"

As she watched in helpless horror, he reached down and parted his robe fully. Reaching out, he caressed her face once more.

"It shall be just as you remember it," he said smoothly. "Long and slow, and again and again. And this time, my sweet, it shall go on for eternity. I may even allow enough of your powers of speech to return so that I might hear you softly whimper." Again the wicked smile came. "Surely you remember how much I enjoyed hearing you weep."

Ragnar held out a finger and pointed it at the bodice of her dress. She heard a slow, deliberate ripping sound, and looked with horror as a rip parted her dress at the top and began to tear its way down. Her body wanted to shake with fear but couldn't, locked as she was within the monster's unyielding warp.

Saying nothing more, his bloodshot eyes gleaming, Ragnar knelt by the side of her bed, placed his wet, pink tongue against the inside of one of her thighs, and began moving it upward.

Screaming, Celeste bolted from the bed and fell to the floor. For a moment she remained on all fours, her chest heaving and sweat running down her face. Then, finally, she dared to look about the room.

Amazingly, everything was just as it should be. The windows were open, and the night breeze was caressing the tree branches outside. The Minion campfires were lit, sending their glow upward into the dark of the night sky.

And there was no Ragnar. It had been another nightmare.

Lowering her head in shame, she sobbed mightily, wondering when she would ever be free of her horrific memories. At last she rose to stand on shaky legs, walked to the mirror, and slowly lifted her head to regard the stranger staring back at her. The eyes were red; the long dark red hair was disheveled; and the woman staring back at her was shaking uncontrollably. She placed her quivering hands over her face so that she couldn't look any longer.

This is what he still does to you, even though he is dead, she heard her mind whisper. Suddenly, though, several more words floated to the surface—unusually defiant, challenging words that, after three hundred years of torment finally transformed her life.

But I will allow it no more!

And then something in her psyche snapped.

She stamped to the door, tore at the doorknob, and sprinted down the hallway. Her newfound rage intensifying with every stride, she went faster and faster, trying to dispel her energy. When she reached one of the secret passageways leading down into the Redoubt, she opened the door, went through, and practically ran down the circular staircase.

Her fury was limitless. Soon she found herself banging on the door of the Hall of Blood Records and screaming relentlessly, demanding to be let in.

A startled Shailiha came to the door, only to have the exhausted, furious Celeste embrace her desperately, the tears coming yet again.

The princess quickly dismissed Abbey and Lionel, and the two women sat and talked until dawn.

CHAPTER

Thirty-one

T he darkness was impenetrable; there was absolutely no sound. For all the lead wizard knew, this place could be either very small, or endless. Uncertain what might lie beneath them, he dared not release the spell that kept him hovering in the air. Floating weightless, all of his senses deprived, Wigg wondered if this was what it was like to be dead.

He could not see his own hand before his face. Only the familiar squeak of Faegan's chair, caused by the crippled wizard's turning it in an attempt to look around, told Wigg that he was not alone.

As Faegan raised his hand to produce some light, the Paragon hanging around his neck began to glow, just as it had done earlier. It flooded the room with its vibrant, red illumination.

The stone chamber in which they found themselves was quite unremarkable. One might even have called it disappointing. It seemed to be little more than a small, square room cut out of the rock, with a matching stone floor and a rather low ceiling. Looking at each other in silent agreement, they gratefully lowered themselves.

When they touched ground, an azure beam shone from the ceiling, illuminating a hole in the floor. They went to it and looked down. It was the opening to a circular stairwell that was barely large enough for Faegan's chair to pass through. It wound its way down into utter darkness.

Taking a deep breath, Wigg looked over at Faegan. "After you?" he said dryly.

Pursing his lips, Faegan looked tentatively down the hole, then seemed to make up his mind. Levitating his chair, he lowered himself into the depths, the wheels narrowly scraping their way by on either side. With a sigh and a concerned shake of his head, Wigg began following Faegan down.

The winding staircase was very small and cramped, lined by walls of solid stone that added greatly to the sense of confinement. It was exactly like being trapped in a cramped, stone tube. Like Tristan, the lead wizard hated being closed in. The farther down he went, the greater his sense of foreboding became. The air grew cold and smelled increasingly damp and musty.

After a while Wigg looked up, trying to gauge how far they had come. He paused, taken aback.

The opening to the stairwell was gone, replaced by another ceiling of solid rock, just inches above the top of his head. In fact, the length of circular stairway they had just descended was gone, too. A solid stone wall had silently materialized only inches behind him, blocking their way back. Between the cramped ceiling, rear wall, and sidewalls, he could extend his hand no more than half a meter in any direction other than downward. The red light from the Paragon around Faegan's neck cast eerie, sharp shadows against the unforgiving barriers and added greatly to the suffocating sense of helplessness.

Wigg felt like a trapped rat. Despite the coolness of the air, he broke out in a sweat, his sense of dread growing by the moment. Looking forward, he saw Faegan continue down the staircase, apparently quite unaware of their predicament.

Wigg took another tentative step down the stairs. Glancing back over his shoulder, he saw the wall just behind him silently, quickly advance by the exact length of the step, while the ceiling closed in by the same margin. And the step he had last stood on had disappeared, leaving only the one he was now occupying and those that lay below him. Someone or something had taken great pains to make sure the two wizards could continue their trek in only one direction: downward.

"I think you had best see this," Wigg said to Faegan as calmly as he could.

The elder wizard turned in his chair and immediately understood the dilemma. His face darkened with worry. But for once he said nothing, and simply turned back around. With no other course of action possible, the two wizards continued downward, into the bowels of the earth.

After what seemed an eternity, they exited at last into another simple, square room of stone. This one was even smaller than the first, and barely large enough to accommodate the two of them. There were no other doorways, or holes in the floor such as there had been in the other room now so far above them.

Suddenly a frightening thought occurred to the lead wizard, and he turned around to find his suspicions confirmed. The stairway they had just come down had vanished, filled in by the wall that had so ominously followed them in their descent. There remained no exit whatsoever, and their only source of light was the Paragon, which seemed to glow even more brightly as they waited.

The silence in the room was oppressive and the air was thin. Wigg tried not to think about the prospect of dying in this unforgiving fortress of stone.

Then a narrow line of azure appeared in the air before them. It snaked toward the wall they faced and pressed itself against the stone in the shape of a rectangle large enough for a person to pass through. The area within its borders began to glow. Then the glow faded, and the section of wall simply dissolved.

Where the stone wall had been stood a tall figure, unmoving, silent. A dark cloak covered the body, its hood pulled up over the head and face. In one of the hands was a long, gnarled wooden staff. Looking closer, Wigg noticed that the hand holding the staff was only a collection of bones.

Wigg finally found his voice. "Who are you?" he asked.

"I am the watchwoman of the floating gardens," the answer came back. It was a woman's voice. But its timbre was ancient, and her words seemed to fight and scratch their way across the distance between them. "But you come at a bad time, for the gardens are not what they once were."

Faegan wheeled his chair a bit closer. She remained motionless.

"And why is that?" he asked anxiously.

"First tell me," she said, "has there been a recent disturbance in the life of the stone?"

"Yes," Faegan answered. "The dead son of the Chosen One was returned from the heavens as a servant of the Heretics of the Guild. He tried to take all of the power of the Paragon into himself, so as to allow the Heretics to return here, to the land of the living. Only at the last moment were we able to stop him and return the power to the jewel of the craft, where it rightly belongs."

"So the Chosen Ones have finally come?" For several moments she did not speak, the silence in the chamber engulfing them all like a shroud. "Tell me," she went on at last, "are the Chosen Ones now the *Jin'Sai,* and the *Jin'Saiou?*"

"What are you talking about?" Faegan asked.

"So you do not know," the watchwoman said softly. "But one day you will. Finally, after eons of waiting, the progression toward joining the two sides of the craft can begin." Her voice was a mere whisper. "Perhaps the Vigors may triumph, after all." Silence reigned again for a time as the two stunned wizards tried to grasp the enormity of her words.

"You still have not told us about the state of the gardens," Wigg pressed. "Our need for your help is very great. Yet another threat to the Vigors walks the land, and has the potential to become the most potent danger we have ever faced."

The figure in the robe glided over to Faegan's chair. Reaching down to his chest with a skeletal hand, she picked up the Paragon and examined it closely. Even at this proximity, Faegan could see nothing within the dark confines of her hood. Finally she let go of the stone, allowing it to fall back into place.

"The gardens are not as they once were because all things of the craft take their sustenance from the power granted by the stone," she answered. "As the stone neared its death, so too did the gardens that I tend. They have only just begun to rejuvenate. Because of this, what you have traveled so far to find may no longer exist, but we shall try. What exactly is the nature of your request?"

"Agents of the Vagaries have mixed our stores of herbs and precious oils," Faegan explained. "They must be separated again, reclassified, and their potency revalued so that they might be employed by our herbmistress to use her gazing flame. The Chosen One is missing, and we must find him. We also seek the Scroll of the Vigors. Can you help us?"

Her answer was both frightening and immediate. "Do you mean to say that the Scrolls of the Ancients have been loosed upon the world?"

"Yes," Wigg answered. "Can you tell us why they are so important?"

"No," she told them, "for I have not been blessed with such knowledge. But I do know that the importance of the scrolls is on a par at least equal to that of both the Tome and the Paragon. For the Vigors to survive you must recover the scrolls at once, or all that we have worked for so long to preserve will perish."

"The Tome mentioned a psychic price to be paid for the knowledge that we seek," Faegan said cautiously. "What does that mean?"

"How long have each of you been alive?" she asked.

Confused, the two wizards looked at each other. "We are each more than three centuries old," Faegan answered honestly. "But why do you need to know?"

"Only three centuries," she mused. "Still so young. Mere children in the intricate tapestry that is the craft. Due to your youth, you may not possess the depth of experiences required to pay the price, and trying to do so might well cost you your lives."

"I don't understand," Wigg interjected. "What do our ages have to do with the psychic price that you demand?"

"To acquire what you seek, the price to be paid is not money nor other physical goods of any kind. The payment demanded is that one of you must leave behind a piece of your very soul. To do so, you must be forced to relive your greatest regret, as if you were experiencing it for the very first time. Therefore, the longer you have lived, the greater the chances that you possess regrets that will satisfy the price. As you make payment, the psychic pain you experience in your soul shall be accompanied by an equally severe, physical pain in your heart—the very seat of such regret. And should your endowed blood not be strong enough to persist, your heart will burst, and you will die. If that occurs, you will never leave this place. I realize your need is great. Therefore the price demanded shall be, also."

"How could you possibly know what each of our greatest regrets might be?" Faegan asked. "We might try to trick you."

"I do not need to know. Only you do."

"But why must we pay such an awful price?" Wigg asked. "Why can't you simply give us what we need? Are our goals not the same—the preservation of the Vigors?"

"That is not my place to say," she answered. "The Ones Who Came Before built these chambers and others like them before they perished, hoping they would be found by those who value only the Vigors, just as you obviously found both the Tome and the Paragon. But in their wisdom they also dictated the price to be paid, so that what might be given to you will not be taken lightly, or squandered. The nature of the price therefore demands that only those of exceptionally strong blood will prevail, and be able to use that which they have been given. As you will soon see, many of your kind have tried over the ages, and failed."

"Do those of the Vagaries know of these chambers?" Faegan asked, practically bursting with curiosity.

"That does not matter just now."

"Why not?"

"Because possession of the Paragon is required to enter, and you are its current wearer," she answered simply. "The others of your race who have come here seeking answers over the eons were, like you, in possession of the stone. It is hoped that finally, after all this time, the Chosen Ones will accomplish what so many others have failed to do, and at the same time will learn all that there is to know of what has gone before. And with that shall dawn a new age."

His eyes alive with questions, Faegan looked into the dark recesses of her hood. "Are you one of the Ones Who Came Before?" he breathed.

"I am, and I am not," she said cryptically. "I have been here in this place for eons, doing their bidding. As you can see, my flesh has fallen away, but my mind remains. But I will tell you that eons ago, I was a woman of the craft. Tell me, do women still practice the arts in the world above?"

"For a long time it was forbidden, but now there are again such women," Wigg answered. "They are known as the Acolytes of Fledgling House. But they are only newly trained, and remain scattered across the land. We would like to call them all home, but we do not know how."

The watchwoman remained still for a time as she considered his words. "If the threat to the Vigors is as great as you say, you will need these women in your service," she said. "I suggest you call them back immediately."

"But as I said," Wigg protested, "we don't know how."

"If you are able to find the Scroll of the Vigors, examine it carefully, looking for the formula that invokes the River of Thought," she told him.

"The River of Thought?" Faegan repeated. "What do you mean?"

"No more talk," she said flatly. "Your questions are legion, and I have accommodated you long enough. It is time for you to make your decision. Do you wish to pay the psychic price for what you seek? Understand that if you agree, and pass this portal into my world, you are bound by your blood to keep your end of the bargain. There can be no turning back."

Faegan looked up to Wigg with questioning eyes. After a long pause, the lead wizard nodded.

"We agree," Faegan said.

"Then follow me," the watchwoman ordered. Turning, she walked into the darkness.

Wigg and Faegan followed tentatively behind, wondering what lay waiting for them on the other side.

Thirty-two

"Can I have one, Marcus?" Rebecca asked. She was fairly jumping up and down, excited almost beyond words. "Please, Marcus," she pleaded, pulling on the sleeve of his shirt. "Please, can I?"

Marcus looked up and down the street to which he had carefully guided them. Like Bargainer's Square, it was teeming with passersby and street vendors. But this section of Tammerland was infinitely more appealing, not to mention safer. The area they were standing in was known as the Plaza of Fallen Heroes, and here and there could be seen marble statues erected to those who had fallen over the centuries in the service of the crown.

By Marcus' side stood the wheelbarrow that had lain up against the shed he and his sister lived in, and lying in the wheelbarrow was the scroll. Marcus was strong for his age. Even so, he found the scroll, with all of its gold adornments, difficult to lift. Finding the discarded wheelbarrow had been a great stroke of luck.

The patterned rug they had stolen was wound tightly around it, hiding it from view. The open ends of the rug were stuffed with rags. Marcus hoped that these simple measures would be enough to hide the scroll—at least until he had concluded his business with the man they were supposed to meet. He prayed to the Afterlife that it would not start glowing again. He and Rebecca had already survived several close scrapes, and they didn't need another one.

The man he was waiting for was supposedly a purveyor of artifacts of the craft. After Marcus had described the scroll to him, the fellow had seemed most anxious to examine it—almost giddy, in fact. Until yesterday Marcus had not known that such vendors existed, and had come upon the fellow's establishment quite by accident, during his latest foray to steal food. Subsequently asking around a bit, he learned that since the demise of the wizards of the Directorate, such places had not only begun to spring up in Tammerland, but were also flourishing.

Some of these purported merchants of the craft were legitimate, it seemed, and some were not. Selling anything they could get their hands on, they all claimed their wares to be of the craft. But what did appear certain was that with the fall of the Royal Guard and the Directorate, there was no shortage of those now willing to take advantage of a newly curious, souvenir-hungry populace. Many citizens had become morbidly anxious to own something that smacked of magic, or its supposed connection to the fallen House of Galland. It was said that anything that had come from the looted royal palace—and had its authenticity verified—would bring nearly its weight in gold.

Marcus looked down again at the rolled-up rug in the dilapidated wheelbarrow, thinking of what lay inside it. He had no idea whether it had come from the palace, but he was certain it was of the craft. Nothing else would glow like that—he was sure of it. And he was anxious to turn it into kisa so he and Rebecca could stop hiding and get on with their lives.

But that was not to say he was willing to sell the scroll to the first interested party who came along. Marcus had made it clear to the man meeting them today that he was merely to give them a price, and that he and his sister were going to entertain other offers before bargaining their item away. If an offer was good today, it would also be good later, he assumed.

Still, he remained nervous, and his palms were beginning to sweat. Reaching into his pocket, his hand found the cool, comforting handle of his knife.

"Come on, Marcus!" Rebecca started pleading again. "It only costs one kisa, and I know you have a few in your pocket. I heard them jangling together as you walked!"

Marcus smiled down at his sister. As he took in her dirty, tattered dress and the clubfoot that she never complained about, he felt his heart slip a bit.

In truth he would have much preferred to carefully spend all the kisa on food. It had been a long time since he had felt the comforting weight of coins in his pockets, even if they were few in number. And acquiring them had come hard. He had been forced to lounge around almost all afternoon yesterday on a nearby street corner before finding the perfect victim to "accidentally" bump into and relieve of his coins. And after all of that, he had only come up with four.

"Are you sure that's what you want?" he asked. "I know it's only one kisa. But when you buy one of those, it doesn't seem that you get much for your money. I worked hard for these coins, you know."

Rebecca just gazed up at him with her big, brown eyes, giving him the forlorn look that she knew he could rarely resist.

As she expected, Marcus finally relented.

"All right, all right," he said, smiling and reaching into his ragged pocket. "But only one, piglet. Do you understand?"

Nodding gleefully, she snatched the shiny gold coin and ran over to the stand, followed by Marcus and the wheelbarrow.

The vendor's stall was a simple, square-roofed affair. An ancient-looking woman sat inside on a stool, taking care of her customers. A young male assistant sat beside her, tending to the wares. Dozens of small wooden cages hung from the roof and lay scattered along the counter-top. As Rebecca looked them over, Marcus smiled, reminded of what a nonsensical custom this was. Not to mention a very bad investment. Still, they weren't the only people standing here, willing to spend their kisa on what the crafty woman offered.

Each of the cages contained a throat lark. The birds were remarkably small: three of them could usually fit into the palm of a grown man's hand. They had presumably acquired their name because of the bright colors adorning their throats. The remainder of the bird was usually a very soft, dappled blue, although that sometimes varied. Well known for their singing voices, they were prized as house pets. As the larks danced happily about in their cages, their twittering combined to create a singularly beautiful harmony, attracting yet more of the curious to the old woman's stall.

Marcus smiled and shook his head as Rebecca picked out a lark of soft powder blue with a deep green throat. Satisfied, she handed the single, precious coin up to the woman on the stool. Then she took the bird, cage and all, over to where her brother was standing.

The highly unusual, implied agreement with the vendor was that once the purchase had been made, the cage door was to be opened immediately, and the bird set free. Then the cage was to be returned to the stall.

Everyone knew, of course, that the birds were trained to fly immediately back to the old woman, only to be caged again by her assistant to await yet another customer. But none of that mattered to the buyers. Eutracian custom said that paying to set a caged creature free, even if for only a moment, would gladden the heart and bring good luck.

The practice had sprung up after the recent hostilities accompanying the return of the Coven. Mourners had begun freeing birds already in their possession to honor the departed souls of their loved ones, wishing them a safe journey to the Afterlife.

Smiling from ear to ear, Rebecca gingerly opened the cage door, releasing the throat lark to the sky.

With a short, clear call, the bird left the cage and went winging straight back to the stall, to land on the countertop. Rebecca turned back to her brother. Her eyes were wet. No one had to tell Marcus whom she had been thinking of when she had opened the cage door.

"Do you feel better?" he asked softly.

All she could do was nod. Then remembering her responsibility to the vendor, she hobbled back to the stall with the empty cage. Watching her go, Marcus couldn't help but think how much he loved her—and that he would do anything to make sure that, unlike the birds in the cages, she stayed free. It was just then that his thoughts were interrupted by a deep male voice.

"Good afternoon. Right on time, I see. I like that in a businessman. Shows proper intent, I always say."

Turning, Marcus took in the man's tall, plump frame, silver hair, and expensive clothes. His name was Gregory of the House of Worth, which fit him perfectly. Gold jewelry flashed at his fingers and wrists, and a thick, white mustache lay elegantly just above the decisive mouth. His predatory eyes were dark, and seemed never to miss a thing.

The moment Marcus had first met him, he had taken the fellow for a shrewd bargainer. After making a few polite inquiries, he had learned that Worth seemed to have an honest reputation. Still, Marcus remained nervous as he tried his best to steel himself against whatever first offer Worth might make. Even at the tender age of twelve Seasons of New Life, he knew that someone's first proposal was never the best, and he had no intention of being taken advantage of. He also had a plan.

With a distasteful grimace, Worth looked down at the rug lying in the wheelbarrow.

"Perhaps I was mistaken," he said slyly. "I didn't come here to buy a rug."

"That's good," Marcus answered calmly, "because I didn't come here to sell one."

Worth smiled. By now Rebecca had joined them, and Marcus bade her nearer.

"Are you alone?" Marcus asked him. He realized that it was a foolish question, for Worth could have any number of confederates waiting here in the plaza to rob him, and Marcus wouldn't recognize any of them. But he hoped the question would set a certain tone, rather than glean reliable information.

"Of course," Worth answered, stabbing his thumbs into the shiny, expensive vest that stretched its way around his prodigious middle. "That was our agreement, was it not?" Looking down at the rug again, he smiled, then twisted one of the ends of his mustache. "It's in there, isn't it?"

Checking to see that no one stood too near to them, Marcus beckoned Worth and Rebecca closer, until they all stood crowded around one end of the rug. From this position, even if someone walked directly behind them there would be little to see.

Slowly, carefully, Marcus removed the rags from the end of the rug, grasped the golden rod at the base of the scroll, then pulled it free a short distance. It was just enough to give Worth a taste of the glories promised within.

Worth gasped. He had never seen such a treasure of the craft. To his mind it was easily worth tenfold the entire contents of his shop. The glistening, golden rod and its end knobs alone were worth a king's ransom, to say nothing of the historical value of the elegant Old Eutracian script.

Knowing he had succeeded in whetting Worth's appetite, Marcus quickly slid the scroll back into the relative safety of the rug. "How much?" he asked, coming straight to the point.

Sweating, Worth ran a pudgy index finger around the inside of his shirt collar. "Six—six thousand kisa," he stammered.

Marcus thought he might faint. Six thousand kisa was a huge sum—more than he might earn in an entire lifetime of honest labor. Still, he tried to retain his composure.

"Twelve," he said sternly. Rebecca's eyes went wide. She was quite sure her brother had just lost his mind.

"You just doubled your price!" Worth exploded. "That's not how we negotiate where I come from!"

"Then we obviously don't come from the same place," Marcus countered boldly. "Besides, I didn't double my price. I never set one. I simply doubled your offer. Saves time."

Looking around again, he moved one corner of the rug back a bit to reveal another hint of the golden end knob, letting it shine in the sun. "You're wasting my time, and you're not the only artifacts vendor in Tammerland." He looked hard up into the man's eyes. "The price just went to fourteen."

"Ten," Worth found himself saying.

"Sixteen."

"Thirteen," Worth answered, hardly believing his own bid.

"Is that your final offer?" Marcus asked him. He began to sense resignation in the other man's eyes.

"I fear it must be," Worth answered. "It is all I have."

"Then I shall consider it," Marcus answered. "But as I told you before, I mean to speak to other interested parties." After replacing the rags in the open end of the rug, he picked up the handles of the wheelbarrow.

Worth took an anxious step forward. "But how will I know if it's mine?" he asked urgently. His forehead was bathed in sweat.

"I know where you work, remember?" Marcus answered. "You will hear from me. But in the meantime, I am leaving. If you ever wish to see the scroll again, you will now leave the plaza by walking away in the opposite direction."

Worth nodded. "But if someone outbids me, you will allow me the chance to make a better offer, will you not?" he asked desperately.

Marcus only smiled. "Why would I bother?" he asked bluntly. "Thirteen thousand kisa is all you supposedly have, remember?"

Marcus watched as the beaten vendor walked away. As they had planned, he and Rebecca headed the opposite way from their shack, ducked into an alley, and waited there for a long while. When they were sure they weren't being followed, Marcus began pushing the wheelbarrow toward home, his mind roiling with the unimaginable prospect of having thirteen thousand kisa. But he also knew he was playing a dangerous game, and that his luck couldn't last forever.

It was just then that the scroll began to glow.

From out of the folds of the rags at each end again came the unmistakable azure hue of the craft. Worried, he picked up the pace as fast as he could with 'Becca limping beside him. As one of the rags in the front came loose, he stole a glance up at the sky, to see that darkness was already falling.

As the glow bled out into the coming night, it would be a miracle if someone didn't notice.

*G*rizelda, Krassus, and Janus stood together on the rooftop of the Citadel, watching the blue streaks of the gazing flame dance in the darkness of the night. Grizelda tossed a few more of the herbs stolen from Shadowood into the fire, and the viewing window in the center started to take form.

Now that she had all of the goods she could possibly need, the only limits on her search for the scroll would be her personal endurance, and Krassus had insisted on her trying every two hours. This most recent viewing was her eighth such attempt in a row, and she was tired. Nonetheless, she did her best to persevere.

As the viewing window came into sharper focus, it changed shape, turning into a ragged circle. From within the circle could be seen not only one of the gold end knobs of the scroll, but also what lay past it. It was apparent that the scroll was at least partially hidden, and someone was taking it through a city. But which one?

And then, finally, Krassus saw a group of unmistakable statues. This was without doubt the Plaza of Fallen Heroes. The scroll was in Tammerland. He had done it!

His joy at locating the scroll was quickly replaced by a sense of dread. Better that the scroll were in any city other than the one still inhabited by the wizards of the Redoubt. He knew that Wigg, Faegan, and Abbey would also be desperately trying to find it, presumably through the same methods he was employing. True, he had set their labors back by destroying those herbs and oils that he had not stolen from Shadowood, but the wizards were exceedingly clever, which meant that there was no time to lose. He turned to Janus and Grizelda.

"The two of you are to leave for Tammerland on the first ship that can be readied," he ordered. "Take the supplies you'll need to continue attempting to view the scroll as often as necessary. I don't care how you do it—just get the scroll back to the Citadel! Anchor well off the Cavalon Delta, and take a small, quiet skiff up the Sippora. Your crew must stay belowdecks, out of sight, while you are gone. Demonslavers have never been seen in Tammerland, and I wish to do this quietly, not start a riot."

"You will not be accompanying us, my lord?" Janus asked.

"I cannot," Krassus answered briskly. "Wulfgar needs my full attention, as do other matters of importance here. The return of the scroll I leave up to you. Do not fail me in this."

He turned on the herbmistress. "Grizelda, do not think for one moment that you will be able to escape me simply because you are out of my sight for a time. I found you once, and I can do it again. If you make me hunt you down, it won't be to employ your talents. It will be to kill you. Slowly. Do you understand?"

Looking back to Janus, he had another thought. "When you discover whoever has the scroll, kill him," he added casually. "Leave no loose ends."

The herbmistress bowed her head in submission, while Janus nodded.

Once the gazing flame was extinguished and Janus and Grizelda were gone, Krassus walked slowly to the edge of the roof and looked out on the Sea of Whispers. The three rose-colored moons were full, painting the sea with their palette. There was virtually no wind, and the ocean looked like a sheet of magenta-colored glass.

Placing his hands into the opposite sleeves of his two-colored robe, he turned and descended the stairs.

Thirty-three

Tristan sat looking with worry at Tyranny as she lay on the sofa in her quarters. The ever-present Scars stood by her side with an equally concerned expression on his face. She had fought bravely and survived, but she had been wounded and had passed out from loss of blood. Tristan and Scars had tended to her as best they could before cleaning and bandaging Tristan's shoulders. Then they had waited.

It had taken some time for her to come around. Like any good captain, her first concern had been for how many of her crew she had lost. Then she inquired about the general condition of *The People's Revenge* and the other two ships sailing with them.

Their little fleet was in bad shape, Scars reported. Nearly a quarter of *The People's Revenge* crew had been lost. A large number had been wounded but were still alive. Many of the sails had been ripped beyond repair, along with much of the rigging. And more than half of the ship's spars were completely destroyed.

The other two vessels had fared no better. Each of them was also dead in the water, drifting at the mercy of the elements. Even Tristan was by now sailor enough to know that if they were struck by a sea storm or a fleet of demonslaver ships while in this condition, they would be finished.

Scars had ordered repairs to begin, but it would be a difficult, incomplete job at best. They needed help. But out here, this far into the Sea of Whispers, Tristan knew there could be none.

Tyranny sat up groggily and took a sip of the wine Tristan held out to her. Then she stabbed one of her rolled tubes of leaves between her lips and lit it from the flame offered up by Scars. Taking a deep draught of bluish smoke, she slowly blew it upward, toward the roof of the cabin.

"What in the name of the Afterlife *were* those things that attacked us?" Tristan asked, unable to contain his curiosity any longer. "I have never seen anything like them."

Tyranny took another sip of wine, then gingerly adjusted her position on the sofa. "We call the creatures screechlings," she told him. She took in another lungful of smoke and blew it out. "This was only the second time we have fought them. Scars named them for the horrible noise they make just before they attack. They began to prowl these waters only recently, about the same time the demonslavers started taking their captives from Farpoint. I think the screechlings must have originated at the Citadel, but no one knows for sure. Did you see how they glowed, just before they began attacking us? That tells me they come from magic. But who of the craft would be so cruel as to create such monsters and loose them on the sea?"

Krassus, Tristan thought. It had to be. He would have wanted something that would protect his slave ships and attack any enemies. No doubt the ability had been provided by yet another Forestallment placed in his blood by Nicholas. Tristan lowered his head and closed his eyes.

"Are you all right?" Tyranny asked softly.

He raised his head and looked into her eyes. "No," he answered. "But I will be." He took a deep breath and forced his thoughts back to the problem at hand.

"I saw many of the screechlings purposely destroying the sails, as well as the spars and the yardarms," he said. "Why would they do that, when they could have been attacking the crew?"

"It seems they are both highly intelligent and well organized," Scars answered for his captain as she took another sip of wine. "They know that if we are sufficiently crippled, they can return at their leisure and finish us off. And unless we can get these three vessels moving again, that is exactly what will happen."

Tyranny looked up at her first mate. "How much undamaged sail did we liberate from the slavers?" she asked hopefully.

"Not nearly enough to do a proper job," Scars answered. "Especially considering the fact that we have three vessels to repair. I have taken the liberty of ordering all three ships lashed together, so that we might share resources and not drift apart on the nighttime sea. Dawn will rise soon, and we can work faster then. But even when we are finished, the best we will be able to do is to limp along. If the screechlings find us again, we shall be easy prey." He remained silent for a moment as he considered his next words.

"Our best bet is to make for the Isle of Sanctuary and hope that we reach it before they return," he suggested. "I know this isn't what you want to hear, but we are already wounded, Captain. Unless we reach the isle in time, the deathblow may not be far off."

Tyranny scowled. Then she looked up at her gigantic first mate. "Please leave us now," she said. "I have issues to discuss with our new friend here. In the meantime, make all the repairs you can with what we have available, and then set course for the Isle of Sanctuary. Even limping along, as you put it, is better than sitting dead in the water as live bait for the screechlings."

After nodding to his captain and casting a questioning glance at the prince, Scars left the cabin, closing the door behind him. A combination of anger and confusion crossed Tristan's face.

"What is this Isle of Sanctuary you are taking us to, eh?" he protested. "I, for one, have never heard of it!"

"You can still trust me, I swear it," Tyranny assured him. "Our bargain remains intact. The reason you have never heard of the Isle of Sanctuary is because it is a secret, known only to a very few."

"Enlighten me," he said shortly.

Tyranny took another sip of wine. "Please go to my desk and bring me back my charts."

Tristan skeptically did as she asked, placing the parchments on her lap. Rifling through them, she finally selected one and spread it out.

"We are here," she said, pointing to a section of the chart displaying open sea. "Or at least that's where we were when we were attacked. Dead on course for the delta, just as I had agreed. Our current position has no doubt changed a bit since we have been adrift. But not by much, since the winds have remained light. Anyway, the Isle of Sanctuary is not far off our direct course to the delta. Look."

Running one finger west toward the Cavalon Delta, she stopped it near a small island shaped like a long, crooked finger. According to the scale it was about four leagues long by two wide. Several natural harbors indented its coast. It was drawn in a darker ink, as if it had recently been added to her map.

"I give you the little-known Isle of Sanctuary," she said. "Scars added it from memory."

"But how is that possible?" Tristan asked. "And why must we go there?"

Sitting back, she looked him in the eyes. "You say that two of your wizards still live?" she asked.

"Yes. Wigg, the onetime lead wizard of the Directorate. And his friend Faegan, from Shadowood. What of it?"

"Because your Directorate, or should I say what's left of it, is supposedly responsible for the isle's existence," she answered cautiously. "Or so the legend goes."

Tristan sat back in his chair. "Even if what you say is true, why must we go there?" he asked. "Why can't we just set a course straight for the delta?"

Tyranny took another puff of smoke and let it out slowly. "There is still a great deal of sea between us and home," she answered. "Much of it is known to be infested with screechlings, as well as slaver ships. Provided we can pay the price, we should be able to procure both spars and sailcloth on the isle. Like it or not, we need those to get to the delta in one piece. Even with our layover, and taking into consideration the time it will take to make our final repairs, we will still arrive at the delta faster than if we simply continued to plow along in our current state. You must trust me on this. I know what I'm talking about."

Her face grew dark again, and she reached out, taking his hands into hers. It was the first time she had ever done so. "I don't like the idea of taking us there, either. I would never have given such an order unless it was absolutely necessary. Nor would Scars have suggested it, brave as he is. It's a very dangerous place. During previous visits there I have always lost good people—crew who chose to stay on the isle, rather than return to the sea with me. I wouldn't like to lose any more of them to that place, but those here with me are here of their own free will. What will be will be." She looked away for a moment. "But there is also a personal reason why I avoid visiting the isle . . ."

Seemingly resigned to her decision, she looked back at him. The commanding eyes of the daring privateer had somehow transformed into those of a lovely, desirable woman who suddenly seemed quite vulnerable in his presence.

"You must believe me," she said, gently but insistently. "At this point, everyone on *The People's Revenge* wants to get home as quickly as you do. But we must have the necessary sails to speed our ship, or we may never make it at all." A small smile crossed her lips. "Unless you'd like to row again, of course."

Tristan found his mood softening. Nonetheless, his mind was still full of unanswered questions. "But why do you say that this place has to do with the wizards?" he asked. "How could you possibly know that? Why is it so dangerous? Why did some of your men choose to stay there?"

She gave a short laugh. "You sound like a schoolboy!"

Tristan felt his face flush with embarrassment.

Suddenly the commanding, calculating expression returned to her blue eyes, and she let go of his hands. "No more questions now," she said. "The Isle of Sanctuary is but one day's sail from here, even in our current condition. You will have all of your answers soon enough. Now please help me up. I'm still dizzy, but I must get topside and look over my ships." The wry smile came again. "The crewmembers need to know their captain is still able to pull her own weight."

Standing, Tristan reached down to help her. As she rose to meet him, she winced at a pain in her left thigh and stumbled against him. For a long, uncomfortable moment, they stared into each other's eyes. Then he turned and helped her up the stairway to go look over her crippled ships.

It would be a depressing sight.

Thirty-four

As Wigg and Faegan followed the ancient watchwoman through the portal, they were engulfed in darkness again, save for the light that came from the Paragon hanging around Faegan's neck. Then the watchwoman stopped. Without turning around she raised one white, fleshless hand in a gesture of warning.

"Follow my footsteps exactly, and do not stray from the path," she ordered. "The fall on either side is endless."

She set off again, tapping her wooden staff against either edge of the stony path as she went along. Tentatively, the wizards followed behind her in single file. Fog loomed up on all sides, and the air was so cold that the wizards could see their breath streaming out before them. Although their minds were still brimming over with questions, neither of them spoke.

At one point, Faegan produced a gold coin from the pocket of his robe and tossed it over the side of the path. Using the craft, he trebled his wizard's hearing and waited for the sound.

None came.

After that, both wizards picked their steps with even greater care.

Finally the watchwoman stopped and indicated that it was safe for the wizards to come up alongside her. When they did, she raised her hands.

Radiance stones lining the ceiling immediately began to glow with sage light. As they grew in brightness, the light from the Paragon faded, until at last the jewel returned to its normal state.

Faegan and Wigg saw that they were standing in a very large cavern. Within the boundaries of its walls lay a small lake, its waters glowing with the hue of the craft. Fog steamed up from the lake surface and encroached onto the jagged shoreline.

All around the lake rose tall, black rocks whose slick sides shimmered in the glow from the lake. On the edge of the shore lay a small rowboat. There were no oars to be seen. A slight breeze rippled the water and rustled the wizards' hair; it felt good on their faces.

Looking out at the azure lake, Wigg was reminded of the azure waters he had seen in the Caves of the Paragon, just before he and Tristan had been bled and taken to Ragnar, Nicholas' servant. He wondered how it was that such waters could exist here, as well.

Without speaking, the watchwoman walked to the boat, pushed it into the water, and climbed into its stern. Raising her staff, she then beckoned the two wizards forward to join her. After exchanging a quick, questioning look with Faegan, Wigg stepped into the boat first. Then Faegan levitated his chair up and over the side, joining him.

Still silent, the watchwoman began using her staff to pole them across the fog-shrouded lake. After a time the fog parted, and the wizards could see the far wall of the cavern, where it plunged down into the azure lake. Seven circular openings had been carved into it in a row, each filled about halfway with water. A light breeze emanated from each of them, softly disturbing the surface of the water.

The watchwoman carefully guided the little boat into the center opening and began pushing them down a long, dark tunnel. She paused only to raise her skeletal hands to illuminate the radiance stones that lined the roof of this place, as well, but though their light was very bright, they revealed little. It seemed to be a stone passageway, nothing more.

At last Wigg thought he could see an azure glow that signified the end of the tunnel. The watchwoman stopped poling the boat, and it slowly came to rest.

"You search for the way to untangle the herbs and precious oils of the craft, you say?" she asked in her raspy voice.

As Wigg turned around to face her, he saw that there was still nothing but empty darkness within the depths of her hood. "Yes," he answered.

"Very well, then," she replied. Pushing down on her staff, she levered the boat forward again. "Behold," she said.

As they exited the tunnel, the wizards were faced with a vision of such serene majesty that it nearly made them weep.

The square, stone chamber was huge, stretching at least one hundred meters in all directions. There was no fog here. The waters of the tunnel spilled out into yet another large lake of glowing azure, this one so bright that its light filled the space and streamed across the stone walls and ceiling.

As they approached the far end of the chamber, a sloped, earthen embankment could be seen stretching completely from one of the side walls to the other. Its surface was covered with variegated vines and dark, strong-looking roots. The sharply sloped embankment rose upward in layered, horizontal tiers. Each wide, flat step of earth held what looked to be dozens of small pools of azure water. Water flowed from holes in the rock wall above the highest tier to tumble gracefully from one pool into the next, all the way down to the lake.

In each pool grew plants of the craft, their stems and blossoms rising just above the surface to create individual, floating gardens. These plants were bursting with every possible color, a vibrant rainbow of living energy. As the brilliant water coming from the wall above ran down and into each of the tiered pools, it burbled happily, the sound bouncing off the stone walls and the surface of the lake.

As the wizards stared, entranced, they became aware of the incredible scents in the air. Each mingled with the next, yet was somehow also singularly distinct to the nose.

If these gardens were not what they once had been, Wigg could not even conceive of what they might have looked like in their prime. As it was, their beauty was so great it made his heart ache.

"The floating gardens of the Chambers of Penitence," Faegan breathed, hardly able to contain his joy. "The Tome was right. They really do exist!" But his delight faded as the watchwoman began pushing their boat away from the gardens, rather than toward them.

"Where are you taking us?" he asked anxiously. "What we require is back there, is it not, in the tiered gardens?"

"Indeed," the watchwoman answered quietly, as her macabre hands continued to steer the boat toward the sheer rock wall to their right. "But before I give you what you need, one of you must pay the price. Then, and only then, am I allowed to grant you entrance to the gardens and provide you with what you seek."

Wigg and Faegan looked at each other tentatively, but they said nothing.

Approaching the shore near the far wall, she gently beached the boat and indicated that they should disembark. Then she began walking along the rocky shoreline. The wizards followed.

She soon came to stand before a plain, square doorway carved into the rock wall. There she turned to them. The darkness within the hood of her robe was as impenetrable as ever.

"Only one of you shall be allowed to enter the chamber," she said.

She pointed her blanched, bony hand at Wigg. "It shall be you," she added coldly.

"Why?" Wigg asked.

"The herbs you request are among the rarest in existence," she answered. "Therefore the psychic price to be paid is exceedingly high. Of the two of you, the cripple has far less chance of survival. I can sense that his mind is always struggling to control the pain in his legs. The added burdens that await in the Chamber of Penitence shall be more easily borne by you—which is not to guarantee your survival, either. The choice remains yours: Decide."

Wigg looked down at Faegan and nodded slowly. If he died here in this place today, then so be it. But no matter what else might happen, no harm could come to the Paragon.

Faegan looked up at Wigg with wet, guilty eyes. "I'm sorry, my friend," he said, his voice cracking. Then he looked down at the stark wooden chair that was at once both his freedom and his prison. "I have far less to lose," he added sadly.

Wigg placed a hand on Faegan's shoulder. "It's all right," he said softly. "But if I never come back, please do all you can to help Celeste come to terms with her past. I have only just found her, and I would like to know that my oldest, best friend will be looking after her. Just as I know you will also care for Abbey and the Chosen Ones."

Lowering his head slightly, all Faegan could do was nod.

Wigg looked back at the faceless woman. "I am ready," he said.

She turned and walked through the doorway and into the darkness beyond.

Taking a deep breath, the lead wizard followed her inside.

Thirty-five

"You're insane," Wulfgar breathed softly, incredulously, as he stared at the wizard. "Even you, in the warped, twisted world of this bizarre island you command, cannot believe everything you have just said! And even if you do, such things are not possible! What you propose is monstrous, and I will have none of it, do you hear? None of it!"

Smiling slightly, Krassus stood from his chair and came to stand by Wulfgar's side. Looking out over the nighttime sea, he saw the running lights of several slave ships approaching the underground pier. Counting them, he saw that there were five. He smiled again. With the exception of the ship Janus and Grizelda had just departed in, most of his fleet was now home. And here in the protection of the Citadel was where they would stay, at least for the time being.

With the discovery of Wulfgar, he had no further need for the taking of *R'talis* slaves. Even before the half sibling of the Chosen Ones had been found, Krassus had already secured more of the endowed captives than he needed to fulfill the other, more esoteric part of Nicholas' plans. Nor did the wizard need more *Talis* slaves, even though they had been brought here for an entirely different purpose. And so he had told Janus to order all of the slaving activities in Eutracia abandoned. Soon his entire fleet and most of his demonslavers and consuls would be back at the Citadel, awaiting his next orders.

From the moment he had first entered these rooms and looked Wulfgar over, Krassus had been pleased. Tall, broad shouldered, and muscular, Wulfgar had intense hazel eyes that burned brightly with both his innate intelligence and the strength of his uniquely endowed blood.

His rugged good looks were not what one might have called classically handsome, but he carried with him a defiant sense of purpose, just as did the other two offspring of the late queen Morganna.

Krassus could barely contain his eagerness to discover just how strong Wulfgar's blood would eventually prove to be.

But first he would need to consult the Scroll of the Vagaries.

For the last two hours Krassus had been explaining his plan in great detail to the unbelieving man seated beside him, telling him why he had been brought here and what was about to happen to all of the other slaves, both *Talis* and *R'talis* alike. Some of it, the wizard had said, was already going forward at the hands of the consuls under his control.

As Krassus had gone on talking, the look of extreme horror on Wulfgar's face had turned to one of pure rage. At one point he had actually tried to attack the wizard. But Krassus had, of course, been able to control him, painfully but gently showing him the error of his ways. After that Wulfgar had simply paced, seething, knowing that there was nothing he could do but listen to the impossible-sounding plans of the wizard with the long, white hair and the strange gray-and-blue robe.

Krassus had fully expected Wulfgar to react this way. In fact, he would have been bitterly disappointed if the son of Morganna had not. But he also knew that Wulfgar's feelings would change soon enough. And there would be absolutely nothing Wulfgar would be able to do to prevent it.

When Krassus had explained that Wulfgar was in fact the bastard half sibling of Tristan and Shailiha, the Chosen Ones themselves, Wulfgar had laughed, calling the wizard insane. But after Krassus had explained to him about the wizards' orphanage and the fact that he had been given over to a couple named Jason and Selene of the House of Merrick, his derisive attitude had slowly subsided. And when Krassus had shown Wulfgar the blood signatures of all three of Morganna's offspring, and then gone on to explain how they had been formed by the craft, for a time Wulfgar had become strangely silent.

"Why Serena?" Wulfgar finally asked, his mood quieter now.

"What do you mean?" Krassus responded politely.

"It was painfully obvious that that freak Janus wanted us together, and in a very bad way," Wulfgar answered. "I had never asked for a woman. Yet there she suddenly was. Presented to me on a silver platter, to supposedly do with however I wished. I now partially regret to say that it worked. I care very much for her, as she does for me. But you know that already, don't you? So tell me, why was it so important to you that we meet?"

"I handpicked Serena for you myself, as the dead son of the Chosen One commanded me to do, just before his ill-fated attempt to empower the Gates of Dawn," Krassus answered perfunctorily. "Serena is not only quite beautiful, but also highly intelligent. The assay rating of her endowed blood makes her an excellent match for you. It is in fact a value of three—very high quality, indeed. And her blood signature leans far to the left, just as your does, making her even more suitable. But as of yet, of course, she is completely ignorant of such nuances."

Still confused, Wulfgar scowled at the thought of how easily he and Serena had been manipulated. But his love for her was real. Now he knew why she had been taken away by the demonslavers this morning: so that the wizard called Krassus could come here and speak to him privately. Suddenly more concerned than ever for Serena's well-being, he glared at the wizard sitting so calmly across from him.

"You still haven't answered my question," he demanded. "Why was she presented to me? It couldn't have simply been for our sexual gratification."

"No, no, of course not," Krassus answered happily, crossing his legs and taking a sip of the excellent red wine on the table before him. "Although an offspring from your union would certainly be useful, that is not my goal. Other, more pressing matters must take precedence. As I have told you, you will eventually become the ruler of not only this island, but a good deal more, as well. And every king needs a queen. The woman behind the throne, as they say. Serena was the obvious choice, and is also the woman you will no doubt bestow this honor upon when the time comes. When all is said and done, you will eventually find that the two of you are compatible in ways you could never have dreamed."

Wulfgar thought for a moment. "Assuming that all of this insanity is in fact true, how can you be so sure that I will choose Serena?"

"Because even though you don't realize it yet, you are a highly superior specimen of the craft," Krassus said calmly. "At some point even you will finally understand that only the best will do. Your position, the quality of your blood, and the left-leaning nature of your signature will eventually demand it. And Serena is without question the most highly qualified woman here."

"So you plan to do to Serena what you wish to do to me?" Wulfgar asked furiously. Guilt that he had somehow helped Krassus draw Serena into all of this piled on top of his anger, and he stood again and began pacing the balcony.

"Oh, no," Krassus answered. "When the time comes, that shall be your task. You will most assuredly want to do it yourself, to make sure her arrival into your new world is perfect in all respects."

"But if she is so important to you, why did you make her an outcast from the other slaves, feeding her fine food in their presence while they starve?" Wulfgar asked. "What possible purpose could that serve except to reinforce your cruelty?"

"Ah, yes," Krassus answered. "You see, it is time Serena began learning how to handle what will soon be her new station in life. As you will learn, the unendowed are little more than a natural resource for the endowed to exploit. Mere cattle, as it were. And becoming immune to the pleadings of those of lesser blood is an essential part of that realization. What better way to begin teaching her than to force her to watch her friends starve while she thrives? Besides, as I understand it, it was you who insisted that she receive better nourishment. Perhaps you should have been more careful with your words, Wulfgar. You know what they say: Be careful what you ask for, you might just get it."

Seething, Wulfgar stopped pacing for a moment to glare at the imperious, self-confident wizard. "And that freak of nature named Janus," he said angrily, "what rock did you find him under?"

Krassus gave a soft chuckle. "Interesting, isn't he?" he commented. "Nicholas suggested that I select a Eutracian of unendowed blood to help oversee the slaving operations. Far easier to kill, you see, than someone of endowed blood should something sour in the relationship. So I went shopping for an assistant in Bargainer's Square. That section of Tammerland is literally teeming with criminals for hire. Janus seemed an excellent choice." The wizard took another sip of wine.

"But I can sense how much you hate him, Wulfgar," Krassus added conspiratorially. "So once you have attained your potential, if you wish to kill him, then kill him. Frankly, I couldn't care less. Janus is merely a means to an end. Thugs like him are a kisa a dozen, so to speak."

A short smile finally crossed Wulfgar's lips. "If I can eventually kill Janus, then how do you know that I won't also kill you, and all of your demonslavers?" he asked. "I would enjoy that very much."

Krassus calmly took another sip of wine. "Because by then you won't want to," he answered. "As you will eventually see, you will need the slavers. And by that time, killing me would profit you nothing. As I told you, I now have a preordained life span. It came to me compliments of Nicholas, in the form of my rather inconvenient but very effective lung disease. A creative incentive granted to me by my master, designed not only to hurry me in my work but also to grace me with the greatest reward of all: to reside for all of eternity in the embrace of the Heretics of the Guild. So once you can, feel free to kill me. My fate is sealed one way or the other."

Wulfgar's emotions reeled between disbelief and hatred. Could this wizard actually be telling the truth? Or was he simply mad? And if it all really was true, then how could he, a simple blacksmith and livery owner, ever hope to stop it? How could one hope to defeat a madman of the craft?

"Why did you bother to come here to me and tell me all of this?" he asked angrily. "Considering the barbaric, inhumane manner in which we were all brought here, not to mention your horrific plans for the rest of the slaves, drinking wine and engaging in conversation is a bit over-civilized, isn't it? If you're as powerful as you say, then why don't you just get on with it all?"

Krassus only smiled. "If that's how you feel, then tell me, Wulfgar: How would you prefer it be done?" He took another sip of wine.

"You could struggle, of course, and I could have my demonslavers beat and torture you," he went on calmly. "But that would be so pedestrian, don't you think? Besides, I need you healthy. You shall need all of your strength to survive what I am about to do to you. In the end, your struggle would only prove a waste of time and energy for us both—and given my condition, time is the one luxury I do not have. Also, should you be entertaining any heroic notions of trying to kill yourself to thwart me, know that from now on at least two armed demonslavers will be here with you, watching you every moment until my work with you is finished. Then our roles will be reversed, and you shall command me. And I shall gladly obey you for as much time as I may have left. But just now, there is something I must do."

Walking back inside, Krassus beckoned Wulfgar to join him. Realizing he had no choice, Wulfgar reluctantly did as he was asked.

Krassus pointed one hand in the direction of the balcony, and the azure glow of the craft started to appear. As it did, the wizard gracefully moved his hand back and forth, and the glow slowly began to cover the entire expanse of the doorway, creating a thin, transparent wall of blue. Krassus lowered his hand.

"A wizard's warp," he said casually. "Designed to prevent you and Serena from doing anything unpleasantly athletic. Such as a lovers' leap, for example. I have made it transparent, though, so that you might still enjoy the view. Given everything else you are about to endure, it would have been quite heartless of me to have taken that away from you, don't you agree?"

Wulfgar looked through the shimmering azure wall and out into the blackness of the night. "I will fight you; you must know that," he said softly, at the same time wondering how he might ever accomplish such a thing. "So will Serena. Somehow we will reach Tristan and Shailiha, and together we will kill you."

Krassus nodded knowingly. "Yes," he agreed. "You will no doubt struggle against all that is about to happen. At first, your blood will demand it of you. But then the left-leaning nature of your blood signature will take over, turning you toward your true calling. In the end it will not matter how much you struggle, for you cannot win. Nor can Serena. Eventually you will both understand, and thank me for the wondrous world I have lain before you. And then I shall die, leaving the rest of Nicholas' magnificent mission in your very capable hands."

Placing his hands into the opposite sleeves of his robe, he turned to leave, but then stopped. "There is still so much you do not know," he said softly, as if he were speaking to an uneducated child. "Things your unprepared mind and untrained blood are not yet ready to embrace. But they soon will be. In the meantime, I will have Serena sent back to you. Even if you tell her all that we spoke of tonight, in the end it will make no difference. So do with your newfound information what you will, and enjoy your time with her. In a few days we will begin our work together. But first there is research I must complete, and for that I need the *R'talis* slaves. Then, when I am finished, I will send for you. Be ready."

With that, Krassus called for his demonslavers. The bolt scratched its way across the other side of the door and three of the monsters sauntered in, armed to the teeth. Saying nothing more, Krassus walked from the room with one of them. The twin doors closed behind him with finality, leaving Wulfgar alone with the remaining two slavers.

As Wulfgar turned to look through the bizarre, transparent wall left by the wizard, his thoughts were again drawn to the hideous plans Krassus had for not only the other slaves, but also for the rest of the world.

For the first time since his capture in Farpoint, a single tear overcame the lower lid of one of his hazel eyes and rolled its way down one cheek.

Thirty-six

S hailiha shifted her weight in the saddle as the bay gelding cantered across the broad, rolling field of barley. The wind created waves in the sea of ripe grain, and the sun, unusually warm for this time in the Season of New Life, lit the tan stalks with sparks of gold and amber. Smiling, she took a deep breath. The field smelled fertile with the promise of a good harvest, and she could hear the rose-colored valley swallows calling out to one another as they swooped through the clear sky, helping to create the seductive but misleading impression that all in the princess' nation was well.

Celeste rode beside her on Pilgrim, Tristan's dappled gray stallion. Since coming to live with them, Celeste had been learning to ride. Now, several months later, she could very nearly hold her own with the best of them.

She had asked Shailiha's permission to use Tristan's horse today, and the princess had gladly agreed, aware that riding Pilgrim made Celeste feel closer to Tristan.

The horrific nightmare Celeste had suffered the night before had clearly been a turning point for her. After her initial terror had passed, an overpowering rage had rushed hotly, suddenly through her veins, and she had hurried to talk with Shailiha. Her feelings—anger, fear, shame— had come pouring out, and at last had finally crumbled away. And for the first time in three centuries, her denial of her past finally departed, as well. In its place had arrived a sense of acceptance. With that newfound acceptance had finally come the freedom and the desire to taste all of the good things available to her in her new life. And the thirst her soul most desperately wished to quench was to tell Tristan how much she truly cared.

And to be with him.

Unfortunately, the best she could do for now was to ride his horse in the company of his twin sister—and her best friend.

Smiling at Celeste, Shailiha suggested that they stop for lunch and a rest in a nearby grove of trees. Celeste nodded her agreement and touched her heels to Pilgrim's flanks, urging him toward the end of the field. Laughing, Shailiha followed.

After securing their mounts and untying the two saddlebags, the women sat down in the shade of the trees. The deep, green carpet of grass was lush and soft, and it felt good to be off the horses for a time. Opening the saddlebags, Shailiha removed some cold seasoned grouse, fresh fruit, and dark bread. She also produced a bottle of very good white wine and two wooden cups. Eating and drinking in companionable silence, they took in the stillness of the countryside and the warm, soft breeze that came visiting from time to time. High above, Ox and his Minion squadron circled lazily in the sky. In truth Shailiha had at first been disappointed to know that she and Celeste were going to be chaperoned. But now, seeing the silhouettes of the powerful Minion wings against the blue background, she felt comforted.

At last Celeste spoke. "You think Tristan's still alive, don't you?" she asked quietly.

Taking a deep breath, Shailiha looked out over the field. "I don't just think it," she said with conviction. "I know it."

"As much as I love hearing you say it, how can you be so sure?"

Shailiha looked down at the glittering medallion lying around her neck. Then she held it up for Celeste to see. "Call it intuition, if you like," she answered. "But ever since I first found this around my neck and I came out from under the awful spells the Coven had placed on me, I have felt far more connected to him than ever before. In my heart I have always thought there is more to these medallions we wear than first meets the eye. They are twins, just as we are. And I believe there is meaning in that." Sighing, she let the bit of shiny gold fall back to her chest.

"Don't ask me to explain it, for I can't," she said honestly. "Tristan is in danger—of that I am sure. But he is also alive and trying to get back home—I just know it. If only the Minion patrols flying over the Sea of Whispers could bring us back some scrap of information—anything that might help us find him! But we cannot lose hope. I *will not* lose hope." She held her face up to the breeze, eyes closed. Then her brow creased as a dark thought crossed her mind.

"And now Tristan and I learn that we have a brother out there somewhere, most probably suffering horribly at the hands of the wizard Krassus," she said quietly, half to herself. "We must someday bring him home, as well." She paused. "There have been so many secrets," she finally whispered. "And, I fear, still so many more to learn."

For a time they both sat there, saying nothing.

"I hope with all my heart that you are right and that we can find them both," Celeste finally said. She pulled her knees up beneath her chin. "Tell me something," she said softly. "What was your husband Frederick like? I'm sorry I was never able to know him."

With Tristan still missing, the princess wasn't sure she possessed the fortitude to speak of her late husband, as well. Frederick had been the love of her life, the father of her only child. When he had been killed at the hands of the Coven, it had been as if the flame in her heart had suddenly been blown out. Sometimes it seemed that the part of her heart the flame had once inhabited had gone cold, never to be rekindled again. She had spoken little of Frederick since his death. But as she thought on it, she realized that she needed to, wanted to. A sad smile came to her lips as she took another sip of wine.

"Frederick was the commander of the Royal Guard," she began. "He and Tristan were best friends, and they constantly teased each other—especially over who was the better swordsman. Frederick taught Tristan everything he knows about combat, yet in some ways, the student eventually overcame the teacher. It was Tristan who taught me to use a sword, and later on he introduced me to Frederick. When I first saw the stalwart officer in the splendid uniform, I was so smitten that I couldn't breathe."

Celeste smiled at her.

"Silly of me, I know," Shailiha continued with a short, sad laugh. "But that's how love is. And now Frederick is gone, but at least he lives on in Morganna. I am immensely grateful for that, and always will be."

The wind came up again, moving through her long blond hair. She pulled the disobedient tresses behind her. Then she turned her eyes back to Celeste.

"You love my brother very much, don't you?" the princess asked gently, already knowing the answer.

Smiling, Celeste lowered her head a bit. "It is really so obvious?" she asked back, blushing slightly.

"Oh, yes," Shailiha answered. "Everyone at the palace sees it. And rest assured, the same sentiment rests in his eyes, as well. But tell me: Now that so much has changed for you, what will you do when you finally see him again?"

It was Celeste's turn to look out over the field. "My newfound heart won't let me wait this time," she said softly, her mind made up. "I will tell him. And then we shall see."

Shailiha smiled as she wondered what the future might hold for Celeste and Tristan, if and when her brother ever came home. Neither of them spoke, for they both knew that there was nothing more that needed saying. Instead they packed up the remainder of the food and mounted their horses.

As they rode back through the field of waving grain, the Minion warriors still patiently circling above, Shailiha closed her eyes and called for Caprice. Silently, softly, the beautiful flier of the field came fluttering down to land obediently on her mistress' outstretched arm.

Thirty-seven

"Drop anchor!" Scars shouted loudly.

The anchor went in with a splash, and *The People's Revenge,* all of her sails furled, drifted for a moment before coming to a halt. Not far from them, the other two ships in their little fleet likewise dropped anchor and came to a rest. Satisfied, Scars looked back to his captain and nodded.

Tristan stood on the bow next to Tyranny, wondering how she could be so sure they had arrived at the Isle of Sanctuary. It was midday, and the sun was high, but a dense fog bank blocked the view ahead of them. But then, through the salty sea air, he was surprised to realize he could distinguish another odor: the smell of land.

Tristan was not the only one who welcomed the chance to stand on firm ground again. Tyranny's crew seemed extremely anxious to go ashore. For some reason still unknown to the prince, Tyranny had ordered the slaves to stay aboard for the time being. A smattering of crewmen, chosen by lot, stayed behind to watch over the ships as they lay at anchor. The others were all joyously clambering into the skiffs hoisted along the length of the hull, lowering themselves down into the water as quickly as they knew how, and paddling off into the fog.

Tyranny stood watching her crew depart with a distinct look of concern on her face. The bandage Tristan had wound around her forehead yesterday had been removed, as had the ones on her hands. Only the cloth around her left thigh remained, since that wound had been deeper and still tried to bleed through from time to time. Tristan wondered what she was waiting for.

"Aren't we going ashore?" he asked her. On hearing his words she seemed to come out of some kind of personal reverie, and she turned her wide, blue eyes toward him.

"Yes, yes, of course," she answered rather absently. At a gesture from her, Scars walked to the gunwale and prepared to lower the captain's personal skiff into the sea. Tyranny started to join him, but Tristan gently took her by one arm, stopping her.

"I think it's time you gave me some answers about all of this, don't you?" he asked, jaw hard with determination.

Tyranny nodded. "You're right," she said simply. "Climb into the skiff, and I will explain on the way."

But as the skiff made its way into the gloom, Scars rowing, Tyranny was silent. The dense fog was cold and clammy against Tristan's skin, and so thick that he could barely see Tyranny next to him. If it hadn't been for the reassuring sound of the oars slicing through the sea, he wouldn't have known that Scars was there at all. Tristan scowled.

"What is it about this place that has unnerved you so?" he asked. "That isn't like you. And why do you seem so hesitant to go ashore, when the rest of your crew was so eager?"

She closed her eyes for a moment, and a short, rather sad smile crossed her face. "You're very observant," she answered. "I don't fear this place, Tristan. There is nothing in this world that I truly fear, including the screechlings that attacked us. But there are reasons why I do not wish to see this place again."

He edged closer and put an arm around her, not only to help ward off the cold, but also, he hoped, to inspire a sense of trust. She did not shy away from his touch. "May I know what these reasons are?" he asked.

"The Isle of Sanctuary is a haven for pirates," she said. "Not privateers such as Scars and myself, mind you, but true marauders of the seas. These men, and in some cases women, make their living by plundering the honest merchant vessels that ply the coast of Eutracia. Whenever they take a ship, those captives who refuse to join them are immediately put to the sword. Because of this practice, their ranks have swollen quickly. On discovering this island they made it their base. Even the name of Sanctuary that the wizards gave to this place suits the needs of the pirates. Ironic, wouldn't you say?"

But something else occurred to Tristan. "How is it possible that you know of the connection between this place and the Directorate of Wizards?"

"A great library was found here—only one of numerous structures. The texts within held the plans for the island. The Directorate was clearly the force behind it. The construction apparently began sometime just after the end of the Sorceresses' War. But although the buildings were finished, it seems they were never occupied."

Stunned, Tristan turned to look back out into the fog. For a moment his mind was teased by the idea that he might find the Scroll of the Vigors here, but then he quickly dismissed the notion. If the scrolls had been hidden here, Wigg and Faegan would surely know. He turned back to Tyranny.

"Tell me," he asked. "Are these records still intact?"

"As of my last visit here, yes," she answered. "The pirates have little use for such things. Many of them can't even read. But now I have a question for you. I have been sailing these waters all of my life, and I would bet my last kisa that despite the evidence contained in the library, this island did not exist until the return of the Coven. So how is it that it has so suddenly sprung up from the depths, so to speak, for the pirates to use?"

"I have no idea," Tristan replied. "All I can tell you is that the wizards often have their own inexplicable ways of doing things . . ." He shook his head. "But you still haven't told me your reasons for not wanting to come here," he reminded her gently.

"First of all, I always lose a number of good crewmembers to this place," she answered sadly. "The temptations here are too great for many of them to resist. That is surely the only reason my ships are allowed entry here—because I lose so many of my people to their cause. It profits the pirates to let me visit."

"If that's the case, then why do you let your crew go ashore at all?" Tristan asked.

Tyranny snorted. "It's easy to see you have never captained a sailing vessel, my dear prince," she scoffed. "Just what would you have me do to stop them, eh? You, Scars, and I certainly aren't enough to keep them from going ashore, are we? These are basically good people, Tristan, and when we are at sea, they follow my orders to the letter. But like all people they have their weaknesses, especially after having been out for weeks on end. When a vessel at sea is stopped by pirates, the crew is forced into service—they have no other option. But here, once a crewmember goes ashore and learns what Sanctuary has to offer, many of them join the pirates willingly. And the pirates are smart enough to know that someone who has joined them of his or her own accord will probably serve them better than one who has not."

Tristan shook his head. "And the other reason?" he asked gently, hoping to finally come to the heart of the matter.

"There is one here who is in charge of it all," she answered softly, sadly. "His name is Rolf of the House of Glenkinnon. At one time he worked for my father, in our fishing concern. That's how we met. Later on, he became not only my partner in my pursuit of the demonslavers, but my lover, as well. But once we found this place and he set foot ashore, all of that changed."

"Is Sanctuary really that alluring?" Tristan asked.

Tyranny nodded.

"I see," he mused. "So this man was persuaded not only to leave you, but to become an important part of what you despise. I'm sorry, Tyranny. That must have been difficult."

Turning to him, she placed a hand over his. "You must be very careful in this place, Tristan," she warned him. "My common crew are welcome, even accepted in this place. But needless to say, you look and act very different. Even though Rolf and I are no longer together, he can be insanely jealous, especially when he is drinking. We will not require his permission to buy our sails and spars from the tradesmen here. But he could just as easily tell them not to deal with us, should the mood strike him. And they would obey him without question. He rules by intimidation and is a quick and efficient killer—the best swordsman I have ever seen. So give him a wide berth, and let me do the talking. I want to be in and out of here as quickly as possible."

She allowed herself a small half smile. "Besides," she whispered, leaning in closer toward his ear, "you and I have business to conclude in Eutracia. I still haven't forgotten about my money, you know. I must admit that I gave serious thought to having Scars tie you up and then leave you aboard with the freed slaves until we could be done with our business here. That way I could have better protected my investment in you. But after coming to know you as I have, I decided that as Scars and I shopped for the things we need, we were safer with you and your strange sword than without you."

This time it was Tristan's turn to give a snort. Tyranny was nothing if not clever, he reminded himself. He turned his attention forward again. As he did, he thought he saw the fog start to thin. Then the skiff plunged headlong out the other side of it, and the Isle of Sanctuary suddenly lay before him.

Thirty-eight

As Wigg followed the watchwoman of the floating gardens down the dark, cramped tunnel, his apprehension grew. He was the lead wizard, his knowledge of the craft second only to Faegan's. As such, he normally had little to fear. But now Faegan was no longer by his side, and Wigg was alone with this strange, dark-robed creature. As she led him along he felt a sense of dread shooting up his spine, coupled with a cold, nervous sweat. As he thought about it, he didn't know which was worse: having to wait to endure the nature of the psychic price he was about to pay, or facing the possibility of dying alone in this strange underground world should he fail to withstand it.

Finally the watchwoman stopped. Coming up beside her, Wigg could see that he was at the exit to the tunnel, standing on a stone landing. A circular stairway led from the landing to a large, simple room below. The radiance stones here provided unusually soft light, making it difficult to see.

The watchwoman beckoned him onto the top step and raised her hands. Almost immediately the circular stairway started to revolve, lowering itself with each turn like a corkscrew disappearing into a cork. As he and the watchwoman neared the floor, Wigg could see that the room was carpeted in skeletons.

They lay everywhere, in no particular order. All human, of different sizes, and probably genders. And, he saw as he looked closer, they all shared one strange characteristic: every single sternum bone had been completely destroyed, as if it had been forcefully blown apart from within. In many cases the ribs had also been rent asunder, even scattered about the room, leaving gaping holes.

"What happened to them?" Wigg asked as he carefully followed the watchwoman through the shining, white skeletons.

"The answer is simple, wizard," she replied. "They failed."

"But how did they fail?" Wigg asked, hoping to gain some precious insight that might help him survive. "Did their hearts burst because they were not strong enough to withstand the regrets you forced them to relive?"

Finally, after having guided him through all of the bones, she stopped and turned to him. "I didn't force them to do anything," she answered sternly. "They came here of their own free will, hoping to acquire certain herbs and oils of the craft so that they might better protect the Vigors against the never-ending wrath of the Vagaries. And they ended up forfeiting their lives. Just as you may. And also like you, they understood that chaos is the natural order of the universe, the very principle upon which the Vagaries thrive. In their cases, chaos prevailed. You are all alike. Those of you who come here always believe that what you are about to endure is a test of the strength of your hearts. It isn't."

Puzzled, Wigg narrowed his eyes. "Then what is it that is being tested?"

"The inherent goodness of your endowed blood, wizard, such as it may be. Your blood signature was verified as right-leaning by the Woman of Stone before you were allowed entry to this place, was it not?"

She turned to face the far wall of the chamber. Then she raised her wooden staff. "Behold," she said.

The air before them started to take on the azure glow of the craft. Then the gleaming began to coalesce, forming into a very large, shimmering cube that began to spin slowly.

"What is it?" he asked.

"Tell me, wizard, what is your greatest regret?" she asked, ignoring his question. "And remember, you must answer truthfully."

Wigg stared at the revolving cube as he considered her question. There had been a great many regrets in his long life. But one stood head and shoulders above all the others. He looked back at the faceless watchwoman.

"My greatest regret is having banished the Coven of sorceresses to the Sea of Whispers, rather than killing them outright," he said softly. "Had I followed my heart that night and drowned all four of them in the ocean as I was tempted to do, I would have undoubtedly been forced from the Directorate for violating their mandate. But that would have been a very small price to pay. For the Coven eventually returned and laid waste to the land, killing as they went. Thousands of innocents died, including most of the royal family and all of the remaining wizards of the Directorate. It was entirely my fault, for I alone could have prevented it, but did not. It was a mistake for which I shall never forgive myself." For a long moment, Wigg lowered his head and closed his eyes.

"Very well," she replied.

He opened his eyes to see that the gleaming cube was still revolving in the air.

"What I say to you now is for your ears alone, and never to be repeated, do you understand?" she asked. Wigg nodded.

"The greatest tragedy of regret is not what one did or did not do to cause it," she said. "Nor is it what we did or did not experience at the time. It is therefore neither the doing nor the omission of some act that causes the greatest pain and suffering, but rather its aftermath that burns longest in our hearts, and eventually in the hearts of others. The aftermath of your regret spirals down through the years like a plague, infecting everyone and everything it touches. It has always been this way, just as it always shall be. It is therefore this part of that aftermath that you shall now see, for that night in the Sea of Whispers was only the catalyst, not the result. You just said so yourself, did you not? That is truly what the Chamber of Penitence is about, wizard. We are here to observe a small part of the results of what you caused, not simply the lone act that caused them. And may your endowed blood and your wizard's soul possess enough inherent goodness to survive what you shall witness, for it is only that same goodness, as it struggles within you against the aftermath of your error, that can keep you alive."

Then the watchwoman turned toward the gleaming, spinning cube and raised her staff. As she did, shapes began to form within it. Then the shapes came into greater focus, forming an all-too-familiar scene.

As the drama unfolded, Wigg was stricken with an intense, excruciating pain that shot through not only his entire nervous system, but cleaved into his very soul, as well. Though transfixed by the view, his pain took him to his knees. Sobbing, he found himself screaming at the watchwoman, begging her to make it stop. But it didn't.

In truth, it had only just begun.

The scene was of Tristan's coronation night—the night that everything in the wizard's world so irrevocably changed. Through his tears, Wigg could see the royal family standing proudly on the dais. Nicholas . . . Morganna . . . Frederick . . . the Chosen Ones . . . And the other members of the Directorate were also there, waiting for him to place the Paragon around Tristan's neck, sealing the prince's reign for the next thirty years.

Then came the smashing of the glass dome high above, its sharp, glass shards raining down as the first of the Minions dropped into the great hall and began slaughtering the defenseless guests.

Blood, screaming, severed body parts, and yet more blood . . . always, endlessly. The blood flowed until it seemed there was an entire sea of it, sweeping across the once-beautiful white-and-black checkerboard floor.

And then, suddenly, he was watching the struggle that had gone on outside of the palace—the one that until now he had never witnessed. The Minions descended on the gathered citizens like madmen, cutting them down as they went. Men, women, and children fell easy prey to the winged monsters wielding the strangely curved swords. By now some of the Royal Guard had begun to fight back, but the Minion army was too strong, and too large.

Some of the monsters picked up severed human body parts and began using their bloody, ragged ends as paintbrushes with which to scrawl obscenities and warnings across the walls. Raising one hand, Wigg tried to summon his gift and stop the vision, but nothing happened. He found himself forced to watch as it went on and on.

Just as had happened the first time, he found himself experiencing the cruel helplessness of not being able to stop any of it.

Then, quite unexpectedly, his mental and physical pain multiplied, searing through his system even more viciously than before. As each Minion sword came flashing down to cut through sinew and bone, as each woman was thrown to the ground and brutally abused, as each husband, wife, sister, and brother bent over slaughtered loved ones and screamed into the night, Wigg was forced to feel their physical and mental agony. His body convulsed with it, his mind was seared by it, and his heart pounded with it.

Crying madly, the exquisite agony wracking every iota of his being, Wigg fell facedown onto the cold stone floor. Nonetheless, some unseen force lifted his face back up so that he had no choice but to continue taking in the horrifying carnival of blood, gore, rape, and death.

And then he heard the beating of his own heart.

As the agony of the victims continued to flood into his being, the beating grew more insistent. Ever louder, ever faster, it became so overpowering that he thought it might burst his eardrums. Blood, pain, the frantic screaming of the innocents, and the pounding of his heart all combined into a massive, unrelenting crescendo that he knew would soon kill him unless it stopped.

But it didn't. It just kept on going and going, seemingly without end.

Then suddenly it was too much for even the endowed blood and the inherent goodness of the lead wizard to bear.

With the watchwoman standing over him, Wigg's face hit the unforgiving stone floor, and the light went out of his eyes.

CHAPTER

Thirty-nine

As Krassus walked into the weapons forge, he could feel the intense
heat from the hearths blast him in the face. He could hear the
constant hissing of the steam as the slaves lowered the red-hot, partially
constructed weapons into the vats of brackish water to temper them.
The sound of their hammers banging down on the hot metal rang out
endlessly. Smoke and soot hung darkly in the air, infusing the entire
place with a hot, charred odor.

As he breathed it in, he was overcome by the urge to cough.
Quickly pulling the bloodied rag from his blue-and-gray robe, he placed
it over his mouth and involuntarily let go several deep, convulsive hacks.
Taking the rag away, he looked down to see his familiar blood signature
twisting its way across the fabric.

His disease was advancing; he had been coughing even more of late.
It was becoming increasingly evident that he must hurry in his work if
he was to successfully complete Nicholas' mission before he died. And
to be certain of his victory, he needed to acquire the Scroll of the Vigors, the only piece of the puzzle still missing.

Angrily stuffing the rag back into his robe, he walked purposefully
up to the demonslaver in charge. The monster bowed.

"Status report," the wizard ordered simply.

"All goes well," the grotesque servant replied. "The store of new
weapons grows daily, and ever more slavers come to take them up. There
have been no further suicide attempts by any of the workers."

Satisfied, Krassus cast his dark eyes around the room, trying to find the slave that Janus had told him about. Finally Krassus found him stand-ing on the far side of the room, his hands tied behind his back.

"Bring him to me," he said simply. The head slaver immediately obliged, walking over to where Twenty-Nine stood supervising another slave. Grabbing him by the throat, the slaver manhandled him over to where Krassus stood waiting.

Krassus walked completely around the loin-clad slave as if he were examining some beast of burden he might purchase. Then he grasped the slave's dirty chin and turned his face this way and that in the orange-red glow of the hearths.

Confused as to why he had been singled out, Twenty-Nine wondered who this frightening man with the long white hair and the piercing eyes was. He just as quickly found himself hoping that he would never have to face him again.

"So you're the one who gave us so much trouble by trying to take your own life," Krassus said softly. "Did you really think it would be so easy, my friend? I'm glad to see that you have been properly restrained and are giving us no further concern. But as you will soon learn, noth-ing here in this chamber, including you and the weapon smiths you su-pervise, will matter very much longer." He turned back to the head demonslaver.

"I was on my way to the Scriptorium on more urgent business, but I decided to stop here to tell you something," he said. "I have ordered that no more slaves be taken from Eutracia, for our requirements have been filled. Therefore, after you have fully armed all of the forthcoming demonslavers, you may shut this place down."

Turning on his heel, Krassus crossed the room and walked out, the door closing behind him with finality.

As he strode down the open halls lining the manicured courtyard, he took in the crisp afternoon air coming in off the sea and listened for the strangely comforting screams. It was not long before he heard them.

The farther he walked, the louder the screaming became, finally reaching its crescendo behind two huge marble doors that he briskly passed by. As he walked on, the insane wailing faded, then disappeared altogether.

There was no need for him to stop and inspect what was occurring behind those doors, because as long as the screaming could be heard, everything in that chamber was going according to plan. Besides, he had other, far more pressing matters to attend to just now, in a different area of the Citadel.

The room he finally entered was in stark contrast to the one he had just left. This was the Scriptorium, the chamber in which so much of his mission had already been accomplished by the consuls in the dark blue robes—those of the craft who had been freed of their death enchantments, turned to the Vagaries by the son of the Chosen One, and left for Krassus to command. This was also the chamber in which so much of his mission was still to take place, and in which long-held, dusty secrets would be revealed.

The Scriptorium was very large, taking up the entire second floor of this section of the Citadel, and its light, airy appearance belied the gruesome nature of the important work that went forward here. Sunlight streamed in through the many wide, open windows lining three of the four long walls, overlooking the restless Sea of Whispers below. The air in the room was odorless, the environment bordering on a cold sterility.

The Scriptorium's size was deceiving. It was in fact a collection of rooms separated by short, curving walls with openings but no doors. In this way, Krassus' consuls could not only move easily from one chamber to the next as they went about their labors, but they could also maintain a high degree of privacy, so that their concentration would not be broken.

The only room that could be sealed off from the others was Krassus' personal study. Large in size but plain in appearance, it held only an ornate desk and bookcases full of texts and scrolls. It was lit by a single window.

Approaching the door to his private chamber, Krassus narrowed his eyes, calling on the craft. The lock turned over once, then twice more, and the door slowly revolved on its hinges. After opening the window behind the desk, Krassus sat down. Almost immediately the consul in charge of the Scriptorium appeared before him, awaiting his master's orders.

The moment he had arrived at the Citadel with the Scroll of the Vagaries, Krassus had turned it over to the consuls so that they might begin the necessary research. Despite the fact that Nicholas had made Krassus fully aware of the purpose of the Scrolls of the Ancients before his death, there was still a great deal of investigation that would need to be done before the Scroll of the Vagaries would give up the particular secret they were searching for. To this end, Krassus had driven the consuls mercilessly. The research had gone on unabated, both day and night.

So far the going had been difficult. Although Nicholas had known what he needed gleaned from the scroll, even the son of the Chosen One had been unaware of where it had been placed among the seemingly countless other calculations and inscriptions so elegantly written on the very long, uniform piece of vellum. Each calculation the scroll relinquished had to be tested on a person of untrained, endowed blood—an *R'talis* slave—to determine whether it was the one they were looking for. The one magnificent calculation that—in its unparalleled, awesome power—would finally and irrevocably smash everything the wizards of the Redoubt stood for had so far eluded them.

Krassus looked up at the consul standing obediently before him. "Your report?" he demanded.

"For purposes of security," the consul answered, "it seems the writers of the scroll chose to bury this most powerful of calculations somewhere deep within the body of the text and leave it untitled. Although hundreds of useful Forestallments have now been mapped and recorded, the one we search for, the one shown to you by Nicholas, still eludes us. To narrow our examination, we are now putting into use only the untitled calculations." He paused. "It seems that the Heretics of the Guild did not make our task a simple one."

Growing ever more impatient, the wizard scowled. Saying nothing, he rose from his desk and left the room, followed by the obedient consul. Striding across the length of the Scriptorium, he stopped before a particular entryway, through which doorway the azure glow of the craft seeped out. Anxious to view the process, he walked in.

The room was large. Along one wall lay a long, rectangular table covered with reams of parchment. More than a dozen consuls were seated there, recording their observations with ink-laden quills.

Hovering before them in the stillness of the room was the glowing, partially unrolled Scroll of the Vagaries.

The engraved golden band that had once been secured around its center had been removed, and the scroll was unrolled to reveal the beautiful, elegant script spread across its ancient surface. One by one the consuls selected portions of the script. The passages began to glow as they were chosen, lifting themselves from the parchment and hovering in the air before the consuls.

The consuls read the Old Eutracian script floating before them, first deciphering and then recording what they read onto sheets of individual parchment. When each was satisfied that his translation was correct, he ordered the glowing words back to the scroll. Then the name and use of the spell, if given, was recorded on the parchment and passed to a waiting demonslaver, who took it from the room. The consul would then begin anew, selecting the next available passage from the scroll.

And so it went, the faithful scribes deciphering and recording the contents of the scroll while their watchful master looked on. Krassus finally walked to the next room.

Constructed of pure white marble, this chamber was much larger than the one he had just left, and the work here had a more intense, deadly feel to it. Demonslaver guards wandered warily about, their white eyes missing nothing. Bookcases covered every inch of the walls, their shelves lined with ledgers that were arranged in perfect sequential order.

From time to time the consuls would come to the shelves either to take fresh volumes, or to replace those they had just finished with.

These volumes contained the information gleaned from the endowed slaves as they had departed the ships at the underground pier. The blood signatures and assay ratings had been dutifully recorded, along with the names, ages, dates and locations of capture, and sex.

Krassus turned his attention to the center of the bright, sterile-looking room. One hundred white marble tables, each a very precise two meters long by one meter wide, stood arranged in neat rows. Upon each lay a live human body—a conscious, endowed slave, bound to its surface at arms, legs, and throat, and covered by a curved dome of transparent azure. Over each of the tables stood a lone consul, carefully going about his meticulous work. Krassus chose one to observe.

After finding the page in the ledger that held the information about the slave lying before him, the consul caused a perfect duplicate of the slave's previously recorded blood signature to rise from its pages. It came to rest next to the deciphered script on the parchment brought to him from the room housing the scroll.

The consul then reached one hand through the azure dome and placed his palm on the slave's forehead. Terrified almost beyond insanity, the helpless slave struggled, but to no avail.

Closing his eyes, the consul recalled the calculations of the still-unidentified Forestallment just gleaned from the scroll. Then he carefully began infusing it directly into the endowed blood of the slave.

The slave on the table began to convulse. Foam ran from the corners of his mouth, and his eyes rolled back up into his head as his body jerked violently: a marionette dancing on someone else's strings. Although he screamed wildly, no sound could be heard through the azure dome.

Such an interesting phenomenon, Krassus reflected emotionlessly. To see one convulse and scream so violently, yet hear no sounds of torment.

And then, finally, it was over. The slave collapsed, eyes closing.

As the consul removed his hand from the slave's head, the azure dome faded away.

"Is he dead?" Krassus asked casually.

"No," the consul answered. "Some of them live, though most die. Interestingly, it seems that those with a blood assay value of four or better often survive, and can be subjected to the process again. Such information may prove useful one day."

Narrowing his eyes, the loyal consul again called on the craft. He caused a small incision to form in the slave's right arm and ordered a single drop of the slave's blood to land on the parchment next to the blood signature.

Reaching into his robes, the consul produced a vial. Opening it, he released a single drop of red water taken from the Caves of the Paragon. Almost immediately the two drops began to move across the page toward one another, quickly becoming one.

As the slave's blood signature formed, the consul removed another piece of parchment from his robe. It held an exact copy of the Forestall-ment branch they all searched for—the one given to Krassus by Nicholas just before his death. After closely comparing the two, he shook his head. They were not of the same length, nor did the various branches match as they trailed away from the blood signatures.

"Negative again, Master," he said. He summoned one of the many demonslavers in this area to come to the table. "Take this one away," he ordered.

Suddenly they heard a shout of unmitigated joy come from the other side of the room. Navigating his way between the busy tables, Krassus hurried over to the consul who had cried out.

"What is it?" he asked, not daring to hope.

"I have found it, Master," the consul breathed, his excitement barely allowing him to get the words out. Krassus looked down at the tabletop to see that the female slave the consul had been using was dead.

"Show me," he ordered. His hands were trembling with excitement.

With a slight bow, the overjoyed consul handed over both his copy of the long, angular Forestallment branch they searched for, and the copy of the blood signature just taken from the dead slave. Krassus ex-amined them carefully. As he did, his heart leapt.

There could be no mistake. This was the Forestallment branch that Nicholas had ordered him to search for. Now the next stage of this amazing journey in the craft could finally begin. He turned to one of the demonslavers, his dark eyes flashing.

"Bring me Wulfgar," he said quietly.

Forty

As the skiff approached the shoreline of the Isle of Sanctuary, the sheer beauty of the island astounded Tristan. The other skiffs had already been beached, and the last of the crew could be seen eagerly headed down a path into the woods.

Steep, sharply pointed hills rose almost straight up from the shoreline, their tops obscured by gray mist. Below the level of the mist, they were carpeted with a dense, emerald growth. He found himself smiling. At first glance, it looked like paradise.

Gnarled, multicolored trees grew wide and tall, and were dotted with colors that could only be fruits and berries. Thick, strong vines stretched between the trees to create an odd sort of twisted, tangled harmony. The air had a pleasant, sweet-sour aroma, the scents from the flowers and plants combining with the saltiness of the sea as it washed up over the sandy shore. The birdsong he could hear was unfamiliar and melodic.

As he clambered up out of the skiff to stand with Tyranny and Scars on the wooden dock, Tristan tried to remember what the captain had said about Sanctuary being both alluring and dangerous. The first part of the captain's warning he now found easy to understand. But as he took in the serene beauty, he frankly found it difficult to convince himself that it could be dangerous, as well.

As if reading his thoughts, Tyranny turned to him, the same look of concern still blanketing her face.

"Where are all the ships you said were stationed here?" Tristan asked as the three of them walked off the dock and onto the shore.

"The ships are usually moored in various coves around the island," Tyranny answered. "That way if Sanctuary is attacked, all of them cannot be destroyed at once, and at least some of them can escape."

As she spoke, she began leading them down a narrow but well-trod path through the dense foliage between two of the hills.

"That is why you anchored on this side of the island, isn't it?" Tristan asked. "So your ships wouldn't be found."

"Yes," she answered, pausing to push a low-hanging vine out of her way. "I want to enter Sanctuary quietly on foot, as I do not know what kind of reception I might receive from Rolf, if he is in port and not out to sea. If he were to commandeer my ships, we could end up here for a long time."

Looking down at his right knee boot, Tristan thought of the small piece of the Scroll of the Vagaries that had been hidden there by his still-unknown benefactor. All too aware that he must get it back to the wizards and their herbmistress as soon as he could, his jaw hardened. He had had quite enough of being controlled by others. He longed to be home again, and he would do anything—including kill, if need be—to get there.

"And where do we get the sailcloth and spars from?" he asked.

"There are merchants and smiths here," Scars told him. "Most of them were part of the pirate group at one time, but decided to go into the business of turning the stolen raw materials into finished goods. Good money, and much less risk. Especially since most of the raiders would rather be out on the sea than sitting here sewing sailcloth and shaving spars. An unusual arrangement, but it works. So unless Rolf objects and orders otherwise, they will do business with us. But I fear their price may be very high, indeed. Too high, perhaps, for our stores of kisa are not what they once were."

Then Scars pulled Tristan closer, indicating that he wanted the two of them to lag a bit behind Tyranny. Curious, Tristan slowed down.

"The truth is that I have my doubts about our overall success, especially where Rolf is concerned," Scars whispered in a rare example of emotion. "I can only imagine how he reacted after the captain finally left him one night without warning, sailing away as she did by the light of the full moons. By then he had begun to beat her, and she wouldn't stand for it. Frankly, I'm surprised she didn't kill him. But love has a way of tempering one's resolve, does it not? And as you have no doubt noticed, she is very adept at hiding the scars on her heart. Had I known what was happening, I would have killed the bastard myself." Scars paused to look sternly at Tristan. "Keep your sword and your knives at the ready. Rolf is used to seeing me around the captain, but he won't take kindly to a newcomer who is friendly with her, and he is very good with his sword."

Tristan's jaw hardened again. *So am I,* he thought.

They walked on in silence for a time. The narrow, rutted path wound back and forth, and Tristan noted by the position of the sun that they were traveling west. After a while, he saw the first pieces of marble.

The huge sections of broken, fluted column were the largest he had ever seen. He estimated that it would have taken at least thirty men, arms outstretched and holding hands, to surround even the smallest of them. They looked very old, and were fashioned of a rare rose marble shot through with swirls of deeper red. Lying here and there on both sides of the trail, they looked as though they had been randomly cast off by giants.

"How did these get here?" he asked Tyranny, quickening his pace to catch up.

"You tell me," she answered, without turning around. "As I told you, it's all the Directorate's doing. They're your wizards, aren't they?"

With a soft laugh, Tristan shook his head and just watched for the marble pieces. They were gradually increasing in frequency and number. There were not only column pieces but entire columns, as well, sometimes standing alone and complete with their decorative capitals, and he could see that they were built to the same proportions as typical Eutracian columns.

He also saw freestanding sections of wall, their surfaces adorned with intricate alcoves and pilasters, waiting to form buildings that would never be constructed. There were statues in evidence, too, representing both animals and humans.

Finally Tyranny slowed and held up one hand. As Tristan and Scars came up alongside her, the prince looked past her and down into the valley before them.

At the far side of the valley, the Sea of Whispers crashed up against the shore. Dozens of ships, their sails furled, bobbed gently at anchor just beyond the wooden piers that jutted arrogantly out into the sea. And nestled in between, in the heart of the lowlands, lay Sanctuary.

It looked to be something more than a town, yet less than a city. With nothing surrounding it, it was as if it had become somehow lodged forever in-between—like a stunted child that never reached adulthood, long since abandoned by its parents and forced to survive on its own.

Expecting nothing more than a series of hastily constructed, ramshackle shanties, Tristan quickly realized that he couldn't have been more wrong. Despite the fact that Sanctuary had apparently been built long ago, its structures, sparkling like precious jewels in the noonday sun, had a timeless, pristine quality about them.

They were laid out in neatly patterned order. A great, rose-colored marble-floored plaza lay at their center, inlaid with a bloodred representation of the Paragon, its image vibrant and commanding.

Tristan could now see people milling about the town. As the three of them finally came closer and began walking among them, he saw that things were not as genteel as they had first appeared from atop the hill. The exteriors of the buildings were absolutely beautiful, but as many of them had their doors open to the sun, he could see what the pirates had done to them. Trash, personal items, and ale bottles lay everywhere. It was almost as if animals lived here, rather than human beings. Tristan felt disgusted.

Men and women alike seemed to be in a constant state of revelry. For the most part, Tristan and his companions were ignored, so he studied the people without interference. By and large the men here were a dirty, slovenly bunch. Most of them wore sparse, brightly colored clothing, often parted to reveal intricate tattoos. They bristled with weapons and shiny jewelry, and were, for the most part, clearly in various stages of drunkenness. But Tristan could see a careful, ruthless glint in their eyes whenever one of them looked his way.

He had been among their kind before, in Tammerland, just after the return of the Coven and the decimation of the Royal Guard. War bred such men like flies. Tyranny had been right, he realized. These pirates were not only thieves of the sea, but cold, calculating killers, as well. Now he could easily understand the attraction that a place like this, far away from civilization and its demands, would hold for such rebels.

As they walked on, the noise level increased. Barkers loudly tried to entice them into wagering on games and contests; from the balconies above, courtesans in various stages of undress called out coy obscenities, trying to entice passersby to come upstairs. Sometimes Tristan could hear the shameless, crude sounds of urgent intercourse coming from the alleyways as he walked by.

The entire city of Sanctuary seemed to be nothing more than one great, roiling mass of perversion, drunkenness, and greed. As far as Tristan was concerned, the sooner they got what they needed and left, the better. Finally, Tyranny led them down a narrower, quieter street and stopped before a nondescript shop.

"This is where we can order our spars," she told Tristan. "Jonah, the owner, was a friend of my father's. We will be safe here for the time being."

Tyranny walked in, Tristan and Scars in tow. As they did, the bell atop the door announced their presence.

The store was small, with a door in the back that looked out onto a woodworking shop. Several men could be seen quietly fashioning spars and other ships' necessities. The pleasant smell of shaven wood came to Tristan's nostrils as he looked at the man bent over the short, businesslike counter.

He was older than the prince had expected, and he wore large spectacles. Fashioned above one side of them was a smaller, more highly powered lens that could be swiveled down for close work. Tan wood dust covered his curly, iron-gray hair and the striped apron that stretched across his abundant middle; arm garters secured his sleeves.

"Jonah," Tyranny said as he approached the counter. "I need help."

Without looking up, he rudely waved her away with one of his fat, callused hands. "Yes, yes, doesn't everybody these days. The whole damnable island needs my services lately. Seems the screechlings have been more active than ever, for some reason. Go away, and come back when I'm not so busy," he said gruffly, his attention still planted firmly between the pages of his ledger.

Tyranny smiled a bit. "Jonah," she said with a bit more insistence. "It's me—Tyranny."

Jonah's head snapped up, his face overcome with delight. He ran from behind the counter and hugged Tyranny so tightly that her toes left the floor. She grinned widely.

"It's so good to see you, my dear!" he bellowed, finally putting her down. "How long has it been? Three, four months?" Then his face darkened. "You should never have come back, you know. Ever since you left, Rolf's anger has been terrible. Have you lost your mind? Why are you here?"

Before she could answer, he looked at Tristan. "And who is this nasty-looking character?"

"He is a friend," Tyranny told him.

Jonah looked Tristan over again, then gave him a nod. Tristan nodded back.

"You need spars, you say?" Jonah asked. He looked concerned. "Screechlings?"

"Three maelstroms at once," she answered. "We barely survived."

His eyes wide, Jonah ran one hand through his hair in disbelief. As he did, bits of shaved wood rained down. "No one has ever survived three maelstroms," he whispered, half to himself. "They have been far more active of late, and no one seems to know why. Do you have any idea?"

Tyranny shook her head.

Taking a deep breath, Tristan held his tongue. He knew very well why, but he also knew that now was not the time to speak of it.

"Do you have your specifications?" Jonah asked her.

Taking a piece of parchment from the pocket of his trousers, Scars handed it over. With a quick, automatic movement, Jonah swiveled the single lens down over one side of his spectacles and looked over the list.

"Hmm," he mused. "Five new spars, all of unequal thickness and length," he murmured. "This will take some doing. But if I put everything on hold, I can have them for you tomorrow morning. Say, two hundred kisa? That's at no profit to me, child. Given Rolf's attitude, you need to be gone from here as soon as you can." He swiveled the single lens back up into place.

Tyranny nodded to Scars. The first mate reached for the leather cinch bag tied at his waist, counted out a down payment of one hundred kisa, and handed the coins over to Jonah. After slipping them into the pocket of his apron, the shopkeeper looked back at Tyranny with concerned eyes.

"If you suffered three maelstroms, you must also require sails, then."

"Yes."

"That may be a problem."

Tyranny's face fell. "Why?" she asked.

"Because a new arrival named Ichabod is now the only sailmaker on the island," Jonah told her. "He paid hired thugs to kill the other two, so as to have a little monopoly of his very own. Things have changed since you were last here, Tyranny. There used to be at least some honor among thieves. But ever since Rolf took over, all that has gone by the wayside. Rolf gets a cut not only of everything Ichabod sells, but from many of the other vendors here, as well. The likelihood of you getting your sails and leaving here without him knowing are slim, at best."

Tyranny's face hardened, and she took a deep breath. "I have no choice. Where will we find this Ichabod?"

"He's always at the Wing and Claw. It seems he has become so prosperous that he can now hire others to do all of his work for him, including watching over his shop."

Jonah placed a caring hand on one of Tyranny's cheeks. "Be careful, my child," he warned. "Ichabod is as slippery and devious as they come. He would love nothing more than to cheat you."

Tristan had a thought. "I think the two of you should stay here," he said to Tyranny and Scars. "This Ichabod doesn't know me. We will have a much better chance of being successful if I go alone." Hoping for support, he looked up at the shopkeeper.

Jonah looked at Tyranny. "Do you trust him?" he asked.

"Yes."

"Then I think you should do as he suggests. I know how much you like to handle your own affairs, but this time it seems the wisest course."

Tyranny turned to look Tristan in the eyes. As she did he gave her an encouraging look, telling her it would be all right. After a nod from his captain, Scars reluctantly handed Tristan the leather purse and the list of required sails. Tristan handed the list over to Jonah.

"How much should I expect these to cost?" he asked.

Jonah swiveled the single lens back down into place and perused the list. "Four hundred kisa would be fair," he mused. "But Ichabod is not known for being a fair man. Make it five hundred for a rush job, which this will have to be. But under no circumstances should you pay more than six, even to him." He handed the list back to the prince.

"Is there enough money here?" Tristan asked Tyranny.

"Barely," Tyranny answered. "It's all I have. You'd best leave half with me. If you come to any agreement with him, pay him a deposit only." Counting out three hundred, Tristan handed the rest back to her and tucked the purse into his vest.

"Stay here," he said. "I'll be back as soon as I can." He looked over at Jonah. "Where do I find this Wing and Claw?"

"Turn right on this street and keep on going," Jonah answered. Then his face puckered up with a look of distaste. "Trust me, you can't miss it."

Reaching behind him, Tristan grasped the hilt of his dreggan and gave it a quick tug, making sure its blade would not stick. Then he did the same with the first few of his throwing knives.

Saying nothing more, he turned and walked out of the shop. But the moment he set foot on the street he heard the door open again, and Tyranny appeared. She had a strange, searching look on her face. Quickly putting her arms around him, she gave him a surprising, soft kiss on the mouth.

"For luck," she said.

Tristan smiled back. "Don't worry," he said. "I want to get home too, remember?" Gently removing her hands from his shoulders, he gave them a final squeeze. Then he turned and headed up the street.

As he walked, he was increasingly hounded by whores, barkers, and thieves. Drunken men lay in the gutters, while others stopped to rifle through their pockets.

The Wing and Claw was a large, dilapidated building, constructed of the ubiquitous rose marble. The double doors in the front lay wide open. A black wing had been boldly painted on one of them, and a black claw on the other, as if daring passersby to enter. A rail stood just in front, with about a dozen horses tied to it. From inside came a combination of laughter, music, argument, and clinking glass.

After first looking around, he cautiously took the leather purse from his vest. Removing one hundred kisa, he placed them into his pocket so that if he was required to make a deposit on the sails, he could do so without revealing Tyranny's remaining cache of coins. With another quick look around, he replaced the purse beneath his vest.

Wasting no more time, he walked up the marble steps and went in.

The moment he passed through the doors, he knew he was in trouble.

Forty-one

Faegan, alone and desperately worried, sat in the small boat by the shore. The oppressive silence of the stone chamber only added to his anxiety. Ever since Wigg and the watchwoman had disappeared into the tunnel, Faegan had been overtaken by a nearly crippling sense of dread. A long time had passed since they had walked away and left him here—at least it *felt* like a long time. Here, alone in this tomb of rock, time had no meaning.

He looked back across the lake at the latticed floating gardens and the azure waters that flowed so peacefully down out of the wall above them. Such an amazing manifestation of the craft, he thought. But would Wigg survive his ordeal, so that they might finally go home and make use of the garden's secrets? Or would he never see his friend the lead wizard again?

Faegan turned back to face the tunnel entrance, and his sharp eyes finally caught some movement. He froze. It was the returning watchwoman. In her outstretched arms she carried the body of the lead wizard.

Faegan's breath caught in his throat. Wigg's face was blanched, and his arms dangled. His head hung to one side; his slack, open mouth was flecked with foam. Faegan immediately levitated his chair over the side of the boat and came to sit before the watchwoman. She laid Wigg down in the sand before him.

"Your friend lives," she said, "but barely. He is one of the very few to have ever survived the psychic price demanded. His regrets run deep, but his heart and blood are of great goodness. It was that goodness which sustained him through his travails."

Faegan reached down to touch his friend's cold forehead. Closing his eyes, he called on the craft. Wigg's heartbeat was faint, and his mind had gone deep. Faegan looked back up at the robed apparition.

"Will he recover?"

"His blood is strong," she answered. "In time, he should return to normalcy. But his soul will forever wear the imprint of what happened to him this day." Raising her hand, she indicated that Faegan should levitate the lead wizard back into the boat.

He did so, guiding Wigg's body to lie on one of the seats. Then, once Faegan also entered the boat, the watchwoman took up her place in the stern and used her staff to push the craft toward the opposite shore. She beached the vessel near the floating gardens and then turned to him.

"It is time to grant what you came for, wizard," she said calmly. "Leave your friend here, and follow me."

Levitating his chair, Faegan followed her as she slowly climbed one of the stone paths that wound its way up and around the latticed, glowing pools. He could hardly contain his excitement at the mesmerizing sight.

Every herb of the craft seemed to be represented here, plus a great many that he had never seen before. Looking closer at the surface of one of the pools, he saw such esoteric plants as muscle root, gingercrinkle, blossom of malcathion, and even a smattering of the very rare everscent. Finally the watchwoman stopped her climb beside one of the largest of the glowing ponds. Faegan lowered his chair.

"Was all this left here by the Ones?" he asked.

"All things of magic are a direct result of either the Ones or the Heretics," she answered simply. "Or of what came even before them— namely the two glowing orbs of the craft. The bright, golden Orb of the Vigors and the dark, sizzling Orb of the Vagaries forever power the twin but opposite sides of magic, always attracting each other, but never touching. Surely by now you have learned to call them into your presence, and have witnessed their majesty and power. Nonetheless there remains much for you to learn. Not only of the craft, but of those masters and their orbs who were here so long before you."

Faegan bent over to study the pool. "And the items I require to separate my herbs, roots, blossoms, and oils—are they here in this pool?" he asked. There were several beautiful plants lying atop the water. But despite his great knowledge, he had to admit that he had never seen any of them before. He could feel the water calling out to his endowed blood. Even as learned and disciplined as he was, he found its allure intoxicating, its entreaty irresistible. His breath coming quickly, his mind nearly overcome, he let his hand creep closer to the pool.

"Stop, you fool!" the watchwoman screamed, just as his fingers were about to break the surface of the water. With amazing speed and surprising strength, she grabbed his wrist with her white, lifeless hand. Stunned, he looked up into the dark, faceless hood.

"What's wrong?" he asked thickly.

Letting go of him, she raised the bones of her hand directly before his eyes.

"Tell me, wizard," she said caustically, "how do you suppose I came to be this way? Do you wish to suffer the same fate?"

And then he understood. The azure waters here in the Chambers of Penitence were so powerful that they were literally toxic, and eons ago her endowed blood had caused her to succumb to the same temptations he had just experienced. She had paid for her mistake with the flesh of her hands, perhaps even with that of her entire body. And so the Ones had somehow asked that she stay here for eternity, to help safely guide other supplicants in their quests.

Saddened for her and humiliated for himself, he swallowed hard. "I'm sorry," he said. "I didn't understand."

"Nor did I, once," she answered back. For a few moments the only sound was the trickling of the water into the glowing pools.

"This is indeed the pool that holds what you require," she finally said. "But for obvious reasons, it shall be neither you nor I who harvest it."

She raised both her staff and her free hand into the air. "Come to me, my pretties," she ordered.

Faegan heard a grating sound coming from the wall behind them. As he turned to look, he saw that one of the holes in the wall had stopped pouring forth its water and was widening dramatically, until it was a full meter in diameter.

A bird popped its head out of the hole, cautiously looked around, and finally took to the air. Three more appeared, and they began to circle overhead. Faegan watched, spellbound. He had never seen anything like them.

The multicolored birds glowed with the azure of magic. Their necks were long and graceful, as were their wide, brightly feathered tails. They stood on long, spindly legs, like storks, but their shiny bodies were more compact, and their feet were webbed and yellow, like those of a duck. They had gullets beneath their long, wide bills, such as one might see on birds that lived near the ocean and fed on fish. The watchwoman slowly lowered her hands. As she did, the creatures landed gently, one by one, next to Faegan's chair and stood there obediently, as if waiting for the watchwoman to speak.

But she did not utter a word. Instead, she pointed to the pool and the birds walked into it and began to swim carefully through the plants, using their long, wide bills to harvest leaves and flowers and stems. Faegan marveled at their quiet, elegant efficiency.

Reaching into her robe, the watchwoman produced a glass vial with a hinged top. Opening it, she handed it down to one of the birds. The bird took it into its bill, the open side of the vial facing away from its head. Then it dipped the vial into the water, collecting the light green oil that lay in another part of the pool.

After a little while, the birds made their way back out of the glowing pool and, one by one, came to drop their treasures at the wizard's feet. With a sure, slow motion of its head, the bird that had collected the oil put down the vial and shut the lid with its bill.

Smiling broadly, Faegan looked back up at the watchwoman. "How is it that they are not affected by the waters, as you were?"

"Simple," she replied. "They are a product of the Ones, placed here for just this purpose. After my tragedy, the Ones conjured them and left them here to help me harvest the bounty of the floating gardens. They have been my only companions ever since." She then looked back at them and nodded.

One by one they took to the air and flew back through the hole in the wall. The opening returned to its original size, and water began spilling out from the hole once more. Faegan looked down at the treasures lying at his feet.

"May I touch them now?" he asked.

"No," she answered. "They are still wet, and are just as dangerous as ever." The watchwoman reached into her robe again and removed a small, azure-glowing bag. She opened it and held it wide before the wizard.

"Use your gift to place the plants and vial into this bag," she told him. "It will protect your flesh from them until you arrive home. It is also enchanted to absorb the water and render it harmless. Later you will be able to touch them. I have cast a spell of accelerated drying over the herbs; they will be usable soon."

Hearing that such a remarkable spell existed, Faegan was almost overwhelmed by curiosity and the desire to learn, but he managed to drag his attention back to the situation at hand. Doing as she bade him, he focused on the plants and vial and, using the craft, caused them to levitate. They slowly entered the bag, and the watchwoman pulled the cinch tight. She placed the bag on Faegan's lap.

"Thank you," he said sincerely. "You have no idea how much you have just helped preserve the practice of the Vigors."

"Your gratitude is not important now," she said. "It is time for you to leave this place and make use of what I have given you. Do not fail, and do not waste what you have been given. There is only enough to make one attempt to separate your herbs and oils. Time is precious."

His mind racing, Faegan looked down at the bag. "And how do I use these gifts?" he asked.

"First make sure the herbs have completely dried. This will require several more days, at least. Then grind them into a fine powder. Mix the powder deeply within your stores, and watch from a distance. Before you do, however, make sure there are sufficient containers waiting nearby. All will be revealed. The oil, however, may be used to separate your other oils right away."

Faegan looked at Wigg, who still lay unconscious in the boat.

"Given Wigg's current condition, I may not be able to levitate him all the way back to the surface," he said, thinking of the narrow, confined stairway they had taken here.

"The Ones understood that anyone who was fortunate enough to survive this place would not possess the strength to leave on their own," she said simply. "There is another way out." She raised her arms.

Light began to flood down from the ceiling, forming a bright, white circle on the floor of the chamber. "Bring the other wizard with you into the light," she said.

Faegan placed the bag she had given him securely in his robe. Then he levitated Wigg's inert body up to his lap and floated his chair into the circle of light. As he did, the white light turned to azure, and his chair began to revolve.

"What is happening?" he asked nervously.

"You are departing the Chamber of Penitence," she answered. "Farewell, wizard."

The chair revolved faster, then rose into the air. As it increased in speed, Faegan feared he would not be able to continue holding onto Wigg. Using magic to augment his strength, he held on as best he could as Wigg's legs, arms, and robe went flying in circles with the dizzying, disorienting revolutions of the chair.

Looking up into the shaft of azure light, Faegan realized that it led all the way to the top, to the fresh air and sunlight of the world above.

Then the watchwoman raised her arms. "Do not forget what I told you of the River of Thought, wizard!" she shouted from far below. "Farewell!"

Faegan desperately wanted to ask her more, but before he could the two wizards soared into the gleaming, azure bolt of light, and were gone.

PART IV

Rebirth

CHAPTER

Forty-two

*In a sense, time has no place in the practice of the craft. For to those who shall
grant themselves the time enchantments, sometimes a year shall seem as a day,
and a day as a mere moment. And the Forestallments granted into their blood
shall give rise to great gifts, some wondrous, and some terrible in their applications.*

—FROM THE SCROLL OF THE VIGORS

As Tristan walked through the double doors of the Wing and Claw
he stopped for a moment, taking in the scene.

The room before him was very large and very dark, lit only by several dim, oil lamp chandeliers. Tables filled the room, and a long bar sat
before the wall to his right. In one corner a stairway could be seen leading to the second floor—to the bedrooms, he assumed. Men and women
were cavorting loudly. Some, already in varying stages of undress, were
locked in passionate embraces. Others were busy drinking and playing
at dice or cards, the losers shouting out obscenities and invectives at the
Afterlife. One man sat on a chair in the corner, a pipe held between his
teeth as he happily ground out ditties from an ancient-looking squeeze-
box. The entire place smelled of sweat and stale liquor.

No one seemed to take any particular notice of Tristan, and for that
he was grateful. As casually as he could, he walked up to the bar. The
one-eyed barkeep was a thin, greasy-looking creature who walked with
a decisive limp. Where his other eye should have been there was only an

empty hole, crudely sewn shut with bits of leather. The stitches looked as if they had been there for a long time.

Forcing down his revulsion, the prince looked steadily into the man's good, blue eye. "Ale," he said simply.

"Don't got none," the fellow said, almost proudly.

"Why not?" Tristan asked skeptically. "They're drinking it on the street."

"Like I said, don't got none," the man repeated. He smiled, revealing the absence of two front teeth. The same man who had taken the bartender's eye had probably gotten the teeth as well, Tristan thought.

"Then what do you have?" he asked.

"Mead," the fellow answered simply, as if it was something the prince should know simply because he was standing in the Wing and Claw. "Produced special on the island, and it's all we sell here."

"Very well," Tristan said. "Mead it is."

"Do you want the cheap stuff, or the good stuff?" the bartender asked.

Tristan reached into his pocket, produced a single kisa, and dropped it on top of the bar. "Cheap," he answered, almost immediately questioning his decision.

Greedily picking up the coin, the bartender bit into it, testing its worth. Apparently satisfied, he walked down the length of the bar a bit and stopped before a great keg that sat atop it. Turning the spigot, he released a dark, amber substance into a tankard that looked as if it had just been dredged up off the floor of the Sea of Whispers. He walked back and unceremoniously deposited the pungent concoction before the prince.

Tristan took a swallow.

Gagging, he immediately spat it back out, sure he was about to vomit. He had had mead before, but never any so vile as this. After a fit of coughing, he glared back up at the man behind the bar. The fellow once again smiled, displaying the dark vacancies between his remaining teeth.

"Takes a bit of gettin' used to, don't it?" he asked happily.

As the prince wiped his mouth, he sensed someone beside him. Turning, he found himself looking directly into the bloodshot blue eyes of a blond woman about his own age. She wore a tattered dress and long earrings, and smelled something like a musty, abandoned candy shop. Smiling, she inched a bit closer, at the same time reaching down to touch his groin.

"You're new here, aren'tcha, love?" she asked. Her hungry, greedy eyes looked him up and down. "Believe me, if I'd been with you before, I'd remember." Brazenly leaving her hand where it was, she looked at Tristan's tankard, then over at the bartender.

"Now, Caleb!" she admonished him, still smiling. "Don't tell me you served this fellow from the community keg!"

The bartender's greasy, perforated grin returned.

Reaching down, Tristan moved her hand away. He was almost afraid to ask. "The community keg?" he inquired, amidst another short cough.

The blond pointed down the bar, to the keg Tristan's drink had come from. "All of the mead from every partially drank tankard is saved, and poured back into that barrel," she explained. "Then it's aged good 'n' proper, and served as the cheaper stuff. Rolf—he's the owner, see— he doesn't let a drop go to waste, ya see. Waste none, want none."

Nauseated, Tristan looked back into her eyes. "I'm not interested," he said simply. "I'm looking for a man."

"Well why didn'tcha say so, love?" she answered. "I can arrange that, too. But such a waste that is, a fellow the likes of you."

"Not that kind of a man," Tristan answered. "I'm looking for Ichabod, the sailmaker. I was told that he might be here."

The whore raised a tattooed arm. "He's sitting right over there," she answered. "Practically lives here now, he does. Loves to play at cards, and always seems to win. You can't miss him. Handlebar mustache and expensive black clothes."

Then she came closer—so close that Tristan could smell the stale mead on her breath. "And if you change your mind, handsome, I'll be waiting."

Quickly nodding his thanks, Tristan left both her and his tankard of mead and sauntered across the room. He stopped short of reaching Ichabod, and sat down at an empty table nearby. He wanted to watch and listen first, hoping to form some idea of what the sailmaker might be like before trying to bargain with him.

Ichabod was seated at a table with three other men, playing a game of dreng. A large pile of coins sat in the center, and the game was very animated. Of the four players, the biggest winner so far looked to be the sailmaker.

He was tall, and dressed in black breeches, jacket, ruffled white shirt, and vest. Rings adorned nearly every finger. Shiny black knee boots were on his feet, and he sported an equally dark mustache that he worried almost constantly by twisting its curled, waxed ends. Unlike the other men at the table, Ichabod looked very prosperous. He also seemed to be unarmed, but the prince knew that in a place like this, that meant nothing. Tristan smiled to himself, realizing that the sailmaker reminded him of a particularly unctuous Eutracian undertaker he had once had the displeasure to know.

Watching the game for a few moments, Tristan could see that Ichabod was indeed a very accomplished player. Almost too good, in fact. Then his eyes caught something else, and he smiled to himself.

Certain he had found his edge, Tristan walked casually over to the table to stand directly behind Ichabod. He looked down at the sailmaker's hand, then over at the values on the front sides of the cards being held by the others.

One of the other players glared angrily up at him, then, after looking Tristan over, went back to his cards. Any moment now, one or more of them would most certainly object to his presence. As the precious seconds ticked by, Tristan held his breath.

Finally the moment came that the prince had been waiting for: It was Ichabod's turn to play a card. Reaching down quickly, Tristan selected one of Ichabod's cards and threw it on the table, amidst the others already lying there.

"Dreng," he said quietly.

Ichabod was up on his feet in no time, as were two of the other players, daggers drawn. For a moment the entire place went silent as a tomb, rife with tension. All seventy-three eyes in the tavern had fallen directly onto the man with the strange, curved sword lying across his back.

"And just who are you to be playing my cards for me, you insolent bastard?" the sailmaker shouted. A vein in his forehead beat noticeably. He looked Tristan over, and his face screwed up at the sight of the prince's unorthodox weapons.

"I'm the one who just made you fifty kisa," Tristan replied calmly, never taking his eyes from the sailmaker's. "Your king over the last player's pageboy."

Tristan gave the man a short, conspiratorial smile that he hoped would soften things a bit. "I won't even ask you for half of the pot," he added craftily. "All I want is a little of your time, and now you can afford to give it to me."

Sensing the possibility of a profit, Ichabod calmed a bit. Glancing back down at the table, a short smile crossed his mouth. "Dreng it is," he said softly, looking back over at the prince. "But that's not good enough. Who are you really, and what do you want? Surely it isn't to give me card lessons. I've never seen you before. Tell me true, or I'll have my friends here cut you from groin to gizzard with a dull deer antler and feed what's left to the sharks."

Tristan looked over to the two glaring pirates who had so quickly risen from their chairs. The light from the chandelier glinted off their weapons. The fact that he had just cost each of them money had only added to their desire to act on Ichabod's grisly suggestion, and he knew it. But he stood his ground, holding his own in the contest of wills.

"I'm a prospective customer," he told Ichabod. "One with money to spend. I need a rush job, and I'm willing to pay extra for it. Is there someplace where we might speak in private?"

Thoughtfully rubbing his chin, Ichabod looked back at his friends. With a decisive grunt he finally picked up his money and directed Tristan to a table in the corner. As the tavern slowly returned to normal, the sailmaker came straight to the point.

"I assume you have a list of your needs?" he asked. Tristan produced Tyranny's list and handed it over.

"This is a very big job," Ichabod mused. "You must have more than one ship in distress."

Tristan nodded shortly, almost rudely. He didn't want much small talk, for that might only trip him up. "We were attacked by screechlings," he explained simply.

"When do you need these?"

"By dawn."

Ichabod tossed the list to the table. "These are unusually large and must be custom-made. Not only that, but you want them very quickly. All of my people would have to put everything else aside and work straight through the night in order to accomplish this. And that is going to cost you."

"How much?" Tristan asked, holding his breath.

"One thousand," Ichabod said confidently, leaning back in his chair. Reaching up, he began twirling one end of his mustache with his fingertips.

"Three hundred, and you deliver them to my ships by dawn," Tristan countered.

Ichabod scowled at Tristan as if he had just descended from another world. "I don't even get out of bed in the morning for less than five."

"Four hundred, then, take it or leave it," the prince said.

Pushing his chair back with finality, Ichabod stood. "You're insane," he said gruffly as he turned to go. But before he could, he found Tristan had taken him by one wrist.

"If you don't accept my offer here and now, you will never be able to visit this place again," Tristan growled quietly. "In fact, you may lose your life over it. Tell me, is it really worth it?"

Bending over, Tristan reached down and stuck his hand into the surprised sailmaker's right boot. He pulled out several playing cards, examined them closely, and casually tossed them down onto the table.

"What do you think will happen to you if I drag you back over to those men by your hair and show them what you keep in your boots? Whose friends do you think those drunken morons with the daggers will be then, eh? Not to mention that you have been cheating your partner's patrons, right under his very nose. And I seriously doubt you've been giving Rolf a cut—that's something he won't take kindly to." Tristan's face turned as hard as granite. "Now sit down, before I cause you some real trouble."

Still unimpressed, Ichabod gave Tristan a confident, arrogant glare. "Go ahead and try," he dared. "I'll tell them the cards belong to you. Who do you think they'll believe?"

Tristan only smiled. "Actually, I think they'll believe me," he said softly.

"And just why is that?"

"Because there is wax on the edges of these cards," Tristan answered casually, as he grabbed one up from the table and held it before the sailmaker's eyes. "The same as that on your mustache. And in case you haven't noticed, I'm clean-shaven. So tell me, sailmaker, now which of us is the insolent bastard?"

Ichabod's face went white. On trembling legs he searched absently behind himself, finally finding his chair. He sat down carefully.

"Four hundred, you say?" he asked, his voice breaking. His tone had suddenly become far more agreeable.

"Four hundred," Tristan nodded. "Far be it from me to swindle a card cheat. And no deposit. Rather, payment in full on delivery to my ships tomorrow at dawn. You'd best not cross me. I wouldn't take it well."

"Where are you anchored?" the sailmaker asked.

"On the eastern shore. In the rocky cove, just off the wooden docks. Do you know it?"

"Yes."

"Then I will see you there at dawn," Tristan replied. "With the sails."

Ichabod's eyes narrowed a bit. "Once you leave the Wing and Claw, how do you know I'll keep my end of the bargain?"

Reaching back, Tristan casually produced one of his throwing knives and held it to the chandelier. The soft light glinted off the dirk's razor-sharp edges.

"Because if you don't, I'll come to you tomorrow night," the prince said quietly. "Sanctuary is a small island, and I'll find you no matter where you try to hide. I'll find you, and I'll cut you." Looking back down into Ichabod's eyes, he smiled. "From groin to gizzard."

Ichabod swallowed hard. "Very well," he said in a much smaller voice. "It shall be as you say."

Remembering what Tyranny had taught him, Tristan spat into his right palm and held it out. After a moment, Ichabod followed suit, and they shook hands. The prince had been inordinately lucky. He also knew that he should leave quickly, before anything went awry.

But as he stood to go, someone else entered the Wing and Claw. Someone he knew. It was Scars.

As might be expected, the giant's frame filled the doorway, blocking out much of the afternoon sun. But as Tristan looked more carefully, he saw that something was very wrong. Scars' hands were tied behind his back, and his face was bruised. He was being prodded into the room by two leering pirates, their sabers held to his back. Tristan froze, trying to act as though he had never seen the colossus before. His mind began to race.

Scars and the pirates finally entered the tavern and slowly walked over to one side. Then, from the sunlight beyond the doors Tristan detected something standing there, its silhouette dark against the afternoon sun. It looked like a man. But it had too many arms and legs to be a man, and some of them weren't where they were supposed to be.

Then he saw the thing start to spin around, and Tyranny came flying through the air to crash into one of the nearby empty tables. It collapsed beneath her, and she went down hard. Dazed and hurt, at first she seemed unable to get up.

Tristan started to go to her, but somehow her eyes found him in the crowd. She gave him a short, decisive shake of her head, telling him to stay put. Understanding, he fought down the impulse to help her and forced himself back down into his chair.

He heard boot heels on the clapboard sidewalk, and a man walked arrogantly into the tavern. Striding over to Tyranny, he reached down and, viciously grabbing a handful of her short hair, wrenched her face up for everyone to see.

"I'm looking for the other man who came into town with this!" he shouted. "It has come to my attention that there is another rooster in my henhouse! Reveal yourself, whoever you are, and I'll let her live!"

Staring at the man with hatred, Tristan's endowed blood began to rise hotly in his veins.

His hand closed automatically around the handle of his knife.

Forty-three

"Tell me, Wulfgar," Krassus asked. "Are you comfortable?"

The hard, white marble table pressing against his back, Wulfgar looked around the Scriptorium as best he could. He and the wizard were alone. He had been forced here by several of Krassus' demonslavers, and they had tied down his hands and feet, making it impossible for him to move.

He was naked save for a pair of emerald-green silk trousers. His long, sandy hair fell down over one edge of the table and stretched toward the floor. As he lay there, looking up into the smiling face of the wizard with the long white hair and the strange, two-colored robe, his heart beat wildly. Sweat born of fear poured maddeningly off his face and body.

Craning his neck to one side, he saw a partially unrolled scroll hovering in the air nearby. It was magnificent, and it glowed with the same strange blue color that he had seen come and go so often since being imprisoned here in the Citadel.

"What are you going to do to me?" he demanded, straining against his bindings for what seemed the hundredth time.

Krassus wiped the perspiration from his subject's brow. It was almost as if he were a healer, compassionately tending to a patient.

"I am nothing if not a man of my word," he said calmly. "I'm going to do exactly what I promised you that day in your quarters. I shall introduce you to something wonderful—something that will change your life forever. In the end you will thank me. And before we are finished, you will find yourself begging for more."

Summoning all of the saliva he could, Wulfgar arched his back and spat it directly into the wizard's face. Unperturbed, Krassus calmly wiped it away.

"I will fight you; you must know that," Wulfgar swore. "One day I will find Tristan and Shailiha, and join them. Together we will kill you— you and all of these monsters that serve you." Exhausted, he lay back down against the hard, almost welcoming coolness of the stone.

"Of course you will fight me," Krassus said. "Given the nature of your blood, I would be very disappointed if you did not. So will Serena, when her time comes. But by then you won't want to kill the demon-slavers, Wulfgar. You will want to command them. I am simply an inter-mediary, doing my late master's bidding." Krassus turned to view the scroll.

"I believe prudence dictates that we begin with one of the simpler Forestallments," he said casually. "Although the process will not be pleas-ant, it will have nowhere near the impact of some of the more powerful ones that will eventually follow. But by then your unique blood will have adjusted. When I finally deem you ready, I will gift you with the one Forestallment that will change the world forever—the one my loyal con-suls worked so hard to uncover in the scroll."

Narrowing his eyes, Krassus called on the craft, and a section of the beautifully elegant, glowing text lifted itself from the scroll and came to hover before his dark eyes. But just as it did, Krassus began to cough again.

Taking his rag from his robes, he covered his mouth. His hacking went on unabated for some time. It was becoming progressively worse, he realized. Finally the convulsions subsided, and he put the rag away. Now it was Wulfgar's turn to smile.

"Perhaps you will die before you can turn me, wizard," he said. "Did your supreme master consider that before he departed?"

"Of course," Krassus answered hoarsely. "But have no fear: I shall easily live long enough to turn you, perhaps even long enough to see you fulfill my master's plans. What a glorious day that shall be! Now then, shall we begin?"

Pointing an index finger at one of Wulfgar's arms, Krassus caused a small incision to form. It immediately started to bleed. Reaching over to a nearby table, the wizard retrieved a small glass vial, with which he col-lected some of the blood. Then he closed the vial and caused it to glide back over to the table. Narrowing his eyes, he watched the wound close, the skin knit back together, and the angry red scar disappear completely.

The wizard committed the glowing words and calculations hovering before him to memory. With a smile, he then placed one of his palms on Wulfgar's head.

Wulfgar began to scream.

His body arched with exquisite pain; drool ran from his mouth. His body jangled mercilessly, relentlessly, against the cold, white marble table. Sweat poured from him, and at first Krassus worried that Wulfgar's violent thrashing might break the bones of all his limbs. But the wizard continued with the process of imbuing the first of many Forestallments into Wulfgar's blood.

When Krassus was done, Wulfgar had gone unconscious from the pain, but he was still breathing. Pointing an index finger at Wulfgar's other arm, the wizard caused another incision to form, then ordered a single drop of blood to rise from the wound and come to rest on the table.

He picked up another container. This one was filled with red waters taken from the Caves of the Paragon by Nicholas, and entrusted to Krassus just before the son of the Chosen One had died at the Gates of Dawn. Opening its top, he released a single drop and watched it fall to the table, landing next to the spot of Wulfgar's blood. Almost immediately the two beads of fluid began to move and join.

Krassus pulled a scope closer and centered it directly over the freshly forming blood signature. He held his breath and looked down.

The newly created Forestallment in Wulfgar's blood signature was perfect.

Looking further, he found the other change he was hoping for: Wulfgar's already left-leaning blood signature now tilted farther yet. Krassus' heart leapt in his chest. He had just proven in practice what Nicholas had told him would work in theory: that the Forestallments inscribed so long ago on the scroll could still be correctly deciphered and imbued directly into the blood of the living.

Looking up from the scope, he gazed out one of the broad windows overlooking the Sea of Whispers. As he did, several realizations came to him.

Failee, Wigg's deceased wife and onetime first mistress of the Coven of sorceresses, must have possessed and employed at least one of the Scrolls of the Ancients. There was no other way that Tristan and Shailiha could possibly have obtained the Forestallments in their blood. Even Failee was not brilliant enough to have woven such wondrous aspects of the craft on her own. And the same held true for Celeste's Forestallments, as well.

But the Coven had not been in possession of the scrolls when Wigg banished them to the Sea of Whispers. So Failee must have either discovered them in Parthalon or hidden them somewhere in Eutracia before leaving and then ordered her second mistress, upon invasion of Eutracia, to return not only with the Paragon and Princess Shailiha, but with the scrolls, as well.

But how had the scrolls found their way back to Eutracia from Parthalon? he wondered. How was it that they both eventually came to be in the possession of Nicholas? And perhaps most importantly, how had Failee come upon the scrolls in the first place?

Then another, even more fascinating realization hit him. If Failee had had only the Scroll of the Vagaries in her possession, and if she gleaned from it the Forestallments that she later placed into the blood of Tristan and Shailiha, then all the still-unrealized gifts of the Chosen Ones would be of the darker side of the craft! If she had had both scrolls, would she even have used anything of the Vigors? If so, why? And what about those gifts in Celeste's blood? Would Failee ever want her only daughter's blood infused with anything remotely associated with the side of the craft that she professed to loathe?

His head spinning with questions and contradictions, Krassus looked down at Wulfgar's placid, sleeping face. He smiled to himself. It didn't really matter if he found the answers, he decided. All that mattered was that he complete his master's mission before his disease took him to the Afterlife.

Closing his eyes, he caused the glowing, hovering calculations he had just employed to return to their places in the scroll. Then he selected another section of text and beckoned it to him. After committing it to memory, he placed his open palm back on Wulfgar's forehead. Wulfgar's eyes snapped open.

His screaming went on long into the night.

Forty-four

"He will live," Faegan said with relief as he removed his hand from Wigg's forehead. "He has been through a great deal, and it was apparently very close. His heart has been deeply strained, as has his mind. But I believe he will make a full recovery," he said. Then Faegan looked over at Celeste.

Abbey, Faegan, Celeste, and Shailiha were surrounding the lead wizard's bed. Shailiha's daughter Morganna sat in an infant's carriage newly made for her by Shannon the Short.

Wigg lay sleeping, the down covers pulled up to his shoulders. His breathing was still labored, and his face remained pale. Reaching out to touch her father's face, Celeste found that his skin was cold. As she withdrew her hand, her eyes became shiny.

Abbey and Shailiha were no less worried. The two wizards had been gone from the palace a long time, and when the Minions had finally landed in the courtyard with the litter the three women had run to meet them, hoping for the best. But what they had found was a stricken lead wizard, and Faegan frantic to have Wigg cared for. That had been several hours ago. At one point Wigg had opened his eyes, looked at them briefly, and then fallen back into a deep, silent sleep.

Once Wigg had been put to bed, Faegan had told the others all he could of their amazing journey. The bag of herbs and the vial of oil that had been taken from the floating gardens lay safely on a nearby table.

"Is it really true that you cannot use the herbs the watchwoman gave you until they have dried out?" Shailiha asked as she rocked Morganna's carriage with one hand. The baby gave a soft coo.

The princess was very anxious for Abbey to try to find her brother by way of the gazing flame. There still had been no news from the flying Minion patrols that stubbornly refused to give up looking for the prince, or from the Minion fleet that had supposedly left Parthalon several days earlier, under the joint command of Geldon and Traax.

But at least Faegan's stores of herbs and oils were now all here in Tammerland rather than remaining in his mansion in Shadowood. Just before leaving for the Chambers of Penitence Faegan had ordered a contingent of Minions to fly Abbey, Celeste, and Shailiha back to Shadowood to oversee the return of the goods.

Abbey had been speechless at what she had seen there. But she had taken it all in stride, helping make sure that everything was packaged up and transported as ordered. Faegan's stores now resided safely below ground level, locked in one of the laboratories of the Redoubt.

As he considered the princess' question, Faegan turned to look at the bag and the vial. Then an unexpected smile crossed his lips, and he turned his chair toward Abbey.

"Tell me," he asked the herbmistress, "can you effectively produce and employ a gazing flame through the exclusive use of oils, rather than dried herbs?"

Taking a deep breath, Abbey searched her memory. "Herbs work much better for that purpose," she answered carefully. "That is why oils are rarely used for viewing. There is one that will work, but the results are often unclear. The oil is called unction of scythegrass root, and it is very rare. Do you know it?"

Smiling, Faegan nodded. "It awaits us in the Redoubt, mixed with the others."

"I don't understand," Shailiha interjected. "I thought we had to wait for the herbs to dry."

"No," Faegan answered. "The watchwoman told me that we could use the oil she gave me to separate the other oils right away." Smiling, he looked around the room. "That being the case, I therefore suggest we descend to the Redoubt."

Celeste turned her attention back to Wigg. "I will stay here, in case Father awakens," she said adamantly.

"Very well," Faegan agreed, smiling at her. Thinking, he turned to the princess. "I think the child should stay here with Celeste," he added. "I am not entirely sure what might happen. Best not to take any unnecessary chances." He turned back to Celeste. "If you need us, you know where we will be."

He gazed down into the craggy face of the wizard who had risked everything for their cause. "Sleep well, my friend," he said softly.

Turning his chair away from the bed, he wheeled himself over to the nearby table and placed the vial and the bag into his lap. Shailiha rolled the carriage over to Celeste. Bending over, she gave Morganna a kiss good-bye. The baby grabbed playfully at Shailiha's blond tresses, causing her mother to cry out in mock consternation. Then the princess and Abbey followed Faegan out of the room.

They had a long way to go to get to the laboratory. Down numerous corridors they went, the oil sconces on the walls surrendering a soft, even glow, the heels of the women's shoes ringing out crisply against the shiny marble floor.

Faegan finally stopped before one of the seemingly innumerable doors of carved mahogany. Narrowing his eyes he called the craft, and Shailiha heard the lock in the door turn over once, then twice more. Abbey opened the door and went through, Faegan and the princess following along behind her. The massive, carved door closed behind them heavily.

The laboratory looked as if it had not been used in some time. It reminded Shailiha of a teaching chamber, complete with text- and scroll-filled bookcases, a long table near the far wall, and rows of dusty mahogany, desk-topped chairs. Shailiha found herself smiling as she thought of days gone by, when the room would have been filled with dozens of eager consuls listening to Wigg or some other member of the Directorate lecturing on some arcane topic of the craft.

Faegan wheeled his chair over to the corner that held the bags of herbs and the vat of oils. Before attempting to use the goods obtained in the Chambers of Penitence, it was vital that he employ his power of Consummate Recollection to recall exactly the instructions the watchwoman had given him. He had to be supremely careful, he knew, for he would only have one chance of returning the oils to their previous states. Taking a deep breath, he closed his eyes. The watchwoman's words came floating back to the surface of his consciousness.

Faegan opened his eyes and looked around the room. They would need many glass containers, he realized. After a good deal of searching the three of them finally found some in an abandoned cupboard, but were forced to scour other nearby rooms to collect the rest. It took some doing, but when they were finished, several hundred glass beakers stood in neat rows on one of the dusty, abandoned tables.

Beckoning the women to one side, the wizard raised an arm and caused the heavy vat of mixed oils to rise and move through the air to land gently just behind the rows of waiting glassware. He caused the hinged top of the vat to open, exposing the oils within, then wheeled his chair to the opposite side of the room, indicating that Abbey and Shailiha should join him.

"What happens now?" Shailiha asked in a hushed tone, as if her voice might somehow upset things.

"Now I am to mix the oil from the floating gardens with those in the vat," Faegan answered softly. He pursed his lips. "After that, even I do not know what will occur, so stay alert."

Raising an arm again, the wizard caused the vial in his lap to rise into the air and float directly above the open vat. The vial opened and slowly poured its contents into the mixture of other oils. Shailiha held her breath.

Precious seconds ticked by, but nothing happened. Then the entire vat took on the azure glow of the craft and began to revolve. At first its movements were slow and gentle, as if some unseen force were trying to stir its contents. But soon it was rocking violently, spinning on the edge of its bottom, occasionally leaving the surface of the table. Faegan's eyes went wide with worry that the vat might spill, rendering his oils forever unusable.

There came a great howling noise, and the contents of the vat rose into the air in a whirling, multicolored maelstrom of oil. On and on it came, until all of it had cleared the vat. Free of its container, it spun faster yet. Then centrifugal force began forcing the oil to fly outward, gradually separating into individual pools that hovered just above the lips of the glassware.

Finally the howling stopped, and the oil pools poured themselves into the various containers all at once. Then things went silent, the oils settling into their containers and finally growing still.

But surprisingly, the vat began to shake again. As it did, elegant, glowing letters rose from it, snaking their way up in a column, like smoke rising from a campfire. On and on they came, separating into groups, each group finally collecting itself before one of the various beakers. Then the groups of letters began to swirl, rearranging themselves into Old Eutracian words that landed on the sides of the glassware. The azure glow finally departed. Stunned, Faegan wheeled himself over to the table. Abbey and Shailiha followed him.

It was a very rare thing to see the master wizard surprised, but he was clearly awestruck by what had just occurred. He picked up one after another of the full beakers and slowly examined them. After reading each of the labels he would hold the beaker to the light, then carefully smell its contents. After randomly regarding about a dozen of them he let go a happy cackle and gleefully slammed one hand down on one arm of his chair. In a display of pure joy, he levitated his chair a bit, then spun it around in the air.

"We've done it!" he shouted. "The oils have been separated and labeled. This is unprecedented! Had I been forced to use the equalizing spoons, the hue harmonizer, and the Chart of Herbal Hues, this task could have taken a lifetime! What we have just witnessed will change herbmastery forever!"

Shailiha was pleased that Faegan was so impressed, but her overriding concern was still the search for her brother. "Can Abbey now use the oil you mentioned to look for Tristan?" she asked eagerly.

"Yes, yes, of course," Faegan answered absently, almost as if he had forgotten the real reason why they had just gone through all of this.

Wheeling his chair up and down the rows of beakers, he began searching for one labeled "Unction of Scythegrass Root." After a good bit of searching he finally gave another cackle and held up a beaker that contained a dark violet oil.

"This must be it," he said. He held it carefully to the light, then took a long, expert sniff. After a moment, he grinned broadly.

"Unction of scythegrass, all right," he announced happily. "I'd bet my life on it!" He looked back at the two women. "Now we go up to the courtyard!" And taking the precious oil, he led the way back up through the labyrinthine passages of the Redoubt.

Once in the open expanse of the courtyard, Faegan turned to Abbey. "A drop of Shailiha's blood should work, shouldn't it?" he asked her. Abbey nodded.

Faegan turned to Shailiha. "Please hold out one hand," he said.

She immediately did so. Pointing an index finger toward her, he caused a tiny pinprick to form, and a single drop of her blood was released. It rose from her finger and came to hover before them in the stillness of the late afternoon air. Satisfied, Faegan handed the beaker of violet oil to Abbey.

"You may begin," he said.

After pouring a small amount of the oil onto the ground, Abbey produced flint and steel from one of the pockets of her dress. As she struck them together, the resulting spark launched itself obediently toward the pool of oil, and a small flame erupted.

After releasing a few more drops of the precious oil down into the flame she stood back, using her gift to force the azure fire higher and higher. When it was at last about two meters wide and five meters tall she crooked one finger, causing the flame to divide into two distinct but unequal-sized branches. Curling her finger again, she pointed to the right, and the smaller of the two flames flattened itself out, coming dangerously close to scorching her hands and her face.

Reaching into the air, she collected the single drop of Shailiha's blood onto one of her fingertips and held it high.

A rectangular window began to form midway up the body of the undulating blaze. Hoping against hope, Shailiha came as close to it as she dared, trying to see what was forming within its midst. Equally mesmerized, Faegan wheeled his chair nearer.

At first Shailiha thought she could see Tristan, sitting in a chair and surrounded by other men and women. But the view was maddeningly fuzzy.

She turned to look at the herbmistress. As she did, the suddenly terrified look on Abbey's face told her that something had just gone horribly, dangerously wrong. For a moment Shailiha saw the herbmistress turn her eyes from her creation to look strangely at the princess; then she immediately gazed back at her flame, her mouth open with horror, and gestured at the blaze as if she were desperately trying to change something about it.

Then, as if in slow motion, she used every bit of her strength to turn and lunge at the wizard and the princess, knocking Shailiha down and sending Faegan's chair tumbling over backward.

Amidst a great thunderclap of heat and fire, Abbey's gazing flame exploded.

Forty-five

Sitting next to the sailmaker, with the deafening, palpable tension of the Wing and Claw raining down around him, Tristan felt his heart racing. Horrified, he helplessly watched the man he assumed to be Rolf pull even harder on Tyranny's hair in an effort to force the prince to reveal himself. Even though she refused to cry out, Tristan could see that she was in desperate pain, and there was nothing that Scars could do to help her. If the three of them were to somehow survive this, it would be completely up to Tristan.

Tyranny's former lover was everything Tyranny and Scars had said he would be. He was tall, hard-muscled, and somewhat older than the prince—perhaps thirty-five Seasons of New Life. Sandy blond hair fell haphazardly down around his face and shoulders. Part of it was woven into two narrow, tight braids that hung alongside the left jaw, their ends capped with small onyx ornaments. His dark blue eyes were hard and unforgiving. He wore a bright red, sleeveless shirt; tight-fitting tan breeches; black knee boots; and a bright red sash around his waist. Numerous tattoos and scars could be seen on his chest and his chiseled arms. At his left hip he wore a saber; an empty dagger sheath was at his right, tied down to his thigh.

"Come forward now!" Rolf screamed again, yanking Tyranny's face a bit higher. Tristan saw Tyranny wince, then close her eyes against the pain.

Remembering the piece of ancient vellum still hidden in his boot, an idea came to Tristan.

He stood up, roughly pushing his chair out of the way. The chair legs screeched loudly on the floor.

Everyone turned to look at the tall, dark-haired man with the strange weapons lying across his back. His eyes never leaving Rolf, Tristan slowly replaced his throwing knife into its quiver, opened his hands to show they were empty, and started across the floor. As he did, many in the crowd smiled greedily. They were sure someone was about to die, and their money was on Rolf.

Coming to stand before the pirate, Tristan looked hard into his eyes. "Let her go," he said. "She's with me now."

Looking Tristan up and down, Rolf let go a derisive laugh. "My men in the street said ya wore a black vest and carried childish lookin' weapons, but they forgot to mention how ugly y'are," he said. Tristan immediately recognized his accent as coming from the Eutracian highlands, just north of Ilendium.

"They also told me that they saw Tyranny kissin' ya in the street," Rolf went on. "So who are ya, then? I would surely like to know, before I order the men in this room to tear y'apart. Then the lass and I would like to be alone." Rolf smiled wickedly. "It seems she and I have some catchin' up to do."

Steeling himself, Tristan decided to take his gamble. He put a snide look on his face, then pointed down at Tyranny. "This bitch and that idiot giant of hers are my partners now, and I want them back."

Tristan held his breath, praying that neither Tyranny nor Scars would say anything. They remained silent.

"What's that ya say?" Rolf demanded, screwing his face up. "And just how did all this come about?"

"The same way everything does," Tristan said calmly, playing up to the pirate's greed. He took another step forward. "I promised to pay for her knowledge, and her ships. She and the giant work for me now."

"Oh, they work for ya, is it?" Rolf asked sarcastically. "Just why should I believe all of this rubbish—not that it matters? And out of idle curiosity, just how much did ya supposedly promise to pay, eh? It would take a fine price indeed for Tyranny to give up her ships, even if she did steal them from someone else!" Smiling, he looked down at her pain-stricken face. "Isn't that right, lass?" he asked her nastily. Then he turned his dark blue eyes back up to the prince.

Tristan smiled at him. "I paid one hundred thousand kisa," he answered calmly.

The moment the words left his mouth, he heard a hush come over the crowd. "If you don't believe me, just ask her for the promissory note

I signed," he added. "She always keeps it hidden between her breasts."
Holding his breath, he hoped against hope that is was still there.

Rolf looked narrowly at the prince, then finally let go of Tyranny's
hair. Bending over, he grabbed her under one arm and roughly pulled
her to her feet. "Is this true?" he demanded.

Confused, uncertain what Tristan was doing, she reached into her
jacket and pulled out the note the two of them had signed that day in her
cabin. She handed it over to Rolf.

Upon reading it, the color drained from Rolf's face for a moment.
Clearly, he was intrigued. But his knife remained steadily at Tyranny's
throat. "And just why would a man of your means want to be out there
on the ocean, eh?" he asked. "Or in a place the likes of Sanctuary?"

"The answer is simple," Tristan said. "She and I have each lost a
brother to the demonslavers. We want to find them. She had the ships,
and I had the money. Even you ought to be able to understand that, you
dumb bastard."

A slight chuckle came from the crowd. Few had ever insulted Rolf
that way and lived to tell about it.

Smiling greedily, Tristan let the insult stand, hoping that he hadn't
just succeeded in getting the three of them killed. A tense silence held
court for several moments.

Rolf turned back to Tyranny. "And just where is this money now?"
he asked.

So far, the greedy pirate was doing exactly as Tristan had hoped he
would. "I'm the only one who knows," Tristan said quickly, before
Tyranny could speak. "It's hidden, buried on the coast of Eutracia. Tyranny has seen it—that was necessary, to prove that I actually had it. But
before I paid her I wanted a first voyage, to see what she could do against
the slavers. That's why I signed the note. Before we set sail I moved the
money, making sure I was the only one who knew the location. But
soon after entering these waters we were attacked by screechlings, and
we had to dock here for fresh spars and sail. Do you really think we
would be here in this dirty hole unless we needed to be?"

Rolf looked narrowly at the prince, then cast his eyes down at the
note.

> This twenty-second day of the Season of New Life, I promise to pay
> Teresa of the House of Welborne one hundred thousand kisa upon the
> successful completion of this voyage.

At the bottom of the page lay two signatures. One belonged to
Tyranny, and the other was the false name Tristan had signed that day in

her cabin, when they had struck their original bargain. His knife still at Tyranny's throat, Rolf looked back up at the prince.

"Assuming what you say is true, what's to stop me from simply torturing the location out of you?" Rolf demanded.

"You could, but how would you know I was telling you the truth?" Tristan countered. "As I said, I'm the only one who knows. And after you sailed me to the coast to prove it, I could lead you all over looking for it. Perhaps even escape in the process. Kill me, and you'll never know. Torture me, and you can't be sure. That's no way to find it, now is it?" He paused for a moment, allowing the pirate's greed and curiosity to build.

"But given my situation, I'm agreeable to letting you have the money, in return for my spars and sails, safe passage away from Sanctuary, and my ships and crews," he offered gamely. Then he looked over at Tyranny. He knew that what he was about to say would hurt her, but if this was going to work, it had to be done.

"I'll even sweeten the deal by letting you keep the girl," he added. "The longer I'm around her, the less she appeals to me, anyway. Someone should tell her that she dresses too much like a man. But I find the giant useful. Give him back to me, and I'll be gone. Agree to my terms, and you win in every way. I'm gone from here, and the money and the woman are both yours."

Believing she had been betrayed, Tyranny's eyes became hard with hate. Then Scars spoke up.

"You liar!" he snarled, pulling frantically at his bonds. "From the first moment I saw you, I knew you couldn't be trusted! The first chance I get, I'll kill you!"

Good, Tristan thought. Even Scars believed him.

"Assuming I agree, just what proof do I have that the location you give me is real?" Rolf asked skeptically.

Tristan's heart leapt. The moment he had been waiting for had finally come. Taking a breath, he tried to calm himself, then took another step closer.

"I have a map," he said. "I drew it for myself, right after I buried the moneybags on the coast. One key to the location is on the map, and the other key is in my head. Neither part is any good without the other. Your proof will be that what I whisper to you will connect up what is drawn on the map."

With Tristan's mention of a map, Rolf's eyes lit up with greed. Even the crowd seemed mesmerized by the stranger's tale, and they inched eagerly closer.

"And after you tell me, what makes you so sure I'll live up to my end of the bargain?" Rolf asked skeptically.

Tristan put a look of concern on his face. "Look around the room," he said. "I don't have many friends here, and I want to live. What other choice do I have?"

Rolf smiled. "None," he answered. "None at all." He greedily looked at Tyranny, relishing the things he would do to her body after this fool-ish rich man standing before him had told him all of his secrets. He would then happily kill him, just to watch him die.

"Very well," Rolf answered. "I agree. Where is the map?"

Tristan shook his head. "First I tell you." He beckoned the pirate closer. Rolf finally lowered his knife.

Tristan came closer and said a few words that Tyranny couldn't hear. Rolf nodded, then smiled.

"And now the map," Rolf demanded.

Tristan reached into his right boot. The parchment was wrapped around the handle of the brain hook, just as he had left it. Losing it to Rolf was a terrible risk, but he had no other choice.

With a single, sure stroke he pulled them both out and slammed the pearl handle of the stiletto into Rolf's jaw, rendering him unconscious. Rolf's knife went clattering to the floor.

In a flash Tristan was behind the pirate, holding him upright, his blade at Rolf's throat. Several of the other pirates from the crowd had al-ready come to their feet, weapons drawn.

There was no time to lose, Tristan knew. What he said and did in the next few moments would surely determine whether he, Tyranny, and Scars lived or died.

"Stay where you are or I'll cut his throat!" he shouted, praying that none of them would come any closer.

"Why should we care?" one of the ones in front shouted back. Sev-eral of them inched forward menacingly.

"Because I am willing to cut you all in on the money!" Tristan shouted. Smiling, he looked out into the crowd. "Even the whores! Tell me, do you think Rolf would ever have done that? And Rolf now car-ries part of the location inside his head. If you try to kill me and I kill him before you do, you'll still have only half of what you need to find the money! He is worth far more to you alive than dead! Now back off!"

Greed won out, and some of the men lowered their weapons slightly.

Tristan looked at the two men still holding their sabers to Scars' back. "Let him go, or Rolf dies. Do it now!"

After looking skeptically at each other, they cut Scars' bonds. But what happened next surprised even Tristan.

Scars whirled on the first of them, pulled the saber from his hands, and then lifted him over his head to send him crashing down on top of the other one.

Tyranny wasted no time either. Grabbing up one of the discarded sabers, she was at the prince's side in a flash.

"Now what, rich man?" the pirate in front shouted at him. It was clear they were nearing the end of their patience.

"You let the three of us go, and as a precaution against your doing anything stupid, Rolf comes with us," Tristan ordered. "I will give you the map tomorrow at dawn, after you deliver my spars and sails to me. Don't worry—our ships are in no condition to sail very far without what we need. If they had been, we would never have come here."

Finding the swindling sailmaker in the crowd, Tristan nodded at him. "Ichabod the sailmaker knows where we are moored," he shouted. "After what we need has been delivered and we have been given time to make our repairs, we are also to be given at least a half-day's start. If we are followed, Rolf dies, and your dreams of wealth die with him. If we are not followed, I will set Rolf adrift in a small skiff along with the map, and then you shall have both parts of the location and can do whatever you want with him—even kill him, for all I care. All the more for you. But mark my words—if you try to double-cross us or take us prisoner, not only will I kill Rolf myself, but I will also destroy the map. At that point, I would have nothing more to lose, and you will have lost the chance of a lifetime."

Pausing, Tristan looked hard into the crowd before speaking again. "Take it or leave it," he said with finality.

Greedy and confused, the pirates started shouting angrily among themselves. Tristan waited and watched, desperately hoping his gamble would pay off.

"I says we take him up on his offer!" a woman shouted, her voice rising above the din. She had climbed up on one of the tables and was gesturing wildly with her arms. Looking closer, Tristan saw that she was the whore who had propositioned him at the bar.

"What have we got to lose except for these three?" she went on. "And we might just make a bloomin' fortune! That sounds like a good bargain where I come from! I say we let them go, and see what happens!"

Tristan smiled and shook his head slightly. It seemed the whore had done him some good, after all.

But at the same time he realized that they needed to take quick advantage of the crowd's hesitancy if they were ever going to get out in one piece; there were flaws in his story, and allowing the pirates time to think things through was certainly not to his advantage.

Looking over at Scars, Tristan nodded toward the door, and Scars nodded back. Reaching down as best he could, Tristan stuffed the brain hook and vellum back into his boot and began dragging Rolf out by his heels. The dangerous, unsure crowd inched forward a bit more, but no one made a move to stop him.

Once through the door, Scars came quickly to Tristan's side and relieved him of Rolf. As though Rolf weighed nothing, the giant tossed him over the front of the saddle of one of the horses tied outside the inn, then freed the reins and mounted. Tyranny and Tristan untied two other horses, jumped into the saddles, and wheeled them around. As they charged away, Tristan looked over at Tyranny, and she smiled at him. Warily turning to look behind him, Tristan finally smiled, as well.

For the moment, no one was following.

CHAPTER

Forty-six

Marcus shifted his weight against the corner of the building as he watched the sun begin to set over the Plaza of Fallen Heroes. It was that special, indescribable hour of metamorphosis when the sky was just starting to change from the turquoise of day to the indigo of twilight. Then the blackness of a full-fledged night would cover everything, the stars peeking out from their distant hiding places in the heavens.

Marcus let out an exasperated breath. He had been waiting here for the last two hours, and he had more than one problem on his mind. As he looked around the hundredth time for a suitable victim, his stomach growled, reminding him of how long it had been since he had last eaten.

Rebecca waited for him at home in the dilapidated shack. She was by now no doubt as hungry as he was, for they'd consumed the last of their food early this morning. Pursing his lips, he thought of her alone with the scroll that lay buried beneath the single, shabby cot. 'Becca must be terrified, he realized. She always was whenever she was left on her own with the strange, wondrous artifact. He only hoped that it had not started glowing again while he was gone.

Marcus had come back to the plaza for two reasons. One was to find a suitable mark whose pocket he could pick. The second was to tell Mr. Worth that they had a deal for the scroll at thirteen thousand kisa, the amount they had agreed upon two days earlier. He assumed Worth would still want the scroll, but a delivery date had yet to be established, and he needed money to feed himself and Rebecca until then.

He looked across the street to Worth's storefront. It was a fairly nondescript place with a glass front and a sign over the door that read ARTIFACTS OF THE CRAFT—ALL ITEMS GUARANTEED AUTHENTIC. Several patrons had left the shop this afternoon, cradling their new possessions as though they had just purchased the greatest wonders of the known world. Marcus had smiled at them with rueful skepticism as they rushed home with their supposed treasures.

Over the course of the last two days he had found and approached two other parties regarding the scroll, but he had not trusted them the way he had Worth. He couldn't put his finger on it, but for some reason he felt that the fat, ruddy-faced artifacts dealer was for the most part honest, while his encounters with the other two had sent a chill up his spine—a warning he always heeded. Deciding his game was fast becoming too dangerous, he had returned to confirm the deal with Worth.

As he looked up the street again, he thought he saw a suitable candidate for pickpocketing. As his target exited a clothing shop several doors down the street, Marcus casually shifted his weight away from the wall and began walking directly toward him.

The man was well dressed and was still counting his coins as he walked out of the shop, his purchases in one hand, his money in the other. Unbelievably foolish, Marcus thought. He had been taught never to exit a place with money still in his hands. Not only could everyone see how much he had, but they could also see which pocket he deposited it in.

Slowing down, Marcus watched as the fellow stuffed his coins into the right inside pocket of his waistcoat. Perfect, he thought.

Squaring his shoulders a bit in order to maximize the impact, Marcus hurried his pace again and walked directly into his mark. As the man twisted in an effort to maintain his balance, his coat flew open. One of Marcus' hands slipped in and out in a flash, then straight down toward the top of his right boot to let the coins fall into it.

"Watch where you're going, you fool!" the man shouted angrily as he juggled his packages. After giving the man a quick, seemingly embarrassed nod of regret, Marcus gracefully stepped around him and kept on going.

But he only took a few carefully measured steps before darting across the street and into Worth's shop. Looking out one of the windows, he smiled. The man he had just robbed was turning the far corner, completely ignorant of how much poorer he had just become. Judging by the weight in his boot, Marcus had done very well. He turned back to look over the shop.

The place was filled with arcane objects, some of which looked very old. Mr. Worth was standing in the back, talking politely to a prosperous-looking man and woman. Marcus walked closer. When Worth saw him his face lit up, and he almost choked on his words.

After taking care of the couple, Worth hurriedly walked them to the door, locked it, and then turned its sign around, indicating that the store was closed. Then he drew the drapes across the windows and walked back over to where Marcus was standing, a hopeful look crowding in around the edges of his face.

"You're back!" he breathed excitedly. "I thought I might never see you again!" Reaching up, he nervously worried one end of his white mustache.

Marcus tried to display his best look of indifference. "The scroll shall be yours," he said. "For the thirteen thousand kisa that we agreed upon. Do we still have a deal?" Holding his breath, Marcus prayed that the shopkeeper hadn't changed his mind.

"Oh, yes!" Worth exclaimed ecstatically. He was fairly bursting with joy. "Yes indeed! But I will need three days to get the money together."

Marcus narrowed his eyes. He didn't like the sound of this. He had hoped to finish his dealings with Worth as soon as tomorrow, and be done with the scroll forever. He looked skeptically up into Worth's dark eyes. Worth seemed even more nervous now than the first time they had met. And if he wanted the scroll as badly as he said, then why didn't he already have the money ready? Marcus wondered. Or did he really have that kind of money at all? A cold sense of dread shot through him.

"Why the three days?" he asked. "I thought you were in a hurry to own the scroll."

"In order to pay you, I must liquidate my entire stock," Worth replied nervously. "I have talked to two other artifacts dealers, and they agreed to buy me out, lock, stock, and barrel. But it will take three days to accomplish the transaction. Then I can meet you wherever you choose."

Marcus thought for a moment, then finally decided that what Worth was telling him made some sort of sense. "Very well," he said finally. "Meet me at midday, in the same spot where we talked before. Near the stand where the old lady sells the throat larks to release. Do you remember?"

Worth nodded.

"Place the kisa into bags, and tie the bags onto a saddled horse," Marcus added. "I'll be moving fast, so follow my instructions to the letter, or the deal is off. My sister will be watching you, so don't try anything stupid. If I receive the wrong signal from her, I'll leave with the scroll, and you'll never see me again." He looked as hard into Worth's eyes as he dared.

"I understand completely," Worth answered quickly. "Everything shall be as you say."

Nodding, Marcus started toward the door. Then he paused and

turned around. Smoothly pulling the knife from his trousers, he touched the button on its handle. It sprang open with a discernible click.

"Don't let my age fool you," he said sternly. "If you do anything to try to cheat me, I'll find you again and you'll be forever sorry."

Worth nodded. Walking the rest of the way to the door, Marcus unlocked it and let himself out.

Back on the street, night had fallen in earnest. Blessedly, he saw no sign of the man he had robbed, so he walked into the nearest alley, pulled off his boot, and counted the coins. Ten kisa. Easily enough to keep them in food until the day he sold the scroll. Happily putting his boot back on, he placed the coins into his pocket and made straight for the farmers' market. There might even be enough left over to buy one of the sweet cakes his sister loved so much. He smiled. 'Becca would be pleased.

From behind a curtain in the back of the shop, two figures came forward. The one painted like a harlequin pulled his dagger from its scabbard and casually placed its razor-sharp tip up against one of Worth's rosy, plump cheeks. The old woman stood next to him, clearly enjoying the anguish that the artifacts dealer was experiencing.

"Well done," Janus said. "You have him completely fooled. Keep doing as I tell you, and you just might live through this."

"Why don't you just follow him and take the scroll?" Worth asked nervously. "Why do you still need me?"

Janus pointed his dagger toward the door Marcus had just gone through. "Despite his early years, that one is exceedingly clever," he answered. "He has probably lived his entire life on the street, and would surely realize he was being followed. I should know, for I was once just like him. Should he suddenly understand that he is being pursued he would run, and we might lose him forever. No, better to let him come to us willingly. I am agreeable to letting you take your three days to raise the money. That adds a sense of well-needed reality to our little game, don't you think? Besides, the boy is smart enough to want to check the contents of your moneybags, so you'd best have them full when the time comes. And then I will keep your kisa for myself when this is all over. I'm sure my master will not mind, since he is well beyond such mundane desires. He may well even compliment me on my ingenuity."

Janus smiled menacingly. As he did the red mask crinkled up at the corners. "And then, once I have both the scroll and the money, those troublesome children shall die."

"How—how did you find me?" Worth asked, his voice trembling. The bizarre man and woman had walked into his shop yesterday and threatened to kill him on the spot. Since then Worth had lived in fear of his life, hoping desperately that Marcus would return.

Janus smiled. "With the craft, of course. You need not know the details."

Terrified, all Worth could do was nod.

Janus ordered Worth and Grizelda back toward the curtain, and let it close silently behind them.

Forty-seven

Geldon felt the sharp sea wind running through his hair as he stood at the bow of the *Savage Scar,* the flagship of the Minion fleet. More than two hundred other such ships sailed with her through the restless Sea of Whispers. The sky was darkening, and the three rose-colored moons had just risen, bathing the froth-tipped waves in their glow.

As the hunchbacked dwarf swayed back and forth with the rhythmic rocking of the vessel, he looked out across the sea and was again reminded of how much had changed since the Chosen One and the lead wizard had first come to his home nation of Parthalon. There were still so many troubles that would have to be surmounted if Eutracia, Parthalon, and the people he cared so much about were ever to find true peace.

Reaching up to his throat, he touched the place where he had been forced to wear the jeweled, iron collar of Succiu, second mistress of the Coven of sorceresses. Then a short smile passed his lips. He owed not only his freedom, but his very life to Wigg and Tristan; and he would do anything they asked of him. Right now, that meant seeing the Minion fleet safely to Eutracia.

Nearly three weeks had gone by since the wizards had sent him through Faegan's portal to Parthalon. Their orders had been explicit: The fleet was to leave their moorings at Eyrie Point immediately, carrying as many of the Minion warriors as they could hold. On the way back, they were to fan out and search for any sign of Tristan.

With so many ships and warriors at his disposal, Geldon could scour large sections of the ocean at a time. Even so, he was enough of a realist to know that they had in fact searched only a small fraction of the Sea of Whispers, and it troubled his heart to think that he might never see the prince again.

The trip so far had been horrific. Several days earlier they had been forced to sail through the area of the sea controlled by the Necrophagians, the beings also known as the Eaters of the Dead. Knowing that there was no choice, Wigg and Faegan had reluctantly granted permission for the Minions to engage in a shipboard battle to the death, an activity guaranteed to provide the forty fresh corpses required to appease the Necrophagians and gain permission to cross these waters.

After the battle, in place of the usual Minion tradition of the burning of the dead, Traax had ordered a short period of respectful mourning. Then the corpses had been lowered over the side to be consumed by the horrible faces that came rising hungrily to the surface of the waves.

The noise and gore that followed had been terrible. Geldon had been unable to watch the once-magnificent warriors consumed by the ever-ravenous, circling maws that prowled the surface of the sea. But at last the Necrophagians, sated for the time being, had disappeared beneath the waves, and the ship had been allowed to proceed with its voyage.

Geldon wondered whether they would ever know just who the Necrophagians were, or why they existed here in the midst of this harsh, cold ocean.

Sighing, he shifted his weight on the barrel he was standing upon, placed his hands on the gunwale, and gazed out again at the ever-changing sea. He felt as much as saw Traax quietly come to stand by his side. For a time neither of them spoke.

From the corner of his eye, Geldon suddenly saw a fleeting shadow cross the deck. Then came another, and yet another. Glancing up, he saw the returning squadron of Minion warriors carefully circle the *Savage Scar,* then land lightly on the ship's decks. They looked forlorn, their wings drooping down tiredly. Seeing this, he frowned. Another unsuccessful search, he surmised.

He watched as the warrior leading this particular group gathered himself up, snapping his wings into place behind his back before he approached. When he reached them the warrior bowed, the heels of his black boots coming together with a crisp, automatic snap.

"Your report?" Traax asked.

"Two more ships were boarded and searched, sir," the warrior answered tiredly. "I am sorry to report that they revealed nothing. And neither of them were slavers."

"Very well," Traax answered.

It was clear by the look on the Minion commander's face that he was disappointed. Traax had fought bravely beside Tristan in the skies over Eutracia just before the collapse of the Gates of Dawn, and the two men now respected each other greatly. Added to this was the fact that Tristan was his sworn liege, and so it was Traax's duty to do everything within his power to find him.

"How many more groups still search the sky tonight?" he asked the warrior.

"Just one, sir," the officer replied. "But I respectfully suggest that no more be sent out until dawn. Heavy clouds are rolling in from the west, making the surface of the sea difficult to observe. It was only by luck that we were able to find the fleet again."

Traax nodded his understanding, his face darkening a bit more. "You are dismissed," he said simply. With another click of his heels, the warrior walked away to take advantage of some well-deserved rest. Traax turned back to look at Geldon.

"Our search continues to go poorly," he said to the dwarf. "The Chosen One's wizards will not be pleased."

"I know," Geldon answered, equally dejected. "We are now just a bit more than two days from the coast. The farther west we sail, the less likely we are to find the prince. But orders are orders."

Saying nothing more, he turned back to the sea and again cast his eyes out over the waves. Traax, too, remained silent, lost in his own maze of concerns.

The silence was broken by the return of the last of the night's Minion search squadrons, coming to land on the deck.

At first glance these warriors seemed even more exhausted than the previous group had been. But then Geldon could see that they were talking animatedly among themselves; they looked almost happy, in fact.

The officer in charge hurried up to Geldon and Traax and bowed, clicking his heels. His name was K'jarr, and he was one of the finest long-distance fliers in the Minion force. Geldon found himself holding his breath in anticipation.

"Speak," Traax ordered quickly. "Do you have word of the prince?"

"Regrettably no, sir," K'jarr answered. "But we have discovered something else that might be of use to us in our search."

"And that is?"

K'jarr smiled. "We found a small patch of fog. It is less than a two-hour flight, south-southwest from the fleet's current position."

At first Traax seemed annoyed by what he viewed to be an inconsequential find. "And this is important because . . ." he said, exercising his considerable authority as he allowed his words to trail off.

"Its nature is highly unusual," the officer answered. "It does not ebb and flow with the winds, as one would expect. Instead it just stays in one place constantly, somehow always retaining its shape. Then, after about an hour of high surveillance, we began to observe the ships."

Geldon's eyes lit up. "What ships?" he asked eagerly.

"A great many vessels came and went from within the depths of the fog," K'jarr replied. "It is difficult to say for sure, but to me they looked like fighting ships. It seemed they were preparing for something. We continued to circle high above, using the clouds for cover. I doubt that we were observed. Instead of soaring down to investigate further, I thought it best to bring the squad directly back, so as to give you my report as soon as possible."

After nodding his approval to the officer, Traax turned questioning eyes toward Geldon. "Does any of this mean anything to you?" he asked urgently.

"No," the dwarf answered. "But if ships are coming and going from the midst of this unlikely haze, there must surely be more to it than meets the eye. If it truly does not move, then it is probably some manifestation of the craft. Magic is afoot."

"Exactly," Traax answered with a menacing grin. It was the first time Geldon had seen him smile since Tristan disappeared. "Do you think your wizards would mind very much if we made a small detour?" he asked conspiratorially.

Geldon thought for a moment. "I'm not sure," he answered. "But we're about to, anyway." He looked back at the officer who had just given them the mysterious news.

"Give the heading to the helmsman, and tell him to make the appropriate course change," he ordered. "We are going to investigate this immovable fog bank of yours. How long do you think it will take the fleet to reach it?"

"If the winds hold, we should be there by dawn," K'jarr answered. "Perhaps sooner."

"Very well," Geldon said. "Go now."

The officer bowed to both of them and clicked his heels together, then left.

"Tomorrow should prove to be a most interesting day," Traax said quietly.

Taking a deep breath, Geldon looked back into the Minion's intelligent, hazel eyes. "And so it shall," he agreed.

Neither of them fully realized just how meaningful Traax's observation was about to become.

CHAPTER

Forty-eight

Serena was worried. Wulfgar had changed.

Not so much that she did not continue to love him, and not in any way that made her fear for her safety. If anything, he seemed to love her even more. But he was more commanding, more sure of himself, more discerning in his thoughts and actions than she had ever seen.

Plus, he seemed to have an even greater desire to be free of the confines of his quarters. He would often stand and stare at the restless sea for hours, saying nothing. And then, without a second's warning, he would begin pacing the rooms like a caged, predatory animal, eager to be released on an unsuspecting world. More than once she had asked him what was preoccupying him so, but somehow he never answered her, distracting her instead with a kiss or by bringing up a different subject.

Since she had come to Wulfgar's quarters to live, he had been taken away by the demonslavers twice, and it was only since then that she had begun to notice the changes in him. She was sure his visits outside of these rooms were the cause of his strange metamorphosis, but she was at a loss as to why and how.

As he continued to pace back and forth before the azure window that Krassus had created, Serena realized that it was as if Wulfgar had been suddenly, involuntarily thrust into something far larger than himself and was being inexorably carried away upon the swelling rise of its tide.

"What is it, my love?" she asked gently. "What troubles you so?"

He stopped for a moment and turned to her, a short smile on his lips. Reaching down, he gently stroked one of her cheeks with the back of his hand. She took his hand into her own and pressed it closer, never wanting to let it go. Lifting her face, she looked into his eyes.

Wulfgar's eyes had always been beautiful. Hazel, compassionate, and strong, they had been one of the first things that had attracted her to him. But since his two mysterious visits to the outside they seemed literally to shine, as if they had been shot full of energy that was waiting to be released. They were mesmerizing, and she quickly found herself lost within their polished depths.

"There is nothing wrong, my darling," he answered softly. "Everything is finally starting to become as it should be. As it was foretold it would be. Only during my last few sessions with Krassus have I finally come to understand. There is much to tell."

"What do you mean?" she asked, still pressing his hand to her cheek.

Sitting down beside her, he looked lovingly into her eyes. "You are to become my queen," he said simply.

His words passed though her heart like a sudden storm. Stunned, she searched his face. "But you are not a king," she answered gently, not wanting to hurt him. She was surely honored by his words, and wanted to be with him forever. But a queen . . .

"I don't understand," she said, finally letting go of his hand. As she did, she found that her own hands were now trembling.

"I know," he answered. "At first neither did I. But Krassus has begun to show me the way. I no longer fear him, or his demonslavers. In fact, I now embrace them. Just as you soon will."

Realizing that she was curious, he turned his right wrist over and narrowed his eyes. As he did, a small puncture formed in his skin. Stunned and frightened, Serena instinctively pulled back. But Wulfgar only smiled, tacitly telling her that it was going to be all right.

He then turned his wrist over again, and a single drop of his blood fell to the silk bedsheets. As she watched, Serena's eyes went wide.

The blood twisted its way into a small pattern with curved lines on the top, and straight, angular lines on the bottom. It also had many smaller lines leading away from it, like branches shooting off from the trunk of a tree. It seemed to stir something within her—something long hidden, and immensely powerful. She looked back up at him, a thousand unanswered questions on her face. Wulfgar pointed down at the bloody signature.

"Within that pattern lies the source of all that there is, and all that shall ever be," he said quietly. "Endowed blood."

Looking at the brand on her shoulder, he rubbed his fingers across it. "*R'talis* blood," he added softly. "The blood you carry, as well." He then allowed silence to speak for a time, as he sensed her trying to absorb the gravity of his words.

"But how is it that you see yourself a king?" she finally asked.

Smiling, he took one of her dark ringlets into his hand and stroked it gently. "Each time I leave this place, I come one step closer to claiming my throne," he answered cryptically. "Just as you shall soon do, for such a seat awaits you, also. All you have to do is reach out and take it, as I am doing." Lost in his thoughts for a moment, he looked away. "I have seen such wonders, Serena . . ."

Suddenly a knock came on the door. It was almost hesitant, as if the person on the other side did not wish to disturb them, but must. Smiling, Wulfgar turned.

"Enter," he commanded. Serena heard the bolt slide away. The huge double doors opened, and a single demonslaver entered the room. Remarkably, he was unarmed. Then the slaver did something she would never forget.

Looking at Wulfgar, the monster bowed.

"Yes?" Wulfgar asked.

"Please forgive the intrusion, but it is once again time," the slaver said simply. "He asks for you." His tone was surprisingly kind. Perhaps even subservient, Serena realized. Wulfgar nodded at the slaver, then looked back at her.

"I will return, and then we can talk more," he said. "I apologize for locking the bolt, my love, but it is for your own good. Soon you, too, will have no need for the chambers to be secured. Just be patient."

Saying nothing more, Wulfgar left with the slaver. They closed and bolted the double doors behind them. Serena stared at the door for some time, still overcome by her lover's words.

Finally getting up and walking to the window, she realized that she had already begun to miss him. The three moons cast their magenta shimmerings upon the waters of the ocean, highlighting the tips of the ever-restless waves. Even though the transparent, azure wall separated her from the outside world, for a moment she thought she could almost smell the familiar saltiness of the sea breeze.

She tried to sort through the mysterious things Wulfgar had told her, but no answers came. As she gazed into the distance the silent waves beckoned, but provided no clues. She shook her head.

A queen, her mind repeated to her over and over again. But a queen destined to rule over whom?

As the sea crashed against the shore below, she stood there for a long time, just as Wulfgar had done, her mind lost in the maze of complexities that had been laid before her.

*L*ying on his back on one of the white marble tables of the Scriptorium, Wulfgar looked calmly up into Krassus' dark eyes. He was not tied down this time, for there was no longer any need for such crude measures. The Scroll of the Vagaries hovered close by, glowing with the power of the craft. Krassus smiled.

"Are you ready?" he asked simply.

"Yes," came the willing, eager answer.

"You're beginning to love the way you feel, are you not?"

"Yes."

"Tell me, then," Krassus asked. "What is it that you want?"

"I want more."

Smiling, the wizard resumed his work.

Forty-nine

As the first rays of dawn crept down through the strange, unmoving fog surrounding the Isle of Sanctuary, Tristan stood wearily against the gunwale of the *People's Revenge*. He had been up all night helping with the repairs, and he was exhausted. Letting out a deep breath, he hoped that their labors would be enough to let them survive another day.

He desperately needed to get the parchment hidden in his boot back to the wizards, but he was beginning to doubt whether he would live long enough to make that happen. So far there had been no sign of the pirates, but he knew that couldn't last much longer. Every moment that passed decreased their chances of escape.

Late the previous afternoon they had arrived back at their ships without incident, Scars still holding the unconscious Rolf over the front of his saddle. After boarding the vessels and tying Rolf securely to one of the masts, Tristan had convinced Tyranny to order her three ships to another location, well within the depths of the fog bank. But when he had tried to convince her of his other suggestion, her face had darkened and she had proven far more stubborn. In a way he understood her concerns, for there were parts of his plan he didn't care for, either. In fact, had Scars not finally agreed with him, he probably wouldn't have made any headway with her at all.

"I won't do it!" she had shouted loudly into the darkness of the nighttime fog, stamping one boot against the deck of *The People's Revenge*. They hadn't dared light the ships' lanterns, but in the rose-colored moonlight, Tristan could easily see the anger on her face. Her sharp jaw stuck out angrily.

"I didn't come all this way just to leave them behind!" Defiantly she folded her arms across her breasts. "Only the Afterlife knows what will become of them if I do! Frankly, you surprise me! What you managed to do back there in the Wing and Claw was wonderful, and I will be forever grateful for it, but what you ask of me now I will *not* grant!"

"I know how you feel, Tyranny," Tristan countered gently, trying to calm her down. "But my story won't hold up long, and I fear they may come for us anytime now, rather than keep their side of our so-called 'bargain.' If we are ever to get out of here in one piece, we must start work right away. If we are forced to try to outrun them in our current condition we are done for—you said so yourself. I know you don't want to leave anyone behind, but you must trust me when I tell you that this is the only way."

Tristan's plan was admittedly desperate. It involved cannibalizing the other two vessels and repairing *The People's Revenge* with what they had stripped from them. Then the remaining slaves and skeleton crews would be brought aboard, the other two ships would be scuttled, and Tyranny's flagship would set sail for Eutracia.

He knew full well that if they did this they would be packed to the rigging with extra crewmen, freed slaves, and provisions, and that that would drastically slow them down. Still, it was all he could think of that might gain them some semblance of a fighting chance. Back in the Wing and Claw he had never really expected the pirates to keep their end of the deal. His entire scheme had only been about getting away safely and buying some time.

But Tyranny would have none of what he was proposing. Knowing they were wasting precious time, he looked over to Scars and silently beseeched the faithful giant to agree with him. Finally, Scars relented and cleared his throat.

"I fear he may be right, Captain. We have just enough material from the two other ships to get the job done. If we start now and everyone lends a hand, we may be able to finish before dawn and leave before the pirates are any the wiser. Sometimes one simply has to know when to cut one's losses and move on. This seems to be one of those times."

Her face still a mask of grim determination, Tyranny continued to glare at them.

"I believe it's what your late father would do, were he here with us today," Scars added.

Tristan looked over again at the first mate, and each of them knew what the other was thinking. In order to get this done, they could simply tie Tyranny up and lock her belowdecks, he supposed, as long as her crew went along with it. But something in his heart wouldn't let him. They were all stronger with her than without her, and he wanted the ship's captain to be a willing part of whatever they did.

When they had first arrived back at the ships, Tyranny had ordered a head count. It revealed that more than fifty of her total crew were still on shore. And she had immediately made it clear that she wouldn't hear of leaving them behind.

In a way Tristan agreed with her, but he also knew that if any of them were going to survive, they had to get going. Any crewmembers not back on board by the time they were ready to sail would simply have to turn pirate—if they hadn't decided to do so already—or otherwise take their chances on the island. Finally deciding enough was enough, he took Tyranny by the shoulders and forced her around to face him.

"And what about your brother, eh?" he asked sternly. "You still remember him, I assume! How much good do you think you can do him if you're dead? Isn't he the real reason you started all this in the first place?"

Letting go of her, he pointed to some slaves sitting on the deck. Sick, ragged, and coughing, many of them looked as though they wouldn't even survive the two days it would take to get home.

"And what about them?" he asked. "Your men still on shore may be left behind, but they knew the risks. If they don't get back in time, so be it. But these slaves you have shed blood to save rightfully deserve their own chance, don't you think? Or have you somehow forgotten about them, too?" His dark gaze didn't give her an inch.

"You trusted me once, and now I'm asking you to do so again," he said, somewhat more gently. Reaching into his boot, he withdrew the ancient slip of parchment and held it before her eyes. "I know this can't look like much to you, but I must get it home at all costs. There are things at stake here that you can't possibly imagine. Things of the craft of magic." Then his mood lightened a bit. "Besides," he added coyly, "wouldn't you like to live long enough to spend that one hundred thousand kisa I promised you?"

Her stance softened, and she looked to Scars for guidance. The colossus slowly nodded his head.

With that, Tyranny reluctantly agreed to Tristan's plan. They had labored hard all through the night, and the decks of *The People's Revenge* were now literally covered with souls from the other two ships. But her spars and sails looked to be in good repair again, and the morning wind was stiffening. Tyranny quietly came to stand next to Tristan at the gunwale. She looked as exhausted as he did.

"Thank you," she said softly.

"For what?"

"For convincing me of what needed to be done," she answered, tousling her hair with one hand. "Sometimes I can be a handful, I know. They don't call me Tyranny for nothing."

Tristan pursed his lips knowingly. "So I've seen," he said wryly. Smiling, he brushed an errant lock of her outrageous hair away from one of her wide, blue eyes.

"You still haven't told me why your blood is azure, or why it glows," she then said, surprising him. "How can that be? Who are you, really?"

Scowling, Tristan looked back out over the ocean. "Even my wizards cannot answer such things," he said softly, sadly. "All I know is that lately I have come to curse my azure blood, and a large part of me wishes that I no longer had it. I long to have normally endowed blood, like Wigg and Faegan. But right now that day seems far away, indeed."

Then he heard footsteps, and turned to see Scars approaching.

"All is finally ready for departure, Captain," the giant said shortly. "May I have your orders?"

Tyranny looked sadly out to where the two stripped, deserted ships lay. They had once sailed proudly beside her, swift and sure in their service. But now they looked for all the world like lost, tattered orphans, fearfully awaiting some unknown fate. Tyranny closed her eyes.

"Scuttle them," she said softly.

With a sad, resigned look, Scars raised one arm and gave the signal to the two crewmen still waiting aboard the other vessels. After signaling back they quickly disappeared belowdecks, only to come up a few moments later. Then they scrambled down into the small longboats that lay tied alongside, and hurried back to the flagship. Once they were aboard and the boats secured, Tyranny turned to Scars.

"Take us out," she ordered simply. The tone of her voice told Tristan that her normally commanding demeanor had returned. "Be quick about it. And be sure to give us a wide berth around the others," she added sternly. "I have no desire to be taken by the undertow as those two frigates go down." Glad to be finally leaving Sanctuary, Scars began barking out orders to make way.

Looking across the fog-covered ocean, she and Tristan watched as the other two vessels began to swallow seawater, their bows slowly nosing down into the waves. Soon the briny, encroaching ocean was crossing them amidships, and the frigates were standing at a sharp angle on their bows. Finally the waves closed in over their aft decks and they plunged toward oblivion. The swirling, dark blue water closed over them, leaving no trace.

Tristan turned to Tyranny. "I'm sorry," he said.

"I know," she replied quietly. They said nothing for a time as they watched the spinning whirlpools slow and finally vanish altogether.

Then he heard the flagship's sails snap open, and *The People's Revenge* started to move. Soon they would be out of the fog and on their way home. So anxious was he to see Eutracia again that he almost thought he could smell the rich, dark soil and the green, waving grasses of the Cavalon Delta. Looking up, he saw his blue-and-gold battle standard snapping back and forth in the wind, and it gladdened his heart.

It was then that he and Tyranny heard the arrogant, hateful voice come snarling across the deck.

"So tell me, lass," the pirate shouted out. "Is it that he's better'n me where it counts, or is it just the money you're after? Know'n ya as I do, it's probably both, isn't it, my little she-cat?"

Turning, Tristan and Tyranny looked over to where Rolf stood lashed to the mainmast, weaponless, hands bound securely behind him. His blond hair was matted, and an angry red welt swelled his chin where Tristan had hit him with the brain hook. His narrowed eyes gazed at Tyranny with an odd combination of hate and lust that Tristan found unsettling.

"You'll never make it home, you know," Rolf added nastily. "Sure'n it was a fine notion to make your ship whole again by robbing from the other two. And even I have to admit that she used to be uncommonly fast. But if I know my boys, they have already surrounded the island. Your new man here may have fooled them back at the tavern, but you'll never beat them out on the open sea, y'have my word on it. Ya should've stayed in the fog, lass, but y'couldn't keep that up forever, now could ya? Worse yet, you're now too heavy to slip by their two hundred ships, and y'know it." Then he cast his eyes lasciviously up and down her body.

"It seems you and I will get to enjoy our little reunion after all," he added wickedly.

He turned to look at Tristan. "And as for you, you clever bastard, I look forward to giving you a taste of my sword," he snarled. "We have unsettled business, you and I. I'm eager to know whether y'really are any good with that ridiculous-looking blade you carry. But time will soon tell, laddie, yes, it will. And time is the one thing ya don't have." Then he smiled. "That and another two hundred ships, of course."

Tristan wanted to untie him and take him on right then and there, but he reluctantly pulled himself back. Taking a deep breath, he looked Rolf in the eyes. "I welcome it," he said quietly.

Just then *The People's Revenge* broke out of the fog. As the stiff, easterly wind filled her sails, Tyranny ordered that the heavily loaded frigate turn west, toward the delta. But before her orders could be carried out, the crewman in the crow's nest started ringing the alarm bell for all he was worth. Looking up, she saw him pointing frantically out over the bow.

Tristan looked quickly to Tyranny, to find that she already had her spyglass to one eye. As she trained it across the western horizon, the blood drained from her face. Saying nothing, she looked over at him and handed him the glass. Tristan put it to his eye and took a quick breath.

What looked to be a line of at least one hundred pirate vessels were tacking back and forth in the wind, quickly converging on their position.

Fearing the worst, Tristan quickly turned astern and raised the glass again. A seemingly equal number of vessels were running before the wind, plowing their way toward them in a battle line from the east.

The pirates' strategy was immediately apparent. The two battle lines planned to meet, trapping *The People's Revenge* in a manmade vise of wood and sailcloth from which there would be no escape.

Tristan knew that all they had now was the superior speed of Tyranny's ship, for the two groups of raiders clearly had the angle on them. But how much speed could she muster, loaded down like this? The best *The People's Revenge* could do was to try to slip through the gap at the northern ends of their lines before it closed. If they could, the open sea lay beyond.

But as Tristan gauged the distances involved and checked the direction of the wind, his heart fell. He was sure Tyranny would give it her best, but he knew they would never make it.

Tyranny gave the expected order, and the frigate immediately heeled over to the north, to begin tacking into the wind. Tristan finally lowered the glass to see that Tyranny's face wore the same sense of defeat that his must.

There would be no way to avoid being captured. And once they were, there would be no clever trick to save them this time, and no wizards to help them avoid their doom.

They were all alone, and they were about to die.

Fifty

Walking gingerly down the hall with his daughter at his side, Wigg cursed both his weakness and the fact that he had been unable to sleep the previous night. Horrific dreams had disturbed him over and over again, causing him to cry out and awaken to find his body covered with sweat, his mind overcome with guilt and terror.

Celeste had stayed by his side the entire night, to calm and reassure him whenever he awakened. He was still weak this morning, but he had insisted on getting out of bed and going to visit his friends. He very much wanted to see Abbey, Faegan, and Shailiha with his own eyes, for only then would he be able to breathe easier about what had happened to them in the courtyard yesterday.

After the unexpected blast had shaken the palace, the Minions had come to his quarters to inform him and Celeste of what had just happened. It had been a massive explosion, but the warriors had finally been able to extinguish the numerous grass fires that had sprung up. Luckily, the palace remained unharmed.

Abbey, Faegan, and Shailiha had survived, but they had been badly shaken. After being carefully examined by the gnome wives, they had been ordered straight to bed. As expected, Faegan had argued, but Shawna the Short had finally prevailed by scowling and shaking one of her pudgy fingers at him. In the end, he had simply been too tired to fight her.

Once he had felt well enough to rise, Wigg had asked that the three others also be awakened, so that he might immediately speak to them. He had not wished to disturb their rest, but he was concerned that what had just transpired could seriously impact their search for both the prince and the Scrolls of the Ancients. Time was precious, and the sooner they met, the better.

After hearing about what had happened in the courtyard, he now suspected that what he had just gone through in the Chambers of Penitence may have been some form of immensely elaborate ruse—one designed to supply him and Faegan with exactly the *wrong* kinds of herbs—those meant to kill them the moment they were employed. Was the watchwoman of the floating gardens somehow in league with Krassus? he asked himself as he shuffled along the polished marble hallways. And if she was, how could they have possibly known that he and Faegan would visit her? There were surely easier, far more certain ways to kill them than that.

None of it made any sense, but he was determined to get his answers. Finally finding himself before the proper door, Wigg knocked once, then let himself and Celeste into the vast library known as the Archives of the Redoubt.

Faegan, Abbey, and Shailiha were already at the mahogany meeting table around a large pot of tea and a silver plate of pastries. The master wizard and the herbmistress were talking in urgent, worried tones. Shailiha was listening to them intently, Morganna held close in her arms. Upon seeing Wigg and Celeste, the baby made a soft gurgling sound.

After Wigg and Celeste took their seats, the lead wizard cleared his throat. Abbey and Faegan finally stopped talking. Looking from them to Shailiha, Wigg realized that they were indeed lucky to be alive. Their faces and hands were decidedly reddened, and parts of their hair and eyebrows had been singed. Abbey looked the worst of the three. Reaching out, Wigg took her hand. She smiled and grasped it gingerly. Her skin felt good in his palm, and he smiled back at her.

"Is everyone all right?" Wigg asked softly.

Abbey looked over at Faegan, then back at the lead wizard. "I think so," she answered. "But it was very close. We have some burns, but Faegan has already enacted a spell of accelerated healing over them. He has also aided our hearing, which was temporarily impaired by the blast. In another day or so, we should be far better. But what about you?"

Placing his gnarled hands flat upon the tabletop, Wigg took a deep breath. "Let's just say that what I went through in the Chambers of Penitence is not something I would ever care to repeat," he said, employing his usual sense of wry understatement. "I should soon be better, as well. But tell me, how did this happen? Was it because of the goods we brought back?" As he looked at Faegan, his face darkened. "Did the watchwoman try to kill us by intentionally supplying us with the wrong items? Was everything I went through for naught?"

"No, I don't think so," Faegan answered almost perfunctorily. "It will, of course, be impossible to know for sure until we again try to use the oils and herbs. But I believe what happened was a result of something we did ourselves, rather than our having been betrayed by the watchwoman."

"How so?" Celeste asked.

"We were actively seeking Tristan," Faegan answered. "And it was the blood of his twin sister that we were employing to do so. Something physical of the subject to be viewed is always required—or at least something as close to the subject as the practitioner can find." Sitting back in his chair, he thought to himself for a moment.

"As I understand it from Abbey, under normal conditions this would never result in the catastrophic results we experienced in the courtyard," he went on. "Since we had nothing personal of the prince's body, we thought a drop of Shailiha's blood might do the trick. But remember, Tristan's blood is now azure—changed in ways that we have yet to fathom. It could simply be that his blood is not compatible with Abbey's gifts, and the process of trying to find him resulted in the flame's destruction. We may never know for sure. In any event, I certainly don't recommend that we use the exact same method to view him again."

Abbey narrowed her eyes with thought. "Actually, there is some mention of such a phenomenon in the ancient teachings of the partials," she said. "I had forgotten about it until hearing what you just said. It makes no mention of Tristan, exactly. But what happened is starting to sound more and more like what my teacher once warned me to be on the lookout for, so many years ago." She paused, and it was clear to everyone that she was trying hard to retrieve the details from her dusty, three-hundred-year-old memories.

Intensely interested, Faegan leaned nearer and placed his long, bony forearms on the table. "And that is?" he asked quickly.

"What we experienced is supposedly called the Furies," Abbey said, as the legend slowly returned to her. "The woman who taught me spoke very fearfully of it, telling me to pass the warning down to any of those partials I might eventually teach. It tells of 'the Two'—those who shall eventually come among us, possessing powers so great that we partials must never try to use our gifts upon them. If we do, we risk invoking the Furies and our spells being returned to us, thereby killing us in return. Much like what happened to us in the courtyard." She paused for a moment as the sudden realization spread across her face.

"The 'Two' the legend speaks of must be Tristan and Shailiha," she said softly. Then the room went quiet, as each of them tried to absorb the gravity of her news.

Faegan, however, wasted no time. Pointing over at the table that held the Tome of the Paragon, he straightened one finger. The white, leatherbound volume rose into the air and came to rest before him. He turned his gray-green eyes to Abbey.

"The 'Furies,' you say?" he asked her. The herbmistress nodded.

Closing his eyes, the wizard called upon his powers of Consummate Recollection. As he concentrated on the single word, a vision began to form in his mind. This time it was only a page number, rather than an entire quotation. Opening his eyes, he looked back down at the great book.

Faegan caused the Tome to open itself, and its gilt-edged leafs started flurrying by. When he found the page he wanted, he caused them to stop turning. After reading it a curious look crossed his face, and he sat back in his chair.

"What is it?" Wigg asked. Without answering, Faegan looked back to the great book and began to translate the Old Eutracian on its pages.

"And there shall come among you the Two, and they shall possess a blood quality so high that those known as the 'partials'—those sole practitioners of certain of the Organics—shall come to dread them. For should those of partial blood signatures attempt to employ their limited gifts upon the Two, the Two's progeny, or others of the same womb from which the Two came, their power shall be reversed upon them a thousandfold, and destroy them. For the blood signatures known as 'partials' shall not be as strong as those of the fully endowed. The Two and their seed may therefore be the partials' mortal enemies, even though the Two may not choose for such a reaction to be so . . ."

Trailing off, Faegan again sat back in his chair, lost in thought.

"What does it mean?" Abbey asked. At first Faegan said nothing. He was ensconced within the caverns of his amazing mind, and his eyes almost seemed glazed over.

"Such a wondrous, dangerous maze is the craft," he finally muttered softly, half to himself. "After three hundred years of trying, we have barely scratched the surface of the knowledge collected by the Ones Who Came Before."

"Faegan," Wigg said forcefully, trying to bring the old wizard's attention back to the rest of them. "What does it all mean?"

Taking a breath, Faegan finally refocused on the people at the table. "It confirms something that I have long suspected regarding the craft," he answered cryptically. "But more about that in a moment." Then he looked intently at Abbey.

"Tell me," he asked her. "Exactly how did you know that something terrible was about to happen in the courtyard?"

"My gazing flame began behaving far out of the ordinary," she answered. "After the viewing window started to form, the top of the flame began to swell. I have never seen one do that before. It was almost as if it was somehow *collecting* energy instead of expelling it, as is the norm. When I saw it, something told me it was about to burst, so I threw myself at you and the princess. Apparently when the flame ruptured, it did so at the top, releasing its energy skyward. Had the rent appeared in its side instead, I have no doubt that the three of us would be quite dead. In all my years I have never experienced a release of such boundless energy."

Faegan smiled at her. "Thank you," he said softly. "And we shall never forget what you did."

"So what does it all mean?" Wigg demanded impatiently. "Aren't you ever going to tell us what's rattling around in that centuries-old, overactive brainpan of yours?"

Faegan only gave them that coy, knowing smile of his again. He enjoyed nothing so much as a mystery of the craft—especially when he was the only one who held its answer.

"Just one more question, I promise," he told the table. "Shailiha, do you remember anything out of the ordinary just before the gazing flame burst? Did you experience any unusual or uncomfortable sensations, for example?"

"Now that you mention it, my heart began beating so fast and so hard that I thought I might pass out," she answered. "But I didn't say anything about it before, because I thought it was just caused by anxiety. Was it significant?"

"Oh, yes, my child!" The wizard smacked his palm down on one arm of his chair in triumph. "Indeed it was!" He looked like the cat that had just swallowed the proverbial canary.

"And so?" Wigg asked, crossing his arms with frustration.

"Abbey is quite correct," Faegan began. "This is further evidenced by the princess' extremely rapid heartbeat. Her blood coursed faster through her body in response to rejecting and further empowering a partial adept's spell. And the energy was returned to Abbey's flame by a factor of one thousand times, so says the Tome. How fascinating!" He paused for a moment to let his words sink in.

"Unfortunately, this dangerous practice was exactly what we were trying to accomplish yesterday, in our benign ignorance out there in the courtyard," he continued. "And we succeeded admirably in making fools of ourselves, didn't we? The fact that Tristan's blood is now azure may have only intensified the effect." He looked around the table. "As we have already said, several of us here are indeed lucky to be alive."

He looked over at the herbmistress. "I strongly suggest that you do not attempt to employ any of your gifts on either of the Chosen Ones again, especially before Wigg and I have had a chance to explore these new revelations further," he added.

Abbey rolled her eyes. "Don't worry!" she said, holding her palms upward in a gesture of surrender. "I have no such intentions; I promise!"

"Tell me," Faegan said. "Do you know of any way to circumvent these Furies, as you call them, so that we might still try to locate the prince?"

"There were always rumors among those in the partial community that such a process existed," Abbey answered. "Legend says that it can be done, provided one possesses the proper calculations for it. But I do not know what the formulas are, or where they might be found. They supposedly involved sending the energy back yet again to the original subject, in its newly constituted strength." She thought to herself for a moment. "The possibility of circumventing the Furies also raises another very interesting question," she added thoughtfully.

"And that is?" Wigg asked.

"Whether such a spell, should it in fact actually exist, would fall within the purview of the wizards, rather than the partials," she answered slowly, as if thinking aloud. "Such uses of the craft would seem to reside well outside the realm of the Organic. It sounds far more like one of the Paragon's facets of the Kinetic, wouldn't you agree?"

Faegan furrowed his brow. It was soon clear to the others that he found this last comment to be even more interesting than what had been discussed previously.

"You're forgetting something, aren't you?" Wigg finally asked from the other side of the table. "Or should I say *someone*?"

"And just who might that be?" Faegan asked.

"Wulfgar," Wigg answered solemnly. Again the room became silent.

Faegan nodded. "Quite right, Lead Wizard," he agreed. "And well done. The quote I just read from the Tome mentioned not only the Two, but also their progeny, and others from the same womb. That would, of course, include both Wulfgar and Morganna." He looked over at Abbey. "For the time being you are to strictly avoid using your gifts not only on Tristan and Shailiha, but on Wulfgar and Morganna, as well," he ordered her. The herbmistress nodded her agreement.

"But still we have failed, have we not?" Celeste asked. "In addition to not finding Tristan, we have no idea where this Scroll of the Vigors may be. It could be anywhere in the world. And unless we find it soon, Krassus will be able to complete at least one portion of the mission originally begun by Nicholas—a mission that we still know virtually nothing about."

Shailiha angrily shook her head. She had been bitterly disappointed again. Her greatest goal continued to be finding her brother, and now it seemed that they were even farther away from it than ever. "I'm tired of sitting here and doing nothing while Tristan is in danger!" she cried out. "Can't you all see that?" Morganna cried a little with her mother's sudden outburst, and Shailiha kissed her cheek to soothe her. "Isn't there anything that can be done?" she asked, trying to keep her voice calmer.

"The herbs and oils we brought back were to have been our solution to that," Wigg said sadly. "However, with this sudden, unexpected appearance of the Furies, I'm afraid we are now forced to discover another way to find him. But hear me when I tell you that Tristan is a very brave and resourceful man, and if there is anyone in this world who can overcome whatever he is up against, it is he. I know that isn't much for you to hold onto right now, but it seems to be all that any of us have." Wigg looked over at Celeste to see a somewhat different, but equally concerned look cross her face.

A growing sense of defeat crept silently over the room.

Fifty-one

K'jarr soared high and fast through the fading indigo of the early-morning sky. He wore his dreggan strapped across his back and his returning wheel securely fastened to one side of his belt; a battle bugle was tied to the other side, waiting to be used. Behind him, the sun rose, bringing a welcoming warmth to his ceaselessly beating wings.

His dark eyes scoured the Sea of Whispers below, and he smiled, blessing his highly tuned senses. He would need them all today, he knew.

He banked to the left slightly, changing course, and the one hundred specially selected Minion warriors accompanying him followed suit. Officers all, they had been handpicked not only for their overall intelligence and superior flying speed, but also for their expert fighting ability. They were the Minion forces' best of the best, and their mission was clear: Find the mysterious fog bank and investigate it. Board and carefully examine the ships they found there. They were to leave no stone unturned in their search for the prince.

They could not have been far from the fog bank when K'jarr saw a line of ships heading west, running before the wind. They were still some distance away, and moving fast. Surprised by their great numbers, he counted them to find that there were just a bit more than one hundred in all. Then his eyes caught sight of a lone frigate desperately plowing her way north, while the line of ships closed in on her from the west. She was clearly trying to make a run for the gap in the northernmost points of the ships' lines. But the prevailing winds were easterly, and tacking back and forth as she was, she would never make it in time.

As he watched from afar, the battle lines were closing together, surrounding the single ship in a deadly, seaborne ring of wood and sailcloth. Sensing a looming tragedy, he flew faster, his wings straining. And there, at last, was the mysterious patch of fog he had been searching for, lying peacefully and unmoving in the blue water, blocking the single frigate's escape to the south.

K'jarr's jaw hardened with hate. Why would anyone commit so many vessels to the capture of a single ship? he wondered. It just didn't make any sense. And then it hit him.

The Chosen One might be aboard.

He watched in horror as the ring closed more tightly around the trapped vessel.

Turning, he called orders to the three officers who were to return to the Minion fleet with the exact location of the fog bank. Immediately they peeled away from the main body and soared through the air, flying hard in the direction from which they had just come.

He returned his attention to the action in the distance, hoping against hope that his sworn lord was not trapped on that lone, desperate ship. It would be many long moments before he and his warriors could reach them—moments that the ones aboard the frigate clearly could not afford. Turning to the officer nearest him, K'jarr began barking out orders.

Just then the lead vessel in the oncoming fleet rammed the lone frigate directly amidships. As he watched, K'jarr's razor-sharp eyes caught something that quickened his heart: At the top of the ship's mainmast flew the blue-and-gold battle flag of the House of Galland.

K'jarr drew his dreggan. Despite the rushing of the wind, he could hear the reassuring ring of his warriors' blades cutting through the air all around him.

He smiled grimly. This was what they had been bred for, had spent their entire lives training for. There was no greater honor for a true Minion warrior than to perish in the service of his lord. Many of them would no doubt meet their final reward here today, somewhere over the Sea of Whispers.

Suddenly snapping his wings closed behind his back, K'jarr held his sword before him and jacknifed into a dive, pointing straight down in a perfect, vertical free fall. The warriors behind him followed suit. Faster and faster they fell, plummeting toward the stricken ship as attackers swarmed over her decks.

The odds were overwhelming, K'jarr knew. But if his lord was indeed here, then there was no other duty, no other choice than the one lying before them.

Narrowing his dark eyes against the wind, he led his forces down.

*I*n a violent cacophony of splintering wood, the lead pirate ship had rammed *The People's Revenge* directly amidships. Then she had swung alongside, her raiders screaming and jumping from their vessel to swarm like ants over the decks of Tyranny's flagship.

One man leapt from the rigging with a knife between his teeth, and swung his saber broadly in an attempt to take the prince's head off.

But Tristan saw him coming. Quickly slipping to one side, he held his dreggan out with both arms and pressed the button on the hilt. The extra length of blade launched forward, catching the pirate across the belly. The pirate's face registered a moment of shock; then the light went out of his eyes. Ignoring the gushing blood, Tristan roughly pushed the corpse off his sword with the heel of one boot. But as he turned to look around, his heart fell.

Tyranny and Scars were lost among all the fighting. All around him, men were dying. Worse yet, the other raider vessels were approaching rapidly. The deck of *The People's Revenge* was a mass of screaming, struggling pandemonium, blades clanging noisily amid the sounds of shouting and groans of pain.

It would be over very shortly, he knew, and they would all be dead. The scrap of parchment hidden in his boot would never reach Eutracia, and Krassus would win. But before that happened, Tristan swore he would take as many of them down with him as he could.

Seeing a pirate raise his sword against one of the slaves, he instinctively reached over his right shoulder and drew one of his knives. Almost before he knew it, the dirk was twirling end over end toward its victim.

As it buried itself into the side of the man's neck, blood rushed out in furious, uncontrolled spurts. Wet, slippery waves of crimson cascaded down the man's left shoulder as he clutched frantically at the handle of the knife. But it was already too late. As blood spewed from his lungs, his eyes became strangely fixed in the distance. His sword dropped noisily to the deck, and he fell stiffly, face forward.

Tristan turned to look up into the rigging from which his first attacker had come. As he did, his heart skipped a beat. All of Tyranny's crewmembers who had remained behind on the Isle of Sanctuary had been captured and hung from the pirate ship's masts and rigging.

Tristan had known some of these people. He had laughed with them, worked with them, and learned the ways of the sea from them. And now they were dead. As he stood gaping up at the bodies that had once been so full of life, a sudden wave of guilt swept over him.

Bending over, he tried to keep from vomiting.

Later he would recall that it was truly a miracle he hadn't been killed then. Finally returning to his senses, he spun around to rejoin the battle.

Almost immediately another of them was upon him. Awash with rising anger, Tristan used all his talents to make sure the pirate died.

*A*s they neared the stricken ship in their headlong plunge, K'jarr's warriors fanned out. They had been ordered to find whether the prince was aboard before joining the battle, and to do so at all cost. K'jarr unfolded his wings and buffeted the air to hover at a point near the mainmast, about ten meters off the deck. He wanted very badly to join the fray, but he had to monitor the progress of his warriors first. If his lord was struggling somewhere on this ship they would soon find him, or die trying.

Finally, in the midst of the battle, they saw him.

*A*s the first of them went soaring by, Tristan thought he must be seeing things. Then one swooped down to land beside him, dreggan drawn, eyes flashing. Then came another and another, until a multitude of them had formed a protective ring around him, slashing viciously at their attackers as they came. Many of the stunned pirates died right there and then.

Tristan's heart leapt in his chest. He didn't know how many of the Minions there were here, or where they had suddenly come from, but now, finally, he thought there might be a chance to prevail after all.

K'jarr landed beside Tristan. After quickly telling him the number of warriors under his command and the location of the Minion fleet, he waited calmly for Tristan's orders. The prince looked out across the waves to see that the rest of the pirate vessels would soon be upon them. Then an idea struck him.

Using precious seconds, he gauged the speed and distance between them and the nearest of the oncoming ships. He leaned toward K'jarr again.

"Take half of your force and fly toward those ships!" he shouted urgently above the din. "Leave the other half of your warriors here to help us secure this vessel! When you reach the enemy vessels, this is what I want you to do!"

Leaning in further, he shouted some final directives to K'jarr. Understanding, the officer smiled. He then took to the air again, half of his warriors following him as ordered, and flew directly toward the oncoming pirate ships. Tristan and the remaining warriors began grimly hacking their way through the raiders on board *The People's Revenge.*

The battle continued to rage, but the prince thought there were now more of Tyranny's crewmen standing than there were pirates. Still, the scene before him was something out of a nightmare. Dead men lay tangled in the rigging of both ships. Body parts were everywhere. The wounded of both sides were screaming pitifully for help, and the decks were slippery with blood.

He desperately needed to find Tyranny and Scars and tell them what was happening. Fighting his way down the length of the decks with his warriors by his side, he finally saw them. Amazingly, they were both still alive.

*A*s K'jarr and his Minions approached the encroaching pirate vessels, they obeyed their lord's orders and climbed higher. Then their leader gathered them into a hovering, eager group and started barking out commands. Only two warriors to a ship, he told them quickly. When they were done with their work, they were to advance to another vessel and then another, always doing the same thing until the task was complete. By then their fleet should have arrived, and the killing could begin in earnest.

Smiling to himself, K'jarr watched them go, as two by two they bravely dove down on the pirate armada. As they did, the pirates began to notice, looking up and staring at the winged ones with wide, unbelieving eyes.

K'jarr smiled. Trying to board these two hundred vessels and kill all of the pirates would have been blatant suicide. Still, had Tristan ordered them to do so, they would have obeyed him without question. But the Chosen One had not commanded his winged warriors to attack the pirates.

He had ordered them to attack their ships.

*O*ut of one corner of her eye, Tyranny saw Tristan coming. Then, for the first time in her life, she saw the Minions. So stunned was she that she literally stopped what she was doing and simply stared at them, her sword hanging limply from one bloody hand. Only at the last moment did one of the warriors step in, expertly slicing away the head of a sash-wearing pirate who had tried to take advantage of her lapse in judgment.

Running up to her side, Tristan shouted out to her, telling her that the winged ones were his, and that she shouldn't be afraid of them. With the fighting on *The People's Revenge* finally starting to abate, he did his best to explain what he had just ordered the Minions to do, and how their fleet was on the way. There were still two hundred pirate vessels bearing down on them, but at least now they had a slim chance. As he told her, he saw a glimmer of hope appear in her eyes. Then he looked over to see Scars.

The ever-weaponless giant was holding a frantically squirming, screaming pirate in his arms. Tristan knew from prior experience that there would be no escape for the man. Seemingly oblivious to everything going on around him, Scars calmly walked the terrified raider over to the gunwale, the pirate's red, telltale sash dragging on the pitching deck as they went.

Without fanfare, Scars lifted the man into the air, then brought his head down sharply against the smooth, polished edge. With a sickening snapping sound, it cracked open like an eggshell. Gray brain matter slipped from within its shattered depths to fall sloppily onto the deck. Saying nothing, Scars tossed the body overboard into the sea. Then he looked up at Tristan and smiled broadly.

*A*s K'jarr's warriors finally reached the oncoming pirates' ships, they drew their swords. Swooping and darting among the vessels, staying aloft rather than taking to the decks, they hacked savagely at the sails and rigging of the ships, bringing them tumbling to the decks in tattered, useless heaps of tangled rope and sailcloth. All the angry pirates could do was to watch helplessly, shaking their fists and cursing the days the winged ones were born.

A few of the more aggressive pirates started climbing the remains of their tattered rigging, to reach the Minions and fight them. But that proved to be a huge mistake. From their superior positions aloft, the Minions easily cut them to pieces, the raiders' mutilated bodies crashing back down to the decks or splashing into the Sea of Whispers.

On and on it went, one ship after the next, as the Minions mercilessly hacked down the sails and rigging. Others of them destroyed the hulls of the ships' longboats and skiffs, making escape impossible. Finally, exhausted but satisfied, the Minion warriors resheathed their dreggans and soared higher, to regroup with their leader.

Looking down, K'jarr smiled broadly. Just as the Chosen One had hoped, the warriors had been able to stop the pirate vessels dead in the water, and now they drifted aimlessly, at the whim of the currents. Their decks covered with white sailcloth, the ships looked rather like oddly shaped clouds that had somehow fallen from the sky to land in the openness of the blue sea. There was no way the pirate forces would be able to reach their comrades in the battle for *The People's Revenge.*

As the pirates screamed invectives at the winged ones who had crippled them, K'jarr knew that he and his warriors had just secured for their lord the one thing he had needed most: time. Time for their fleet to arrive, under the dual command of Geldon and Traax. That would not be long now, he knew. Then the real killing could begin. In true Minion fashion, his blood sang with the promise of slaughtering the enemies of his sworn lord.

K'jarr turned his sharp eyes toward the eastern horizon. To his great delight, he could finally see the sails of their fleet approaching. Then another dark, fleeting shadow passed over the ocean below, and he smiled.

The sky above him was suddenly swarming with Minion troops. Traax was leading them, and six of them were carrying a litter that presumably transported Geldon.

Traax waved K'jarr's forces up, and the two groups combined. After a quick word of explanation from K'jarr, the warriors left the pirate ships in their misery and began flying as fast toward Tyranny's stricken ship as their wings would allow.

Despite their initial success, Traax's face darkened. Their lord wasn't safe yet, and every passing second mattered.

Tyranny, Scars, and Tristan stood together back to back, fighting against the remaining pirates who still dared to take them on. Tyranny had already been wounded in one shoulder, and Scars in his right thigh. Neither of their injuries was mortal, but they needed attention, or they would both soon become weak from blood loss.

Tristan was still unscathed. He continued to fight like a demon, even though his arms were becoming so heavy he didn't know how much longer he would be able to raise his dreggan. Fortunately, their attackers were becoming fewer, and at last all three of them were able to stop fighting.

Their chests heaving, Tristan and Tyranny took a moment to rest on the hilts of their swords. Using a shirt taken from a dead pirate and ripped into strips, Scars temporarily bound Tyranny's wound and then his own.

Then a voice rang out across the deck, causing Tristan's blood to run cold.

"I said that you were a clever bastard!" Rolf shouted. "And what you just did to my ships proves it, doesn't it? These winged monkeys of yours can certainly use a sword, I'll give them that! But what ugly things they are! Sure'n it's just you and me now. What say you, laddie—are you up for a little fun?"

At some point in the battle, one of the pirates must have cut Rolf free from the mast. Looking out across the ship, Tristan could see him standing arrogantly on the far side of an empty patch of bloody deck. He beckoned Tristan forward, the red sash around his waist fluttering in the wind. In one hand he held a bloody pirate saber, and in the other a dagger. Smiling, he wiped the sword blade clean on one leg of his trousers. Then he raised it, expertly twirled it around in his hand, and pointed its tip directly at the prince's face. For a split second Tristan wondered how many of Tyranny's men the pirate had just killed.

"Are you going to hide behind that traitorous bitch's skirts forever, or come to me like a man?" Rolf shouted. Then he smiled and bowed sarcastically to Tyranny. "Sorry, lass, but I forgot—you never wear skirts, do you? Still, that never kept me from finding my way in, did it now?"

Enraged, Tristan stalked toward the pirate leader. He knew that they had already won, that this didn't need to happen. And in his heart he knew that Rolf understood that as well as he did.

But Tristan's supremely endowed, azure blood was overcoming these sentiments. Both he and Rolf had their reasons for what was about to happen, and neither of them would be denied. He paused by Tyranny, his eyes still fixed squarely on Rolf.

"If he kills me, you must see to it that the vellum hidden in my boot gets back to the wizards in Tammerland," he said quietly. "My fleet will be here soon. When it arrives, give the paper to the warrior named Traax. He will most probably be in command, and he can be trusted. Do you understand?"

Tyranny nodded. Reaching out, she squeezed his arm. "Be careful," she whispered. "He is very, very good."

"I know," Tristan answered softly, without looking at her. Reaching behind his back, he removed one of his throwing knives. Then, temporarily holding the dirk in the same hand that held his dreggan, he used his free hand to unbuckle the knife quiver, which fell to the deck. His baldric, scabbard and all, followed. He returned the knife to his left hand.

Although almost without equal with a sword, Tristan was no expert at this kind of dual-bladed fighting. He had trained in the art briefly, and knew he possessed the basic skills. But watching Rolf's sword and dagger whirl around in the bright morning sun, he realized that this was the pirate's chosen specialty. Tristan would have to be good—very good—if he was to have any hope of staying alive. But the die was cast, and there was no going back now.

As he moved forward again, he and Rolf warily began taking stock of each other in the center of the slippery, bloody deck. A strange kind of quiet came over the ship. Crewmen, slaves, pirate captives, and Minion warriors alike watched intently as the deadly scene unfolded.

Rolf acted first. Lunging sharply at the prince, he slashed diagonally with his saber. Stunned, Tristan realized that he had never before encountered such raw speed—not even that day when he had killed Kluge, the previous commander of the Minions. Only at the last moment did Tristan understand that Rolf's first blow had been a feint, designed to distract attention from the dagger as it came stabbing straight out from underneath.

It was a miracle that he saw the dagger come out at all. But as it emerged from the shadow created by Rolf's body, it flashed for a split second in the sun. Only at the last moment did Tristan violently swivel his torso to avoid the strike. Rolf's dagger sliced through the side of his leather vest, narrowly missing his skin.

With Rolf now off balance, Tristan rushed back in and stabbed his dirk directly at one of Rolf's eyes. But the pirate was too fast, sidestepping immediately, almost as if he had been expecting that very countermove. At the same time, he parried Tristan's strike with his sword, and its greater weight nearly knocked the dirk from the prince's tired hand.

Holding their weapons high, they circled each other again, each looking for an opportunity to strike. This time, however, Tristan decided not to wait. If he wanted to stay alive, he would have to go on the offensive and stay there, no matter how exhausted he was from his previous battles.

Using both weapons at once, Tristan windmilled them with everything he had. Rolf was able to keep parrying them as they came, but just barely. The sound of the clanging blades became an almost continual ringing out of steel against steel. Tristan's arms moved with lightning speed. He was finally gaining ground, forcing Rolf over near the port gunwale, just across from the mainmast. But Rolf seemed to be answering Tristan's blows more confidently, as he was beginning to get a feel for the prince's fighting style and for his equally amazing speed. Tristan could only hope that Rolf was tiring, as well.

But then the pirate surprised Tristan. Backing away as he parried and struck with his saber, the pirate placed his dagger between his teeth. He then grabbed the nearby rigging and ascended one-handed with practiced ease, continuing to fight Tristan with his sword.

Three rungs up, Rolf halted his climb and moved to the far side of the ropes, where he smiled tauntingly down. Then he wrapped one arm through the rigging, leaned back almost casually, and spread his arms in an arrogant gesture of welcome. It was clear the waiting spider had just dared the fly to come and enter his web.

Seeing this, Tyranny almost cried out. But not wanting to divert Tristan's attention from anything Rolf might do, she held back. She closed her eyes for a moment. She had watched her former lover single-handedly kill over a dozen demonslavers with this very ruse, back before he had succumbed to the temptations of Sanctuary and had become a pirate. Rolf was a very different man now, but his fighting skills were as sharp as ever. She had never seen any of his unsuspecting opponents survive what he was about to do.

She looked over at Scars, who shook his head. Understanding how inexperienced Tristan still was at shipboard fighting, they both knew in their hearts that he had just committed suicide.

No sooner had Tristan climbed up to meet Rolf than the pirate dropped his sword, grasped the far side of the rigging with both hands, and kicked his feet away from the ropes, launching his body out into space. Using the tension in the ropes to add power and momentum to the maneuver, he swung around behind the opposite, flat side of the rigging, straightened out his legs, and sent his boots plunging through the gaps between the squares of rope and smashing directly into Tristan's chest with tremendous force.

Tristan lost his grip. He went crashing back down to the bloody deck, hitting his head hard.

In a flash, Rolf followed him down.

Looking up through a cloudy, concussive haze, Tristan saw Rolf raise his dagger as if in slow motion, his green eyes flashing with hate.

Then, Tristan glimpsed a flash of silver, and Rolf's expression changed from one of conquest to one of surprise. Tristan watched as a bright red line appeared around the back of Rolf's neck.

Then the pirate's head literally fell off his shoulders, tumbling to one side and crashing to the deck. His body followed suit, landing hard next to the prince.

Just behind where Rolf had been standing stood Tyranny, her sword covered with fresh blood.

Tristan felt hands under his arms, pulling him to his feet. He stood, wobbly and dazed, for several moments, trying to understand what had just happened. The silence was complete except for the gentle creaking of the ship's hull. Finally, Tyranny looked Tristan in the eyes.

"I'm glad I killed him," she said softly, her voice little more than a whisper.

"*You're* glad . . ." Tristan answered, rubbing the back of his head.

A strong, familiar laugh rang out behind him. Turning, the prince found himself looking into the clear, predatory eyes of Traax.

"If she hadn't gotten that bastard in time, I would have done it for her," he said. Sheathing his dreggan, the Minion warrior smiled broadly.

"But it seemed she really wanted to kill him herself. And who am I to contradict such a beautiful woman—especially one who seems to care so much for our lord!"

Dazed, Tristan looked around. The decks of *The People's Revenge* were overflowing with Minion warriors. Still more circled in the skies above, their numbers occasionally blotting out the sun. A Minion litter sat on the deck nearby.

He cast his eyes out over the sea. Not only had the pirate fleet been immobilized, but the Minion vessels had by now completely surrounded them, as well.

Thankful to be alive, he took a deep breath. It seemed they had done it, after all. But there were still difficult decisions to be made, and he knew it. Then he saw Geldon.

The hunchbacked dwarf was waiting patiently near the gunwale, his dark, intelligent eyes taking in everything. Tristan went to him on still-shaky legs, and they gratefully embraced one another. Smiling, Geldon looked up into the prince's eyes.

"We were very worried," he said simply. "We have been tearing our hair out trying to find you. The Sea of Whispers is a very big place." He smiled again, at the same time giving Tristan a knowing wink. "In case you didn't already know, the Minions can become very irritable when they are concerned for the safety of their lord."

A look of worry crossed Tristan's face. "And what of everyone at the palace?" he asked, his mind finally starting to clear. "Are they well?"

"As far as I know, yes, they are," Geldon answered. "But I have been at sea for nearly thirty days, bringing the fleet across. In any event, you will soon see them for yourself."

Looking back to the very confused Tyranny and Scars, Tristan beckoned them forward. But as he was introducing them to Geldon and Traax, he saw Tyranny's face turn dark.

"What's wrong?" he asked. "We've won. You should be happy."

Then he understood. She had just noticed her dead crewmembers hanging from the rigging of the pirate vessel that had rammed them.

Without speaking, she walked over to the nearby gunwale and looked up. No one followed her; no one spoke. After a time, Tristan walked up and put one arm around her, and she laid her head tiredly on his shoulder.

"I'm sorry," he said. "But at the same time I must tell you that if I were forced to make that same decision again, I would."

For a moment she did not speak. "I know," she finally answered. "And I am not angry with you. But no amount of kisa in the world can remedy this."

Tristan turned to Traax. "Have them cut down immediately," he ordered. "And have the bodies covered with sailcloth. Their remains are to be respected, and buried at sea." With a sharp click of his heels, Traax turned and began barking out orders.

Raising her head from Tristan's shoulder, Tyranny looked up into his dark eyes. "Thank you," she said softly. "For everything." Knowing there was little more to be said, Tristan only nodded.

Then another Minion officer approached, and Tristan recognized him as the one he had ordered to destroy the pirate sails and rigging. The warrior went to one knee, his head bowed.

"Permission to speak, my lord?" he asked politely.

"Granted," Tristan said.

The Minion stood. "My name is K'jarr, and I wanted you to know that it was my great honor to serve by your side in the skies over Farplain, just before the destruction of the Gates of Dawn. It was also my privilege to fight alongside you again here today."

Tristan smiled at K'jarr. Sometimes it seemed that the horrific battle over the fields of Farplain had been many years ago, rather than mere months.

"Thank you, K'jarr," he said with feeling. "I will not forget you in the days to come."

Traax reappeared then at Tristan's side, his face showing uncharacteristic concern.

"Forgive me, my lord, but my news is urgent. *The People's Revenge* is taking on water—a direct result of having been rammed. The leak is slow, but our shipwrights tell me that it is irreparable. It is imperative that we transfer all of the survivors to our other vessels, and that we do so quickly."

Looking forward, Tristan could see that Traax was right. In the heat of all the fighting, he hadn't noticed. But the ship was going nose-down, her bowsprit already nearing the waves.

"How long do we have?" Tristan asked.

"No more than one hour," Traax answered.

Tristan turned to look at Tyranny. He could use the Minions to force an evacuation, but he wouldn't. This was her ship, and it would be her decision.

Closing her eyes for a moment, Tyranny finally nodded.

Tristan turned back to Traax. "Very well," he answered. He looked back at Tyranny. "Is there anything you wish to take?" he asked.

"Only my charts and navigational tools," she answered. Looking over at Scars, she gave the faithful giant some silent commands with her eyes. In a moment, he was gone.

As Tristan cast his gaze back down the length of the stricken ship, another thought came to him. Pulling Tyranny nearer, he whispered something into one of her ears.

A relieved look came over her. "Of course," she said gratefully. "Especially if you think it will help. How could I have been so forgetful?"

Tristan gave her a smile. "You've had rather a lot on your mind lately, I'd say."

He beckoned K'jarr back to him, and the warrior was by his master's side in an instant. After hearing his new orders, the warrior selected two other officers to help him, and they walked dutifully away.

"Forgive me, my lord, but there remains one final issue to be dealt with," Traax said. Knowing full well that his lord understood what that was, he said nothing more.

Tristan's face darkened. He had to make his decision about the fate of the pirates. Walking over to the gunwale, he looked out to sea again.

The pirate vessels were clearly helpless, but the seething, violent men aboard them were not. They were killers and thieves of the highest order, and they had to be stopped. If he chose to, he could order his Minions to attack them, and they would no doubt prevail. But some of the Minions would lose their lives—as would all of the pirates, unless they surrendered. Deep in his heart, he knew he simply couldn't authorize a slaughter like that. Besides, he reasoned, he would likely need every single Minion he could muster in what might very soon become a struggle with Krassus and the demonslavers. Looking back, he beckoned to Tyranny and Traax to join him at the gunwale.

"I want you to take the pirates alive, if at all possible," he ordered Traax. "There is a sizable island just to the south of us, hidden in that fog bank. Take the pirates there and maroon them. I also want you to station enough Minion warships around the island's perimeter to ensure that none of them can escape. The remainder of the fleet is to make for Eutracia at the best possible speed. And tow the pirate vessels back with you—they're too valuable to waste. Anchor just off the Cavalon Delta, and then come to the palace with your report. Together with my wizards, we will arrive at some conclusion regarding the pirates." He looked back out at the opposing fleets for a time as he carefully considered his next words.

"If the pirates reject your terms, and it becomes a case of you or them, then you have my permission to kill them in a fair fight," he said quietly.

"It shall all be as you say," Traax replied.

Tyranny watched as Traax walked away. "They are amazing," she said. "I wish they had been at my side when I was hunting down demonslavers."

Upon hearing this, one corner of Tristan's mouth came up. He knew it may yet come to that.

"Where in the name of the Afterlife did they come from?" she asked quizzically. "And how is it that they obey you so unerringly? I have never seen anything like them."

Shaking his head, Tristan gave a short laugh. "That's a long story," he answered her. "One that I shall be happy to share with you on the way home."

"You should have plenty of time to tell it to me," she reflected. "It's still a two-day sail to the coast."

Tristan gave her an odd, knowing look. "Actually, we shall be in the palace by sunset, at the latest."

She watched, confused as Tristan turned around and faced the decks of her ship again. Two Minion vessels had come up along the opposite side, and the evacuation was already in progress. Minion warriors were taking the weak and the wounded into their arms and flying them across the sea to the waiting ships.

Then she saw Tristan grin and point to the litter that sat waiting on the deck, not too far from them. Realizing what he intended, she felt the blood rush from her face. She raised her palms up in a desperate gesture of defiance.

"Oooh, no!" she shouted.

"Oooh, yes!" he ordered her. "You, me, Scars, and Geldon." Then he smiled again. "I admit it takes a bit of getting used to, but your prince commands it."

Without giving her another chance to argue, he took her by one arm and pulled her over to where the litter stood. They were clearly running out of time, and they needed to go.

By now, Scars had reappeared with the maps and tools. He looked tired, and was soaked from the waist down by the seawater that was already flooding hip-deep through the lower decks. With a word from his captain, he tentatively got into the litter, finding that he had to stay bent over slightly to keep his head from hitting the roof. At a word from Tristan, Geldon entered next. When it finally came Tyranny's turn, she turned and gave him a look.

"You'll pay for this, you know," she said coyly.

Smiling, Tristan raised an eyebrow. "And as you already know, my good captain, that has always been my intent," he replied. "But first we have to get home." Looking for Traax in the melee, he finally found him, and walked over.

"Tyranny, Scars, and Geldon are coming with me," he said. "I grant you three days to carry out my orders. After that, I expect you and the fleet to return to Eutracia with all due haste."

Traax was holding Tristan's weapons. Smiling, he handed them back to him. "Three days, then," he answered. He held out his arm. Reaching out, Tristan heartily slapped the inside of his forearm against Traax's and grasped it. Neither of them spoke more, for there was no need.

Tristan turned away and walked back to the waiting litter to find K'jarr standing there with two large packages, both wrapped in sailcloth. "Well done," Tristan told him. He ordered the Minion to lash them to the top of the litter. As the last to get in, Tristan found barely enough room for himself and his weapons, but he managed. He looked back out at K'jarr.

"I want you and fifty of your finest warriors to escort us home," Tristan ordered. "What I carry is of the greatest importance, and it must reach there safely. Make your course directly for the palace. And we shall need a few additional bearers, because of the extra weight."

Honored to have been given the privilege of seeing the Chosen One and his entourage to Tammerland, K'jarr clicked his heels together, and went to select his warriors.

At last the litter rose from the deck of the sinking ship. Leaning back, Tristan closed his eyes. He was drained and exhausted, but his heart sang with the knowledge that he was finally going home. Home—to see Wigg, Faegan, Abbey, and Shailiha and her baby.

And Celeste.

Fifty-two

S tanding in the midst of the white, silent Scriptorium of the Citadel, Wulfgar looked lovingly down at the subject sleeping on the marble table. Krassus stood by his side. The Scroll of the Vagaries hovered nearby, glowing brightly. Wulfgar's hazel eyes danced with the power of the craft.

"You have done well," Krassus said quietly. "Your use of the Forestallment calculations provided by the scroll proved even faster than mine. I have now done all I can for you, because your blood and your current gifts already outshine mine by a considerable degree. Even greater, I daresay, than the combined talents of the two wizards of the Redoubt." Pausing for a moment, Krassus took his eyes from the subject on the table and turned to Wulfgar.

"And that is to say nothing of what you will both eventually become," he added. "After today, you and Serena will no longer need my powers to gift one another with additional Forestallments, the calculations for thousands of which can still be found in the scroll. But for now, far greater, more urgent plans await your newfound talents. The work for which you have been prepared is about to commence."

The transformation of the bastard half brother of the two Chosen Ones had easily exceeded the wizard's wildest dreams—even more so than his late master Nicholas might have guessed, he surmised. Wulfgar stood tall and unflinching in his newly realized gifts. His mind and blood were alight with the power of the craft; his determination to see Nicholas' work through to its glorious end had become even more resolute than Krassus'.

He wore emerald-green silk breeches and a short, matching jacket that lay partially open to reveal his chest. Black leather sandals adorned his feet. The hard, smooth muscles of his body rippled every time he called upon them, as if even they had somehow also been enhanced by his recent transformation. His sandy blond hair was still tied behind his neck, but the old worn leather strap had been replaced with a narrow, flat band of solid gold.

His sessions with Krassus finally complete, Wulfgar was now protected by the time enchantments. He was also fully committed—heart, blood, and mind—not only to the exclusive practice of the Vagaries, but also to the work that his nephew Nicholas had begun, but was unable to finish. As yet, however, the dying wizard had not told him what that was to be.

Krassus reached down and gently placed one of his palms on Serena's abdomen. As he closed his eyes, a smile came to his lips.

"She is pregnant," he said, opening his eyes again. "Well done. Your firstborn is to be a daughter."

"I know," Wulfgar answered quietly. "Serena has been with child for only a few hours. I saw the azure glow gather around her the moment conception took place. It is good that this happened during, rather than after, the gifting of her blood. For now the child will be born with many of her mother's Forestallments intact, and will thereby be spared the painful process of their installation."

Wulfgar looked again at the woman he so loved. Serena's strong, beautiful face was placid in sleep, framed by the dark ringlets that spilled gracefully down over her shoulders and breasts. She wore a black, full-length gown of the finest satin, with matching, bowed slippers on her feet. Pure gold adorned her delicate throat, wrists, and fingers.

She was a true queen, Wulfgar thought. Worthy of standing by his side in their coming struggle with the Chosen Ones.

"She will command powers of the Vagaries that are virtually unheard of," Krassus said. "Only you will be more powerful." Picking up one of Serena's hands, Krassus held it as though it were made of the finest porcelain.

"It is now her time in history, as well as yours," the wizard continued softly. "Awaken her, Wulfgar. Let her finally see the world through her newborn eyes."

This time it was her lover's turn to touch her. Placing his palm on her forehead, Wulfgar watched her eyes flutter softly and open. Immediately she looked up into Wulfgar's face and smiled. He reached out his hand. Grasping it, she slowly sat up on the table. Then she placed her satin slippers on the marble floor and stood up.

Without hesitation she threw her head back and stretched her body like a cat. Breathing deeply, she smiled again, clearly reveling in her new-found power. Without hesitation, she purposefully walked closer to Wulfgar, placed her arms around him, and kissed him on the lips.

"Thank you, my lord," she said simply as she drew one of her long, freshly painted nails down his cheek. "Thank you for granting me the time enchantments. And for so generously opening the psychic portals of the Vagaries and exposing their many wonders to my mind. Now I am able to serve you not only with my heart, but also with my endowed blood. I shall be forever grateful." Suddenly her eyes went wide, and she took a quick breath of realization.

"Oh . . . ," she exclaimed, as she placed one hand on her belly. Then she looked back up to him and smiled again. "A girl. It truly seems there is no end to the gifts my lover has bestowed on me."

Krassus held his hands out to them, and they each took one. "Come with me," he said simply. Walking them over to a pair of marble double doors, he employed the craft, and they swung open.

Still holding hands, the three of them walked out onto a broad balcony overlooking the Sea of Whispers. The red-orange ball of the sun was descending into the ocean, and the night birds called softly to one another. A gentle sea breeze swirled up, bathing everything in its fresh, clean scent.

Turning around, Krassus looked them both in the eyes.

"From this point forward your lives and your blood are inextricably bound to each other," he said solemnly. "And all of what you see before you I bequeath to you and your heirs, just as my late master Nicholas told me to do if he perished in his travails at the hands of the Chosen Ones. This Citadel, the fleet, the demonslavers, the Brotherhood of Consuls, and the island that provides them safe haven are all yours, as are all of the many creatures of the Vagaries that call this sacred isle their home, whether they be of the surrounding earth, sea, or sky. Protected by the time enchantments, from here you will forever perpetuate the Vagaries and strive to destroy the Vigors. Never forget that your enemies—the so-called Chosen Ones and their wizards—shall endeavor to annihilate you from their lair in Eutracia. And so you shall do the same to them from your new home, here in the Citadel." Smiling at them both, Krassus took a deep breath of the sweet sea air.

Almost immediately his coughing began.

This time it was far worse than Wulfgar had ever seen. Krassus leaned weakly against the short balcony wall as his hacking went on in great, uncontrollable spasms. Finally, after what seemed forever, it abated.

Krassus turned around to face them again. His chin and the front of his blue-and-gray robe were covered with blood. Concerned, Wulfgar reached out to steady him, but Krassus waved him away.

"Do not be concerned for me," he said hoarsely as he produced a rag from his robes and began to clean himself. "As far as my existence in this lesser world is concerned, all is as my master said it would be. This malady I am stricken with—my fatal gift from Nicholas—will soon completely overtake me. I estimate that I have scant time remaining before you two are left here without me, to accomplish all that has been ordained by the son of the Chosen One. Only two duties remain for me now before I go to the Afterlife: to secure the Scroll of the Vigors, and to instruct you in your mission." Letting go another short cough, he slowly turned back toward the sea.

"Grizelda and Janus remain unheard from, however," he said softly, the concern showing in his voice. "But even if they already had the scroll, it would take them fifteen days to return it to us. Therefore, we shall use the time wisely." When he turned back to them, it seemed he had regained a bit of his strength. He smiled and looked to Wulfgar.

"First I suggest you show your new queen the wonders of this place," he said. "She will be seeing it all as if for the first time, and there is much to learn about its workings. After you have finished, please join me in my private quarters for dinner, and we will begin the first of our discussions regarding your futures. Tonight, finally, you are to learn why you have been brought here, and why all of this has come about."

Looking across the room, Krassus pointed one hand at the still-hovering Scroll of the Vagaries. It stopped glowing and then rolled itself up. As soon as it finished collecting itself, the familiar golden band with the Old Eutracian engraving rose from a nearby table and floated across to slide down over one end of the scroll. Then the bound scroll flew across the room into the wizard's arms.

Satisfied, Krassus gave them both a short bow. "As I said, the Citadel, and everything in it, is now at your beck and call. Until later." Without further ado, he walked slowly from the room.

After the wizard had left, Wulfgar took Serena's hand. "We shall take Krassus up on his suggestion." Looking into her eyes, he could see that they were alight with curiosity, just as his had been after Krassus had finally turned him to the Vagaries and first shown him the true wonders of this place.

"Come with me," he said gently. He ran the back of his fingers down one of her cheeks. "There is much to show you." Leading her from the stark Scriptorium, he took her down a flight of stairs.

Arm in arm, they walked for a long time. As they went, they would occasionally come across armed demonslavers who bowed deeply to them. The same was true of the blue-robed consuls they passed. Wulfgar would often stop to talk to them. Without exception, they seemed honored to be in his presence.

But it was far more than that, she thought, as she walked beside her powerful lord. The entire Citadel seemed different to her. It was far more alive, more beautiful, and more comforting then she remembered. On the surface, at least, it now seemed a wondrous, enchanting place. Or perhaps it was only she who had truly changed; she didn't know. Regardless, the fortress was a wondrous sight to behold.

Rather than being constructed of marble or brick, the entire Citadel had been hewn from the gray rock that comprised much of the island. It looked quite ancient. It was as if the workers of so long ago had started at the top of a great stone mountain rising up from the sea and then chiseled away what they didn't want, to reveal this massive collection of walls and buildings.

The island itself was angular, and much larger than the area upon which the Citadel stood. A wide spit of fertile land reached its way east from one end, stabbing its long finger out into the Sea of Whispers. This was where the crops were grown, and where the livestock was bred, tended, and eventually butchered for food. Wells dotted the island, supplying fresh water.

The exterior of the fortress was dark and foreboding. It completely belied the beautiful, graceful nature of its interior rooms, columns, and halls, most of which were constructed of elegant colored marble. Taken as a whole, the Citadel gave one the impression of a great, self-sufficient city. Pilastered, crenellated walls surrounded the entire fortress, protecting both the inner ward and the various central buildings. A single portcullis granted access to the outside.

The interior of the Citadel was made up of many keeps, towers, and other structures, most of them hundreds of feet tall and adorned with leaded stained-glass windows that could be swung open to the sea. Elegant catwalks extending from balconies connected many of the towers to one another. The inner ward surrounding them held magnificently manicured gardens complete with stone walkways. Magnificent, illuminated fountains danced both day and night.

In the center, rising above everything else around it, stood a tall spire. Within its center was a circular stairway leading to the top. At its peak there was a broad, exposed walkway that completely encircled it. From here, demonslaver guards could see many leagues out over the Sea of Whispers in any direction. A warning bell was attached to the spire wall, waiting to be rung.

Demonslaver warships patrolled the surrounding sea constantly, their graceful, white sails full as they caught not only the wind, but also the last rays of the setting sun. Many more lay peacefully, sails furled, at anchor just offshore. So many, in fact, that their numbers virtually filled the waters surrounding the island.

The sight of so many vessels brought reassurance to her heart. But they also brought more questions, as well. As she and Wulfgar walked along one of the many torchlit porticos lining the gardens, Serena found she could no longer contain her curiosity.

"Tell me, my lord," she asked him. "Who are the demonslavers that serve us? Where do they come from?"

Wulfgar smiled. After he had been turned to the Vagaries, this had been one of the first questions he had asked Krassus. The answer had both surprised and delighted him.

"The demonslavers serve us in much the same way the Minions of Day and Night serve our enemies, the Chosen Ones," he explained. "Krassus has told me of the Minions. He explained how they were first brought into existence by Failee, the late wife of Wigg, the lead wizard. And how Tristan came to become their current lord and master. While it is true that our demonslavers cannot fly, they are at the very least just as ruthless and loyal."

Wulfgar finally stopped before a pair of double doors. "But before I answer your question about the demonslavers, there is first something I wish to show you," he said.

Pointing one hand to the doors, he caused them to open. He then took Serena by the hand and led her into the room. As he did, some of Krassus' words of explanation came back to him.

Despite her transformation, she would retain all of her former memories, Krassus had told him. Just as he and the many others over the centuries who had been so blessed as to have tasted the joy of the Vagaries did. And if she truly became one of us, the wizard had gone on to say, she would love only the Vagaries and those practitioners equally devoted to its cause. Just as the Heretics of the Guild meant it to be.

As they entered the room, he carefully watched her face.

They were standing in the room that held the *R'talis* slaves—the same stark prison in which Janus had once forced Serena to take her meals, in plain view of the poor unfortunates starving before her. The chamber was illuminated by many bright wall torches, their shadows crisscrossing the beige marble walls. Even the magnificent table and chair she had been forced to sit at was still here, complete with its tablecloth, elaborate setting for one, and matching gold candlesticks.

Serena slowly walked toward the cages. Many of the captives started shouting insults at her and waving their arms with rage. By now, most of them were little more than skin and bones.

But something was different now, Serena realized. Both *Talis* and *R'talis* slaves were here, and the cages were no longer filled to overflowing.

Wulfgar watched Serena as she left the slaves and walked the short distance over to the table. She ran her fingers over the fine gold plates and utensils as if she loved them, revered them. Then she looked back at the slaves.

This time, instead of weeping for the slaves' plight as she had done in previous days, she only smiled. As Wulfgar came closer to her, he realized that the Vagaries swirling in her blood had truly become a part of her soul. He and Krassus had succeeded, he realized. He took her hand.

"And now that you see the world for what it truly is, what say you, my love?" he asked.

Serena nodded slowly. "These puny, untrained beings, many of whom do not even have endowed blood, mean nothing to me," she told him. "I see now that they are no more than human resources for us to mine. Indeed, if my lord would allow it, I would like to once again take some of my meals here, if for no other reason than to see the looks on their faces. It should prove most entertaining. Do you think you could let me do that, my love?"

Wulfgar smiled. "Of course," he answered. "But it may not be possible. The sand in the hourglass of their lives is running short."

"I don't understand," she said.

Taking her by the hand, Wulfgar led her to a door on the other side of the room. As they walked through it, Serena felt an intense, searing heat blast over her, and charred, dense air came suddenly to her nostrils.

The demonslaver forges were still in use, but would not remain so much longer. The slaves, dressed only in their soiled, torn loincloths, worked tirelessly, forging the instruments of sudden death that Wulfgar's demonslavers would soon use in the service of their master. The incessant clanging of the slaves' hammers and the stale, telltale smell of human sweat filled the smoky air. The orange-red coals in the hearths glowed brightly, casting an ocherous aura over everything in the room.

As they walked purposefully through the chamber, the demonslaver guards there bowed obediently. Then Serena noticed one slave whose hands were tied behind his back. She stopped to look at him. He seemed to be supervising the others as they fashioned the various weapons. Curious, she turned to Wulfgar.

"And what of this one?" she asked. "Should he not also toil in the service of his lord?"

"A troublemaker, nothing more," Wulfgar answered. "They tell me his number is twenty-nine. He will soon be dealt with, as shall all of the others here in this chamber."

When Twenty-Nine finally saw Wulfgar, he immediately recognized him as the same man he had stood next to on the docks the day they first disembarked. Seeing the slavers bow to the man, Twenty-Nine realized that he and the woman he was with had somehow become of great importance here.

Knowing he was risking his life, he brazenly hurried over to Wulfgar. The slavers reacted immediately, grabbing him and roughly pushing him to the dirt at Wulfgar's feet. With a shiny trident pressing into his back, he could raise his face only enough to look up into his new master's eyes. Wulfgar was intrigued by the slave's wanton display of insolence.

"You know me!" Twenty-Nine pleaded hoarsely. "In the name of the Afterlife, tell these monsters that you know me! We were together at the docks! You looked into my eyes! Don't you remember? Why don't you help us?" His words trailed away as the three sharp tips of the trident lightly punctured the skin of his naked back.

After emotionlessly examining Twenty-Nine's face, Wulfgar looked back up at the slavers. "I have seen him before," he answered coldly. "But I don't care for his welfare. When this group has finally finished their labors and you are ready to dispense with them, bring this one to me. I want him to be one of the forty." The slaver holding the trident to Twenty-Nine's back smiled wickedly and nodded.

"The 'forty'?" Serena asked quizzically.

Wulfgar smiled. "You will understand soon enough," he answered, and he guided her to the doorway at the far end of the room. Without looking back, Serena followed him through.

The next room lay some distance below where they were standing, and it was very large, its brightness in direct contrast to the room they had just left. Like the Scriptorium, this chamber was also littered with white marble tables. The walls and floor of the room were constructed of a very pale green marble, and the many ornate stained-glass windows in its walls lay open to the night. The breeze coming off the ocean filled the air with a cool, welcoming scent.

Consuls were busy at work here. A great pile of what seemed to be demonslaver clothing lay unexplained in one corner of the room, with several slavers standing next to it. Taking her by the hand, Wulfgar led Serena down to the shiny green floor via a long, curved series of steps.

Then a door opened in the wall to their left, and a large, menacing squad of slavers began roughly herding a group of terrified slaves into the room. Nine-tails cracked out in the air, and shiny tridents and swords poked and prodded the unfortunate captives as they moved haltingly along.

Serena recognized some of them as those who had shouted insults at her in the room of cages. As she looked at them, she smiled. They didn't seem so arrogant just now. She wondered what Wulfgar had meant about the sand in the hourglass of their lives growing short.

Wulfgar snapped his fingers, and slavers immediately brought over two luxuriously upholstered red velvet chairs. Motioning to Serena, Wulfgar bade her sit in one, and he took the other. Then two more slavers appeared, bearing goblets of red wine that they offered to their lord and lady. Wulfgar tipped his glass in Serena's honor and took a sip. After joining him in the excellent wine, his queen turned her attention back to the helpless slaves being paraded before her.

The group contained both men and women, and the brands on their shoulders told her that they were a mixed group of endowed and unendowed blood. As the slavers began pushing them toward the marble tables, the confused slaves cried out frantically in terror. Blatantly ignoring their wailing, the slavers began hoisting them up onto the tables and tying them down. The consuls, silent and foreboding in their dark blue robes, carefully watched the proceedings unfold.

When all of the slaves were secured, one of the consuls walked forward to stand obediently before Wulfgar. Lowering the hood of his robe, he looked up into the commanding, hazel eyes of his new master.

Smiling back at the consul, Wulfgar nodded. The consul turned to face the rows of tables. Then Wulfgar's servant bowed his head and raised his arms.

The torches in the room began to dim, their light slowly replaced by the azure glow of the craft. As the glow encompassed the entire room, Serena heard soft tearing sounds that gradually became louder and louder. As the unusual noise increased, so did the screaming of the slaves, the two disparate sounds combining to create a bizarre chorus of anguish. Smiling, the consul standing before them lowered his hands and calmly placed them into the opposite sleeves of his robe.

Then Serena realized what was happening. The twisted loincloths of the men and the simple, one-piece frocks worn by the women were being torn apart by the craft. They fell to the floor, leaving the terrified people on the marble tables naked, humiliatingly exposed.

The consul standing before Wulfgar and Serena turned back to look at Wulfgar. After taking another sip of wine, Wulfgar nodded. Returning to his work, the consul again raised his arms.

The azure glow in the room increased to a brightness that almost made it difficult to keep one's eyes open. The slaves began to writhe painfully in their bonds and scream even louder. And then their transformations began.

First the color of their skin changed into the stark, blanched white so characteristic of demonslavers. Serena watched, her mouth agape, as the slaves' hair began to fall out, sliding from their skulls and bodies to drift down onto the various tabletops and the green marble floor.

Then, surprisingly, their genitalia began to disappear. The women's breasts flattened, coming to resemble those of the males. Gasping with disbelief, Serena realized that what she had long assumed about the demonslavers being male had not been true. They were asexual beings, made that way by the craft.

As she watched, the slaves' fingernails and toenails began to fall away, drifting silently to the floor. In their place talons emerged. Suddenly, still screaming and struggling against their bonds, they all closed their eyes. When they opened them again, their eyes had been replaced with the white, lifeless-looking orbs of the demonslavers. Then their muscles began to bulge, becoming hard and strong. Their ears lengthened to points, and as the victims twisted their mouths with agony, Serena could see that their teeth had become pointed and black.

The azure glow slowly faded, and the room became strangely quiet as the subjects on the tables finally stopped wailing and lay still, their metamorphosis complete.

Turning to look at Wulfgar's profile, Serena smiled. The creation of the demonslavers was ingenious, she thought. First the consuls of the Brotherhood had been turned, and now the Chosen One's subjects, as well—all aligned against them and their wizards.

"How is this possible?" she asked Wulfgar. She took another sip of wine.

"It has to do with something called Forestallments," he answered simply. "And they have to do with the craft. But for now, suffice it to say that the spells for the creation of the slavers were passed from Nicholas to Krassus, who will soon show you how to use your Forestallments, as I am now able to do." He ran a hand down her cheek. "And when that happens, my love, it is a wondrous moment of realization. Your blood will sing. I very much look forward to sharing that day with you." He leaned over and kissed her, then straightened again.

"And now that Krassus has found the particular Forestallment he wanted so badly, and has placed it into my blood signature, he is free to convert all of the remaining slaves, both *Talis* and *R'talis* alike, into demonslavers. We have nearly completed transforming them all. He also tells me that only I, of all the endowed beings in the world, carry this special Forestallment in my signature. In my heart I know this single Forestallment, more than any other, is the one upon which our struggle with the Chosen Ones shall soon turn, but he has yet to inform me of its nature. Perhaps tonight he shall."

Then the consul approached Wulfgar and bowed. Wulfgar nodded.

"Permission to continue, my lord?" the consul asked.

"Of course. When you are finished, you all may leave."

After a low bow, the consul returned to the tables. With a wave of his hand, the bindings holding the newly created demonslavers vanished.

As they did, the beings sat up and came to stand on the floor. They were directed to the large pile of clothing in the far corner of the room, which they used to dress themselves. Then the newly minted slavers filed quietly out, presumably to take up the weapons that were still being constructed in the forge. The consuls and senior demonslavers followed in their wake, leaving Wulfgar and Serena alone in the great room.

Rising from his chair, Wulfgar walked over to one of the open stained-glass windows and looked out. Lost in thought, he took a deep breath and leaned against the window frame. The three rose-colored moons were up, and the sea below was calm.

Concerned for him, Serena stood and went to join him, linking her arm in his. "Tell me, my love," she asked, hoping to take his thoughts away from whatever was troubling him. "What is Krassus' part in all of this to be?"

Wulfgar took a deep breath. "For now, we still need him," he answered, his eyes still leveled on the Sea of Whispers. "But not for much longer. I believe Nicholas only meant for Krassus to be a tool, an instrument of victory as it were, rather than to preside over the victory himself. That is to be our task. As Krassus said himself, very soon now he will be dead. And when he is, we alone will be left to carry the battle to the Chosen Ones, and prevail against their practice of the Vigors."

He turned away from the window and looked around the deserted room. "Very soon now, all of the remaining slaves will have been transformed, and the struggle can begin. But what concerns me the most is that we are still not in possession of the other scroll. Nicholas and Krassus have deemed it important that we have them both in order to ensure our victory. And still I do not know why."

She could see the worry in his eyes. "Krassus asked us to join him for dinner, did he not?" she asked. "Perhaps tonight you will finally get the answers you seek."

Wulfgar nodded his silent agreement and escorted her from the room.

The walk back to Krassus' quarters was pleasant, and the new master and his pregnant queen talked of many things as they walked along, arm in arm. The Citadel was quiet now, the only sounds coming from the lighted fountains as they danced and played in the manicured gardens of the inner ward, and the quiet, careful footfalls of the demonslavers on patrol. Finally arriving at the door to Krassus' private quarters, Wulfgar knocked lightly once, then twice more.

An armed demonslaver let them in. Krassus was sitting alone at an elaborately decorated table, his back to them as he gazed thoughtfully out to sea. Enticing aromas drifted up from the sumptuously laid table.

Turning to look at Wulfgar and Serena, Krassus smiled. There was genuine admiration in his eyes for these two magnificent beings of the craft he had been so privileged to help create. Lifting one hand, he beckoned them nearer.

"Come in, my children," he said softly. "Sit with me this night, and we shall talk of the wondrous things to come."

As Wulfgar and Serena took their places at the table, the demonslaver bowed once more. Walking out the door, he closed it behind him and took up guard in the hall outside.

Fifty-three

"I still can't believe you're actually here!" Shailiha squealed happily to her brother for what seemed to him to be at least the hundredth time. She gave him yet another affectionate hug, nearly squeezing the life out of him and causing him to spill his wine. On the prince's other side sat an equally ecstatic Celeste, who had embraced him closely when he descended from the litter.

The hour was late, bordering on dawn, Tristan guessed, and he was tired beyond all measure. Still bloodied and exhausted from the recent fighting, he had already eaten several healthy portions of the gnome wives' wonderful cooking, washed down with a serious amount of red wine.

Not ones to stand on ceremony, Tyranny and Scars had done the same, Scars eating so much so quickly that the diminutive cooks had been forced to make five separate trips back and forth to the kitchens just for him. Of course the territorial little women had fussed worriedly over everything, but Tristan knew that deep down they were secretly delighted.

Looking around the massive oak meeting table in the Hall of Supplication, the prince realized what a disparate group of people had been gathered here. It included himself, Shailiha—with Morganna playing on the floor close by—Celeste, Abbey, Geldon, Wigg, Faegan, Tyranny, and Scars. Or, put another way, he thought wryly, the group consisted of a prince, a princess, an herbmistress, a hunchbacked dwarf from Parthalon, two irascible wizards, a three-hundred-year-old beauty, a female pirate captain, her giant first mate, a baby, and Faegan's blue cat, of course.

Tristan shook his head. Telling everyone his story would probably last well past sunrise. And he needed to hear of all that had transpired while he was gone, as well.

The Chamber of Supplication was the great hall in which Tristan's father and the late Directorate of Wizards had from time to time heard special, urgent requests from the populace. Sometimes, if the petition was worthy and within the wizards' ethical and magical purview to provide, it would be granted. The chamber was made of dark blue Ephyran marble. Patterned rugs adorned the floor, and light flooded the room from wall torches and the great oil-lamp chandelier that hung over the table.

When Wigg and Faegan had suggested this room in which to talk, Tristan had quickly agreed. He knew that the wizards would not want strangers poking about in the Redoubt below. And despite the fact that he trusted the pirate captain and her first mate implicitly, Tristan went along with the wizards' request.

Tristan's arrival by Minion litter had been joyous, to say the least. Upon reaching the coast, he had ordered K'jarr to fly ahead and tell everyone they were coming. As a result, every person in the palace had come running out to greet them at once, including as many Minions, male and female alike, as could wedge their way into the courtyard.

Being the first one out of the litter, Tristan had been immediately pounced upon by Shailiha and Celeste. Then Ox had taken him up in his great arms like a vise, hugging him tightly and lifting him high off his feet. As he did, the other warriors cheered. Tristan could scarcely breathe.

"Ox so glad to see Chosen One!" the huge warrior bellowed. "Ox worried!"

Geldon exited next, followed by Tyranny and Scars. When the sea captain and her first mate appeared, things became a bit awkward, to say the least.

First there had been the issue of Scars. Tristan had known for some time that he had earned the giant's grudging respect, and with that had come a certain attitude of protectiveness. When Scars saw Ox go for Tristan, his first instinct had been to free him. Caught in Ox's arms, Tristan had barely managed to wave Scars off.

But once Ox had put Tristan down, the two giants had begun menacingly sizing each other up. Not knowing what else to do, Tristan had impetuously stepped directly between them and made the necessary introductions. When both backed off, Tristan was greatly relieved. He could scarcely imagine the outcome had these two giants actually gone after each other.

And then Tyranny had stepped from the litter. Seeing her rather provocative striped pants and short, low-cut leather jacket; her dark, urchinlike hair flying every which way in the breeze; her gold hoops dangling from her ears; and her sword slung low down over one hip, Shailiha and Celeste raised skeptical eyebrows. Shailiha's mouth puckered slightly, and she gave her brother a quizzical, not altogether approving glance. Celeste simply crossed her arms over her breasts and began tapping the ground with one foot.

As Tyranny descended the litter, she coyly held out one hand for the prince to take, and he had no other choice but to do so. Immediately sensing Tristan's discomfort, she couldn't help but take advantage of it—presumably as payback for having made her ride in the litter, Tristan assumed.

Surmising that one of these two women—probably the redhead, she thought—must be the famous Celeste, Tyranny leaned over, gave Tristan a short kiss on the cheek, then linked her arm through his and smiled cattily at the two other women.

Later on, a grinning Wigg would tell Tristan that when all of this happened, the prince's face had become as red as the lead wizard had ever seen it. For his part, Faegan had simply covered his mouth with one hand and let go a quite unnecessary cough. After the rather stiff introductions had been made, they had all adjourned to the palace.

Now, his dreggan and throwing knives hooked over the back of his chair, Tristan told them everything. In between bites of food and cups of wine, he described in great detail his capture, his time rowing, and his meeting with Krassus and the herbmistress Grizelda. He went on to tell them of his rescue by Tyranny, the attack by the screechlings, their time on Sanctuary, and their fight with the pirate fleet only hours earlier. He also explained how he had marooned the raiders on Sanctuary rather than killing them, and that he had ordered a small contingent of Minion warships to stay behind to guard them.

He did not, however, demand answers from them regarding the mystery surrounding the existence of Sanctuary, for he realized that the two secretive wizards would not wish to discuss it in the presence of two relative strangers.

Wigg and Faegan listened to his story intently. They asked questions from time to time, but for the most part they remained still. When Tristan finally finished, the room went completely quiet, the only sound the purring of Nicodemus, Faegan's blue cat. It was Wigg who finally broke the silence.

"It seems we have much to thank you for, miss," he said, turning to Tyranny. "But tell us, why did you decide to go demonslayer hunting in the first place? It seems like a particularly dangerous occupation to take up, even for a person as capable as you appear to be."

Tyranny's face darkened. "They took my brother," she answered, "and killed my parents in the process. I escaped, and I have been searching for my brother ever since. My family name is Welborne, and we lived in Farpoint. My father ran a fleet of fishing vessels there. Scars and I know the Sea of Whispers as well as anyone alive." Then she looked over at Tristan, and a smile crossed her lips. "Besides," she added, "I am not so easily captured."

A look of recognition flashed over the lead wizard's face. "The Welbornes of Farpoint?" he said. "A very long time ago, I knew such a family. There was once a privateer, Isaac Welborne, who sailed in the service of the Directorate. But that was more than three hundred years ago, during the Sorceresses' War."

"Isaac Welborne was one of my ancestors," Tyranny said proudly. "My father used to love to tell the story of how, just after the end of the war, Isaac loaned his battered ship to the newly formed Directorate, so that they might use it to banish the sorceresses from Eutracia. The ship was a galleon named the *Resolve.* But that was a long time ago."

It might have simply been the retelling of the story, or it might have been due to the lead wizard's recent, heart-rending experiences in the Chamber of Penitence, but for whatever reason, Wigg's eyes grew shiny. He wiped them with the sleeve of his robe.

"Tyranny has brought you a pair of gifts," Tristan added softly. "She agreed with me that they probably belong here in the palace, where they could be protected."

He gave Geldon a nod, and the two of them left the room for a moment. When they returned, they were helping each other carry two rather unwieldy packages. Each was wrapped in bloody sailcloth and tied securely with ship's rope. They placed them on the table before Wigg, then sat down again.

The lead wizard raised an eyebrow. "What are they?"

"The only way you're going to know is by opening them," Tristan answered, a smile on his face. "As far as I know, even you and Faegan can't see *through* things."

From the other side of the table, Faegan gave one of his wry cackles. "Don't be so sure."

Wigg looked down at the crudely wrapped packages. He couldn't imagine what they might be. Nor could he remember the last time anyone had given him something, for that matter. Narrowing his eyes, he called on the craft. Almost immediately, the sailor's knots began to untie themselves. As they did, Tristan looked over at Tyranny and Scars to see that their eyes had become as big as saucers.

As the sailcloth was unwrapped, it revealed a worn ship's wheel—the one Tristan had ordered taken from *The People's Revenge* just before she went down. The other package contained the wooden-and-brass plaque that listed not only all the names of those who had commanded the *Resolve,* but also the various other vessels the wheel had been passed down to over the centuries by the Welborne family.

Rather high up on the list, it said, WIGG, LEAD WIZARD OF THE DI-RECTORATE OF WIZARDS. COMMANDER OF THE *RESOLVE*. The last entry read, TYRANNY OF THE HOUSE OF WELBORNE. CAPTAIN OF *THE PEOPLE'S REVENGE.*

The wizard's eyes welled up with tears as he ran his ancient fingers over the engravings. He then looked up at Tyranny with genuine affection.

"My greatest thanks, child," he said softly, his voice cracking. "I couldn't possibly know how to repay you."

Pushing his tongue against the inside of his cheek, Tristan looked over at Tyranny. "Actually," he began, "there is a way . . ."

"And that would be?" Faegan asked suspiciously.

Tristan indicated to Tyranny that she should hand over the promissory note. When she gave it to him, he unfolded it and passed it over to the lead wizard.

As Wigg read the note, his eyes went wide. He remembered all that Tristan had just told them about his recent adventures, though, and his expression softened a bit. Still, he wasn't convinced that such a huge amount should be paid.

He finally passed the note over to Faegan, who scanned the page. With a cackle, he handed it to Shailiha. Everyone around the table eventually read it. After they had, quiet settled in as they all waited for the lead wizard to speak. Wigg looked down at the ship's wheel and plaque again, then back up at the sea captain.

"Forgive me, Tyranny, but I simply must ask," Wigg said quietly. "Did you give me these gifts just to soften my mood?"

"No," Tristan interjected firmly. "It was all my idea." Then he smiled. "Still, I didn't think it would hurt."

Wigg shook his head adamantly. "Tristan, surely you must realize what a huge sum this is!" he countered. "I fully understand that it is the identical amount that was once offered for your capture, and as such it may therefore possess some small degree of justification. But such a sum is without precedent in the entire history of Eutracia! Such a reward would make Tyranny the wealthiest woman—nay, perhaps even the wealthiest *person*—in the entire nation!"

But Tristan wasn't about to back down. She had saved his life twice. And he had given her his word. A deal was a deal. Leaning over the tabletop, he looked Wigg directly in the eyes.

"Then it's a good thing we're all sitting in the Chamber of Supplication, isn't it?" he asked Wigg seriously. "What better place to grant such a request?" He leaned back in his chair and looked around the table again. "Besides," he said shortly, "there are other things I wish her to have, as well. Things that are now in our own best interests to provide."

"And just what might those be?" Faegan asked.

"I want the two of you to grant her letters of marque, just as you once did for Isaac," Tristan said. "These times we live in are no less dangerous than then—perhaps even more so. I want you to draw the papers up immediately. They are to validate her rights as a privateer to prowl the waters off the coast of Eutracia, and to attack and commandeer any demonslaver vessels she might run across, and any pirate ships that might have slipped away during our recent battle. Despite the efficiency of the Minion fleet, given the great scope and confusion of yesterday's confrontation I would be very surprised if at least several of the raiders' vessels hadn't eluded us. In return, Tyranny is to give over three-fourths of whatever booty she collects to the monarchy. The remainder she is free to do with as she wishes."

Wigg looked over at Tristan. "Is this all you want?" he asked sarcastically.

"As a matter of fact, there is one more thing," the prince answered boldly. "But it is no less important." He glanced over at Tyranny to see a look of surprise on her face. "She and I haven't discussed this last issue, but I hardly think she'll mind." He faced Wigg again.

"Of the pirate vessels that were captured and are now being escorted home by the Minion fleet, I shall give her one dozen," he went on. "I shall also order my Minions to make whatever repairs the vessels might require, while Tyranny goes about hiring the additional crewmembers she will need." He looked back to Tyranny again, and now it was her turn to smile. Tristan gave her a wink.

Stunned, Wigg sat back in his chair. As usual, Faegan produced a broad smile at Wigg's discomfiture.

"I hope you have a very good reason for all of this," the lead wizard finally replied, his voice little more than a whisper.

"As a matter of fact, I do," Tristan replied. Reaching down into his boot, he withdrew the ancient scrap of vellum and unceremoniously placed it in the center of the table.

"A simple piece of vellum?" Wigg asked quizzically. "I don't understand."

"I believe this came from the Scroll of the Vagaries," Tristan said. "I found it hidden in my boot. It was secretly placed there by someone while I was unconscious. It matches identically the color and texture of the Scroll of the Vagaries I saw atop Krassus' desk on board his ship. It was clear that pieces had been cut away from it, and I believe this to be one of them. I think the pieces are being used by Grizelda, Krassus' herbmistress, in an attempt to find the Scroll of the Vigors. If that's true, it puts them far ahead of us in this race, I'm afraid. Indeed, for all we know they may have already found it. Someone is trying to help us— that much seems certain. But I don't know who that might be. In any event, had Tyranny not saved me, this would not be in our possession. We may eventually have more to thank her for than we can ever know."

Faegan leaned forward over the table, his eyes flashing with curiosity. "Do you mean to say that you have actually seen one of the scrolls?"

"Yes."

"Please describe it for us."

"It was approximately one meter long, about half as wide," Tristan answered. "It seemed very tightly wound, and a golden rod ran down through its center. Golden knobs adorned each end of the rod. What I could see of the parchment was covered with Old Eutracian. A solid gold band, also engraved in Old Eutracian, secured the document around its middle. And as I said before, it appeared that blank pieces had been cut away from its exposed corners, presumably to aid Krassus' herbmistress in her search for the other scroll."

Faegan asked Shailiha to hand him the parchment. She did so. After feeling it, smelling it, and examining it in the light of the chandelier, he placed it carefully down on the table and sat back in his chair. As was so often his habit, he stared out at nothing, mindlessly stroking his cat.

"Well?" Wigg asked impatiently.

"This is made of the same material as the Tome of the Paragon," Faegan said. "Therefore, this ages-old sample may well have been produced by either the Ones Who Came Before, or by the Guild of the Heretics. But no matter which faction produced it, this ancient scrap adds weight to Tristan's argument that it was taken from the actual Scroll of the Vagaries."

He sat back in his chair. "Amazing . . . ," he added softly, his words trailing off.

Wigg asked to have the scrap passed to him. After examining it, he handed it to Abbey. "What do you think?" he asked her gently. "Can you use this to find the other scroll?"

"Perhaps," she mused as she looked it over. "But needless to say, the process must go as planned. I have no desire to repeat the calamity that occurred in the courtyard."

"What calamity?" Tristan asked.

"That is a topic best left for later," Wigg answered, making it obvious that he did not want to speak of it before Tyranny and Scars. "Right now, however, I would like to make my decision regarding your captain friend."

Several quiet moments passed as the lead wizard weighed his options. Then he turned his brilliant, aquamarine eyes toward Tyranny, and she felt their power go straight through her. Tristan held his breath.

"I will grant all that Tristan asks in your behalf," Wigg said to her solemnly. "As he says, it is probably now in our own best interests to do so. But before I do, you must agree to two provisos."

"And those are?" Tyranny asked.

"First, that you conduct all of your nautical activities under our aegis alone," Wigg answered sternly. "This shall also be spelled out in your letters of marque. The news that piracy has resurfaced in Eutracia is disturbing, to say the least. So far, your unsolicited services to the monarchy have been exemplary. Therefore, I will grant all that the prince has asked for on your behalf. But should we receive any word that you are using your funds or your newly acquired fleet to violate Eutracian law, or to enhance your own wealth outside of what shall be allowed by the letters of marque, we shall take swift and decisive action against you. In addition, you are to visit the royal palace no less than once every three months, at which time you shall relinquish our percentage of whatever bounty you have taken, and give us your written reports."

Sitting back in his chair, Wigg placed his hands flat on the tabletop. "My second condition is that all of your expenses—including the purchase of further vessels, their maintenance and repair, and the payment of your crews—must come either out of your share of the booty, or the funds that have come your way as a result of this bargain," he added. "As part of this agreement, we may rescind our letters of marque at any time of our choosing, and for any reason we deem necessary. That is how it has always been, even going as far back as Isaac. But until you see fit to retire, or *we* see fit to retire you, it seems you now work for us, young lady. As does your rather huge, very quiet first mate."

Tyranny had barely dared dream that the things the prince had told her might be true, much less that she would be granted such gifts and privileges. She looked over at Scars, and he nodded his approval. She turned back to the table.

"Thank you," she said softly, her voice cracking. "Thank you all."

"Oh, don't thank me quite yet," Wigg answered with a sigh. "I haven't written out a proper letter of marque in over three centuries. I'm not even sure I can remember how one goes. For all I know, I may end up giving you the recipe for pheasant under glass."

Everyone at the table laughed. Then Tristan decided that it was time for him to reveal what might be Tyranny's most valuable secret of all.

"There is something else that our new friend has agreed to provide us with," he said as the table finally quieted down. "She believes she has actually seen the island fortress where Krassus is keeping the slaves. She has marked it on her charts, and is willing to make duplicates of them for us."

"Is this true, child?" Faegan asked breathlessly.

This time Scars decided to speak. "It is indeed," he answered for his captain, in his booming voice. "When we first came upon the fortress, I marked out our position and entered the location on the charts myself."

Everyone except Geldon, Tyranny, and Tristan turned toward the war-torn, bare-chested colossus.

"Uh, thank you, Scars," Wigg said awkwardly, as this was the first time he'd heard the eloquent first mate speak. "I should like to receive those copies of your charts at your earliest convenience."

The newly minted privateers nodded back.

Dawn would soon be creeping through the windows, and everyone around the table was clearly exhausted. Still, there remained things that Wigg desperately wanted to tell Tristan—things that couldn't wait, and that could only be said in private. He looked up at the group.

"Geldon, I would be very thankful if you would escort our two new guests to their rooms, where they might finally get some rest," he half asked, half ordered. "Faegan and I must speak to the prince in private now."

Geldon, Tyranny, and Scars all stood.

Wigg looked up at them and smiled. "Sleep well," he told them. "Tomorrow there will be much more to discuss."

An ear-to-ear grin on her face, Tyranny walked over to Wigg and bent down to kiss his cheek. The lead wizard turned red. Then she turned and followed Geldon and Scars to the door. But before going through, she stopped and walked back to where Tristan was sitting.

Raising her right hand to her face, she spat into her palm. Understanding, the prince stood and did the same. He then slapped his palm into hers. "Done," he said.

"And done," she answered back. "And thank you." Turning on her heel, she walked out the door.

With Tyranny and Scars finally gone, Wigg turned his aquamarine eyes toward the prince. He didn't waste any time getting started.

"Much has happened while you were away," he said solemnly, "and very little of it has been good."

Tristan listened intently, and for the next two hours the people he cared for so much told him of all that had happened in his absence. When they were done, Tristan slumped back into his chair, stunned. There was so much new information to absorb, his mind didn't know where to begin. Then Faegan gave him the most recent piece of news.

"The Minion patrols have informed us that no demonslaver activity seems to be taking place anywhere in the kingdom," the ancient wizard said. "None of their slave ships have been spotted within the Minions' flying range from the coast. For the time being, at least, we seem to be free of them." Thinking for a moment, he gave Nicodemus another stroke on the head. "But that can only mean one thing."

No one had to tell Tristan what that was. "If they have given up taking slaves, that means they have finally found Wulfgar," he said softly, sadly. He looked over at Shailiha and clasped her outstretched hand. "And if Krassus now has both the Scroll of the Vagaries and Wulfgar, our futures will be very dark indeed."

For a moment his thoughts went to the half brother he had never seen, had never even known existed until only a short time ago. What was Wulfgar suffering at the hands of the wizard Krassus? Tristan wondered. Were they soon to become mortal enemies? Finding his reflections too painful to cling to, his mind sheered away.

"What about the Isle of Sanctuary?" he finally asked. "Tyranny says that there were papers left behind that seem to indicate the Directorate's involvement. And there are some extraordinarily beautiful buildings there. Some of which, I'm sorry to say, have been desecrated by the pirates. How is it that we have never heard of this place until now?"

Sighing, Wigg looked over at Faegan and waited for the inevitable reaction. It wasn't long in coming.

"Yes, please do explain," Faegan said with a frown. It was suddenly clear to everyone that even he did not know about Sanctuary. And if there was one thing Faegan couldn't abide, it was being left in the dark—especially when the subject had to do with the craft.

"The Isle of Sanctuary was not 'created' by the Directorate," Wigg explained. "At least not in the sense that we could cause an entire land mass to suddenly rise up out of the Sea of Whispers. We do not possess such gifts, I'm sorry to say. The island already existed. It was uninhabited, of sufficient size for our needs, and had not yet been charted. It therefore seemed perfect. Faegan had already been taken prisoner by the Coven at that time, so he had no knowledge of it."

"But why would you require such an island, Father?" Celeste asked.

"The Tome ordered us to create a secret place of the craft," Wigg answered softly. "A 'sanctuary' for the Vigors, as it were—hence the name. It was to be a place far away from prying eyes. It was to be a sacred place, to be used only by the Chosen Ones who would eventually come into our world. Given that description, this site couldn't very well be the Redoubt, now, could it? As I said, the island seemed perfect for our needs. The buildings were constructed soon after the formation of the Directorate. The moment the buildings were completed, a strange, immovable fog bank surrounded the island. To this day I neither know how, nor why."

"Yes, I remember now," Faegan said to himself as he reached back into his amazing memory. "There is such a command in the Tome. But as far as I knew, it had never been carried out."

He leaned back in his wheeled chair, thinking further. "Sanctuary must be the sacred place from which the Chosen One finally combines the two sides of the craft," he finally exclaimed. He trained his gray-green eyes on Wigg. "I'm right, aren't I?"

Faegan's words suddenly, painfully reminded Tristan of the fact that the wizards still refused to train him in the craft or allow him to wear the Paragon, because of the unknown nature of his azure blood. He thought of the savage whipping he had suffered, and how the strangely colored blood dripping down onto the filthy deck had caused fear and distrust among the other slaves.

"I believe you are," Wigg told Faegan. "But as yet, there is no way to validate this hypothesis. Now, given what we have learned here today, where does this knowledge lead us?" He sat back in his chair, patiently awaiting the answer.

Silence reigned again until Morganna, tired of her toys, fussed for Shailiha to pick her up. As Shailiha lifted her daughter into her arms she grasped the implications of Wigg's riddle.

"Krassus' fortress," she said, so softly that the others could barely hear. "It is meant to be the direct antithesis of Sanctuary, isn't it? The secret asylum of the Vagaries. The place from which the Heretics of the Guild mean to have their servants stop us from attempting to combine the two sides of the craft." She hugged Morganna closer to her chest in a protective embrace.

"The Citadel," Tristan breathed to himself.

"What?" Wigg asked curiously.

"The Citadel," Tristan repeated. "That's what it is called. We know this because Scars was able to force it from one of Tyranny's captured demonslavers."

"Yes, of course," Faegan said to himself. "I understand now. Sanctuary—a sacred place of the Vigors, where Tristan's process of combining the two opposing arts might go forward in peace. And the Citadel—an equally sacred place of the Vagaries—a place of darkness, from which the process shall be killed."

"Indeed," Wigg replied. "And now Wulfgar and the Scroll of the Vagaries presumably reside there, both of them under Krassus' control. If all that we have just deduced is in fact true, it now seems that the crisis before us is of even greater magnitude than we first thought."

Tristan looked back down at the piece of vellum he had risked life and limb to bring home. "We have to find the Scroll of the Vigors," he said thoughtfully. "It seems the only chance we have of unraveling what this is all about." He looked tiredly over at the herbmistress. "Can you really use your gifts to find it?" he asked her.

"If the sample you brought back is genuine, then yes, we have a chance," she answered. "But it will not be simple, and it will require all of my powers to accomplish."

Turning to Wigg, she placed one of her hands over his. "But I'm tired, and I need to rest before I try." She rubbed her brow. "If you like, we could all reassemble at midday, in the courtyard. Then we shall see what we shall see."

"And what about the herbs you said Abbey needs?" Tristan asked Faegan. "Have they been separated again? Will they work this time, or blow us all sky high?"

His fatigue also beginning to show, Faegan closed his eyes and shook his head. "The plants and roots Wigg and I brought back from the Chambers of Penitence finally dried out, and we were able to use them to separate and categorize my other stores," he answered. "It was a long, amazing process to behold. But whether they will work properly is still anybody's guess. I suppose at midday, we'll find out."

Wigg stood. "Then I suggest we all try to get some rest. It seems that in a few hours, we may need it."

Testing the sleepy muscles in his legs, Tristan also stood. He felt as if he had been awake his entire lifetime. After retrieving his weapons from the back of his chair, he walked over to Shailiha and Celeste and gave them each a kiss.

"It's good to have you home," Celeste whispered into his ear. "And when you have the time, there is something I would like to tell you." She hugged him again and held him close, as if never wanting to let him go. The myrrh in her hair drifted up to him, reminding him of so much he had thought he might lose forever.

"It's good to be back," he answered her sleepily. "You'll send someone to wake me?"

Smiling at him, Celeste nodded.

He walked to the door, turned to smile at them all again, then gratefully left the room, his dreggan and throwing knives draped loosely over one shoulder. The serpentine hallways of the palace yawned back at him as he went. The heels of his knee boots rang out sharply, reminding him of how lonely life could sometimes be in this massive, overpowering place. And of how many people had once constantly come and gone through these beautiful halls, and of how relatively few did now. From time to time he would come across a lone Minion sentry, silently standing guard at one of the many hallway intersections. Each sentry bowed and snapped his heels together as Tristan passed, but it was all he could do to nod back in return. Finally he found himself back at his own quarters.

Dropping his weapons into a nearby chair, he pulled off his clothes and tossed them aside. Then he walked to the open stained-glass windows and looked out for a moment. The first rays of dawn were finally scratching their way up over the horizon, and the birds had begun to sing. Smoke rose lazily from the Minion campfires, curling its way into the sky. Finally closing the windows, he drew the heavy, red velvet draperies across them.

Naked, he slipped in between the cool, silk sheets of his bed. Paradise, he thought.

In mere moments, the Chosen One was fast asleep.

Fifty-four

"Come with me, my love," Wulfgar said to his queen. "There is still more I wish you to see."

Dawn had broken over the Citadel several hours earlier, bringing with it the promise of a fine day. The sea was high again, and the white sails of the constantly patrolling warships dotted the ocean like so many floating daisy petals.

After sharing their evening meal with Krassus the previous night, both Wulfgar and Serena were now fully aware of all the details of their impending mission. As he walked alongside his queen, the new lord of the Citadel could feel his endowed blood almost sing with the promises such a venture held. And soon, very soon now, it could all begin.

Wulfgar led Serena across the magnificent gardens of the inner ward. As they passed down one of the many stone walkways, bees buzzed, birds sang, and the beautifully blooming flowers, trees, and shrubs filled the air with their scents. Finally reaching the western side of the compound, Wulfgar walked along the shaded portico lining the inner wall, then came to a stop before two imposing doors guarded by armed demonslavers. As he and Serena approached, the slavers bowed deeply. Calling upon the craft, Wulfgar caused the doors to open. He took his queen by the hand, and they walked in.

Serena had seen many wondrous things here at the Citadel, but none compared to the splendor that lay before her now. The room was huge, and its entire western side lay open from floor to ceiling to reveal both the sky above and the sea below. The floor was fashioned of dark green marble, shot through with swirls of the palest gray. A series of black columns rose from the floor, to support the rather low ceiling. In one corner of the room stood Krassus, in his blue-and-gray robe. Turning his thoughtful gaze from the sea, he bowed. Serena acknowledged his presence with a nod.

Then she heard the sounds of splashing water. Looking to her right, she saw several women of about her own age, naked except for the flowers in their hair, happily bathing in a descending series of ornate marble pools. The scented water splashed down from a wide, curved trough in the wall above.

Seeing Serena, the women stopped what they were doing, stood, and bowed to her. Turning, Serena looked questioningly back to Wulfgar.

"They are your new handmaidens," he said to her. "I selected them myself, from the few *R'talis* slaves who remain alive. Their minds are now ours, and they have been granted the benefits of the time enchantments. They are yours to command for all of eternity."

"My lord's gifts are truly great," she said, smiling. She took one of his strong hands into hers and kissed it gently.

"Come," he said, beckoning to her. "There is more."

He led her toward the open side of the room, where two thrones of black marble sat overlooking the sea. On either side of the thrones stood a huge, freestanding column of dark red marble. Each of them was circled by garlands of violet flowers, and topped by a shallow black urn in which burned a bright flame.

From the edge of the shiny floor a series of wide, dark green marble steps led down to the sea. The stairway was lined by more freestanding columns, each topped with a flaming urn. The steps emptied out onto a broad terrace that lay just above the waves that continuously rolled over its leading edge. The clean, salty sea air drifted up to Serena and stirred her dark ringlets.

The train of her magnificent black gown snaking along behind her as she went, Wulfgar's queen walked tentatively over to touch the smooth, cool marble of one of the thrones. As she did, it was as if the massive seat of power suddenly sparked something deep inside her. She could feel her *R'talis* blood, graced as it was by the presence of so many Forestallments of the Vagaries, begin to swirl hotly, quickly through her veins. And like her lord, she was filled with the urgent need for their sacred mission to begin.

Krassus walked over to touch Serena's arm, bringing her back to the moment. Smiling, the wizard walked her back over to Wulfgar, and the three of them looked out over the sea.

"Come," Krassus said to them simply, and they descended the marble steps to the terrace. There, Serena could see that their entire fleet of slaver warships had stopped patrolling and had formed a massive, protective ring in the sea before them. Within the ring lay a great expanse of open water.

"Bring them, Wulfgar," Krassus said quietly. "Bring them all. They're yours to command now, by way of the gifts I have imbued into your blood. Bring them, so that your queen may know the many that now do your bidding."

With a nod to the wizard, Wulfgar turned to face the sea and raised his arms.

Almost immediately the vacant area of ocean surrounded by the demonslaver vessels seemed to come alive with huge, swirling eddies. Then the watery tornadoes rose from the ocean and into the air: dark, impenetrable maelstroms. As Serena watched breathlessly, they started to glow and turn colors, spinning so fast that they became fluid riots of alternating hues. Wulfgar spread his fingers.

As he did, several of the screechlings that made up one of the packs spun off and flew to where the three of them were standing. After circling them for several moments, the screechlings returned to the maelstroms that continued to whirl just above the waves.

Suddenly, another area of the sea began to churn, and Serena saw hundreds of menacing serpentine heads rise up slowly out of the sea. Their eyes were yellow and slanted with vertical black pupils. Each of the menacing heads was covered with dark red scales, and was a good two meters across. Pink, forked tongues slipped in and out of mouth slits as the creatures tested the air. Occasionally the beasts' forked tails would rise up out of the water, only to submerge again as they slithered their way through the waves.

Suddenly, Serena noticed a softly distant pounding. It grew in strength, soon blotting out every other sound, even the crashing of the waves against the edge of the terrace. Looking up, she saw the source of the rising cacophony.

In their eagerness for their mission to begin, the thousands of white-skinned demonslavers aboard the warships were standing at attention on the decks, relentlessly banging their swords on their shields.

Wulfgar finally lowered his arms and turned to his queen. She saw a determined, powerful look in his eyes that she knew could never be conquered. As the ceaseless pounding continued, she turned back to the sea and took his hand. Krassus smiled.

CHAPTER

Fifty-five

When Tristan first heard the knock on the door, he wanted whoever it was to go away and let him sleep in peace. Why couldn't they all just leave him alone? Hadn't he done enough?

He rolled over, hoping whoever it was would go away.

The knocking came again, even more insistent this time. Tristan realized that it sounded more like someone kicking at the door, than knocking on it. Shannon the Short, he thought, sent by Wigg to come and wake him up.

He threw off the sheets and hobbled stiffly over to the chair in the corner, where he grabbed up his trousers and pulled them on. Then he went to the door and opened it.

Celeste stood there, smiling at him. She was dressed in black, form-fitting riding breeches, black knee boots, and a low-cut, yellow silk blouse that was ruffled at the neck and wrists. Her dark red hair tumbled down over her shoulders. Tristan could smell the familiar fragrance of myrrh, and it helped to awaken his senses. In her hands she held a large silver tray, its contents covered with a lid.

She gave him an unnecessary, highly coquettish curtsy. "Are you going to make me stand on ceremony all day, Your *Highness*, or are you going to let me in?" she asked. Then she nodded at the tray in her hands. "After all, I bring gifts."

"Oh, over here," Tristan said. He led the way to the opposite side of the dim room, where he drew back the drapes and opened the stained-glass balcony doors, revealing a bright, clear day.

Celeste, her eyes on the tray, followed him and carefully placed the food on the balcony table.

"How much of the day has gone by?" he asked sleepily.

"It is nearly midday. You have had only five hours of sleep, but I'm afraid it's going to have to do. We are due to meet the others in the courtyard in one hour."

She lifted the lid from the tray. "Spotted quail's eggs," she said with another smile. "Poached, just the way you like them—or so the gnome wives in the kitchens tell me. Cured ham slices, gingerwheat toast with violetberry jam, and tea—extra strong and extra hot. And all enough for two."

She placed her hands on her hips and turned to look at him. Then she puckered up her mouth and shook her head.

"You're a mess," she said, giving him a grin. She took in the shadows on his face from not having shaved, the comma of dark hair lying down over his forehead, and the dirty trousers. "Shall we eat first, or do you wish to bathe?"

"Eat," he said with authority as he poured himself a brimming cup of the dark, hot tea. He took a sip and felt its warm goodness go all the way down. "Bless you," he said as he gingerly sipped some more.

Suddenly remembering he was still half naked, he put his cup down and walked back over to the chair to fetch his vest. As Celeste watched him go, for the first time she saw the angry, still-healing scars across his back, and her eyes went wide with concern. As he walked back to her, he looked up from lacing his vest and immediately understood.

Taking her hands into his, he saw that her eyes had become shiny.

"It's all right," he said softly. "They don't hurt as much as they once did." Reaching out, he touched her cheek.

"Did Krassus do that to you?" she asked, her face darkening with anger.

"In a way. These marks are from my time on the slave ship. One of the demonslavers did this."

Celeste looked down for a moment. "Then he shall have to answer for what he has done," she said, so softly he could barely hear her.

"That won't be necessary." Placing one hand beneath her chin, he raised her face back up to his. "He has already answered," he added gently. "To me." Silence reigned for a few moments.

"You lead such a dangerous existence," she said bravely, trying to hold back her tears. "It would be safer for you if you stayed here in the palace."

One corner of Tristan's mouth came up. "It would be safer for me if I were someone else altogether," he answered with a smile. "But we can't do much about that, now, can we?"

"No," she said, a hint of a smile returning. "I suppose not."

"Come and eat," he said, leading her back out in the sunshine. "I, for one, am famished."

"I'm not sure I've ever seen you when you weren't," she chided as they sat down across from each other.

As they sat and ate in the sunshine, Celeste told him a bit more of what she knew about Abbey, and the prince expanded on his experiences with Krassus, and the pirates of Sanctuary. As they talked, Tristan couldn't help but notice a very discernible change in Celeste. She seemed more alive, more spontaneous, happier than he had ever seen her. As he took another bite of the gingerwheat toast, he innocently told her so. When he did, a more thoughtful look came over her.

"Does this have anything to do with what you said you wanted to talk to me about?" he asked gently.

Celeste put down her teacup and looked into his eyes. "I'm finally free," she said softly.

"Free?" he repeated.

"Free of Ragnar," she answered. "I will, of course, never forget my time with him. But my horrific memories and nightmares no longer haunt me. While you were away, he came to me in a dream. It was so real that I was sure I was awake. He had returned from the dead somehow, and had used the craft on me so I couldn't move. He was going to abuse me again, right there and then, and return me to the Caves. But when I awakened from my dream, my mind fought back this time, and my anger finally came flooding out. When it did, something inside of me just snapped, and the grip of his terror over me was broken." Taking his hands, she closed hers lovingly around them.

"I'm finally free, Tristan," she said softly. "Free to live, laugh, and love." Her eyes anxiously searched his face, trying to discern what he was feeling. "The way it was rightfully meant to be," she added. "The way it should be between a man and a woman."

His heart full, Tristan stood, bringing her up with him. Pulling her close, he held her for a long time. When she finally took her face away from his shoulder, he saw the tears in her eyes again.

"Is it too late?" she asked softly.

At first Tristan didn't understand. Reaching up, he dried one of her eyes. "Too late for what?" he asked.

"Does Tyranny mean anything to you?" Her body trembled slightly, and her voice was barely audible. "Is it too late for you to love me?"

Closing his eyes for a moment, he pulled her closer. "Don't you know by now?" he asked her. "It has always been you. From the first moment I saved you at the edge of that cliff and looked into your eyes." Feeling her body rise up to meet his, he looked down at her open mouth and realized the time for words had ended.

Reaching into her hair, he gave it a sure but gentle tug. As he did, her body bent willingly beneath him, and he put his mouth down on hers.

He looked into her eyes. She smiled, and cried, and laughed, and cried again. Her tears coming freely now, she rested her face against his chest and held him so tightly that he thought she would never let go. With his hands, he turned her face up and pressed his forehead against hers.

At that moment, Tristan understood that he had never truly loved before. Certainly not in just this way, nor ever with so full a heart.

"And just what do you suppose your father will have to say about all of this?" he asked with a little laugh.

"I have no idea." She laughed, too. "But I know I love you with all my heart, and nothing in this world will ever change that, I promise you."

"And I, you," he answered softly.

Taking a deep breath of self-discipline, she tore herself away. "I have to leave," she said. "And you need to clean yourself up!" Her sapphire eyes seemed to stab right through his heart. "I will see you in the court-yard."

With a final smile of good-bye, she walked to the door and left him alone with his thoughts. Long after she was gone, he could still smell the myrrh in the air.

Tristan walked back out to the balcony and looked down at the re-mains of the breakfast she had brought him, and then stared out over the peaceful countryside. Realizing his lips still held the memory of her kiss, he slowly grazed his fingertips over them. It was then that the long-awaited understanding finally came whispering its way into his mind.

And so it begins.

Fifty-six

By the time Tristan had bathed, dressed, and finally reached the courtyard, the sun was nearing its zenith. Abbey, Wigg, Faegan, and Shailiha were already there, waiting for him. Caprice, Shailiha's violet-and-yellow flier of the fields, was perched calmly on the princess' outstretched arm. Shailiha had left her daughter in the care of the gnome wives, Tristan assumed. As he joined the group, he gave Celeste a knowing smile.

Seeing Tristan, Wigg scowled and loudly cleared his throat. "And now that we're all finally here . . ."

Tristan paused in midstride. Glancing at Wigg, he sighed and pursed his lips.

The lead wizard turned to Abbey. "Are you ready?" he asked.

Running one hand worriedly through her thick salt-and-pepper hair, the herbmistress nodded. "Perhaps this time our luck will hold." She looked over at Faegan. The Paragon, hanging around his neck, sparkled in the sun.

"But given the fact that we still do not completely understand the Furies, I suggest we take some protective measures," she added. "We have postulated that the Furies arise only when the blood of the Chosen Ones is involved in this process, but we also must admit that our understanding of this remains limited. I have no desire to relive what happened the other day. To that end, I have a suggestion."

Faegan looked up from his chair. "Indeed," he replied. "What is your idea?"

"Can you use the craft to fashion something to contain my gazing flame?" Abbey asked him. "Something that would be strong enough to shield me from the Furies, if need be, but that my hands and my gifts might also be able to actually reach through, so that I still might accomplish my work?"

Faegan nodded. "There is a variation of the wizard's warp that should do."

Raising his arms, he called the craft. As he did, the familiar azure glow appeared. Then the glow coalesced into a gleaming, transparent cube sitting silently before them on the grass of the courtyard. Open at the top, it was about five meters high, and another five meters across on each side.

Tristan guessed that Faegan had left the cube's top open purposely, so that if the process erupted the force would go upward, harmlessly releasing its power into the sky.

Faegan lowered his arms. "That should suffice," he said thoughtfully. "I have fashioned it to be as strong as I know how, yet also accommodate your other demands. But what you need to understand is that whenever a warp is constructed so that one may pass any part of his or her body through it, by necessity some of its inherent strength is lost." He went quiet for several moments. "I certainly hope it will be enough," he added casually, his sense of understatement not lost on the others.

"Then it is time for me to begin," Abbey said quietly. She held one of her arms out toward Faegan. "The herbs I specified?"

Faegan untied the leather cinch bag from around his waist and handed it over to Abbey. Then the herbmistress turned to Wigg. "And the fragment from the Scroll of the Vagaries?"

As Wigg took the vellum from within his robes, he looked down at it, and a look of concern crossed his face.

"Tell me, Abbey," he asked her. "Do you need all of the vellum to view the other scroll?"

"While the relative size or quantity of the matching item is important, it is not so critical to the process as the quality and quantity of the herbs," she answered. "Why do you ask?"

"Because if this thing blows up in our faces, I would prefer that we only risk half of the vellum, rather than all of it. Do you think you could be successful using only one half?"

"Perhaps. We won't know until we try."

Nodding, Wigg looked over at Faegan. "What say you?" he asked.

"I think we should proceed," Faegan said knowingly. "But we must also tell them the other reason we wish to divide the vellum in half."

"And what might that be?" Shailiha asked quizzically.

"Consider the following," Faegan said as he pushed his chair closer. "While it's true that Tristan brought us the vellum, and that we believe it came from the Scroll of the Vagaries, we still have no way of knowing who put it into his boot. Or even why, for that matter. Since only Krassus and the woman Tristan describes as Grizelda supposedly had access to the scroll, logic would dictate that it had to be one of them. But why would they do such a thing? They certainly do not wish to aid us in our search for the Scroll of the Vigors. But there is one thing Krassus and his herbmistress very much *would* like to see us accomplish on our own," he added wryly.

"And what is that?" Celeste asked.

"To die," Tristan said softly, half to himself. He looked over at the wizard in the chair. "That's what you're getting at, isn't it? You and Wigg believe that Krassus and Grizelda have somehow enchanted the vellum to destroy us, should we try to use it to view the other scroll. An enchantment set to enact with the onset of Abbey's flame." Angrily, he shook his head. "How could I have been so blind!" he groaned. "I might have gotten us all killed."

"Don't be so hard on yourself," Wigg said, laying one hand on the prince's shoulder. "Faegan and I came to this hypothesis only hours ago ourselves, as we were examining the vellum."

Tristan scowled as he thought about it all. Then he suddenly realized that part of the wizards' theory made no sense. "But how could he know I would escape?" he asked.

"From the story you told us, there was no way he could have," Faegan answered. "But you're a very resourceful individual, and your reputation precedes you. We believe he may have enchanted the vellum and then placed it into your boot as an additional strategy, should you somehow actually find your way out of your predicament. Think about it. Why else would Krassus show you the scroll? As anyone in your position would do, you immediately associated the piece in your boot with it, and tried to bring the vellum back to us as quickly as you could." Pausing for a moment, Faegan cast his ever-curious eyes over at the vellum Wigg still held in his hand.

"If you failed to escape, it wouldn't matter," he continued. "If you did, he was prepared. Given the desperate nature of our situation, he is no doubt counting on the fact that we will hurry in our attempts to employ his little gift without first considering the consequences." Faegan took a deep breath. "And he was very nearly proven right."

Deeply discouraged, Tristan shook his head. "So what do we do now?" he asked.

"We do what we came here for," Wigg answered. "Provided, of course, that Abbey is still willing to try. After everything she has just heard, we can hardly condemn her, should she choose to decline."

"And so the other reason why you want to divide the vellum in half is to lessen its deadly effects, should Krassus have actually enchanted it," Tristan surmised.

"Well done," Wigg replied. He looked concernedly over at Abbey. "Are you still willing to try?"

Abbey shook her head. "Just how strong is this warp of yours?" she asked Faegan.

"As powerful as I could make it," Faegan answered. "But there are no guarantees."

Sighing, Abbey rubbed her brow. Then she looked up at Wigg and gave him an ironic smile. "I just *had* to come back to Tammerland with you, didn't I?" she said ruefully. Glaring back at Faegan, she raised her eyebrows. "Is there nothing else that can be done to help protect me?" she asked. "Surely that legendary brain of yours can come up with something."

Looking up at the sky, Faegan took a few moments to mull it over. "There might be something," he said finally.

"And what is that?" Wigg asked.

"If I begin to see the cube eroding, Wigg and I can try to shore it up again," Faegan answered slowly, thinking out loud. "Though by then it might already be too late."

He looked up into Abbey's eyes. "Do you trust me to keep you alive?" he asked seriously.

Obviously unsure, Abbey hesitated. "Is there any other choice?" she finally asked resignedly. When neither of the wizards answered, she gave a short, derisive laugh. Then she bent over and put her mouth near Faegan's ear. "If you let me die, I'll kill you," she said, fully realizing the absurdity of her words.

Faegan let go a soft cackle. "If you die, I'll let you," he answered. "Now then, shall we begin? But first I suggest that the rest of you retire to a much safer distance. Wigg, if you would."

Wigg nodded, then turned to face the new brick wall he and Faegan had conjured that morning, upon coming to their disturbing conclusions.

Raising one arm, Wigg loosed an azure bolt against it. When the bolt reached it, it flattened out, encasing the wall entirely. Apparently satisfied, the lead wizard dropped his arm.

"Just another little precaution in case something should go wrong." Faegan winked. "Now then, I want everyone except Abbey and myself behind that wall."

Wigg watched them all go, then gave Abbey a kiss on the cheek. "Good luck," he said quietly. Then he joined the others. The wall was just tall enough for the three of them to see over.

When Faegan was satisfied that the others were safe, he looked at the herbmistress. "Please give me the scrap of vellum." Once she did so, he used the craft to divide the ancient skin in two. He returned one piece to her, then nodded. "You may begin whenever you are ready," he told her. "And may the Afterlife look over us."

Taking a deep breath, Abbey opened the leather cinch bag Faegan had given her and removed two smoke-colored bottles. Taking a pinch of herbs from the first bottle, she tentatively reached through one side of the cube, watching as its azure wall closed in around her arm. Finally satisfied, she dropped the herbs to the floor of the cube and withdrew her arm.

Closing her eyes, she bowed her head.

Almost immediately, the familiar golden flame erupted, slowly snaking its way toward the open top of the cube. Abbey reached back through the side and cast a few more of the herbs into the flame. Roaring even higher, the gazing flame gained strength and color. Abbey removed her hand from the cube and backed away a bit. Raising one arm, she silently commanded the flame to split into two separate branches. The smaller of the branches angled toward her.

Opening the other bottle of herbs, she carefully measured some out, then reached into the cube again and dropped the herbs into the nearest of the branched flames.

The two branches rejoined, returning to the vertical. Placing the two bottles on the ground at her feet, Abbey took the piece of vellum in both hands and raised it high.

As she watched the fire, a rectangular, azure window appeared in its midst. Within its confines, an image slowly formed. Faegan wheeled his chair closer to the edge of the cube and peered in.

A street scene was unfolding. It looked like a plaza of some kind. But which city? Faegan wondered. And for that matter, which country? Eutracia or Parthalon? Trying to examine the image was maddening—like trying to solve a shimmering, constantly moving puzzle with several of the pieces missing. But then Faegan saw the familiar statues.

The Plaza of Fallen Heroes! he realized. The Scroll of the Vigors was there in Tammerland, right under their noses!

But suddenly the piece of vellum in Abbey's hand began to quiver and turn azure. Nearly beside herself with fear, the horrified herbmistress turned to Faegan.

"Get out!" she shouted. She shoved her arm into the warp, and dropped the ancient scrap inside. Immediately, she hiked up her skirts and charged toward the protective wall. Shaking off his shock, Faegan levitated his chair and soared over the courtyard to join her and the others.

As they all watched in horror, the vellum in the cube began to emit strange pinpricks of light. With the birth of the lights came great screeching sounds, so loud that the people behind the wall could barely stand the pain in their ears.

The pinpricks became shafts, and the shafts increased in size and began ricocheting against the inner walls of the cube. Some of them soared up through the open top, screaming their way into the empty sky above. The entire cube shook and jumped violently on the grass.

And then the walls of the cube began to crack.

Like sharp, threatening crevices wending their way through melting ice, the fissures in the walls of the cube started to lengthen. Levitating his chair over the top of the wall, Faegan hovered there and raised his arms. Then he loosed an azure bolt at the disintegrating cube, trying to shore it up against the power of the shrieking beams of light. Straining with effort, Faegan began to shake.

Tristan watched in dread as the walls of the cube continued to shake, split, and crack. Hurrying out from behind the wall, Wigg shot another azure bolt against the cube. But even with the lead wizard's added power, it was clear that Faegan's warp was deteriorating. It wouldn't be long now, Tristan realized, before more of the beams of light were unleashed.

Then he heard Faegan scream something out to Wigg. The lead wizard quickly nodded. As one they both sent out azure bolts to lift the cube from the ground, the piece of vellum still inside it. Using all their power, they began moving it over to one side of the courtyard, near the northern wing of the palace.

Transfixed, Tristan realized what the wizards were about to do. His jaw dropped. Were they insane?

With a great, final heave, the wizards shoved the cube toward double, side-by-side stained-glass windows. It tore through them as if they were made of paper, and kept on going.

Tristan watched, aghast, as the flashes of light screamed within the castle chambers. They lit up the rooms with what looked to be lightning strikes. He heard furniture being rent apart, glass breaking, and interior walls tumbling and crashing. Sections of the palace roof heaved, throwing marble pieces high into the air. Some of the beams of light escaped and tore their way across the courtyard to slam into the opposite wing of the palace.

At last, it was over. Dust and debris choked the entire courtyard. Into its midst, swarms of concerned Minion warriors landed, dreggans drawn. Coughing deeply, Tristan, Shailiha, and Celeste walked out from behind the wall to rejoin the wizards.

"Faegan!" Tristan exclaimed. "What in the name of the Afterlife just happened?"

"Never mind that now!" the wizard shot back, anxiously waving his arms. Tristan wasn't sure he had ever seen him so animated. "The Scroll of the Vigors is in the Plaza of Fallen Heroes, I'm sure of it! But it's on the move! And it seems to be wrapped in something, as if its current owner is trying to hide it! This may be our only chance to bring it back!"

Then he looked over at Abbey. "I want you to remain here," he ordered her. "You've done all you can for now. The rest of you come with me! We have to get to the stables!"

But Tristan had a question, and he urgently grabbed Faegan's arm. "What about the Minions? Shouldn't they help?"

"No," Faegan said thoughtfully. "This must be done very carefully." Pausing for a moment, he looked over to Shailiha to see that Caprice was still perched on her forearm. Wasting no time, he quickly beckoned the princess to him.

Faegan whispered something to her. Shailiha raised the arm holding Caprice and closed her eyes. After several moments the flier launched herself into the air and flew away.

Abbey watched in silence as Wigg, Tristan, Shailiha, and Celeste sprinted from the courtyard. Faegan levitated his chair again and went soaring along beside them. In mere moments they had rounded the corner of the partially destroyed palace and were gone.

Completely exhausted, Abbey stared out over the hissing rubble and tried to fathom what had just happened. No quick answers came. Turning back, she looked apprehensively toward the corner where her friends had disappeared.

Slowly, tiredly, she began making her way back to the palace.

Fifty-seven

As Tristan sat atop Pilgrim at the edge of the Plaza of Fallen Heroes, a sense of foreboding crept over him. Finding the scroll was going to be difficult at best, and for all he knew Krassus might also be here. Searching the sky he finally found Caprice as she soared gracefully above, all of her senses on alert. Ordering any of the fliers this close to ordinary citizens was always a risk, but Faegan obviously thought the stakes were too high not to employ her talents.

On the way to the plaza, Faegan had shouted out his orders. Tristan, Wigg, Celeste, and Faegan would approach the square from different directions, then wait quietly on horseback at its outer edges. Shailiha would walk calmly to the center and wait. From above, Caprice would have an excellent view of the scene and, it was hoped, would silently inform Shailiha when she spotted the scroll. When Shailiha moved, the rest of them would quickly follow her, and converge on the scroll from different directions.

Assuming it was still here, Tristan thought.

He could just make out Wigg, Faegan, and Celeste as they waited nervously atop their horses at different spots on the plaza's outer edges. They were wearing dark blue consuls' robes to help hide their identities. To the wizards' great consternation, Tristan had refused to wear one, claiming it would interfere with quick access to his weapons.

He glanced back at Faegan, and one corner of his mouth came up in admiration. Since their battle with the demonslavers at the docks, Tristan had learned that it was very painful for the crippled wizard to sit a horse. But somehow Faegan was able to partition his mind and control the pain. And the prince knew that the inquisitive wizard wouldn't have missed being here for the world.

As he stared out across the plaza, his jaw hardened. This wasn't much of a plan, he thought. Then again, there hadn't been much time to formulate one.

Reaching behind his right shoulder, he grasped the hilt of his dreggan and gave it a short tug, making sure its blade would not stick if called upon. Then he did the same with the first three of his throwing knives. As Pilgrim shifted his weight beneath him, Tristan leaned one arm down on the pommel of his saddle and glued his dark eyes on his sister.

"*A*re you ready, piglet?" Marcus asked Rebecca encouragingly. He could see that she was very afraid.

In truth, Rebecca wished that Marcus would just forget about the silly old scroll. But she also knew that this was the day he had worked so hard for, and when his mind was made up, it was made up.

Leaning against the brick wall of the alley, she took the weight off her clubfoot and looked down at the old wheelbarrow. In it lay the scroll, wrapped once again in the rug that Marcus had stolen. Maybe this was for the best, she finally thought. At least after today she wouldn't have to watch it glow anymore. She looked tentatively up into her brother's hopeful green eyes.

"I guess I'm ready," she said softly. "What do you want me to do?"

Marcus smiled. "That's my girl," he said. He pointed out into the plaza, to the booth where he had purchased the bird for her to release.

"Do you remember that stand?" he asked her. "And the bird I bought for you?"

Biting her lip, she nodded.

"Very soon now, a man will lead a horse over next to it. He's big and fat, and has a white mustache. There will be several bags tied to the saddle. Once I think he is alone, I will walk out with the wheelbarrow, speak with him for a little bit, and then exchange the horse for the wheelbarrow. That will be all there is to it. But when I leave the plaza with the horse, you must do something for me. From where you will be standing, you must watch and see if anyone is following me. If you're sure they are, I want you to run to me straight away. I'll hoist you up on the horse, and we'll make a run for it. But if no one is behind me, then we'll meet later, in our usual spot. Do you understand?"

Rebecca nodded. Her foot ached, and she just wanted all of this to be over. "Where do you want me to stand?" she asked quietly.

"Do you remember the place I showed you earlier this morning? The one by the corner?"

"Yes."

"Stand there. From that spot you should be able to see everything."

Marcus glanced out into the plaza. Time was getting short, and if the artifacts dealer was truly coming, he would be here soon. Only within the last hour the scroll had glowed again, and Marcus found himself as anxious to be rid of it as 'Becca was.

Bending down a bit, Marcus took 'Becca by the shoulders and looked into her frightened brown eyes.

"You can do this for me, can't you, piglet?" he asked as he searched her face. "Your part is awfully important. I couldn't do it without you, you know."

Looking up at her brother, Rebecca did her best to smile.

Marcus looked nervously out into the plaza again. "I think you should go now," he said. "And try to remember everything I told you. Very soon this will all be over, and we'll be free."

Taking a deep breath, Rebecca stood away from the wall and limped out into the sunlight. After taking only a few steps, she turned and looked back at her brother for a moment. As she did, Marcus held his breath.

Then she turned back to the teeming plaza and kept on going. He watched the back of her tattered plaid dress for as long as he could, until it finally melted away into the crowd.

His breath coming quickly now, Marcus leaned against the wall, closed his eyes tight, and desperately hoped that he had just done the right thing. Turning back to the bird booth, he fingered the spring-loaded knife in his pocket and waited.

*G*rabbing Mr. Worth by his expensive, sweaty collar, Janus slammed him up against the nearest wall of the empty artifact shop. Worth shook with fear. Grizelda smiled.

Then the painted freak looked down at the three heavy canvas bags lying nearby on the otherwise barren floor.

"It's time," he whispered nastily. "Time for me to obtain what I came all this way for." As he smiled, his red mask crinkled up at the edges.

Reaching down to his belt, he removed the twin iron spheres and held them up before Worth's frightened eyes.

"I am deadly accurate with these," he hissed. "Emphasis on the word 'dead.' And my friend and I won't be far away. So don't get any bright ideas about double-crossing me, or your head will soon be lying all by itself on the bricks of the plaza." He smiled. "You could then be called one of the Fallen Heroes! How deliciously ironic! Do you understand my instructions, you fat bastard?"

Sweat running down his face, Worth nodded.

Janus let Worth go, and he and the shopkeeper wrestled the heavy moneybags outside and onto the waiting horse.

*M*arcus looked out from the darkness of the alleyway. Right on time, Worth was leading a bay mare over toward the bird booth. Three bulging bags were tied to the saddle.

Marcus forced himself to wait for a few moments before going out with the wheelbarrow. Let the artifacts dealer sweat a bit, he thought. Might make him easier to deal with, should he have suddenly acquired any new ideas.

Slowly, carefully, Marcus picked up the handles of the wheelbarrow and pushed it out into the light.

As Marcus approached, the shopkeeper seemed almost overjoyed to see him. Marcus carefully put down the wheelbarrow and looked around. Then he trained his skeptical eyes on Worth. "Is it all there?" he asked simply.

"Uh, er, yes—yes, of course," Worth stammered, as if he didn't know what else to say. "All thirteen thousand."

Reluctantly leaving the scroll for a moment, Marcus walked over to the mare. Uncinching the first of the three bags, he pulled it open and worked one hand all the way to the bottom to pull out a coin at random.

After carefully examining it in the sun, he bit down into it, testing its worth. Then he repeated the procedure with the other two bags. Finally satisfied, he tied them back up and looked at the sweaty shopkeeper.

"Now it's your turn," he said quietly.

No one had to tell Worth what the young man meant. Walking to the wheelbarrow, he unrolled part of the rug to expose a large section of the magnificent scroll. As he did, Marcus winced. Whether out of greed, stupidity, or some other foolish reason, the idiot was exposing far too much of his newly acquired treasure to the world. But that wasn't Marcus' problem any more.

Sensing victory, he looked back into Worth's eyes.

*I*t is here, Mistress.
  Where?
  In the center of the plaza, near the booth with the captive birds. It is hidden in a wheelbarrow. You must hurry.
  Well done.

Gathering up her robes, Shailiha quickly looked around. Then she started to make her way toward the booth.

At the same time, a strangely dressed man with a painted face, and a grizzled old woman in rags began moving in the same direction.

Tristan didn't hesitate. As soon as he saw his sister move, he walked Pilgrim out into the busy plaza. Looking around, he saw that Faegan, Wigg, and Celeste were already converging on her. Tristan saw Shailiha come to a stop near a wooden vendor's stand, and watched as she looked around, searching for the scroll.

Then the prince finally saw it. The scroll seemed to be partially wrapped in something—a rug, perhaps—and it was lying in an old, dilapidated wheelbarrow. A fat, red-faced man was bending over and about to make off with the scroll, barrow and all. Knowing he had to hurry, Tristan spurred Pilgrim into a gallop across the cobblestoned yard.

That was when everything started to unravel.

Faegan had also seen the scroll and was quickly nearing the man with the wheelbarrow. As he did, the fellow seemed to suspect something and began to run, pushing the barrow as fast as he could. Raising one arm, Faegan sent a bolt of the craft toward him, forcing him to drop the barrow. Amazed, all Worth could do was to look up with horror as the prize he so coveted literally floated away on the air.

Citizens standing nearby began to scream and point. Then they began to scatter, running away from the frightening azure bolts of the craft.

As he charged toward the center of the plaza, something else suddenly caught Tristan's attention. He saw a young man, eyes wide with terror, mounting a bay horse. His saddle was loaded down with what looked to be heavy canvas bags. The boy whipped his mount in an attempt to get away.

Turning Pilgrim hard, Tristan raced to catch the boy, who was just passing a wooden booth laden with birdcages.

Then the boy's overloaded mount slipped on the cobblestones and went down hard, sliding directly into the side of the wooden booth. With a great noise the spindly booth shattered, sending pieces of wood flying everywhere. Many of the birdcages were destroyed, and the larks inside them flew out in every direction in a maelstrom of fluttering wings.

Surprised by the birds, Pilgrim reared. As he had done so many times before, Tristan automatically shifted his weight forward in his saddle and confidently rose with his horse. But he hadn't seen the spinning orbs that were already flashing their way across the plaza. Nor did he realize that the stallion he loved so much was about to save his life.

The orbs Janus had thrown were meant to take the prince's head from his shoulders, and if Pilgrim had not reared up at the last moment that is exactly what would have happened. Instead of the orbs finding the prince, they found the stallion.

Winding their connecting cord around Pilgrim's raised forelegs, the orbs viciously drew them together and cracked them in two as if they had been matchsticks. As he came back down to land on his front legs again, the sharply fractured bones ruptured the skin. Screaming insanely, Pilgrim went down hard on his left side, trapping Tristan's leg beneath him.

Still unsure of what had just happened, Tristan tried desperately to free himself but couldn't. He instinctively reached back for his weapons, but to his horror he found them gone. With his fall they had all scattered and lay just beyond his reach.

That was when he first saw the painted face leering down at him.

The man was dressed like a bizarre harlequin, and he held a shiny dagger in one hand. Saying nothing, he calmly walked around Pilgrim to come and stand over the helpless prince. He smiled as he raised his dagger, its blade twinkling in the midday sun.

The wizards would later say that the azure bolt that tore across the plaza was among the brightest they had ever seen. It tore into Janus' back and exploded with a force so great that it nearly killed Tristan, as well. Janus literally blew apart, organs and bones flying for meters in every direction. Then what was left of him dropped sloppily to the ground next to the prince.

Opening his eyes, Tristan found himself littered with blood and offal. The dagger that had nearly killed him lay nearby, still clutched in the harlequin's severed hand.

Then he felt a strong pair of hands beneath his arms, pulling him free. Finally rising up on shaky legs and still dazed, Tristan steadied himself and looked around.

The plaza was almost completely deserted. Celeste stood a short distance away. The fingertips of her right hand were scorched and red, and smoke rose from them softly, curling its way into the sky. Next to her stood Shailiha, who wore a tragic look on her face. On her outstretched arm sat Caprice, the giant butterfly gently opening and closing her wide, diaphanous wings.

Wigg stood near Tristan. In his craft-strengthened grip the wizard held the collar of the young man Tristan had seen trying to escape on horseback. The three canvas bags floated beside him in the air. A young clubfooted girl was also with him, desperately clutching the young man Wigg held and sobbing hysterically.

Next to Shailiha stood Grizelda, Krassus' herbmistress. Held prisoner inside a wizard's warp, she was angrily waving her arms and shouting vile curses at them. With a wave of one hand, Wigg promptly took away her powers of speech.

Looking further, Tristan saw that the fat man who had tried to make off with the scroll lay dead, facedown on the cobblestones, a knife sticking out of his back. Then the prince felt a comforting hand on the back of his shoulder.

He looked up to see Faegan. The wizard was still atop his horse. In his arms he cradled the Scroll of the Vigors. But, like everyone else, the wizard looked upset, not triumphant.

"What is it?" Tristan asked softly, sensing that something was very wrong.

One simple, awful word came down to him: "Pilgrim."

Tristan's daze evaporated, and he whirled around to find the stallion still lying on the ground, an unfamilar weapon tangled around his legs. Tristan felt his heart tear in two.

Both the stallion's forelegs were smashed and bleeding. In horrific pain, Pilgrim whinnied weakly as he saw the prince look at him. Dropping to the ground, Tristan gently cradled the horse's head in his lap.

His face stern, Wigg gave the care of the young man and the crying girl over to Faegan. Then he placed his hands into the opposite sleeves of his robe and came to stand next to the prince.

Tears flooding his eyes, Tristan looked beseechingly up at his old friend and mentor. But deep in his heart, he already knew the answer.

With a tear in one eye, Wigg slowly shook his head.

Crying freely now, his body shaking with grief, Tristan held Pilgrim closer. "Can you make it painless?" he asked, his voice cracking.

Coming nearer, the lead wizard placed a hand on Tristan's shoulder. "Of course," he answered softly.

For what he knew would be the last time, Tristan gently stroked Pilgrim's velvety muzzle.

"I will never forget you," he whispered. As if somehow understanding, Pilgrim whinnied back to him softly.

Without looking up, Tristan nodded. Wigg raised his right arm.

The dappled stallion closed his eyes.

Uncontrollably, shamelessly, Tristan raised his tear-streaked face to the sky and cried like a child.

Fifty-eight

"Come back to me safe, my love," Serena said to Wulfgar. Placing one hand on her abdomen, she looked up into his hazel eyes. "Both I and your unborn daughter will be anxiously awaiting your return."

As he stood with her on the stone terrace overlooking the ocean, Wulfgar reached out to touch her face. "Wish me luck," he said softly. "For it is all about to begin."

Then he turned to look at Krassus. The ailing wizard was sitting in a chair, taking in the last rays of the slowly setting sun.

"We both thank you for all of our gifts," Wulfgar said to him. "If I never see you again, rest assured that I will not stop until I have accomplished all that I have been charged with. Thanks to you, the Chosen Ones shall soon suffer a fate even they could never have imagined."

Smiling, Krassus looked up at his two magnificent creations. "It is not me whom you and your queen should thank for your gifts," he answered weakly. "Nor for the mission with which you have been entrusted. It is the Heretics of the Guild upon whom you should shower your gratitude and undying loyalty. For they, in all their glorious wisdom, are the ones who are ultimately responsible not only for your powers, but also for the mission you have been honored to carry out." Taking a short, painful breath, the wizard cast his dark gaze back out over the sea.

"And do not weep for me," he added softly. "I am only thankful that I could live to see this day, and entrust all the wonders of this place to you." He lifted his head and looked wistfully up at the sky.

"Very soon now I shall go to them, and I do not fear it. It is my reward, and I welcome its coming."

Wulfgar walked over to the wizard, bent down, and gently kissed his creased, weathered cheek. Then he turned and embraced his queen.

He had no need to remind Serena that by now all of the remaining slaves had been turned to their cause, save for the forty who had been placed in confinement aboard his personal ship. Or that a specially selected group of demonslavers had been left behind to guard the Citadel, as had the consuls under his command. For these things his queen already knew. Wulfgar had by now enacted all of Serena's Forestallments. In his absence, his servants would obey all of Serena's orders as unquestioningly as if they had been his own.

Krassus had at first been against Wulfgar starting out on his quest so soon, for they were not yet in possession of the Scroll of the Vigors. But in truth, Wulfgar was now far beyond the wizard's control in such matters. Besides, the consuls had recently come to him to say that the Scroll of the Vagaries had glowed suddenly and unbidden, and Krassus knew exactly what that meant.

Krassus' senses told him that Wigg and Faegan had employed the vellum he had slipped into the prince's boot. By now they had most probably perished in the attempt due to the enchantment he had so ingeniously placed upon it. If the wizards of the Redoubt were dead, Wulfgar's chances of success had increased exponentially, especially since neither of the Chosen Ones was trained in the craft. But he had told Wulfgar that there was no way to be certain, until he arrived in Eutracia. Even so, it seemed the future now belonged to Wulfgar and Serena. And so, he had finally given his blessing to the early commencement of Wulfgar's mission.

The new master of the Citadel reached out and snapped his fingers at a pair of armed demonslavers, who approached immediately. They briskly escorted him to the end of the terrace and down the short steps to the sea. The three of them climbed aboard the skiff tied there, and one of the slavers set it adrift. Then the creatures began rowing their master out toward his waiting flagship.

Placing one hand over her eyes to shield them from the setting sun, Serena looked over the scene. It was an awe-inspiring sight.

The moored demonslaver fleet stretched nearly as far as the eye could see. Each was heavily loaded with arms and provisions, and slavers by the thousands could be seen amassed on the decks. Their sails furled, the vessels swayed peacefully in the water, the gentle movements belying the deadly nature of their purpose.

Vast numbers of screechling maelstroms darkened the surface of the waves. And beneath them, mere shadows, writhed the hordes of sea slitherers.

As she watched, the sails of Wulfgar's flagship finally unfurled and snapped open to the wind. The flagship snaked its way amid the others and began to lead the way west, toward the open sea. The sails of the other vessels followed suit and filled with wind. One by one, the warships of the great armada began plowing their way toward Eutracia, the screechlings and slitherers following obediently in their wake.

Serena and Krassus stood there for some time, watching the departing fleet disappear over the horizon. After finally bidding good night to the wizard, the queen of the Citadel walked up the marble steps that led to the throne room and proceeded on to her private quarters.

*K*rassus continued to sit silently as the night gathered around him. Shivering from the cold, he pulled his gray-and-blue robe closer and thought of all that he had been able to accomplish, and of the wonders that Wulfgar and Serena would yet live to see.

It was then that he finally felt the oncoming sensation, and he knew that it was over.

Finally giving way to their disease, his lungs ruptured once and for all, and he began drowning in his own blood. It flowed warmly from his mouth and splattered down on the floor of the terrace.

As if in slow motion Krassus fell gently from his chair.

With his passing came a sudden wind. Then lightning tore across the night sky in unbelievable streaks, its branches seeming to reach everywhere. As the howling wind increased, it roiled the sea, causing the waves to smash violently into the edge of the terrace.

And then the wind and the lightning slowly abated, leaving the dead body of the wizard silent and still in the pale, rose-tinted moonlight.

*A*ll of her oil lamps extinguished except one, Serena was about to retire. Then she saw the lightning flashes, and she knew. Raising one hand, she caused the transparent wall that had once barred her entrance to the balcony to vanish. Carrying her lamp out onto the balcony, she looked over the ocean. As the wind and the lightning finally relented, she smiled to herself.

Taking a breath, she blew out the light.

PART V

Retribution

CHAPTER

Fifty-nine

It is not for myself that I go forth to do this thing, but for all of those who came before, who tried but failed in their attempts to ensure that the Vagaries shall one day rule supreme.

—WULFGAR

Glad to be home finally, Tristan sat drinking wine at a butcher's table in the palace kitchens. It was early evening, and Wigg and Faegan sat there with him, along with the young man named Marcus. The massive hearths were directly behind them; copper pots and pans hung overhead, dangling from iron hooks.

When the gnome wives had first seen the two dirty, half-starved children, they had insisted on feeding them immediately, regardless of whatever the wizards might have to say about it. The wonderful smells of the women's creations still hung stubbornly in the air.

Tristan felt mournful. The loss of Pilgrim had been a shock that he knew would take a long time to recover from. At least the stallion had not died in vain: They had successfully secured the Scroll of the Vigors, and for that he was glad. The document was safe and sound, locked below the palace in the Hall of Blood Records. But before they examined it, the two wizards wanted some answers, and they were determined to get them as soon as they could.

After Tristan had removed Pilgrim's saddle and bridle, Wigg had lowered his head to call the craft and set fire to the horse's body. At first

Tristan couldn't bring himself to watch. But in the end he had finally looked over, tearfully doing his best to honor the companion that had seen him through so much.

Then Wigg had respectfully done the same thing with the body of the artifacts dealer and what was left of the harlequin. As Wigg went about his work, frightened citizens had begun to mill tentatively around the edges of the plaza, but upon seeing the lead wizard's use of the craft, none of them had approached.

On the way back to the palace, Wigg had explained to the prince what had unfolded in the plaza. Wigg had been the first to see Rebecca run away. Suspicious of such a young, obviously terrified girl running through the square, he had ridden his horse over to her and scooped her up. As for the artifacts dealer, it seemed that it had been Grizelda who had so conveniently plunged the dagger into his back. They still didn't know who the bizarre harlequin had been, but they hoped that the herbmistress would soon shed some light on that subject, as well. For now, she was securely locked behind one of the hundreds of doors deep in the bowels of the Redoubt.

The clubfooted girl named Rebecca had been too terrified by what she had seen to be of much help with the wizards' questions. Seeing this, Shailiha and Celeste had requested—and received—permission to take her away to feed her, bathe her, and reassure her as best they could.

Now the wizards wanted to hear from the young man named Marcus. His knife had been discovered and taken from him on the way to the palace. So far, the dirty, curly-haired redhead had barely stopped eating, and there seemed to be no end to the amount of food he could consume.

"Now then," Wigg began. "What is the name of your family house?"

"First things first," Marcus answered arrogantly, as if he owned the palace he was sitting in. He kept on chewing as he talked. "Where is my thirteen thousand kisa?"

Reaching out, he rudely swiped up yet more of the sliced lamb and stuffed about three bites' worth into his mouth all at once. Chewing hurriedly, he washed it down with another glass of goat's milk. After wiping his mouth with his sleeve, he turned to look greedily at Tristan's wine goblet.

"Give me some of that, and I'll gladly tell you who I am," he said confidently. "It seems the least you could do. I didn't ask to come here, you know."

With a brief snort, Faegan smiled and shook his head. But it was clear that the lead wizard didn't think any of this was particularly humorous.

Knowing that Marcus was still hungry, Wigg called on the craft. Almost immediately all of Marcus' precious food and drink rose into the air. The young man's eyes went wide. Then Wigg caused all of the dishes to go flying out the kitchen door and into the adjoining hallway. Without taking his eyes from Marcus, Wigg folded his arms across his chest and calmly leaned back in his chair. With that, everything fell crashing to the hallway floor—the dishes smashed, the food ruined, and the drinks spilled.

Frozen in place, Marcus stared at Wigg as if the wizard had just descended from one of the moons. Leaning in, Wigg cast his aquamarine eyes sternly at the young man and lowered his voice.

"Now that I have your full attention, let's try again, shall we?" he asked quietly. "What is the name of your family house?"

Lowering his face slightly, Marcus scowled and placed his greasy hands on his lap. "Stinton," he finally answered. "The House of Stinton."

"And where are you from?"

"Ilendium."

Wigg raised an eyebrow. "And the girl you travel with. She's your sister, is she not?"

Marcus nodded. "Rebecca." He added softly, "I call her 'Becca."

"I see," Wigg said a bit more compassionately. "And your parents. What of them? They must be worried about you."

"They're both dead. Killed by the great birds that came one night. 'Becca and I are orphans."

On hearing about the "great birds," Wigg looked at Tristan and Faegan. They nodded back. Marcus had to be referring to Nicholas' hatchlings, the winged beings that had so ruthlessly destroyed the city of Ilendium just before the construction of the Gates of Dawn.

"I'm sorry," Faegan said softly from the other side of the table. He was beginning to have genuine admiration for the brash young man, even if the boy was a thief. Master Stinton was nothing if not resourceful, he decided.

"How was it that the two of you were not also killed?" Faegan asked.

" 'Becca and I had gone fishing at the head of the Sippora River. We used to like to do that sometimes. And it was helpful, especially when father wasn't doing so well. But the fishing had been good, and we were very late getting home that night. By the time we did, everything was gone."

"I'm sorry, too," Wigg said earnestly. "But what did you mean about your father not doing so well? What was his trade?"

Marcus smiled again and puffed out his chest with pride. "My father was a pickpocket—the best in Eutracia. He could slip one hand into your drawers and come back out holding your private parts if he chose to, long before you felt the draft. And I'm just as good, if I do say so my-self."

Sighing, Wigg placed one hand over his forehead, closed his eyes, and leaned his elbow on the table. He shook his head slowly.

Tristan tried hard not to smile.

"And where did you get the scroll?" Wigg asked without look-ing up.

"We found them in one of the broken marble sections, left over from the destruction when those monuments, or whatever they were, fell to the ground," Marcus answered simply. It was clear he did not understand the importance of the site he and his sister had visited.

"Everything there stayed so hot, it took a week before 'Becca and I could do a proper search of the place," he went on. "We were on our own by then, and looking for food." Then he smiled again. "But that wasn't what we found."

Wigg's face shot up. "You said 'them'. Do you mean to say that both scrolls were there when you first went in?"

"Yes. But they were so heavy I could only take one. And there was no way 'Becca could handle the other, especially with her bad foot. Later I came back for the other scroll, but it was already gone. Somebody beat me to it."

"How did you get the scroll to Tammerland?" Tristan asked.

"In the rowboat we always used to fish out of. It was my father's. On the way down the Sippora we fished, so as to eat. Kept us alive."

"And was it always your intention to sell the scroll?" Tristan asked, his admiration for Marcus also growing.

"Of course. What would I want to keep the damned thing for?"

Tristan smiled. "And how did you find the artifacts dealer?"

"I asked around. It wasn't hard. I had an appointment with him today, to finally exchange the scroll for the kisa. He was the only one I trusted. But he won't be doing any more business, will he? From that point on, you know the rest." Then Marcus' face darkened. "I'm sorry about your horse," he added.

"Thank you," Tristan replied. "So am I."

Wigg had apparently heard all he needed. He stood and walked over to one side of the kitchens, to give a tug on a velvet pull cord. In a few moments, a Minion warrior appeared.

"Take this young man to the princess' quarters so that he may rejoin his sister," Wigg ordered. "See to it that he is cleaned up and given some decent clothes. I want one of you to keep an eye on him and his sister

at all times. They seem to have an unusually high predilection for lar-
ceny."

The warrior clicked his heels together. "As you wish."

Wide-eyed at his first glimpse of a Minion, Marcus was slow to rise
from the table. Before leaving, he turned around and looked back at
Wigg.

"I'll make a deal with you," he said.

Sighing, Wigg shook his head again. "I am the lead wizard of the
Directorate," he answered. "And I am not in the habit of dealing with
pickpockets. Especially young ones."

"Can you cure 'Becca's clubfoot?" Marcus asked. "For as long as I
can remember, it has been her dream to come into your Chamber of
Supplication and request an audience for your help. If you cure her, I'll
even let you keep the bags of kisa."

"As I remember, you no longer have the money," Wigg answered.
"It rests with us now. But leave it to you to bargain with something you
don't have. However, I did notice Rebecca's foot. If it is within our
powers to help, we will. But right now I want you to go, Marcus. We
have urgent business to attend to." Wigg then nodded to the Minion,
and Marcus was escorted from the room.

"I'm assuming our urgent business is now with Grizelda," Faegan
said.

"Indeed," Wigg answered. "And it should prove most interesting."

The three of them stood from the table and headed for the Redoubt.

*O*n the way Tristan requested that they go by the Great Hall, the
room into which Faegan's warp and Krassus' destructive beams of
light had been tossed. He was very curious about how much damage had
been done. As they approached the room and walked in, the sight before
them was disheartening, to say the least.

Krassus' powerful light shards had caused the walls to crack and tumble in many places, and the ceiling was torn by a number of great, ragged
holes through which the encroaching night sky could be seen. Glass,
dust, and smashed furniture lay everywhere. A work party of male and
female Minions was already going about the business of trying to return
the room to its former glory, but that would take time, Tristan realized,
if it ever came about at all.

Wigg walked slowly through the rubble, bits of glass crunching beneath his boots. With a great sigh, he shook his head and turned back to
Faegan and the prince.

"Such a shame," he said. "But at the time it was all I could think of to contain the lights. Even then I had no way of knowing whether Krassus' enchantments might take the entire palace down. In a way, we were very lucky."

"The power behind his spell was great indeed," Faegan added thoughtfully. "And very cleverly wrought. Your solution worked. Had the shards impacted anything softer than stone, the results would have been catastrophic." After a last look around, the three of them finally proceeded to the Redoubt.

As they came to stand before the doors, Faegan called the craft and unlocked them. Inside, Grizelda was still trapped within the azure wizard's warp. When she saw them enter, her lips turned up into a sneer.

Tristan looked at the herbmistress. She had changed little since that day on Krassus' flagship. He took in the long, dry, gray hair that hung haphazardly down around her weather-beaten face; her long, hooked nose; and the tattered, dirty brown robe wrapped around the gaunt body. She glared back at the prince with venom in her eyes.

"Good evening," Tristan said politely. "I hope you find the accommodations to your liking. At least here we don't force anyone to row. But should you prove uncooperative, I'm sure something like it could be arranged."

"So you escaped after all." Grizelda sneered. "My compliments. But your capture of me won't do you any good, Chosen One. I will never give up the things you so desperately need to know. I have a new lord now, and I won't betray him. Your days are numbered, and are dwindling rapidly. Soon I shall be free again, and *you* are in wizards' warps." To emphasize her point, she spat wetly against the inside of her cage.

"Your manners leave something to be desired," Tristan answered back. He turned around to face the wizards for a moment. "Charming, isn't she?"

Faegan and Wigg came the short distance to Tristan's side. "Is Krassus holding Wulfgar prisoner at the Citadel?" Faegan asked her bluntly. "Has the lost brother of the Chosen Ones been turned to the Vagaries?"

Grizelda smiled again. "That much I will answer, because of the joy I shall feel when I see the looks on your faces. Besides, it does not matter, for you can never stop him now." Obviously relishing her next words, she paused for a moment.

"You are quite wrong in assuming that Wulfgar is a prisoner of the Citadel," she answered at last. "By now he is most certainly its master— as well as the master of all the demonslavers and the other creatures of the Vagaries that have been newly conjured for his use." Raising one of her long, thin arms, she pointed an accusatory finger at the three of them.

"Blasphemers!" she whispered ominously. "Would-be destroyers of the sacred side of the craft! You can never defeat Wulfgar, for he already possesses powers that you could only dream of! He will soon set things right, just as they should have been eons ago. Things have been set into motion that you, in your feeble, exclusive practice of the Vigors, couldn't possibly begin to understand. Things that even Nicholas himself left undone. Wulfgar is coming for you, of that you may be assured. And no power on earth can stop him."

"Why is it that you follow the Vagaries?" Wigg asked.

Grizelda smiled. "You are familiar with the concept of Forestallments?"

Wigg nodded.

"Krassus imbued my partial signature with the Forestallments that finally brought my blood and mind to the light," she answered proudly. "Just as I am sure he has also done for Wulfgar by now. And Wulfgar may do the same for you." Pausing, she smiled again. "Assuming he doesn't kill you outright, of course."

She looked at the prince, and her smile widened. "It seems we shall soon see whether endowed blood is truly thicker than water."

"Who was the Harlequin?" Tristan asked. "I had never seen him before."

"Merely an unendowed servant of Krassus'," Grizelda replied. "He had his uses, but was of no real consequence. In truth, I cannot say I am sorry he is dead."

"What purposes do the Scrolls of the Ancients serve?" Wigg asked urgently.

Grizelda shook her head adamantly. Then she smiled again and made a clucking sound with her tongue. "Clearly, you haven't been listening," she answered. "No more questions."

Wigg looked over at Faegan.

"Would you like to do the honors, or should I?" Faegan asked.

"I will," Wigg answered. "Because she is only of partial blood, it shouldn't prove too difficult."

The lead wizard walked closer to the gleaming cage. As he did the herbmistress' eyes widened, and she scrabbled toward the back of the cube.

Wigg closed his eyes and began to call the craft. Tristan recognized what the lead wizard was doing: He was employing his powers to probe her mind, in an attempt to glean the answers to their many questions. Fascinated, Tristan watched the process unfold. As Grizelda felt the power of the wizard's consciousness entering her own, a look of horror crossed her face. And then, somehow, things started to go terribly wrong.

Placing her hands on either side of her head, she screamed. On hearing her cry out, Wigg opened his eyes and immediately ceased the spell. But by then it was already too late. Tristan watched in horror as the herbmistress shook her head violently and screamed again, insanely. He couldn't believe his eyes.

Her face was beginning to melt away.

Tristan gasped. As Grizelda bent over in exquisite agony, the skin ran from her face in steaming rivulets to reveal the barren, white skull beneath. Her green eyes drooled their way out of the sockets and flowed down what was left of her cheeks. Dead, she collapsed to the floor of the warp. Then her blood started to run from the remains of her mouth, ears, and empty eye sockets, to gather in steaming pools on the floor of the cube.

The blood rushed from Wigg's face. Stunned, he took a halting, tentative step toward the cube. "What have I done?" he gasped. "What in the name of the Afterlife just happened?"

Wheeling his chair closer, Faegan looked carefully down at the roiling blood, and then examined the rest of what used to be Krassus' herbmistress. Apparently satisfied, he wheeled his chair back a bit and looked up at Wigg.

"It wasn't your fault," he said. "This would have happened no matter which one of us had employed our gifts on her."

"What do you mean?" Tristan asked.

"I suspect that this was yet another of Krassus' safeguards, designed to keep us from getting too close to the truth," he answered. "Do you see how her blood steams? She admitted that Krassus laid a Forestallment into her signature to bring her to the Vagaries. I now think he gave her another one, as well—one specially designed to make her blood boil the moment her mind was invaded. Particularly the blood that was collected in her brain—the very seat of the answers we needed so badly, but will now never possess." Pausing for a moment, he thought to himself.

"How clever," he added softly. "The Tome makes mention of such blood-boiling devices of the craft, but I am not adept at them. Had I been, I might have been able to stop this. But even then, I doubt that what would have been left over could have been much good to us."

Tristan finally tore his eyes away from the horror in the cube and looked at the wizards. "Krassus has been ahead of us every step of the way, hasn't he?" he asked sadly.

Placing his hands into the opposite sleeves of his robe, the lead wizard nodded slowly. "And if Grizelda was telling the truth, then Wulfgar is now of the Vagaries, and returning to Eutracia with his demonslavers."

"Do you believe what she said?" Tristan asked anxiously.

With a deep sigh, Wigg nodded. "I believe her because it's too dangerous not to."

Saying nothing more, all three looked at one another. Then they made their way out of the Archives and back to the palace above.

There were plans to be made, and they were clearly running out of time.

CHAPTER

Sixty

Standing atop a grassy knoll, Tristan gazed out over the Cavalon Delta and the sea beyond. The wind was high again, just as it had been for the last seven days. A contingent of Minion warriors led by the ever-faithful Ox stood some distance away by the litter that had carried Tristan here, waiting obediently in the midday sun.

The Minion fleet had arrived four days earlier with the captured pirate vessels in tow, and all of them were now anchored offshore. More than four hundred ships—some long, narrow, and built for speed, and others wide and slow, but made for carrying heavy loads—lurched gently up and down against their moorings. All of the red banners that had once graced the pirate ships' mainmasts had now been removed, and the ships had all been repaired.

For her part Tyranny had not been content simply to stand by at the palace, like some dainty lady-in-waiting. Three days of uselessly prowling the rooms and grounds had been quite enough for her, despite finding herself immersed in their relative luxury. Tristan smiled. It seemed that no matter how much Tyranny hated traveling by Minion litter, the wonders of the palace had clearly been no match for the constant, intoxicating lure of the sea. Scars had, of course, accompanied her here.

Tristan had been here for the last three days as well. He had brought with him not only the kisa he had promised Tyranny, but also the letters of marque the lead wizard had prepared, both of which were now safely aboard the frigate she had chosen as her personal flagship.

In truth, Tristan had been glad to come here, for there had been little for him to do in Tammerland. With Grizelda and the Harlequin dead and Marcus already questioned, there was no one left to interrogate. Since Wigg, Faegan, and Celeste were the only three among them who could read Old Eutracian, they had vanished into seclusion in the depths of the Redoubt in order to attempt to unravel the mysteries of the Scrolls of the Ancients. They were all desperate to discover the purpose it served, and why Wulfgar was on the way with his demonslaver fleet.

As he looked out over Tyranny's fleet, Tristan smiled. The mainsails of the twelve frigates she had chosen now carried a bright red image of the Paragon painted squarely in their centers. In addition, each also flew his blue-and-gold battle flag high atop its mainmast.

He took a deep breath of sea air and knew he would miss being out there again. A part of him longed simply to cast away his responsibilities and go with her and Scars. The sea had quickly become a part of his blood, and he had greatly enjoyed the freedom and sense of adventure that had come with it.

Looking down the knoll, he saw Tyranny and Scars approaching. As she came nearer, the privateer smiled.

"Traax told us we'd find you here," she said quietly as she turned to look out over the fleets. The breeze was having its way with her short, dark hair. "We'll be leaving soon," she said, her voice cracking a bit. "I want to clear the delta before the evening winds abate."

"I understand," Tristan answered quietly.

There was a genuine look of both sadness and admiration in Scars' eyes as he held out one of his huge, meaty paws. "It has been a pleasure," he said sincerely.

Taking the giant's hand, Tristan gripped it firmly. "And for me," he said. Then he smiled. "If you come across any more demonslavers, twist a couple of them apart for me, will you?"

Smiling, Scars nodded back. Then he turned and walked slowly back toward the shore, where Tyranny's personal skiff lay waiting.

"Have you picked out a name for your new flagship?" Tristan asked her.

"Yes," she answered. "She is now the *Reprisal*. Appropriate, don't you think?"

Looking down to the sea, Tristan's eyes finally found the ship. She was tall and proud, just like her new captain, and his battle flag snapped back and forth atop her mainmast.

"Yes," he answered softly. "Yes, I do. Where will you go first?"

"Farpoint. It is a short sail from here. There we will release the slaves and hire the additional crew we need to man the ships properly. It shouldn't take long. Then it will be on to the open sea to search again for my brother and begin patrolling for you and your wizards. Whatever demonslavers or remaining pirates we run across we will do our best to make short work of, I promise you." Then she looked down at the ground and began using the toe of one boot to push some grass back and forth, as if she suddenly needed something to do.

"She's lovely, Tristan," she said softly, as if it was suddenly difficult for her to get the words out. "Celeste is a very lucky woman."

Not quite knowing what to say, Tristan nodded.

Then Tyranny smiled again, and looked back up. "But this isn't good-bye forever, you know," she added. "You can't get rid of me that easily. I still have to come back to the palace every three months to split the booty and give you my report, remember? So it seems I'll still occasionally be in your hair. At least for a while, anyway."

Then she came closer, looked deeply into his eyes, and gave him a soft, slow kiss on one cheek.

"Farewell, Chosen One," she said softly. "I shall always remember you." Saying nothing more, she turned and followed Scars to the shore.

Tristan stood on the knoll and watched as they climbed into the skiff, and the giant first mate rowed them out. Shortly thereafter, the freshly painted sails of the *Reprisal* snapped open, and she gracefully moved away from the delta. The eleven others in the newly formed fleet followed suit, as one by one they heeled southeast, toward Farpoint. Slowly the Paragon image on their sails shrank, until they finally crept over the horizon and were gone.

*B*y the time the Minions returned him to Tammerland, night had fallen. Tristan walked from the courtyard into the palace and directly down into the Redoubt. Eventually he found himself standing before the doors of the Hall of Blood Records.

Just before Tristan had departed for the coast, Wigg and Faegan had mentioned that they were going to enchant all of the doors in the Redoubt to temporarily open without the use of the craft, so that Celeste might be able to come and go among these chambers more freely, without out a wizard present. They had also made mention of the fact that they would do the same for the thousands of drawers containing the blood signature records, should they need someone to fetch one or more of the documents for them. Time was precious, and the wizards were striving to be as efficient as they could.

Hoping that the two mystics had been true to their word—but also that he would not find them here working—Tristan grasped one of the gold doorknobs and gave it a turn. The massive mahogany doors obediently parted, and he walked in. There was no one there.

As he had expected, all of the oil lamps in the great room were burning. Looking over to one side, he found what it was he had come to see: the Tome of the Paragon.

The massive, gilt-edged, white leather book lay open on its pedestal, the special light in the ceiling shining down on it as always. As he ran his hand lovingly over the ancient, wrinkled pages, he tried both to understand everything that had happened to him, and to beat back the disappointment he felt in his heart. The beautifully penned words in Old Eutracian stared back up at him uselessly, their meaning completely hidden from his mind.

He had, of course, known he wouldn't be able to read it without wearing the Paragon around his neck; that was not why he had come. But for some reason he had suddenly felt an unexplainable, irresistible urge to be near the great book. And as he stood there looking down at it, he realized that this was the first time he had ever been truly alone with it.

He finally took his eyes from the Tome and looked over to the many long, flat drawers that held the blood signatures. After staring at them for several quiet moments, he decided to give it a try.

"Prince Tristan of the House of Galland," he said loudly, much the same way he had heard Wigg and Faegan do several times before. At first he felt immensely foolish, speaking out alone into the room this way. Foolish, that was, until one of the drawers obediently opened and a sheet of parchment rose from it, to float over and land on the nearby meeting table. Tristan sat down in front of it.

Taking a deep breath, he looked at the azure signature on the page. It was the one made most recently, when Wigg and Faegan had been trying to determine whether Nicholas had indeed been Tristan's son. He immediately recognized the soft, fluid lines at the top that had come from his mother Morganna, and the harder, sharper lines at the bottom from the blood of his father, Nicholas I. But no one else in the world possessed a signature that was azure.

Except for Nicholas, he reminded himself. And he is dead. As Tristan continued to regard the swirling, azure lines, the feelings of disdain for his blood surfaced again.

Then he heard the door hinges creak a bit, and he turned to look. Wigg stood quietly in the door frame. There was no telling how long he had been there.

"Tristan," he said gently. "Are you all right?"

The prince nodded.

"I was walking by and saw the open door," Wigg went on as he came to sit next to him. He looked down at the parchment on the table. "What are you doing here all by yourself?"

As Tristan turned to look at him, Wigg could see the concern in his eyes. "There are things you need to know," the prince said softly. "I've changed, Wigg. And I have to tell someone."

"I'm listening," Wigg answered compassionately.

"Part of it is about my azure blood," Tristan said quietly. "I have come to hate it. Not only can my enemies immediately recognize me by it, but it also makes me feel distinctly isolated from the rest of the world. And the fact that it is azure keeps you and Faegan from training me, and also from allowing me to wear the Paragon, so that I might finally read the Tome. And as long as that is the case, my destiny can never be fulfilled. Nor can that of my nation." He rubbed his brow in frustration.

"I don't blame the two of you for not training me," he went on softly. "How could I? But sometimes my blood makes me feel like an outcast, especially when I am among the ones I love the most. I'm not angry that my blood is endowed. I still cherish that fact with all my heart. And my desire, my *need* to learn the craft burns as hotly within me as ever. But if I don't soon find a way to return my blood to what it once was, sometimes I think I'll go mad." Leaning back in his chair, he looked to the ceiling. He suddenly realized that simply telling all of this to someone he cared about had made him feel a bit better.

"I understand," Wigg said. "I can see it in you. We all can. But there simply hasn't been time to properly search for the solution to your problem. And to tell you the truth, we don't really know how. But I know your answer is out there, somewhere. And together, one day we will find it. But just now I must tell you that we have far greater concerns to worry about."

Tristan placed his forearms on the table and looked into the wizard's eyes. "You're talking about the Scroll of the Vigors, aren't you?" he asked. "What have you learned?"

Wigg's face darkened. "We would prefer to inform everyone at once, after we are sure," he answered. "As you know, during her time in the caves, Celeste was forced by Ragnar to learn Old Eutracian. We will never know what use for that he had planned—but it is without a doubt the single good to come out of those years of torture. Anyway, she, Faegan, and I have been deciphering the scroll for a week now, and we have never seen anything like it. It is absolutely amazing. It opens up entire new vistas of the craft that had been previously closed to us. But please be patient for just a bit longer. We hope that by tomorrow's dawn, we will be sure. And if what we suspect is true, then what we have found in the scroll represents the greatest peril we have ever faced." A short silence followed as Tristan looked down at the azure signature again and considered the import of the wizard's words.

"You intimated that there was more than one thing you wished to discuss," the lead wizard said. "What is it?"

As Tristan looked into Wigg's aquamarine eyes, he knew that once it had been said there would be no going back. But he also knew in his heart that he had to be truthful. He closed his eyes for a moment, then opened them again.

"I love your daughter," he said softly, irrevocably. "Forgive me, Wigg, but I do."

Wigg smiled. "I know," he answered gently.

"You do?"

"Of course. Everyone in the palace knows. They also know how she feels about you. Only a fool could miss the way the two of you look at each another."

"I'm sorry," Tristan replied carefully, not knowing exactly what to say. "I know how damaged she was. And I stayed away, because I wanted to respect that. But she tells me she is much better now. I'm glad for her, and I've never seen her so vibrant and alive. But I also know how little time the two of you have had to come to know each other, and I didn't want to intrude on that, either." Pausing, he looked down at his hands. "Despite how much I cared, being with her seemed impossible. For so many reasons.

"Still, I couldn't help but love her," he went on. "When I first saw her that night on the cliffs, the feeling swept over me like a storm, and it simply won't go away."

Wigg looked over thoughtfully at the man he loved so much. From the time he had watched Tristan come into the world, he had done everything in his power to prepare him for the teachings he would eventually impart into his blood, and for the destiny the prince was chosen to fulfill. But not even the lead wizard could have foreseen the turmoil and loss that would accompany Tristan and Shailiha on their unexpectedly dangerous journey to enlightenment. And now, in the midst of it all, had come Celeste. Reaching out, Wigg put a hand on Tristan's shoulder.

"You have my blessing, if that's what you're asking for," he said quietly. "Nothing would make me happier than to see the two of you together. And I mean that. She loves you, Tristan. And with an ardor I have seldom seen over the course of my three centuries."

As Tristan looked up, Wigg could see a tear in his eye. Realizing that the same thing was about to happen to him as well, the wizard promptly stood, cleared his throat, and busily rearranged his robes.

"Now then," he said, his wizardly demeanor apparently having retuned, "I must get back to Faegan and Celeste. They'll be wondering where I've been." One eyebrow came up. "And you know how Faegan can be."

As Wigg turned to go, Tristan reached out and gently took the wizard by one arm. "Thank you," he said softly.

"There is no reason to thank me," Wigg answered back. "In truth, I doubt there is any power on earth that could keep the two of you apart. All I ask is that you continue to treat her well."

"I will," the prince answered back, his voice cracking a bit.

With a final, comforting smile, Wigg left the room.

His mind awash with the memories of everything he had been through and thoughts of all that might still lie ahead, Tristan remained there in silence for some time before he finally ordered the parchment back to its drawer. Suddenly exhausted, he left the room and began the long walk to his chambers.

Very soon now, he knew, he and the others would hear what the wizards had to say about the Scrolls of the Ancients.

CHAPTER

Sixty-one

From his place in the bow of his warship, Wulfgar watched and listened as the oncoming waves split noisily against the prow. Looking higher out over the breadth of the nighttime sea he felt his long, sandy hair sway behind his back in the wind, in time with the ceaseless rocking of the ship.

The voyage of the last seven days had been uneventful, and the cold winds had remained brisk, allowing his fleet to make good time. The screechlings and sea slitherers had kept pace well, following dutifully behind in the wake of his vast armada. Demonslavers prowled the decks, the ships' running lamps pointing up their lifeless white skin. As the ship swayed beneath him, Wulfgar took a deep breath of the crisp sea air.

Looking at the reflections of the rose-colored moons in the ever-surging waves, his thoughts turned back to Serena and Krassus. He had no doubt that the diseased wizard was dead. Watch for the lightning and the wind, he had told Serena. Then shall you know that he has truly expired. When it happens, order a contingent of slavers to lay his body in a small skiff and set it ablaze as they push it out to sea. Wulfgar and Serena owed everything to Krassus, and he deserved to be well remembered. Then Wulfgar's thoughts drifted to his beautiful new queen.

He loved her deeply, and missed her as he missed nothing else in the world. Since she had been turned to the Vagaries, she had never been away from his side until now. He missed how she looked, how she smelled, and the supple touch of her skin. He wanted to hold her in his strong arms and take her over and over again, making her beg, then gasp, and finally cry out in joy, just as she always did. And already he missed the daughter she carried, even though her pregnancy was still without outer evidence. He would finish Nicholas' work quickly, and return home to the Citadel in triumph.

Nicholas, he thought. The nephew he had never seen. What a magnificent being he must have been! How he would have loved meeting him, conversing with him, planning with him. Part of Wulfgar could even understand how Krassus had been so willing, almost eager, in fact, to die and go to him, even though it had been Nicholas himself who had made it so.

But Nicholas' plans lived on—first in the blood of Krassus, and now in Wulfgar's. He would reign supreme, he swore. The practitioners of the Vigors would soon know the exquisite sting of their defeat, as would the entire world.

Then the wind stopped completely, and he knew. Even though there was no land in sight, Wulfgar's fleet had arrived at the first of their destinations. And the new lord of the Vagaries was prepared.

Wulfgar turned to his first mate. "Furl the sails, tie off the wheel, and signal that the same be done to every other ship in the fleet," he ordered. "There are to be absolutely no exceptions. Have the forty remaining *Talis* slaves brought up out of the hold." Pausing, he smiled. "We are about to have guests."

With a nod, the first mate went off to perform his duties.

Then the fog rolled in over the night sea from seemingly nowhere and everywhere, quickly engulfing the entire fleet. Thick and gray, it clung to his clothes and his skin. With the arrival of the fog, the temperature plummeted, and soon Wulfgar could see his breath.

The fog coalesced into hundreds of great columns that rose up out of the sea. And then, just as Krassus had told him would happen, the columns morphed into giant hands, each pair of them grasping a ship by the opposite ends. All his ships were thus caught. The demonslavers looked up in awe but remained disciplined, ready to carry out any commands their master might order.

Wulfgar stood in sheer joy at this example of the Vagaries. To his enlightened mind it was not only magnificent, but was also something to take advantage of—and he would be the first being in the history of the world to do so.

Turning to look down the deck, Wulfgar saw that the forty *Talis* slaves had been brought topside. They stood in four neat lines of ten each, shivering from both the cold and their sense of foreboding.

As Wulfgar expected, the sea around the fleet began to bubble and roil, as if something was trying to come to the top. Then faces began to form on the surface of the ocean. They were the Necrophagians—the endowed, ages-old Eaters of the Dead.

And I am the only living being who both truly knows what they are and can also call them into his service, Wulfgar thought as he greedily looked over the side of the ship.

He stared at the faces. There seemed to be hundreds of them, their flesh a horrible mixture of sea green and dark red, streaked with ancient wrinkles and boils. Where eyes and mouths should have been there were only dark, empty holes. And then came the expected demand.

"Pay us our bounty, or we shall take both your bodies and your ships," the faces whispered in the strangest of voices. There were many speaking at once in complete conformity, yet so softly that they could barely be heard.

The new lord of the Vagaries knew full well that the Necrophagians were referring to the forty cowering slaves on deck. To allow safe passage across the sea, the Eaters of the Dead were demanding to be fed. It was known as the bargain of tenfold times four—the pact made with them by Failee, first mistress of the Coven, as she tried to save her life and the lives of her sisters after having been banished by the Directorate of Wizards more than three centuries before. But this time, Wulfgar knew, things would be different.

Leaning over the side of the vessel, Wulfgar raised his arms. "Eaters of the Dead!" he shouted out over the sea. "I honor you, and come prepared to pay your bounty! Or you may choose a different path this day. I suggest that a new bargain be struck—one that will release you from your ages-old bondage and allow you to follow me!"

A deathly silence followed as Wulfgar's entire fleet waited, dead in the water. Finally, the eerie whispering came again.

"Who are you to bargain with us?" came the voices. "And who are you to speak of our freedom? Even Failee, the one with whom we struck our agreement so long ago, did not possess such power. No one can free us of our torment except he or she who shall eventually command the Scroll of the Vagaries."

"I am that man," Wulfgar replied calmly. "I am also the only living being in the world who knows who you truly are, and why you were condemned to this purgatory in the sea. I and the Heretics of the Guild need you now, and your penance can finally be over, should you choose. But first you must follow me, and serve me in my mission." Silence reigned again.

"Do you mean to say that the Scrolls of the Ancients have finally been loosed upon the world?" the voices asked, their combined tones even more hushed this time.

"Yes," Wulfgar replied, determined to stand his ground.

"We require proof," the voices replied. "It is said that he or she who would eventually command the sacred Scroll of the Vagaries would have the proof of it in his blood. Show us your proof now, or be devoured for wasting our time. If you are not that person, we tire of your foolishness."

Smiling, Wulfgar narrowed his eyes and called on the craft. Raising his arms, he levitated himself up and over the warship's gunwales and came to hover only inches above the sea, directly over the horrific faces in the water. Extending his right arm, he turned up his wrist and caused an incision to form. A single drop of red blood dripped from the wound and hovered in the air.

Almost immediately Wulfgar's blood signature began to form. Raising his arms, he caused it to increase in size until it seemed to take up the entire night sky. Hundreds of Forestallments could be seen branching away from the main body of the signature, but there was one among them that clearly stood out, its massive length and width overshadowing all of the others. The magnificent Forestallment seemed to surge with life, as if impatient to fulfill its destiny.

This was the Forestallment Krassus and the consuls had worked so long and hard to find in the depths of the scroll—the same one Wulfgar would soon unleash upon his unsuspecting enemies.

"What say you now, Eaters of the Dead?" Wulfgar asked calmly.

"Are you truly the *Enseterat*?" the voices asked reverently. "Has he finally come to us?"

"He who was to have been the first *Enseterat* is now dead," Wulfgar answered. "He was the son of the Chosen One. I am the brother of the Chosen Ones, and have inherited both the mantle and the glorious, unfinished work of the *Enseterat*."

"What would you have us do in return for our freedom, *Enseterat*?" the voices asked.

For several long moments, Wulfgar explained his mission and the rewards he would give them for traveling in his service. Another long silence followed.

"We will serve you, *Enseterat*," the Necrophagians finally whispered with one voice.

Wulfgar turned to look over at the forty cowering, shivering slaves. "Will you be requiring the offering I brought?" he asked.

"That will not be necessary this time," they whispered back. "For we now have a new master, and where we are going, there shall be many such offerings. If we succeed, we shall no longer need them. And if you fail we shall soon consume all that you are, in any event."

"Very well," Wulfgar answered. Raising his arms again, he levitated himself back aboard.

With the new bargain struck, the hundreds of foggy hands released the ships, and the temperature returned to normal. Wulfgar ordered the fleet's sails unfurled. They snapped open to the easterlies and began moving the ships forward. The terrified slaves were ordered chained below-decks once again.

As the fleet plowed through the sea, the screechlings, the slitherers, and the Eaters of the Dead, all under the command of the *Enseterat,* followed dutifully behind in its wake. Wulfgar gazed west, toward the sacred home of his prize.

Everything was going according to plan.

Sixty-two

After sleeping like the dead, Tristan opened his balcony doors to find that a beautiful day had arrived. While bathing and dressing, he realized how hungry he was—not only for a good breakfast from the gnome wives, but for the company of Celeste, as well. He was walking down a hallway contemplating a plan to find her after breakfast when he turned a corner and literally bumped into her, along with Abbey and Shailiha. Celeste was dressed in shiny black knee boots, black riding breeches, a white, low-cut blouse, and black riding gloves. She was holding a basket. Shailiha was pushing Morganna's ornate carriage. Caprice circled lazily overhead, in the spacious heights of the hallway. All three women smiled at him as if they all knew something that he did not. The moment he looked into their faces, he knew what it was.

Celeste had told her friends about the change in her relationship with him. One more thing for Shailiha to tease him about. Things would never be the same.

Celeste came closer and gave him a kiss on the cheek. The other two women grinned. Tristan blushed.

"I knew we'd find you on the way to the kitchens," Celeste said happily. She held up the basket. "So I took the liberty of putting some breakfast together for us."

Tristan's eyebrows went up. "Again? You're going to make me fat. Besides, I'm on my way to see the wizards. I want to know what they have discovered about the scroll."

"Yes, my prince, breakfast *again*," Celeste growled back comically, giving him her best look of feigned ferocity. "But a picnic this time. I thought we could go for a ride." Then her face darkened a bit.

"In truth, this was Father's and Faegan's idea," she admitted. "They knew you would be demanding answers as soon as you awakened, and they asked me to keep you occupied for a bit. They have released me from my translation duties, but they said that they would like to see us all on the balcony of your late father's quarters at midday. That's all I know."

"My father's balcony?" he asked, baffled. "Why in the world would they want to meet us there?"

Shailiha shrugged. "We don't know. But they are in a very somber mood—of that there is no doubt. I suggest the two of you get going. Be back by midday at the latest."

Tristan never had liked having his day arranged for him by others. But he *had* wanted to see Celeste, and his stomach was growling. Besides, if the wizards wouldn't see him, they wouldn't see him; that would be all there was to it.

Then he remembered Marcus and Rebecca. "What about the two children?" he asked. "Where are they?"

"They're in the combined company of Shawna the Short and a Minion overseer," Abbey told him with a quick laugh. "Rebecca is so sweet. But Marcus has proven to be quite a handful. He has already tried to make off with some of the palace silver. But you know Shawna. She put him back in his place quickly. I think he's more frightened of her than he is of the Minions." She smiled. "I don't think Marcus likes it here very much."

Sighing, Tristan gave Abbey a little nod of acknowledgment. Then he turned to Celeste. "Well, I suppose if we're going to go, then we should do so," he said. He relieved her of the basket and took one of her arms into his. Whatever she had packed smelled wonderful, and his stomach growled again.

After pursing his lips at Shailiha, he gave a patronizingly deep bow to his sister and the herbmistress and began guiding Celeste down the halls of the palace. Head high, he pretended he didn't see the wide grins on Shailiha's and Abbey's faces.

The walk to the stables was short and uneventful. Geldon was there as usual, tending to the horses. He saddled a bay mare for Celeste, while Tristan, his face somber, began a rather sad, quiet search for a new mount. When Geldon made a move to help him, Celeste touched the dwarf's arm and placed one finger over her lips. Sighing, Geldon nodded. Celeste was right, he realized. This was something Tristan would want to do—need to do—on his own.

Finally selecting a sturdy tan stallion, Tristan glumly avoided the familiar saddle and bridle he had always used on Pilgrim, and chose others instead. As he turned with the reins in one hand, he saw Celeste tying the basket to the back of her saddle. He looked at her quizzically.

"What's going to keep everything from breaking?" he asked as he mounted. "Or at the very least getting all mixed up?"

Smiling, Celeste gave him a wink. "Father enchanted the containers," she told him. Placing one boot into a stirrup, she easily mounted her horse, then grinned at him. "Want to race?"

Without waiting for an answer, she wheeled her mare around and galloped out of the barn, her red hair flying. Laughing out loud, Tristan spurred his stallion and went after her.

Tristan had never seen Celeste ride, and he was impressed by how confidently she sat her horse. She galloped hard across the stable yard and the palace grounds, then pushed her mare noisily up and over the drawbridge. Several Minion warriors gaped at her as she went by. Then came another quick, skidding left, and she went tearing off into the countryside, charging away so fast she nearly lost him.

Tristan's stallion was not as quick as Pilgrim; in truth, few had ever been. But the horse was surefooted, and it felt good to Tristan to be away from the troubles of the palace and feel the wind hitting his face.

Celeste pointed her mare across an open meadow, Tristan following. The tall grass teased the bottoms of their stirrups, and they left two lanes of crushed grasses in their wake. Then she leapt directly over a section of broken rail fence, splashed unerringly across a small stream, and ran along its opposite bank for a time. As she approached another bend in the river, she stopped, her mare panting hard.

Tristan pulled up next to her. Her chest heaving, Celeste leaned one arm down on the pommel of her saddle, looked at him, and laughed lightly.

Jumping down, Tristan held her reins as Celeste dismounted. She untied the basket from her saddle, and he walked the two panting horses to the stream, allowing them to drink a small sip of water. Later, when they'd cooled down, he'd allow them to drink their fill. After tying the horses to two trees that were a good distance apart, he walked back to Celeste. By then she had removed her gloves, laid out a plaid blanket, and set out the food.

Tristan removed his weapons, tossed them to the ground, and sat down on his heels next to her. He saw spotted quail eggs again—hard-boiled this time—fresh fruit, cheese, dark bread, and what looked like unfermented mintberry juice.

He took an egg and began to peel away its shell. As he did the morning breeze came up, the stream burbled, and they could hear the songs of the triad larks. Looking around at the idyllic scene, Tristan wished he could stay here with Celeste forever, with no wizards, magic, or enemies to interfere with their lives.

"You spoil me," he said quietly. "I could become quite used to this." He popped the tiny egg into his mouth.

"Good," she replied, as she handed him a cup of the light green juice. "Spoiling you is one of my favorite pastimes, you know. Besides, someone has to do it. You're still too thin from your time in captivity."

Seeing his face darken, she immediately regretted her remark. She reached out and touched his hand in apology. Silence passed between them for a time.

"It was awful, wasn't it?" she asked finally, softly.

Turning his face away for a moment, Tristan looked out over the meandering stream. "Yes," he replied simply. "It was. But I was one of the lucky few. I was saved. And what I suffered does not begin to compare with your treatment by Ragnar." Then he remained quiet for a bit longer.

"You were the one thing on my mind as the demonslaver whipped me, just before I passed out," he continued softly. "I will always carry these scars on my back. But I had vowed that I wouldn't scream, and I didn't. Without knowing it, you helped me accomplish that."

Celeste lay down on the blanket, her beautiful, dark red hair splayed out around her face. Tristan lay down on his side next to her, propped up on one elbow. He heard the wind rustle the tops of the trees, and he could smell the myrrh in her hair.

Reaching up, she toyed briefly with the laces of his vest. "What is going to happen to us?" she asked. "Do you really believe Wulfgar is coming with his demonslavers?"

"I don't know what to believe about a brother I have never met," he answered thoughtfully. "Much less one who has supposedly been turned to the Vagaries. But I do know one thing: If there is a way out of our troubles, your father and Faegan are the ones to find it. You helped them with the translation; is there anything about the scroll that you can tell me?"

"I wish I could," she answered sadly. "But the truth is that the translations I did for them were nothing but gibberish to me. They were almost exclusively calculations of the craft. I couldn't understand them. My translations only made their more important work go faster. I not only fear whatever it is they might tell us today, but I am also at a complete loss as to what it might be."

He was about to tell her of his conversation with her father the previous night when Celeste placed her fingertips gently across his lips. As she looked up at him, her face slowly changed. She placed one palm alongside his cheek, and the lids of her sapphire eyes lowered slightly.

Her breathing came a bit harder. Her lips parted as her eyes searched his face. Tristan's heart beat faster. He was sure he had never seen such a beautiful woman in his life.

Celeste raised up a bit and kissed him on the lips. As she did, one hand slid down and touched him.

"Please," she asked him softly.

Leaning gently over her, Tristan ran one hand into her thick hair and gazed sharply into her wide, blue eyes. "Are you sure?" he asked.

"More so of this than anything else in my life," she answered. Her mind made up, a look of needful surrender crossed her face.

"Please, Tristan . . . my love . . . please teach my desire to fly . . . to fly on the wings that you alone bring . . ."

Leaning down closer, he touched his lips to hers.

The wind wafted through the trees, and the birds sang.

*L*ater, Tristan awakened to find the plaid blanket covering them both. Celeste's naked body felt warm as she slumbered beside him with her head on his shoulder. What had passed between them had been more wonderful than he could ever have imagined.

It was then that he first noticed the soft, azure glow of the craft quietly surrounding them. But it was gone before he could really focus on it. Perhaps he had imagined it, he thought sleepily. It must just have been a dream.

He closed his eyes and felt himself begin to drift off again.

CHAPTER

Sixty-three

By the time Tristan and Celeste had returned to the palace and found their way to the late king's quarters, everyone else who had been asked to attend was already there. As the prince walked across the rooms, a profound sense of sadness went through him. He had not visited these chambers in a long time, and part of him—the part that still cried over what he had been forced to do to his father—did not wish to be here now.

As he approached, Tristan could see that the wizards had arranged to have a large meeting table and matching high-backed chairs placed out on the balcony. The Scroll of the Vigors sat on the table, its golden center rod and engraved middle band gleaming in the midday sun. Another table sat nearby holding an abundance of tea and scones, telling the prince that they all might be here for some time. He took a seat, and Celeste sat next to him.

Looking around, he saw Wigg, Faegan, Abbey, Geldon, Traax, and Shailiha. Morganna's baby carriage sat by his sister's side, and the princess gently rolled it back and forth with one hand. For the life of him, Tristan couldn't imagine why they were meeting on his father's balcony. It was pleasant here, to be sure. But knowing the wizards as he did, he knew that couldn't be their reason.

Puzzled, Tristan was about to ask Wigg what was going on, but the lead wizard jumped in first, his face somber. Clearing his throat, Wigg placed his ancient hands flat on the tabletop and came straight to the point.

"It is my sad duty to inform you all that the danger we now face is the most grave in our history," he said quietly. Everyone around the table became quite still, eyes focused steadily on him.

"I will put this as simply as I know how," Wigg continued. "As we speak, Wulfgar, the lost half brother of Tristan and Shailiha, may be returning to Eutracia with an army of demonslavers. Faegan and I believe it is his intention to permanently destroy the Orb of the Vigors. In a matter of mere days, all we know and cherish may disappear from the face of the earth."

Stunned, Tristan sat back in his chair. He could clearly recall that day on the mountain not so long ago, when Wigg had called the two orbs to appear so that Tristan might view them for the first time. The Orb of the Vigors had been bright, shining, and golden, while the Orb of the Vagaries had been black, and literally dripping with the destructive energy of the dark side of the craft.

"But how could such a thing be made to occur?" he breathed across the table, scarcely able to get the words out. "And why?"

"The Scrolls of the Ancients make it possible," Faegan answered. "They're what this whole thing has been about from the beginning."

"Is that what the scrolls are meant to teach us?" Shailiha asked. "How to destroy the orbs?"

"That," Wigg answered, "and a good deal more. In many ways it is easier to tell you what the scrolls *cannot* show us, rather than what they can. In essence, the scroll before you holds the calculations for virtually every known Forestallment of the Vigors, just as we believe the scroll in Krassus' possession does for the Vagaries. By employing the calculations gleaned from the scrolls, one can identify any already existing Forestallment branch that shoots off from a person's blood signature. The Forestallment branches can now be 'mapped,' as it were. In addition, whoever is in possession of the scrolls can actually not only decipher the calculations required for any Forestallment he or she desires, but can also imbue the blood signature with it and activate it at any time of his choosing."

"But there is even more to the puzzle," Faegan said, leaning over the table. "The scroll also reveals the answers to many of the mysteries of the craft that have plagued us for centuries. In truth, we have only had enough time to scratch the surface of what the scroll may tell us. Reading the document is an amazing experience—like looking into the very souls of the Ones Who Came Before. We now believe it was they who wrote the Scroll of the Vigors, and the Heretics of the Guild who wrote the other. Neither side expected to use the information to destroy the orb that supported their side of the craft, of course. But by including the opposite formula in each one, it seems they could assure themselves of mutual mass destruction in their struggle against one another, should the need arise. Simply put, each scroll was meant to be both a safeguard and a weapon for future generations of the craft to protect themselves with, should its opposite ever be found and used against them."

"What do you mean by 'mysteries of the craft'?" Abbey asked.

"For example, we could never understand how Nicholas had circumvented the death enchantments of the consuls of the Redoubt," Wigg answered. "But now, after reading part of the scroll, we do. We believe the calculations for their reversal must be contained in the Scroll of the Vagaries. Nicholas imbued them into the consuls' blood, thereby allowing them to participate in the construction of the Gates of Dawn without violating their oaths and perishing. The Forestallments no doubt exist in their blood to this day, thereby allowing them to serve their new master Wulfgar on the isle of the Citadel."

"I'll give you yet another example," Faegan added. "I believe each of you is familiar with the phenomenon that accompanies the deaths of certain endowed individuals and creatures of the craft. Most of us have seen the lightning and sudden wind that accompanies these events, such as occurred with the deaths of the mistresses of the Coven. The Directorate had always believed these phenomena to be a way for those who had perished to signal their demise to those of their cause who might still live. We now believe we might have been wrong about this—that the atmospheric events might have something to do with only the death of one's blood, rather than the death of both the blood *and* the body. Forestallments are, of course, a part of one's endowed blood. But unlike endowed blood, which is present at birth, Forestallments are conjured and added later. Each is the physical embodiment of a spell—a very potent and complicated one. But I digress. The truth is that we have far greater problems to solve now."

"So Wulfgar wants to destroy the Orb of the Vigors," Tristan said, half to himself. "And that is why Krassus so badly wanted the Scroll of the Vagaries, isn't it? He needed it so that he could imbue Wulfgar's blood with the proper Forestallment, among others."

He looked up in horror at both of the wizards. "That's what this is really about, isn't it?" he asked. "That's what it has always been about."

"Yes," Wigg answered. "Had he survived, it now seems that Nicholas' plans were to have gone much farther than simply releasing the Heretics from the heavens. Do you remember how Krassus talked about wanting to carry on Nicholas' work, but we could never fathom what he meant by that? Well, now we think we know."

"But how can you be so sure that this is his mission?" Tristan countered. "With so many Forestallments recorded in the scrolls, how can you know that the destruction of the Orb of the Vigors is Wulfgar's intent, and not something else?"

"An excellent question," Wigg answered. "While Faegan and I must

admit that our conclusions are more educated guesswork than substanti-
ated fact, one thing stands out about the scroll that convinces us we are
right."

"And that is?" Celeste asked.

"Of all the calculations, one seems to rise head and shoulders above
the rest in its relative importance and complexity: the formula for the
destruction of the Orb of the Vagaries. We must surmise that the scroll
in Wulfgar's possession contains the formula to destroy the Orb of the
Vigors."

With all of this talk of Nicholas and the orbs, Tristan sensed a recent
memory trying to float to the surface. He knew it had to do with the day
he had visited the Caves of the Paragon, when Nicholas had not only revealed that he was Tristan's son, but also what his plans were. Finally
Tristan took a quick breath of realization and looked over at Faegan and
Wigg.

"You're not wrong," he said quietly to the table at large. "The destruction of the Orb of the Vigors is exactly what Wulfgar has in mind."

Wigg looked carefully at the prince. "And you are certain of this because . . ."

"Because Nicholas told me so himself, that day in the Caves when
he first revealed to me who he really was, and why he had been sent here
by the Heretics," Tristan answered. "He did not tell me of his orders to
Krassus should he perish, or of the existence of Wulfgar. Those intrica-
cies of his mission he must have wished to keep secret, should all else fail.
But he did tell me of his eventual plans for the orb."

Closing his eyes, Tristan did his best to recall Nicholas' words of that
day. As they came back to him, he spoke them aloud as best he could remember.

" '*After the return of the Heretics, we shall eliminate all the others of the
earth . . . Our world shall become one barren of all human life other than that
which is sufficiently gifted . . . Together we shall then destroy the Vigors and their
orb forever, leaving only the true, sublime teachings of the Vagaries that we have
so come to love . . .*' "

"The other half of Nicholas' mission," he murmured. Not only to
destroy the Orb of the Vigors, but also to kill anyone—other than the
consuls he was corrupting—with a right-leaning blood signature, as well!
But first Krassus needed two things, didn't he? He needed Wulfgar because of the quality of his blood and the fact that he has a severely left-
leaning signature. Wulfgar was the perfect choice because he would be a
far easier subject to turn than Shailiha or I, yet he still possesses the blood
of Morganna, the mother of the Chosen Ones. And Krassus also required the Scroll of the Vagaries to provide him with the calculations for

the Forestallments he needed to gift into Wulfgar's blood, the most important of which shall grant Wulfgar the ability to destroy the orb."

Wigg looked over to where Faegan was sitting, to see that his old friend's face had become a mask of grave concern. Then, sensing what the prince was feeling, he reached out compassionately and placed one hand on Tristan's shoulder. "From what you tell us, it seems we were right after all," he said softly.

"Indeed," Faegan replied. "This is one of the few times in more than three centuries that I can honestly say I am sorry my deductions have proven correct. But there is most certainly another reason why Wulfgar will come."

"And what is that?" Tristan asked, lifting his head.

"He will try to take the Scroll of the Vigors from us—if for no other reason than to keep us from gifting your blood signature with more Forestallments. The more power you gain, the greater the danger to him and to what he wishes to accomplish."

"And Grizelda and this Harlequin, whoever he was, were supposed to retrieve the scroll for him and take it to the Citadel," Wigg added soberly. "But they failed, and are both dead."

"What do these orbs look like?" Shailiha asked. "And what purpose do they serve? I have heard you speak of them before, but I don't really understand them."

"Nor do I," Celeste added. "What are they, exactly?"

"Magic is everywhere," Wigg answered. "Even though it cannot be seen. In this aspect it is very much like the air we breathe, constantly surrounding us but invisible. In truth, however, magic has substance and shape, as does the air. Let me be clear: I'm speaking of the craft itself, of what it *really* is. There is a true, interwoven consistency to its energy and its existence, and it can be literally seen, each of the two sides, both the Vigors and the Vagaries. This is the reason we asked you to meet us here on the balcony, rather than in the depths of the Redoubt. So we could show you this wondrous thing firsthand, that you might better understand what it is we must bend every effort to try to protect." Wigg then closed his eyes and raised his arms, as if in supplication.

The sky began to lighten. As it did, a gigantic glow began to coalesce before them in the air of the courtyard. Slowly it started to spin and turn on its axis. It was becoming a brilliant, golden orb, with offshoots here and there of the palest white radiating outward from its center. From time to time golden droplets of energy would trickle down from the revolving orb and fall to the courtyard, dissipating into nothingness. For the second time in his life, Tristan found himself looking in awe at the Orb of the Vigors.

Wigg raised his arms again, and a darker image began to form. As it grew in size to match the other orb, it too began to coalesce into an orb and spin, but rather than being beautiful and awe-inspiring, the dark orb gave off a distinctly menacing aura—frightening, even horrifying.

As they watched the dark orb grow to the size of the Orb of the Vigors, it began to try to push the other orb aside, as if attempting to make room for itself. It was as frightening as the Orb of the Vigors was beautiful. Droplets of dark energy dripped from its pitch-black, shining sides, and bright scratches of lightning shot through the ebony orb's center. The Orb of the Vagaries, Tristan thought. The dark side of the craft in all its ghastly splendor.

Completely entranced, the people at the table watched as the two great orbs began to move about the afternoon sky. They would slowly, repeatedly attract one another, as if somehow needful of each other. But then, just as they were about to touch, they would unexpectedly, violently repel one another, and the process would continue. In some ways it was almost a pitiful thing to watch, the never-ending attempts to join, only to be thrust apart, over and over again.

Wigg opened his eyes. "Each thing in nature has its opposite," he explained. "Male and female, light and dark. And so it goes through the entire scheme of the world as we know it. The two sides of the craft are no different. For as long as we have known of their existence they have been in this perpetual state of struggle with each other." Pausing, he looked around the table at the amazed faces.

"It is believed that the two orbs must never touch," he continued. "Should that happen, the result would be calamitous—a rent, or tear, if you will, in the fabric of each. If the tears were large enough, it is believed that their powers would be released, to join uncontrollably, and that such an occurrence would be the end of all we know. It is also believed that there are invisible corridors in the fabric of the craft that might one day be called upon to finally, safely join the orbs, and that until these corridors are traversed by one or more of the Chosen Ones, neither side of the craft, no matter how powerful it may seem to be individually, has even a smattering of the dynamism it would if properly joined with the other." Lifting his arms again, Wigg closed his eyes, and the two orbs began to dissipate, finally vanishing altogether.

"What will happen to the craft if Wulfgar is successful in destroying the Orb of the Vigors?" Abbey asked.

Reaching out for the cup of tea before him, Faegan thoughtfully took a sip and then replaced it on its saucer. "In truth we cannot be sure, for so many of the concepts of the craft we once thought to be inviolate now seem subject to review—such as our long-held theory that one side of the craft couldn't exist without the other, for example. But at the very least the Vigors would cease to exist. As will you, Wigg, Celeste, and myself, for our time enchantments are each supported by that side of the craft. Not a very happy prospect." He took another sip of the tea. "At the very least, the world would be plunged into the dark side of the craft, perhaps forever, with Wulfgar as its master."

Another thought occurred to Tristan. "Why can't we simply beat him to it?" he asked hopefully.

"I don't understand," Wigg said, his expression skeptical. "What are you talking about?"

"You believe that the scroll in our possession contains the calculations for the destruction of the Orb of the Vagaries, correct?"

"Yes."

"Then why can't we destroy the Orb of the Vagaries first, and render Wulfgar powerless? That would solve all of our problems, would it not?"

Wigg sighed. "We thought of that, and it is a very tempting proposition. But it wouldn't be wise. Assuming, of course, that such a situation is even possible."

"How so?"

"You're forgetting something," Wigg explained. "The Tome states that it shall be your mission, and then the mission of your sister should you either fail or perish in your attempt, to combine the two sides of the craft for the good of all humankind. If we purposely destroy the Orb of the Vagaries and thereby allow only the Vigors to exist, you will never be able to fulfill the destiny that the Tome says you must." Wigg gave a small sigh and looked down at his hands.

"Perplexing, isn't it?" he continued a moment later. "It seems we have been placed in the unwelcome position of having to preserve *both* sides of the craft, no matter how repellent we find the Vagaries. While Wulfgar, on the other hand, is left completely unbridled, and quite untroubled by such a conflict of interest. In many respects, his task is far easier than ours."

"How will it happen?" Geldon asked.

"How will what happen?" Wigg responded.

"When Wulfgar employs the Forestallment to destroy the orb, I mean," Geldon answered. "What will actually happen?"

Wigg laced his long fingers together. "That is impossible to say," he replied. "The Scroll of the Vigors provides the calculations, but does not actually describe the unfolding of the event. It does, however, make mention of something called the 'Isthmus.'"

"What is that?" the dwarf asked.

"We're not sure. Perhaps more research will tell us. But for now we believe it to be a manifestation of the craft that somehow allows the partial joining of the orbs, without the two of them actually touching each other. And we believe this Isthmus may be an inherent part of what Wulfgar has planned. But there is one advantage we do have over Wulfgar in all of this."

"And what is that?" Tristan asked, eager to hear a scrap of good news.

"Over the centuries, it has been our experience that the two orbs reside only over the landmass of Eutracia," Wigg answered. "Although they exist within the fabric of the craft, and we believe the craft to exist everywhere, every attempt to move the orbs either out over the Sea of Whispers or over the heights of the Tolenka Mountains has always failed. We never discovered why, but it seems quite impossible to do. The only reason we could ever discern was that the Tome stated that Tristan and his sister would one day arrive in Eutracia, and for the Chosen Ones to fulfill their destinies, eons ago the orbs were somehow enchanted to remain imprisoned here, in our homeland, thereby helping to ensure Tristan's or Shailiha's success. But that is still only a theory; as with so many things of the craft, no one can be absolutely sure. But this is why Wulfgar cannot simply call the Orb of the Vigors to the Citadel and destroy it there."

Traax's strong, commanding voice rang out. "We will beat him back, I swear it," the Minion said sternly. "No fighting force on earth can overcome our warriors. We will give him a reception he shall never forget."

Tristan looked over at him. "Forgive me, my friend," he said with concern, "but that may not be the case. I have seen the demonslavers fight. While they do not have the gift of flight, they are nonetheless ferocious adversaries, and they care absolutely nothing for their own safety. Our forces were drastically weakened during the battle with Nicholas' flying creatures over the fields of Farplain. Even worse, the demonslavers will have a full-fledged wizard of Morganna's blood leading them." Thinking to himself for a moment, he looked out over the balcony, then back to Faegan and Wigg.

"If the Minions cannot keep Wulfgar from reaching the coast, can your combined gifts beat him back?" he asked them bluntly. "Is there any way we can win this?"

"There will be no way of knowing that until it happens," Wigg answered grimly as he placed his hands into the opposite sleeves of his robe. "The powers of the *Enseterat* will be great, indeed."

Tristan narrowed his eyes. "What are you talking about?" he asked. "What is the *Enseterat*?"

"*Enseterat* is a word found in the scroll, and is the title by which Wulfgar will no doubt wish to be known. It is Old Eutracian for 'lord of the Vagaries.' The scroll says that once the Chosen Ones finally mature, and their blood has been gifted with Forestallments, then they are to be known by such names."

Tristan looked over at his sister. "So what are Shailiha and I supposed to be called?" he asked softly.

Wigg looked carefully first at Tristan, then Shailiha. "Tristan, you are to be known in the craft as the *Jin'Sai,* or 'The Combiner of the Arts'. And Shailiha is to be known as the *Jin'Saiou,* the feminine version of the same phrase.

"We first heard these words spoken by the watchwoman of the floating gardens," Wigg said. "But when she realized that we were unfamiliar with them, she would tell us no more. Now we know. Or should I say, at least we know more than we did."

"But why?" Shailiha asked. "Why would the Ones give us such names?"

"As is the case with so many things of magic, we do not know," Faegan answered. "We have theorized that it may be so that future beings of the craft you encounter in your struggles to join the two sides shall know you for who you now are, and therefore willingly accept your aegis over them. Or there may well be deeper, even more meaningful reasons for this. Only time will tell. And time is the one thing we don't have."

Despite all that Tristan had heard, the thought that had been going through his mind since he had sat down needed to be addressed before anything else was done. Wulfgar and his fleet could be there at any time, and they had to be as ready for him as they could.

"We must deploy the fleet," he said sternly. "And we need to set up a system of warning, should they see Wulfgar and his slavers approaching."

"Our thoughts exactly," Wigg said. "What do you suggest?"

Tristan turned back to Traax. "What you must do is to keep the fleet concentrated in strength, so that it can be ordered to move as a unified force at a moment's notice. I want the fleet maneuverable, without having our backs up against the coastline. Sail east from the delta, but venture no farther from Tammerland than your best warriors can fly without stopping to rest. Hold your position there. Then order a small contingent of scout vessels farther east, but again no farther than the warriors can safely fly back to the main body of the fleet. Send warriors flying out from the decks of the scout vessels to scour the sea as far to the east as they can. When the slavers are finally sighted, send a message to me at once. If we can destroy his fleet and keep him from reaching the coast, we may be able to save the orb."

Tristan looked over at the wizards. "Agreed?" he asked. They both nodded.

Tristan thought to himself for a moment, then looked back over at Traax. "Do you remember the officer named K'jarr?" he asked. "His intelligence and bravery impressed me during the sea battle with the pirates."

"Of course," Traax answered with a smile. "He is one of my best. Still a bit young and impetuous, but very capable."

"Good," Tristan answered thoughtfully. "When you return to the fleet, find him and keep him by your side. He is not to participate in any of the flying search parties. When I finally join you I may have a special use for him, and I want him available. I may also want a special litter built. I will tell you about it later."

Traax bowed his head slightly. "I live to serve," he said. Then his strong, rather menacing-looking smile emerged again. "It shall all be as you order, *Jin'Sai*."

On hearing himself called that for the first time, Tristan sighed and shook his head. He had never been one for titles, and now it seemed that still another one had been heaped on him. He looked over to Shailiha, and saw her smile slightly.

"And for your part, what will you be doing?" Tristan asked the two wizards.

"What we have been doing for the last week," Wigg answered. "Specifically, trying to find a way to combat the Forestallment gifted to Wulfgar that will result in the destruction of the orb. But I must tell all of you here that given the quality of his blood and the still-unknown nature of the various gifts he has surely been imbued with, the likelihood of our stopping him will be remote, at best. And if we fail, all that we know and love may soon vanish." As he finished speaking, a tense silence descended over the table.

Tristan looked over at Traax. "Go now," he ordered. "Take the fleet out, but leave a sufficient number of troops here to defend the palace, should it come to that. Once at sea, follow my directions to the letter. I will await your word."

Nodding, Traax stood. He walked a short distance to the side of the balcony, snapped open his wings, and took to the air.

Looking down at the scroll on the table, Tristan took a deep breath. Rising, he stretched his long legs and walked over to the balcony wall. He kept his dark eyes on Traax as the loyal warrior became smaller and smaller against the backdrop of the sky, then finally vanished.

He knew that if they were not exceedingly fortunate, they would lose this fight. Then the warrior K'jarr crossed his mind again. There might yet be a way—one that he had not discussed with the wizards.

Suddenly, despite the loved ones sitting just behind him at the table, the newly anointed *Jin'Sai* felt very much alone.

Sixty-four

T he baby girl coughed yet again as she lay struggling for her life in the plain, wooden crib. As she did, the woman in the robe sensed that this gentle but sinister convulsion would be the child's last. Long past grief, the baby's mother and father huddled helplessly near their child, their eyes red and crying as they watched her die.

Closing her eyes, the woman called upon the craft yet again in her efforts to help the infant breathe, at the same time trying to make sure the familiar azure aura did not form, thereby alerting the parents of her secret abilities. But she knew she was losing this battle, and the end would come soon.

Almost as quickly as she had thought it, the child's deep, brown eyes closed, her soft eyelashes fluttering for the last time, like tiny butterflies' wings. Then came the delicate death rattle from her exhausted lungs, and her head slipped quietly over to one side. The woman slowly stood back up.

With tears in her eyes, the woman named Adrian lifted the worn blanket up over the baby's face. Turning to look at the parents, she shook her head sadly.

Refusing to believe, the frantic mother snatched the dead child up in her arms, as if by holding her close, she could somehow imbue her with new life. Adrian left the mother to her grief and walked to the father. His name was Inar, and he hadn't eaten or slept for three days. Near collapse, he leaned his head against the wall and sobbed openly.

"Please know that I did all I could," Adrian said softly.

Reaching out from the sleeve of her hooded robe, Adrian gently touched his hand. It felt cold and lifeless, just as his heart now surely did. Tears running down his face, the father could only nod.

Knowing there was nothing left to be said, Adrian quietly left the room. Going to the cottage door, she let herself out onto the street, where a light rain had begun to fall. She walked to where her horse was tied, pulling up the hood of her robe as she went.

As she mounted her roan gelding, she took a final look back at the modest cottage. Smoke wisped up out of the chimney, and she knew that the traditional black silk ribbon of mourning would soon adorn the door.

What a difference only a few seconds could make, she thought. A body could be warm and alive one moment, and then, in the twinkle of an eye, it was not. After closing her eyes for a time, she slowly opened them again and turned her horse up the slick, cobblestoned street.

Had the child's parents somehow had the occasion to see Adrian's upper left arm, they would have noticed her tattoo: a square, bloodred image of the Paragon. Still, that would not have entirely revealed Adrian's secret, the one she had promised never to divulge since the age of five, when the wizards of the Directorate had granted her father's humble request that his only daughter be accepted for training in the craft. But Adrian was more than simply another person of endowed blood.

Adrian of the House of Brandywyne was of the craft, and a graduate of a place known only to a privileged few. A place called Fledgling House.

Listening to her horse's shoes strike the cobblestones, she regarded the drab city of Tanglewood as it passed slowly by. It was not one of Eutracia's more prosperous places, and probably never would be. And since the unexpected return of the Coven of sorceresses and the deaths of the wizards of the Directorate, she feared the city's plight would only worsen.

The houses in this section were made of dark wood and had shabby thatched roofs. They all seemed to look the same somehow, and had a crooked, fragile, ramshackle quality about them. It was almost as if they needed to lean up against one another just to remain upright, and if the first of them fell, the rest would also give up the effort and tumble down with it.

She had been trying to save the dying infant all night, and it was now just after dawn, the rising sun smothered somewhere just over the horizon among inky, dark rain clouds. Around her, Tanglewood seemed to be slowly waking up. Low, muffled conversation could be heard here and there, and smoke was rising from the tops of the chimneys. The occasional chamber pot could be seen held out of a window, its contents unceremoniously dumped on the nearby ground. Men in worn work clothes began appearing from doorways to kiss their wives good-bye and go about their daily labors. The enticing aromas of peasant food—plain, but good—hung in the damp morning air.

Adrian's stomach growled, reminding her of how long it had been since she had eaten. Trying to save the baby girl had taken all her strength, and she was exhausted. She reached into one pocket of her robe and counted her kisa. There should be enough, she reasoned. She would stop at the first inn she came across, allowing herself a rest before returning to her village.

Sometimes she felt very alone in the world, despite the number of people she always seemed to encounter who needed her help. At thirty Seasons of New Life she found herself neither young nor old. She was not yet married, but that did not trouble her too much. And she had been an only child, her mother dying while giving her life. Her father had not visited her modest cottage—the one he had built for her with his own two hands—for nearly a year now, and because of that she feared greatly for him. He was a consul of the Redoubt, and it had often been said that he knew the lead wizard personally. But for some time it had been widely rumored that Wigg was dead, along with all of the other wizards of the Directorate. A shudder went through her as she wondered anew about the fate of her father and the other members of his discipline.

She had not come across any of the Brotherhood for some time now, and that was unusual. She would certainly have known them, just as she always had, by their simple dark blue robes, quiet manners, and the tattoo of the Paragon on their shoulders, should any of them deign to reveal it to her. It seemed something sinister had happened not only to the Directorate but to the Brotherhood as well, leaving her and her sister acolytes lost and alone in the craft.

But Adrian was a hardy, stalwart woman. And she would continue to uphold her vows, regardless of the nation's plights. She would gladly perform the good deeds she had promised the headmaster and matron of Fledgling House the day they had pronounced her trained and set her and her classmates free at the age of twenty-one.

She had been a proud member of the first such group to be given their tattoos and then sent forth. She had always yearned to return to Fledgling House, to see again the modest, charming castle sitting next to the base of the northern Tolenka Mountains. But she never had. She also longed to see Duncan again—the wizard with the long gray hair who had taught her so much. And Martha, Duncan's wife—the kindly, rotund matron who had always seen to the girls' other needs. She remembered the couple fondly and hoped they were both well. Fledgling

House was the only real home she had ever known, and Duncan and Martha were more her parents than her father and late mother had ever been.

Perhaps I will return one day, she thought. When times are not so cruel, and the need for my gifts is not so great.

As she rode along, Adrian clutched an errant lock of her hair that had somehow escaped the hood of her robe and hooked it behind one ear. As she did, she smiled gently to herself. She knew she was not beautiful. But she possessed the strength of heart to know that the quality of her femininity mattered far less than the quality of her service to the craft. What she may have lacked in appearance she more than made up for with not only her intelligence, but with the goodness of her heart.

Adrian was rather short and plain. Her wide, level eyes were deep brown. Her sandy, curly, shoulder-length hair always seemed to be getting in the way. The sleeves of her dark red acolyte's robe fell loosely down around her wrists, and the hem gently swished across the tops of her boots when she walked. A black, knotted cord secured the robe at its middle, its tasseled ends falling down along the outside of her right thigh.

Finally she saw an inn, with a sign proclaiming it THE BEAR AND FINCH. But as she approached it, she felt a strange sensation and pulled her horse up short. Breathing heavily, she began to sweat noticeably, even though it was certainly not warm on the street. She had never felt anything remotely like this. It was not painful. It was more . . . needful. Yes, she thought. That was the word she was looking for: needful. But needful of what? she asked herself.

As if suddenly possessed, she turned and looked southeast, over the roofs of the houses. Tammerland, she thought. The royal palace was there. She felt compelled to go to the palace. She had never been so drawn to anything in her life.

But visiting the royal residence was forbidden to acolytes. The wizards' punishment for such a transgression was said to be severe. But how could something her heart of hearts was so desperately telling her to do be so very wrong? She didn't know, for what she was experiencing went against every iota of her training. But the urge was irresistible, and she realized that if she did not go, her heart might burst from the longing.

As if in a dream, Adrian found herself turning her horse around and pointing him down the road leading to Tammerland.

She could not know that all her sisters in the craft were experiencing the same thing—being drawn to Tammerland, the country's capital and seat of the craft.

*E*xhausted, Wigg opened his eyes and lowered his arms. It was just after dawn, and he and Faegan had been working through the night, trying to make use of one of the calculations they had found in the scroll. The lamps of the Redoubt burned brightly, and the Scroll of the Vigors hovered nearby, partially unrolled, glowing with the power of the craft.

"Is it done?" Faegan asked quietly. He sat at a nearby table, in his wheeled chair. Nicodemus lay across his lap, purring contentedly.

"It is as done as I can make it, old friend," the lead wizard answered tiredly. Shuffling his way around the table, he took a seat next to Faegan. "Only time will tell whether it will truly work."

Faegan decided to change the subject. "Have you talked to them yet?" he asked. "Have you told Tristan and Celeste about the warning we found this morning?"

"No," Wigg answered with a sigh. "Frankly, I don't know how to bring myself to do it. They love each other so much . . ."

Faegan's face darkened, and he rolled his chair a bit closer. "You cannot wait any longer, Wigg!" he said sternly. "You know it as well as I! I will do the deed for you, if you cannot. But either way, they must be told. I know it will break their hearts, and that they have already suffered far more loss than any two people should ever have to endure. But we owe it to them, nonetheless."

The lead wizard looked down at his hands, as if wishing to somehow avoid the issue entirely. A tear came to one of his eyes. Tristan and Celeste had both been through so much already, he thought. How could he do this to them? Still, for the good of the craft, he had to.

Finding his resolve, Wigg stood. He walked over to one corner of the room and tugged resolutely on a velvet pull cord. In a few moments the expected knock came on the massive, double doors. With a word from Wigg they opened, and a Minion warrior appeared. Upon entering the room, he clicked his heels together.

"I live to serve," he said.

Wigg looked back at Faegan, but knew he would win no reprieve from his old friend. Faegan glared back at him sternly and nodded. His mind finally made up, Wigg turned back to the obediently waiting warrior.

"Bring the *Jin'Sai* and my daughter here at once," he said simply.

The warrior clicked his heels again and promptly left in search of the prince.

Wigg walked sadly back to the table, sat down heavily next to Faegan, and waited in silence.

Sixty-five

When the strong, familiar knock came on the door, Wigg stiffened. Looking over at Faegan, he took a deep breath, then glanced back toward the doors again.

"Enter," he said simply.

The prince and Celeste walked in. For some unknown reason, Tristan seemed especially eager to see them. Removing his weapons from his shoulder, he slung them over the back of one of the chairs and took a place next to Wigg's daughter at the table.

Taking a deep breath, Wigg looked over at them. "I'm glad you're here," he said quietly. "We need to speak with you. There is something I must—"

"And I need to speak to you," Tristan interrupted excitedly. "Had you not asked for me, I would have sought you out myself."

"What is it?" Wigg asked. "Is something wrong?"

"I have an idea," Tristan answered quickly. "And I'm afraid that whatever you wanted to say will have to wait for the moment. What I have to tell you is vitally important. But first, please tell me—have the two of you found any possible way to stop Wulfgar?"

Sitting back in his chair, Wigg raised his eyebrow. "No," he said. "And time grows short."

Reaching into a pocket of his trousers, Tristan took something out. He gently placed it on the table. "This may be our answer," he said softly. "I was reminded of it yesterday, during our meeting on the balcony."

Faegan looked at the item on the table, then back over at the prince.

"Of course we recognize it," he said, as he stroked Nicodemus. "But I still do not understand what you have in mind."

"You told us yesterday that the orbs cannot be coaxed out over the sea. And also that if we could keep Wulfgar's fleet of demonslavers from reaching the coast, we would have a much better chance of stopping him from destroying the Orb of the Vigors, correct?"

"Yes, that's true," Wigg answered, his curiosity growing. "But what are you driving at?"

For more than the next half hour, Tristan explained to Wigg, Faegan, and Celeste exactly what he wanted to do, and how he would do it. As he spoke, the wizards could hear the optimism rising in his voice. When he was done, the two mystics sat back in silence as they considered his plan. Long moments ticked by as the prince awaited their opinions.

"I'll admit that it has its merits," Faegan finally answered. Tristan could see the wheels turning in the old wizard's head. "But the logistics and execution would be daunting, to say the least. The timing would have to be perfect, and your idea carries with it absolutely no guarantee of success. Still, it's the best plan I have seen so far." He smiled at the prince. "Frankly, I'm impressed."

"I agree," Wigg said. "But tell me, does anyone outside of this room know of your idea?"

"No."

"Good," the lead wizard said adamantly. "Keep it that way. And leave what you brought here with us. We will consider your plan, and let you know if it is viable."

"If that's what you feel you must do, then so be it," Tristan countered. "But you'd best hurry. The warning from the Minion scout ships could come at any time, whether you're ready or not."

Satisfied for the time being, Tristan crossed his arms over his leather vest. "Now then," he asked politely. "What was it you wished to tell us?"

As was his habit, Wigg placed his hands into the opposite sleeves of his robe. "There are two things, actually," he began. "And they both have to do with the Scroll of the Vigors."

Tristan and Celeste both looked over to where the scroll was hovering in the air. The azure glow of the craft flowed from it, and it was partially unrolled to reveal the elegant, flowing Old Eutracian words and symbols inscribed on it. Its golden center rod and end caps gleamed in the light.

"What about it?" Celeste asked.

"Do you remember Faegan and I telling you about something the watchwoman of the floating gardens mentioned to us? She called it the River of Thought."

Tristan's brow furrowed. "Yes, I do," he answered. "But frankly, I had forgotten. You said little of it."

"That's because at the time, there was very little to say," Faegan replied. "We wanted to be sure the calculations for it actually existed within the scroll. And we finally found them."

"And just what does this so-called River of Thought accomplish?" Tristan asked.

"Used properly, it can stir certain feelings or sensations in one or more endowed persons at the same time," Wigg replied. "Faegan imbued its Forestallment into my blood only this morning, and I just used it for the first time."

"To do what?" Celeste asked, her voice a whisper.

"To call home all of the acolytes of Fledgling House," he replied. "The Redoubt has been empty for far too long. It needs to be used for the reason it was built—the further training and safe harbor of those who have devoted their lives to go forth in our name and perform good deeds of the craft. As you both know, whatever consuls may still exist have been freed of their death enchantments, turned to the Vagaries, and taken to the Citadel. Sadly, they are now all subject to Wulfgar's control. But they are not the subjects of our efforts." Pausing for a moment, he looked into their surprised faces.

"Instead, we have employed the River of Thought to summon the acolytes here, to what will be their new home," he went on. "What better place to harbor these valuable souls during such troubled times than the depths of the Redoubt? Their mission will be to take the place of the consuls who have betrayed us." He looked sadly at Tristan.

"This was your mother's lifelong dream," he added softly. "Equality for women in the craft. Faegan and I wanted to call the acolytes home sooner, but until we learned of the River of Thought, there was no practical way of doing it. Now there is. We are about to make Morganna's vision for the future come true. The circle shall be complete again, for the first time in more than three centuries."

Tristan stared at the two wizards, then smiled broadly, happy beyond words that they had finally arrived at this crossroads in history. But then another thought came to him. "This is wonderful news," he told them. "Still, how will we know they are who they claim to be? Anyone can acquire a red robe. Couldn't there easily be traitors among them? This seems like a very dangerous time to be taking strangers into the palace."

"First, of course, they will all be women," Wigg answered, "the oldest of whom should be no more than thirty Seasons of New Life. And, as you point out, each of them should also be wearing the dark red, hooded robe of her station. But clearly, those things alone are not sufficient proof. We shall therefore also be checking their blood signatures against our records for final confirmation before any of them are shown the secrets of the Redoubt. We shall also check them for the presence of Forestallments, to see whether their blood has been tampered with. There should be none. But if any of the acolytes are found to posses them, those women will be segregated and held for questioning." Pausing for a moment, the lead wizard laced his long fingers together.

"Tristan, with your permission I want to order the Minions now stationed before the palace entrance to move their campsites immediately," he said. "I want them out of sight. I think we can safely assume that few of the acolytes have ever seen one of our winged friends before, and I don't want to scare the women away. Their hearts will already be filled with enough trepidation about what they are doing as it is. For all they know just now, they are breaking their vows simply by coming here. We can only hope that the River of Thought is strong enough to overcome those feelings in them and keep them continuing on the path home. They will be very conflicted when they arrive. They must feel welcome, and know that it was we who called them here."

"Forgive me, Father," Celeste began, "but are you sure this is a good time to be doing this? What about Wulfgar and his fleet?"

"Now is the best possible time," Faegan answered. "In other ways, it is also the worst. And Wulfgar is the reason behind both. If he truly is on the way, we want to get the acolytes to safety as quickly as we can, before he can influence them. And if Grizelda was lying and Wulfgar is not advancing on us, then why wait? Your father and I thought long and hard about this, and finally decided to go ahead."

Tristan looked over at Wigg, and the lead wizard's face darkened. "And the other thing you called us here to discuss?" Tristan asked. "What is it?"

Ignoring Tristan's question, Wigg looked sternly at both of them. "We are sorry to have to ask you this, but we must know if the two of you have been intimate. And if you have, how many times this occurred."

Tristan and Celeste stared at him, shocked. "How could you ask such a thing?" the prince demanded. "Besides, this really isn't the time for—"

"Just tell us," Wigg interrupted sternly. "Trust me when I say that we have our reasons. It is vitally important that we know."

Had any other man asked him this, Tristan might well have knocked him down. But these were Wigg and Faegan, and the wizards always had their reasons. Still, he scowled.

"Once," he answered. Annoyed, he crossed his arms over his chest. Celeste blushed.

"When was it?" Wigg asked.

"Yesterday morning."

"And during your time with one another, did either of you see an azure glow form, then disappear?"

Tristan looked over at Celeste. He took her hand, then looked back at Wigg. "I may have," he said tentatively.

"That's not good enough," Wigg shot back impatiently. "Either you did, or you didn't."

"I was half asleep," Tristan answered. "And that's the best answer I can give you. Even now I cannot be sure whether it was a dream or whether it was real."

"What is all of this about?" Celeste asked anxiously. "Is there something wrong?"

Wigg's expression softened a bit, and he held one hand out to her. "Please stand, and come to me," he asked her quietly. She did so.

Wigg looked to the table at large. "Everyone please be still," he asked. "What I am about to do is very important."

Reaching out with his free hand, he placed his palm onto Celeste's lower abdomen and closed his eyes. Silence reigned as Wigg gently moved his long fingers to and fro, as if searching for something. After a time he removed his hand, opened his eyes, and bade Celeste to sit back down.

Faegan leaned anxiously over the table and looked at Wigg. "Well?" he asked.

A sad look overcame the lead wizard's face. "I can't tell," he answered softly. "My attempts were blocked, exactly as the scroll said they would be."

Wasting no time, Faegan wheeled his chair over to where Celeste sat. Placing his hand upon her as Wigg had just done, he also closed his eyes. When he opened them again, his face registered an equal look of surprise.

"Do you now see?" Wigg asked him sadly. "Just as I told you. Inconclusive. And to my knowledge, this has never happened before."

"But how can that be?" Faegan whispered, half to himself.

Cleary frustrated, Wigg ran his hands down his face. "I have no idea," he answered slowly. "But the influence of Tristan's presence has clearly been at work here. Did you sense it? It was almost as if our powers were being overcome somehow. It seems that once again, as has also been true with so many of the questions concerning his azure blood, we can find no clear-cut answer."

Tristan looked quizzically at Celeste, then back to the wizards.

"What in the name of the Afterlife are you two talking about?" he asked. "What were you doing to Celeste?"

"The two of you have done nothing wrong," Wigg said compassionately. "But you have been caught up in something not of your own making, and there are things that must be said. Things the two of you will find very difficult to hear. And they have to do with the scroll." Turning to Faegan, the lead wizard nodded. Faegan nodded back.

Wheeling his chair away from the table a bit, the old wizard raised his arms in the direction of the hovering scroll. Almost at once a short section of text in Old Eutracian lifted itself from the body of the scroll and came to hover over the center of the table. It glowed magnificently.

Looking over at Celeste, Tristan saw that she was reading the text. Then a sudden look of horror overcame her, and the blood ran from her face. She placed her hands over her eyes, as if looking at it had somehow become unbearable. Not knowing what else to do, Tristan put an arm around her.

"In the name of the Afterlife, will one of you please tell me what is going on here?" he shouted at the wizards. "Can't you see you're upsetting her?"

"Perhaps the best way is to read the passage for you, since you cannot do so for yourself," Faegan answered him softly. Turning his chair, he looked up at the glowing, hovering script and began to read aloud.

" '*And should the Chosen One make use of his gifts before he is trained to do so, the ordeal shall alter the nature of his blood, changing it from red to azure. But with this change shall come a price. For should his seed then mingle with that of any female, the child they might produce would be horrible beyond description, for the blood of the* Jin'Sai *shall be tainted. And no endowed female in the world, except for the twin of the* Jin'Sai, *shall carry a blood signature strong enough to keep such a child from possessing the left-leaning signature that shall without question emerge. Such shall always be the case, until the blood of the* Jin'Sai *can be returned to red. Thus, no seed of the* Jin'Sai *may be allowed to walk the world at any price, and no practice of the craft shall be able to determine whether the* Jin'Sai's *mate is with child. Only nature's way of revealing the answer shall be available to those who shall both worry, and wonder . . .'* "

His mind stunned and drifting, Tristan slumped down into the chair. Finally, slowly, he looked over at the wizards. Their faces were very concerned.

"Why didn't you tell us sooner?" he breathed, scarcely able to get the words out. "We could have prevented this . . . That's why you were examining her, isn't it? You needed to see if she was carrying my child." He paused tentatively for a moment. "Is she—"

"We don't know," Wigg interrupted softly. "We only discovered this message in the scroll this morning, and then called for both of you straight away. It was the best we could do."

"But I thought the scrolls were only a compilation of Forestallment formulas," Tristan countered softly. "Do you mean to say that they speak of other things, as well?"

"Yes," Wigg answered. "The scrolls are much more than they appeared to be at first glance. Not only are they the repository of the Forestallment calculations, but they are informative, as well, much like the Tome of the Paragon."

"And you are unable to use your gifts to tell us if she is with child?" Tristan asked.

"That's right," Faegan answered. "It is just as the scroll said it would be. The only way we shall know is by the appearance of the traditional, natural signs. And that will take some time. I also regret to say that until Tristan's blood is somehow returned to normal, the two of you must refrain from physical intimacy. I'm sorry, but being of the craft sometimes also means making sacrifices. For now, that is how things must be."

Faegan took a deep breath and let it out slowly. "Aside from the impending arrival of Wulfgar, it now seems that our most pressing concern is the search to unravel the mystery surrounding Tristan's blood." Pausing for a moment, the brilliant wizard thought quietly.

"Who knew?" he asked. "Who knew that Tristan's answer to defeating the Coven of sorceresses—the only answer available to him, and achieved with such great self-sacrifice—would in turn somehow become the greatest, most dangerous riddle of the craft?"

Finally removing her hands from her face, Celeste looked out over the table. Tristan fully expected to see her eyes full of tears, but they weren't. Instead, a look of grim determination had overtaken her. Reaching out, she took both of Tristan's hands into hers and held them tight.

"There has to be a way to remedy this, and we shall find it," she said softly. Despite the gentleness of her tone, her voice carried so much weight that her words sounded like an oath. She looked deeply into Tristan's eyes.

"If I am carrying our child, we shall find a way to safely bring it into this world, regardless of what the scroll may say. I swear it to you, my love," she added.

Tristan tried to speak, but was so overcome he found he had no voice. Narrowing his eyes against the coming tears, he simply nodded.

Then the familiar, hated feeling for his azure blood crept up on him again.

He looked away for a moment, his jaw hardening. And now, it

seemed, his blood had caused pain not only to Tristan, but to the woman he loved, and to the child she could be carrying.

His eyes full of tears, he took Celeste into his arms and held her for what seemed forever.

Sixty-six

The Minion warrior's name was Osiv, and as his strong wings carried him through the air, his sharp, dark eyes searched the ocean beneath him. About fifty meters away and matching his pace stroke for stroke flew Takir, his scouting partner. The midday sky was only partly cloudy, but heavier, darker clouds loomed to the east, directly across their flight path. Soon, Osiv knew, they would have to turn back to the scout ship from which they had come, empty-handed once again.

Looking down, all Osiv could see were the reaches of the Sea of Whispers. Five days had passed since the main body of their fleet had taken up its position off the coast and the scout ships had been sent on ahead. This was Osiv's and Takir's fourth such mission. They had come upon other vessels, to be sure, but none of them had proved to be slaver ships.

Just then Takir saw a lone frigate plowing her way due west. Running before the wind, she was making very good time. She carried no identifying flag. He signaled his find to Osiv, and the two warriors folded their wings behind their backs and rolled over into free fall, plummeting down to take a closer look.

As Osiv unfolded his wings to slow his descent and make a first pass over the frigate, he thought he must be seeing things. The ship seemed to be completely deserted. There were no sailors on her decks. Nor were there any to be seen in the rigging or in the crow's nest. Even the ship's wheel was unmanned. Still she plowed gamely on through the waves as if tended by the best of seamen, her course never varying.

Despite the fact that he was a Minion officer, Osiv felt a shiver go down his spine. *A ghost ship.* He had listened to stories about them all his life around Minion campfires, but had never dreamed he might actually see one. Only the graybeards among them had claimed seeing them. As he remembered their stories, one corner of his mouth turned up. As he had grown and become wiser, he had come to realize that the elders always told such stories, the next one always more improbable than the last.

Signaling to Takir, he indicated that they should investigate. Osiv drew his dreggan from its scabbard. Nodding, Takir did the same and warily followed him the rest of the way down.

Buffeting his wings, Osiv landed lightly, carefully, on the pitching stern deck. Takir came down next to him. Still the ship sailed obediently on. The masts and rigging swayed peacefully, and the hull groaned slightly in continual protest as she plowed her way along, the waves parting across her bow. Otherwise, no sound whatsoever came to their ears.

Then they heard a sharp banging noise and they spun around, dreggans held high.

But all they saw was an open stairway, its unsecured door swinging back and forth in the wind. A set of steps led down from the doorway, to the lower deck.

His hand tightening around his dreggan and all of his senses on alert, Osiv went to the door. Takir followed behind. Osiv winced as the boards of the steps creaked, traitorously announcing their presence.

The hallways below were not darkened, as Osiv had somehow expected them to be. All of the wall sconces were burning brightly, making it easy for them to find their way. As they walked forward from the stern, they saw all of the usual trappings of a ship at sea. The larder shelves were stocked with food, and there were signs of crewmen having recently eaten. Freshwater barrels, their contents partially consumed, stood securely roped against the starboard hull in several neat rows. Next they found the crew's sleeping quarters. The traditional rope hammocks were all still hanging from the rafters, swinging back and forth with the ceaseless rhythm of the abandoned ship.

A further search revealed that there were absolutely no crewmen aboard, anywhere. Yet everything was in its place, just as it should be on a well-run vessel. What strange fate could have befallen them? Osiv found himself wondering. Could the Eaters of the Dead be responsible for this? But if they were, then where was all the blood?

Seeing another set of steps heading topside, he led Takir back up, into the sunlight and the breeze. The scene was just as they had left it. The sails were still full and properly trimmed, and the ship remained duly on course, making her way toward some unknown destination.

Relaxing a bit, Osiv lowered his sword. Looking around, he saw a nearby keg. He went over and sat on it, then placed his dreggan across his knees. Takir came to stand beside him, placing the point of his dreggan on the pitching deck and leaning on the hilt. The wind moaned hauntingly through the lonely, unmanned sails.

"I don't understand it," Osiv said quietly. "Where could they all have gone? And this ship! She's still on course somehow, as if nothing was wrong. How is such a thing possible?"

"I have no idea," Takir replied. "It's as if they have all—"

Suddenly Takir heard the familiar, unmistakable sound of a sword blade ripping through bone and flesh. When he looked at his friend, he froze in disbelief.

A long, vertical wound had opened up in Osiv's head. It literally split his face in two, a vertical cut from chin to top of skull and back down to the nape of his neck. The two halves of his head slowly began to separate and fall away toward the shoulders. Osiv's eyes went blank; blood and brain matter began to slide from the wound and run down onto his body armor.

Osiv's body went crashing sloppily to the deck, his dreggan clanging noisily down.

On pure instinct, Takir lifted his dreggan high and turned full circle, searching for Osiv's murderer. But no one was there. The empty, pitching decks simply yawned back at him, in silent ridicule of his foolishness.

"Show yourself!" Takir screamed in anger as he whirled about again. He viciously slashed his sword through the surrounding air, but its razor-sharp blade bit into nothing. Suddenly, something told him he should unfold his wings and take flight. But the impulse came just a fraction too late.

"If you insist," a voice said calmly from somewhere. It was a strong, commanding voice.

Takir felt a strange sort of shudder go through him.

Looking down, he saw a vertical slit in his body armor. Then his blood began rushing from it. He absently, drunkenly, reached down and placed one hand over it, but this last act was to serve no purpose. Everything went black and he fell forward.

As the blood from the two Minion corpses joined to run slowly across the deck, the azure glow of the craft appeared. Then it faded in intensity and finally vanished altogether, to reveal Wulfgar.

His long, sandy hair swaying behind him in the wind, he looked casually down at the two dead bodies. He raised one arm, and his demon-slaver crew materialized, all of them heavily armed and standing stiffly at attention, awaiting their master's orders. The sword of the one nearest him dripped with fresh blood.

Wulfgar bent over and picked up the dreggan that had belonged to

Osiv. Holding it high, he examined it carefully as the sun bounced off its shiny blade.

"Such fine craftsmanship," he said, half to himself. "These swords really are a marvel. It is said that even the *Jin'Sai* himself carries one." With a sneer on his face, he strode purposefully to the gunwale and threw the beautiful weapon overboard. Pointing back to the slavers, he singled two of them out.

"You!" he ordered sternly. "Throw these dead bodies overboard. The rest of you return to your duties." With dutiful nods the two monsters he had chosen went about their work.

Wulfgar's tactical gamble had worked perfectly. He gave silent thanks to Nicholas for providing invaluable information about Minion abilities and customs. Now he had an excellent idea of how far away the Minion fleet was, without them knowing the position of his own. Two days' flying time, he guessed. One day from the scouting vessels to here, and another from the scout ships to the Minion fleet. That put the Minion position near the coast.

Looking over the side, Wulfgar watched as the slavers tossed the Minion bodies into the sea. The water ran red with blood, and he heard the snuffling, hungry grunts come as the pieces were greedily consumed. As he continued to watch the feeding frenzy, he smiled.

"I'm sorry there wasn't more, my children," he said softly. "But soon now, you will have your fill." Looking toward the stern, he saw the supposedly empty sea behind him, and he smiled. Even the wakes of his ships were unseen.

He silently thanked the late Krassus for gifting him with the Forestallment of invisibility.

Wulfgar closed his eyes. He raised his arms, and the familiar azure glow engulfed his flagship. When it faded away, all that remained was the cold, restless sea.

Sixty-seven

The thirteen confused women sat side by side in the Hall of Supplication, each waiting her turn to approach the lead wizard. Wigg and Faegan sat at a table before them. On the table was a tall stack of parchment documents, and an odd-looking device the likes of which none of the women had ever seen. A group who had already passed the wizards' exotic tests sat off to one side.

As she waited for her turn to be called, it was plain to Adrian that so far, none of her sister acolytes had failed the wizards' examinations. Still stunned by the beauty of her surroundings, she looked around again at the sumptuous room. Fledgling House had been beautiful, to be sure, but she had never seen a place like this. Huge stained-glass windows had been swung open slightly to let in more light and fresh air. The black, variegated marble floor was covered with multicolored patterned area rugs, and an ornate mahogany throne sat on a dais at the far end of the room. The room still smelled faintly musty, leading her to believe that it had seen little use of late. She could only imagine what the rest of the palace must look like.

She and the other women had arrived only this morning. They had discovered one another on the way here, and as they shared their experiences, they learned that every single one of them had been overpowered by the same sudden, unexplained compulsion to make the journey to the royal palace in Tammerland.

Adrian, as the senior among them, had been selected to lead them through the palace gates. There they had been greeted by a hunchbacked dwarf who had introduced himself as Geldon. He had explained that the lead wizard himself was responsible for their undeniable need to come here, and that they had done the right thing by doing so. No harm or punishment would befall them.

Greatly relieved, the women had followed the dwarf across the drawbridge, through the courtyard, and into the palace proper. Once in the Hall of Supplication, Geldon had recorded their names and family houses on a piece of parchment, handed it to the wizards, and directed the women to their seats.

Still taking in the grandeur of her surroundings, Adrian was startled when the lead wizard called out her name.

"Adrian of the House of Brandywyne, please approach."

Standing, Adrian took a deep breath and ran her palms down her robe, smoothing it out. Then she walked to the table and looked down at the lead wizard. Not knowing what else to do, she gave him a slight curtsy. The lead wizard smiled.

"Please sit down," he said. "And do not be afraid, my child. No harm will come to you here, I promise."

Adrian took a seat in the high-backed, upholstered chair across the table from the lead wizard.

Rifling through the pile of parchments, Wigg finally pulled one out and placed it before him. After examining it, he looked back up at Adrian and smiled.

"Welcome, my dear. I knew your father. He was one of the best of the consuls."

Was, she thought. The single, harsh word went straight through her heart. "Begging your pardon, Lead Wizard, but do you mean to say that—"

"Forgive me, Adrian," Wigg interjected quickly. "I do not mean to imply that your father has died. In truth, we do not know. But more of that later. Now then, how many years have passed since you graduated from Fledgling House?"

Somewhat relieved, Adrian let go the deep breath she had been unconsciously holding. "Nine," she answered.

"That would make you one of the first class to do so, would it not?"
"Yes."
"Have you married?"
"No, Lead Wizard."
"Do you have children?"
"No."
"Please show us your tattoo, if you would."

With a nod, Adrian slipped her left arm from the sleeve of her robe and lifted it to show Wigg the Paragon on her shoulder, just as the other acolytes before her had done. After the lead wizard nodded, she placed her arm back into the robe.

"And now, please demonstrate some small use of the craft," Wigg asked her. "If the azure glow appears, that is permissible. But as a test of your talents, please try not to produce it."

Adrian looked around the room. Seeing the cold fireplace along one wall, she raised her arm and spread her fingers. The logs immediately jumped ablaze. No azure glow was evident. She closed her fist, and the fire went dead. She turned back to the lead wizard just in time to see one of his eyebrows arch up thoughtfully.

"Well done," he said. Beside him, Faegan smiled and stroked his blue cat.

"Please extend one wrist," Wigg said, placing a blank piece of parchment on the table.

Adrian did so. Wigg caused a small, painless incision to form in her skin, and a single drop of her blood fell onto the parchment. Almost immediately the droplet began to writhe its way into her familiar blood signature. For some time the two mystics compared it to the document Wigg had pulled from the pile. Finally, the lead wizard nodded his approval.

Reaching out, he pulled the odd-looking device toward him. It seemed to be a tripod, with a glass lens mounted at its top. Placing it directly over Adrian's blood signature, he looked down through the lens. After a few moments he nodded again, and passed the entire affair over to Faegan, who went through the same process. When the crippled wizard nodded, Wigg looked up at her and smiled.

"Welcome, Adrian," he said to her. "It is a pleasure to finally meet you. Were your father here, he would be very proud. As one of the first class to graduate Fledgling House, your senior status will be very much appreciated. Please take a seat with the others of your sisterhood."

With a nod, Adrian walked to the side of the table and joined those upon whom the two wizards had already passed judgment.

It took close to two hours for Wigg and Faegan to interview the remaining women. In the end, all were accepted.

Then Wigg stood and spoke to them as a group. He told them a brief history of the return of the Coven of sorceresses, the destruction of the Gates of Dawn, and how and why he had summoned them here. Prince Tristan had wished to greet them personally, Wigg said, but was on urgent business elsewhere. He also told them not to fear the menacing-looking Minions of Day and Night, whom they would soon see in and about the palace.

When he had finished, Wigg placed each hand into the opposite sleeve of his robe. His aquamarine eyes seemed to see right into the hearts of the assembled women.

"From this day forward, you are no longer to be known as the acolytes of Fledgling House," he said solemnly. "You are now the acolytes of the Redoubt, and your place is here, with us. You are hereby accorded all the rights and responsibilities associated with your new positions. As more of your sisterhood arrive, they will be examined as you have been. If they are found to be true acolytes, their blood also unpolluted by the Vagaries, they too will be blended into the fold." Then the lead wizard smiled.

"Welcome, ladies," he said with obvious feeling. "This moment has been too long in coming. It is truly a historic day."

Sixty-eight

As Tristan paced back and forth across the deck of his flagship, his mind was overcome with concerns both new and old. The scout ships had gone farther east into the Sea of Whispers days earlier, but still their patrolling warriors had little to tell. There was nothing to see but water, they kept on reporting as they tiredly returned to their vessels.

Have I ordered us all out here for nothing? he found himself wondering. Had the herbmistress Grizelda lied to them, simply to throw them off track? And if she had, then where was Wulfgar? Were Wigg and Faegan even correct in their assumption that his bastard brother was out to destroy the Orb of the Vigors?

The prince had gone to join the fleet as soon as he had learned that two of his warriors had gone missing. Although their disappearances proved nothing, he could sense that Wulfgar was out there somewhere. Soon, very soon now, things would come to a head.

It felt good to be at sea again. His newly acquired love of sailing was truly a part of him now—a part he hoped he would never have to give up completely. As the brisk westerlies moved through his hair, he casually grasped a line of rigging and leaned against the gunwale, his mind lost in thought.

Wigg, Shailiha, Traax, Abbey, and the warrior K'jarr were all here aboard the *Savage Scar* with him. Two days had passed since Wigg had accepted the acolytes into the Redoubt. Geldon had been left in charge, to greet any others of the sisterhood who might also make their way to the palace. Shawna the Short and a Minion warrior continued to watch over Marcus, Rebecca, and Morganna, while Ox and the remainder of the

Minion forces had also been left behind as a palace guard. Faegan and Celeste, too, remained at the palace, in case their gifts were needed to protect the Scroll of the Vigors. These measures gave Tristan a modicum of comfort. But as he continued to look out over the deep blue sea, the prince was both anxious and worried.

Traax came to stand next to Tristan. The Minion second in command laced his fingers and leaned his muscular forearms on the gunwale. As the *Savage Scar* cut through the waves, for several long moments neither of them spoke.

"Where in the name of the Afterlife are they?" Tristan finally breathed, his gaze still locked on the waves. "Are Wulfgar and his fleet of slavers really on the way, or is this all just some kind of elaborate ruse designed to draw the bulk of our forces away from the palace? Could they have already gotten by us?"

Looking for answers, he finally turned and searched the warrior's face. He valued Traax's opinion greatly, and he needed to know his thoughts.

"I do not know, my lord," Traax answered solemnly. "All I can say is that if the roles had been reversed, I would be doing exactly what you are now. Only time will tell. As Wigg said, we have no choice but to believe what the dead herbmistress told us, because it is far too dangerous not to."

"Yes, yes, I know," the prince replied. "But I just can't escape the feeling that—"

He stopped short as he realized that his breath was streaming out of his mouth in the form of a short, white, vapor trail. The temperature had dropped so quickly that neither he nor Traax had noticed at first, but now it was so bitterly cold that both of them had begun to shiver. Then the *Savage Scar* lost all of her forward momentum.

Fearing the worst, Tristan looked up to the sails. They had all gone completely limp, their lower hems nearly touching the decks. Turning, he desperately looked out over the sea and was horrified to find that its surface had become as smooth as glass. His flagship and every other vessel in the Minion fleet were dead in the water.

By now Shailiha, Abbey, and Wigg had come running, and the decks were awash with sword-wielding warriors, all shouting to one another and wanting desperately to help, but not knowing what to do.

From out of nowhere, Tristan was suddenly reminded of something Tyranny had said to him during their first meeting together, that day in her private quarters aboard *The People's Revenge*. As he replayed it in his mind, his blood ran cold.

Speed is the one thing that keeps us alive out here.

Tristan turned to Traax. The expression on the warrior's face had become as hard as granite.

"What is it?" the prince breathed. "What is happening?"

"It is the Necrophagians, my lord," Traax answered sternly. "The Eaters of the Dead. They have somehow found us. And nothing I know of can stop them."

Then another cold realization shot through the prince—the Necrophagians had never been known to venture this far west! Wasting no time, he reached out and grabbed Traax by both shoulders. As he did, he could see that a strange, dark gray fog had already begun to form. It was snaking its way up from the sea to surround his fleet. Soon the enemy would be here, he realized. And they would be more than just the Eaters of the Dead.

"Order all of the sails furled!" he shouted. "And signal all of the other ships in the fleet to do the same!"

"But my lord!" Traax exclaimed in a rare display of protest. "That will do no good! It would be a waste of precious time! With no wind, it does not matter!"

"Don't argue with me!" Tristan shouted angrily. "Just do it! And have K'jarr found and brought to me immediately!"

Traax snapped to attention. After going to bark out the orders, he returned to stand resolutely at his master's side, his dreggan drawn.

"What is it?" Wigg called urgently. "What's going on?"

But before Tristan could answer, the fog began to coalesce into hundreds of pairs of huge, gnarled hands that came rising up out of the sea. As he watched in horror, they began to cut their way silently through the smooth, still ocean, positioning themselves in pairs near each of the Minion vessels. Then the hands reached out and grasped the bows and sterns of the ships, holding them helplessly in place. Sections of gunwale and railing began to crack apart under the immense pressure.

Tristan felt his heart sink. He looked up urgently to the masts and spars to see the Minion crewmen trying to furl the sails as fast as they could. Some were done already.

Suddenly, the sea all around them seemed to come alive. As it began to burble and roil, he looked over the side and saw the horrible faces of the Eaters of the Dead surfacing. Then he saw the first of the maelstroms.

From beyond the Eaters of the Dead, dozens of glowing waterspouts rose from the sea, turning with a speed so fast he found it dizzying. Their great heights soon dwarfed his ships. The maelstroms flattened out at their tops, then dissolved into thousands of individual, flying creatures. There could be no mistaking them.

Screechlings.

And then Tristan gasped as he saw the first of Wulfgar's demon-slavers. The white-skinned monsters had seemingly materialized out of thin air to land crouching on the decks of his ships, their swords and tridents at the ready. Screaming wildly, they began hacking into the surprised Minion warriors with suicidal fury.

Tristan tried to shout orders out to Wigg and Traax, but each of them was already locked in individual combat. Pulling his sword from its scabbard, Tristan raised it just in time to ward off a blow from a demon-slaver that appeared from nowhere. Then he slipped to the right and slashed his dreggan low, tearing the flesh of the monster's left thigh with the point of his double-edged blade. As the slaver bent over in agony, Tristan raised his blade again and took the thing's head off with a single blow.

Using a few precious seconds, Tristan turned desperately to look for Shailiha. When his eyes finally fell on her, he saw that she had drawn her sword and was fighting off a slaver. But the monster was gaining ground on her, pushing her backward across the already bloody deck. Reaching behind his shoulder, Tristan grasped the first of his throwing knives and sent it spinning end over end. The dirk buried itself into the slaver's neck and the monster fell over.

Across the deck, Wigg was throwing azure bolt after azure bolt against the demonslavers, killing as many of them as possible the moment they materialized. Then there seemed to be a short lull in the fighting, and for a wonderful, fleeting moment Tristan almost believed they might somehow survive the carnage. But he had forgotten the screechlings.

The thousands of large, three-winged, brightly colored flying fish descended on the Minion fleet all at once. Deftly avoiding the demonslavers, they soared over the decks, and tore into sails, spars, and Minions alike with their razor-sharp teeth. Many of the warriors took to the air and tried to hack the deadly things from the sky. But it soon became clear that they were outnumbered.

Spars and rigging came crashing down, and whatever sails had not already been furled were systematically shredded. Minion warriors by the dozens were being viciously torn apart by the screechlings and then hoisted ruthlessly over the side, to be consumed by the wailing, ravenous Eaters of the Dead. Despite all of the screaming, clanging sword blades, and mayhem, the sickening tearing of Minion flesh could be heard rising from waters that were quickly turning red with the crimson stains of death.

Traax and K'jarr reached Tristan's side, and the three of them slashed violently with their dreggans. Tristan was about to shout to Traax, when he saw the warrior's face suddenly fall—a rare sight indeed, even in combat. Whirling around, Tristan looked to see what had so stunned his second-in-command. As he did, his mouth fell open.

All around them, the warships of Wulfgar's fleet were materializing. There must have been hundreds of them, Tristan realized, and they had clearly been the launching points of the demonslaver attacks. As endless swarms of demonslavers continued to use swinging lines and gangplanks to land on his decks, Tristan saw that his troops were not only hopelessly outnumbered, but completely surrounded, as well.

The prince's heart fell at the thought of how easily they had been led into the trap. Wulfgar must also be here, he thought as he struggled with a screaming slaver, pausing only to raise his dreggan to slash a screechling out of the air. But if Wulfgar was there, then why hadn't Wigg detected his blood?

There was only one thing to do now. It had only a small chance of success, and if it was ever to happen it would have to be soon, for the odds against their survival were climbing by the second. The prince shouted out his orders to Traax and K'jarr.

"Traax, I want you to find Wigg, Abbey, and Shailiha and get them safely into one of the litters! Leave the other litter empty! Tell them it is time, and they will understand! I will join you soon!"

With a nod, Traax was gone. Reaching down into the top of his right knee boot, Tristan withdrew a small oilskin pouch and carefully handed it to K'jarr.

"Do you remember your orders?" he shouted to the Minion.

"Yes, *Jin'Sai*," K'jarr shouted back. "It shall be done!"

Despite the madness and turmoil going on all around them, Tristan took a few precious seconds to look deeply into K'jarr's dark eyes. "All of our lives and the life of your nation depend on what it is you now do," he said. "You must not fail us in this!"

K'jarr unflinchingly returned Tristan's gaze. "I live to serve!" he shouted.

With a final nod from his lord, the warrior hid the small package beneath his leather body armor, took to the air, and slipped over the side of the ship. Tristan ran toward the bow, desperately fighting his way through demonslavers and screechlings as he went.

By now the situation had become so critical and the number of demonslavers so great that a thick horde of Minions had to surround him simply to ensure he would reach his goal. Many of them died. Blessedly, by the time he made it there the others were waiting for him inside one of the litters.

With Tristan finally aboard, the Minion bearers lifted the litters into the sky and soared upward, just as they were overrun. Some of the screechlings tried to follow, but were cut down by Minion escorts. Then the remainder of the warriors soared from their stricken vessels and followed suit, climbing into the sky after them. As they did, the demonslavers left on the bloody decks cheered and waved their swords in celebration of their great victory.

Wondering whether his plan would work, Tristan looked silently over at his sister. She was dirty and disheveled and her left arm was bleeding, but Wigg had apparently been able to close the wound for now. Tristan gave her a small smile, and she smiled back.

Looking down at the fleet he had just ordered abandoned, Tristan desperately wondered whether he had done the right thing. It was out of his control now, he knew. As he waited and watched, he closed his hands tightly around the hilt of his dreggan.

K'jarr soared low over the waves, desperately staving off the screechlings that tried to force him down into the dark, waiting maws of the Eaters of the Dead. Four times they nearly took him, and four times he fought them off. But the battle on the decks had tired him, and he wasn't sure how long he could continue searching for the right opportunity.

Finally, after several long moments of circling the waterline of the *Savage Scar*, he found a place clear of screechlings and Necrophagians.

Hovering near the bowsprit he took a supreme chance and turned his back to the sea. Reaching into his body armor he withdrew the oilskin pouch, then carefully stuffed its contents into the gap between the bowsprit rail and the hull, taking extra care to make sure it would not come loose.

Turning away from the hull he soared up and away, in search of the *Jin'Sai*'s departing litters.

*W*hen Wigg thought they were finally high enough, he nodded to Tristan. Then the prince gave his litter bearers a prearranged signal and they stopped climbing, instead hovering in place. They were high in the sky, directly above the two opposing fleets. The bloody Minion decks were now empty of warriors, and the demonslavers were still swarming over their decks, raucously rejoicing in their victory.

Tristan anxiously waited for Traax to lead the remainder of his forces up. As they came, he was dismayed at how few of them had survived. Then K'jarr finally caught up with them.

"Is it done?" Tristan shouted out nervously.

"Yes, my lord!" the Minion answered proudly. "All is as you requested!"

A look of relief crossed the prince's face. Wasting no time, he gave orders for the two litters to separate and to put a good distance between one another. Then he looked back over at Wigg and Abbey. It was time.

"You can do this," he told them.

"If I can both hold the litter in place long enough and also sustain a warp, and if the process will actually work in reverse," Wigg replied. "But as Faegan and I told you before, there are so many variables—"

"This is no time for a lecture about the craft!" Tristan countered quickly. "We're out of time! You need to start now!"

Nodding, Wigg looked over at Abbey, and then out at the distant litter the Minions were still holding. Taking a deep breath, he steeled himself and raised his arms in its direction.

Azure bolts shot from his hands and flew toward the other litter. As the azure glow engulfed the litter, the bearers let it go and flew away from it. Two of the warriors were badly burned, but it couldn't be helped.

It was plain to see that the lead wizard was straining with all his might to keep the empty litter from crashing into the sea, while at the same time maintaining the azure warp he had placed around it. Beads of sweat broke out on his forehead, and his arms shook.

Glancing over into Abbey's terrified eyes, Tristan gave her a look of encouragement. Then he looked out of the litter toward Traax.

"Now!" he shouted at the warrior.

Traax flew around to Abbey's side. The herbmistress stood up shakily, and Traax lifted her into his strong arms. Then he flew her toward the empty litter.

As she lay hundreds of feet above the waves in Traax's arms, Abbey carefully opened the leather cinch bag that hung from a strap around her neck. It held the ingredients required to start a gazing flame. Removing a pinch of herbs from it, she reached through the warp, dropped them over the side of the litter, and watched them fall onto the hot embers already burning on its specially constructed, metal floor. She then bowed her head.

As expected, almost immediately the familiar, golden flame came alive and started to burn away the sides and roof of the litter, leaving only the metal floor. Abbey cast a few more of the herbs into the flame and it roared higher, gaining color and strength. Raising one arm, she silently commanded the flame to split into two separate branches. The smaller of the two then obediently angled itself over toward her.

After carefully placing the first bottle of herbs back into the cinch bag, she removed the second one. Opening it, she took another pinch of herbs and dropped them down into the nearest of the two branched flames. The two branches rejoined, returning to the vertical. Placing the second bottle back into the cinch bag, she gently removed yet another precious item. Closing her eyes, she held it high.

It was a piece of vellum recently taken from the Scroll of the Vigors.

When the viewing window in the gazing flame started to form, Abbey opened her eyes again. Looking into the window she saw what the piece of vellum in her hands was searching for and had finally found: the same item K'jarr had just hidden in the gap between the bowsprit and the hull of the *Savage Scar.*

It was the other half of the vellum that Krassus had enchanted and hidden in Tristan's boot—the vellum the wizard of the Vagaries had hoped would destroy them all, but hadn't. It was also the item Tristan had shown the wizards that day on the balcony, when he had outlined his battle plan for them.

As Abbey watched, the vellum in the window—the twin image of the one on board the *Savage Scar*—began to emit pinpricks of azure light. With the birth of the lights came great screeching sounds, their noises so great that she and Traax could barely stand the pain in their ears.

Knowing the time had come, Traax immediately turned around and flew them both back to the waiting litter. As he did Wigg lowered his hands, and the remains of the other litter and Abbey's gazing flame fell into the sea. After Abbey was helped back inside, everyone looked down at the *Savage Scar.* Hoping against hope, Tristan held his breath.

From the bow of the flagship the screaming shafts of light broke free of the enchanted vellum and tore into everything around them. They lit up the sea and sky with massive, azure strikes, twisting and turning relentlessly as they sought out whatever they could find and destroy.

The *Savage Scar* went up first. The shards of light shot through her from stem to stern, and with a great, torturous shudder, she blew apart. Her masts and spars came crashing down, her decks ruptured mightily, and what was left of her rolled over, capsizing in the sea.

As she went down, the hordes of screaming demonslavers still on her decks fell overboard. The careening shafts of azure light struck them, killing them instantly, providing fresh carrion for the hungry Necrophagians below the surface of the water. Finally, the *Savage Scar* slipped beneath the waves.

The shards continued on, tearing into the remaining ships, both Minion and demonslaver alike. One by one the other vessels exploded and turned over, spilling the slavers into the sea. The blood on the ocean seemed to stretch on forever.

Meanwhile, the azure lights had found the screechlings and were tearing into them in midflight. As the shards struck them the screechlings exploded, torn offal and thin red blood tumbling sloppily into the sea to join the carnage.

And then, finally, it seemed to be over. The faces of the Eaters of the Dead had vanished, and all the ships of both fleets had sunk, leaving only wooden debris bobbing up and down on the restless, crimson waves.

But as the occupants of the litters and the warriors hovering along-side it were about to learn, Krassus' enchantments were not finished. Pausing for a moment, the azure shards began to regroup and hover just above the surface of the waves, as if still searching out life-forms to destroy.

And then they began soaring upward, directly toward Tristan and his companions.

"Get us out of here, now!" the prince shouted to Traax.

Traax ordered the warriors to fly the litters higher in a desperate attempt to escape the twisting, screaming shards.

Climbing ever higher, the litter ripped through an oncoming cloud bank. Tristan held his breath, looking back to see whether the deadly shards were still following them. Then the hundreds of light streaks also tore out of the cloud, still racing unerringly toward the litter.

Tristan gritted his teeth. Krassus' shards were gaining on them, and in a matter of moments it would all be over.

Then he felt Wigg push him to one side, and the wizard looked out of the litter. His robe flying in the wind, Wigg raised his arms, ready to throw his own bolts at the relentlessly pursuing shards.

But just as Wigg was about to attack them, the shards started to fade. One by one, as their power died, Krassus' enchantments finally slowed, then tumbled end over end into the waiting sea. As they struck the waves they caused the ocean to bubble and roil for a time, and then they were gone. Closing his eyes, Tristan took a deep breath and sat back in his seat.

When he opened them again, he found the lead wizard staring at him. Saying nothing, Wigg raised an eyebrow. Tristan smiled at him, then ordered the litter to turn west, toward home.

Sixty-nine

"Do you really think they'll be all right?" Celeste asked anxiously as she searched Faegan's face for what must have been the hundredth time. "There has been no Minion messenger from the fleet today, and that's not like Tristan. Something is going on out there on the Sea of Whispers—I can almost smell it. Not knowing what is happening is driving me mad."

She and the wizard were in the Hall of Blood Records, deep in the Redoubt. Faegan had been ensconced there for the greater part of the day as he studied the record of Wulfgar's blood signature, looking for answers. Regrettably, none had come to him.

He feared for the lives of his friends but was trying not to reveal his concern to Celeste. Already she paced the sumptuous room like a caged animal. Faegan's ancient violin—one of his most prized possessions—lay beside him on the table. Playing it sometimes helped him to concentrate, and today had been no exception.

For her part, Celeste had grown tired of being left to her own devices in the lonely palace above and had come to search Faegan out. It wasn't about being frightened. She was ready to face the worst, should it come to that. It was more about being left behind with nothing to do while Tristan and the others were out at sea, looking for Wulfgar. Being marooned at the palace had made her feel impotent and alone.

The wizard raised his face from his research and smiled slightly. "We were left here for a reason, you know. But do not worry, my child. Wigg, Abbey, Tristan, and Shailiha are four of the most resourceful people I have ever known, and if anyone can stop Wulfgar's demonslavers, it is they. Besides, we still do not know whether Grizelda was telling the truth. For all we know, Wulfgar may not have even left the Citadel."

"I know that," she responded. Some composure had crowded its way back into her husky voice. "But the truth be known, I just can't help feeling—"

She stopped as the wizard suddenly stiffened and raised one arm, bidding her to silence. His face had suddenly become very grave and searching.

Furrowing his brow, Faegan cocked his head and swiveled his chair, as if he was looking for something. Then he looked upward. Celeste's eyes followed his, and saw that one corner of the ceiling was glowing with the power of the craft, just as it had not so long ago in the card room of the palace above, when Krassus had first revealed himself to them.

But the glow gathered far more quickly this time; so fast, in fact, that neither Faegan nor Celeste had time to react before a man's form coalesced, clinging to the walls and ceiling just as Krassus had. As Faegan raised his hands to use the craft, a single, terrible bolt of azure confined him within a wizard's warp. Dread shot through him as he realized he could neither move, nor speak.

Celeste didn't hesitate. She raised both hands and let loose terrifying bolts that seared across the room. But the man only laughed and launched himself to the opposite side of the room. Celeste's bolts exploded against the empty wall in a massive crash of marble, noise, and dust.

Raising her arms as fast as she could, she attacked him again. But again he was too fast for her. He launched himself into the air, leaving her bolts to tear into one of the massive bookcases. With a great crash it toppled over, spilling texts and scrolls onto the floor. The room began to fill with dark, acrid smoke, which made her cough.

Then the man vanished again. Celeste took a hesitant step forward. As she did, from the depths of the smoke came a dark, knowing laugh.

Suddenly twin bolts came slashing out of the gloom and struck her squarely in the chest. The force of the impact lifted her high off her feet and threw her across the room as though she were a rag doll. Red hair flying, she smashed against the hundreds of drawers containing the blood records and fell unconscious to the floor.

ooking around the room for a moment, Wulfgar seemed to make up his mind. With a single wave of one hand, the smoke disappeared and the fires went out.

He placed one of the chairs from the meeting table before Faegan and sat down. Then he lifted his long legs onto the table and crossed one over the other.

After regarding Faegan for a few moments, Wulfgar reached out one hand and arrogantly snapped his fingers. Faegan immediately found his voice had returned.

"You're Tristan and Shailiha's half brother, aren't you?" the old wizard growled from within the azure warp.

Wulfgar smiled. "How astute."

Faegan looked with concerned eyes at Celeste. "What have you done to her, you bastard!" he demanded. "Is she dead?"

Crossing his arms over his chest, Wulfgar leaned back in the chair. Lazily, he glanced over at Celeste.

"In truth, I do not know," he answered unconcernedly, as if he were discussing the weather instead of the survival of a fellow human being. "She is the daughter of Wigg, is she not? Krassus told me of her. Such a rare beauty! Were I not otherwise involved, I might be inclined to take her for myself." Then the menacing eyes turned back and found Faegan again.

"But she is not the reason I have come," Wulfgar said. "I have far greater goals to attain, and you are going to help me. I have come to accomplish what Krassus tried to do but failed, that day he visited you. Things have finally come full circle."

The amiable expression melted away from Wulfgar's face. As his upper lip twisted its way into a sneer, he leaned forward and glared at the helpless wizard.

"Now then," he asked softly. "Where is the Scroll of the Vigors?"

"Tristan and Wigg will return," Faegan countered gamely, trying to buy all the time he could. "You have very little time to destroy the Orb of the Vigors."

A knowing look overcame Wulfgar's face, and he gave Faegan a short, menacing smile. "Krassus told me that the two remaining wizards of the Redoubt were exceedingly clever. How right he was." Then the look on his face turned deadly again, and he removed his legs from the table.

"Anyone who was with your fleet is by now quite dead, I assure you," he continued. "Even the gifts of the lead wizard could not have overcome both my creatures and the overwhelming surprise I arranged. If by any bizarre chance any of your people did escape, however, they will be caught by the small contingent of ships I set to guard the entrance to Cavalon Delta. I'm so glad you decided to stay behind, though, because that gives us this little chance to chat." He sat back in his chair.

"Now then, where is the Scroll of the Vigors?" he asked again.

"This is your last chance to answer without consequence. I suggest you think it over well. Your arrogance is about to cause you a great deal of pain, old man."

"The Minions surrounding the palace will come and take you," Faegan said boldly. "Even you will not be able to kill them all." Sweat was running down his face as he desperately tried to break free of Wulfgar's warp. But it was completely unforgiving—like sitting in a tight iron cage that had no door.

"Oh, yes, yet more of my brother's warriors to be dealt with," Wulfgar answered dismissively. "But I've brought an entire host of demon-slavers here with me by cloaking my flagship and sailing up the Sippora. They outnumber your remaining Minions by more than two to one, though they have remained quite invisible until this point. At the same time I appeared before you, my slavers also materialized, and they are engaging your very surprised troops as we speak. Even your vaunted flying warriors cannot overcome my demonslavers' superior numbers unless they choose to fly away. But that would go against everything their strict warrior code stands for, now, wouldn't it?" The twisted smile came again.

"In some ways it could be said that your Minions are actually killing *themselves*," Wulfgar added thoughtfully. "It seems there will be a great many Minion funeral pyres lighting up the sky tonight, wizard."

"How did you get into the Redoubt?" Faegan growled, still trying to stall. He desperately needed to free himself somehow and regain the use of his powers. But the more he tried, the more impossible it became. He had never felt such raw power. The sweat ran down from his brow to tease his eyes maddeningly.

"How did I enter the Redoubt, you ask?" Wulfgar responded. "Why, that was the easiest part of all. I cloaked my blood and followed you here, you fool! I have been following you all day, hoping that you would lead me here. And you did not disappoint. I had cherished the thought that you might unknowingly show me where the scroll is hidden, but you did not. So now we are forced to do this the hard way. I know you have the answer, and I will get it from you, one way or the other."

"Why do you need it so badly?" Faegan demanded. "You already have the other one. You do not need the Scroll of the Vigors to destroy the orb. Isn't that why you have come?"

"I wish to possess them both for another reason," Wulfgar answered calmly. "What you have failed to grasp is that the Scroll of the Vigors holds the secrets to my brother's unique, azure blood. Yes, wizard, that's right. My dear brother—the only being in the world who might one day challenge my powers. Without the scroll, the secret of how to change his blood back from azure to red will never be known, and I will always reign supreme."

His eyes shining with the anticipation of imminent success, Wulfgar leaned closer. "Now, tell me, old man," he said menacingly. "Where is the other scroll?"

Knowing full well that he was condemning himself to death, Faegan shook his head. "We know you possess a left-leaning blood signature, but how can you willingly do such a thing? He's your brother!"

A look of disdain crossed Wulfgar's face. "I am the *Enseterat*. My brother is the *Jin'Sai,* and his sister is the *Jin'Saiou*. They are of the Twos, and I am of the Heretics. It was preordained eons ago that we should eventually become locked in conflict, and so we shall." Wulfgar's patience was wearing thin.

"Now then," he whispered. "I ask you for the final time: Where is the other scroll?"

Clenching his jaw, Faegan shook his head again. He had already begun partitioning his mind in an attempt to keep Wulfgar from gleaning the location of the scroll. It had been hidden well, and only he and the lead wizard knew where. If he could keep Wulfgar out of his mind, he was relatively sure that the scroll would not be found. The fate of the world would soon boil down to a contest of endowed wills.

And blood.

"Very well," Wulfgar answered softly. "You leave me no other choice."

Then Wulfgar did something unexpected. Reaching through the warp he had created, he lifted the hem of Faegan's robe, exposing the crippled wizard's destroyed legs.

Twin bolts of shock and horror went through Faegan.

Sitting back in his chair, Wulfgar carefully examined Faegan's mutilated legs. "My, my," he murmured as he looked closer. "The late Coven of sorceresses did quite a skillful job on you, didn't they?"

Faegan's legs were a gruesome sight. The skin was almost completely gone, and much of the muscle mass looked as if it had been shredded away by some terrible beast attacking the legs with teeth and claws. The remaining bright red muscles throbbed visibly, and what looked to be exposed nerves and blood vessels ran up and down their lengths. For over three hundred years they had been this way, and even given his immense knowledge of the craft, Faegan had never been able to heal them. Only his wizardly self-discipline had kept him from going irretrievably mad from the pain.

The sight of his legs brought memories flooding back—the same three-hundred-year-old nightmares that he had tried so hard to forget. The Coven had tortured him for information and left him to die, only to be found later by the gnomes of Shadowood and nurtured back to health. And now the same, unspeakable torment was to begin anew. But this time there would be no one to help him, and he probably wouldn't survive.

Hoping against hope, he looked over at Celeste, but she was still unmoving. Gathering up his courage, he looked Wulfgar in the eyes. "Why not simply enter my mind?" he asked.

"I could," Wulfgar answered. "But when Krassus told me of the nature of your infirmity, I realized that this approach would prove infinitely more entertaining. And with your friends all dead, and my demonslavers in control of the palace, we have all the time in the world to amuse each other. Besides, should this prove unsuccessful, I can always walk through your thoughts later." The wicked smile came again.

Looking across the table, Wulfgar spied Faegan's violin and bow. Calling the craft, he caused them to rise. The bow stroked the strings, and the melody they produced was sorrowful and forlorn.

"Some music to help drown out the noise?" Wulfgar asked. "Personally speaking, I don't like screaming. It's so . . . common."

Narrowing his eyes, Wulfgar caused the violin to play louder. He leaned forward eagerly in his chair.

"Now then," he said softly. "Shall we begin?"

Seventy

As Tristan soared along in the litter, he still couldn't let go of his dread. The enemy fleet had been defeated, but he couldn't escape the feeling that Wulfgar and Krassus had not been with it, as there had been no atmospheric disturbances that would have accompanied their deaths.

It was entirely possible that Wulfgar and Krassus had been aboard one of the ships that had been farther out to sea when they sank, but in his heart the prince didn't think so. And he didn't think the lead wizard believed it, either.

Looking across the litter, the prince saw Wigg staring out of the window, lost in thought. Shailiha and Abbey gave Tristan comforting, supportive smiles, but he knew what they were all thinking.

This wasn't over.

Suddenly Traax appeared, flying beside Tristan's window. The warrior had a very concerned look on his face.

"Permission to enter?" Traax shouted out. The prince nodded.

With a single, sure motion, Traax grabbed the roof of the litter, snapped his wings closed, and hoisted himself in. Landing abruptly on the seat next to Shailiha, he looked over at Tristan. Wigg took his thoughtful gaze from the Sea of Whispers and turned his attention to the Minion second in command.

"There is news," Traax said simply. "Our scouts have sighted vessels near the mouth of the delta. They say they are demonslaver warships."

Tristan froze.

"How many?" he asked.

"Fourteen, my lord. But there are a dozen or so other ships fighting them. They carry the image of the Paragon on their sails and fly your battle standards atop their masts. That means they belong to the woman privateer, does it not?"

Tristan's breath caught in his lungs. "Take us there immediately!" he barked. "I want the warriors to fly as they have never flown before! Those who arrive first are to join the battle immediately! When the litter arrives, search out the *Reprisal* and take us down! Then I will issue further orders!"

With a nod of his dark head, Traax dived headfirst from the speeding litter.

Tristan stared over at Wigg, his eyes searching the ancient wizard's face for some reassurance that they might get there in time. Wigg looked down at the floor of the litter for a moment, then back up at the *Jin'Sai* and sadly shook his head.

*H*ad Scars not been watching his captain's back, Tyranny would have died immediately. As a screaming demonslaver raised his trident, Scars came up behind him and hoisted the white-skinned monster into his massive arms. With one arm wrapped around the slaver's throat and the other pushing sideways against its hairless skull, Scars viciously forced the monster's head over to one side until he heard the neck bones grate, then give way and crack apart altogether. As the light went out of its eyes, Scars hoisted the dead slaver over the nearby gunwale and tossed it into the sea.

But instead of the body sinking beneath the waves, another fate awaited it.

Wulfgar's dark red sea slitherers combed the waters around the struggling vessels, their long, smooth, scaly bodies slipping over and under each other as they sought out their next mouthfuls of warm flesh. Scars didn't know what these creatures were, or how they had come to be here. Nor did he care. All that concerned him was the survival of his captain and her crew. But the battle was not going their way, and unless the tide turned soon, he knew that they would all perish.

He grabbed another screaming slaver, viciously broke its back against the gunwale, and dropped it into the sea.

The screams and the muffled, snarling grunts of the gorging sea slitherers seemed to go on forever.

*A*s the moments passed torturously by, Tristan's knuckles turned white around the hilt of his dreggan. It had been more than half an hour since the Minion forces and the litter had turned toward the delta, and still there was nothing to see other than waves. But a report had come back through the Minion lines that some of the fastest warriors had finally reached the fighting and were starting down. For that much, at least, Tristan was thankful. He knew Tyranny needed them.

As the cold wind lashed his face, he searched the waves for a sign that Tyranny and her little fleet of privateers might still be in one piece.

And then, finally, there they were.

Her twelve ships were lying adrift amidst the slaver ships, their decks bloodied. The *Reprisal*'s spars, sails, and rigging had been damaged in the fight, but she seemed to be in no danger of sinking.

As the litter went down, Tristan could see that the fighting seemed to be over. Hundreds of Tyranny's crew, Wulfgar's demonslavers, and Minion warriors all lay dead. He could not tell what the outcome had been. Body parts from both sides could be seen everywhere. A strange sense of quiet prevailed, despite the horrific nature of the scene. As the litter finally hit the deck, Tristan jumped out, his dreggan held high.

"You're late!" he heard Tyranny's voice call out from somewhere behind him. Then he heard her laugh. "I told you I'd still be in your hair for a while!"

Tristan spun around to see her standing there, the hilt of her sheathed sword still dripping blood. In one hand she held a bottle of red wine, and in the other was one of her small cigars. After swallowing a healthy swig of wine, she took a draught of smoke, inhaling it deeply. With a satisfied sigh she raised her lovely jaw and blew the smoke toward the sky. Then her expression softened a bit, and she smiled at him.

"You didn't think for one moment that I was about to let you have *all* the fun, did you?" she asked coyly.

Tristan immediately went over and embraced her. Her face was smudged and bloodied, and her short hair was even more tousled than usual. Looking over her shoulder, he saw that Scars was still alive, helping to direct the tossing of slaver corpses into the sea. Those that had survived the battle were on their knees, waiting to have their throats cut. There seemed to be no shortage of crewmen volunteering for the task.

By this time Wigg, Abbey, Traax, and Shailiha were all standing beside them, and the bulk of the Minion forces were landing on the decks of the other vessels, dreggans drawn. A few surviving slavers tried to fight them off, but were quickly dealt with.

"What happened?" Tristan asked anxiously.

"We were returning to the delta when these slaver ships suddenly appeared out of nowhere," Tyranny answered. "Thank the Afterlife there weren't more of them than this! They had completely surrounded us, and we had no alternative but to stand and fight. For some reason it seemed imperative to them that they not allow us any closer to the mouth of the Sippora, and they fought like they were insane. Had your warriors not arrived when they did, we probably wouldn't be standing here talking to each other." She took another drink from the bottle, then smiled again.

Something she had said to Tristan struck a nerve. But before the prince could answer her, Wigg's voice cut him off, separating him from his thoughts.

"Tristan!" the lead wizard called out. "Come here and look at this!"

The prince turned to see Wigg standing beside Scars at the starboard gunwale, staring down into the surrounding sea. Tristan and the rest of them walked over to join him and looked down as well.

Scars and a handful of Tyranny's crewmen were tossing demonslaver corpses and body parts into the sea. For the first time Tristan saw the horrific, serpentine sea slitherers as they hissed viciously at each other, competing for the next mouthful of warm flesh.

"What in the name of the Afterlife *are* those things?" Shailiha breathed, her voice little more than a whisper.

"They are certainly a product of the Vagaries," Wigg mused, "although in all my three-hundred-plus years I have never seen their kind before. I suspect they were meant to follow Wulfgar's fleet as an additional form of protection. Much like the screechlings. Very clever, when you think about it. One beast to serve him in the sea, and another to serve him in the sky."

Tristan looked at Traax. "Before we leave here, select a contingent of warriors to stay behind and deal with these abominations," he ordered.

Traax came to attention and snapped his boot heels together. "It shall be done," he replied quickly.

Tristan had an important question for Tyranny. But before he could ask her, Scars reappeared by her side. There was a strange look on the giant's face.

"Begging your pardon, Captain, but during their searches of the demonslaver ships, our crew made an unexpected discovery."

"What is it?" she asked.

Turning, Scars pointed one of his huge paws toward the bow deck. "More slaves," he said quietly.

Tyranny snapped her head around. Forty filthy, emaciated slaves, men and women alike, had appeared before them on the deck. Shackled together by hand and foot, many of them could no longer stand. Some were on their knees, while others simply lay on the bloody deck, slowly dying. A few stood, looking at their saviors as though they had just descended from some long-forgotten dream.

Tyranny took a slow step toward them, then another and another, her eyes on a male slave. His hands were crippled and his face and body were covered with soot, as if he had just come from some kind of forge. Dressed in only a tattered loincloth, he had a long, filthy beard and hair that nearly reached his shoulders.

Then the wine bottle dropped from Tyranny's hand, and she began to walk faster, then faster still. Finally she was running for all she was worth across the bloody deck.

"Jacob?" she breathed, not daring to believe. "Jacob . . . *Jacob!*"

As if locked within some kind of dream, Twenty-Nine simply stared at her as she came running toward him. With tears in his eyes, he fell to his knees sobbing. As she reached out her arms, Tyranny's face reflected exultant joy.

Dropping to her knees, she placed a hand on either side of Twenty-Nine's face and looked into his eyes. Tears cascaded freely down his cheeks, and he wrapped his shaking arms around her and held her close, as though he never wanted to let go. Pulling him to her, she closed her eyes and began gently rocking him back and forth as she ran one hand down over his long, dirty hair. After what seemed forever, he looked back into her face.

"Mother and Father?" he asked, his voice little more than a hoarse whisper.

Tyranny shook her head. "No," she whispered back.

Hearing boot heels, Tyranny looked up to see Tristan standing beside them. "Your brother?" he asked softly.

Tyranny nodded. "Jacob," she said, turning her eyes back to him. "I had almost given up hope."

Tristan was about to speak again when a quick, dark shadow passed over the deck. Looking up, he saw a Minion warrior half flying, half tumbling down out of the sky. His chest and arms were covered with blood, and one of his wings seemed to be injured.

He was flying from the direction of the palace.

Traax and two others immediately took off, reaching their wounded comrade just as he was about to give up and come crashing to the deck. Holding him in their arms, they landed gently and laid him down. Everyone crowded around.

The warrior's wounds were grave. Wigg immediately knelt down and placed one palm on the Minion's forehead. The wizard closed his eyes. Upon opening them again he stood up and, looking sadly over at Tristan, shook his head.

Kneeling down, Tristan looked into the warrior's face. His eyelids were heavy, and his breathing was labored. Blood ran from his wounds to mingle with that already on the deck. Tristan lifted the warrior's head up.

"Can you hear me?" the prince asked gently.

The warrior nodded weakly. "Yes, my lord."

"Did you come from the palace?"

Another nod.

"What happened?"

Reaching out to grasp Tristan's forearm, the Minion tried to bring his face closer. Tristan leaned farther down—so close that he could hear the death rattle starting to build in the warrior's lungs. The Minion's body was shaking; a trickle of blood ran from one corner of his mouth.

"Demonslavers," he whispered. "Too many of them . . . so many of us dead . . ." His face constricted with pain, he looked up into Tristan's eyes. "You must hurry, my lord . . . Celeste and the wizard Faegan . . . They're . . ." With a final, wheezing rattle, the last breath escaped from the warrior's lungs, and his eyes closed.

Gravely, Tristan laid the warrior's head down on the deck of the *Reprisal*. Standing, he stared for a moment into Traax's eyes.

Then he ran toward the litter. Shailiha, Abbey, and Wigg followed him. He helped the others safely inside, then was about to get in himself when Tyranny brushed by him and began to climb in.

Grabbing her by the arm, Tristan gave her a hard look. "What about Jacob?" he asked.

Stopping, she turned and looked at him. "I'm coming with you," she said flatly, as the wind moved through her hair. "I owe you this. If you hadn't seen to it that I had been given these ships, my brother would still be out there, somewhere. And as for Jacob, he couldn't be in safer hands. Scars will care for him as he would care for me."

"Besides," she added, "I have a feeling that you're going to need all the swords you can muster."

As she started to climb in again, Tristan pulled her back. "There's something I have to know," he asked her urgently. "Did you see any humans during your fight with the demonslavers? Anyone of the craft?" When Tyranny shook her head, Tristan's heart sank.

Quickly the two joined the others in the litter. As the litter rose from the decks of the *Reprisal,* the sky around it became dark with Minion warriors. Like a strange cloud, it turned to the southwest and sped across the sky. Soon the rich, green grasses of the Cavalon Delta appeared below them.

As Tristan looked out of the litter, a single, burning thought kept crowding out all his other fears.

Celeste.

CHAPTER

Seventy-one

With a wave of one hand, Wulfgar caused the hovering violin and bow to change the tune they were playing. Listening to the new haunting melody, he closed his eyes and leaned back luxuriously in his chair. When he finally opened his hazel eyes again, he began to speak in an even, measured tone; just as a father might speak to a son whom he had decided needed to be punished.

"You're making this far more difficult on yourself than need be," he said quietly, almost compassionately. "Simply tell me where the Scroll of the Vigors is, and I will grant you a quick, painless death. And the woman, as well, should she still be alive. Doesn't that sound wonderful? Just think of it—no more agony in your legs, and no more misplaced loyalty to a group of so-called friends who seem to have foolishly left you here in my care. Just a perfect, forgiving, and peaceful sleep that will last forever."

Faegan slumped over in his chair, his head lolling to one side. Drool dripped from one corner of his mouth, and his robe was folded up over his lap, exposing his crippled legs. He was soaked with sweat, and his entire body shook uncontrollably from time to time like a marionette dancing at the ends of some unseen master's strings.

The torture had been going on for more than two hours now, and twice Wulfgar had been forced to use the craft to bring his subject back to consciousness after the wizard had fainted.

And Wulfgar's patience was wearing thin.

The *Enseterat* turned to look at the still-inert body of Celeste, lying facedown like a broken doll beneath the pile of records drawers. He gave a short laugh. He had not bothered to determine whether she was still alive, but he really didn't care. Who was she, he thought, to think that she might challenge his powers?

He turned back to regard the azure, serrated knife that hovered in the air near the wizard's right calf. He had chosen to conjure this particular instrument not only because it could yield its results slowly and with great precision, but also because the simplicity of the concept amused him.

Leaning forward, Wulfgar smiled. "Sometimes less is more, wouldn't you agree?" he asked Faegan. Eyes glazed over, the crippled wizard tried to lift his head, but couldn't.

"I will . . . never tell . . . you," he said thickly. "No matter what you do . . . to me."

"As you wish," Wulfgar answered casually. The *Enseterat* narrowed his eyes, and the serrated edge of the knife moved closer to Faegan's calf.

Then it began to slowly scrape its way down along the raw, exposed flesh and nerves of Faegan's leg.

Faegan screamed. His eyes bulged and the cords in his neck knotted, standing out in sharp relief. Then the blade stopped about halfway down, and Wulfgar pursed his lips. Crying and babbling incoherently, Faegan's head slumped forward onto his chest.

Wulfgar sighed. "I may have to enter your mind after all," he said casually. "Even though that was not my first choice. I now ask you for the last time: Where is the scroll?"

Slowly opening his eyes, all Faegan saw was a blur sitting across from him. Blinking hard, he desperately tried to get his mind working again. He had been holding out for as long as he could. But he feared that if he rebelled much longer, Wulfgar would walk through his mind, trying to discover the location of the scroll. And if that happened now, weak as Faegan had become with the torture, all of their planning would be for naught. For then the bastard brother of the Chosen Ones would possess a secret far more precious than even the Scroll of the Vigors. The secret that he, Wigg, and Abbey had discovered and wished to keep hidden no matter the cost.

He would do his best to endure one more use of the azure knife, he thought drunkenly. And then he would give Wulfgar the scroll. That was what Wigg and Abbey would want—to sacrifice the scroll in order to keep the secret.

Raising his head, Faegan did his best to look into Wulfgar's eyes.

"No," he said bluntly. "Do your worst." Gathering up all of the saliva he could muster, he spat it directly into Wulfgar's face.

Calmly wiping away the spittle, Wulfgar gave Faegan a menacing smile.

"As you wish," the *Enseterat* said softly.

Narrowing his eyes, Wulfgar caused the knife blade to press up against Faegan's right leg, and the crippled wizard cried out insanely. As the blade made its slow, torturous way down, waves of hot, searing pain shot through his nervous system. The wizard knew that if the torture continued, he would be only a few heartbeats away from death. That was when he finally allowed himself to beg.

"Please," he sobbed. His voice was little more than a whisper. "I'll tell you . . . just don't do that any more . . . I beg of you . . ."

The knife stopped and moved over to one side. Wulfgar smiled. "That's more like it," he said quietly. Leaning forward, he folded his arms over his chest. "I'm waiting," he whispered.

"The far wall," Faegan answered. "At the end of the bookcase . . . The three variegated swirls in the marble . . . Touch them all at once . . ."

Wulfgar stood and walked to the wall. He reached up with his right hand and placed his first three fingers on the smooth, cool spots Faegan had described. As he did, the azure glow of the craft surrounded the area.

With a soft click, a section of the marble wall revolved on a pivot to reveal a deep, square vault. The Scroll of the Vigors lay inside, one end pointing toward him. Carefully, almost reverently, Wulfgar pulled it from its resting place.

He cradled the scroll triumphantly. He did not need the Scroll of the Vigors for his personal use. His only need was for the Scroll of the Vagaries, and the secrets it contained. But by keeping this scroll away from the mentors of the *Jin'Sai* and the *Jin'Saiou,* he could keep Tristan and Shailiha perpetually untrained.

And in doing so, he would ensure that he would rule supreme forever.

He turned to look back at Faegan, another smile crossed his face.

"When the Orb of the Vigors is destroyed, the life enchantments sustaining you and the lead wizard will vanish, so I must now bid you a final good-bye. I shall leave my warp in place, so that you don't run off anywhere."

On his way out of the room, Wulfgar turned back. "Before I go, please let me ask you one final question," he said courteously. "Tell me, traitor, how does it feel to have betrayed everything you once held so dear?"

Without waiting for a reply, Wulfgar smiled again, and the azure glow of the craft surrounded him. Then the glow disappeared, and both he and the scroll were gone. After a few moments the door to the Hall of Blood Records opened, then closed again.

Sobbing, Faegan looked over at Celeste. Then he looked at the empty vault in the wall, its door still open and yawning at him. Tears ran down his cheeks, and he lowered his face in shame.

CHAPTER

Seventy-two

By the time Tristan's litter and its accompanying Minion forces reached Tammerland, night was falling. Little had been said during the trip, and it had seemed to the prince that for some reason Wigg and Abbey had remained especially distracted. But he had to admit that he, Shailiha, and Tyranny had all been quiet as well, their hearts heavy with concern about what might have become of Faegan and Celeste.

Tristan was about to give the order to take them down when Wigg leaned out of the litter and looked around. After a time, it seemed he had found what he was searching for. "Have the Minions land us on that rise coming up!" he said firmly. "There is something we must do before going any farther!"

Scowling, Tristan glared at the wizard. "Are you mad?" he shouted. "Celeste and Faegan might be fighting for their lives for all you know! We have to get to the palace!"

"No!" Wigg shouted back. He reached out and took Tristan by the shoulders. "You must trust me! There are things that Faegan, Abbey, and I have not told the rest of you!" For a moment Tristan actually thought that the wizard might go so far as to use his powers, if need be, to enforce whatever he had in mind.

"Now do as I say!" Wigg shouted. "And have them land the litter on that rise below us! And don't send your troops into the fight until I have done what I came here for!"

His jaw clenched in anger, Tristan looked out of the litter and shouted some orders out to Traax. Almost immediately the litter and the Minion host started toward the rise. As they reached the top, the palace grounds came into view below. Tristan looked down and took a short breath. The blood and bodies of both Minion and demonslaver alike littered the palace grounds. The survivors were still battling. The Minions, greatly outnumbered now, were clearly losing this fight. Most of them had been forced into the courtyard, their backs up against one of the inner walls as the demonslavers rushed them time and time again.

Some of the demonslavers were also dying, but it seemed that for every one of them that went down, two or more Minions died just as quickly. There were so many demonslavers upon them that the Minion warriors could not even take to the air.

His heart full of rage, Tristan spun around and glared at Wigg with angry, beseeching eyes as they landed.

"What's wrong with you?" Tristan shouted as he thrust one hand out, pointing at the ongoing massacre. "Can't you see that if I don't release my warriors, the ones down there will be cut to pieces?"

Wigg grabbed him by the shoulders again. "What I am about to do must be done!" he said harshly. "There is no time to explain! You simply must trust me! What do you want to save the most, eh? Some of the Minions who have sworn to defend you, or the very craft itself?"

Letting go of the prince's shoulders, Wigg turned to Abbey. Tristan watched as the lead wizard took a piece of parchment from his robes and handed it to her. It was covered with what looked to be Old Eutracian. Then he touched the locket she always wore around her neck and kissed her cheek. Fear on her face, she stood and exited the litter. Wigg waved his arms at the Minions. "Well don't just stand there!" he shouted. "We must go now!"

As the litter and the Minions climbed back into the sky, Abbey lifted her head and watched her lover depart. One tear of concern fell down her cheek.

*B*y the time the litter reached the palace, Tristan, Shailiha, Tyranny, and the Minions were spoiling for a fight. But by now Wigg had convinced them of why they must not participate, and also of their need to stay close to him.

Looking down into the courtyard from the roof on which they had landed, Tristan saw his Minions finally go flying down and begin tearing into the surprised demonslavers. Before landing he had given Traax orders to leave none of the white-skinned monstrosities alive. Grinning broadly, the Minion second-in-command had nodded in agreement.

Wigg stepped from the litter and glanced up toward the sky. He was greatly relieved to see that the twin orbs of the craft were not visible; that meant that if Wulfgar was indeed here, he had not yet conjured them.

But it was imperative that they find Morganna's firstborn before he was able to enact the Forestallment that would allow him to destroy the Orb of the Vigors.

If Wulfgar was cloaking his blood from Wigg, and he had also been gifted with the powers of invisibility by Krassus, trying to find him could be a nightmare, if not a complete impossibility. Their only hope lay in the fact that Wulfgar had clearly not yet destroyed the Orb of the Vigors, for Wigg still possessed his powers. And so if they could not find Wulfgar, Wigg would force him to come to them.

There was only one way to do that.

Wigg would conjure forth the twin orbs of the craft before Wulfgar did. For wherever the orbs were, Wulfgar would also have to be in order to carry out his plan.

Wasting no time, Wigg raised his arms.

As the four of them watched, a gigantic glow coalesced in the inky night sky. The glow began to spin, quickly becoming the Orb of the Vigors, the massive, golden globe of energy that sustained the altruistic side of the craft. The pale white beams that radiated from its center lit up the night sky for what seemed to be leagues in every direction. Tristan suddenly realized he had never witnessed the orbs at night. It was an awesome sight.

Then the darker, menacing Orb of the Vagaries took shape, its blackness scratched through by bright lightning.

Tristan glanced down to see that the battle in the courtyard below was winding down at last. The surviving demonslavers were being systematically beheaded, just as he had ordered. Traax and Ox landed quietly by his side. Ox looked exhausted, and one leg was wounded. Traax gave his lord a nod, and Tristan nodded back. Satisifed, he looked up at the sky again.

Then Wigg lowered his arms, and a strange sense of quiet descended over everything. The night larks and tree frogs stopped calling out to one another, and the branches of the trees below were no longer swishing to and fro, for the wind had suddenly stopped, as well. The orbs continued to hover silently, as if waiting for something to happen.

And then they changed.

Tristan glanced over at Wigg and saw the lead wizard shake his head, telling him that it was not he who was causing this phenomenon. *Wulfgar,* he thought.

The orbs had moved closer to each other than he had ever seen. Shards of lightning had begun to shoot back and forth between them, and the orbs themselves were shaking. Tristan glanced at Wigg to see that the lead wizard's face had blanched as he watched, spellbound.

A band of azure light took form between the orbs. It slowly extended itself from the side of the Orb of the Vigors, growing hauntingly until it reached the Orb of the Vagaries and attached itself.

Then this new connection between the orbs transformed itself from mere light into what looked like a tangible mass. It glowed ever brighter, until it became almost impossible to look upon. Suddenly, Tristan knew what it was.

The Isthmus: the bridge between the two sides of the craft that would somehow allow the destruction of the Orb of the Vigors.

And it had been conjured by Wulfgar.

A deep, commanding laugh shattered the silence. Tristan, Shailiha, and Tyranny drew their swords, blades ringing loudly as one through the air. As they did, the laugh came again.

"Tell me, Brother," a voice said. "Do you really think you can kill me with a weapon as crude as that?"

They all looked around, but they saw nothing except the magnificent orbs. The laugh came yet again, mocking them.

Then an azure glow began to build on one side of the roof. Turning, his hand clamped tightly around the hilt of his sword, Tristan watched as the glow took shape. As it coalesced, he and Shailiha found themselves staring at their long-lost sibling, the half brother they hadn't known existed until only a short time ago.

Wulfgar was wearing emerald silk trousers and a matching jacket that lay partially open, exposing his muscular chest. His sandy hair was pulled back from his forehead.

In his arms he held the Scroll of the Vigors.

If Wulfgar had the scroll, that meant he had found Faegan, Tristan realized. Was the wizard dead? And what had happened to Celeste?

Placing the precious scroll down on the roof, Wulfgar gave them all a menacing smile and took several brazen steps nearer.

At that moment, Wigg raised his arms and sent twin azure bolts at Wulfgar.

Casually, almost lazily, Wulfgar also raised his hands and caught a bolt in each. Then, placing his hands together, he joined the two bolts into one and took another step forward. As he did he looked squarely at Wigg and smiled again. Then he spread his fingers.

The azure bolt went screaming back toward Wigg and struck him squarely in the chest, throwing him high into the air, and across the roof. He landed hard on his back, unconscious. The front of his robe was scorched and smoking, and his arms were outstretched, as if in supplication.

Tristan, Shailiha, and Tyranny ran to him and knelt down. Wigg didn't seem to be breathing. Standing slowly, Tristan glared back with hatred at the monster that had just dared call him brother.

"Is he dead?" he asked, his body shaking with anger. He wanted to attack Wulfgar then and there. But after all he had just seen, he knew it would be hopeless.

Wulfgar simply smiled.

"I asked you a question, you bastard!" the prince raged. "Is Wigg dead?"

On hearing the insulting reference to his parentage, Wulfgar's face fell for a moment, and his gaze hardened. Then his composure resurfaced again.

Wulfgar pursed his lips. "Probably," he answered shortly. "I don't really know. Nor do I care, any more than I care about Faegan, or the daughter of the so-called lead wizard." Then the smile came again. "Don't you see?" he asked. He gave a sarcastic laugh. "I'm still rather new at all this."

Completely beyond anger, Tristan took a determined step forward, but Shailiha grabbed his arm. Tristan stopped, but continued to stare into Wulfgar's eyes.

"You had best listen to our sister," Wulfgar said. "You are untrained, and I could kill you with a single thought."

"Then why don't you?" Tristan snarled.

"I may do that yet," Wulfgar answered softly. "But as you have apparently guessed, I have other, more important business to finish first. A mission that your late son first entrusted to Krassus, and then Krassus entrusted to me." A new thought seemed to cross his mind, and he smiled at Tristan.

"Tell me, *Jin'Sai*," he said nastily. "What does it feel like to know that you have not only murdered your own father, but have also lost your only child, as well?"

Tristan took a slow, measured step forward. "The same way it will feel when I kill my only brother," he growled quietly. "Sad, but necessary."

Wulfgar shook his head. "Krassus told me you would be inordinately stubborn in your beliefs," he said. He looked down into the courtyard to see that the prince's Minions were finishing off his demonslavers. Strangely, he seemed quite unconcerned.

"Don't you care about what is happening to them?" Tristan asked.

"Why should I?" Wulfgar answered. "You have apparently done away with my fleet, or you wouldn't be standing here. I don't know how you did it, and I don't care. None of that matters any longer, for neither of your wizards can help you. The demonslavers, the screechlings, and the sea slitherers were only a means to an end. Besides, the slavers were all originally your subjects, not mine.

"And by the way," he continued, "order those Minion warriors behind you to go back down into the courtyard and tell the others not to come up. If any of them approach, our lovely sister—your famous twin—will die."

Turning, Tristan looked at the warriors and gave them a nod. Reluctantly they jumped from the edge of the roof and soared toward the courtyard.

Trying hard not to look up at the hill above them, Tristan turned back to Wulfgar. He could only hope that after hearing what Wigg had told them in the litter, Shailiha and Tyranny would have the good sense to do the same.

He thought desperately, as if by willing it hard enough he could somehow make them hear him. If Wulfgar turned his gaze there, they would all be finished.

"Now then," Wulfgar said, almost politely. "Shall we begin?"

Raising one arm, he encased everyone before him on the roof in a wizard's warp. Tristan couldn't move any of his limbs, but he found that he still controlled his powers of speech. Apparently satisfied, Wulfgar stared calmly at the people trapped in his warp.

"You're going to destroy the Orb of the Vigors, aren't you?" Shailiha asked. "That's what this has been about all along!"

"Of course," Wulfgar answered calmly. "But before I do, there is something I would like the two of you to know. It will pain you to hear it, I'm sure. But then again, making my brother and sister happy isn't really why I have come."

"What is it?" Tristan asked.

Looking over to one side, Wulfgar pointed down at the Scroll of the Vigors.

"That scroll," he began, "the one you held in your possession so briefly, holds many of the answers you seek. Yes, *Jin'Sai,* it even tells of the potential coming of your azure blood, and of how you might eventually rid yourself of it. But now, with the scroll in my possession, none of those things will ever happen. For until your blood reverts you cannot be trained, cannot wear the Paragon, and cannot read the Tome, and you will be unable to fulfill your so-called destiny. You will even be barred from siring children, for your tainted blood would be far too dangerous for any woman's to join with. Have your friends the wizards told you that yet? Your famous, all-powerful blood that was to have empowered you above all others is now the very thing you must most despise." The wicked smile came again.

"Aside from me, of course," he added knowingly. He turned to look at the orbs.

"How can one of our blood be so evil?" Shailiha shouted at him. "Doesn't any part of you care about the horrific, irreparable damage you are about to cause?"

Turning back from the orbs, Wulfgar looked directly into his sister's eyes.

"*Evil,* you say?" he asked her. "Don't you understand? I have no concept of the word 'evil.' As Krassus was so fond of saying, we of the Vagaries simply have a different point of view."

Turning again, he raised his hands. Almost immediately the orbs began burning brighter.

Never taking his eyes from his bastard brother, Tristan turned his thoughts toward the hill.

*A*bbey saw Wulfgar turn toward the orbs and saw them glow even more brightly. She levitated the parchment Wigg had given her so that it hovered in the air before her. Opening the cinch bag at her waist, she took out a pinch of precious herbs and placed them on the tinder she had prepared and lit. Then she stood back and used her gifts to force the fire higher and higher. When it was at last about two meters high and a meter wide, she crooked a finger toward her, ordering the flame to divide into two unequal branches. Curling her finger again, she pointed to the right, and the smaller of the two flames flattened out, coming dangerously close to scorching her hands and face. Looking down, she blessed the Afterlife that Wulfgar's back was still toward her.

She threw another pinch of herbs into the branch of flame, then reached for and opened the silver locket that hung around her neck. The usual dark locket of hair, the one belonging to the lead wizard, still lay inside as always. But now there was another with it. It was sandy colored, and secured around its center with a red ribbon.

It was Wulfgar's—the lock of hair that she had first seen in the Hall of Blood Records when Wigg had explained Wulfgar to them and shown them his blood signature. The lock of his hair that his grand-mother had taken from him before her daughter gave him over to the or-phanage, thirty-four years ago.

She removed the ribbon and divided the lock of hair into two halves, than dropped one half into the lower of the two flames and held the other half high. She was ordering her flame to find Wulfgar, even though he was in plain view.

She knew she was risking her life by doing so. She was only a par-tial, and so her attempt to find Wulfgar, one of those of the womb of Queen Morganna, would undoubtedly call forth the Furies—the same phenomenon that she had experienced that day in the courtyard when she, Faegan, and Shailiha had nearly been killed while trying to find the prince by employing a drop of his twin sister's blood.

But this time, she prayed, she had the answer.

*A*s the orbs and the Isthmus joining them glowed ever more brightly, Wulfgar smiled. Even though the Forestallment required to accomplish his task was immensely refined, the concept behind his mission was exceedingly simple. He could still hear Krassus explaining to him how it was to be done, as though it were only yesterday.

First, call upon your blood and conjure forth the Isthmus. When the Isthmus has appeared and the orbs seem stable, then use your mind to open the gate at the end connected to the Orb of the Vagaries, and allow its dark energy to trickle through. As it begins to reach the Orb of the Vigors, open the other end of the Isthmus and force the dark energy inside the Orb of the Vigors without allowing it to return to its source. The Orb of the Vigors shall therefore become polluted, while the Orb of the Vagaries shall remain pristine. When enough dark energy has finally been transfused, however, the cataclysm will wish to commence, and you must be exceedingly careful lest you risk the destruction of the world, for chaos is the natural order of the universe. But if done correctly, before the great cataclysm occurs the controlled nature of your work will cause the Orb of the Vigors to explode in a great ball of fire and light, and your mission will be complete. The Vigors will be no more, Wulfgar, and you may return to the Citadel and rule in splendor forever.

Closing his eyes, Wulfgar used his mind to open the floodgate at the end of the Isthmus touching the Orb of the Vagaries. As he did, its destructive energy trickled into the Isthmus and flowed down the length of its interior, making it darker as it went. Any second now, Tristan saw, the energy of the Vagaries would reach the Orb of the Vigors, and everything they treasured would be gone forever.

*J*ust as it had done that day in the courtyard, the top of Abbey's gazing flame began to swell. The viewing window also began to form, but that was not her main concern this time.

Looking at the parchment hovering in the air before her, she began urgently reading aloud the formula that Wigg and Faegan had found in the Scroll of the Vigors only days before—the formula that the community of partial adepts had for centuries whispered would countermand the action of the Furies and send the energy back to the subject a thousandfold.

With a great explosion her gazing flame burst, throwing her to the ground. But unlike the previous time, that was not the end of it.

Sheets of pure energy shot from the exploding flame, illuminating everything for leagues around. The night sky erupted in a cacophony of noise and light as the energy streaked down the hill, searching out the subject that was to have been viewed.

Wulfgar.

Sensing that something had gone terribly wrong, Wulfgar turned for a moment to look up the hill. As the light shards came nearer, his face contorted into a mixture of confusion and terror. Then the Furies, magnified a thousandfold, found him.

Ignoring the orbs, Wulfgar turned to confront the Furies in a desperate effort to save his life. Frantically he sent azure bolts against them. But to no avail.

As the bolts slammed into the energy cascading down the hill, they simply fizzled away against it, dissipating into nothingness. Unaffected, the Furies continued toward him. Tearing across the roof, they passed over the Scroll of the Vigors and headed unerringly for Wulfgar.

As they approached their target, they began to produce a whirling maelstrom that soon surrounded him, trapping him within its confines. As it closed in on him, Wulfgar could feel the intense heat it emitted. He knew that if he remained inside, he would die. For a few precious moments he turned his hateful gaze on Tristan and Shailiha.

They heard him scream insanely. Then the scream died away. The maelstrom closed in hard—and exploded.

As the force of the blast tore through the night air, Tristan, Shailiha, and Tyranny felt the searing heat and power of the dying Furies from the confines of Wulfgar's deteriorating warp. Trees from the nearby hill were uprooted and sent flying into the air, and parts of the palace roof exploded, sending marble pieces high into the sky. Then the warp finally vanished altogether, and Tristan, Shailiha, and Tyranny collapsed to the roof. Tristan could barely move. Craning his neck, he looked over to see that the two women were either unconscious or dead.

It was all the prince could do to look up at the glowing orbs of the craft. Wulfgar's Isthmus had vanished, and the orbs seemed to be undamaged. Suddenly, they were gone.

Using what strength he had left, Tristan looked over at the scroll. Blessedly, it still lay on the palace roof, where Wulfgar had left it.

In horror he saw that the Scroll of the Vigors—the only known document in the world that could provide the answers he so desperately needed about himself—was burning. He tried to crawl toward it. But his strength gave out, and he collapsed back down to the roof.

The last thing he remembered before passing out was his Minion troops finally landing on the roof beside him, and Traax and Ox running toward the burning document.

CHAPTER

Seventy-three

"In the name of the Afterlife, hold still!" Wigg shouted at Rebecca. He had been extremely cranky for the last three days, and it seemed to him that every bone in his three-hundred-plus-year-old body still hurt.

"Tristan!" he growled softly, trying not to frighten the young girl any more than she already was. "Can you get her to calm down somehow? I simply cannot do this properly if she won't stay still!"

Smiling with one corner of his mouth, Tristan took Rebecca by the shoulders and gently pushed her back down onto the table. Then he whispered something into her ear, and she giggled. She promised to remain still as best she could, then gave Wigg a curious look and giggled once more.

Narrowing his eyes, Wigg called the craft and again started employing the process that would begin healing her clubfoot. As he did, Rebecca seemed to calm down. He cast a wary eye toward the prince. "What did you say to her?" he asked.

"Oh, nothing," Tristan answered casually. "Just that whenever you become irritated, the vein in your forehead starts to throb. I suggested she watch it to pass the time, and count how many times it did before you finished."

Sighing, Wigg shook his head, then snorted a laugh and went back to his work.

Tristan, Wigg, Faegan, Abbey, Shailiha, Celeste, and Tyranny were all in attendance here, in Wigg's personal drawing room. The stained-glass windows had been swung open to let in the fresh morning air and the songs of the birds.

Marcus stood next to the lead wizard, and Shailiha held Morganna on her hip. Shawna stood to one side, watching the process unfold. She had become quite attached to Rebecca and her brother, even though Marcus had proved to be quite a handful. Looking around the room, Tristan felt a great sense of thankfulness. He wondered briefly how the wizards would react to what he had planned.

They had all somehow managed to stay alive during their recent ordeal, but just barely. Tristan, Tyranny, and Shailiha had acquired some burns with the onslaught of the Furies, but had been protected for the most part by Wulfgar's warp. Abbey had also been burned, but not more so than the first time the Furies had erupted. Wigg, Faegan, and Celeste, however, had suffered far worse.

Wigg had been deeply injured by Wulfgar's bolts; beneath his robes he was a mass of black and blue, and would be for weeks. But after a few sessions of Abbey's healing skills he was finally feeling better and would continue to improve.

Celeste had also survived, but her left forearm had been broken in Wulfgar's attack, and it was wrapped in a sling. It was only the high quality of her and her father's blood, it was later assumed, that had kept the lead wizard and his daughter alive. Celeste sat in a chair along one wall as her father tended to Rebecca.

Faegan's case was different. His injuries had been physical, to be sure. But they had also been psychological. It was plain by the look on his face that he was ashamed at having been broken by Wulfgar's torture, even though he had succeeded in keeping secret their plan with the Furies. Knowing Faegan as they did, the others realized that it would take the old wizard some time to get over what he considered to be so great a personal failure. Then Tristan was reminded of the time enchantments, and he smiled slightly. If there was one thing the wizards had plenty of, it was time.

As for the Scroll of the Vigors, it had been once again locked away in the Redoubt, awaiting further research. And true to form, ever since Wulfgar had been defeated the two wizards had chosen to rest, rather than make explanations.

Tristan was determined to get his answers, as soon as Wigg finished with Rebecca and while everyone was still here, whether the wizards felt like talking or not. And he had a special request to put before them, one that had been on his mind for some time now. But for that he would wait until the three of them were alone.

Almost a full hour later, Wigg finally stopped what he was doing. After another quick examination of Rebecca's foot, he seemed pleased.

"You may get up now," he said to her. "Place your weight on your foot, and see how it feels."

Rebecca sat up, slipped her legs over the side of the table, and tentatively stood. As she did, her face registered pure joy.

"Marcus!" she shouted gleefully. "Come and look!"

Marcus ran to her side of the table and looked down. His sister's misshapen foot looked completely normal. For the first time in her young life, Rebecca was finally without pain. With tears of joy in her eyes, she began skipping around the drawing room.

She finally stopped in front of the lead wizard. She looked up into his eyes with a humble expression. Then she crooked a finger at him, beckoning him closer. With a characteristic rise of one eyebrow, he did as she asked. Before he knew it she had wrapped her arms around his neck and kissed him on the cheek.

"Thank you," she said softly. "I will never forget what you have done for me."

"I won't, either," Marcus added. "And I'm sorry if I've been a lot of trouble."

"You're quite welcome," Wigg replied simply. As he did, Abbey came up beside him and linked one of her arms through his.

"Three hundred and sixty times. I'm sure of it," Rebecca said unexpectedly.

"I beg your pardon?" Wigg asked.

"Three hundred and sixty," she answered back. "That's how many times the vein in your head throbbed." Then she looked innocently over to where Faegan sat in his chair, stroking his cat, Nicodemus.

"If I asked him real nice, maybe Mr. Faegan could fix that for you," she said helpfully. "Despite how long everybody says you've been around, it seems that you haven't been able to do it for yourself."

The entire room roared. Even Wigg, embarrassed as he seemed to be, gave up and erupted into laughter. Abbey leaned over and placed her lips close to his ear.

"That will be the day . . ." she whispered coyly.

"Uh, er, that won't be necessary," Wigg finally answered Rebecca. "But thank you for offering, just the same."

Deciding it was time to get back to business, Tristan looked over at Shawna.

"Would you please take the children back to their quarters?" he asked her. "We have some matters to discuss."

With a quick nod, Shawna herded Rebecca and Marcus from the room, softly closing the door behind them. Wasting no time, Tristan walked over to stand next to Celeste, and then trained his dark eyes on Wigg. Determined, he folded his arms over his chest.

"I already know that you and Faegan must have found the calculations for reversing the Furies somewhere in the Scroll of the Vigors," he said. "It's the only answer that makes any sense. But what I don't know is when."

"And why didn't you tell us until the last minute, Father?" Celeste asked. Using her good arm, she reached up to take one of Tristan's hands. "Wouldn't it have been better if we had all known?"

"Actually, no, it wouldn't have," Faegan answered as he wheeled his chair into the center of the room. Reaching into his lap, he gave Nicodemus a scratch under the neck.

"Why not?" Shailiha asked.

"Because the fewer of us who knew, the better," he answered. "You, Tristan, and Wigg were about to leave, to search out the demonslaver fleet. At the time, Wigg and I thought that we might be at least partially able to fight off Wulfgar's use of the craft on our minds, should it come to that. But if you, Celeste, or Tristan had been captured, you never could have resisted his probes, for none of you have been trained to do so. Therefore, we did not tell you of the secret location of the scroll, or the discovery of the calculations. What you did not know could not be tortured from you, no matter how hard Wulfgar might have tried.

"And as it turned out, even I was unable to resist his torture," he added softly, "and he ended up taking the scroll anyway. Still, that was better than revealing to him the calculations of the Furies."

"But you took a great chance, did you not?" Shailiha asked. "You could have been killed."

"True," Faegan answered. "But remember, at that time we still did not know whether Wulfgar was even coming, or by what route. That is why we decided to leave me and Celeste here, to guard the scroll." Then he looked down at his hands again.

"I want to apologize to everyone," he said softly. "And especially to Tristan. If Wulfgar had not been given the location of the scroll, it would still be intact. But I held out for as long as I could, to make him believe that the location of the scroll was all I had to give him."

"And the condition of the scroll?" Tristan asked softly, not daring to hope. "What of that?"

Placing his hands into the opposite sleeves of his robe, Wigg sighed. "As best we can determine, about two-fifths of the Scroll of the Vigors has been completely destroyed," he answered sadly. "We have forever lost what were surely some of the most important secrets of the craft. But we will do what we can with the parts that remain."

"And do you believe Wulfgar to be dead?" Abbey asked. Snaking her arm a little farther underneath Wigg's, she edged closer to him.

"Yes," the lead wizard answered flatly. "Neither Faegan nor I can see how anyone, no matter how powerful he or she was in the craft, could have survived that. He was undoubtedly vaporized by the Furies."

"What about the traitorous consuls he commanded?" Shailiha asked. "They remain a threat to us, do they not?"

Faegan scowled. "That is impossible to say," he answered grimly. "We must accept the possibility that, in addition to those he controlled at the Citadel, some of them remain in Eutracia. With Wulfgar dead, there will be a power vacuum within their ranks. Sadly, that may make them even more dangerous than before. There are few things as unpredictable as a zealous army without a leader."

Tristan looked over at his sister to find the same mixed expression on her face that he knew was on his own. Wulfgar had been a monster—that much was certain. But part of Tristan wanted to believe that somewhere, sometime, Wulfgar had once been a kind, honorable man, before Krassus' demonslavers had come for him.

Silence reigned for moment, and then Tyranny spoke up. "Forgive me, Tristan," she said. "My brother awaits me, and I need to check on the condition of my wounded crewmembers and my ships."

Smiling slightly, Tristan looked over at the highly competent, tousle-haired privateer. "I understand," he said quietly. "But before you go, I have something for you. Several things, actually, that I believe will come in handy. They should be here by now."

Walking over to the door, Tristan opened it and looked out into the hallway. At a sign from him, K'jarr led six Minion warriors into the room.

Tyranny's mouth fell open. Everyone else in the room seemed equally surprised. Wigg scowled a bit, and Faegan gave a soft cackle.

"Do you mean to say—"

"Yes," Tristan interrupted her. "I am giving you command of these six warriors. They were each handpicked by Traax, chosen by him from a large group of volunteers. It seems, dear lady, that you have made quite an impression on them. They are to sail with you, two weeks from now, and not before. For reasons you will discover later, I do not wish you to depart until then. I also ordered the construction of a special litter for you, and it awaits you in the courtyard. K'jarr has kindly offered to be an ongoing part of this, both to act as an overseer of the warriors in any orders you might give them, and to more fully brief you on Minion customs and tactics. These warriors are to be rotated with others every six months. You will find that they make especially good scouts. But I have a selfish motive in all of this, as well. With both these warriors and a litter aboard the *Reprisal,* you will be able to reach the palace far more quickly, should you need to." Seeing her still-amazed expression, he gave her a short, knowing smile.

"And given your natural proclivities for trouble, I think you will need them rather a lot," he added slyly.

Still stunned, Tyranny walked over to him and embraced him

warmly. Then she looked into his face. "I don't know what to say," she said softly.

Smiling, he raised his right hand and spat into his palm. "Yes, you do," he said. He raised his hand a bit higher. "Done," he said.

Smiling broadly, Tyranny spat into her right hand and slapped her palm into his. "And done," she answered back warmly.

Tristan turned back to face the room. "And now, I wish to be alone with my wizards," he told everyone. Then he looked at Faegan and Wigg and grinned widely. "I have a proposition for them."

Wigg raised an eyebrow, and Faegan's normally impish, curious countenance returned. The remaining people in the room walked to the door. As they did, the prince gave Celeste and Shailiha a smile of good-bye.

After they had all left, Wigg scowled and folded his arms over his chest.

"What is this about?" he asked skeptically.

Saying nothing, Tristan bade the two wizards to join him out on the sunlit balcony. As they did, he took a chair at the table, crossed one of his long legs over the other, and poured himself a cup of tea.

And then, in quiet, measured tones, he told them of his plan.

CHAPTER

Seventy-four

As Tristan walked down the colorful hallways of the Redoubt, his boot heels rang out against the marble floor, once again reminding him of what a lonely, massive place this underground labyrinth could be. While it was true that many of the previously wandering acolytes had passed the wizards' examinations and now called this place home, their numbers were still too few even to begin returning the Redoubt to its former level of activity. Still, he realized, it was a start.

New beginnings, he thought to himself as he crossed through yet another of the Redoubt's intersections. Snapping his heels together, the Minion warrior on guard came to stiff attention as his lord passed by. Not wishing to be late, Tristan only nodded and kept on going.

Two weeks had passed since the day when Rebecca's foot had been cured, and Tristan's subsequent time alone with the two wizards had gone well. He had spent the remainder of that morning with them out on Wigg's balcony explaining in great detail what he wished to do. It was time, Tristan had told them, and in the end they had agreed.

When he had finished, the prince thought he had seen some shininess in their eyes. But being the indomitable mystics that they were, each had caused it to vanish as quickly as it appeared. The wizards had then informed everyone of Tristan's decision and asked them all to meet at the appointed day and hour.

Finally approaching the elaborately carved double doors, he saw the two Minion warriors standing guard on either side. Each of them held a long, gold-tipped spear in one hand, the spear's end planted firmly by the heel of his foot, the point held away from his body. As the prince approached they snapped their heels together and pulled their spears toward them, into an upright position. Stopping before them, Tristan nodded his approval.

"Has the furniture I ordered been brought here?" he asked.

"Yes, my lord," one of them answered. "Minion artisans finished it only this afternoon, and it was moved into the room several hours ago."

"And everyone who was asked to attend," Tristan said. "Are they present?"

"All except for Commander Traax," the warrior answered.

"And where is he?" Tristan asked.

"Right behind you," Tristan heard Traax's voice ring out. As Traax walked up, he seemed to be trying to force down a smile. "I apologize for being late."

"Where have you been?" Tristan asked.

Smiling, Traax shook his head. "It seems that a situation has developed that required my attention," he answered wryly.

At first Tristan stiffened, wondering whether they all might be in danger again. But he realized from the expression on Traax's face, that he could relax.

"And what might that be?" he asked.

"It's about the two children, Marcus and Rebecca."

"What about them?" Tristan asked.

"They're gone. And so is the thirteen thousand kisa."

Tristan's eyes went wide. At first he didn't know whether to laugh or cry. Then he looked at the infectious expression on Traax's face again, and he decided to laugh.

"How?" he asked. "And when?"

"We still don't know how," Traax answered. "Shawna is beside herself, of course, but she'll get over it eventually. Feeling that she could finally trust them, she had dismissed the warrior who usually watched over them. What a mistake! As to when, well, it happened sometime during the night. I think that Marcus had this planned for some time now, and the only thing he was waiting for was for Wigg to cure his sister's foot so that for the first time in her life she could run away as fast as he could!" Pausing for a moment, Traax smiled and shook his head again.

"Thirteen thousand kisa is a great deal of money," he said quietly. "But you know, in an odd sort of way, I think they both earned it."

Rubbing his forehead, Tristan couldn't help but laugh again. Partly, he knew, because he found Traax's news so amusing. And partly because it simply felt so good to laugh long and hard again, after so long. He looked back up at Traax.

"Do you wish me to send out search parties?" the warrior asked.

"No, no," Tristan said with a wave of one hand. "I think they've earned it, too."

"Then may I request a favor?" the warrior asked.

"What is it?"

"Whenever you finally tell the wizards, might I also be in attendance? The looks on their faces will be worth every bit of that thirteen thousand kisa."

Tristan laughed again. "Yes!" he answered. "But until then, this stays just between the two of us."

His mood turning more serious, Tristan turned and faced the door. "Are you ready?" he asked Traax. "From this moment on, so many things will change."

"Yes, my lord," Traax replied gravely. His face had suddenly become full of both respect and gratitude. "This is a great thing you have done, and I thank you with all my heart."

Tristan nodded at the two warriors flanking the doors, and they obediently opened them. Then the prince and Traax walked in and took their appointed seats with the others.

The magnificently carved table Tristan had ordered two weeks ago was ten sided, and a matching, high-backed chair sat at each station. An image of the Paragon had been beautifully inlaid in its center. Each chair held a person he cared for very much and who possessed, each in his or her own way, talents that would no doubt serve them all well into the future. Their seating arrangement alternated by gender. Their names had been carved into the tops of their chairs just as the chair of the ill-fated Directorate of Wizards had been. As Tristan looked around the table, he was reminded of why he had selected each of them.

Wigg and Faegan were here, of course, as full-fledged representatives of the craft. Wigg was wearing his golden ceremonial dagger around his waist, and from Faegan's neck hung the Paragon, its bloodred facets dancing in the light of the fireplace. Between them sat Abbey as a representative of the partial adepts, the mysterious men and women of the craft whom the prince still knew so little about, but hoped to learn so much more. On Faegan's left sat a very stunned Adrian of the House of Brandywyne, whom Wigg and Faegan had selected to represent the acolytes of the Redoubt. And on her left was Traax.

Next to Traax sat Shailiha. Caprice perched quietly at the top of her mistress' chair, gently opening and closing her violet-and-yellow wings. After her came Geldon, whose knowledge of Parthalon had no equal. At Tristan's right was Celeste, the love of his life.

And finally, on the prince's left, sat Tyranny. With the Minion fleet smashed, she and her small squadron of privateers now represented the only seaborne defenses Eutracia had.

Looking up, Tristan nodded to the Minion still waiting by the door.

The warrior walked into the hallway, closed the door behind himself, and took up his post.

"By my order, the Directorate is no more," Tristan said solemnly. "We are now the Conclave of the Vigors."

ABOUT THE AUTHOR

Robert Newcomb is the author of *The Fifth Sorceress,*
Volume I of The Chronicles of Blood and Stone.
He traveled widely in his youth as a member of the
American Institute for Foreign Study, studying at the
University of Southampton, England, and aboard a
university-sponsored ship in the Mediterranean Sea.
After graduating from Colgate University with a B.A.
in economics and a minor in art history, he enjoyed a
successful career in business. He lives in Florida with
his wife, a neuropsychologist and novelist. His Web site
is robertnewcomb.com.